P

THE

After working on local newspapers in Devon and in the East End of London, Diana Norman became at twenty years of age the youngest reporter on what used to be Fleet Street. She married the film critic Barry Norman, and they settled in Hertfordshire with their two daughters. Her first book of fiction, *Fitzempress's Law*, was chosen by Frank Delaney of BBC Radio 4's *Bookshelf* as the best example of a historical novel of its year. She is now a freelance journalist as well as a writer of biographies and historical novels.

THE
VIZARD MASK

Diana Norman

PENGUIN BOOKS

PENGUIN BOOKS

Published by the Penguin Group
Penguin Books Ltd, 27 Wrights Lane, London W8 5TZ, England
Penguin Books USA Inc., 375 Hudson Street, New York, New York 10014, USA
Penguin Books Australia Ltd, Ringwood, Victoria, Australia
Penguin Books Canada Ltd, 10 Alcorn Avenue, Toronto, Ontario, Canada M4V 3B2
Penguin Books (NZ) Ltd, 182–190 Wairau Road, Auckland 10, New Zealand

Penguin Books Ltd, Registered Offices: Harmondsworth, Middlesex, England

First published by Michael Joseph 1994
Published in Penguin Books 1995
1 3 5 7 9 10 8 6 4 2

Printed in England by Clays Ltd, St Ives plc

To Bertie and Oliver Norman

Author's Note

THERE *was* a Restoration actress called Peg Hughes and she was the first woman to play Desdemona on stage. She became Prince Rupert's mistress and bore him a child, Ruperta. I have adapted and elaborated what little is known about her life to my purposes, including in it a few – though by no means all – of the humiliations imposed on those real-life first actresses.

William III, while still a very young Prince of Orange, was made roaring, door-battering drunk during his first visit to England.

The King Philip War as it was called, between the New England settlers and the Indians in 1675, is said to have cost proportionally more lives than any war fought by Americans since.

Judge Jeffreys's treatment of the rebels is true to the record, though I've swopped the trials' locations here and there. He died in the Tower.

Aphra Behn's title should be more than that of the first woman to earn her living by her pen. *Oroonoko* was translated into French and German and became popular in France during the French revolutionary period. In England it was reprinted repeatedly during the eighteenth century and, along with the play adapted from it by Southerne, helped form part of the literature of the abolitionist movement which became a political force a century after Aphra's death.

Like all women who break out of the stereotype she was subjected to the process that begins with detraction and ends in oblivion. The nineteenth century, when she was mentioned at all, found it necessary to apologize for her. By the beginning of the twentieth she had all but disappeared. An article in 1913 by a Mr Ernest Bernbaum declared that she never went to Surinam, never spied on the Dutch for Charles II – despite evidence in the State Papers that she did — virtually, that she didn't exist.

The lines on her tombstone in the east cloister of Westminster Abbey are typical of the smart, uncaring age she lived through and are said to have been written by John Hoyle:

> Here lies proof that wit can never be
> Defence against mortality.

A more accurate memorial is in Virginia Woolf's *A Room of One's Own* where she points out that genius is a succession: 'Jane Austen should have laid a wreath upon the grave of Fanny Burney, and George Eliot done homage to the shade of Eliza Carter ... all women together ought to let flowers fall upon the tomb of Aphra Behn, for it was she who earned them the right to speak their minds.'

Incidentally, there is no evidence for the fight between her friends and the Chapter of Westminster Abbey over that same tomb.

But she should have been buried in Poets' Corner.

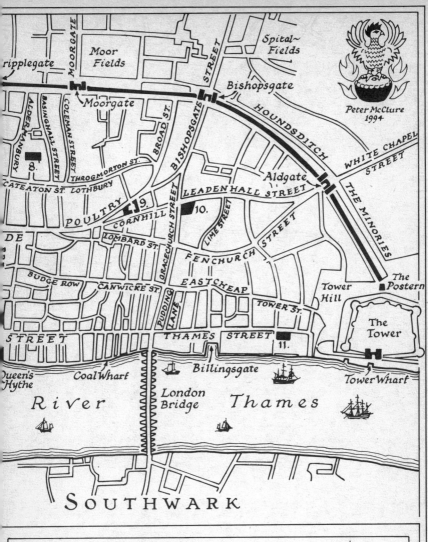

Peter McClure
1994

LONDON ~ *circa* 1665

Key ~

1. St. Paul's Cathedral
2. St. Paul's Churchyard
3. The Fleet Prison
4. Bridewell
5. Baynard's Castle
6. St. Bartholomew's Hospital
7. Charterhouse
8. Guild Hall
9. Royal Exchange
10. Leaden Hall
11. Customs House

A Scale of Half an English Mile

0   ¼   ½

Map labels:

Cripplegate
MOORGATE
Moor Fields
Spital~Fields
STREET
Moorgate
Bishopsgate
HOUNDSDITCH
WHITE CHAPEL STREET
ALDERMANBURY
BASINGHALL STREET
COLEMAN STREET
8.
THROGMORTON ST.
BROAD ST.
BISHOPSGATE
CATEATON ST. LOTHBURY
Aldgate
LEADEN HALL STREET
THE MINORIES
POULTRY
9.
CORNHILL
10.
GRACECHURCH STREET
LIME STREET
FENCHURCH STREET
LOMBARD ST.
STREET
BUDGE ROW
CANWICKE ST.
EASTCHEAP
PUDDING LANE
TOWER ST.
Tower Hill
The Postern
STREET
THAMES STREET
11.
The Tower
Queen's Hythe
Coal Wharf
Billingsgate
Tower Wharf
London Bridge
River   Thames

SOUTHWARK

BOOK I

Chapter 1

PENITENCE HURD and the Plague arrived in London on the same day.

Penitence was eighteen and carried a beaded satchel.

The Plague travelled by fur-lined carriage and was as old as sin. It had been to London before – part of it had never left – but this time conditions were perfect for its purpose. The summer of 1664 had been the hottest in living memory and an overcrowded population was being swelled daily by workers in the luxury trade catering for the merry monarchy of Charles II – the number of ribbon-makers alone ran into thousands. In the poor areas people were crammed so close they breathed in air that had just been breathed out by everybody else.

Master Endicott, captain of the *Deliverance*, was being flustered by Customs men. 'Thee wait now, Pen, until I can take thee to the minister.'

Penitence had no intention of waiting, especially for a minister. Her experience with the Reverend Block back in Massachusetts had rendered her fearful of all ministers. She stood still until Master Endicott took the Customs men into the hold and then she scurried down the gangplank.

From another ship further along the Plague was carried down a hawser to the wharf.

A rat whisked across Penitence's path, but she barely noticed it. She'd encountered rats before, it was London she was new to. The smell along this piece of its river frontage was a combination of dockside and country; the stink of fish, tar and dirty water was almost wiped out by the manure rotted on the towering heaps of dung gathered from the streets, ready to be shipped to the gardens of Whitehall.

But it was the noise. Drivers of wagons going down to the

wharf altercated with the drivers of wagons coming up. Wheels rumbled as dockers yelled, ships and cranes creaked, rigging flapped and water-boatmen called 'Ho's' eastward and westward. Beyond it all, like a titanic millwheel, was the resonance of a city that shook with the vibration of half a million people.

Deafened, Penitence just in time jumped out of the way of a wagon carting strong-smelling wool. '*Some trust in chariots, and some in horses,*' she scolded it, '*but we will remember the name of the Lord our God.* Psalm 20, verse 7.' She glanced up at the sun to take her bearings. It was setting now, and London Bridge with its houses was a black cut-out against vermilion.

'*West.*' To go west she had first to go north along the narrow, loomed-over street that had led up from the river, but she turned left as soon as she could. Politely, she dropped a curtsey to everyone in her path, but, since that meant bobbing up and down like a sanddipper and nobody saluted her back, she became tired of the exercise. '*They have mouths but they speak not: eyes have they but they see not. Noses have they and they smell . . . awful.*' The school joke was to cheer herself up. Master Endicott, bless him, had tried to tell her. 'Thee cannot contain the thought of it, Pen. 'Tis a Leviathan. Thee could put all Boston in one of its parishes and lose it.'

He was right; she had been unable to imagine it. She was used to distant horizons. Here the few open spaces were cross-angled by buildings that blocked in her vision, buildings that bent over her, seeming to shuffle up and claim her attention with beautiful woodwork and worn gargoyles. Overhead a forest of signboards splattered her face with raindrips from an earlier shower as she gawped up at them.

She was an odd figure, her neatness pointing up the chaos through which she moved. Her black dress covered her thin body from her throat down to the tops of her ploughboy boots and showed that she had no breasts to speak of and was stiff-backed. Her walk was ungainly for a woman, the lope of one who covers long distances easily. Plainer women were more attractive than she was because Penitence Hurd not only was not aware that she had beauty, but would have been ashamed of that fact if had she known it.

4

Even without the high-crowned hat — its buckle exactly centred — covering every inch of her hair, she would have declared herself a Puritan by her care to avoid physical contact with passers-by and the purse of her lips as she looked about her. London had known that look during the days of the Commonwealth; it had toppled maypoles, cancelled Christmas, closed theatres, killed its king and forbidden sin. Now it had set up a new king along with the maypoles, the bears were back, sin was in fashion, and no disapproving sniff from Penitence Hurd's nose was going to get rid of them, thank her kindly. She sniffed on, occasionally jeered at as an oddity by rude boys, though no more than they jeered at beggars, madmen, amputees, soldiers, richly dressed women and jugglers in this modern Babylon. Men and women openly tumbled each other in the doorways of taverns. Others fought, some vomited. A lady in a carriage passed by with her bosom exposed and was not arrested.

'Tis an habitation of dragons.' Crime she had expected, but not this engulfing wickedness, not foul words from men as she passed, not a flaunting of sin that was an aggression aiming itself at her, as if hers alone was the innocence it meant to destroy.

'The souls of the righteous are in the hand of God, and there shall no torment touch them.' Clutching her righteousness and her satchel, Penitence travelled on. The sun had long gone down, but, instead of retiring to bed like a Christian, London lit the flambeaux in its streets, illuminated its windows and intensified its wickedness.

A crowd at the top of Ludgate Hill stopped Penitence's progress and in trying to press through it she was trapped between a wall and a well-covered gentleman. Penitence's hat had been pushed to the back of her head and, glancing round, the well-covered gentleman saw her eyes. 'Keep close.' Unable to do anything else, Penitence kept close as, shouting 'Make way', the gentleman whacked a path with his staff for them both through to the front. 'Get along there.'

His was the first amiable countenance she'd seen since leaving Master Endicott and, as she couldn't move anyway, Penitence stayed by him.

'Sir John Lawrence, heard of him?' asked her new acquaintance.

Penitence shook her head.

'He's our new Lord Mayor, Sir John. Queenhithe man. Being chaired today. And what do you think of our little city?' It was a rhetorical question. Penitence's acquaintance was revelling in unfolding the wonders of it to this country bumpkin.

Trumpets and drums sounded in the distance, the crowd began cheering the empty street in anticipation until runners in the King's livery and carrying torches filled it. 'Now then,' said the well-covered gentleman, 'here they be.'

The City and Charles II were still on their honeymoon, and a wild affection suffused the crowd as coaches carrying the court presaged that of the King's. Penitence's acquaintance showed off, sweeping his hat to each coach, listing his familiarity with the great in a litany of names for his own benefit as much as Penitence's. 'Count Cominges, the Frog. Hyde, the old devil. Duke of Buckingham. Albemarle. Southampton. Arlington. Ormonde . . . and here he is, bless him. Got the Queen with him tonight.'

Ignoring the presence of the Queen, the crowd emitted rutting noises in appreciation of its king's libido. Forearms imitated the sexual act as voices in the cheering advised him to 'Swive 'em, Rowley'. The loudest calls, however, were for war with the Dutch. 'Blow the butterboxes to hell.'

Charles Stuart himself. Shall I spit? Turn my back? Who else in this mass of sinners would reprove the man? It was Christ the Lord should be ruling England, not this Papist-sympathizing wencher. She risked a peek at Satan rampant. No smell of sulphur, no forked tail. Penitence's nose sniffed perfume, and for a second her eyes, instead of the hackneyed evil she'd expected, saw something more complex and more awful.

Sobered, she followed her new friend through the dispersing crowd. 'Now then, young lady, where do you want to go?'

Penitence delved into her satchel-bag and brought out the slate she had prepared with the words: 'I do search for my aunt. Last known address, the Rookery, St Giles-in-the-Fields.' She held it up.

The gentleman was pitying. 'Dumb eh? Poor maid, poor maid.' Then his expression hardened. 'The Rookery? You don't want to go to the Rookery.'

But the girl's expression too had changed, the eyes he'd admired were dull with the obstinacy often observed in the afflicted. 'Very well, I'll show you your way, but I warn you . . .' He warned her all down Ludgate Hill to the gate and up Fleet Street. Civilization was the City: its extension into the Strand, Covent Garden, Whitehall and Westminster was still the home of gentlemen, but half-way up Drury Lane things became dubious and by Holborn, and especially St Giles, downright barbaric.

That his beloved city had no charitable alternative to offer the poor girl made his warnings increasingly angry, so that by the time they had reached Drury Lane he shouted: 'I have a care for my purse, mistress, if you have not', and stumped away, giving her no chance to thank him. After a few paces, however, he paused and watched the strange small person in its dreadful hat and boots lope out of sight. Her chances of reaching her destination without assault were slim, her chances of staying unraped once there were non-existent. Well, he'd told her, done his best, gone out of his way, couldn't think why he'd bothered. The memory of her eyes put him out of temper the rest of the night.

By a quicker route than Penitence's the Plague's carriage took itself to the Fleet Ditch by the time Penitence and her companion crossed it. It could have settled more than once, but a force stronger than itself twitched the rat on towards even greater congestions of people. It liked the habitation of people, the more crowded the better.

Finding itself in the gardens of Bedford House, it sensed there was nothing for it in these spaces. Its teeth couldn't gnaw marble and stone, it couldn't breed in roof-tiles. Its shadow elongated as it slipped along a gutter at the edge of Covent Garden Piazza. It turned left and north.

Better. Better. Thatch, and rotten wood, open cesspits, the warmth of human bodies living close. There was no point in going on; its flickering whiskers brought the message that not far away habitation thinned into fields which were no use to it.

It was glad to stop. It wasn't feeling at all well.

As her acquaintance had noted, there was a stubbornness under Penitence's apparent vulnerability which had been formed as a protection against a religion, guardians and a community demanding absolute obedience. Penitence approved of the religion, had dutifully loved her mother and grandparents — and just as dutifully grieved for their sudden death; she had done her best to conform to the community, but to preserve an unbroken spirit under such an upbringing had necessitated reserving a place in her mind and soul against the lot of them, and in that place had grown the obstinacy which had brought her three thousand miles against all advice.

All at once Drury Lane's smart roofs lowered, becoming tile or thatch rather than slate. Its traffic was as thick as it had been further back, but here it consisted of single horsemen and pedestrians, and the jollity was cruder. Penitence's mouth gaped as she was turned this way and that by the entertainment on offer. There was singing and dancing everywhere. A seven-foot giant was teetering along on stilts which put his head on a level with upper windows while a dwarf ran alongside collecting pennies in a hat. From the windows ladies showing too much of their anatomy leaned out, screaming and laughing, to try and push him off. *'She painted her face, and tired her head, and looked out at a window.* Kings II, chapter 9.'

Everywhere she looked there was evil, and, more appalling, the *enjoyment* of evil. She broke into a run. At any moment the Lord would destroy this Sodom and Gomorrah with fire.

It was darker further up, what light there was showed meaner houses and fewer people, but it was quieter and she could slow her pace. Back home she could have walked ten times as far and not felt as tired.

I'm in peril. The familiar sense of danger cut through her fatigue and was immediately trusted. She knew it well.

Penitence's twice-weekly journeys to school had involved

paddling a canoe five miles down the Pocumscut and a subsequent walk of three miles through forest. She'd carried a satchel of books and a primed flintlock. Attack by men was unheard of, unless you counted the occasional Iroquois raid, but bear, moose and wolverine, especially wolverine, posed a threat that required instant reaction to the inexplicable shadow or the leaf moving when there was no wind. Reading the signs had become an instinct that had twice saved her life. Now, here, in this dark lane, there was a wolverine.

She had no flintlock, but she slipped the knife from its sheath on her wrist in one concealed movement, as Matoonas had taught her to do.

Just as the Drury Lane beadle's nose could detect a possible charge on his parish, so the Reverend Robert Boreman, rector of St Giles-in-the-Fields, had suffered enough from Puritans in the Interregnum to smell them at forty paces. The one at his gate was young and female, but stank of bigotry. 'What do you want?'

Penitence was no more amicable towards the Reverend Boreman than he to her. To be seeking assistance at the gate of an Anglican church was nearly as bad as asking help from the Pope. However, she knew she'd been lucky to get this far. In the walk between Drury Lane and here she had been pestered, pawed and propositioned. Two women, one old, one young, had tried to enrol her for Lord-knew-what. ('Put you in the way of riches, dearie.') A man had tried to steal her purse and she had been forced to jab her knife at him.

From this high point above the river, she had looked around at the jumbled roofscape and known that unless she had a guide she was defeated. She'd made for the spire.

The Reverend Boreman groped for his spectacles and took the proffered slate to the lamp by his lych-gate. '"Penitence Hurd."' He was right, only damned Puritans could have called a child 'Penitence'. Searching for her aunt, last address St Giles Rookery. Despite himself he was touched. 'My child,' he said, 'go home. Go back to where you came from. Where *do* you come from?'

The girl retrieved the slate and wrote: 'New England.'

New England. What was wrong with the old one? Stiff-necked, hypocritical heretics calling themselves pilgrims sailing off to create their joyless Zion and plague the poor savages. New England indeed. Still, he could hardly send her back there.

'Was your aunt born here? Married here?' Another shake of the head that wobbled the ridiculous hat. No, of course not. Her aunt was probably not married at all; indeed, if this was the child of Dissenters, she was a bastard whose parents imagined that some words said over them by a magistrate rendered them married. Nothing the Puritans had done had upset the Reverend Boreman more than denying the sacraments of the wedding service. On the other hand, if the aunt was a Puritan, what was she doing in the Rookery? He found himself curious. 'Are you dumb?' Obviously, she wasn't deaf.

'Shall I try to tell him?' She was tired, it would be too hard, and she wanted no involvement with a church that had persecuted her people. Besides, he was the height and shape of the Reverend Block back home, dressed in black, white tippets to his collar just like the Reverend Block's, only older. The sooner she got away from him the sooner her stomach would stop heaving. Insistently, she pointed to the slate.

The Reverend Boreman shrugged. 'On your own head be it. I must warn you that the Rookery is the lowest sink of sin, and that if your aunt is still in it she is undoubtedly defiled or dead, probably both.' He didn't believe in sugaring the pill, and merely having to admit the existence of such a place in his parish shamed him. God knows he'd done his best. 'Ah, Peter Simkin.'

His clerk joined him at the gate. 'I'm away to alert the Searcher, Rector.'

'Peter, here is a person from the Americas trying to find her aunt. Last known address the Rookery.' The two men exchanged looks.

Peter Simkin turned to Penitence: 'What's her name?' It might be that the Rookery woman was a member of the congregation, though unlikely; precious few were.

10

As Penitence wrote, the rector said acidly: 'Our young friend from the Americas, though not dumb it seems, does not deign to speak to us.'

'"Margaret Hughes,"' read Peter Simkin. 'Plain. Also unknown.'

'Oh, take her along to the Searcher,' said the Reverend Boreman. 'If anyone knows this woman, she will.' It had been a long day and he wanted his supper. 'And don't forget to get Sexton to toll the bell and ask John Gere to dig the grave.' Reluctantly, he added to Penitence: 'If you don't find your aunt, you'd better come back.' He'd have to procure her employment, or put her in the workhouse if she was indigent, which he was sure she was.

He lingered to watch Penitence and the slightly shorter figure of his clerk disappear along the High Street into the shadows. Another bit of jetsam washed into this penance of a backwater. How long, O Lord, how long before he procured a decent parish? How had he offended? He did his best, badgering the authorities for drainage, an almshouse, more help to save souls. And what did he get? Jetsam. By the day more poor were coughed out by the overcrowded city to turn this once pleasant suburb into a Gehenna.

Whores, pimps, beggars, buggerers, playwrights, even Jews – and poor Jews at that – washed up in St Giles-in-the-Fields. Fields indeed. He remembered the fields, he'd walked there with his wife, God rest her soul. And now they were a laystall and had gained their first American Puritan. Well, she'd have to take her chance with the rest.

He strode off to the rectory and the supper provided by his housekeeper. First he washed his hands, as he always did, and wished he felt less like Pontius Pilate while doing it.

'There's a death in the Buildings, see.' The neat little clerk was brightly informative. 'Lucky for you, else you'd have had to wait for another corpse. Can't call on the Searcher except to view the corpse for the cause of death. Against the rules. Mind you, you wouldn't've waited long. They die here pretty frequent.'

Penitence could believe it. The difficulty would be not to. Her boots were fouled with the excreta, mud and rubbish of the alley they had turned into. The only light, apart from Peter Simkin's lantern, was a moon that came and went between cloud. The few shutters were closed; where they'd rotted or broken off, scraps of sacking hung between the night and the even darker interiors.

'They retire early round here,' said Simkin, 'saves candles.'

Here and there the holes emitted the cries of a baby or an altercation, but otherwise there was the quiet imposed by hopelessness. Her home had been in a wilderness miles from other human habitation and it hadn't been as silent as this. Penitence bent over in a sudden cramp that was part hunger and part homesickness for river sounds, a nightjar, her grandmother humming a psalm.

'Careful,' said Simkin, 'falling down here ain't recommended.'

They went deeper into the maze and stopped before an afterthought of a house squeezed in between two others, with a door that was at least intact, if small. The clerk hammered on it.

'Threepence a corpse,' he said to Penitence. 'Penny under the going rate, but she gets more business than most. Stand back if I was you.' He stood back himself as shuffling footsteps approached the other side of the door and it opened.

Penitence had been expecting something horrible, but even worse was the shrouding of the old woman's face so that neither then nor later did she see it, leaving her to imagine leprosy, or even a blank.

'Harrison. The Buildings,' said the clerk. 'And this young lady's looking for a Margaret Hughes, last seen in the Rookery.'

There was a wheeze from within the shawl. 'Tuppence.'

Peter Simkin turned to Penitence. 'She wants paying for finding. You got tuppence?' Penitence nodded. 'Off you go then.' He left.

After much wheezing and muttering within the house, the Searcher emerged, more be-shawled than ever and carrying a white staff. A movement of the bundle that was her head indicated that Penitence should fall in behind her and she went off at a brisk shuffle. It was almost the nastiest of all the nasty walks Penitence had taken that day. She wasn't interfered with – the few pedestrians pressed against walls as the Searcher went by – but every step took her deeper into this unclued labyrinth until they were going along tiny alleys so dark that the Searcher's white wand was the only thing visible and moved as if with a life of its own. Some inhabitant, a woman, was screaming but it was impossible to locate the sound.

This was the Rookery. As they passed each closed door, the Searcher whispered. Reluctantly, Penitence caught her up to listen. The whisper wasn't for her benefit; each building was eliciting a response of memory from this basic brain. 'Top floor, convulsions.' 'Second floor back, childbed.' 'Basement, frightened.' 'Worms, attic.'

They passed 'Palsy, third floor front', and stopped before a door. A frightened-looking man opened it and retreated before the Searcher. From outside Penitence could see a candle held over a bed in a room that contained little else. The Searcher went to the bed and drew back a cover. Penitence heard children crying and a woman's voice, weeping and pleading.

The Searcher came shuffling back to the door, followed by the man who was begging: 'It ain't the you-know. You'll say it ain't. It's rickets, she had rickets.'

'Shilling,' said the Searcher, and the man counted some coins into her hand.

As they continued up the alley, Penitence heard more wheezing. The Searcher was laughing. 'Ain't Plague, but Tom Fool thought it were.' The shawls caught sight of Penitence, the voice stopped talking to itself and addressed her: 'Rickets. Ain't Plague.' Penitence, hypnotized, shook her head. 'Rickets and hectick fever. They're frit of Plague round here. Had it bad in the 'twenties.' She pointed ahead: 'Dog Yard.'

Penitence pressed ahead into a courtyard of light and noise so welcome that it took time to absorb how sinful it was. Here, in a broken-cobbled area about sixty feet long and thirty wide, was the Rookery's largest and only professional alehouse and, therefore, its social centre. Here, every human degradation which London had forced on Penitence's attention was represented in the women drinking on the doorsteps, their knees wide apart, their mouths loose and shrieking, in the men who staggered and lolled, in the children who dabbled in the guttered sewers. A young woman sitting at an open window fed a toddler from one breast and clutched a bottle against the other. A cock-fight was exciting wagers and shouts in one corner, a dice game in another where, high above it, an altercation was in progress between two women over the washing-line strung between their windows.

Penitence saw no good in the place; she had gone beyond seeing good at all in this terrible capital city. Quick to recognize and resent disdain, the Dog Yarders didn't see much in her either. Catcalls commenting on her appearance and making suggestions as to her hat broke out — until the Searcher emerged beside her, at which they stopped.

Everything stopped. Like a small, muffled Gorgon, the Searcher hobbled through a crowd frozen in mid-movement into a tableau in which the only sound was the flutter of cocks' wings and the tap of the Searcher's wand.

Nobody followed them as they climbed steep street steps to the high north side of the Yard and stopped outside a door on the edge of it. The shawls whispered to Penitence: 'Margaret Hughes.'

Three thousand miles of anticipation, and she was here. She had expected a feeling of the momentous, but it escaped her in fatigue and confusion. She was not sure she was here at all; any reality she recognized had been left behind on Master Endicott's ship. The Searcher grabbed her arm. 'Tuppence.'

Penitence had no idea of the rate of exchange, but in the circumstances she was prepared to overpay. She felt in her satchel and brought out her smallest string of wampum. The shawls directed their attention on it, and said again: 'Tuppence.' Penitence pressed the wampum, the shawls rejected it. 'Tuppence.'

Penitence panicked. Back home this many shells, a fifth of a fathom, would be worth five shillings. True, she hadn't seen any wampum changing hands since she'd been in London, but her grandfather and other merchants had traded in little else. If its value hadn't survived the Atlantic crossing, she was in extreme trouble, unless her aunt had money, which, considering the surroundings, was unlikely.

The Searcher had turned nasty and was spitting words with which Penitence was unacquainted. Penitence held open her satchel and shrugged. 'Wampum or nothing.' The Searcher sniffed at the satchel, sniffed again and was suddenly scrabbling like a burrowing animal at earth.

Relieved that she had means to pay the old woman after all, Penitence held her off with one hand while managing to open the box inside her satchel and extract one of its carefully packed contents.

The Searcher took the pipe into her disfigured hands, sniffed the tobacco in its bowl with the reverence of a communicant receiving the host and hobbled off with it, leaving Penitence to knock on the door.

Down below, Dog Yard relaxed at the departure of the Searcher, but much of its interest remained on Penitence. She sensed a change of mood; the catcalls redoubled but with a difference. Where before the Yarders had merely resented her as an uppity stranger, now they appeared to have placed her. The mewing to which she was subjected was as derisory as the hoots had been, but more amicable. The words, as far as she could understand them, were definitely filthier, with a tinge of contempt. The Yarders seemed to have gained advantage over her.

One of the washing-line quarrellers remarked: 'I thought I seen all the quiffs there was, but that's a new one on me.' She called down to Penitence: 'Here you. Under the tile. Her Ladyship running a new line?'

Even had she been able to answer it, Penitence did not understand the question. She knocked more smartly and made a show of studying the house before her.

It was a peculiar house, the biggest in Dog Yard, and the only one in good repair from what she could see of it. In height and breadth it was reassuringly like the large farmhouses back home that the settlers of Massachusetts had built for themselves, copying the medieval halls of England. It was the wrong way round. Impatiently pacing, Penitence peered down the alleys on either side and saw that it continued irregularly backwards for at least fifty feet. Its age suggested that it had once stood in solitary grandeur, looking over the fields of St Giles, until tenements accommodating the City's overflow had sidled up on its back and front so that its southerly side was now the frontage that faced her and the Yard.

What was bizarre was the addition to this frontage, a rectangular extension of brick which stood out from the main wall of the house by what seemed only four or five unnecessary feet. It was like a shield, windowless and with a door that could have withstood a battering ram. Its only ornamentation was a red lantern hanging above the door and, along its top, which rose over half-way to the house's gable, six china medallions containing life-sized portraits of ladies. The inevitable sign protruding from above the door showed a cockerel rampant on the crust of an enormous pie, though the words beneath it read, confusingly: 'Her Ladyship'.

Presumably her aunt had gone into the catering trade, since the place didn't seem to be an inn. *What will she say when she reads my name?* Penitence got out her slate and rehearsed several enjoyable possibilities in all of which her aunt ended by weeping tears over the niece who had come to save her.

'Thy aunt fell from grace, child. We have cast her out. Let thee be silent.' Thin-lipped, her mother and her grandparents had refused to tell her anything more, always the same answer in the same words since she'd been old enough to ask.

In Puritan terms a fall from grace could involve anything: adultery, murder, dancing round the maypole, celebrating Christmas, or using starch. It must have been for one of the deeper sins, probably you-know-what. How deplorable, how shameful, how *different*.

The young Penitence had obediently condemned this fallen aunt, but her censure had been tinged with curiosity and the older she got, the more curious she became. Her own adolescent falls from grace, though petty, had made even more

16

intriguing an aunt who had fallen on a grand scale. She had begun to dream that naughty Aunt Margaret would one day arrive at the Hurd trading post; sometimes she imagined her as being rowed up the Pocumscut in a scarlet barge, dripping jewels and wickedness, sometimes as emerging from the forest, a thin, dying figure begging forgiveness with its last breath.

Whatever she needed forgiveness for, Penitence, as one of the saints of the Pure Church, had come three thousand miles to save her from it. And she needed to do it quickly. There were footsteps prancing up and down behind her in what she guessed was mimicry and might, at any moment, become attack. *Pray thee hurry, Aunt.* She knocked again. There was an impression that life was going on in the house's deeper recesses, but it wasn't coming to the door.

At last, footsteps approached from inside. The door opened, not to let Penitence in, but to allow half a dozen black-clad gentlemen out. In the glow from the shop's interior their clothes had the unmistakable sheen of richness, a phenomenon almost as sinister as the holes where their faces should have been. All of them were masked. They passed the shrinking Penitence so that she saw their glossy, contained shapes against the rags of the crowd and the untidy clutter of the Yard buildings. It flashed into her mind that these, predatory and beautiful, were the Rookery's rooks.

Migratory rooks. From the shadows around the Yard emerged a succession of attendants carrying sedan chairs; a fat one turned back. There was a glimpse of flesh and teeth as the mask said 'Most interesting, Your Ladyship.'

'Come again, my lord.' The chairs were trotted across the court, be-ringed hands through the windows scattering coins on the cobbles. In an instant Dog Yard became patched with heaps of struggling bodies.

Penitence turned to the lady in the doorway, who was a large-scale burst of colour from her black-rooted golden hair to her surprisingly tiny jewelled slippers. In between was an acreage of scarlet satin topped by black and white lace lying so low round her shoulders that Penitence's Puritan fingers twitched to hitch it up.

17

The twitch lasted until she met the lady's eyes, which were of such a light blue as to be nearly colourless, and cold enough to freeze fingers in their sockets. 'What?'

Penitence held up her slate. Her Ladyship's eyes didn't bother with it. They penetrated Penitence's bag, assessed its contents, stripped her and made an educated guess at the price of her body and soul. Her Ladyship was tired, it had been a long night, but she was a professional, and here were professional possibilities. 'Down on your luck, pippin? Come in. Who sent you?' The voice contrasted with the eyes, being reminiscent of warmed molasses. She put her arm round the mopsy's shoulders and guided her gently through the red-lit ante-chamber, fingering the bones beneath the dreadful dress. With a bit of feeding-up, there were definite possibilities, and all of them unexplored. Her Ladyship advertised virgins, but it was a long time since she'd been able to offer her customers a real one.

As they went through the double doors of the salon, she paused for the effect. The salon always impressed her novices.

It impressed Penitence, though not favourably. Here was the large hall promised by the exterior of the house, here great oak pillars that held up the roof strode its length in two rows, but they had been striped like a barber's pole in scarlet and yellow and bore gilded plaster capitals of fruit-and-vine design. Hiding the inevitable saddle beams was a much lower false ceiling of pinewood panes painted with poor execution and an overheated imagination.

A gallery ran along the four walls with its open side pillared, like a clerestory, but it obtruded so far on the left side in order to provide space for the row of rooms behind it that it gave the hall a lop-sided air. Where a ladder had once led up to the solar, there was an imposing staircase with a much-curlicued banister.

The furniture consisted of low tables, a few gilded chairs and many couches, these last a novelty to Penitence who had been taught that you lay down only when you slept. Gaudy cushions and hangings made the unexpecting eye blink.

Despite all that had been done to its dimensions and

dignity, the country house such as Penitence had grown up in was there under its tawdry paint, like a whiff of Massachusetts air detectable in cheap scent. It was occupied by young ladies relaxing in various stages of undress, but again – and this was the eerie thing – she was reminded by their poses of her grandparents and mother after a hard day in the fields. One had taken off her high-heeled shoes and was rubbing the joints of her feet, just as Grandmother used to, another was loosening her corsets and scratching, another had flopped down on the couch with her feet up and eyes closed.

Her Ladyship guided her to a couch and sat her down. A couple of the young ladies turned tired, incurious eyes in her direction.

'What's your name, pippin?'

She held up her slate, showing it round the room. It had no effect. They couldn't read. What sort of city was this that it allowed itself to turn out illiterates? She was going to have to speak, *Help me, Lord*, she would have to speak. The familiar mountain reared up in front of her. She clenched her fists, hunched her shoulders and ran at it: 'Umm P-p-p-ppp. Umm P-p-pp—' *Why didn't they call me Hannah?*

Outwardly the effort was as unsightly as it was inwardly difficult. In order to produce her first words on English soil Penitence's mouth compressed so hard that her neck cords protruded. One shoulder came up like a hunchback's, her hands clawed into her skirt as her body heaved, like a dog vomiting, to relieve itself of words.

'Ummm P-p-p-p. Umm P-p-p-p-P-Penitence Hurd.'

One of the young ladies said: 'Gawd help us. Ought to be Patience the time it takes', and there was giggling from some of the others. They began to gather round.

She never got over it. She saw compassion extended to unfortunates, she heard preachers urge charity towards the blind and the lame, but for her there were only jeers.

Nobody she'd ever met had made the mental leap to join her behind this oral barrier and realize how high it rose between her and the rest of the world. At first there might be sympathy, nearly always embarrassment, but both inevitably declined into irritation, as if her stammer were an option she had chosen in order to be annoying. Her mother, seeing the Devil everywhere, had suspected his presence in her daughter's tongue and designed a splint for it so that it stuck out of her mouth, like a gargoyle's, kept in place with strings that looped round her ears.

On and off, she'd spent months in that instrument, her tears shrinking the strings so that they cut into her cheeks.

Her Ladyship was frowning at the young ladies. 'I'll take your coat, will I, Penitence, while you tell us about it? This is Alania, this Phoebe, and this is Francesca and this is Dorinda, here's Fanny and this is Sabina . . .' She desisted in the attempt to take off Penitence's coat when the mopsy drew away. Her Ladyship had recognized her mistake; the dummy had wandered here by accident, looking for somebody. She'd need careful angling before she was landed, but it would still be worth it; the eyes alone . . . the stammer wouldn't matter. The clients wouldn't be demanding conversation.

Her Ladyship looked round into the dimness behind the pillars, and jerked her head at Job to close the doors. 'Alania, little pet, go and ask Kinyans to bring some supper. Penitence looks starved. And STOP THAT.'

The giggling ceased. Her Ladyship's fat hand patted Penitence's. The dummy was taking fright; any more and she'd run for it.

I'm in peril. Wolverines were in this appalling room. A shape, a big one, had moved out from behind the pillars and was blocking her escape.

Penitence's ignorance of life was a deficiency of upbringing, not judgement. She was naive, but she was nobody's fool. That she hadn't recognized a brothel when she saw one was because she hadn't been aware that prostitution could be wholesale. She knew of individual harlots, like Jezebel, the Whore of Babylon, Goody Manning – who'd gone into the forest with the pedlar and had her ears clipped for doing it – perhaps her own aunt, but had thought them rarities in the scheme of things. Whoring as a corporate activity hadn't arisen in Puritan Massachusetts.

She was learning. The air was heavy with the stink of sin. Sin was painted on the walls, incorporated into the pillars, steeped in the floor, sucking at her. This evil Ladyship trapped girls into you-know-whattery. The Searcher was in her pay, a procuress who had never heard of Margaret Hughes. She must get out of here.

An acolyte, Kinyans, an ugly little man, had entered the salon with trays and was setting out food that made her mouth water. Whatever was wrong in this temple of sin, it didn't extend to its kitchens. And she was famished. If she was going to have to make an escape, she wasn't going to be able to do it unless she ate.

Carefully, she watched Dorinda and the others eating, then grabbed a chicken leg for herself.

Kinyans had picked up her slate. '"I do search for my aunt. Margaret Hughes",' he read. His eyebrows went up. 'Well, well.'

'Never heard of her,' said Alania through a full mouth.

'Before your time,' said Kinyans. 'But we knew her, didn't we, Ladyship?' There was something in the man's voice. Penitence's hastily swallowed chicken caught in her throat.

'Was she one of them Cromwell shipped to the West Indies, Ladyship?' asked Sabina.

There had been a change in the room, some of its menace had withdrawn. Her Ladyship was stroking the beads around her thick, white neck and not looking at anything. *She knows. Where's my aunt?*

'Bloody Cromwell,' said Dorinda.

Penitence moved over to stand square in front of Her Ladyship.

Slowly, the woman's eyes moved into focus on Penitence's face. There was still calculation in them, they were no less cold, but it was a different calculation and a different cold. 'She's dead.'

Penitence sagged.

Her Ladyship stood up. 'Can you sew?'

'*What?*'

'Can you sew? Pull yourself together. Can you sew?'

Penitence nodded.

'I'll give you board and lodging. Kinyans, get the skivvy to make her up a bed in the attic. Dorinda, take her up and see her settled.'

'Isn't she going to——?' began Alania.

'I said take her up. I'll talk to her after.'

Penitence followed Dorinda up the curving staircase that led out of the salon because she didn't know what else to do; the object that had motivated her life these last months had gone, leaving it directionless.

Had Her Ladyship maintained her menacing sweetness, she might still have attempted to leave, but the woman's voice had reverted to a brusqueness at once more natural to it and reminiscent of the shortness with which Penitence had been addressed for most of her life. She was responding to dislike as the safer emotion. She was too tired to do anything else.

'Them's *our* rooms.' Dorinda shifted her shoulders to indicate that they were better than the attic. They were progressing along the clerestory around the top of the salon. The six or so doors leading to 'our rooms' were closed, each of them distinguished by a china name-plate which Penitence was too depressed to read.

'You're up here,' said Dorinda. She opened a door on to a tiny, curving wooden staircase. Here, on its third storey, the house reverted to an ungilded, untidy maze. The light from the candelabra Dorinda carried flickered into little passages which led off from the landing at the top of the stairs. There were unexpected windows and others that had been blocked in, steps ran up and down to different floor-levels, ceilings were low at some points, at others were replaced by the high rafters of the roof.

'The skivvy sleeps here,' said Dorinda, with disdain. She led on and lifted the latch of a small door: 'You're here.'

Penitence had to stoop to enter. Dorinda's candelabra revealed a large oblong room in which the only decoration was cobwebs. Plywood packing cases were stacked one side. The height and shape of two shuttered windows, one to her left and another in the wall opposite, suggested they had once been sack hoists. There was a faint, comforting smell of grain, but mainly the place smelled of age. Even the cobwebs were old and hung in flimsy black strings from the rafters, as if the spiders who'd spun them had died too dispirited to breed a new generation.

Behind her, Dorinda's voice said: 'And a dummy like you ain't welcome.' The door closed and her footsteps retreated, taking the light with them.

Penitence collapsed on to a packing case. Drearily, she repeated the Puritan formula for adversity. *'Count thy blessings, Pen.'* But where were they? Her aunt was dead. She had come three thousand miles to save from a fate worse than death a woman who was dead already. She felt ill. She was facing knowledge of the grossest self-deception. Her aunt hadn't had need of her, it was she who had needed, and needed badly, her aunt.

Aunt Margaret. Underneath all the opprobrium her mother and grandparents had heaped on the name, it had carried a kindness which had not been present in her mother, nor her grandparents. There had been no father to provide it; he had died fighting for Cromwell before she was born, but since he, too, had been a Hurd – her mother had married a cousin – and also a strong Puritan, it was doubtful if he would have instilled warmth into that enclosed family even if he had lived.

She knew now that in her need for parental affection she had, unconsciously, transferred it to the fancied figure of the unknown aunt. For all her fault, and through a mysterious proxy of siblings, Aunt Margaret would possess the maternalism that was lacking in her sister. As an outcast through frailty, she would have fellow-feeling for the girl who was outcast through handicap. Disguising her need as beneficence, Penitence had come three thousand miles to find love, and the aunt who should have given it had died without so much as a by-your-leave.

The door opened and a weary-looking girl came in backwards, dragging a plank bed heaped with bedding. She pulled it into the centre of the room and bad-temperedly began making it up. 'Don't help, will you?'

Penitence didn't; she was barely aware the girl was there, and when she'd gone, she sat on. What was she going to do? Suddenly she stood up, staggered to the bed, still clutching her satchel, fell down on it and went to sleep.

Chapter 2

SHE WAS in Massachusetts. In the minister's house again, in Springfield, still grieving for the death of her mother and grandparents. The Reverend Block was kneeling in prayer beside the bed, preparatory to getting into it.

She fought him off. Screaming. She was running away.

How *could* he? Every Sabbath she could remember, his voice had filled the meeting-house under the oak tree with fulminations against sin. The community had applauded his Christianity in taking her in when her grandparents' trading post had burned with her grandparents and mother in it.

Was it her? Had her gratitude been misconstrued? Had she, without knowing it, led him on? She was stuttering to Goody Fairchild and Goody Fairchild was saying she *had* led him on. The Reverend Block was a good man, one of the saints. Goody Fairchild's anger was voicing what would be the community's opinion. To believe that its minister was prey to the sins of the flesh would rend its structure; better to disbelieve Penitence of the cursed tongue, Penitence the misfit.

Running away again, she was following a trail that had been worn twenty inches below the forest floor by generations of moccasined feet. It led her to the familiar lodge filled with wood- and tobacco-smoke, to an old woman smelling of bear grease. As always, her tongue had no trouble with the sing-song of the Algonquin language. As always, Awashonks's eyes, like boot-buttons sewn into creased leather, accepted everything while condemning nothing. They hadn't condemned the Reverend Block even.

'You Owanus,' Awashonks was taking her pipe out of her

mouth to spit, 'you dam up your bodies' rivers and when they leak you curse them. He wanted. You didn't. Where is the problem?'

'It wasn't me then?'

'No. He wanted Nagret when he came here to preach his religion.'

'What did Nagret do?'

'She gave it. She liked him. She said he sweated strong.'

She was aware of nothing, warned of nothing, except relief that the Reverend Block fornicated wholesale. She was wrapping herself in deerskin, lying down to sleep the sun round in the thick, warm air of Awashonks's lodge. In the morning she would go off with Matoonas and hunt moose.

But there was no sanctuary. A deputation, led by the Reverend Block himself, had come to get her back.

'Deliver the person of Penitence Hurd to us, O Awashonks, sachem of Squakheag.' The Reverend Block was speaking with the loud precision that the Puritans used to the Indians on formal occasions.

From her hiding place behind the rock she could hear the voice as clearly as she had heard it every Sabbath at meeting.

'She is not here.'

He wouldn't believe Awashonks. He didn't. 'Deliver her or soldiers shall come and force her from thee. She has transgressed and must be punished.'

'What have I done?' What had she done? Except refuse you-know-what with the Reverend Block. Matoonas was nudging her to keep quiet.

The flames of the dancing ground's ceremonial fire were flickering on the Indians' gleaming skin and their beads and were absorbed into the matt clothes of the Puritan embassy. She had known these faces, red and white, all her life but in the upward light of the flames they had become equally monstrous.

'What do you say she has done?'

'She is a witch. Her tongue is witness to the Devil. How did the trading post burn down, killing those good people, except by her agency?'

25

'No. No. No.'

NO. NO. NO.

'Sit up.'

Penitence sat up. A large shape was blocking the light of dawn that was trying to creep in through the opened shutters of the side window. A hot beaker of milk was being pressed into her hands. 'Drink this.'

'Now then.' Her Ladyship had put on a mantua which hung straight down to her feet from the prow of her bosom. She sat down on the end of the bed, nearly tipping it. 'Who sent you here?'

Penitence searched in her bag and brought out her Bible. After the fire, her neighbours had found her grandfather's iron box among the calcified spars and ashes. Inside, among the heat-curled flakes of paper, had been a scrap on which the words 'Yr affct dautr, Margaret Hughes. The Rookery, St Giles-in-the-Fields' were just distinguishable. Below the words was a cross, against which was written: 'Margaret Hughes, her mark'. She opened the book at the beginning of the New Testament and carefully held it for Her Ladyship to see the crumbling pieces arranged on the page.

'I see. Well, she's dead. Died in the West Indies.'

Penitence was aware that harlots had been transported to the West Indies by the Commonwealth. The Puritan community in New England had rejoiced and sent letters of praise to Cromwell for cleansing Old England of its sinners. But there was strangeness here. Her Ladyship was lying. The Squakheag, who had developed lying to an art form, had taught her to listen for the nuance that bespoke falsehood and she'd just heard it.

It may be true she's dead. It is not true about the West Indies. She blinked enquiry at Her Ladyship.

'A letter,' said Her Ladyship, defiantly. 'Friend of hers out there sent me a letter and wrote she was dead. So she's dead. How old are you?'

Her Ladyship's face was intimidating. If Penitence hadn't seen the mouth stretched into a smile the night before, she would have thought the heavy, handsome flesh incapable of any expression other than the bitterness that came naturally to it. Her Ladyship's head cocked sideways as if, whatever it was, she didn't believe it. Her pale eyes looked indifferently out through barricades of fat at the omnipresent frailty of mankind.

'You can speak,' said Her Ladyship impatiently, as Penitence drew the figure 18 in the dust of the floor, 'I heard you. So speak.'

Compelled against her better judgement, heaving, grimacing, going into ludicrous diversions around words that began with 'p', 'b' and 'c', Penitence answered questions about her parentage and her reason for coming to England.

'Very well,' said Her Ladyship at last, getting up. 'You shall have lodging and two meals a day. In memory of Margaret Hughes.' She paused for a moment. 'But for that you do our mending and making, and when we're busy you'll serve the clients with their drink.'

Penitence shook her head. 'I'll s-s-sew, th-though I'll s-serve no s-s-sinners. And I'll n-not w-w-work on the S-Sabbath.'

'You'll do as you're bid.'

'I'll n-n-not s-sin.'

'Sin?' Her Ladyship's hand clutched the neck of Penitence's gown and almost lifted her off the bed. 'What do you know of sin?' If the woman's face had been intimidating before, now it was dreadful. 'Sin's hunger. Sin's cold. Sin's rape. Sin's dying out there on the streets and nobody caring. Don't you talk to me of sin, you sanctimonious little bitch.'

Penitence shrank away from the breath that was being puffed into her nostrils. Her Ladyship released her with a shove that sprawled her back on the bed. 'Penitence,' she said, and spat. 'They called you Penitence, did they? I'll give you penitence. You'll work for your penitence, like I did.' The room vibrated as she stamped out of it and slammed the door.

Behind her, a wavering voice said: 'N-not on the S-Sabbath, I won't.'

Penitence spent most of the morning on her knees in search of the Lord's guidance, and the afternoon sitting upright arguing with it.

At first the Lord was adamant: 'Thee shall leave this house of abomination on the instant.'

'I agree with thee, Lord. Where shall I go?'

'Just go,' said the Lord, 'I shall provide.'

Desperately, she wanted to believe him. But her careful soul and its experience of the London streets demanded a more realistic assurance. As she had learned, wampum was not in currency in Old England. Therefore, she was moneyless. She was also homeless and friendless. Her only allies were red men and women three thousand miles away, but to go back to them would put them in peril. It would imperil her even more. While the Reverend Block was alive it was impossible for her to return to New England; his assertion that she had burned down her grandparents' house would put her on trial, and who would believe her stammering word against the word of that stalwart in the Lord, Ezra Block?

'I might starve to death, Lord.'

'Then die and receive eternal life.'

But she'd only had eighteen years of the old one. In agony, she looked around the attic. There was no comfort for her here, but there would be less on the streets. Would it endanger her soul to stay for a while, until she could find respectable employment? Her Ladyship had as good as promised that she would not force her into you-know-whattery, and on this matter Penitence was prepared to believe her. Besides, for all her animosity – and animosity had always been a constant in Penitence's life – Her Ladyship had known Aunt Margaret, indeed seemed to have been under some sort of obligation to her. To leave here would be for ever to break contact with that fancied, though now departed, figure of whom she would still like to know more.

'Joseph served the Egyptians when he was in thrall to Pharaoh, Genesis, chapter 39,' she pointed out, 'and his soul retained its honour.'

'True,' admitted the Lord.

'Potiphar's wife didn't tempt him into you-know-whattery, nor shall Her Ladyship tempt me.'

'True again,' admitted the Lord.

'If I have no truck with its sinners, if I observe the Sabbath, if I leave as soon as circumstance permits ...' promised Penitence.

'Thee hast no other choice,' agreed the Lord.

Her Ladyship left Penitence to her attic all day, knowing hunger to be the best compromiser of principles. So it was. When Mary, the Cock and Pie's maid-of-all-work, put her head round the door at five o'clock and said: 'Her Ladyship says come and get your peck', Penitence followed her down-stairs — to find that Her Ladyship herself had compromised. She was to work in the kitchen with Kinyans, releasing Mary for the more immediately sinful task of serving the Cock and Pie's clients with their drink.

'And anyway' — this was dark-haired Dorinda, as they all ate their dinner round the big table in the kitchen — 'our gentlemen don't want a crow like her handing them their malmsey, do they, Ladyship?'

'Civility don't cost nothing, Dorinda,' said Her Ladyship, levelly.

Dorinda's grimace indicated that she found it expensive, but from then on she kept her observations to herself, contenting herself with a covert kick at Penitence's ankle.

Penitence kicked back. At school in Springfield, where she'd been bullied by the best, she'd learned that turning the other cheek merely got that one hit as well. Besides, a true Puritan boot could inflict more damage than a harlot's slipper. She munched on while Dorinda's eyes watered.

'She'll need a change of duds, though, won't she, Ladyship?' asked Phoebe. 'Hers ain't suitable, and besides they're dirty.'

Suitable for what? Penitence clutched the collar of her best durance coat more closely to her neck. Travel-stained it might be, but a wash-tub could better that, and she wasn't exchanging its bulwark thickness for the flimsy drapes of her fellow-diners.

'We wear raiment, Phoebe, not duds,' corrected Her Lady-ship. 'Penitence shall be provided with cloth of her choosing. No spitting, Sabina. And Fanny, we do not wipe greasy hands on the table. What are the finger bowls for?'

Penitence, who'd thought they were for thin clear soup, was glad she hadn't yet had time to quaff hers. She was confused by the manners in evidence, even while she was prepared to condemn them as effete. The girls were skilled in the use of the fork, an art still in its infancy in Massachusetts. They dabbed their mouths with clean linen napkins. They drank — from glasses, not beakers — with the little finger elegantly raised. All this, she saw, was in close imitation of Her Ladyship, whose eye was quick to notice a breach in etiquette.

Even more confusing was the conversation. These females were preparing for a night's pursuance of the most abominable of sins, but instead of the lewdness she had expected, Her Ladyship led them on to topics ranging from the weather to the proposed war with the Dutch.

'Is the Dutch the same as the Frogs?' asked Fanny.

'More attention, Fanny, please,' said Her Ladyship. 'Supposing the Dean chooses you again tonight? Suppose he wants to discuss the war? What'll you say?'

'If he does what he done last time, discussing won't come into it,' said Fanny. It was the first reference to their trade, the first confirmation that it *was* their trade, and it appalled Penitence by its lightness. She studied Fanny's round, young features for the mark of Satan and failed to find in them anything more diabolical than oafishness.

Her Ladyship rapped on the table. 'May I remind you ladies it's Saturday? Tableau night. And His Lordship has requested "The Savage".'

There was a general groan. 'Not "The Savage", Ladyship,' said Phoebe, 'them feathers gives 'em ideas.'

From the bottom of the table Job complained: 'And that tannin don't half aggravate my pimples, Ladyship, and weeks 'a wear off.'

'Then set to it, young man. There's the dais and all to get ready.'

Penitence had been at a loss to fit Job into the scheme of things. At one point her neighbour at the table, Phoebe, the most friendly of the bawds, had nodded her head in his direction and said: 'Job's our apple-squire', which left Penitence no wiser. In the shadows of the salon his vast frame had been unnerving, a troll, but the thin, high, unexpected squeak of a voice that came out of his mouth would have shamed any self-respecting troll, while direct candlelight revealed that, though of an alarming brown colour, he was only a little older than herself with an amiability of expression that bordered on the vacuous.

Next to him, Mary, the skivvy, was bouncing up and down with the first animation Penitence had seen in her. 'Can I be the Maiden, Ladyship? Can I?'

'No.'

Mary relapsed into a sulk. 'I obliged last week.'

'We was busy. Francesca will be the Maiden.'

Dorinda said nastily: 'Francesca's always the bloody Maiden.'

Penitence didn't understand what they were talking about, but if Francesca was the girl opposite her, fair-haired and delicately boned, she would be the natural choice to imperson- ate a maiden. The other female faces round the table, even Mary's, though the skivvy could have been no more than fourteen, wore a hard-bitten awareness which, Penitence sup- posed, was the result of sinning. Francesca's had the ethereal absent-mindedness of an angel. *Surely, she be not a harlot.*

Francesca turned her head towards Dorinda and opened her lovely mouth: 'Fuck yourself, Dory.'

When supper was over and the two of them were left clearing the table, Kinyans caught Penitence's glances around the kitchen. 'What you staring at, Goggles? Didn't expect this, did you?'

She hadn't. The place was as well kept, larger and better equipped than her grandmother's. Like all the best farmhouse kitchens, its windows faced east and north, though where, presumably, they had once looked over fields they now faced brick walls and chimneys. The west wall contained a big open fireplace flanked by two brick ovens above which hung every conceivable form of pan and cover, kettle, trivet, skillet, skewer, rake, sieve and mould, all of them burnished to a shine. Hams were smoking in the recesses of the chimney, herbs hung in branches from overhead beams.

Hastily, to show she was unimpressed by anything in this house of sin, she reassumed the disdain which had become her natural expression since she'd entered it. It annoyed Kinyans into giving her a tour of his kingdom. From what he had learned of Penitence's background from Her Ladyship, he was pleased to employ the fiction that the settlers of the New World had adopted a life of savagery among the Indians. Poking an aggrieved finger into her arm at each revelation, he introduced her to seven variations of roasting jacks and spits, 'No gobbling your meat raw here', the salting-table, the brine tubs, the dough trough, and 'one oven for pastries. See? P-ay-strees. And another oven for bread. What d'you redshanks do? Wind flour and water round a stick and toast it?'

Penitence thought of her grandmother's manchet, white as a swan's breast and as soft, of the Indians' hundred ways of cooking corn, all of them delicious.

Leading off from the kitchen was a two-roomed larder, one for an extensive range of ales and wines as well as butter and milk, the other, which was icy-cold, hung with fowls, fish and joints of meat. The cold – and this *was* impressive – came from the mouth of a large well.

'Yah,' crowed Kinyans, at last seeing the effect, 'had to scoop your water out the stream, didn't you?'

They hadn't, but during the course of her life she must have tramped hundreds of yoked miles to fetch and carry from the inconveniently placed well down by the vegetable patch. On the other hand, she spotted glaring omissions from the Cock and Pie's utilities. Where was the laundry? The brewhouse? The hen-run? And where was the privy?

Returning to the kitchen she stepped out through its back door. Separated from the houses around by a high brick wall were a few square yards of sour earth being made sourer by a family of cats. A spike-topped gate stood open to the alley on her left and revealed what had been playing a discordant counterpoint to the wholesome fugue of the kitchen. A laystall was niched into the wall of the house opposite spilling rotted vegetables, flies and human excreta into the alley itself.

As she watched, a cat jumped on a dark, sinuous shape and carried the rat back into the Cock and Pie yard to gnaw it.

Can I suffer this? Could she? It was not the filth she objected to but its proximity. Back home the privy had been a decent little lean-to, thirty yards away from the house, containing a bench with backside-shaped holes through which one voided one's waste into the stream that took it, chuckling, into the Pocumscut which in turn pounded it down the falls and loftily swept off its minuscule remnants to the great Connecticut River and the sea. Back home she could stand at the kitchen door to look out on to hundreds of miles of virgin forest and sniff an air full of pine and balsam. Even when they'd locked her in the wood cellar for some peccadillo or another, she'd known that outside the darkness was the space of a near-empty continent.

Walls, excreta, rats and cats moved in to form a box, enclosing her, covering her face. She began to gag.

'Enjoying yourself?' shouted Kinyans. 'Get in here and work.'

The Cock and Pie catered, in food, drink and women, for the carriage trade, or, rather, the sedan-chair trade — carriages finding it difficult to manoeuvre in the alleys that led to it. Penitence had thought Her Ladyship's references to deans and lords to be pretentious nicknaming. Kinyans disabused her. As they worked, he elaborated at length on the fact that the clientele came from what he called 'the high-game', much of it ecclesiastic.

'Here, your hands cold? Then rub them pastry crumbs. Fine, mind. Only last week the Bishop, he says to me, Kinyans, he says, your pastry's ambrosia bedecked with gold. And that's a proper bishop. And the Archdeacon, he's one for my pernollys. Kinyans, he says, you keep fatiguing your rolling pin on these little coffins, he says, for no egg has a finer burial. That's noble, that is. No reason why pulpit-drubbers shouldn't have their froiseys same as other gentry.'

There was no mention of girls, of what went on in the

salon and the bedrooms. To hear Kinyans, his cooking was the only reason gentlemen visited the Cock and Pie at all. Penitence could have forgiven them if it had been. The man was an artist.

While Penitence kneaded, sieved, stoked and sweated, instruments jumped into Kinyans's knobbled hands like magic. A cut, a twist and he'd made a pastry lattice fine as lace. A woodpecker rat-a-tat of chopping, and parsley, sage and mint turned into emerald powder.

Brought up on sustaining, wholesome Puritan cookery she looked amazed on his quivering orange-flavoured creams, the virginal junkets, the godcakes, slices of golden-fried batter on cherries, the pale toffee-coloured gauffres, the oysters, crayfish on their beds of watercress, prune-stuffed chicken slices on their sallet, sticky gingerbread slabs stuck with gilt-headed cloves, the amber marvel he called 'Open Apple Tart After The Pig'.

As Mary piled them on trays to take them through to the salon where artificial welcoming cries from the girls indicated that their clients were arriving, Penitence resisted the temptation to snatch. *Devil's food*, she thought, even as she drooled. To titillate sensual appetite, not to supply good nourishment; finger food for dalliance, sin's platter — else why should it tempt her into this gastronomic equivalent of lust?

Watching her as she sanded down the chopping block, using elbow grease and both hands, as they cleared up, Kinyans said grudgingly: 'They taught you to work, them redshanks, I'll say that. Come here. I got something for you.'

The Reverend Block had said much the same thing, in much the same tone. Carefully, Penitence edged round the table to put it between her and the cook. Kinyans advanced and held out his hand, to reveal he was offering nothing more sinister than a savoury wafer. Loftily, Penitence shook her head. It would enhance her credit with the Lord to deny herself something that was at this very moment being partaken by sinners, however delicious. Indeed, the more delicious, the more credit.

Kinyans was stung. 'Don't you go lifting your nose at my

froiseys, Miss Prinkum-Prankum. Don't lift your nose at any of us. Know where you'd be if Her Ladyship hadn't taken you in? In the shitten-cum-shites. She knows. She's been there, her and me. Two Somerset dumplings lacking gravy.' He was whipping himself up. 'Iffen she'd turned up her nose, we'd be there yet and I ain't having a vinegar-pissing bare-bones like you look down on her or me. She done what she had to, and she done it wonderful. She's as rare a woman as ever twanged and the day you better her will be when dead men fart . . .'

The violence of his anger took Penitence aback, even while she decided it was defensive. *Thee is ashamed, Master Kinyans. And rightly.* It was time she went to bed. She lit a candle and went.

The route to her attic from the kitchens was by way of a cupboard staircase that came out on the north end of the clerestory. The walkway was in deep shadow but down below there was light, tobacco smoke and the quiet that had human breath in it. They were fornicating down there. Should she look? A true Puritan would pass right along, eschewing the sight of fornication. But what exactly did you do when you fornicated? You-know-what, of course, but what else? She peered over.

She had expected scenes from the farmyard; what she saw was surprisingly sedate. Half a dozen or so men were lounging on the couches, all fully and finely dressed. Two of them wore masks, the others had abandoned them to display faces that were no better and no worse than she had seen judging cattle at Springfield market. They were all old, her grandfather's age, fiftyish. One was older than that, white-haired, gently featured, not unlike the Reverend Trubridge at Hartford. The Bishop? The Dean? She could imagine his ascetic face above a pulpit sorrowfully condemning the sin of an adoring congregation.

Her Ladyship was holding a lighted taper to a pipe being smoked by a man whose fat jowls bulged from around the edges of his mask. Dorinda, looking bored, was eating a froisey. The Cock and Pie women, Penitence was relieved to see, had their clothes on, though Fanny and Sabina had regrettably loosened the front of their gowns and seated

35

themselves on two male laps, which they were kneading in a desultory way.

None of them was being paid attention. The men's eyes were fixed on something hidden from her view by the clerestory's overhang. The fat man's masked jaw was so slack his pipe drooped. The ascetic appeared to be contemplating his God. There was a fixed, masculine, breathy silence which made Penitence uncomfortable, reminding her of the Reverend Block before he'd jumped.

Quietly, she crept along the clerestory and leaned over the balustrade to see what godlessness was commanding such concentration.

At the head of the salon a dais had been slid in the space between the staircase and wall and on it, lit by sconces, were Job and Francesca.

She had been expecting some awful idolatry. *Oh, what nonsense.* Francesca, in wispy white, was stretched on the dais, her hands raised in steepled prayer as if in terror of the figure that bent over her with upraised whip. The impression of fear was abated by her expression which, though lovely, was as bland as it had been at dinner. Penitence wondered how, looking at Job, she could keep a straight face at all.

A bear-skin was slung over one shoulder of his undoubtedly magnificent, if smeary, torso which, in this light, shone orange. His bottom half was in tights, strings of beads hung everywhere, and on top of his shaved head had been stuck a large, somewhat wobbly, plume of yellow feathers. Another plume stuck out from his belt at the back, as with a cock's tail. If the grimace on his face was meant to be threatening, it wasn't succeeding. He looked like a badly pruned laburnum.

What nonsense. Her contempt was complete. How could presumably educated men contemplate such mummery to excite themselves? She knew instinctively that was what they were doing; there was a heat rising from the salon that had nothing to do with temperature.

What sort of men took pleasure in a woman threatened? For, despite his absurdity, Job was meant to look threatening. Apart from the whip there was a tomahawk in his belt . . . a tomahawk. *He's meant to be an Indian.* She gripped the balustrade and a great cry came up in her throat. 'N-n-no. They're n-n-not—'

Her Ladyship's head turned up and a cold beam from her eyes sliced across Penitence's open mouth. 'Go to bed, pippin,' she said softly.

As Penitence turned away, she glimpsed Dorinda knuckling her temple, indicating that they had been interrupted by a madwoman.

She limped into her attic, put the candlestick on the floor, and lowered herself on to her bed as if she'd been physically wounded. Nothing she'd seen since she came to this benighted country had lacerated her soul as deeply as the travesty she'd just witnessed, implicating in its tawdriness an innocence which its audience wasn't fit to understand.

She was homesick for them. She had loved them so much; it had taken exile to realize that they were all she *had* truly loved.

The candlelight showed the dust on the elm floorboards and gave distorted shapes to the saddle beams overhead. Knowing the power of her memory, she had tried not to dwell on thoughts of home, afraid she would be undone, but they crept in with the shadows . . .

She was in the threshing barn, the playhouse and refuge of her childhood. She could hear the voices of the neighbours and the swish of flails as they helped thresh the Hurd grain. Sun streamed through the barn across the threshing floor and on to the notches cut on the cruck to mark the passage of time and tell her grandfather when to call a halt for dinner. When they went she did not go with them, but climbed up into the straw manger, watching the chaff float in the sunbeams, letting herself turn into the eagle god, Tookenchosin, so that she could flap through the door and up over the orchard until she circled above the river.

It was a magic river, the only one in Massachusetts to flow northwards. Her wings shovelled her up and forwards until she rode the wind without effort and it was the river that ebbed away beneath her. The smell of its depths and the warm pools where weed grew drifted up to the tiny holes above her fierce nose.

Below her a red-brown figure stood on a rock in absolute stillness, its back in a lovely curve as it held a fish-spear poised above the water which reflected it. That would be Wahunsona. Further along, Wetatonmi was singing to a birch tree as she stripped it of its bark to cover her canoe. The Squakheag sang explanations and apologies to trees they were about to hurt.

Now she was high above the Squakheag village on the wide bank where the river began its turn east. From up here the lodges of the village looked like little brown chrysalises. She began the circles of her descent out of cold air into that warm, wood-smoked, bear-greased fellowship.

Oh God, oh God. She shouldn't have allowed herself to go back. She was being pierced not only by homesickness, but remorse. Why hadn't she enjoyed them more while she'd had them? There'd always been the remove of superiority, a weighting-down by her responsibility to spread the Word of the Lord among the savages.

With her status among her own kind so low, she had tried to lord it over the Squakheag, imagining herself walking down the main, and only, street of Springfield leading a file of red men and women converted to the pure religion by the fluency of Penitence Hurd.

It hadn't happened. She had preached to them, often translating word for word the latest of the Reverend Block's sermons. They had listened with their usual courtesy and then told her of their own gods, who could fly, who walked on four legs and conversed with humans and beasts alike. As far as interest went, the Squakheag won every time. Her starved imagination fell on their stories like a wolf on a leg of pork.

'If thee must make friends of the tawnee, Penitence Hurd, let it be the praying tawnee, not the savage,' said her mother. But it was the savages who were fun.

The praying Indians were merely diminished versions of the Puritans who had converted them. They lived in broken-down huts on the edge of white villages, wore the Puritans' cast-offs, attended services at the meeting-house and shouted obedient hallelujahs. The Puritans patronized them, used them as labourers and fined them when they got drunk, which they frequently did.

The unchristened Indians lived in their own places, outnumbering the whites, hunting their old trails, tilling their fields, skimming up and down their rivers, interlacing the New World with an ancient ownership which uneasily reminded the Puritans that, though the Lord had provided them with Zion, they were still interlopers in it.

There had been goodwill on both sides, despite the knowledge, perhaps because of the knowledge, that it was fragile. Her grandfather had paid a fair price for the land on which he'd built his trading post, as the General Court of Massachusetts had insisted he should.

But the two cultures were impossible to reconcile. The Squakheag, like other Indian tribes, were incapable of understanding the Puritan concept of land ownership. How could earth and water belong to anybody? You hunted it, fished it, tilled it, but you couldn't keep it to yourself.

When she was six her grandfather had taken her downriver to view the pasture he'd bought the year before, and found Umpachala and his family weeding the Indian corn they had planted on it.

Her grandfather prayed for patience. 'Tell these heathens this is my pasture.' He had never mastered Algonquian. Penitence delighted in a language in which she didn't stutter and had learned it from the post's Indian customers almost before she could speak English. She sang: 'My grandfather reminds you, O my uncle, that he paid Awashonks for this land.'

Umpachala had acted amazement, staggering back with his arms out wide. 'He was not using it, little one. How, therefore, was it his?'

The incident passed without trouble that time because the Squakheag were suppliers of the furs Ezekiel Hurd sold in his trading post. He was an ambitious man and in depending on the Squakheag for much of his business he was forced to depend on Penitence. More than once he kept her away from school to take her with him into Indian territory so that she could interpret trade agreements. When he was overtaken by the rheumatics which plagued his later years, he sent her in alone. Her mother and grandmother disapproved, and the Reverend Block had warned against it. 'Fraternizing with the heathen imperils the child's soul, Ezekiel.'

'The Lord has freed the child's tongue to talk easily with the heathen,' Penitence's grandfather pointed out. 'Through her I may spread the Word among them. And wilt thou deny me the instrument He has provided in order that I may flourish in this wilderness?' The Reverend Block would have done so if he could, but Ezekiel was a powerful man in the community. The neighbours were censorious at first, though they got used to it and even called on Penitence themselves when they needed some translation. They were frontiersmen; sexual demarcations broke down where all hands, whether male or female, were needed. Tagging women as the weaker sex was difficult in a country where they laboured in the fields and had to carry guns against depredations from bear, an enraged moose or an Iroquois raiding party.

And it had to be acknowledged that socializing with the Squakheag, while it would do Penitence no moral good, wouldn't harm her physically. Rape of a white woman was unknown; they occasionally beat their own women – and as frequently got beaten back – but there was a strong taboo against rape. It was one of the few crimes of which the Puritans couldn't accuse even the dreadful Iroquois.

Already set apart by her stutter, through her liking for the Indians, and theirs for her, Penitence increased the suspicion in which her community held her. She was peculiar. One might trade with the savages: one did not have to be sociable. Her classmates called her 'Squaw-squaw Pen'.

Denied companionship by her own kind, she found it among the Squakheag who called her Taupowau, the wise talker, and adopted her into the tribe.

At the end they'd offered to fight for her.

They had sat in a circle outside Awashonks's lodge – Indians always made a circle – Awashonks, Penitence, Matoonas, Sosomon, the chief, and Quequelett. Sosomon was still angry at the Reverend Block's threat to bring soldiers. 'He has insulted me, the bandy-legged *wotawquenange*.'

'He insulted *me*,' said Penitence. She was trying to maintain the calm necessary to an Indian council, but she was beginning to panic. The fire at the trading post had killed her family and might well kill her by extension. The Puritan community had known her all her life. It hadn't liked her much, but it couldn't, she was sure it couldn't, be made to believe she was a witch. Could it?

It had been a bad year. A murrain had killed a third of the cattle, lack of rain had rusted the wheat, there had been a string of accidents. The Springfield community was nervous. Even before the fire the Reverend Block had said the Lord was punishing them, ascribing it to the usual transgressions, sabbath-breaking, unclean thinking, etc., but if he now put it to the congregation that the cause was due to a witch in its midst . . .

The sun was coming up over Pemawachuatuck, outlining the twisted mountain in a fringe of yellow. Women were lighting their breakfast fires and the smoke was rising in undisturbed threads all over the village.

'Do the Owanus kill witches?' asked Awashonks.

'Yes.' They'd burned one over the other side of the Bay Colony the year before. The woman had also been a heretic, a Quaker, and her execution had been greeted with general approval. Now Penitence panicked. 'He can't. He knows I'm not. He knows I didn't fire the house. It was an accident. I wasn't there. I was here. Grandmother was always knocking candles over.'

Young Matoonas leaped up. 'I am a *pniese*. I drank the bitter herbs, disgorged, and drank them again in my own vomit. I have made covenant with the god Hobbamock. I am known by my courage and boldness. I shall challenge the Owanus' priest to combat with hatchets to prove my sister's honour.'

'Oh, be quiet,' everyone said. He was Penitence's spiritual younger brother, he'd taught her hunting, fishing, woodcraft; she loved him, but he could be a pain when he started boasting.

'He can't burn me,' Penitence said again. 'Can he?'

'He's frightened of you,' said Awashonks. 'He might.'

He might. The Puritans could not allow the impropriety of one of their number living among Indians. They were forcing the Reverend Block to get her back, but Awashonks was right — he was afraid she would denounce him as a lecher. He had to get in his own denunciation first.

The council relapsed into silence. She smelled wood-smoke, dung, river, the grease on her companions' hair. She was being isolated here by her own people. They'd trained her to feel revulsion for these Indians and sometimes she did. She felt it now. Sosomon looked ridiculous with black paint on his face to disguise his amiability; Matoonas was ridiculous in his pride in an initiation which involved beating his shins with a stick until he could hardly stand, running through snow from sun to sun and drinking his own drugged vomit. And how could she trust in the wisdom of Awashonks, an old woman who wore a sachet of asafoetida round her neck to ward off evil spirits?

Sosomon said: 'Hear me. Taupowau is my adopted grand-child. She has helped us in the past and now she appeals for help. If the soldiers come to take her away, we shall fight for her. I have spoken.' But like everybody else, he looked at Awashonks out of the corner of his eye and waited to see what she said.

'She can stay and we will fight,' said Awashonks. She had the high voice that belonged to very old women and very small children. 'If that is what she wants.'

Down on the river bank the calls of waders were breaking into the nothingness of dawn. The sky hadn't yet gained colour and the moon was an eerie disc waiting to disappear. Penitence dragged her eyes away from it to look at the face of Awashonks the sachem. *She looks like a pickled onion.*

It will be war, said Awashonks's button eyes. Neither side wants it: each side knows it will come. Sooner or later white and red will become tired of wondering how much better it would be if the other disappeared. Something will snap the tension in which we exist. Will it be you?

The Puritans would win. Awashonks had always known it; Penitence knew it in that moment. They might be fewer in number, but their intensity was greater. So was their god. Perhaps not now, certainly not over her, but soon the untidy duality of culture in which she had grown up would disintegrate and out of it would come a neat, unvaried world.

If she went away now and left them all behind she wouldn't see it happen. If she didn't see it, it wouldn't happen.

Politely, she'd got up and declined their offer. She'd thanked them. 'But I shall go back to the Old Country and search for my aunt.'

They had equipped her with the bead bag and packed it with pipes and their best tobacco, with the small hunting bow Matoonas had taught her to use, with Sosomon's best knife and all the wampum they had.

The Farewell had taken an entire day. She'd sat impatiently by the fire in the ceremonial ring while they danced the Quatchet, the going-away dance. At the feast they'd fed her with sustaining food, sutsguttahhash with green squash, Jerusalem artichokes with walnuts, fish chowder with wild leeks, and juicy, black thimbleberries.

Hurry, hurry. Let me go before you disappear.

That night she'd lain down on the wide shelf that ran along three sides of Awashonks's lodge, watching the light from the embers of the fire outside on the crazy patterning of baskets, gourds, turtleshell scoops and baked clay pots hanging from the rafters, the fetishes of children's gods. The silence from the mound of blankets on the far-side shelf suggested that Awashonks couldn't sleep either.

In the morning she and Matoonas had loaded his canoe with beaver pelts and gone north to the river's confluence with the Quintatucquet where they'd turned south and slipped past the tiny Puritan settlements on the banks until they reached the estuary.

Master Endicott, an old trading partner of her grandfather, had given her passage in return for the beaver pelts. The Lord re-established Himself among the pretty, white spires of the meeting-houses standing against the enamel blue of the sky.

His commands were audible in the Customs bells ringing out to announce ships' arrivals and departures and in the guns from the blockhouse warning incoming vessels to anchor for inspection.

Returned to the society of black-clad, high-hatted men and women, she'd become ashamed of the heathenish bead pectoral on Matoonas's bare chest and the eagle's feather drooping from his hair, and had refused to let him see her off. She'd given him one wave as he'd started the long journey back up the Quintatucquet and then turned away.

The Penitence now lying on an attic bed moaned in spiritual pain at that Penitence's ingratitude.

Somebody else moaned, as if in sympathy. She sat up. There was squeaking too; steady rhythmic squeaking like a bed-frame protesting when you jumped up and down on it. She got out of bed and picked up her candle. The noise was coming from beneath her floorboards, from the next floor down where . . . oh, where the harlots' bedrooms were.

The moans became a wail, then an excited crescendo of profanity.

Penitence covered her ears to shut out the sound. *Obliterate them, Lord. Send down Thy bolt and pierce these sinners in their uncleanness. Punish these deans and bishops who call the Indians savages.*

She fell on her knees. *And, Lord, in Thy infinite mercy, guard the people of the Squakheag from all harm.*

Though she'd been late going to bed, Penitence, commanded by the habit of a lifetime, woke up as the night sky began to respond to a sun still below the horizon. During her dreams the previous day's experiences had enmeshed into an almost frantic need to be clean.

I must wash. This attic, her clothes, her very soul were mired.

She got up, used her chamber pot, then, having wrapped herself in a blanket, carried it downstairs, feeling her way with her other hand.

The greyness coming through the high, east windows of

the salon lighted her way along a ghostly clerestory. The place smelled of tobacco, scent and food. The doors of the harlots' rooms were shut. Were the male fornicators still in them? Did they stay all night or did they return in the early hours to their palaces and cathedrals?

She went through the door at the far end, locating by the snores the room where Kinyans and Job slept, and negotiated the dark cupboard stairs to the kitchen where the embers of a fire in the grate threw out warmth and glow. Something soft touched her leg and she saw that the cats had been allowed into the kitchen and were waiting for her to let them out. Putting the pot on the floor, she drew back the bolts and smelled the air that might have been fresh before it passed the laystall. There was utter silence from the buildings around her, re-emphasizing the Rookery's godlessness; by this time back home the trading post would have been awake and working.

Cautiously, she crept out into the alley, emptied her pot and left it in the yard while she went into the cold larder to draw water from its well. She returned to the yard and scoured out her pot.

She drew two more buckets from the well, stoked the fire, poured the water into a cauldron and hung it from a jack to warm. Wondering again where the Cock and Pie did its laundry, she sniffed out a clove-scented tub in a cupboard and took a ball of its storax soap.

When the water was ready she lugged it upstairs, bolted her door, stripped, plunged her head into one of the buckets and washed herself from top to toe. After she'd finished she set her undergarments, cap and dress to soak and put on the fresh ones she'd brought in her satchel from America. She felt better; cold, damp – she'd had to rub herself down with the blanket – but better.

The horrors that had manifested themselves the previous night had changed her mind yet again. *I must go.*

But Penitence Hurd had a careful soul. Undoubtedly she was in the frying pan of Hell; however, before she jumped out of it, she had to be sure what temperature of fire awaited her.

She went to her unglazed west window and opened its

shutters. Less than six feet away the upper storey of a house loomed towards her. It contained a shuttered window exactly facing hers. She leaned out, looking north along the alley between the houses, and saw it passed the Cock and Pie's back gate and the laystall before losing itself among more houses. In the other direction were the steps leading down into Dog Yard.

She padded over to the south window. For a moment, as she opened its shutters, she thought she was again facing a brick wall, this time only three feet away. She stepped up and out on to the platform to find that in fact she was on a balcony. The wall, now waist-high, was a parapet formed by the upper part of the Cock and Pie's peculiar frontage; immediately below her were the medallions, she could see the curve of their blue, pottery tops. Further below and to her left was Dog Yard, but a great deal more compelling than that was the view.

The Cock and Pie was the tallest building in the Rookery, and its parish of St Giles the highest point of the West End. The prospect before her, beyond a rickety roofscape, was a panorama of London.

On her few visits to Boston with her grandfather, its multiplicity of white-spired churches had been impressive enough; she saw now that it had been a puppy. What lay before her here was the splendid, muscled adult, a coiled, silver-scaled dragon of a city.

The sun rising like a giant orange was giving the morning air such veil-like texture that she could almost rub it between her fingers. Here and there were open spaces where the tops of autumnal trees provided palettes of colour. In between, stacked geometrical confusions of roofs became denser as her eye was led east to where, loomed over by the cathedral and the prissy uprightness of the Tower, they became a squeezed mosaic held by the mould of the City walls. Only the Thames had clear definition; along its bank directly to her south, the streets and gardens were indistinct in a haze from which emerged the chimneys and cupolas of the Strand's palaces.

She was transfixed by the sense of being waited for. In one

of these magical towers there lay an expectation, some marvel, something that accorded to an unknown capability within herself if she could only find out what it was.

But not yet. Contempt had gone, to be replaced by unwilling respect. Sinful it might be, but it was the sin of the very old, a city negligent with wisdom and riches, a city with too much history to care what anybody thought of it, and still worth ferreting in for the wonders it contained.

She felt negligible, provincial, yet excited. To discover whatever it was that beckoned her would need sophistication; London was excluding her and, by excluding her, stimulating the desire to join . . .

Could she start from here?

Unwillingly, she looked down to see if Dog Yard had been improved by daylight. It hadn't.

It was too early in Penitence's experience for her to know that what the area around St Paul's was to the City of London, Dog Yard was to the Rookery. Anyone with the physique, will-power and sheer luck to survive a Rookery childhood regarded Dog Yard as the next move up. It was its hub, its bourse, the place where you strolled to pick up news and gossip. Just as most of the world's trade was conducted in the colonnaded loggias of the Royal Exchange, the Rookery's commerce was concentrated on the cobbles of Dog Yard. The fact that nearly all of it came from theft was neither here nor there; as Will Tippin, Dog Yard's late pickpocket, had remarked in his speech from the gallows, so did the Royal Exchange's.

Its eminence arose mainly from the Rookery's only two solid pieces of architecture: the Ship Inn and the Cock and Pie. The Ship was Elizabethan, a building with the raked, be-windowed frontage of a galleon. That it was occasionally patronized by gentry who wanted to see low life while tasting good ale and without having one's throat cut, was due to the muscle and intelligence of its landlord, Sam Bryskett.

The emergence of the Cock and Pie as a brothel – it had led a varied career since its days as a Tudor farmhouse – had at first been an affront to Dog Yard where prostitution was on a freelance basis. More affronting yet had been Her Ladyship's barring of would-be customers living in the Rookery itself, and her prices, which would have barred them anyway. Behind her back the 'barge-arsed bitch' was resented, along with her girls, for her pursuit of the genteel both in clientele and manners.

However, Dog Yard had benefited from Her Ladyship's aspirations. It watched her purchases with interest, noting that she patronized only country sellers of the freshest food, sent her linen to the laundry in Holborn, bought wine at St James's, and sprinkled fresh sawdust on her kitchen floors every week.

In the entrepreneurial spirit for which it was famed, Dog Yard adapted to the situation, Sam Bryskett improved his own cellar and sold direct to Her Ladyship, thereby saving her transport charges.

The country vegetable- and meat-suppliers were persuaded, mostly at the point of a knife, to hand over the retail of their produce to certain Dog Yarders. The Tippin family, who lived in the Stables on the Yard's south side, considered the feasibility of either blackmailing or robbing the Cock and Pie's clientele, but in the end decided against killing the ganders who were laying the golden eggs, and instead instituted a practice of demanding protection money, known locally as 'angel's oil', from the sedan-chair carriers for the privilege of waiting for their masters unharmed. By raiding the nearest woodyard at night, the youngest Tippin gained the sawdust concession.

Her Ladyship fought off — literally — Pont Tippin's attempt to fill the post of the Cock and Pie's apple-squire in exchange for a proportion of the profits, at the same time rejecting his offer to sell her two of his daughters, but she was astute enough to allow all other changes in the interest of goodwill, a commodity always in short supply in Dog Yard.

She also entrusted her washing to the undoubtedly capable hands of Mistress Palmer after two occasions on which it came back muddied from the Holborn laundry, Jethro Palmer having twice tripped up the Holborn laundrymaid who carried it.

Owing to the Dog Yarders' preference for drinking and gambling their profit rather than investing it in brick and mortar, none of their enterprise was evident to Penitence Hurd as she looked down from her balcony that late autumn day. She saw only squalor; irregular patches of lath-and-plaster where rendering had fallen off the walls, broken tiles, thatch on which grass grew in profusion, though none grew on the ground.

The Cock and Pie's threshold, like the Ship's further along, led out on to stone setts which formed a platform running along the high, north side of the Yard and was served by steps. In more ways than one, everything went downhill from here. The Yard itself formed a sink.

With the glory of the Ship hidden from her view unless she leaned out, and unable to see the Cock and Pie's daunting but dignified frontage, her impression was dire. Down and diagonally across from her, the arches of what had once been a decent stable-block were barricaded by criss-crossed planks of wood, though people lived inside – she could see smoke emerging from a decrepit chimney. Next to that, and nearer, was the Buildings, actually one building shared by twelve families, a rectangle of rendered wattle-and-daub which an apologetic mason had ornamented with a castellated top and Italianate, though rusting, balconies. Its bravery was accentuated by lines of Mistress Palmer's washing hanging from the crenellations.

The far west side of Penitence's view was blocked by a high, thin, wooden loft which she knew, from slighting references by the Cock and Pie girls, to be Mother Hubbard's, a brothel which had set itself up in imitation of the Cock and Pie to take local trade or, as Alania had put it with a sniff, 'oblige a billy-goat if it paid 'em tuppence'.

Wherever there was a space between the houses, somebody had filled it with another, so that habitations no wider than nine feet across squeezed in at crazy angles with their roofs and upper storeys tipping frighteningly over the Yard, shading it from all but determined, midday sun. Had the tiny alleys leading into it been wider they would only have been repositories for more detritus and sewage than they were already.

The few persons in evidence were as unprepossessing as

the place; pale children with heads shaven against lice so that it was impossible to sex them, since their rags gave no clue. The front of a vat opened to reveal itself as the home of a man without legs – Penitence later learned that the Yard, in its jolly way, knew him as 'Footloose'. With considerable expertise he hauled himself into a bucket on wheels and propelled himself off for what she assumed would be the day's begging.

Somewhere in the east a church bell began to chime. The sound was taken up by St Giles's on the west, then by the towers and steeples with which the view of London bristled. The call to Anglican prayer had no effect on Dog Yard, but it reminded Penitence what day it was.

Bartholomew, 'tis the Sabbath. Whether she go or stay must be put off until tomorrow. Today was the Lord's. Singing Psalm 121, she took her black Bible out of her satchel, sat herself down on her bed and began to read.

She was still reading and singing two hours later when the Cock and Pie began to stir.

Dorinda came into the attic, yawning, with a bodice in her hands and threw it on the bed. 'Give this a mend, will you.'

Penitence put her forefinger on her place and looked up. ''Tis the Ssa-Sa-Ssabbath.' She returned to the Bible.

'What if it is the Sa-Sa-Sabbath? Get my ballocking mending done.'

Penitence continued to read.

'You're a crophead,' said Dorinda, creeping towards the bed. 'You're a ballocking Leveller, that's what you are. Let's see your crophead.'

She snatched off Penitence's cap. Penitence snatched it back, and kicked. Dorinda gave a return kick and grabbed handfuls of Penitence's short, fair hair. They fell on the floor, fighting.

'Whose dog's dead?' demanded Phoebe from the door.

Dorinda rolled away, jerking a finger from between Penitence's teeth. 'She's a ballocking Sunday saint and she won't do my ballocking mending. I'm going to tell Her Ladyship of her, and then I'm going to darken her ballocking daylights.'

Phoebe and Sabina between them restrained Penitence from pursuit, and sat her down. 'See,' said Phoebe, gently, 'we need mending Sundays. Most of our gentlemen, they spend Sundays pummelling pulpits and tomorrow they'll come back wanting quiff badder than ever. Be a good fubsey, eh?'

Panting, Penitence looked at Phoebe's kindly face and saw she was older than the others, perhaps no more than twenty-four, but ageing rapidly. She shook her head. ''Tis the Ssa-Sab-bath.'

'See,' went on Phoebe, 'it was rare good of Her Ladyship to take you in like she done. Especial if you ain't to be one of the game. Afore, she sent out the mending. Now she's letting you at it. Roof over your head, good pan and peck twice a day. Can't ask more than that, eh, Sabby?'

'That you can't,' said Sabina. 'Don't you go crossing Her Ladyship, Pen. She's a terror when crossed, Her Ladyship. Ain't she, Pheeb?'

Still persuasive, Phoebe patted Penitence's hand. 'And don't you mind Dorinda. She's jealous at Her Ladyship favouring you. Loves Her Ladyship, does Dorinda.'

Sabina nodded. 'More than a mother to us, Her Ladyship's been.'

Penitence stared at her, wondering what their real mothers could have been like.

'Dorry's bark's worse than her bite,' said Phoebe, 'and she obliged a lively 'un last night, didn't she, Sabby? A robe-ripper.'

'Thank Gawd I didn't get him.' Sabina spoke with feeling.

Dorinda's bark might not have been as bad as her bark, but her teethmarks were still hurting Penitence's shoulder, as much as Phoebe's and Sabina's converse was offending her ears. She shook her head once more. ''Tis the Ssab-Ssabbath.'

Sighing at the retribution soon to fall on her, the two girls left the attic hand in hand.

Penitence adjusted her cap and dress, rubbed her shoulder, returned to her Bible and braced her courage against Her Ladyship's wrath.

It didn't come. Later, Dorinda poked her head round the door: 'Her Ladyship says no work, no food.' Her tone spoke satisfaction, but her dark eyes showed disappointment at the mildness of Penitence's sentence.

While going hungry allowed Penitence pleasure in being martyred for righteousness, it was hardship for a girl with a good appetite. Still, as Phoebe had pointed out, it was also hardship for the brothel not to have its mending done. On the one hand, Penitence did not want to contribute to the practice of licentiousness; on the other she would soon have spent two nights under this roof and her Puritan ethics demanded she pay for them.

I'll mend her Bartholomew bodice on the morrow. Then I shall go.

But on the morrow there was other mending than Dorinda's to do, and there came a heavy fall of rain flecked with snow which battered on the roof and poured down the steps outside into the blocked plughole that was the Yard. Looking out, Penitence imagined herself splashing through it with nowhere to go. She was hungry and the smell of Kinyans's beef hare was already wafting through the damp air of the attic.

She felt trapped and aggrieved. *Thee must help a bit, Lord.*

As she and Kinyans cleared after dinner, he said: 'Shall I tell ye about Margaret Hughes?'

She spun round. He'd been indulging in a bonalay of his own concocting, 'to keep me feet warm'. It made them unsteady. He was winking at her and tapping the side of his nose.

'That had ye. Don't know everything, Miss Prinkum-Prankum, but Kinyans do. Old Kinyans do come from Somerset too. Died in the West Indies? So did my arse. Want to know—'

'One more word, Kinyans.'

Her Ladyship stood in the doorway, jewelled in purple, with her face painted for the night to come, but beneath the cupid's bow she'd drawn round her mouth her lips were thin, and colour gave out at her eyes, which were blank. For all its heat, the kitchen fell chill on its two occupants.

Her bulk on its tiny feet moved forward, and Kinyans retreated before her fat, upraised finger.

'One more word,' she said again, 'ever.'

'I weren't going to—'

'Ever.' She went out.

Penitence, by winking and making encouraging noises, tried to reanimate Kinyans into conspiracy, but the old man had sobered and didn't speak again.

Questions kept interrupting Penitence's prayers as she knelt by her bed that night. Kinyans had now made two references to Somerset. His accent reminded her of home, where many of the settlers, like her own family, had originated from the West Country, that hotbed of Nonconformity. Had her aunt come to London with him and Her Ladyship? He'd indicated that she had not died in the West Indies. Had she died at all?

Her imagination dwelled on an Aunt Margaret grown so rich that an envious Ladyship was keeping her niece from her out of malice. Or was she in prison? Hanged? Did Her Ladyship, out of pity, shield her from shame?

Neither case seemed likely, yet the idea that her aunt was alive rooted itself in Penitence's lonely soul, wildly bringing hope at the same time that it dismayed her with the knowledge that the only key to Margaret Hughes's whereabouts was held by the Cock and Pie. The next day it began to snow. Winter had come early.

So Penitence Hurd stayed on at the Cock and Pie and made everyone's life a misery.

Each girl coming to the attic for a fitting at her hands endured a biblical warning with it. It wasn't easy with a stutter and a mouth full of pins, but Penitence had rationalized her dependence on the brothel as a mission. If the Lord had marooned her on this island of evil, it was for His purpose.

Alania got Isaiah, 'O that thou hadst hearkened to my commandments.'

The inseparable Phoebe and Sabina got the Beatitudes, while Dorinda, Penitence's bête noire, got Kings II, Chapter 9 – the death of Jezebel.

She reduced Mary, the skivvy, to such hysterics with a selection from the Epistle to the Romans on the carnally minded that Her Ladyship, in a fury, paid one of her rare visits to the attic. 'I'll not have a chit like you bothering my girls.'

Her hand clamped the scruff of Penitence's neck, dragged

her to the front window and lifted her on to the balcony, forcing her to look over the parapet. 'See down there?'

They had all been down to see it. Dawn had revealed a pile of clothes bunched against the Ship's steps which had not been there when night fell, more detritus the wind had blown into the sink of Dog Yard, human detritus – a woman clutching a baby, both dead.

They were still there, decently covered by one of Mistress Bryskett's sheets and surrounded by Dog Yarders awaiting the arrival of the parish coffiner. The Searcher was just rising from her knees by the bodies.

Her Ladyship called down to Mistress Palmer: 'What she say done it?' Nobody questioned the Searcher directly.

Mistress Palmer looked up, flapping her crossed arms against her sides to keep warm. 'Quinsies, she says.'

'And my aunt's my uncle,' scoffed Her Ladyship. 'Anyone know 'em?'

Mistress Palmer shook her head. 'Not from round here.'

'Then suppose you get my sheets done,' suggested Her Ladyship.

Without a word spoken, and glimpsed as it was through snow, Mistress Palmer's expression managed to convey that Her Ladyship should try drying sheets in this weather, that if circumstances were different she, Mistress Palmer, wouldn't demean herself washing for a brothel, whatever airs it gave itself, and that once Her Ladyship had got them, Her Ladyship could stuff them up her fundament. Nevertheless, she returned to the Buildings where her window steamed droplets into the freezing air.

'Quinsies,' spat Her Ladyship again, releasing Penitence's neck. 'And cold. And no work. And nowhere to go.'

The coffiners had arrived, two men carrying a pine box on a hand-cart. The edges of the unknown woman's skirt stuck to the ice when they lifted her body, and they jerked it to get them free. The baby was a foetal-shaped ball as they dropped it into the coffin on to its mother.

Tears froze on Penitence's eyelids. *Lord, Thee sees each sparrow that falls.*

'And weak,' whispered Her Ladyship. In her blue-mauve mottled face her eyes were dry. She turned them on Penitence. 'See?' Penitence nodded.

At the door her Ladyship looked back. 'And leave pestering Kinyans about your aunt. She's dead.'

Dorinda swaggered in: 'She beat you?' Penitence picked up her sewing, a flowered muslin gown for Francesca, feeling for the needle with her frozen, mittened fingers. 'She should've,' said Dorinda. 'She's good at it. Beats her clients, does Her Ladyship. Beats the Bishop.'

At last she'd got her response. Penitence looked up, amazed.

Dorinda grinned. 'Didn't know that, did you, you prinking crophead. You don't know nothing. He likes it, don't he. Brings him to the brim.'

There was much Penitence didn't know; unwillingly, she was learning. Shocking her became a pastime, the harlots' revenge on her piety. They insisted on enlightening her as to what 'obliging' entailed. The revelations were dreadful. 'Don't you pray at me, Prinks,' said Fanny — Kinyans's name for Penitence had been generally adopted — 'I got enough praying last night. My gentleman likes praying while he's poking.'

She tried to shut her ears against the stream of professional secrets poured into them, tried not to show her nausea at the undreamed-of variations on the sexual act demanded by the girls' clients; the fulders, the rancums, the pissers, the floggers, the Athanasians, the fumblers, suckers, rippers, fugoists — insight into human frailty at its most contorted was laid before her. With detail.

The one thing the girls did not divulge was the clients' names. 'We got our honour,' Alania told her loftily. Some, Penitence knew, protected their identity by remaining masked, even while abandoning all other apparel; she had seen for herself on 'The Savage' night that others did not. Whether these reverend gentlemen could relax in the knowledge that their mutual sinning inhibited each from denouncing the others to their parishioners, Penitence did not enquire. She didn't want to know.

At first she had rammed her bed against her door each night in fear that Her Ladyship should send one of these appalling men up to her attic. But this didn't happen, and the girls resented what they regarded as nepotism.

'Living off our backs, you are,' complained Dorinda. 'Just because Her Ladyship knew your ballocking aunt.'

In fact, Penitence more than paid for her keep. In the Puritan tradition, careless work was an offence against the Lord and Penitence could no more sew a crooked seam than she could fly. Cock and Pie couture was now in better order than it had been in the days when sewing had to be sent out to jobbing needlewomen, yet by and large its girls remained unappreciative. They were jealous of what appeared to be her special standing with Her Ladyship, who was their nurse, provider, instructress, adviser and confessor.

'Favoured, ain't you?' sneered Alania. It took time for Penitence to realize that being permitted to retain her virginity *was* a favour. Apart from Job and Kinyans, there were no other exemptions from the Cock and Pie's trade. Fourteen-year-old Mary was called on to oblige when the house was busy and even Her Ladyship provided the occasional service to established clients who had special, and painful, requirements.

It was useless for Penitence to point out to the girls that they were being exploited, though she did. 'B-b-better for her that a m-ummm-m-millstone were hanged about her neck.'

'Don't you hang no m-m-millstones round Her Ladyship,' warned Dorinda, repeating what Sabina had said: 'She's been a good mother to us.'

And one day — it was Christmas Day — Penitence was amazed to reflect that, in a sense, it was true.

Phoebe put her head round the door. 'Ain't you coming down to dinner?'

Penitence shook her head. She was reading her Bible.

'There's goose,' wheedled Phoebe, stepping inside, 'and cider meat and mutton sausages, and Kinyans's made his sugar pigs.'

Penitence swallowed. From outside came the chimes of bells celebrating the birth of their churches' Lord.

'Her Ladyship's asking. And Dorinda, she wants you to an' all.' At Penitence's look of disbelief, Phoebe sat herself down on the bed. 'Don't be hard, Prinks. You think Dorry obliges acause she likes it? Any of us like it? There weren't no choice.' She sighed. 'Maybe it's different in the Americas.'

It was. Sin was sin in the Chosen Land. You didn't do it. Well, the Reverend Block had tried, but if you did do it, you certainly didn't excuse it as the only choice. Stonily, Penitence read on.

'Poor old Dorry got done by her granddad when she was four,' mused Phoebe.

'N-n-no.' It was forced out of Penitence. 'She's l-lying.'

'Her mum used to let him because it kept the old bugger off her.'

'She's l-l-lying. She's l-umm-lying.'

Phoebe shrugged. And the shrug was proof. It was so true that it didn't matter who believed it or didn't.

'Won't you come down?' pleaded Phoebe, patiently.

'I c-cca-ccan't.' Christmas was a heathen festival. Puritans didn't celebrate it.

Phoebe got up, sighing. 'Don't then.' She looked around the scrubbed, undecorated attic and at the scrubbed, undecorated girl who sat in it, and was moved to drop a kiss on her head. 'Merry Christmas, Prinks.'

Alone, Penitence sat on, unseeing. Was Phoebe right? Did the Cock and Pie girls dislike what they did? Were they not, after all, the separate genus of her teaching, *harlotis vulgaris*, a garish plant which flourished in ordure? Were they as human but less fortunate than herself?

Ordure was the bed of their trade, but they didn't flourish in it. Most of them had already developed the first stages of syphilis, the weeping ulcers around their private parts which would eventually kill them.

Penitence recalled the times they'd forced details of their professional lives upon her – and saw faces intent on punishing themselves as much as her. She recollected conversations, sentences casually let slip during fittings, which had vouchsafed glimpses into their past. At the time she'd deliberately shut her mind to them as further attempts to appal her; now she allowed it to rove over them, wandering along a dark corridor in which doors gave glimpses into Hell.

Beggary, abandonment, beatings, starvation; for most of the girls there had been the accompaniment of sexual assault so persistent that it made the Reverend Block's attempt on Penitence's virtue appear almost benign. She had been able to fight off one guilt-ridden clergyman, she realized; they'd been subjected to violation by men in that darkly hopeless wolf-pit, the lowest stratum of humanity, where the rays of Christianity, even the basic taboos against incest, hadn't penetrated.

No wonder, then, that to them the Cock and Pie was sanctuary. No wonder the woman who insisted on standards for them and their clients had become an adored commander-in-chief. Any client who flouted Her Ladyship's requirements of behaviour was turned away, however good his money. Unwilling conscripts in a dirty war the girls might be, but now they had at least joined a crack regiment.

It became too dark to read her Bible, even if she'd been reading it in the first place.

Frowning, she got down on to her knees to say her nightly prayers and, for the first time since she'd arrived in it, Penitence included in them one of true charity for the girls of the Cock and Pie.

Chapter 3

THE PRINTING shop in Goat Alley had the blue-black smell of ink mixing with dust, sweat, lye and hot lead that brought back memories of the shed where her grandfather had kept his press. There was no signboard outside; the shop's trade, like most in the Rookery, was illegal.

An apprentice, who was contributing more than his fair share to the sweat, grimaced as Penitence climbed the last steps up to the door of the garret. ''Ware stranger, Dada.'

The printer looked up from the screws he was adjusting on the press head. 'Out. Nobody allowed, women especial. Orders taken downstairs.'

Penitence had pared her sentence to the bone — 'Have you work?' — and wobbled only slightly on the 'w'.

The printer advanced on her. 'The wife cleans round here. Out.'

Penitence shook her head. 'I'm a per-per-umm-per—'

'Puritan?' guessed the printer. 'No God-botherers allowed. Out.'

'I'm a per-per-um-per—'

'Peach? Pest? Pushy?' The son was getting the hang of it.

'Pp-printer,' said Penitence. 'Grandfather took me on as a pp-pp—'

'Pox doctor?'

'— prentice,' finished Penitence. 'Also I can umm I can porr-proooumm-proo ...' *Oh, Bartholomew the trade.* '... pp-proof-read.'

'What you think *I* do?' asked the apprentice with resentment.

'G-get it wr-rong.' Penitence held out the theatre poster she had taken off a wall in Drury Lane. Apart from giving even unstandardized spelling a bad name, some sentences were upside-down.

The printer followed Penitence's forefinger along the errors, then cuffed his son round the ear. 'No wonder they never paid us.' But to Penitence he brazened it out. 'What's it to you, Goody-boots? Four-line capitals and Roman they wanted, four-line capitals and Roman they got.'

Ezekiel Hurd had been a master printer before he'd been forced out of England by Charles I, and he'd made a profitable sideline from his press in the Americas, teaching Penitence everything he knew. However, if this idiot here wouldn't admit his need for help, she was wasting her time.

'They got four-line capitals and p-p-pica,' she said. She was at her best when she was angry.

Out in the alley again, she tapped her hat more firmly over the scarf she'd wound round her ears. She was in one of her must-leave-the-Cock-and-Pie phases. As the long, cold winter wore on, her contempt for its girls was being replaced by something nearer pity, but her contempt for herself in remaining there was unabated. Kinyans steadily refused to disclose any more information about Margaret Hughes, and she was beginning to lose hope that he ever would.

Broaching that unlicensed Bartholomew of a printer for employment had been an impulse brought on by the familiar smell issuing from his window as she'd passed it on her way back from buying threads at the drapery in St Giles's High Street.

Be not downcast, Pen. All things work for good to them that love God. And standing around here wouldn't buy baby a new bonnet. Her feet were losing feeling, the winter evening setting in. The High Street had been lively with traffic – she could still hear it – but there was none in this alley, no flambeaux either. The cold was one more enemy in its inhabitants' fight for survival and had driven them indoors. She was getting to know her way around the Rookery, but she didn't trust it after dark.

Icicles like the Sword of Damocles hung over her head as she loped past quiet, gimcrack houses where the whiteness of the roofs indicated that if the rooms beneath them were warmed at all the fires were too pitiful to send up warmth to the rafters.

New England's winters had been colder than this, but its houses had been built to withstand them. Matoonas had shown her how to use snowshoes . . .

Her mind was in Massachusetts and her body proceeding along Butcher's Cut when two figures barred her way. They had rags tied across the lower halves of their faces. A muffled, very young voice said: 'You know what we want, lady.' Boys, but dangerous boys.

She shifted the basket she was carrying to her left arm and got ready to flip her knife out of its sheath on her right. 'N-no.' *Why did I say that? Can I take on two?*

Driven to the lie by desperation, she quavered: 'I'm a f-friend of the T-t-tippins.'

One of the boys said: 'Who's the fucking Tippins?' He was advancing.

Strangers, then. Young footpads from outside the area. If they'd been local, they'd have known this was Tippin territory, with only Tippins allowed to rob it.

If it came to it, she could throw her knife into the leg of the biggest and outrun the scrawny, shoeless one. But she'd rather it *didn't* come to it. She began to back up the Cut, shouting 'Help'.

Nothing happened, except that the buildings around her became more silent, as if huddling away from trouble. The youths were coming at her. Carefully, she stood up on a step to give herself the advantage of height, rapping the knife in her hand on the door behind her and shouting 'Help' again.

Nobody, nothing. She was on her own.

No, she wasn't. From some way behind came an unsteady thump of footsteps and a voice making anticipatory 'Oh ho' noises.

She turned to see whose it was, and slipped on the ice of the step.

Her spine jarred but instinct rolled her over as the boys grasped her ankles and she kicked, crawling in the direction of the newcomer, her head raised like a deer with a wolf on its hindquarters – and saw, coming towards her, the gentleman.

For all her fright, she classed him immediately. More to the point she saw he was on her side. And he was big.

The grip on her legs relaxed. Above her, the gentleman waveringly faced her attackers, smiling as if he loved them: 'How now, you secret, black and midnight bastards,' he said. 'That's not nice. Don't do it.'

Without taking his eyes off her attackers, he proffered a hand to Penitence and she hauled herself up by it.

The youths had stepped back. She saw their eyes calculate ratios of cudgels to the half-drawn sword in the gentleman's scabbard, lengths, heights, needs and possibilities, and come to a conclusion. They ran.

She let go the hand and, despite the pain in her coccyx, sat down on the steps to relieve her shaking legs. The gentleman was having a lovely time, shouting, 'Down, down to hell; and say I sent thee thither', after the retreating backs, bowing to the heads which, now they weren't needed, had emerged from windows. He returned to Penitence and swept off his hat. 'At your service, mistress. Are you hurt?'

She shook her head and hoped he'd go away now. She *hated* fusses. She was grateful for the rescue but he didn't have to be loud about it.

'Does this happen often?' From under his cloak he produced a leather bottle and offered it to her. She shook her head. It smelled of liquor. So did he. He took a swig himself. 'What did those noblemen want?'

Wearily, she pointed down at her boots.

He studied them. 'Why?'

How rude. They'd seen better days, but they were solid Massachusetts boots, and desirable in a district where half the population went barefoot. And his own were nothing to write home about. She knew now why she'd assessed him as a gentleman. In her community it was not a title of respect; it applied to the despised representatives sent out to the Massachusetts Bay colony to represent the English government. From her few glimpses of them on visits to Boston and from her grandfather's unflattering descriptions, she had built up a picture of braggadocio and here it was. In spades. Everything about the man had flourish, his cloak trailed over his shoulder and on to the ground, his sword bobbed with the swing of his legs, his wide hat boasted an outrageous feather and performed a parabola when he twirled it off to bow.

Also, he was drunk. She was about to get up, but he bumped down on the step beside her. 'Let us sit upon the ground and tell sad stories of the death of kings,' he said companionably. He took another drink from his bottle. 'And how you can't trust any of the buggers.'

Embarrassed, still shaken, nervous of his peculiarity and his swearing — even at that early moment, Penitence caught the contrapuntal moan of hurt underneath the gibberish, and relaxed in recognition. Miserable men had no harm in them. He was impersonal with the self-absorption of drunkenness; she was an incident he'd happened on, nothing more.

He wagged his finger at her: 'Put not your trust in princes, madam. Well, possibly Rupert. But the next time a king asks you a favour . . .'

She smiled placatorily and stood up.

'No, no,' he scrambled unsteadily to his feet, 'here wast thou bay'd, brave heart; here didst thou fall: and here thy hunters may still be lurking about. We go together.' He took another swig, replaced the bottle beneath his cloak and offered his arm. Feeling a fool, she took it.

Their progress was erratic and noisy: he sang all the way.

As they were approaching Dog Yard, he stopped. 'I am lost in this forest, fair maid. Tell me which of its palaces is the Cock and . . .' he squinted at some writing on the back of his hand. '. . . the Cock and *Pea*?'

There was giggling from above their heads where the girls of Mother Hubbard's establishment were leaning out of their back window. 'Pie, darling,' said one of them, 'Cock and Pie. And we'd oblige you better. For free.' From the way she was ogling, she meant it.

Penitence couldn't think why. Admitted, the man had panache, but he was ugly. His overlarge nose, which the cold had turned red, contrasted with a livid, pockmarked face, his eyes were baggy and he was definitely down on his luck. There was a split in his doeskin boots, the edge of the cloak was ragged where it dragged on the ground and his hat, like her boots, had seen better days, but not recently.

He was doffing it to Mother Hubbard's: 'Gracious ladies, forgive a poor actor; I'm spoken for.'

Penitence pressed on. An actor, was he? Spawn of the Devil's playground. In Massachusetts they'd have cropped his ears for him, and rightly. Irony was new to her, but she resented the gentleman's use of it. He was ridiculing all about him. The moment he called her 'fair maid,' she'd known what a scarecrow she looked, just as his address to the Mother Hubbard girls disguised the loathing for their trade. *And his own little better.* For the first time she felt protective of the Rookery; he might think himself too good for it, but patronage of the Cock and Pie showed he was not — her growing tolerance for the Cock and Pie's whores had not lessened her loathing for their clients. And if he thought he would be obliged cheaper at the Cock and Pie than in the brothels of Drury Lane, he had a shock coming.

Descending the steps into the well of Dog Yard, she pointed across at the Cock and Pie's signboard and held back, unwilling to be taken, even by this man, for one of its obligers. But he was insisting on seeing her home.

She stumped up the steps to where the lantern above the door glowed into the mirk and turned defiantly. She saw the actor's wide mouth go down and his eyebrows up as he looked from her Puritan hat to the red light. He was amused.

She opened her mouth then closed it. She would not expose her stutter to this man. Not ever.

Dost care what a sinner thinks of thee, Penitence Hurd?

Yes, she did. In this case, she did.

He was consulting his hand again: 'Left, left.' After an elaborate bow, he was walking on to stop outside the house on the other side of the alley that ran past her west window. His destination wasn't the Cock and Pie: it was Mistress Hicks's.

He knocked on the door and, when it opened, swept off his hat. 'Ah, madam, I am informed your delectable establishment has rooms to rent.'

He *had* fallen on bad times. Mistress Hicks rented on the principle that if you were desperate enough to take one of her rooms you deserved everything you got. Penitence's mouth twitched. Interested in this encounter, the Yarders came to their windows.

'What trade?'

'A poor actor, ma'am, an unfortunate follower of Thespis who—'

'Resting?' Mistress Hicks's voice, which could have gravelled driveways, indicated that she had taken in actors before.

'I am assured of employment at the Cockpit, ma'am,' said the actor, humbly

'Name?'

'Henry King, ma'am, at your service.' Listening ears at the

windows round about caught the split second of thought that preceded the announcement. Arrivals in Dog Yard rarely used their own names.

Mistress Hicks's nose, which knew a thing or two about liquor on its own account, analysed the actor's breath. 'Shilling a week. Fire, pan and peck extra. And no spewin' in the room. Take it or leave it.'

'Done.'

Going upstairs, Penitence remained irritated. The swaggerer had done her a good turn, but he had diminished her in doing it. Of course, one could not expect someone of his debasement to recognize a woman whose moral fibre made her anybody's equal. On the other hand, he might have found it difficult; her hat rammed on top of one of Her Ladyship's swathing shawls, thick boots, old coat, made it hard to divine somebody's sex, let alone their moral fibre.

For the first time in her life, Penitence considered her appearance.

Mary met her on the clerestory. 'Gawd, Prinks, where you been? Dorinda's roaring. One of her gentlemen's due soon, and you promised a fit of her new jacket.' Mary vibrated like a tuning fork to the house disturbances and her present tizzy indicated that Dorinda's temper was special.

Dorinda could Bartholomew off.

A yawning Alania emerged out of her bedroom on her way downstairs. 'Did you see any, Prinks?'

Penitence nodded. In her capacity as Cock and Pie dress-maker, she had that morning walked down to Hyde Park to examine the fashions of the high-society skaters on its lake. 'M-m-muffs are in.'

'Always were, dear,' said Alania, languidly adding another to the apparently infinite number of euphemisms for the female pudenda. 'Make me one if I buy the silk?'

Penitence nodded.

'You're not a bad old bundle, Prinks.'

She'd left the door of her room open, and in going past it Penitence hesitated. All the girls' rooms, though small, were equipped with large mirrors which she now knew — another piece of knowledge she could have done without – had other functions than to see if one's hair was tidy.

Standing by the open door, Penitence battled with the temptation to look at herself. *Not a bad old bundle.* Was this how she seemed to others?

Until now, glimpses of her own reflection had been in buckets of water. Mirrors were vanity. 'The Devil stares back from the looking-glass.' Who'd said that? Oh, Reverend Block, the old Bartholomew. On the other hand, though she had cast out the teachings of the Reverend Block, she had not abandoned his God. She was merely in the process of reassessing Him.

Sternly, she resisted the mirror's temptation and took herself off to her attic. She would not imperil her soul by narcissism because some coxcomb hadn't noticed its worth.

Instead, she went to her balcony. Despite the cold, she had taken to standing here every evening to watch the sun go down over London.

This time at the end of every day transfixed her. Misery, vileness, crime – nobody knew better than she what went on in the hidden streets. Yet in these moments they were wiped away by distance and a sunset that magicked frosted spires and roofs into pure amber and sent a golden wave along the Thames. Again, tonight more than ever, she felt the sense of expectation.

A shuffle and tap below drew her attention downwards, back to Dog Yard and its depressing mortality. The Searcher was crossing the court to the Ship Inn steps. It occurred to her that the Searcher was much in evidence these nights.

Behind her, the attic filled with invective and Dorinda's bad temper. 'What are you doing out there, gawdelpus? Get your fun in here. And where's my ballocking jacket?'

But by the time Penitence had climbed back into the room, the girl had stopped and was staring out of the side window. 'Well,' she said to herself, slowly, 'and how's *your* poor feet?'

Penitence peered with her. The room across the alley, which had been shuttered since she'd arrived, had become an oblong of candlelight. An unsuspected grate in its far wall held a fire before which they could see the actor. He had divested himself of cloak and hat and was sitting on a chair, his arms behind his head, apparently lost in an unhappy exploration of the cracks in Mistress Hicks's ceiling.

Dorinda was appreciative. 'And who's that bit of butter and bacon?'

Penitence shrugged. 'S-some actor.'

Firmly, Penitence closed the shutters. Dorinda's eyes didn't move. 'He looks like he looks, and my gentlemen look like my gentlemen. And they say there's a God.'

It happened again. She kept getting stabbed by pity at the girls' weariness with their profession; now even Dorinda, most unlikeable, foulest-mouthed of the trollops, was gnawing at the jaws of the trap.

She could give the girl a pious 'Go and sin no more'. But if Dorinda asked: 'Go where?' she would be answerless. She'd searched the Bible only to find no solution to that one. The soles of her boots were wearing out in her own attempt to find somewhere else to go, and the jaws of her trap were padded compared with the teeth that held this girl where she was.

Mildly she said: 'I've near f-f-finished the jacket', and Dorinda, recovered, said: 'About time.' She stood quiet while Penitence put it on her, smoothing and patting. Dorinda's jealousy was subsiding; Her Ladyship's attitude towards Penitence, a wariness that verged on hostility, gave it no cause. It was puzzling; Penitence knew she was repaying Her Ladyship's charity by hard work; the hostility must be connected not so much with herself as with her aunt. Undoubtedly, Her Ladyship owed a debt to the memory of Margaret Hughes, but had not liked her much.

The woman's exploitation of her girls seemed less appalling as Penitence found out what it had saved them from, and there were times when, in her loneliness, Penitence very nearly envied the Cock and Pie's camaraderie, the sisters-in-arms spirit, which Her Ladyship fostered between her girls and herself without allowing it to lapse into disrespect.

'Not pulpit-bashing tonight?' asked Dorinda.

Penitence shook her head. She'd stopped preaching. Sometimes it worried her; was she guilty of what her grandfather had denounced as 'Anythingarianism', becoming so tolerant that she no longer possessed any fixed views on right and wrong?

Well, if she was an Anythingarian, she was still closer to Jesus's teaching than the Reverend Block's Cut-their-ears-off-and-brand-them school of divinity. She'd learned that much.

Lord, she was tired; tired of confusion, and the girls who caused it, tired of this cold attic.

She stood back. 'P-p-perfect.'

Dorinda looked round for a looking-glass and found none. She marched over to the shutters and flung them back. 'Hey, Play-actor.'

Penitence rushed forward to stop her, but the man was already looking in their direction. He bowed from his chair.

'This is my friend, Penitence,' said Dorinda.

The actor bowed again.

'Like my new jacket?' asked Dorinda, twirling.

He squinted blearily and nodded. He wanted to be left alone.

Horrifyingly, Dorinda said: 'Why don't you leap over and take it off?'

He stretched and came to the window. 'Madam, between you and me is a great gulf fixed: your honour, mine, and that bloody great drop down there. I wish you and your friend richer pickings tonight than my old carcase.'

He bowed, reached for his bottle, and went back to his chair.

'Well,' said Dorinda, 'he put it nice.'

Penitence wrested the girl's hands from the shutters and banged them to. 'H-how c-cccc-could you?'

Dorinda's mouth was twisted 'Let him know he's neighbour to a cat-house right away,' she said. 'Gentlemen like him, they get that look when they find out. So I tell 'em. And ballocks to them.'

Again that unsuspected vulnerability, and this time complicated with self-punishment. The girl had declared herself a whore on the principle that, being attracted, she must kill the likelihood of attracting. She thrust her face towards Penitence's. 'Fancy him yourself, do you?'

She most certainly did not. But it rankled that such a man should think her a whore. When Dorinda went, she wondered if she should go back to the window and explain. *Prithee, sir, I am no prostitute.*

She practised it. 'Prithee, sir, I am no prostitute.' It was a peculiarity of her affliction that when she was alone she did not stammer. The 'p's came out in beautiful puffs of sound.

But the statement hung ludicrous in the air, and how much more ludicrous would she appear as she heaved out the terrible syllables in delivering it from her window. Pri-prri-pri, pro-ppro-pro.

Damned if she did; damned if she didn't.

She got angry. Who was this busking mountebank to pity her, either as stutterer or strumpet? What did she, whose soul would be saved on the Day of Judgement, care for the opinion of one who would be sucked, screaming, into the Pit?

A beautifully enunciated, soul-endangering phrase spoke itself into the attic, alarming its utterer even as she uttered it. 'Ballocks to him,' it said.

Chapter 4

MONDAYS were Bills of Mortality days. On Mondays Peter Simkin took himself, an ink pot, a quill, a ruler and paper into the vestry of St Giles's church and copied from its register of births, marriages and deaths the names of those who had died in his parish in the previous seven days, and why.

He drew lines for the columns, then checked through the register list for the deaths to write them down in alphabetical order which, since death did not come alphabetically, meant arranging them on a slate before he could make the final fair copy. His comfort lay in the fact that all over London, parish clerks like himself were going through the same procedure, though St Giles's parish, being overcrowded, poorer and more frequently visited by death than others, involved greater work for less pay than theirs.

Like the rector, he was ashamed by the number of times he had to write 'Pox' in the column detailing the cause of death.

Usually the job took him not quite an hour. On this first Monday of April it took him nearer two. He counted the number of deaths again. Thirty-one. Usually they averaged out at nineteen. He went to the vestry door and called in his rector to show him the list.

'I know,' said the Reverend Boreman. 'It's been a bad winter.'

'Eight fevers,' Peter pointed out. 'A deal of fever.'

The Reverend Boreman shrugged. They were dependent on what the Searcher told them. 'And how many with the pox this week?'

Embarrassed, Peter Simkin moved his eyes. Following them, the Reverend Boreman looked over to a dark corner of the vestry where a prim figure sat under the choir surplices. She was here again. Peter Simkin had told him she was inhabiting the Cock and Pie, in which case she'd be cognizant with the word 'pox' by now, even though she was not, again according to Simkin, taking part in its *raison d'être*. He was even inclined to believe it; in that Puritan get-up she could inspire lust only in the religiously deranged. He nodded 'Mistress' and received a frigid curtsey in reply.

'The cold,' he repeated. 'Things will improve now spring's here.'

Doubtfully, Peter Simkin rolled up his list, adjusted his hat and set off for the City, with Penitence loping along at his side. Their acquaintance, renewed by a meeting in the High Street, had led to mutual weekly forays to the City, he to deliver St Giles's Bill of Mortality to the authorities, she to try to look for new employment.

At first he'd suggested she approach London's Puritan communities. 'They ain't popular, I grant you,' he'd said, 'but they'd find you work.'

She'd rejected the idea. It was possible the Reverend Block had sent word from the Americas that a certain Penitence Hurd, a stuttering woman, was an arsonist and a witch. She was safer with Peter Simkin, for all that he belonged to the wrong church. The little man had an undemanding, motiveless kindness; in his company she was emboldened to venture the odd sentence. She ventured one now: 'Rats, t-t-too. A lot of d-d-dead rats.'

He hadn't noticed the rats; it was dead humans that worried him.

Should I tell him about the Searcher? To her certain knowledge, the Searcher had taken two bribes – she was Dog Yarder enough nowadays to think of them as 'angel's oil' – in the past week; one from Dog Yard's pawnbroker whose lodger had been found dead in bed, the other from Sam Bryskett, who'd had a customer fall dead on Ship premises. Word had it the corpses were pustulated. Afraid for their business, both men had crossed the Searcher's palm with silver to report the causes of death as non-infectious.

But the Plague had died out, surely. And she knew from her own experience that the Searcher could pretend to diagnose Plague in order to encourage silver across her palm. *Let sleeping dogs lie.* Sleeping corpses, anyway. She liked Sam Bryskett and his red-headed family, and, she was surprised to find, her loyalty to Dog Yard made her reluctant to betray it to an outsider like this parish clerk, nice man though he was.

Anyway, it wasn't a day for talking death. Today she would live for ever; everybody would live for ever. She always enjoyed these Monday walks; it was a pleasure to stroll past buildings that gladdened the eye instead of threatening to fall down, to smell coffee-shops and bakeries instead of laystalls. And today London had erupted into spring, as if an apologetic God was trying to make up for His bad winter.

What had been a stone city became a garden in which buildings dwindled to ornaments set among the greenery; London regained its countryside as drovers came in from the home counties and grazed their flocks of sheep and geese on its open spaces, and cocks crowed the alert to warm, soft dawns.

She sniffed appreciatively at the combination of blossom, new grass and horse-dung as she and Peter Simkin made their usual detour to Hyde Park, because Peter liked to be able to describe to his wife – a large lady tied to their house in the High Street by an even larger brood of children – what the fashionable were up to. In winter they had gone there to watch the skaters swoop and circle like brilliant-coloured swallows over the frozen Serpentine. Today she was shocked by the maypole, even as she tapped her foot in time to the flutes accompanying the Mayday milkmaids dancing round it and plaiting its bright ribbons.

Peter Simkin pointed as riders went by. 'There's Lady Castlemaine, look, Pen. The King's friend.'

The King's trollop more like. 'She's in m-m-m-man's attire.'

'Fashion, Pen. Fashion.'

Foppery. Extravagance. Look at the sheen on that plush. Even as she sniffed, Penitence noted the lovely cut of the long-tailed coat for future reference. It would suit Francesca.

All the way into the City, her Puritan egalitarianism warred with appreciation of beauty; the new stage-coach stations were attracting passengers now that the roads were passable again, even at a shilling per five miles. Mouth-watering pigskin luggage with brass locks was piled on the coach roofs while ladies, clambering inside, lifted gowns to reveal brocaded petticoats and high-heeled, pom-pommed shoes. In the India shop languid men and women sipped tea in an exotic-smelling cave while rolls of Smyrna cottons and Persian silk were flung down for their inspection. Next door, the lace shop frothed with Burgundian, Holland, cut and point-work that shaded from clotted cream to May blossom. 'I'll have some of the Flanders for baby's bib,' a female customer was saying. 'Eighteen shillings a yard? Extortion. Oh well, if one must, one must.'

Eighteen shillings. With eighteen shillings the unknown mother and baby who'd died in Dog Yard would be living yet.

At Bride Lane they parted. Peter Simkin entered the curlicued portals of the Worshipful Company of Parish Clerks Hall and handed in the list. The secretary who took it gave it a glance and said: 'St Giles up again, Master Simkin? More pox, I'll be bound.'

But as he dined off steak pie and porter at the Ring o' Bells in the Vintry, Peter Simkin heard his fellow-clerks from St Martin-in-the-Fields, Westminster and St Clement Danes admit that their lists were up too.

'Like our Searcher says, the cold nipped 'em,' said St Clement Danes, and the others agreed.

The talk turned to the war against the Dutch, but it seemed to Peter Simkin that the steak pie and porter lacked their usual flavour.

Outside, Penitence was waiting for him. He handed her a thumb-bread he'd saved from dinner. 'Any luck?'

Munching, Penitence shook her head. 'P-p-printing's out.'

The week before she had abandoned the idea of sewing as an employment prospect; London was awash with Huguenots escaping from Louis XIV's persecution, and all of them, as far as she could tell, were in the clothing trade. The answer was always the same: there were more seamstresses than there was work.

Today she'd tried peddling her other expertise and gone round every printing shop in the area of St Paul's, to be told they rarely employed journeyman printers and didn't employ women at all.

She'd been surprised to discover how few master printers there were. The recent Licensing Act, it appeared, limited their number to thirty-six. 'Is that L-London?' She'd asked at Stationers' Hall. The porter, who was ushering her out, shook his head. 'Country-wide.'

A country with only thirty-six printers. *And them only allowed to print what they're told.* There'd been more in New England; admittedly they'd mostly been small, apart from the one in Cambridge, but they'd been free. Small wonder there were so many illegal cock-robin shops, like the one in the Rookery's Goat Alley. She blamed it on the King. *Cromwell wouldn't have stood for it.*

'Ain't you got no other skills?' asked Peter Simkin, sympathetically. She hadn't; at least, none that would give her employment. There wasn't much call in London for tracking moose.

From her balcony that night Penitence Hurd watched the sun go down. Then she went to bed. Then she got up again and watched the moon come up.

What is it? What was calling her? What demon down there in the scented night was whispering this itch into her veins?

Perhaps it was the war. The City that day had throbbed with hatred against the Dutch; merchants grumbling that Norway was nothing more than the United Provinces' forest, that the Rhine banks and the Dordogne were just Dutch vineyards, that Spain and Ireland grazed Hollandish sheep, that the Bank of Amsterdam dominated trade between the Old and the New Worlds.

Bartholomew the Dutch. She didn't give a fig for them, or the war. Some older battle was pulsing in her blood, some unchristian thing which this night had rolled up all the springiness of springtime into a cowslip ball and tossed it into her lap.

She crossed her attic and opened the shutters of the other window merely to let in more air, and happened to notice, not that she was interested, that the play-actor's window was in darkness. He hadn't come back from Drury Lane yet.

The man was making a considerable impact on Dog Yard, which had taken to him, or, as Penitence thought, been taken in by him. His elaborate speech, which the Yarders would have called 'high-sniffing', i.e. supercilious, in anybody else, was offset by his poverty and boozing, familiar conditions which matched their own.

Mistress Palmer smuggled his washing into the Cock and Pie's, so that his linen was now laundered at an unknowing Her Ladyship's expense. Footloose ran or, rather, trundled his errands, Sam Bryskett allowed him free ale on condition he brought his fellow-Thespians to drink at the Ship, which he did. Fulker, the pawnbroker, advanced him cash without pledge and the Tippins not only didn't rob him, but saw that nobody else did either.

The most astonishing victim to his charm was Mistress Hicks, though there the conquest was mutual. On the morning when he'd been found slumped over the table at which he wrote far into the night, too drunk to go to the theatre, Mistress Hicks had hauled him downstairs by his hair, dunked it and the rest of his head in the horse-trough and then personally accompanied him to Drury Lane where she had kicked his backside through the door of the Cockpit Theatre. Her threat to do it again had kept him sufficiently sober to do his work ever since.

Joyfully watching the dunking from her balcony, Penitence had assumed Mistress Hicks was merely protecting her rent, but Dog Yard saw it as love pure and simple.

Phoebe, watching it with her, said: 'Gawd Almighty, anyone else she'd 'a' ground him for mustard and thrown him out.'

Dorinda and Alania, both infatuated, followed him to the Cockpit. They spent their spare time hanging round the theatre and swallowed, if not the anchor, a large part of the stage; both adorned their faces with patches and drawled my dears at every opportunity. They were seriously thinking of becoming theatre orange-girls. 'Killigrew took him on, my dear,' Alania told Penitence in the lofty, non-explanatory way of one who knew who Killigrew was to one who didn't, 'to help him with a French play that our Henry's translated by Molly someone. Did you know our Henry speaks French? My dear, like a native.'

The French being a people associated with Papistry and now, apparently, one which suffered women to write plays, did little to raise Penitence's estimation of the actor. She was at a loss that others were unable to discern, as she did, the contempt for the Rookery and its people which underlay the man's supposed charm.

She confided her puzzlement to Phoebe.

'He don't belong here, Prinks,' Phoebe said. 'If you ask me, he don't belong in the theatre, neither. One of them as lost their place under Cromwell, I wouldn't be surprised, and can't get it back. Acourse he don't like it. But it ain't us he looks down on. It's hisself.'

Penitence recognized the wisdom, though she preferred her dislike. She was discomfited that, as tonight, the thought of him took up so much of her attention. She must uplift it.

She sat down on her bed and took up her Bible, allowing it to fall open where it would. It chose the Song of Solomon, pages the Puritans of her community had regarded as one of the Lord's oversights and turned over quickly. She had not read it before.

The words wound themselves round her before she could stop them; spikenard and saffron, calamus and cinnamon, frankincense and aloes wafted her into the enclosed garden with its sealed fountain. Sometimes it was a woman speaking the words, sometimes a man — and a man with a very unsound attitude to his sister. The beloved came leaping over the hills like a hind to look forth at the windows, showing himself through the lattice.

She shut the Bible with a snap. The only enclosed garden round here was Dog Yard through which the Searcher was even now tapping her way. And the only lattice was the play-actor's.

What is it? Perhaps the sight of Hyde Park's beautiful women in beautiful clothes tonight made her want to imitate beauty. Perhaps, tomorrow, she would beg some material from Her Ladyship and make herself a new gown. Black, of course, high-necked, but new.

The impulse to go out into the scented night to find what was calling her was strong, and had to be resisted. Instead, unable to express her agitation in any other form, she laid herself down on her bed, put her hands behind her neck and sang.

Singing had always been her joy. When she sang she didn't stutter, a phenomenon that had brought more than one beating from her mother who'd argued that if she could sing freely it was perversity on her part to stutter when she talked.

Usually, she sang psalms, but not tonight. Psalms held no outlet for the unchristian beat in her veins.

When, later, the actor came home, he entered a Dog Yard whose residents sat on their doorsteps in the moonlight, listening to a strong young soprano echo round its court and alleys in a throbbing minor key, singing of corn-planting in a language they did not understand, of a god, Cautantowwit,

provider of harvest three thousand miles away, of young
men's return from winter initiation to a people they had never
heard of.

He sat down next to his landlady on her step. 'Who's that?'

'Puritan cat next door,' said Mistress Hicks. 'Where's my
rent?'

He handed over the money. 'Cat?'

'Cat. Tart. Whore. The one in the hat.'

'Ah, Mistress Boots.'

'Don't know her name. Wauling like a bloody cat, though.'

But they sat on. Springtime had struggled through even to
Dog Yard in clumps of valerian sprouting between the cracks
in its stones, and in an unsuspected hazel showering catkins
over Footloose's vat. The beggar was propped in the mouth
of his huge barrel, swinging his stumps in time to the song.
Mistress Parker leaned against a washing-draped crenel on the
roof of the Buildings. In a window further down, Mistress
Fairley was dreamily breast-feeding two babies at the same
time. Along to the left, the Cock and Pie girls had pulled
stools on to the flagstones, the better to enjoy the air. Even
such Tippins as weren't off burgling had gathered in unusual
silence to drink their ale on the steps of the Ship. It was a rare
moment.

'Odd,' said the actor. He produced his leather bottle and
proffered it to his landlady.

Mistress Hicks drank. 'Takes all sorts,' she said. 'Must be
some as fancy her or that Ladyship wouldn't keep her. She
ain't in the charity business.'

'I'm sure. But when I was in Paris there were missionary
priests from Quebec who had brought back some of their
Indian converts to show King Louis. They made them sing.
Their song wasn't dissimilar to hers. Odd that a poor little
whore in a Rookery brothel should sing a song of the
Iroquois. Rather gloriously, too.'

'Life's odd,' said Mistress Hicks.

They drank to that philosophical pearl.

'An' don't go boozin' in the Ship for a bit. They got illness.
Sam Bryskett's called in the 'pothecary.'

They drank to Sam Bryskett's continued health and sat on together, listening.

So passed one of Dog Yard's rare nights of peace. Its last.

The next day, the collated Bill of Mortality for all London, its liberties and out-parishes that week was on the desk of the Lord Mayor.

> Abortive: 4 ... Aged: 45 ... Broke her skull by a fall in the street: 1 ... Childbed: 28 ... Dropsie: 32 ... Gout: 1 ... Grief: 3 ... Lethargy: 1 ... Purples: 2 ... Quinsie: 5 ... Suddenly: 2 ... Vomiting: 10 ... Wind: 4 ... Worms: 20.

The infinitely varied ways in which people could die always fascinated Sir John Lawrence. 'What's Purples?'

'I don't know, my lord.'

'No more do I. And Suddenly could mean anything.' He checked the total. 'It's up.'

'Somewhat, my lord,' said the clerk to the Worshipful Company of Parish Clerks. 'Been a hard winter.'

Sir John ran his finger down the 'p's. 'Pox in plenty again.'

'St Giles,' said the clerk, smugly. 'It's always them.'

'They're the only ones honest enough to admit it.' Sir John's finger went up the column a notch. 'No Plague.'

'No, my lord.'

'Why not?' Sir John leaned forward over his desk, tapping it. 'Nat Hodges personally told me he attended three mortal cases in Westminster last Tuesday week. They're not down here. Why not?'

The clerk to the Clerks shuffled. Cripus, how he hated new brooms; the old Lord Mayor had passed the Bills without a glance. 'Manifestly, my lord, Westminster's Searcher said different.'

'Manifestly,' said Sir John, catching the word and bouncing it, 'manifestly, Westminster's Searcher, like all searchers, couldn't tell the difference between Plague and Phthisis. *Manifestly*, for two groats she'd say they were carried off by the choir invisible.'

The clerk to the Clerks wondered why he'd been backed into defending a system which manifestly had its flaws. Because it *was* the system; always was, always would be. Doctors didn't record deaths, searchers did.

But Sir John was like that; aggressive, a little man with large ideas. Out to make his mark. He'd try reason. 'My lord, it's twenty year since the last bad outbreak. Manifestly' — oh, Cripus — 'there's doctors never seen a case of Plague. The Searchers is old women and they got long memories.'

'They've got long pockets.' The Lord Mayor glared. 'You listen to me, Master Clerk. This will be a good mayoral year for London, a great year. If there's Plague, I'm nipping it in the bud. One clerk hiding a plague spot and I'll Barbados him so fast he won't have time to say goodbye. They tell me, as Chief Magistrate. And me first. Is that manifest enough?'

When the Clerks' clerk had gone, the Lord Mayor's secretary, who was also his nephew, said gently, 'Hard on him, my lord.'

'Him and his manifestly.' Sir John Lawrence went to the window of the Guildhall, holding up a hand to ward off reproach. 'It's not his fault, I know isolated cases crop up occasionally, I know all that. But the thing comes in twenty-year cycles, I know *that*.' He whirled round on his little shoes. 'And so do you. In '25, again in the mid-'40s. How many thousand?'

Young Simmons said: 'Before my time, my lord.'

'It wasn't before mine.' He remembered the terror. 'Men dug their own graves and laid in them to die, knowing their wives couldn't carry them. Nobody else would touch them.'

Every twenty years. Not this twentieth, for Christ's dear body. He'd worked for this; alderman, sheriff, staying loyal to young Charles in exile. The first civic dignitary to be knighted after the Restoration — and he'd deserved it. Now with the rightful king back on the throne, and himself — between them they'd give London such days as it hadn't seen since the time of Dick Whittington. He wouldn't be robbed of it.

In the rectory of St Giles-in-the-Fields, the Reverend Boreman broke a long silence. 'And there's no possibility it was fever?'

William Boghurst shook his head. 'The tokens were plain. I was apprentice to my father in the '25 outbreak. One saw them then.'

The Reverend Boreman persisted. 'The Searcher says it was rickets.'

'She's wrong.'

'They do say,' said Peter Simkin, almost to himself, 'they do say as the Searcher buys meat every day now instead of once a week.'

'God damn the hag,' shouted the Reverend Boreman. 'So it could be rife.'

'Undoubtedly,' said the apothecary, calmly. 'The Ship is the most popular inn in the Rookery. And the largest.'

The Reverend Boreman got up and strode to the rectory drawing-room windows which were open to let in the May scents of his garden. It was at its best this time of year. His wife had planted it. 'Plague,' he said. He realized he was rubbing his thumb and third finger together, a nervous habit Janet had tried to cure him of. He'd christened all the Bryskett children. Eight? Nine? Red-headed every one. Sad, sad Sam Bryskett, a better fellow than most in the Rookery. God help him.

'The Lord Mayor's instructions was to tell him immediate, Rector,' said Peter Simkin. 'So's he could isolate it.'

'Isolate it? How? The parish hasn't even a pest-house.'

'The Worshipful Company's clerk was telling me as Sir John had plans to take all the healthy *out* from a plague parish and move all the sufferers *in*. If it came. Isolate it, like.'

The Reverend Boreman snorted. 'Easier said than done.'

'But,' went on the parish clerk, doggedly, 'I was also told as how the Privy Council's sent down orders for shutting-ups.'

The Reverend Boreman was receiving too much information too quickly, but one thing stood out: 'You mean to tell me, Peter Simkin, that the Privy Council has suspected an epidemic?'

'Looks like it, Rector.'

'One imagines that St Giles is not the only parish to have more deaths than usual,' said the apothecary. 'It has been suspected, but concealed. Myself,' he continued, 'I recommend my electuary antidote, an infusion first compounded by my father which proved highly efficacious. Eightpence an ounce.'

'Make some up,' the rector told him. 'A lot.' He was putting off the moment that would solidify the phantasm into reality. Suffering, work, responsibility, would come crashing in. He was too old; perhaps he should retire now and let a younger man . . . die. Oh, God, that was what he would be doing. He was afraid. Christ in Heaven, he was afraid. 'Well, Peter Simkin, be off and alert the Lord Mayor. And the wardmote. Sexton, of course. Tell the parish officers to be here tonight.'

As Simkin went, the rector turned to the apothecary. 'We must inform Doctor Whaley. He'll be needed.'

William Boghurst laced his fingers. 'I called in at the good doctor's house on my way. He has been called away. Suddenly. With his family. A visit. To his sister who is ailing. In the North.'

'I see.' The wall between his garden and the churchyard was covered with Janet's favourite pink rose. If she'd been alive and the children still at home, would he have emulated Whaley and run for it? But she wasn't. They weren't.

The apothecary's self-righteous little voice was saying: 'I must take issue with the Privy Council's policy of shutting up, if that is intended. It did no good in '25, it will do no good again. It results in even more concealment, to say nothing of flight. Above all, it is unchristian. I go so far as to say it is murder.'

'No ailing sister, then?' He turned round and saw the apothecary blink behind his spectacles.

'As it happens I do have a sister who is, indeed, unwell. She has the rheumatics. Unfortunately, she lives in the parish.'

'You'll stay?'

'Oh yes.'

Boghurst and Boreman, thought the Reverend Boreman. Defenders of St Giles. And who would remember them? Ah well, perhaps God would.

He crossed over to where the apothecary sat and pressed his hands on the thin, prim shoulders. 'Let us say our prayers, my son,' he said.

'G-g-go?' Penitence stared at Her Ladyship. 'W-where shall I g-go?'

'Listen, will you? We're busy. A-first Leadenhall Street. Number forty-two. Ask for Master Patterson. He's a scrivener and my legal man. Say you've come for Her Ladyship's papers. Understand? Her Ladyship's papers. Then back here and pack your bag. Tomorrow you go.'

'B-b-but w-where shall I g-go?' asked Penitence again.

There was knocking from below, and Her Ladyship hurried out.

Penitence stood where she was, waiting, oddly shocked. It was one thing to have been trying to leave the Cock and Pie under her own volition; quite another to be ejected. *What have I done?* Her sewing had been more than adequate.

It had been a shock in itself to be summoned to Her Ladyship's bedroom. After the first glance she'd kept her eyes away from the flounced pink voile which framed the chains and fetters decorating the wall beyond the bed.

She winced at Her Ladyship's agonizingly ladylike vowels floating up the staircase. 'Not at all, my lord. I understand perfectly. This way, my lord. Can I suggest our Mistress Fanny? Prime of all my rosebuds.'

The busy click of the woman's heels and the slower march of male boots passed outside the boudoir door on their way along the clerestory.

Her Ladyship came back, puffing, but before she could return to the room there was another knock on the great outside door. She went downstairs again and ushered another client up – this time for Sabina.

Penitence found it puzzling. It was so early. The Cock and Pie's clientele usually visited under cover of darkness.

Her Ladyship came in and lumbered over to a walnut bureau from which she took a purse. 'There's two guineas in that. It'll keep you till you find work.'

'W-w-umm-where?' Penitence asked again.

Her Ladyship's lips went thin with irritation. 'Away from London. Go to Taunton and join the rest of the God-botherers. Your aunt came from Taunton. Mention her name at the George in Fore Street.'

It was disconcerting to have her dearest wish materialize in this fashion. She was grateful, but now that it came to it she was floundered by the prospect of change. 'W-why?'

'Why what?' snapped Her Ladyship. She shoved the purse under Penitence's nose. 'Here's your wages. Take it. There won't be no more.'

Penitence went into her stammering attitude. Her head went down, her hands fisted. 'Bu-bu-b-b-umm-bu-but why?'

'Acause trade's finished, is why. No more gentlemen, is why. No more sewing, is why.' Her Ladyship sat down on a stool with a pink cushion. She stared at her hands. 'From here on the clientele we get won't care iffen we're ragged.'

There was another thunderous knock on the outside door. Angrily, Her Ladyship heaved herself up and went to the balustrade outside. 'You answer it, Job. If he's sober and can pay, let him in. Tell Mary to show him up to Francesca. It's her turn.'

Penitence persisted. 'B-b-but it's so b-b-b-busy.'

Her Ladyship shut the drawer of the bureau. 'We're busy all right.' She turned on Penitence, who flinched back. 'You want to know why? We're busy acause the gentlemen's got wind of Plague.'

'P-p-plague?'

Her Ladyship did what she'd never done; she imitated Penitence's stutter. 'P-p-plague. Oh, they don't know there's Plague at the Ship. But they know there's Plague around town somewheres.'

Bewildered, Penitence caught at the most immediate fact. 'The Ship?'

Her Ladyship let out a deep breath. 'Sam Bryskett's littlest. Died in the night.'

The littlest. That would be Jenny. Was Jenny. Unseeing, she stretched out her hand and took the purse Her Ladyship held.

She was frightened and she would go, of course she would go, and quickly, but this woman, wicked as she might be, had provided a rock for her to cling to these past months.

She found herself saying: 'W-why don't you come too?'

Something happened in the brothel-keeper's large face; she went back to the bureau and stood before it for a second or two before she turned around. Penitence flinched again. How had she offended?

'You bird-witted barrel of treacle.' Her Ladyship's fingers bit into the flesh of Penitence's upper arm as she dragged her out on to the clerestory. 'Hear 'em?' she whispered. 'Hear them beds going? Hear that one brimming?'

She could. She tried to draw away.

'Know what they're doing?'

Penitence dragged her hands up to cover her ears. 'All t-too well.'

'No, you don't. You don't know *anything*. These ain't my regulars. These have been recommended. These gentlemen have come for to get the pox, that's what they're doing.' Her whisper was more terrible than if she'd screamed it. 'Get the pox, you don't get the Plague. That's what them fine gentlemen want and that's why I'm charging double today. For the pox.' She looked along the corridor. 'God rot you, fine gentlemen,' she said, and smiled. 'As undoubted He will.'

She was still smiling as she shoved Penitence back into her bedroom. 'Come too?' she said. 'Pippin, they'd love us in Taunton.'

She became businesslike. 'There's a drayman delivering at the Ship and spending the night there — he don't know about the Plague, either. He'll lift you to the Great West Road tomorrow. Take a rattler to Taunton from there. Or walk. I don't care. Just go. But get the papers first.'

Pushing her way through Drury Lane, Penitence saw male crowds at each brothel door. Outside Mother Bennett's they were waiting in line.

Until then she hadn't been able to believe what Her Lady-ship had told her, but it was obviously, appallingly true. With hideous deliberation, without the excuse of lust, the gentlemen back at the Cock and Pie, no less than these common men here, were deliberately seeking to inoculate themselves against disease by contracting another of delayed effect that they would take back to their wives. *God damn men.* God DAMN them. She began to run to get to Leadenhall Street quicker, to get to tomorrow faster, so that she could leave London and never come back.

There was a touch on her arm. 'Where's the fire, Pen?'

She looked into the sober face of St Giles's parish clerk; automatically they fell into step, but for once she was repelled by his company. He was a man. Who knew but that even he had been attending the Drury Lane brothels?

Peter Simkin looked cautiously around, then muttered: 'You heard about the "P", Pen?'

The pox? No, he meant the Plague.

Born into a generation and an area of New England which had escaped the American Plague, the word did not carry the terror for Penitence which she had seen in Her Ladyship's eyes and now saw in Peter Simkin's; nor had her grandparents, always uninformative about their past in England, made much of any experience they might have had during the '45 outbreak. It was a bogeyman word, alarming but belonging to the out-there. She had never been ill; she could not imagine being ill. She was armoured by her own magnificent health and her trust in the Lord. And it was another lovely spring day.

Nevertheless, alerted, she noticed little eddies in London's confident streets that indicated an undercurrent of alarm. All through Cheapside there were more sellers of hares' feet than there had been the week before. The window of a dark apothecary shop was newly strung across with wooden cabalistic letters 'to be hung round thee necke'.

A jeweller was standing in the street holding an emerald between tweezers with which he angled it to catch the light. A green beam danced across the wall, and Penitence and Peter stopped to watch it. 'See, master,' the jeweller was saying, to his well-dressed customer, 'a sunbeam passing through this will extract all malignant humours from the body.'

Tobacconists were doing a roaring trade. 'No tobacconist ever died from the "P", well-known fact,' whispered Peter Simkin.

A lady and a small boy emerged from one such shop, both puffing on pipes. When the child broke into coughing and complained, 'But I don't like it, ma'am', his mother cuffed him: 'It's good for you.'

The magnificent gateway of the Guildhall was choked with carriages. Penitence arranged to meet Peter back there, and hurried on to Leadenhall Street, all her dread now concentrated on the next few minutes during which she must face strangers and request Papers from a Patterson.

'Her Ladyship's papers, please, Master Patterson,' she practised. No good. Too many p's together. Her hands were beginning to sweat. *Documents, I'll ask for Her Ladyship's documents.* She was better on 'd's. *And I'll leave out the 'please'.* It would make her sound churlish, but she was used to that; stammerers couldn't afford nuances of courtesy. 'Please pass the salt' had to be pared down to the peremptory 'Salt'.

Can I leave out the 'Patterson'?

A woman buying a chicken outside the Market was staring at her. Penitence glared back: 'Master Lawyer, I require Her Ladyship's documents,' she said. *Oh, Bartholomew. I sound like a highwayman.*

Here was Number forty-two, a thin, elegant house with a brass plate at the door, and here she was, a perspiring wreck. *Why don't I go back to the Yard and get Pa Tippin to burgle the place?*

It was worse than she'd imagined. The porter was deaf or stupid or both and made her repeat the request to see his employer three times. Master Patterson, a careful Scot and a typical lawyer, proved reluctant to hand over papers without Her Ladyship's written request, despite his knowledge of Her Ladyship's illiteracy. Penitence had to stammer answers to questions designed to test her bona fides.

At last, and reluctantly, she was given a box and shown to the door. Even there, the lawyer delayed her: 'Eh am surpraised that a gairl of your ... pairsuasion is ... May eh enquire what is your capacity in Hair Ladyship's employment?'

She'd had enough, 'W-what's yours?', and stamped off, careless of the existence of all plagues but her own. Until she saw Peter Simkin's face.

'The B-b-bill? Is it up?'

He was as precise as ever, though his hands shook. 'The total Bill of Mortality for London is nine.'

Nine. One of them little Jenny Bryskett. But for all London it didn't amount to disaster. 'N-not b-bb-bad then.'

'No,' he said, 'ain't bad at all. Only it ain't true.' He lifted his hat to wipe his forehead, then replaced it. He had a newspaper in his hand — he always bought the weekly quarto-page *Newes* so that he could read it to his wife, who liked to know what King and court were up to. 'There's a special Privy Council committee been set up.' He read her the names: 'General Monck, Duke of Albemarle — he's the one got the King back on the throne, Pen. Lord Arlington, he's the Head of State. Earl of Southampton, he's Lord Treasurer. The Lord Chamberlain. The Duke of Ormonde. The Earl of Bath. The Comptroller. The Vice-Chamberlain. Mr Secretary Morice.'

He looked up. 'Nine,' he said. 'That's nine very grand gentlemen for only nine deaths.'

They began walking. 'Know what I reckon, Pen? I reckon it's been creeping up all winter, and now it's at the gates.' Peter Simkin was looking around him as if seeing everything for the first time. 'It's a rare city, Pen,' he said.

As always, they cut through the nave of St Paul's down to Ludgate instead of going round by Carter Lane. Penitence never minded, though Cromwell had condemned the cathedral as papistical. She regarded the nave as a secular thoroughfare — as did most of London.

Steeling herself to squeeze through the stalls selling every-thing saleable and push away pedlars selling a great deal that wasn't, she was taken aback when Peter Simkin said 'With your permission, Pen' and slipped off into a side chapel. She saw him go down on his knees.

Embarrassed, she went back out on the steps to wait for him. *He's acting as if it's the end of the world.*

From here she could see over the churchyard, over the

jumbled roofs beyond it to the Thames where the eel ships scudded upriver, their brown sails bellied out by the May breeze in satisfying, pregnant curves.

To her left the thin tower of the Exchange rang the bell to end trading just as, beyond it, the clock on the ornate lantern of St Mary-le-Bow chimed the hour. Between the flying buttresses behind her, the booksellers began gathering up their texts, poems, broadsheets and translations and dismantling their trestles.

From here Southwark, across the river, looked like a rural village instead of the continual alehouse-cum-brothel it really was.

Dutifully she thought: *Woe unto you, Jerusalem.* But it had become *her* Jerusalem, a city of energy and beauty and a promise it hadn't yet fulfilled. In contrast, the unknown Taunton assumed the qualities of Puritan Springfield in Massachusetts: ordered, worthy, loveless — and dull. She would stay there only until she had discovered what there was to discover about Aunt Margaret; then, somehow, she would come back.

All the way home Peter Simkin chattered about the Orders. Doctors to examine suspected cases and report, all needless concourses to be prohibited, the poor to be given relief and work, houses to be kept clean, ordure to be removed from the streets, pest-houses to be built, none allowed to travel in the kingdom without a certificate of health, the College of Physicians immediately to advise on medical procedure . . .

She barely listened. 'Reasonable,' she said. *What a fuss.*

'That's reasonable if put in hand, Pen, but old Johnson — he's St Martin's — he says as the same Orders was issued in '25, and look what happened then.' Peter Simkin sucked on his teeth. 'And reasonable if they got the cash for it, Pen. But Parliament's only voted money for war against them damned Dutch, if you'll pardon my French. Now it's gone and prorogued itself and when's it going to meet again, that's what I want to know? If they put the charge on the parishes — well, St Giles ain't got it, and that's a fact. And it's the poorest parishes'll get the "P" worst, you mark my words.'

He looked around him in case anybody was listening, and

touched her arm, speaking low: 'And young Pettit – he's Houndsditch – he said as how the King's issued secret orders as how the Tower's got to be garrisoned in case of panic and riot.'

What a fuss. As they passed the alley leading to the Cockpit, she happened to glance down it but saw nobody she recognized.

Full of his news and duties, Peter turned off to the High Street while she wandered on to Dog Yard – and found the place in tumult.

They were shutting up the Ship.

Have the Dutch invaded? Her first impression was of a battle; but that was ridiculous. The first hostilities on English soil weren't likely to be fought in Dog Yard. But it was a war all the same. On one side soldiers armed with pikes and parish officers lashing out with their white wands, all commanded by a small magistrate in a big hat on a white horse, waving and shouting. On the opposing side Dog Yard.

The Dog Yarders were impeding, screeching and fighting. Two Tippins were pummelling a beadle lying on the cobbles. Mistress Parker was trying to kick the shins of a soldier, who was holding her off with one arm.

Penitence saw Footloose propel himself and his tub into the path of two more beadles going to their fellow's rescue. One fell over him, but the other, an enraged fat man, plucked the beggar out of his tub, looked round, spotted a cresset-holder sticking out of the Buildings and hung him up on it by the back of his jacket.

In the shelter of the Stables chimney, a young Tippin was tearing tiles off the roof, dodging out to throw them at the soldiery, then dodging back. The Cock and Pie and Mother Hubbard's had joined forces. She saw Dorinda clinging like a monkey to the back of a man who was attempting to do something to one of the Ship's windows while hampered by a Mother Hubbard girl swinging from his arm.

From her window, Mistress Hicks was emptying her boarders' pots over the head of any member of the opposing army who happened in range, following up with well-aimed throws of the pots themselves.

The noise was horrific. In the encircled court it was like being trapped with yowling cats in a bucket battered by bricks. Between, under, through the chaos ran children, dodging and yelling: among them the hair of the Brysketts streamed like torches.

One ran up to Penitence and flung his arms round her waist. 'Don't want to be shut up, Pen. Don't let 'em shut me up.' She put her arms round him. It was the second littlest Bryskett.

A pikeman strode up. 'Let's be having him, mistress.'

Convulsively, she hugged the child closer. 'N-n-no.'

Behind the face-bars of his lobster-tail helmet, the pikeman's look was not unsympathetic. 'Orders, mistress. Plague-houses to be shut up with all inhabitants.'

A muffled voice came from the middle of Penitence's coat. 'I ain't got it. Jenny had it. Ma wouldn't let us see her.'

'No,' said Penitence again.

'Come on, son,' said the soldier. Leather gauntlets manoeuvred the boy firmly out of Penitence's clutch, carried him across the Yard, up the steps, and handed him in at an upstairs window of the Ship to the pale-faced, red-headed Mistress Bryskett.

The Ship's door was already stapled with a chain fastened by a padlock. A large figure trapped on the inside was struggling to get his shoulders through the tiny gap the door offered, bellowing a desperate litany of complaint. 'That's not right, maister. I'm clean. Hertfordshire man, me. Just delivering. You let me *out*. I got wife and children in Potters Bar. What of me hosses? You let me OUT.'

No one was taking any more notice of him than of the magistrate on the horse, whose voice had gone into the higher register of scream.

Click, click, click-click-click. Light, ordered sound did what shouting couldn't and impinged on everybody's consciousness. One by one, parish officers and Dog Yarders turned their head towards it.

The pikemen had drawn up in a crouched line with their backs to the Stables and the Buildings, the base of their pikes on the ground in a neat line sloping towards the riot.

The man who had taken the second littlest Bryskett away from Penitence went on tapping his pike on the cobbles until there was silence. He stepped forward. He was tall; only tall men could carry the eighteen-foot pike with grace.

'My name,' he called, conversationally, 'is Corporal Forbush. These gentlemen squattin' here is a troop of His Majesty's Pike. They are in the position what is adopted to repel chargin' horse.' He had everybody's attention. 'Now then,' he went on, 'when this here troop charges, they stand up, like what I'm doing, and they level the pike. Like this.'

Dog Yard's eyes became riveted on a steel-sharp tip.

'Now then,' said Corporal Forbush, '*they* don't want to do this. I don't want 'em to do it and *you* don't want 'em to do it. So what I suggest is, we all stay very quiet and listen to what Magistrate Flesher here's got to say.' He saluted in the direction of the little man on the horse, whose mouth was still open.

So that's Flesher. Known to the Rookery with reason – and among other things – as Flogger Flesher.

'I'll arrest the lot of you,' he was screaming. 'Constables, get those men.' He pointed at the spot where the Tippin brothers had been punching the beadle. The beadle was sitting up, feeling his jaw, but the Tippins had disappeared, and with them had gone much of Dog Yard's attempt to defy the inevitable. Corporal Forbush strode up, and under cover of quietening the magistrate's horse, offered some muttered advice.

Reluctantly, Flogger Flesher took it. He put his sword into its scabbard, straightened his hat and, producing a scroll, began to read: 'By the authority invested in me by His Royal Majesty . . .' The audibility of the warrant was marred as much by the clove-studded orange he now held to his nose as by the drayman, who was still shouting.

Penitence turned to the figure next to her, which turned out to be Phoebe stemming her bleeding nose on her petticoat.

'*How* l-long d-did he s-say?'

'Forty days,' said Phoebe. 'Fuckers. That's finished me with the King.'

The Ship, those children, shut up for forty days? 'C-c-can't,' she said. 'They c-c-can't.'

They were. Such younger Brysketts as were still outside were rounded up and lifted in.

As, one by one, the diamond-paned ground-floor windows were boarded over, the imprisoned Bryskett children ran to the next. Outside, Dorinda followed them, her hand raised to clutch theirs, like someone saying goodbye to a passenger in a moving coach. When the planks went over the last window she leaned back against the wall, then slid down on to her hands and knees.

Penitence ran to help her up. The girl was sobbing. 'The little 'uns. I can't bear it.'

'I know.'

Mistress Parker was still trying to effect an entry into the Ship as forcibly as the drayman was trying to make an exit. 'You got my old man in there, turd-brain,' she screamed.

Magistrate Flesher urged his horse to the Ship steps. 'Who's in there?'

The beadle on the door saluted: 'Landlord and his lady, sir, eight childer, two potboys, one tapster, one drayman, a skivvy – and a person still asleep with a pint pot in his 'and.'

'That's him,' shouted Mistress Parker.

'All persons found on the premises stay on the premises,' said Magistrate Flesher. He dismounted and strode up the steps. 'Give me the chalk.'

There was squealing from the back of the Ship and a constable came marching round to the front, his hand clamped on the thin shoulder of a girl. 'Nelly Ogle, sir, spinster of this parish. Skivvy to the Ship. Caught trying to escape.'

Magistrate Flesher considered Nelly Ogle and his options. If he opened the door the drayman, a very big man like all draymen, would get out. 'Get a ladder and tip her in.'

In silence Dog Yard watched twelve-year-old Nelly Ogle, spinster of its parish, hauled up a ladder, watched her helped in by Mistress Bryskett, watched Mistress Bryskett's face, watched Magistrate Flesher draw a red cross on the Ship's door and chalk words above it. He turned round, planted his short legs apart and addressed the crowd: 'Anyone violating this order will be subjected to the severest penalties. Consider yourselves lucky I have not imposed them already. Constable.'

Ill-will was something Magistrate Flesher was used to, but he preferred facing it from the height of his Bench. He waited at the top of the steps until the pikemen had formed two protective lines around his horse before giving the signal for the company to move off.

As he marched out of Dog Yard, Corporal Forbush reached up, plucked Footloose off his bracket and popped him tenderly into his tub. 'God Save the King,' he said.

It was a salutation usually eliciting a cheer from the Dog Yarders among whom a sovereign of legendary naughtiness had been an icon. 'To Charlie, may he bust a thousand bellies' was a toast that had raised many a loyal tankard in the Ship. Today they remained silent.

Between them, Dorinda and Penitence helped a weeping Mistress Parker to her feet. 'What's them words say?' she asked, pointing at the Ship door.

Penitence read them: 'Lord Have Mercy Upon Us.'

Mistress Parker wept again. 'He always wanted to die with a tankard in his bloody hand,' she said, 'I reckon he's got his wish.'

They took her to the door of the Buildings and returned to the Cock and Pie, threading through a yard full of people who were being joined by others from the alleys of the Rookery, all staring in the direction of the Ship.

'There'll be trouble,' said Dorinda.

How much more trouble can there be?

Plague was as yet merely one of the immeasurable diseases the Rookery lived with; on the other hand, intrusion by royal authority was here and now. As far as popularity went, the King couldn't hold a candle to Sam Bryskett, who provided employment and entertainment in an area where both were scarce. Penitence heard one man say: 'Whosis Fornicating Majesty with his jools and fancy women to shut up our fucking inn?'

Gaining the attic, Dorinda sank on to the bed, Penitence on

to a stool. The last vestiges of daylight were coming through the front window.

'My bread's baked,' said Dorinda. With her eyes closed, the girl looked vulnerable and exhausted. 'I ain't never been taken medicinally before.'

Penitence remembered the men who'd been tramping up and down to the clerestory all day. The Plague sign on a nearby door would keep them away from now on. 'Th-that's over, at l-least.'

The sympathy in her voice stirred Dorinda into sitting up and reclaiming ground lost by her show of weakness. She looked round the attic and sniffed. 'Smells like a new-baked turd in here.' She got up and swatted a stem of St John's wort hanging from a beam — Penitence had gone out into the country near Tottenham Court to pick herbs after spring-cleaning the attic. 'Think a bunch of weeds'll keep off the Plague?'

Penitence shook her head. 'F-f-umm-fleas.'

'Fum-fleas,' said Dorinda, with contempt. 'Fleas won't kill you. Plague will. But I forgot, didn't I? Miss Prinkum-Prankum won't get it. Her Ladyship's sending Miss Prinkum-Prankum away.'

'N-n-no m-more w-w-work.'

'That's what she said.' The old viciousness was back. 'She's favouring you, you ballocker. She's always favoured you.' She glanced towards the actor's window, found his room empty, and went.

Upstairs after dinner, Penitence emptied her bead satchel on to the bed, ready to repack it. Her Ladyship, with surprising generosity for the imprisoned drayman, had told Job to take the man's team back to his wife in Potters Bar in the morning. Penitence was to go with them.

She considered the small pile of belongings; useless strings of wampum which she would take with her because they were reminders of the Squakheag, as were the little hunting bow and quiver of arrows Matoonas had made for her. The tobacco and pipes she would give to Kinyans, who was a fumer when he could afford it. Clean underwear and dress, her old coat, clean but threadbare – thankfully, she would have little need for it with summer coming on – a pair of Phoebe's cast-off slippers and a new cap she had made from a linen cut-off.

Even with Her Ladyship's two guineas, it was little enough for the months she had spent in this attic. On the other hand, she was taking other things away with her: a compassion for the life of whores, a reluctant admiration, even fellow-feeling, for the spirit of an indigent people who, half a year before, she would have condemned as worthless. Whether these changes of attitude were advances, or merely destructive Anythingarianism, she could not have said. The God she'd believed in when she arrived here would certainly have disapproved, but He had undergone a bit of a sea-change Himself.

She heard movement from the play-actor's room and saw light from his window flicker on her sill. Lately, he'd taken to sitting at his table, writing into the early hours. The scratch of his quill had been audible through her shutters and kept her awake. Alania said he was writing a play.

It occurred to her that he might not know there was Plague at the Ship and ought to be told. Personally, she didn't think there was danger; but he ought to be told.

Immediately the thought of exposing her stutter sent her into a panic. There was no avoiding the word 'Plague', it being the *raison d'être* of the warning, but it would block her. Was there no other noun for it? Only Pestilence, another insuperable 'p'.

Bartholomew the man. What did she care what he thought of her? And who was he to cavil at the messenger? He should be grateful she was telling him at all.

Whipping herself into a fury, she went to her half-open shutters and pulled them wide. He'd taken off his cloak and hat and was studying the papers on his table. 'Hey,' she shouted.

He looked up. 'Ah, Mistress Boots.'

At once, her anger left her and she went into the worst stutter of her life. 'There's P-p-p-pl-p . . .' It wouldn't come out. It stayed reverberating behind the compression of her lips. *Give up. Run and hide.* Her clenched knuckles dug into the sides of her thighs as she fought with it. 'There's P-p-pl . . .'

Instead of turning away, or helping her out, he looked at her with interest. 'Why do you do that?'

She was so surprised, she said: 'I s-st-stutter.'

'So it seems. You know it can be cured?'

So casual. As if she'd caught it, like a cold. How dare he. She was angry enough to get out: 'There's P-plague at the Ship.' *Let him cure that.* The last glimpse she had before she slammed the shutters and went to bed was of his grimace as he reached for a bottle on his table. He'd get drunk. It was all actors were good for.

Chapter 5

THE REVEREND BLOCK knelt by her bedside, muttering profanity and prayer. This time he'd brought reinforcements. A dozen lecherous clergymen were outside the door, shouting obscenities. The noise pinioned her arms to the bed like clamps. She wouldn't be able to fight him, them, unless the noise let her arms go. *Stop it, stop it.*

She sat up in bed, drenched in sweat. There *was* noise, like that produced by the riot earlier, but magnified ten times over. Pulling the bedspread over her night-shift, she hurried to the front window.

The scene below *was* like the evening riot magnified ten times. Yet not like. One hundred or more figures milled in and out of the flickering light thrown by Dog Yard's only cresset. Where before there had been anger, now there was hate, unfocused, generalized hate. It scalded through the Yard like boiling steam.

It took a while for her to realize that the resentment which had erupted in Dog Yard that evening had spread to the rest of the Rookery as its men — and the swarming crowd below consisted mainly of men — emerged into the night to find their favourite inn closed against them.

Imprisonment of the Brysketts, fear of the Plague, bitterness against authority, drunkenness, had sparked the fuse of terrible deprivation and burst into a huge, illogical explosion.

One man standing upon Footloose's vat, weaving perilously, was urging a march on Whitehall. 'Let's go wake up the King. Let's go 'n shut up Old Rowley's inn.'

Nobody was listening to him, having better things to do, like trying to kick in the doors of the Stables, or claw up cobbles to throw at windows. The Dog Yarders, having shot their bolt that afternoon, had retired indoors to protect their homes.

The Ship's doors were open, and so were the flaps to its chute; barrels were being passed up and broken open. There was no sign of the Brysketts – Sam was probably trying to defend his cellar. No sign, either, of the two watchmen who had been left on guard; perhaps gone for reinforcements. *They could be dead*. The mob was capable of killing.

The only faces she recognized were the drayman's, who was drunk and dancing, and Mistress Parker's husband, who was just drunk and ignoring the pleas of his wife from her balcony to come home.

There was thudding immediately below. She leaned over the parapet and saw a phalanx of men rhythmically ramming a plank against the Cock and Pie's door. One of them spotted her. 'Come down here, you cat, or we'll come and get you.' More amiably, somebody else shouted: 'Come on down, chucky, and give us the pox.'

Over at Mother Hubbard's another group had broken in. There were screams coming from inside. Whores screamed in pretended admiration, but not like that. The Mother Hubbard girls were being raped.

A torn-up cobblestone cracked against her parapet. As she ducked back, she heard the noise of triumph and splintering wood. The outer door had given in. If the inner door gave, what was happening at Mother Hubbard's was about to happen to the Cock and Pie.

She ran to tip out the satchel's newly packed contents, feeling for her knife. Her fingers came across Matoonas's hunting bow and quiver, and grabbed them. At the door it occurred to her that a swordsman would be useful, and she rushed to her side window.

'Actor. ACTOR.' What was his damned name?

She heard a groan: 'Leave me alone.' A guttering candle on his table allowed her to see that he was lolling over it, still clutching his bottle.

She picked up her ewer and threw its water in his direction, hoping to sober him. He'd help or he wouldn't. There was no time to see. Outside, in the corridor, she bumped into a shivering Mary and pushed her out of the way.

On the clerestory she looked over the balustrade into the salon. It was dark, but lights from the flares outside came through the high windows. Job, with his back to the door, was spreadeagled like Atlas holding the world up, but he was being jerked forward every time something heavy crashed into it. The mob would be in any second.

Everybody else was facing the door; Kinyans and Francesca had raided the kitchen for cleavers, Dorinda, Alania and Phoebe were holding chairs at shoulder level, Sabina and Fanny both had pokers.

Her Ladyship, representing her profession, was wielding a whip, though at the moment she was cracking it above her girls' heads. 'Upstairs, get upstairs. Job can't hold. Jump over to Ma Hicks's.' She drove them towards the stairs.

As the girls came up, Penitence took a position from which she could shoot downwards. She wasn't adept with a bow and its arrows were only lethal against small animals, but she might administer a sharp enough sting in arms and legs to give the invaders pause for thought.

If she'd had time she'd have given way to the terror inspired by the screams from Mother Hubbard's; instead she found herself obeying an instinct to protect not only herself but the Cock and Pie. Sinful it might be, but the brothel was her home; its girls were fellow-women. *And no bastard's going to abuse them.*

Even so, her hands were shaking and she had difficulty notching the first arrow.

Job went sprawling as the door fell inwards and men

trampled over it. Penitence loosed off an arrow, but she only did it because she'd planned to do it; nothing, no whip, no cleaver, no arrow, could keep this mob at bay. Its individual faces were giggling, shouting, lusting, drunk, but it wasn't twenty or so individuals, it was a forty-legged, forty-armed, twenty-headed monster that compounded a violence greater than itself, reducing even Her Ladyship to an ineffective pigmy. Penitence saw her crack her whip across the first of the monster's faces, saw Kinyans throw his cleaver, before both of them turned and ran. The thing ran after them. It had never been allowed into the high-and-mighty Cock and Pie before, another deprivation in its dreadful life for which it was about to take revenge.

That Her Ladyship and Kinyans gained the stairs was due to Penitence's arrows and missiles from the girls on the clerestory, but the confusion of light and dark aided the enemy; those who weren't hit were unaware that others had been and came on regardless of counter-attack.

'The attic,' Penitence yelled. Kinyans had reached the top of the stairs, Her Ladyship was lumbering, dragging with her a man who was clutching the back of her skirt. It was difficult to see. Penitence leaned over and shot. The man's hands released Her Ladyship and flew to his backside. He caused enough of an obstruction to give the Cock and Pie contingent time to get behind the door to the attic stairs. In the narrow, dark space at the foot of the stairs they stood on each other, fumbling to hold the door against a battering of kicks that thudded it inwards.

There was a tiny gleam of light above them and a voice used to carrying said: 'Allow me, ladies. This way if you please.'

The actor was coming down the stairs towards them, gesturing with his sword for the girls to squeeze past him. The door kept being thrust in and Penitence, Her Ladyship and Kinyans exerted their whole weight to thrust it back while one by one the girls escaped to the attic.

At last the beautiful voice said: 'Leave it now. This is for me.'

The strong scent of perfume (Her Ladyship) and cooking (Kinyans) receded and a smell of leather and wine took its place. 'Go.'

She stood back. She had a half-second glimpse of the actor's face as she turned and the door gave way. She felt him lunge, heard a scream, then he was out on the clerestory, swearing lyrically. With his free hand, he felt for the door behind him and slammed it shut.

Penitence would have opened it again, but at that moment a fat hand grasped her collar and dragged her to the top of the stairs.

'He'll be all right,' said Her Ladyship, which was more than Penitence knew.

In the attic a plank had been laid from her side window over the alley to his. Most of the girls were peering back at her out of the actor's room, extending advice and arms to Mary who was crawling precariously over. Dorinda was still in the attic, pushing Mary from her side. The noise from the bottom of the stairs was fading. Kinyans went back to the fray now that he'd seen them safe. Mary was across, being lifted in.

'Now you, Ladyship,' commanded Dorinda.

Her Ladyship shook her head and sank on to the bed. With Dorinda beside her, Penitence made for the front window and looked over. Rioters were running out of the Cock and Pie. One skidded into her view on his back. Job, it seemed, was alive and well and chucking out. She saw half a dozen more men backing into Dog Yard as the actor emerged, his sword snicking at their jerkins, left hand elegantly raised.

There were flares moving to the sound of marching feet over by the Ship steps. The Watch was back with reinforcements. She slumped on to the stone balustrade.

But it wasn't over yet. The rioters on this side of the Yard were making too much noise to know that authority was on its way, and their pride had been pricked by their ejection on the end of a sword.

There were a lot of them, some with clubs. Their cropped heads crowded into a half-circle just out of sword-reach as the actor, his long hair bobbing, swept his sword from side to side

100

in a crouch. Job was wrestling with two; the rest were getting ready to rush forward.

As one woman, Dorinda and Penitence turned to go down and help, but a deep baritone growl from below brought them back to the parapet. The play-actor had been joined by an ally more potent than them both. A frightening figure was standing by his side in the half-circle.

'What you fuckers think you're doing?' asked Mistress Hicks.

More daunting even than Mistress Hicks's anger at the disturbance was Mistress Hicks's attire, which, contrary to local opinion that Mistress Hicks hung upside-down all night from a beam, showed she retired to bed in grubby green lace and curl papers.

A voice shouted: 'Who's this fancy bastard to turn us out of our own bloody cat-house? An' you keep out of this, Ma.'

Mistress Hicks advanced. 'He's my fucking tenant, that's who he is, and he pays his fucking rent, the which is a bloody sight more than I know you do, Rob Whinney, an' you, Abel Smith. An' you, Parky Potter.'

The naming was genius, taking away the mob's anonymity. There was more cursing and club-waving for the look of the thing, but, accepting Mistress Hicks's invitation to fuck off home, the men started to disperse.

Penitence put her head down on the parapet and began to laugh, to weep with laughing. *Corporal Forbush and Mistress Hicks. Savers of situations.* She drummed her fists on the parapet top.

Below her the play-actor, standing at a loss beside Job, looked up, saw her and shrugged.

Whooping, she sat down and rocked. *Lord, when did I last laugh? Did I ever laugh?* Dorinda was shaking her, but rape, riot and ridiculousness in one package was too much for her. She went on laughing and then she cried.

Half an hour later everybody gathered in the salon for a Bumpo. Bumpo was a lethally alcoholic concoction of Kinyans's, but at the Cock and Pie the word applied not only to the drink but to the occasions when Her Ladyship gathered her girls to discuss, remonstrate, celebrate, or console.

The salon had suffered. Its mirror and candelabra had been shattered along with most of its chairs, though the few candles Kinyans had lit were not sufficient to show the worst damage to its giltwork. Everyone found seats where they could and sipped the steaming Bumpo in a lassitude of companionship and shock.

Phoebe, Sabina and Francesca had accompanied Her Ladyship over to Mother Hubbard's to enquire after its workers' welfare and see what assistance was needed. They came back, white and sobered, leaving Her Ladyship still there; some of the girls had suffered multiple rape and were in a bad way. 'Could have been us.'

'Would have been,' said Alania, simpering at the play-actor, 'if it hadn't been for Henry.'

THAT was his name. Henry King.

'Leaped across the alley, he did,' went on Alania, 'leaped. Then tore up one of Prinks's floorboards to make a bridge for us with his bare hands. His bare hands.'

What else would he use? The man was magical, no doubt, sitting there with his long legs stretched out, his ugly face amused, his good hands, his better-days clothes, but if the girls thought his rescue had been to save them personally, they could think again.

The glimpse of his face as he'd pushed her behind him to confront the men at the foot of the attic stairs had shown love of a fight, some bred-in concept of chivalry which did not exist in her world. He hadn't done it for her, not for any of them.

Glorying in his agility and the odds, murmuring abuse, one hand with a sword, the other gesturing the mob towards him: the picture was framed in her mind. Now and always. Like a good actor, he had provided an image so beautiful to impose on the other pictures of the terrible night that it might even outlast them. She would take it with her when she set out tomorrow.

Her prejudice had gone, to be replaced by that strange recognition she'd felt as they'd sat on the steps of the Cut together. Whatever history had blown him into Dog Yard, he was familiar to her. Underneath the bravado was desperation at his entrapment in the Rookery; she knew, because it had been her own. There was a level on which she understood the man. She wished she'd had time to dress; wrapped in her bedspread she must look typical Cock and Pie; well, not as typical as Alania and Dorinda who were allowing theirs to fall open in the area of the chest and legs, but certainly not respectable.

Her Ladyship came in from the Yard. Unpainted, her fat face looked featureless and, for once, her hair was dishevelled. 'The Watch is rounding them all up for the basket,' she reported. 'Jethro Parker and the drayman are back inside the Ship, poor bastards.'

There was a snuffle from the shadows under the clerestory where the only disconsolate, and biggest, figure of the party sat with its head on its knees, sucking raw knuckles. Penitence regarded it with disfavour, finding in it a scapegoat since the mob, the real villain, had been elemental, as blameworthy as an earthquake. Job, the brothel's physical force, its supposed protector. *Much protecting thee did.*

She had always considered it disgraceful work for a grown man and now, grown man that he was – and few grew larger than Job – he had failed in it. She'd never forgiven him for 'The Savage'.

Her Ladyship waddled over to the one remaining table, poured a beaker of Bumpo and took it over to her apple-bully. 'Weren't your fault,' she said. 'They was too many.' Wiping his eyes, Job shambled behind her as she walked back to the sofa and sat by her feet, her hand on his head.

Her Ladyship settled herself and looked around her wrecked salon. 'Well,' she said, 'that were a to-do.'

The deliberate litotes released a post-mortem. Though the actor was the hero of the hour, there had been other triumphs. Sabina, Dorinda and Phoebe had scored direct hits with their missiles from the clerestory.

'And what about Prinks with her arrers?' Penitence found herself the centre of the Cock and Pie's respect, which warmed her – Dorinda actually patted her admiringly on the back –

even while she knew it would confirm her as one of its own in the eyes of the actor.

He was looking at her. 'O tiger's heart wrapped in a woman's hide,' he said. 'More Mistress Amazon than Mistress Boots, it appears. You come from the Americas, I believe?'

Fanny put a heavy arm round Penitence's shoulders. 'All the way from New England,' she said, and she meant well. 'Right little Puritan when she got here, but we changed all that. One of us now, ain't you, Prinks?'

'I am sure she is,' said the play-actor.

The conversation passed on.

Sir, I am the needlewoman of this establishment. No prostitute, but brought here by circumstance as unfortunate as your own, whatever that may be. She couldn't say it. For one thing she *couldn't* say it, and for another her pride demanded he have as much percipience with regard to her as she for him.

Anyway, it would hurt the girls. Anyway, come the morning they would never see each other again.

Mistress Hicks's boots clumped on to the floor. 'Come on, Henry. Take me home. I need me beauty sleep if you don't.'

Without a blink the actor rose to say his farewells, which he did with much hand-kissing and deprecatory shrugging at the applause.

Her Ladyship curtseyed to him and reverted to her best accent. 'Any time you wish to avail yourself of the courtesy of the house, sir, my girls will be happy to oblige.'

Penitence, turned away, heard his 'You are too good, madam, but I am rewarded enough to have been of service'. He offered his landlady his arm. 'Come to your sleep, Titania.'

When they'd gone, Dorinda said: 'Gawd, I could eat him.'

Her Ladyship looked at her sharply. 'Don't you make no mistake, my girl, he despises us.'

'He don't,' protested Alania. 'He rescued us. Chatted lovely and all.'

'He's a proper nobleman, doing his noblesse obleedge, and God bless him for it. But he still despises us.'

She knows. How does she know?

The brothel-keeper was ushering her brood to bed. 'Come

104

on, now. Ma Hicks ain't the only one needing beauty sleep.'
She looked around: 'Where's Mary? She ain't had her Bumpo.'

A search discovered the skivvy to be absent.

'Last I saw her was when we got her over to Ma Hicks's,'
said Sabina. 'She was a trouble on that plank. I thought she'd
fall.'

They went out into Dog Yard where constables stood
guard over a group of now-quiet rioters waiting in hobbles to
be marched off.

'Where were you when we needed you?' demanded Her
Ladyship. 'And who's going to pay for my damage?'

The constable she addressed shrugged.

'You seen my skivvy?'

Just then they all saw her, emerging from Mistress Hicks's,
staggering so that for a moment they thought she was drunk.
She appeared to have gone blind, feeling the air with the
palms of her hands as if it were a wall.

'Mary.'

She turned towards them and fell down.

A constable held Her Ladyship back. 'Careful.' Another
went over to the figure on the ground and gently lifted the
top of the shift with his halberd. He crossed himself. 'God help
us, look at them rings. She's got it right enough.'

Carefully manoeuvring their halberds under Mary's armpits,
they lifted her to the Cock and Pie and slid her inside its door.

Within the hour, the shutting-up of the Cock and Pie and
Mistress Hicks's, with all their inhabitants, had begun.

Chapter 6

IT WAS the poor's plague. Like a river obeying gravity in
always finding the lowest ground, the Plague observed social
laws and did not bother the rich. Approaching the grounds of
great houses occupied by few people, it washed back and set
off once more along the streets of overcrowded tenements.

Trickling out from St Giles's, it avoided the meadows that lay north and west, and followed the lines of population down Holborn, through Drury Lane, into St Clement Danes at the City's western gate, into the parish of St Martin-in-the-Fields which, at the end of its long arm, included the royal palace of Whitehall.

On its way along Chancery Lane it passed Lincoln's Inn only to find that the students, lawyers and barristers had been too quick for it, discharging the readings and fleeing elsewhere, leaving servants in charge. The Plague killed the porter at the gates, and proceeded on its way towards the City.

'Item,' wrote Peter Simkin, 'a board for the carrying of the dead: 3s.

'Item. To Harry Weedon, smith, for 108 locks for shutting up: £3 11s.

'Item. Pails for the carrying of water to shut up persons: 5s 9d.

'Item. To Mr Mann for links and candles for the night bearers: £2.

'Item. Shrouds . . .'

His quill jolted as the Reverend Boreman loomed over his shoulder. 'What do the damned bearers want links for?' The apothecary was with him.

'If there's no reply, Rector,' said Peter Simkin, not looking up. He was badly behind.

'No reply to what?' snapped the Reverend Boreman.

'No reply from a plague-house,' explained William Boghurst. 'It's becoming all too frequent. There's no reply to the bearers' call at night so they have to enter. It usually means all the occupants are dead.'

'That's why links and candles. Order of the Examiner,' added Peter Simkin, still writing.

'Is it,' said the Reverend Boreman, flatly. 'Let us hope the Examiner pays for it.' The still-living needed the parish's funds, not the dead.

It was cool in the little vaulted vestry; he'd brought the apothecary in here because it was the only place that was, apart from the church itself — and there the huffing and grunting and creaking and counting from the bell tower as John Gere pulled at the sally got on his nerves. The bell got on his nerves. Tolls for dead men, dead women, dead children. It was tolling away his parish.

At first, when the deep, clear, regular strokes of the passing bell had rung out, men out in the streets had removed their hats in time-honoured courtesy to the dead, but as June came in it had begun to toll nearly all day. On the second of June it was joined in its insistence by the bell of St Martin-in-the-Fields and, further away, that of St Clement Danes, so that men got tired of putting their hats on and off and no longer bothered.

He longed to sit down, but if he did he'd never get up again. 'Well?'

The apothecary seated himself in the great chair kept for episcopal visits and swung his short legs. Despite the heat, the strings of his close-fitting ancient leather cap were tied in a bow under his chin. 'I fear I must ask you to extend my apologies to the emergency meeting tonight. I am not at leisure to attend. And I must ask you, Rector, to issue a protest to Magistrate Flesher on my behalf.'

'Master Flesher *will* be pleased,' said the rector.

'Whether he is or not, I wish my opinion to be on record that as soon as a house is infected, all sound people should be had out of it and not shut up to sicken in their turn. Shutting up is murder. It is against humanity and religion, above all it is against common sense.' His light voice was unemphatic.

'We know that. But there's no money.' Striding around the vestry, the Reverend Boreman dragged the choir surplices from their pegs. With the choir cancelled for the Plague's duration, they could be laundered.

'We are not containing it, Robert.' William Boghurst might have been commenting on the weather. He was getting on the rector's nerves.

'I know that, don't I?' Damn, Emmy Smith had died yester-day. Who could he get to do the church laundry now? He bundled the surplices up and kicked them into a corner. 'What's the bill this week?'

The parish clerk kept on writing. 'Near two hundred, Rector.'

'Where is it?' It was unlike Simkin to be inexact. 'It's Monday. You should be taking it in.'

'I am, Rector. But until Master Elliot's back on his feet there's the churchwardens' accounts to be finished.'

'George Elliot won't be getting back on his feet.' He'd just come from his churchwarden's death-bed. The nine tolls John Gere had just rung were his. 'Where's the damn Bill?'

Wearily, the parish clerk turned round on his stool. He had ink on his nose. 'Master Elliot gone? I'm right sorry, Rector. God rest him.'

'Indeed. What about the Bill?'

'I farmed it out, Rector. There weren't no time to copy it proper, it's got so big, what with being up all night seeing to the relief . . .'

The Reverend Boreman pulled himself together; they were all doing their best. 'Nobody blames you, Peter. Who to?' The number with literary skill had never been high in St Giles, and the Plague was diminishing it fast.

He saw Peter Simkin's exhausted face crumple. 'It's been difficult coping, Rector . . . I been giving it to Mistress Hurd to write out for me.'

Who the hell was Mistress Hurd? 'Not that Puritan slut? I thought she was . . . Good God, man, she's shut up with the rest of the Cock and Pie.'

William Boghurst intervened. 'She passes the Bill down in a basket and I have advised Peter Simkin to bake it in his oven to rid it of infection before handling it.'

The Reverend Boreman reminded himself not to breakfast off any more loaves baked by Mistress Simkin. Then he thought: With all the dying, Plague-ridden hands I've held these last weeks, what difference does it make?

'She's got a neat hand, Rector,' pleaded Peter Simkin.

Nevertheless, a Puritan who had chosen to live in a notorious brothel . . . He took a deep breath: 'Very well, but we will keep this matter from Magistrate Flesher.' He had to adjust to the inconceivable. He was living through it. 'And the Bishop,' he added.

As they walked together through the church, the apothecary said: 'Master Simkin is in need of rest.'

'So are you. So am I.'

In the porch they braced themselves before going out into the sunlight. The weather was getting on the rector's nerves. This June was so damnably . . . jolly. Out of kilter. Like some brash soul being determinedly festive long after the party spirit had gone out of the other guests. The grass needed cutting, but old Ben White had been scythed down himself last week. He said: 'So you've been visiting the Cock and Pie, Master Boghurst.'

'Professionally.' The apothecary was undisturbed. 'My profession, not theirs. As a matter of fact, it is a case in point. It has suffered one death, yet ten souls are imprisoned within it awaiting the inevitable.'

'Guilty souls.' The rector looked with disfavour at the dust which was turning his yew trees grey and clouding up from the endless procession of horses and coaches going past his gates on the flight from London to the country. The sound of horses and wheels very nearly drowned the sound of the tolling bell. No wonder that even when he got time to sleep, he couldn't.

Some of Janet's roses trailed over the wall from the rectory garden. He should be able to smell them, smell the lavender along the church path that the bees were busy with. Instead the warm air reeked of horse manure and the rank stink of earth from the mounds outlining the two great pits disfiguring this once-blessed place.

He held mass funeral services at night, unbelieving that he was doing it, but doing it. Rebuking the bearers for tipping the bodies in like sacks of rubbish, yet himself becoming more callous, every night more accepting of the unacceptable.

There were so many dead he barely had time for the living. And no money. The 1s 6d a week they paid out of parish funds to the sick and needy wouldn't keep a cat alive.

A woman framed in the window of a pretty carriage held up by a delay in the traffic was craning her neck to look over the wall at the pits, drumming her gloved fingers on the side of her door. She had rings glittering over her gloves and a scarf over her mouth.

Talk of guilty souls. 'Have you contributed to the relief of the poor you leave behind, madam?' he shouted. It had cost 4s 9d – three days' work – to get those pits dug. Startled, the woman pulled down the carriage blind. They could hear her urging her coachman to drive on. Damn her. He looked up the road, crowded with luggage-laden carriages. Damn them all. 'I get so angry.' His heart was pounding.

'You should rest. Surely, some of them have been generous to the out-parishes. Prince Rupert, the Duchess of York.'

'Some.' It was the sense of abandonment. Every time he had to dodge a carriage with a coat of arms on its door, its occupants goggling at the pits as they passed on to safety, he struggled against the impulse to pull them out of it, take them into the sickrooms, make them watch the terror. And sometimes he could have begged them to take him with them.

The Rookery had gained a fresh rash of red crosses overnight. Along Butcher's Cut, Peter Simkin had already counted twelve. Iffen it goes on like this, he thought, it'll be cheaper to mark houses as don't have it.

He walked softly, trying not to attract the eyes that would plead through gaps in the boards over the ground-floor windows, and the voices that swore because he wasn't the apothecary or the relief cart bringing food.

It was hot. The sun made a ragged track of light along the middle of the Cut, intensifying the shadows under the over-hang of the upper storeys. One thing, he thought, the Rook-ery ain't never been cleaner. The Examiner insisted that laystalls throughout the parish be regularly emptied and rub-bish cleared – 'Item: Street-cleaning: £4s 2d'. The Cut was empty and the quiet outside intensified the sounds coming from each muffled window, the murmuring, the occasional quarrel, children crying and being shouted at.

He tried to imagine those interiors and pictured a squirming dormouse nest. How to afford the food to keep these people?

When they obligingly solved the problem by dying, how to afford the cost of burying them?

At the end of the Cut, the figure of a man crossed from one side to another, then back again. He walked with his hands up, his legs jerking him forward in a corkscrew motion on to his own shadow.

Where's the Watch? Peter Simkin looked round, saw a side alley and escaped down it. He found two watchmen sitting chatting on a stile by the pond in Cow Lane when they should have been patrolling.

Sharply, he ordered them to go and see to the poor soul in the Cut. 'Another bloody walking corp,' one of them grumbled. They picked up their grappling hooks and strolled off to do their duty. He'd complain of them to the magistrate at the meeting tonight, but what was the good? The sort of men who were prepared to do their sort of job for the pay the parish was offering were unlikely to be the flower of England.

And they were right; the man in the Cut was a corpse, stumbling its way to its own grave. The Plague was ambulatory; spasms moved its host's arms and legs like a puppet's, impelling the dying out of their beds to the open air in a possession that wiped away the personality of the possessed, the last bid of the spirit to keep the body upright and escape the poison which was altering every organ of the body. If they got out into the streets they wandered until they dropped. There'd been one in the High Street yesterday, scattering the few passers-by, causing coaches to stop.

Peter Simkin clenched his hands on the rough wood of the stile. 'I'm so frit, so *frit*, Lord.' Every morning he and Mary scanned each other's and the little ones' bared upper parts for the tokens, and got down on their knees in gratitude for unblemished skin. But for how long? Day before yesterday it took the littlest of the Evans family, two doors down. 'Tell me what to do, Lord, anything, and I'll do it. Only spare us that cross.'

The level in the pond was low and covered in duckweed; there was another cost – bringing water in carts to the shut-ups.

A loud bang from a street or two away made him jump. They'd started then. 'Item. Powder and shot for killing vermin: £6 0s 9d.' He'd better get on. The thought of the trudge to Parish Clerks' Hall was daunting, but not as daunting as the hostility when he got there. St Giles-in-the-Fields had become synonymous with Plague and he its scapegoat. His fellow-clerks had made it clear they didn't want him dining with them in the Ring o' Bells any more. He ate with the other pariahs, St Martin's and Clement Danes.

And he'd been upset by an article in his *Newes* last week which, trying to calm the City, assured it that there were only nineteen Plague cases within its walls; it was St Giles where the infection raged, and that, it said, due to poverty and sluttishness. The tenor was that St Giles had made its bed and could lie in it.

He'd been shamed. For his parish. For his favourite newspaper's lack of charity. It didn't mention that more and more servants and journeymen, left with no work by their employers' flight from the City, were swelling St Giles's overcrowding and contributing to its sluttishness. He hadn't shown it to Rector. The poor man was in enough of a taking as it was.

Ahead of him the tall, boarded shape of Mother Hubbard's looked so like a windmill that, as always, he found himself mentally sketching in the missing sails. Two girls hung out of its high side window and he braced himself for the calls – 'Want some fickytoodle, dearie?' – with which Mother Hubbard's advertised its wares. None came. Surprised, he looked up and saw the girls' eyes were lacklustre, watching him pass because he was there to be watched, like a beetle.

He understood as he turned the corner and saw the red cross on their door. Apothecary Boghurst was wrong then. He'd said whores were protected against Plague by their pox. Lord have mercy.

He paused on the west steps of Dog Yard and waved across to the figure peering over the balcony opposite. There she was, her old domed hat shading her face from the sun.

Lord have mercy on her and all. Ever since that night when he'd led her to the Searcher, he'd felt responsible for her somehow. Rector said she'd be defiled by now. 'The Cock and Pie is pitch and she has touched it.' But he'd swear she was still a maid. Probably always would be. A born old maid, for all her pretty eyes. All straitlace and stumbling tongue, though a neat hand with the quill.

As he went down the steps to cross the Yard, the heat trapped in its well of gimcrack houses enclosed him like an oven. Red crosses everywhere. He held his breath until he'd climbed the steps to the walkway below the balcony. The Yard watchman, sitting on them, nodded a greeting and shifted his halberd so that he could pass.

The basket was already hanging down on its string. Almost guiltily, he put a glove on his right hand and took out the slate on which the deaths had been scrawled as they'd been reported, and the columned paper on which she'd categorized them in her neat, small writing.

'All well, then, Pen?' His voice echoed discomfortingly around the Yard. He could hardly see her face as he squinted up into the sun, but the hat nodded. 'Not long now, eh?' She spread and closed her fingers. Eyes watering, he counted. Twenty-six more days. Twenty-six if the Cock and Pie stayed healthy; forty more on top of that if it didn't.

Awkwardly, he searched about for something to say. 'They'll be coming round to shoot cats and dogs in a while. Don't be frit of the bangs. Sooner the vermin's gone, the sooner it'll be over.' Another nod. He pointed down the side alley in the direction of the laystall. 'They clean out the you-know satisfactory?' He'd told them to. Another nod.

That was it, then. He didn't know what else to say and he daren't put off the City any longer. 'Keep you, Pen.' He felt her eyes, all their eyes, follow him until he'd turned the corner by the Stables.

Suffering the heat, Penitence stayed on the balcony, facing the direction the little parish clerk had taken. At nights she fetched her mattress out here and slept on it, the stars helping the illusion that she was in Awashonks's hut with the raised door-flap leading to unlimited space.

By day she pretended she could step out into the view and

113

down to Hyde Park where deer flicked their tails under the trees, or walk along the river. She knew London was emptying; every morning when she carried her night-pail downstairs, she passed the window at the back of the attics which looked across the roofs to the beginning of the countryside, and saw the dotted snake that was the Tottenham Court road crammed with traffic going north. The Thames was sparse of boats, and at every dusk fewer and fewer windows lit up in the towers of the Strand palaces.

But distance kept reality at bay, and so did she, or else go mad.

She'd made an exhibition of herself during the shutting-up, fighting to open the door that three constables on the other side were holding closed. 'Not me, not me. I don't belong.' The coffin lid was closing down. Any sense of companionship with the others had gone. It was a mistake, she was here by mischance. She couldn't die in the Cock and Pie, she was no sinner. *I don't belong*. She was too panicked to feel shame.

She was spun round and given a slap across the face that rocked her sideways. 'Get to your room,' said Her Ladyship. 'And don't come down.'

The sunny attic dissipated some of the claustrophobia, but it was like the bridge of a ship of which the lower decks were already under water, retaining light and air until it, too, went under.

She'd thrown herself on her knees. *Take me back, Lord. I'm sorry, I'm sorry*. She had connived at wickedness. How had she been so careless of a God who had this vengeance at His disposal? How had she forgotten the plight of Sodom and Gomorrah? Rummaging frantically in her bag for her Bible, she heard shouts across the alley. The actor was striding his room, venting his own despair, calling on his God.

She blamed him. Her neighbourly feelings to him had kindled the wrath of the True Puritan Being. She'd slammed her shutters to pray her way back into the Lord's favour in peace. They were shut still.

But as the days went by with no more deaths at the Cock

and Pie, though more crosses appeared in Dog Yard, the Plague accrued its own normality. A macabre imitation took over from the bustle of life as it had been.

The tramp of the Watch's patrol replaced everyday foot-steps. Instead of barrels rattling over the cobblestones to Sam Bryskett's cellar, there was the clatter of keys turning and re-turning in padlocks as the food-and-water carters made their deliveries on long poles. Before the Plague, she'd woken up to old Hannah at the bakery round the corner shouting her muffins: now there was the morning cry of 'Bring out your dead' and the inevitable response 'Here', and turning of more keys.

Every other day saw a coffin carried out of the Ship – first a child's, then another child's, then Nelly Ogle's – until Penitence became immune to sadness and wondered irritably why they couldn't arrange to die all together and save this hideous prolongation.

Loyally, Dog Yard followed each coffin to the churchyard on behalf of the shut-up landlord and his wife, and with equal loyalty raided the Ship's depleted cellar for a wake afterwards. The processions were dwindling. More and more Yarders were being shut up themselves.

Yesterday, for little Nelly Ogle, there had been just three mourners, one of them Footloose, propelling himself along in his bucket. Why didn't he trundle himself off to an uninfected part of the City? If she had his liberty *she'd* go, she'd crawl.

He waved at her and she waved back. The movement brought spots shifting before her eyes. *Lord. Preserve me. Is it now?*

Not this time, just the heat. The sun right overhead beat down through her hat and made her head swim, but, God, how she did *not* want to go inside.

On Her Ladyship's orders all the girls kept to their rooms, with Kinyans setting trays of food from his fast-diminishing store outside their doors. Occasionally she could hear him in the kitchen, otherwise there was silence – apart from the strokes of St Giles's bell which at first had been a hideous *memento mori*, then an unstopping, brain-scarring assault.

Her Ladyship had nursed Mary alone and was the only one to see her die. Penitence on her balcony had watched the small pine coffin carried away. There had been nobody to follow it.

Today, apart from Mistress Palmer's cat lapping at a puddle which had been dripped by the water cart, the Watch nodding in the sun, and Footloose sitting in the mouth of his vat, the Yard was empty. Any longer out here and she would faint. She went inside, closing her eyes to accustom them to the gloom. Around her the shadows waited with the unfillable hours of twenty-six more days.

At nights the Plague assumed human, murderous personality. She would jerk awake; it was in the house somewhere, a creak suggested it was creeping up the stairs to kill her. She couldn't get away. By day it became a vast, smothering, soft eiderdown of tedium that baffled the walls of the attic so that sometimes the only sound was the hum of her own listening.

Automatically, she picked up her Bible, threw it down. To stay still enough to read was to be suffocated; she began to pace the length of the attic, one, two, three . . . fourteen, fifteen and a half. The asymmetry of the half always annoyed her. Turn, lengthen pace to lose it. One, two, three . . .

An echo to her footsteps came through the side shutters from across the alley where the play-actor paced his own room. Being longer-legged and in a smaller room, he took six steps before he turned. She'd counted. She'd counted everything, the attic beams, the patches where plaster had fallen off her walls, the revealed laths, the unremitting strokes of the bell.

Seven more days until Peter Simkin brought another life-saving, death-counting Bill for her to write out. There was no more thread or she could sew something . . . fourteen. And a half. She'd lengthened her pace too much. One, two, three . . .

There was noise outside in the Yard and she went back on to the balcony. Two constables carrying guns were standing on the Mother Hubbard steps. One of them was aiming his musket at Mistress Palmer's cat which, having had its drink, was now sitting on the cobbles with one leg sticking up into the air, grooming its chest. It was brindled, scrabby and blind in one eye, not a nice cat, but she'd become used to seeing it. Mistress Palmer was fond of it.

The activity had attracted the attention of those with upper, unboarded windows. Mistress Palmer was on her balcony, alternately pleading with the constable not to shoot, and shouting at her cat to run, which it wouldn't

'Sorry, ma,' said the constable. 'Orders is orders.'

Penitence put her hands over her ears. The musket barrel exploded and so did the cat.

Rubbing his shoulder from the recoil, the constable walked into the well of the Yard, picked up what was left of the cat by its tail and put it in a sack.

From every window, boarded and unboarded, the Yarders loosed their wide repertory of obscenities. Mistress Palmer was crying.

The other constable pointed to the alley that ran between the Cock and Pie and Mistress Hicks's boarding house. 'There's a nest of 'em along there.'

Kinyans's cats. She turned and hurried out of the attic. Along the clerestory the whores were in their doorways. Only Her Ladyship's door was shut. 'What's them bangs?'

'Shooting. K-K-Kinyans' c-c-cats.'

They followed her. In the yard outside the kitchen, Kinyans was already arguing with the inevitable. 'They're doing no harm, bor.'

'They been promulgated. Vermin. All cats and dogs to be killed.'

'Who's going to kill the bloody rats then? Ain't rats vermin?'

Rats weren't on the constables' brief. 'Orders is orders, granfer. Just get inside.'

Desperately, Kinyans looked round. In the high-walled yard his cats lay in sun-drenched contentment on upturned barrels; one had its paw over its eyes. 'What about the kittens? You going to shoot them and all?'

'Don't make this difficult, granfer,' said one of the constables, wearily. 'Just get inside.'

Fanny put her muscular arm round Kinyans's shoulders and led him gently into the kitchen, closing the door. The old man was sobbing. Outside the shooting began. In between the shots they could hear scrabbling.

'What you sluts think you're doing?' Her Ladyship, awful in anger and a peignoir, had woken from her nap and come downstairs.

'They're shooting Kinyans' moggies,' said Phoebe.

'I'll shoot you if you don't get to your room. Now get.'

In her attic, there was a new ingress of sun. Her side shutters had been pushed open and the actor, stretching across the alley, was tapping at them with his sword. 'What's happening?'

In the first blast of religious terror, Penitence had forsworn commerce with the man as she had forsworn every other vice she could think of. The man was an actor, probably a Papist and, *ipso facto*, a sinner. In the interest of her soul, she had laid him on the altar of the Plague-sending God. But the attrition of a fortnight's isolation made the sacrifice ridiculous, if sacrifice it was. It could do no harm, surely, to answer. The Lord didn't require incivility. 'They're sh-shooting c-c-cats.'

'You're weeping for a bloody cat?'

She hadn't known she was weeping. It wasn't for cats.

From very far away, under the tolling of the bells, came a new sound, a deep percussion resulting in the faintest vibration of air.

Thunder. Perhaps it will rain and wash the Plague away.

The actor was on his feet. 'They're using cannon on cats? What's happening?' He became furious. 'Well, go and ask.'

He had no prospect into Dog Yard, his only window stared straight into hers. Cannon? He was unhinged. Then it occurred to her that there had been no cloud a moment ago, and to judge from the lancing paths of sunlight coming into her attic, there still wasn't.

She went out on to the balcony. The sky was as clear as blue enamel. Unusually, the Watch was standing alert, listening to the distant reverberation. They saw her. 'Reckon it's our fleet firing on the Dutch at sea.' They couldn't keep still with the excitement. One kept stabbing at the air with his halberd. 'Up the navy. Blow the bastards out the water.'

Oh, war. She wandered back to the actor and stuttered it out, to be amazed by his agitation. That men could fire metal balls at each other at a time like this was an irrelevance barely warranting attention.

'What about France?' he demanded. 'Is she maintaining her neutrality? Courtin's over here as ambassador. What's he doing? Ask, woman, ask.'

She shook her head. In the first place she doubted if the watchmen knew, and in the second place her stammer wasn't up to it.

Her refusal brought an outburst of oaths. War with France was likely any minute. Trapped in a pest-ridden hell-hole. At the mercy of common idiots as well as disease. Knowing nothing. Nothing to do.

And your wine bottle empty. She saw that his hands were shaking. Parish relief didn't include wine on its menu and she doubted if he had the money to send Footloose for more. *That'll teach you.* Proverbs chapter 20, verse 1: *Wine is a mocker, strong drink is raging.*

From the lack of it, so was he. He literally stamped in a temper which was now, illogically, turning on her. He threw himself down in his chair by the window table. 'And with you,' he said, 'you as my line of communication. It's your fault. You offend me.'

Such rudeness. She should slam the shutters, but she didn't. 'M-m-umm-my f-f-f-fault?'

He wagged his finger. She had illustrated her offence. 'Your fault. Good God, girl, you're heir to the language of Chaucer, Shakespeare, of Jonson, of ME. Yet you let yourself be walled in within a few inches of this glorious landscape. Talk about shut up, you're not even trying to find the key to the bloody door.'

The imagery of imprisonment was so exactly her own experience that she was intrigued. 'H-how?' Curiously, she found herself more at ease with him when he was like this than with his ornate artificiality. She was at home with bitterness; with her family, she'd had to be.

'How? Well, I suppose I could teach you.' He stared gloomily at his boots. 'There's damn all else to do.'

She stared at him. The man was a mountebank. On the other hand, speech was his business. *Suppose* ... No, she couldn't. Besides, she'd be dead soon and so would he; the far-off thunder was the Lord telling her to spend her remaining hours in prayer lest she be damned.

She said: 'There's n-no t-t-time.'

His eyes stayed on his boots. 'Oh, I agree. One's social engagements make too many demands. Cut off to 'em then, and leave me alone.'

She considered. Again, he wasn't proffering help for her sake, but his own. As desperate for distraction from terror and tedium as she was, he needed occupation. Her massacred words grated on his ear; like a houseproud woman with a sluttish neighbour he was offering to straighten her up.

She was stood in the sun of an autumn schoolyard, outside — she was always outside — a ring of children dipping for a game of Tom Tickler. Fern edging the hard-baked, foot-scuffed yard was turning rust-coloured, the shade of the great maple under which they played dappled the girls' caps red and orange. *'Inty, minty, tuppety, fig.'* Charity Trumblett's voice chanted the magic gibberish and her finger jabbed horizontally round the circle. *'Delia, dilia, dominig.'*

'I want to p-p-play.'

'Otcha, potcha, dominotcha.'

'Let m-m-m-me p-p-pum-play.'

'Hi, pon, tusk. Huldy, guldy, boo. Out goes you.'

A tall black figure was casting its shadow across her boots. 'Why do thy schoolfellows shun thee, Penitence Hurd?'

A rhetorical question; he knew. His shadow was long; it reached the ring of children under the maple tree. She curtseyed the right answer. 'My t-tongue is c-c-cursed, sir.'

'Verily, it chatters too freely with the tawnee and too little with Christians. I reprimanded thy grandfather, Penitence Hurd. I reprimand thee.'

Standing in an attic eleven years and three thousand miles away, eighteen-year-old Penitence watched the small, grubby, be-snivelled hand of seven-year-old Penitence reach up in a daring grab at the immaculate white cuff-band. 'I w-w-wish to b-b-be c-c-cured, sir.'

In those days the Reverend Block still spoke for God. In the distant rumble of guns she could hear his voice: 'Shall the clay say to Him that fashioneth it, What makest thou? Woe unto her that striveth with her Maker. Thou wast afflicted for God's purpose, child, not thine.'

And from that day to this God's purpose had not been revealed to her. In sending little coffins out of the Ship, it still wasn't revealed to her.

Otcha, potcha, dominotcha.

Her gaze focused back on the actor's face. He'd closed his eyes. She knew what she would be letting herself in for by exposing her stammer to this man: domination, quite possibly the wrath of the Lord her God, and most certainly humiliation. But what else had she endured all her life? She could stay outside the circle no longer, she had to be dipped in by somebody, even this sinner.

Huldy, guldy, boo. Out goes you.

The actor became aware that the clear eyes of the next-door whore were still watching him, and opened his own. 'Well?'

She nodded.

Chapter 7

'BREATHE, for God's sake.'

'I a-am.'

'From the stomach, like I told you.' The actor in the window across the alley put his hand across his lower ribs. 'Like this.'

'I'll g-get the P-Pla-Pl-umm-Plague.'

'Well, it's too late now. Breathe.'

She took in a lungful of alley air and nearly burst before he let her release it.

121

'Now.' He took up his quill as a sign of his schoolmasterly status. It formed another in the vertical lines of which he consisted; lank hair to his shoulders, long cheeks and nose, the points of his stuff shirt-collar over the slashed leather jerkin, the excellent hands protruding into the sunlight which reached his table in the mornings leaving the rest of him in shadow. 'Talk.'

'Uh?'

'Talk. I've got to hear what you do when you talk. Tell me your name, tell me anything. It doesn't matter. Just say it.'

It doesn't matter. There was the trouble, or part of it; his disinterest in who she really was. To him she was the prostitute across the alley he was trying to improve because improvement was possible and because it passed the hours of shut-up. She had been right to expect humiliation from these lessons and already it was being doubled by his indifference.

Dorinda tripled it. From her window immediately below them came her voice: 'Her name's Pen Hurd. She's our American whore.' With the precision of the jealous, Dorinda had located the crack of misunderstanding and was whittling it wider.

'Madam, I don't care if she's the Witch of Endor. Don't interrupt.' He frowned across at Penitence. 'Talk.'

Shall I suffer this? Better to retreat into the dignity of loneliness, stay on the outside of life where she belonged. But it wasn't life behind her in the shadows of the attic, it was the slow death of listening to the daily round of the Plague and waiting for it to suck her into its anonymity. She got ready, balled her hands, lifted her shoulders, sucked in her breath . . .

'Don't *do* that. Relax your hands, let your body go. And for the love of God, will you BREATHE. Tell me your name.'

'P-Pe-Pp-e-Ppe—' The plosive reared up against the hedge between them, tried to leap and tangled itself in invisible foliage. 'I c-c-can't.'

'Look,' he said, patiently, 'I heard you singing the song of barbarians. Where did you learn it?'

'N-nn-no-ot ba-ba-bar-bumm-bar-barians.' *Such ignorance.* 'Alg-gonquin.'

'The French priests told me the Algonquin were barbarians. They said the only good Indians were Iroquois.'

She knew what he was doing, riling her into speech, but she couldn't stop her rise to the bait. French priests sent to convert the Iroquois were trouble-makers and liars, the Iroquois themselves vicious savages, unfit to lick an Algonquian moccasin.

Writhing, she tumbled into a panegyric of Awashonks, Matoonas and their people, scrambling through thickets of stutter, watching words she had to abandon fall into the alley, crawled up syllables, persisting in the truth about her Indians because it had to be told and because telling it brought a whiff of Pocumscut air into her Plague-ridden nostrils.

He was pleased. 'There you are, you see, Boots. Your main trouble is at the front of your mouth. You stutter on everything, but mostly at the closure of the lips, the p-urrs and the b-urrs.'

He doesn't hear a word I say. Only the way I say it.

She heard the rumble of the burial cart. She got up. 'I m-m-must go.' As the only one with an outlook into Dog Yard, she had been deputed to act as the Cock and Pie's Plague-watcher and report the night's toll.

He gave a disgusted 'For God's sake' at her defection and slammed the shutters shut.

Penitence crossed the attic and went out on to her balcony.

The chalk of the first Plague crosses had been replaced by official red paint and gleamed against nearly every one of Dog Yard's doors with alien smartness. The burial cart had drawn up against the pawnbroker's on the far left corner, in the mouth of Pincher's Lane.

One of the bearers was putting nosebags over his horses' bridles; they would be here some time. Beside him, his fellow was ringing a bell and shouting 'Bring out your dead' as casually as if he were calling for rags and bones. She thought drearily: *I suppose he is.*

She tensed herself for the answers. 'Here.' 'Here.' 'Here.' 'Here.' 'Here.' 'Here.' *Lord, let it stop.* It didn't. 'Here.' 'Here.' 'Here.' 'Here.' How long before there was a response from behind the door of the Cock and Pie? Or Mistress Hicks's? The upper rooms in the Buildings were still free of it, but the Stables was answering; Pa Tippin must have gone.

Oh God help us. She sank down on her knees as one of the bearers raised a finger in acknowledgement of a call from the Ship's window. *Not again.* She stayed as she was, not to pray, but to escape the sight of another coffin being carried out of the inn's door. *Why are You doing this?*

Crouching, she listened to the silence from the Ship, to the Jewish ritual wail of grief from the pawnbroker's wife as her family was carried away, to the scuffle at the Stables as the Tippin boys tried to rush the door and follow their father to his ill-deserved rest, listened to panic, grief, anger and bewilderment form an elaborate motet out of the responsory of pestilence.

When it was over, she dragged herself up again and let Soper, one of the watchmen, tell her the toll. Then she went down to the clerestory. Her Ladyship stood in the doorway to her room: 'Well?'

She gave the list. '. . . and t-two more from M-umm-M-Mother Hubb-Hubbard's. The paw-pawnbroker's gone, and his s-son.' Her stammer worsened in ratio to how well the dead had stood in Her Ladyship's regard. 'And M-M-Mistress C-Cr-Craw—'

'Jenny Crawford?' Her Ladyship's face never altered.

'And the b-b-babies. I'm s-s-ssorry.'

'Ma Palmer? Ma Hicks?'

'N-no. Th-they waved.' It had become a ritual; the living signalled to each other. Men who'd punched one another's noses, matrons who'd shrieked at next door's children, now waved and exchanged news in the weary comradeship of survival. The sight of Mistress Palmer flapping a piece of morning washing towards her once mortal enemy, Mistress Hicks, and the rag in the brawny fist of Mistress Hicks — the view of her neighbour's contiguous frontage was hidden from Penitence's balcony — flapping back, reassured her that there were some things the Plague could not kill. Yet.

'Is that all of them?'

Reluctantly she said: 'An-n-nother B-Br-Bry-Bry-umm-Brys-kett. S-S-second oldest.' 'She tensed herself for the moan from the open doors along the clerestory, and for the sobbing from Dorinda's room. It came.

'You bitch. You ballocking cow, you. You corpse-sniffing crow. Ain't you got better things to do?' Dorinda's grief invariably confused the message with the messenger.

Penitence went slowly back to her attic and sat herself down on the stool facing her side window. *What does it matter?* Stammer, cure, pride, sin, were nothing. The minutes tolled away by the passing bell had become so fragile that they made even humiliation a precious awareness of living.

'Boots.' The command always sounded as if he were calling a servant, it was always at his convenience, not hers. She always answered it.

'Right, now. Polly pours the porridge. And *breathe*.'

She took in breath, let it out, tried to let her hands go limp. *Polly pours the porridge.* Easy. 'P-P-P-P-um-Polly p-p-po ....' It was worse; her lips compressed so hard that only muffled grunting crossed the alley.

'Not *more* poxy porridge.' From below came Dorinda's monotonous but effective sabotage.

'Silence down there. Boots, I've told you. The ambush lies between the words. We don't leave gaps. We are a good general in enemy territory, we keep our file close. We-keep-the-troops-together. Like that. All one utterance, no gap.'

In the privacy of her room, progress was excellent; Polly poured porridge as bravely as brindled bullocks bellowed. Her tongue clicked smartly against the roof of her mouth in the t-urrs and d-urrs – 'Terrible Duke of Tonbridge died in Dorset.' Jh's and ch's made exits as easily from the sides of her tongue and teeth as the k-urrs and g-urrs from clicks at the back of tongue and throat. S's slid through the attic like snakes in wet grass.

That speech could be subject to analysis was exciting in itself. So was his insistence that the stutter was an invading force; not a weakness, not an inherent fault, but something outside. 'It's the enemy, Boots. It attacks us, so we counter-attack.' She thought that, for an actor, he was surprisingly heavy on military metaphor. But they were both learning that the enemy was stronger than she was.

She was losing hope. He was losing patience.

One thing: she had become crafty in diverting him into illustration which, with luck, developed into a performance.

Unknown to herself, Penitence Hurd had become an obsessive and escapist playgoer. Today she managed to nod him into giving her examples of speech patterns. Diverted, he got carried away and acted through the gamut of his fellow-lodgers at Mistress Hicks's. From the fat and Cockney orange-seller with her variously fathered brood in the basement, to the juggler-cum-rope-dancer and the pipe-makers on the first floor, they made their appearance in the proscenium arch of his window in their differing shapes and accents.

'And MacGregor, he's in the room next to mine, he speaks up and down, like his truly dreadful bagpipes which, thanks be to God, he has now sold. Like this: "Now Master King. Will ye be leehnding me. A grooat. For a wee. Sup of ale?"'

The figure of a thick-set man with the amiable, bulbous eyes of a drunk wavered and realigned itself into a tall, thin, regretful actor. 'Poor bastard, I know how he feels. I'd kill for a drink myself.'

But it had been a *tour de force*. From the windows of Alania and Dorinda, the theatre aficionados, who had been able to listen though not see, came applause. 'Better'n Charlie Hart, you are.'

Not knowing who Charlie Hart was, and caring less, Penitence was unable to make a comparison. Amazed by the performance, almost fearing it as witchcraft, she knew nevertheless that she had witnessed a display of skill, but only skill.

She was beginning to think that the play-actor was not a real actor. Acting was something he did because it gave employment at the present time; it was a proficiency like swordsmanship, dancing, or playing the lute, prerequisites of a culture which she only knew about from hearing it condemned. It was a stop-gap, not his life.

There were his occasional unguarded references to military matters, to the political situation, to the mysterious and unexplained sojourn in France, a familiarity with court circles, that reference to the King he'd made on the day he rescued her in the Cut.

Knowing nothing of the theatrical world herself, it might be that all actors were polymathic as he was, but she doubted it. After all, she knew nothing of him, not his parentage or background, nothing.

Had Alania and Dorinda learned from theatre gossip that the man was an exile from the moon Penitence would not have been surprised. What did, and constantly, surprise her was how well she knew the important things about him: his longing for whatever it was that had been denied him, scorn for his present position – and the gallantry with which he endured it. He was making a better fist of it than she was.

It was beneath him to reveal such emotions to her, but they came across the alley like a bow-wave.

He louted to the unseen, applauding girls, then settled back in his chair. 'You've got good teeth, Boots,' he said. 'Smile more often.' He wagged the quill. 'Now then. Hands. Breathe. Begin ... No, no, *no*. We do not suck in on the p-urr, we breathe out. In the name of God, will you BREATHE.'

Her head ached. So, apparently, did his: he was clutching it and calling on someone named Pygmalion. 'His part was easy; he just had to make a woman from a block of stone. I've got this, this—'

She slammed the shutters before he could say it, and heard the answering slam of his own.

The City was losing definition. Peter Simkin kept being disorientated by the lack of human buoyage that had always marked his passage in it. The lavender-seller on the Fleet Bridge was missing. So few people were gathered at St Paul's that he heard his own footsteps echoing back from its high, plain vaulting.

The cobbled sweep of the Poultry was empty, its one occupant – a woman with a lone hen in a crate – making it emptier. He had expected it; large markets were banned for the duration, as were all fairs inside fifty miles of London. Nevertheless, not usually an over-imaginative man, Peter had a fleeting but overwhelming sense of basilisk responsibility, as though he were vanishing these people and that, if it had been somebody else who passed them by instead of himself, they would still be there.

The new porter at Parish Clerks' Hall wouldn't let him in. He was made to put the Bill of Mortality in a warming pan held through the bars of the gate and told to wait.

Last week's Bill on the gate-board declared the Plague total to be 1,089. Next to it the sixteen quarto sheets of the *Newes* had been tacked into a large square.

Peter no longer wasted his penny on it, reckoning that no *Newes* was good 'Newes', but he was prepared to read it for free. It still rejoiced at the victory off Lowestoft three weeks before, the twenty line of battle that English ships had sent to the bottom, the Dutch admiral, Opdam, blown to the skies in his own flagship, ten thousand Dutch seamen drowned and slain.

Considerably more space was given to advertisements for sovereign remedies against the Plague than to news of the Plague itself. However, the editor had utilized a few paragraphs to be still pleased that the dead were mainly in the out-parishes. Although forced to recognize fifty-six in the City, he pointed out that they were 'but in the close and blind alleys'. Also, 'I am warranted by good authority to advertise that partly by taking cold and small drinks in the heat of the fever those who have perished in this dreadful mortality have hastened their own destruction.'

The porter returned to find Peter Simkin still reading. 'You don't want 'a bother with that,' he told him. 'Old L'Estrange prints what the King tells him. And where's our good King Charlie now?'

'Where?'

'Gone.' The porter nodded. 'Or goin'. Off to the greenams without so much as a tra-la-la or kiss-me-arse. Off to bloody Cupid's Arms, and I wish I was with the bugger.' Peter's disapproval of the *lèse-majesté* turned the man surly: 'Clerk says: you done a copy as ordered?'

'Yes.' Not for the first time, he blessed Penitence Hurd.

'Then he says get over to Whitehall and give it to General Monck. Old George's in charge of you bloody out-parishers now and 'a hell with the lot of you.'

Peter Simkin turned round, dragged the seam of his coat away from his sweating armpits, and had obediently set off west when he realized that he was sobbing, not for the defection of his king, not for the spaces where there should have been familiar faces, but because he was too tired to face the extra detour. He reached the top of Ludgate Hill before he could go no further and hauled himself into the Black Bush to sit on a settle and have a drink while his legs stopped trembling. It was cool inside. The contrast with the sunlight outside made the cavernous interior darker than usual, a shadowed, low-canopied grove of ancient wood and brass fittings. Down the far end, a drawer tapped barrels by candle-light.

Soothed by ale and oysters, Peter Simkin went back into the blinding streets. Not being as familiar with this area as with his usual route, he found no gaps to disturb him. Business seemed as usual, though scaled down; there were fewer people but they hurried by with typical City purposiveness, looking no more worried than they always did. It must be him, transferring his anxiety from St Giles, that overlaid everything with wrongness.

The only reminder of Plague was the occasional glimpse of a burial cart down a side street; red crosses were rare on the main thoroughfares and ceased altogether as the palaces reared up on either side of the Strand. He had no resentment against God, whose son had been an upholder of the poor, for so patently favouring the rich; it worried him that his rector got so het up about it. It was the scheme of things and there you were. He was just sorry, as he passed by great gates, to see that fountains weren't playing and that weeds were untidying the ornamental flower-beds.

That was what was wrong; the glittering thread supplied by

the upper classes had been withdrawn from the fabric of London, leaving it workaday stuff. How many times had he disapproved of a group of wonderfully dressed rakes shouldering through the streets or being disgraceful in the coffee-houses, the gilded coaches showering coins and insults? Now they had gone, taking style with them, and he missed them.

His boots puffed up dust. Even under the branches of chestnut trees leaning over the walls it was hot; flies clung tenaciously to his face. The complexities of delivering the Bill in a palace the size of a small English town towered into an enormous problem. He must sit down again, find some shaded grass, before he faced it. But when he turned off, it was to find St James's Park's gates locked against the public for the first time.

A little further south, at the gate to the Privy Garden, Sir John Lawrence, Lord Mayor of London, and George Monck, Duke of Albemarle, waved their hats until the champing, shouting, luggage-encrusted cavalcade and its last trumpet-blowing outrider was out of sight, then became conscious of the silence.

'He had to go,' said Sir John, refuting an accusation nobody had made.

'Should have gone afore,' said the Duke, 'I didn't put him on t'throne to rot of the Plague.'

The Lord Mayor's face twitched — it had developed a tic — as he fought another surge of irritation. God Almighty, Old George wasn't the only one who'd assisted Charles to the throne ... *and* he'd held off with his army to make sure the tide was flowing for the Restoration of the monarchy before he did it, *and* before that he'd been loyal enough to the bastard Cromwell ... yet to hear him talk ... The Lord Mayor got himself under control. Fatigue, that's what it was. To do Old George credit, he was prepared to stay and help — the only bugger in the government who was.

They crossed the road and started the tortuous walk through upper Whitehall towards the Duke's residence.

'Was that Castlemaine I saw dressed up in men's clothes?'

The Duke shook his massive head. 'Stewart. Castlemaine's pregnant.'

'Again?' The Lord Mayor's short legs skipped to keep up with the lumbering stride of the Duke. Through the open windows of the Treasury, he could see clerks still at their desks, but a sense of impetus was missing. Elsewhere large rooms were empty. Perhaps, he thought, one should rejoice at the birth of any child in a month when the Bills of Mortality had already recorded 2,050 deaths, if only the little bastard wasn't going to be a charge on the country's finances.

Money was much on Sir John's mind. He said: 'He's subscribed ten thousand pounds for the relief of the City.'

'Oh aye?'

'Only I haven't seen any of it yet.'

'Oh aye.'

'The Queen Mother, the Duchess of York, Prince Rupert, they've given. But the King . . . he means well, we know . . . it's just that we haven't actually had it.'

The Duke said: 'Castlemaine lost nigh on a thousand pound at basset last night', and he wasn't changing the subject.

Sir John used several words to describe the King's mistress without finding one adequate. A thousand pounds from what, ultimately, was public money, when the sailors who'd fought the Dutch still hadn't been paid, when he himself was at his wits' end as to how the shut-up were to be fed, the sick nursed, the dead buried.

'Some spark left a right little poem on her chamber door t'other night,' the Duke was saying. 'How'd it go? . . . "Why by her must we be plucked, because she is by Caesar fucked?" . . . Some farrago like that.' His chuckles brought back a hollow echo from the emptiness of the Tennis Court. 'Very fit, I thought it, very fit.'

You would, thought Sir John. In your own way you're as vulgar as she is. Lord Jesus, what have we come to that such a thing can be posted in a royal palace? And the Queen in occupancy a few yards away?

'But t'lad's our king.'

Sir John looked up at the big man sharply. Who'd suggested

131

he shouldn't be? Upstarts might shuffle kings around as it suited them, change this one, chop the head off that one, but Lawrences stayed loyal regardless.

At the entrance to Albemarle's apartments he wondered if the Duchess was to be inflicted on him. He didn't feel up to Xanthippes today. But their progress through the suite to the Duke's office was mercifully unimpeded by Lady Monck.

'Now then, Lord Mayor, distribution of relief.' Seated among the Duke's heavy furniture, sipping on over-sweet malmsey, they discussed it.

Sir John, by right of office, would administer the City itself; the Duke to take over the out-parishes. The pest rate levy that had been ordered would depend on how many people in each parish were left untouched by the Plague to pay it. 'Then there'll be private gifts and subscriptions from other cities.' The Duke looked hard at the Lord Mayor. 'Thee'll be expecting thy share of that for the City I don't doubt.'

'The major part, certainly,' said John.

'Aye, but dost thee know thy City's population?'

He didn't. Estimates varied. 'Half a million? A million? Bigger than out-parishes' at any rate.'

'Is it now? Is it? Look at this.' The Duke produced a rough map of the City and out-parishes. He drew a ring round the City making a solid central block surrounded by a ragged fringe.

'It's still bigger,' said Sir John.

'So it do look, but thee needs a soldier's eye. Watch now.' He drew a grid of equal-sized squares over the whole area. 'Thee counts t'squares over t'City, then count t'squares left outside.'

The City had twenty-seven squares, the outlying area twenty-eight. 'I tell thee, Lord Mayor, there's as big a mass of people outside as in.'

Sir John was devastated; he'd had no idea London had spread so wide. Nor was it any use to say, as he was tempted, that the City's population was more concentrated; he knew the overcrowding of the out-parishes.

He felt the now-familiar anger seize him. 'I know what

132

you're asking and I won't do it. Bloody foreigners, swarming in from the country to live like rats, nobody asked them.'

'Aye, but they're not foreigners, are they? They're English men and women as couldn't find work elsewhere, and thy City was glad enough of their labour in t'good times.'

Damn the man and his soldier's eye and damn, damn the Plague. Into Sir John's own eye came the picture of the monument which he'd hoped would have been erected to himself. He'd have dearly liked future ages to know that John William Lawrence's mayoralty had left London more wonderful than it had found it. Now it would be remembered as the Plague Year. He made the bravest decision of his life. 'I shall consult my Aldermen,' he said, 'but you may take it that only money raised in the City will be spent there.'

'God will reward thee, John,' said the Duke, quietly.

'He'd better,' said Sir John.

The Duke's steward came in: 'The parish clerk of St Giles-in-the-Fields is here, my lord, with his Bill. I have baked it, my lord.'

The Duke rose. 'I suppose I'd better be acquainted.' He turned to the Lord Mayor. 'Any road, he's t'lad who's swallowing most of the funds. Do thee like to see him, John?'

'I'd like to see him in Hell,' said the Lord Mayor, sincerely, 'I'd like to see him buried alive in one of his own pits. I'd like to see him screaming on the rack. Him and his whole damned parish.'

Peter Simkin, waiting with his head bared, fingering his hat, saw a small man rush past him who, he thought — near-fainting with the heat as he was, he couldn't be sure — wore the necklace and insignia of the City of London. The Lord Mayor, if it was the Lord Mayor, seemed to be shaking his fist at him.

Like most windows in the Rookery, the actor's was unglazed, a square wooden frame inset with shutters through which woodworm supplied ventilation. The shutters punctuated his moods, slamming to when she enraged him, nudging open to show he'd forgiven her, remaining closed when he was sick of her, bursting outwards for a fresh start.

Today was a fresh start. 'Today,' he said, 'I have a good idea.'

Not another one.

Today he'd acquired a recorder. 'We will sing the phrase.'

She was amazed by his persistence. She had long given up hope for improvement; the lessons were an end in themselves. *We might just as well play chess.*

At the first note, the girls below popped their heads into view. 'Singing now, is it?' And, from Dorinda: 'Pen likes singing to her gentlemen, don't you, Pen?'

'I c-cc-can't.'

'You can.' The shutters would slam to any moment, she knew. Quickly, she weighed embarrassment against another stifling day with nothing to do. She opened her mouth . . .

He kept trying to get her to look at him. 'Look at me. See how my lips move.' But she wouldn't. Like most stutterers she avoided the face she addressed, unable to bear the grimace that reflected her own. She b-urred and p-urred to his right shoulder.

'What you two doing?' Penitence was in the process of sending a near-perfect b-urr across the alley to the pitch of middle C. She unpuckered her lips and looked down.

The new watchman, a former butcher's assistant, was regarding the two of them with suspicion. The Plague had taken Soper two days ago. Watchmen, in the Yard's view, were either knaves or fools and this, Soper's replacement, was promising on both counts. He used his powers under the Plague laws with tyrannous attention to detail. Yesterday he'd wanted Mistress Palmer prosecuted on the grounds that her washing hanging on the pulley line between the Buildings and the Stables' chimney was 'agin promulgation'. It had taken the intervention of Apothecary Boghurst to convince him it posed no threat of infection.

Irritated, the actor removed the recorder and sent down a 'What?' which would have pierced a sensitive man like a shard of glass.

The watchman remained unpierced. 'Blowing kisses. Agin promulgation.'

The actor raised his eyes and waved the man away. 'Again. B-urr.'

'B-b-bbu-umm-b.' Her face was in tics of self-consciousness.

The actor growled. 'You see what you've done to her, you bacon-faced buffle? Go away.'

'Don't you call me a buffle.' The watchman was indignant. 'This is agin promulgation this is and I'll report you to the magistrate.'

'Do it.' The actor hammered on his window-sill. 'But go. This lady must have calm.'

'I know what the Cock and Pie is. That's a lady, I'm a Dutchman.'

The recorder was laid down on the table, very slowly. 'No,' said the actor, 'you're not a Dutchman, you're a pig-eared, dough-brained, privy-stinking dogbolt and you will apologize. You . . . you Dogberry.'

'I'm going to report this.' The watchman lumbered off.

The actor scratched his chin. 'Dogberry,' he said, 'Dogberry, Dogberry, Dogberry.' His chair scraped back and he vanished into the shadows of his room.

He shouldn't swear. But it was nice of him. Is it worth it?

He was back, with a book in his hand. 'Listen to me, Boots. There's an actor in Paris with a stutter like yours. He's one of Molière's company, Jean Béjart.' He was looking at her intently. He was having another idea. 'But when he is on the stage his speech is perfect. Perfect absolutely.'

She nodded with tired indulgence and he became cross. 'For God's sake, when Jean is himself he stutters: when he's some-one else he doesn't.'

She understood what he said; she just couldn't see its application.

He threw the book and she caught it, looked at it, then dropped it when she saw what it was. 'It's a play.'

'A play, yes. It doesn't explode.'

It can injure the soul. The childhood-engrained horror of the conjuring, mocking, delusive mummery that was theatre was strong in her.

She was puzzling him: 'You read, don't you? I've seen you read.'

The Bible. 'The B-Bb-umm-B . . .' Did he think harlots read the Bible? Didn't he know it was the Bible? How could he persist in understanding her so little when she knew him so well? 'The B-Bbb . . .' *Let me tell him. This one word, Lord. I beg you.* 'B-By-Bb-umm . . .'

'God Almighty,' he said, 'do you want to stay in a brothel for ever? Read it.' He slammed his shutters.

Church bells rang all afternoon, adding to the din in Penitence Hurd's brain where the Pure Church thundered its denunciation of acting and actors. It wasn't until evening that she realized it was speaking in the Reverend Block's voice. *And how pure were thee?* The question silenced it, though the bells went on. She sat listening to them and compared two men; one who thought she was a whore and didn't treat her as one, the other who'd known she was not and had.

She went out to watch the sunset. There were lights in the Strand that she couldn't account for, until her nose twitched at a new smell. They were burning disinfectant in the streets to keep off infection.

Below her the neat black figure of Apothecary Boghurst crossed the Yard to the Ship where the Night Watch opened the door for him.

The Yard's living were at their windows, Mistress Palmer on her balcony, a few Tippins on the roof of the Stables. Footloose hauled himself out of his vat and into his trolley. They waited.

After half an hour the knot of watchmen by the door lit their lanterns. One left the group and headed for Butcher's Cut.

The Yard waited, knowing who would come back with him.

The tramp of the returning watchman's boots were accompanied by the shuffle of the Searcher.

Footloose hotched himself across the Yard to the Ship's door; they could hear his high-pitched voice ask a question, a lower reply. Footloose began his round of the Yard, but the news travelled the round quicker than he did. It was whispered from the pawnbroker's to the roof of the Stables, went up and down the windows of the Buildings, leaped across the gap of Butcher's Cut to Mother Hubbard's.

On Penitence's side of the Yard it moved along the houses between the Ship and the Cock and Pie, but it was getting held up at the window of Mistress Chalkley, who was deaf. Nobody shouted it.

From Mistress Hicks's window on Penitence's right came a hoarse 'You there, Pen?'

'Yes.'

'It's John Bryskett. The oldest. That's six.'

Wobbling wheels creaked themselves towards the Cock and Pie's steps. She could hear the puff of Footloose's breath. 'Pen?'

'Yes.'

'There ain't no God, is there?' In the Yard her hat made her the religious authority.

'Yes there is,' she said. *And He crucifies mankind for His pleasure.*

She felt her way down through the sleeping house to the kitchen, lit a rushlight from the ration of coals that now burned in a brazier, and took it back, with a supply, to where the actor's book still lay by the side window. It was quarto-sized and looked as if it had belonged to several people in its time, none of whom had been kind to it.

With one finger, she flipped back the stained cloth cover and the title-page, knelt down and crooked her head round so that she could read without touching it. It was vilely printed and much scrawled. Some minutes later she put out another finger to turn the page and angle the book to a better position. Then she lay down on the floor. When the rushlight went out, she lit another and made herself comfortable on her bed, without knowing she was doing either of those things.

Just before dawn she put the book down and sat up with her arms round her knees. The pith of Kinyans's last rushlight was a twig of ash of which only the bottom quarter sent out a circle of light beyond which existed grief and suffering and a God who cared about neither.

Within the circle it was still Messina. Hand in hand a man and a woman danced out of her sight to the sound of pipers; an insubstantial, foolish couple for whose company, however long or short a time she lived, she would be grateful. There were tears in her eyes to watch them go, though she had them, here, in this smudged book. She opened it at the title-page to see what it was called, and nodded. The author had known, had blown his fragile bubble and let it shimmer, iridescent, into an attic in a plague spot for her, who had never played, to know what play meant.

When the bearers came she was on her balcony to watch John Bryskett's coffin taken away on the cart with only Footloose to follow it. Then she went to her side window and waited for the actor's shutters to open.

He yawned and stretched. 'Did you read it?'

'Yes.' She had it in her hands.

'Well?'

She said: 'It is r-ri-ri-ridiculous.' Too flimsy to warrant the charge of being sinful, it had no moral, no religious purpose. Stripped down to its basic plot it was absurd.

'It's not his greatest. On the other hand . . .'

On the other hand. Whoever this Shakespeare was, he had clothed the feeble bones of his play in starlight. Words so luminous had lit up her attic that, unfamiliar as she was with play form, she had been able to see the movements of the men and women who spoke them as they cavorted around her.

'Did you like Beatrice?'

'Yes.' Last night the lump that was Penitence had found the form it was prepared to sell its soul to be fashioned in. 'H-how d-did he d-do it?'

'Do what?'

'H-how d-d-did he m-m-make you kn-kn-know th-the-they l-loved each other f-f-from the b-be-umm-be-beginning . . .' It was almost the longest sentence she had spoken to him and it was too difficult. They hadn't known they loved each other, everybody else thought they hated each other, the ludicrous devices with which their friends tricked them into declaring love – all that was the plot – but the author had reached over and, in the battle of words between Beatrice and Benedick, had said to Penitence: 'You and I know their attraction, even if

138

they don't. Let us watch them fall off the knife-edge of passion they teeter on.'

'Genius.' He shrugged. 'It's a bauble, I grant you. In dealing with true situation Molière outstrips him. But our Will undoubtedly had genius. Nearly as much as I have.'

She ignored that. 'Had?'

'He's dead, woman. What did they teach you in New England? He died in 1615, 1616, something like that.'

She'd felt his breath on her cheek and he'd been dead when her grandfather was a boy.

Dogberry slouched down the alley towards them. He looked disgruntled.

'All right,' he said, 'so it's not agin promulgation. But I'm watching you two.' He leaned his halberd against Mistress Hicks's wall, then himself.

'So,' said the actor, 'you'll play Beatrice. I'll be Benedick.'

Play Beatrice? How could she, an inarticulate, play a mistress of repartee? Automatically, she said: 'It's d-did-dis-umm-ddissembling.'

'Dissembling,' agreed Dogberry from the alley.

'Of course.' He was surprised. 'Dissemble. Pretend. Imagine. Why not? When you read it, did you think for one moment about the Plague? No, you didn't. Were you sad? No, you weren't. It's a trifle to amuse.' He picked up his quill. 'The lessons are the infantry, step by step. The play's our cavalry. Now then, we'll begin where Beatrice and Benedick meet.' He gestured to Penitence to find the place in the text.

As she ruffled through the pages, she felt nerves snatching at her breath. She breathed as he had taught her, surreptitiously wiping her hands one after the other down her skirt, trying to relax them. She could do this; she could join the cavalry.

'What, my dear Lady Disdain! Are you yet living?'

Immediately, she was thrown. He'd sat himself in the angle of the window, one knee drawn up so that his boot rested on the sill, the sun catching a face that had grown younger. The voice was negligently Benedick's as she'd heard it in her head last night. One finger beckoned Beatrice's line.

'Is it p-p-po-umm-possible D-di-dummdi-ddisdain . . .'

139

She had thought Beatrice's words would speak themselves, that because they were somebody else's they would have their own volition. *What a fool.* Penitence's tongue was patented to stumble whatever it spoke. Dumbly, she looked down at the book in her hands and closed it.

'Breathe.'

She shook her head. It wasn't the breathing. 'It's m-m-me.'

'Ah ha.' He was the play-actor again. 'But you are not you, are you? You're not poor little Pentecost or whatever you call yourself.'

Penitence, she thought miserably.

'You're a grand lady, with spirit, presence. You're cleverer than Benedick; you best him every time. Come on, Boots, you've seen great ladies in their carriages, haven't you?' He flirted his hand across his face, like a fan. 'Imagine what it's like to be one, roasting your maid, cuckolding your husband . . .' He closed his eyes. 'Jesus, I could do with a drink.' He looked down at Dogberry: 'Why don't you toodle off and get me some ale?'

'Why don't you give me the gelt?' asked Dogberry.

The actor looked back at Penitence. 'Will you wear the diamonds today? Boots, you must have imagined what it would be like.'

She most certainly had not. Contempt for the trappings of wealth had been built into her. *Pentecost or whatever you call yourself.* He couldn't even get her name right. But that's what she was, poor. Poor and dumb. She'd never be anything else.

She heard Dogberry say: 'Take some imagining that would. She looks like the cat dragged her in.'

'Her gentlemen like the churchy style,' called Dorinda.

But the actor was thoughtful. 'Dogberry,' he said, 'you are not the fool you look.' He peered beyond Penitence into her attic. 'Those boxes. What's in them?'

She shrugged. *What does it matter?*

'Open them up. We'll get rid of that, that *thing* you're wearing. Beatrice must dress as Beatrice.'

She fought back, defending her habiliment's moral worth. 'It's c-c-clean.'

'Also an atrocity. I don't want to speak ill of the dead, but even I can't act attraction for that. Open.'

Spiritless, she dragged the first chest to the window and rummaged through it, releasing clouds of pennyroyal long turned to dust. *Do this, do that. Put a hat on the monkey. He'll be wanting to paint my face next.*

The clothes were a job-lot from the pawnbroker's where they had lain unclaimed until Her Ladyship bought them cheap, hoping they could be refashioned for her girls. Most had proved forty years old with tight bodices and waists impossible to alter into the flowing, modern, natural line. What was usable had already been used, the rest kept for purses or patching. To Penitence, who had never worn a colour more garish than grey, they were hideously over-bright. She chose the least gaudy thing she could see, a faded primrose partleted bodice still attached to a black skirt.

'Up. Up.' Slouching, she held it up.

'Into the light if you please.'

She shambled to the window, clutching the material to her shoulders. The actor shook his head. Below in the alley, Dogberry considered and then shook his: 'Nah.' Penitence glared at him. A sober, green jacket was rejected by the two of them, so was a more daring magenta pelisse.

The actor considered. 'It's the hair.'

'What hair?' asked Dogberry.

'Exactly. That abortion on your head. Off.'

She clutched her cap. She'd never appeared capless in public in her life. This was her best. 'It's g-g-gumm-good l-linen.' Her hair was her worst feature. It was light yellow. Her mother had called it wilful and cropped it close in an effort to subdue its wave. Penitence had neglected it, meaning to cut it every time she was reminded of its length when she washed it, but hadn't, bundling it into her cap instead.

The play-actor lost his temper. He grabbed his sword and, holding on with one hand, swung outwards. Penitence's cap twitched off her head. Her hair, heavy and warm, fell over her face. Peering through it, she saw the actor regain his room, her cap on the tip of his sword, saw him turn and look at her.

'Rip me,' said Dogberry.

The actor put his chin on his fist. 'The blue,' he said.

Trailing from one of the boxes was an old silk shawl the colour of a peacock's neck. She put it round hers.

'Like this.' He swung his own cloak across his front from shoulder to shoulder. Penitence swung hers.

'Rip me,' said Dogberry.

'Well, well,' said the actor. 'Who'd have thought it? Have you a looking-glass? Then permit me to say "Behold, thou art fair, my love; thou hast doves' eyes within thy locks." Boots, my little Galatea, thy speech shall be as fair as thy face. If we're ever released from this rat-hole, I'll make thee Empress of Cathay, princes shall fawn upon thee, thou wilt be the mistress of kings. Now then. "What, my dear Lady Disdain! Are you yet living?"'

Forced to rely on Penitence's cavalry, the Model Army would have had a bad war. She was just Penitence Hurd with her hair down and a bit of old blue silk across her front. She felt exposed and silly.

The day got hotter. Dorinda got nastier. Dogberry got bored and sat down for a sleep. The actor, persistent in his good idea, waxed long on the techniques of acting, which she failed to grasp.

Eventually, she stuttered them both into an exhausted silence.

She broke it with the final admission of defeat. 'C-c-an I h-have m-my c-ca-cum-cap b-b-back, p-pp-pl-umm-please?' Her head ached and the unstopping tolling of bells expanded and contracted it with each stroke.

The play-actor slumped in his window, fingering her cap. 'Perhaps.'

'P-pl-pl-umm-pplease.'

He stood up and went to the back of his room.

I shall manage. I am no worse off than I was. Something soft fell across her shoulder. She picked it off. It wasn't her cap, it was a scrap of black satin with strings. She looked enquiringly across.

'A vizard mask. People wear them at the theatre. Put it on.

And here.' A gleaming object arced across the alley and she caught it. It was a gentleman's travelling mirror, a small silver oval embossed back and front with a coat of arms.

Penitence took both objects away to the front of her attic; to look in a mirror was still a shameful act — to be done in private, if at all. The mask was made to cover the lower half of the face, leaving only eyes and forehead exposed. There was a slit for the mouth, and a raised area to go over the nose.

Here, then, was the ultimate in deception, the capstone of guile; to put it on, the final severance from God's grace.

The example of God's grace clanged in her ears.

Suddenly, she clapped the mask to her face and tied its strings under her hair. The slipperiness of the material moulded to the warmth of her skin. At once she felt oddly concealed and powerful, as she had not since hunting days when she and Matoonas had waited in hides along the deer runs, spears at the ready.

She picked up the silver oval and slid aside its front. The interior of one side held a miniature of the play-actor when he was younger and richer. She looked into the glass set in the other side.

The eyes of a strange woman looked back at her. They were long, stretching almost to the temples. A strong blue. The lashes were dark — a contrast to the appalling colour of the hair above them — and also long. Above the black anonymity of the mask, they were compelling. It was no vanity to consider them; they were disembodied, unrelated to anything outside the mirror. For the first time that she could remember, Penitence looked somebody straight in the eye. The eyes looked straight back, intelligent and, *Lord*, amused. Beatrice's eyes.

Power was a new sensation for her; she felt it so strongly that she shut the mirror and took the mask off to examine it for witchcraft. No runes had been stitched along its seam which, if anything, was carelessly sewn. She put it back on again, opened the mirror, looked, and took it off again, being careful not to glimpse her bare-faced reflection; she had no interest in Penitence Hurd. She did this several times.

When it hung from her hand the vizard mask was a shaped piece of satin. When she put it on, it was a cap of darkness that vanished Penitence and replaced her with a new and potent being. Nothing, nobody would ambush the woman behind the mask; it was she who lay in ambush. It was a cloak of invisibility allowing the wearer to be whoever she wanted.

She tied it on and ducked out on to the balcony into hot air polluted by the slow chime of bells and smoke from disinfectant bonfires. A fine time to come into possession of a city, but it was hers. She stretched, raising both arms above her head in acknowledgement of fealty.

From below her came a gasped 'Oh my Gawd.'

She looked down. The only two people in the Yard were Dogberry, who had resumed his patrol, and Footloose, sitting in the mouth of his vat and baring his stumps to the sun. Both were staring at her; Footloose had crossed his two forefingers in front of his face to ward off evil.

Beatrice spoke through the mask-shaped hole in the barricade of Penitence's stutter. 'Cousins, God give you joy.'

Footloose patted his heart: 'Gawd, Pen, you didn't half give me a turn. I thought you was a demon.'

I am.

She turned back into the attic.

She was agin promulgation, a thing of darkness, a shapeshifter, a changeling to spin her mother and grandparents in their grave; the Pure Church would wash its hands of her and call in the witch-finders. She'd sold her soul. But the price was right.

I am a voice.

She raised it: 'But then there was a star danced, and under that was I born.'

The voice whipped round the room. It found everything funny. It was a voice surprised to find itself where it was. Its echo slid over the planks of the floor as if expecting to find them marble. It ran a vocal forefinger over the beams and raised its eyebrows at the dust. Clear, used to command, it was the voice of the governors' daughters who had viewed New England settlers as backwoodsmen.

144

The masked woman cocked her head to listen to it. Not quite right.

As a child her mind had escaped into the animal spirits of the Indians, becoming an owl, an eagle, a fish. The woman's mind swooped into Beatrice.

These men went off to their enjoyable wars, they came back, ignorant of the boredom that existed without them. Were she of a resentful humour, which she was not, she would be piqued, just as she was piqued by the changes in her breathing when she looked at him — some devilish aberration for which he must pay. Since he was here, she'd have his attention.

She swept to her side window, wiggling Beatrice's be-ringed fingers.

Benedick still sat in the angle of his window. His hat was over his eyes, so that his face was in shadow, but the light caught his throat where it rose from his shirt. A linen cap dangled from his fingers.

She said crisply: 'Is it possible Disdain should die, while she hath such meet food to feed it as Signor Benedick?'

For a moment he still seemed asleep until, very slowly, he raised a finger and tipped back his hat . . .

Somebody was knocking on the front door of the Cock and Pie, from the inside. Alania's voice was shouting for the Watch to fetch the apothecary.

There were running footsteps on the stairs to her attic and Phoebe fell into the room. 'It's here, Prinks. Oh, what we going to do?' She ran to the window and repeated the shout for the apothecary, then turned back. 'It's here, Prinks. It's in *here*. Kinyans has got it.'

Penitence's eyes met the play-actor's for one long minute. Then she held out her hand for her cap.

She was to remember his hand clenching on the piece of linen as if he could not bear to let it go, and that he said: 'No.'

She knew his concern was not for her as such but for the promising pupil he was about to lose but she was always grateful.

She'd known. For one moment she had experienced such

145

appalling joy that it was only to be expected that the Puritan God would make her pay for it.

She smiled at the play-actor and held out her hand again. Bad-temperedly he threw the cap across.

She caught it, took off the vizard mask and put her cap on her head to go downstairs, tucking in her hair as she went.

Chapter 8

THE GIRLS were gathered on the clerestory, trying to catch what the apothecary was saying over Kinyans's screams. Below them, Her Ladyship and Job struggled to hold the old man down on one of the salon's couches.

They managed to hear Master Boghurst say: 'This is the fear stage.'

Kinyans was attempting to crawl away from something only he could see, though his horror made it vivid enough for Job, his great hands clasped like manacles round the old man's wrists, to keep glancing in the same direction in case it had taken shape.

Her Ladyship snapped: 'How long does it last?' She wasn't paying out half a crown to be told the obvious.

'Four, five hours. Sometimes longer.' He raised his voice without changing its tone. 'After this will come vomiting and the flux. I advise you to have pails ready. Has he the buboes yet?'

The Cock and Pie's front door was open for the first time in three weeks and late afternoon sun was making a path sideways across the salon to the east wall, letting in fresh air. As Job and Her Ladyship fought to strip the patient, Kinyans's hands batted at their faces as if they'd become monstrous. He kept crying out with pain. The apothecary stepped closer and peered. Job kneed the couch into the path of the sun coming through the Cock and Pie's front door. Kinyans's sparse, yellow body was covered with pinhead spots, some of which had run together into rings the size of a fingernail. Dark lumps were forming in each armpit and the groin, giving the impression that giant black beetles had lodged themselves under his skin.

The apothecary pointed at the buboes. 'Hot mustard plasters to gather the poison. They must burst, or be burst. How old is he?'

'Sixty, sixty-five,' puffed Her Ladyship.

The apothecary said without inflection: 'Then he may survive. This is a young person's plague. So far I have been unable to save a single child.'

Oh God. Oh God. This is normal to him. This is what Plague is. She had counted up names with the abbreviation 'Pla.' beside them and transferred the totals to the Bills of Mortality and thought she knew the extent of the disaster upon them all.

It was brought home to her now; every name on Peter Simkin's list had been prefaced by this scene from Hell. Behind every padlocked, red-crossed door this had been enacted, often in multiplication, with noise, with convulsions, with victims evacuating their bowels on the bed-sheets as Kinyans was doing now. One by one the Bryskett children had screamed on this rack while their parents watched, unable to stop the turn of the screw.

She had listened to bells ringing out orderly, sanitary messages of deaths that should have been recorded in jangles of pandemonium.

'I do not recommend a nurse,' the apothecary was saying, 'unless you would take in a sot and a thief. If you wish to choke the patient you may purchase some of the more preposterous physics on offer, or you may prefer my electuary at eightpence a bottle. Keep him clean, warm and, as you love him, no cold drinks until the sweats are gone.'

He spoke through the screams to some inner measure that could not be hurried, as if exercising his profession was an end in itself.

He's lost hope. For us, for him, for everybody. The apothecary's emotions had stopped being kindled by fear, by love of man, love of God, by disapproval for harlots. She saw through him the presence of wholesale annihilation. How to await it was a matter of choice – in gibbering terror or, as this little man was, in a dignified continuity.

There was another shriek under which Her Ladyship asked a question. The girls couldn't see her face; she had her back to them.

The apothecary didn't bother to lower his answer: 'Mistress, I cannot tell. Since this man has had the run of the house I see small purpose in continuing isolation. Let them check their bodies each morning, take my electuary with a little wine each day and permit them to be of help.'

I can't. Lord forgive me, but I can't. Let the others. Not me. Only minutes before she had found the key to life itself. *I can't die now.*

Puritan duty was one thing; she'd been prepared to soothe brows, to comfort, to spoon gruel. But to approach the stinking, raving thing that Kinyans had become, for herself to die like that ... her arm touched against Sabina's and she found she had been sidling back along the clerestory towards the door to the attics.

The apothecary nodded to Her Ladyship and went out, walking through the sunlight to the open air. They heard the clatter of Dogberry's keys and the sun was shut out with a slam. Immediately the salon reverted to twilight where three shafts of fading light came through the high east windows on to the pillars, showing up dust on the peeling gilt, the yellow tone of the old man's naked body, resting on Her Ladyship's lustreless dyed gold hair and the thick bend of the dowager's hump where her neck disappeared into the collar of her robe.

The tawdriness, the smell, the heat, combined into a nausea of suffocation. *I can't.* She could hear the other girls' quick breathing.

Everybody stayed as they were, waiting for Her Ladyship to move. Kinyans's screams were weakening; each jerk of his body increased the smell. Job held him, crouching on the other side with his eyes on Her Ladyship's face. After a while she lifted her right arm and wiped her face along its upper sleeve.

148

'Well,' she said. Kinyans kicked, and she leaned her weight on his ankles. 'Phoebe.'

'Yes, Ladyship.'

'You and Sabina heat some water so we can get this old rasher of wind cleaned up; you'll be in charge of laundry. Fanny.'

'Yes, Ladyship.'

'You and Job get Kinyans' bed down here. Francesca and Alania, start tearing up rags. Clean, mind.'

'Yes, Ladyship.' The woman had brought order back into the universe. Gratefully, the girls scurried off.

'Dorinda, you'll be in charge of the kitchen, Gawd help us. Dorinda.'

There was no reply. Her Ladyship turned round and saw Penitence standing, solitary, on the clerestory. 'What you think you're doing? Get back to the attic.'

She'd been about to slink there; now she was irked to be excluded from the structured industry. 'I c-c-can h-help too.'

'JESUS.' The near-hysteria of the woman's shout jerked Kinyans's body into another fit. 'Why don't you do as you're bloody *told*? I don't *want* you here. I *never* wanted you here. You and your bloody eyes and your stammering gob. Don't you UNDERSTAND?' Her arms flailed at Penitence. Her hands were shaking and she stared at them. Slowly she curled them into fists and brought herself under control. Quietly she said: 'Get Dorinda. Send her down to the kitchens. If you want to help, get and wheedle fresh straw and rushlights out of that bottle-headed watchman. But I don't want to see you down here again. Is that clear?' She turned back to Kinyans.

Penitence rested her hand on the latch of Dorinda's door, dismal with the return of an old pain. Her mother had stood in the kitchen of the New England house as Her Ladyship had stood now. At her feet were the shards of a favourite Delft bowl that Penitence had just dropped. 'I *never* wanted thee. Thee was spawned of the Devil. I'll not have thee in my HOUSE.'

Dorinda was in her room, lying on her bed with her thumb in her mouth. Her eyes were open but when Penitence spoke to her they didn't move.

Francesca and Alania looked in. They were carrying one of the chests from the attic. 'Has she got it?'

'I d-don't know.'

'Oh Gawd. Look, then.'

And because they were expecting her to, she put out her hands to force Dorinda's huddled arms apart and pull down her robe.

The girl's skin was clear. There were no swellings under her armpits.

'I th-think she's j-just afraid.' Dorinda had chosen to meet the end of the world gibbering. Penitence couldn't find it in her heart to blame her.

'Ain't we all. Well, she's no loss in the kitchen, that's for sure.'

'I'll m-manage the k-k-kitchen.' She knew enough of the Cock and Pie girls' slatternly backgrounds to doubt if housewifery was numbered among their skills, whereas it was the one challenge she was equipped to meet. Her mother and grandmother had organized the provisioning of their remote household — during harvest-time when neighbours gathered to help it had numbered more than sixty — with an efficiency that would have put an army sutler to shame. Good housewifery was the only lesson Penitence had learned from them with any pleasure.

Other lessons had been harder: how to cling on to a knowledge of self-worth in the face of women who'd given her none, how to use stubbornness as a resistance against discipline verging on dictatorship. They availed her now. She pulled the bedspread over Dorinda's hunched shoulders and went out on to the clerestory, her mouth set in a line her mother and grandparents would have recognized.

In the salon Her Ladyship was washing Kinyans who had relapsed into unconsciousness. As if he was a baby, she'd got his thin ankles in one hand, lifting them high while she laved the ordure off his buttocks and thighs with a cloth in the other.

Penitence watched her. Two images, a thin woman screaming at a child in Massachusetts, a fat woman screaming in a brothel's salon, moved into each other and fitted into one. The same note, the same rejection. The question of why the Searcher had brought her unhesitatingly to this address all those months ago was answered.

Penitence said: 'I'm m-managing the k-kitchen.' If this was the end of the world, she was going to face it busy. As the woman jerked her head up, she went on: 'You n-need m-me, Aunt M-Margaret, w-want me or not.'

The state of the kitchen indicated that Kinyans had been neglectful of his duties for many days. It was a mess and buzzed with bluebottles. Either he'd been feeling ill for longer than suspected, or, Penitence thought, the killing of his cats had put him into a lassitude.

It had enlivened the rats. Clattering down the wooden staircase from the clerestory she saw a wave rustle through the rushes on the kitchen floor. A big black one in leaping to escape from a shelf in the pantry knocked over a wooden salt-shaker. As she rushed to right it and stop the escaping flow of luck, her foot stubbed into another rat's stiffened corpse. Yet another had died near the well.

Penitence threw a pinch of spilled salt over her left shoulder to blind the Devil, grabbed the nearest broom and set to work. There wouldn't be any more rushes; she'd have to make sure there weren't any spills. From the look of the place, there wouldn't be much to spill. The flour barrel was half empty, the remaining flitch of bacon heavily carved into, and the smell from the meat safe indicated that its contents should have been cooked yesterday if not earlier. The only just-usable joint was a leg of beef which she put in a mixture of water and vinegar to take away its highness. Stew it for supper and Kinyans could have beef tea. She thanked the Lord that there were good supplies of oats, dried peas and beans.

Even so, they'd have to be rationed to one meal a day, and with isolation now pointless they might as well resume the custom of eating it together.

Cleanliness obsessed her and she was worried at finding only one small bar of soap; if Kinyans's condition was anything

151

to go by, they were going to need a lot of it. She'd have to make some. When Job came into the kitchen she took him out into the yard to show him how to burn the swept-out rushes and save the ash, at the same time using the fire to render down the fat she'd shaved off the putrid meat.

Horrified, she stared at the large tub by the gate into which the Cock and Pie emptied its chamber pots. It was overflowing. A humming, shimmering blue-green mass of flies replaced the lid, which had fallen off.

'Lord's sakes, haven't the n-night-soil men b-b-been?' She rattled at the gate to find it padlocked on the outside. 'G-get that lid on.'

She stamped upstairs to give Dogberry a piece of her mind from the balcony. As she passed her side window, she noticed that the actor's room was empty. Just as well, she didn't have time for mummery now.

Considering the time and ingredients at her disposal, Penitence produced a very passable meal that evening. It was spoiled when Francesca pushed her platter away untasted.

Almost shamefacedly, she lowered her fichu to display a chest that had developed a rash. 'Just come up,' she said. She looked round the table. 'It ain't the Plague,' she said, 'I feel well. Can't be the Plague, can it? Not when I feel well. It's a measle, ain't it? They ain't coloured like Kinyans'. Must be a measle.'

Everyone hastened to agree that it was. The spots were less concentrated than Kinyans's and pinkish where his were brown. 'Measles,' pronounced Her Ladyship. 'Go lie down a spell. Don't be afraid, pippin.'

Francesca was shivering. 'I ain't,' she said. 'A bit cold is all.'

Phoebe put her arm round her and helped her up the staircase.

Nobody else moved.

It's here. In this kitchen. Now. There was a spurt of surprise. Even in watching Kinyans's suffering there had been a remove; he was old, male, down there, part of another tableau. But the thing had sat at the table, on Francesca's young flesh, eating supper with them. Next to *her*.

Sabina's spoon was rattling where she rested it on her platter. Her Ladyship leaned over and moved it. 'We'll bring her bed down to the salon,' she said. 'Save running up and down stairs. But eat first.' She frowned at the table. 'Penitence, you've forgotten the finger bowls.'

'Water,' begged Fanny.

'You're n-not s-supposed to have it,' said Penitence, wearily. 'Water.'

From the darkness Her Ladyship's voice said: 'What difference do it make? Fetch it.'

Penitence put her hands on her knees to lever herself out of the little gilt chair by the side of Fanny's bed. 'Shall I g-get s-ssome for the others?'

'Yes.'

She weaved her way to the kitchen. The few coals in the grate gave her enough light to locate the bucket by the well in the room beyond. Her Ladyship was right, she was always right; whether they gave Fanny cold water or withheld it, as Master Boghurst urged them to, she would die just the same. They'd followed the apothecary's instructions with Kinyans and Francesca, giving them only sips of electuary mixed with wine, and fought to keep them covered with blankets during their fevers. Kinyans and Francesca had died.

The Plague had picked up their corpses and slung them on the cart. The Plague had attached so many things to its personality, the stink of the bodies it attacked, the scarcity of food and light, the bells, that now the bearers had assumed the role not of parish servants but of goblins that came at the command of their unseen master to complete the process he had begun. They lived by Plague, died by it, cooked it, regarded the view it allowed them. It had moods and, like the slaves they were, they pandered to them.

It had turned on the three untouched houses in Dog Yard, the apartments next door where Mistress Chalkley lived, the Cock and Pie and Mistress Hick's, infuriated at having neglected them for so long. They'd cowered while it lashed. Kinyans was dead, Francesca was dead, Fanny was dying,

153

Alania and Job were going through the process that led to death.

It had paused for the moment. She could see it, standing back, puffing. She could hear it playing its counting game: 'Otcha, potcha, dominotcha. Hi, pon, tusk. Huldy, guldy, boo.'

Out goes who?

This wouldn't get baby a new bonnet. She attached the bucket to the rope on the windlass and pushed against the heavy handle. The air coming up from the well struck wonderfully cold on her perspiration-soaked dress.

The Indians didn't treat fever like Master Boghurst. They sponged down their patients with cool water from the river. The River . . . It came, lapping about her feet. She felt the cool membrane of its surface trickle up her ankles and the coloured pebbles against her toes.

Baby's bonnet. Keep winding. Was it yesterday it had carried off Mistress Chalkley? This morning? No, yesterday. This morning was the orange-seller and her eldest. This morning the actor had said that Mistress Hicks had got it.

Don't think of him. She began turning the handle fast to keep her mind away. The Plague could catch a thought, it was so clever. It would step next door to carry him off.

Don't even plead with it. She'd pleaded for Francesca.

There'll be nobody left to close my eyes. That worried her very much; Francesca's eyes had been half-open, giving her an appearance of unaccustomed slyness, Kinyans's had been balefully staring. Master Boghurst said most victims died with their eyes open. Unreasonable perhaps, but it bothered her that she would flop, staring, on to the other bodies in the cart with an improper expression . . .

God, I'm so tired. The Indians didn't treat fever like Master Boghurst. The Indians sponged down the sick with cool water from the river. The River . . .

It didn't come this time. The cold shock was her mother's voice: 'Thy aunt sinned, Penitence Hurd. Touch ye pitch and be defiled.'

You didn't understand, Mother. You didn't understand anything.

The action of winding became purpose in itself, cocooning

her in a hiatus between past and future. When the full bucket appeared above the well-head, she stared at it in surprise.

'Penitence.'

'Coming, Ladyship.'

She pulled the bucket, still on the rope, so that it rested on the well-head edge, unhooked it and lugged it through the kitchen.

She wasn't frightened for Her Ladyship as she was for the actor. Her Ladyship was the Plague's match. In other houses there were fights among the dying, screaming attempts to escape, nurses stole their patients' clothes and tipped the corpses, naked, from the window to the burial cart. Not at the Cock and Pie.

The Plague's plan was to steal dignity. Job turned his face to the wall and cried as he involuntarily excreted, Francesca, who'd endured agony with courage, spent her penultimate hour in a temper because Sabina forgot to bring her another pillow. But Her Ladyship overlaid all of it with a gravitas that made those who nursed and those who received nursing aware that they were involved in events of monumental importance.

She'd neither confirmed nor denied being Aunt Margaret and Penitence had not pursued it. It was enough that Her Ladyship knew she knew. As she did; it all fitted. Now listening for it, she heard her mother's voice in Her Ladyship's every pro-nouncement and saw in the woman who had built up a successful business in the most shameful area of London the same unbending capability as in the one who'd faced down a wilderness in Massachusetts.

It concerned her that under Her Ladyship's hardness lay more true charity than had been under her mother's.

I'm proud of her, Mother. What do you think of that?

It took an effort of will to enter the salon. They were lucky to have a large sickroom at all; what conditions were like in the small apartments of places like the Buildings didn't bear thinking about it. But even in daytime the salon's gloom and stagnant air were reminiscent of a mausoleum. At night, still heavy with the day's gathered heat and with the economy of only one candle, it shrank into a tomb.

Her Ladyship said: 'Get another glim, Penitence.' Fanny's breathing was rising into gasps of pain. She put down the bucket and hurried back to the kitchen to fetch a candle, hurried back.

One of Fanny's buboes was bursting. Thick grey-yellow matter oozed through the lint they had put over it and dripped on to the sheet as she twisted.

Not the sheet. Going into the battle of heating water, carrying, scrubbing, rinsing, drying . . . she couldn't do it again so soon. Then she was ashamed of herself. She poured water into a beaker and helped Fanny drink while Her Ladyship cleaned the wound. The emission of poison brought relief; the girl's breathing returned almost to normal. 'Better,' she said.

Penitence went to the other beds. Alania moaned in her sleep. Plague dreams were terrible. It left its victims nothing. Not any good thing.

Job was awake. She wiped the sord off his lips with a rag and helped him drink. 'Fanny better?'

'Yes.'

'That's good.'

She nodded to comfort him. Fanny's was only a remission. The Plague was standing back to consider its handiwork before setting to work again.

'Gawd, Prinks.' Job twisted. 'It's fretting at me gizzard.' She held his hand tight while the spasm lasted. 'Ferrups. Oh Cripus.' He tried to smile at her. 'I'm an old gammer, ain't I?'

'You're bravest of b-brave,' she told him. He had been a revelation. She'd been so contemptuous; helping a male body to use the pot, cleaning it afterwards, was more disgusting than doing it for women. Yet he'd proved more aware of those outside the circle of his distress than any of the others, thinking and feeling for them in a way that showed he always had. She hadn't noticed her stammer was diminishing until his grey, sorded mouth whispered: 'Speaking nice, Prinks.' He was an undemanding sufferer, constantly apologizing with: 'I'm a bother, ain't I?'

Yesterday, in one of the false-hope remissions, he'd said: 'You're a reader, Prinks. Teach me when I'm better, eh?' She'd promised, unsettled at finding someone she had classed as undeniably degraded and even more undeniably stupid should cherish such ambition, but she doubted that he would live to claim the promise. Every gland was swollen to the point where it looked as if marbles had been stuffed under the skin of his joints.

He was little older than the girls, about nineteen; a country boy, Her Ladyship said, who'd blundered his way into the town, 'made a bad job of begging, a better one of starving', until he'd gone to sleep in the Cock and Pie doorway one night where Her Ladyshop, impressed by his size, had given him the job of apple-bully.

On the Plague's present form, he had two more days before he died, each one worse than the last.

Through force of habit, she prayed for his survival. *He's too valuable*. But they were all valuable, and they were all going. Too late, she wished she'd been open to the diversity of character existing around her these last months, appreciated it instead of condemning. Each illness, Kinyans's, Francesca's, Fanny's, Job's, Alania's, drew her into its own private world, each one appallingly the same, yet each one different from the others because beneath it was the palimpsest of the personality that endured it.

'Penitence.'

She disengaged her hand and ran to Fanny's bed. Her Ladyship's voice signalled a change. Fanny's once-heavy legs prodded up and down on the bed, scraping her heels in a steady digging motion. Her Ladyship lifted her feet on to her lap to ease them. They left blood on the sheet.

Suddenly Fanny doubled up as if some animal had bitten into her stomach, and then her head went back to turning on her pillow, left, right, left, right, on and on as it had for days. Her raw, griping heels made bloody lines on Her Ladyship's apron.

Stop it, stop it. If you can stand it, I can't. She took Fanny's hand and tried to will something of her own untortured self into the girl.

Fanny's breathing became short and harsh. Her hand clawed

at her heart. They lifted her shift and saw that the skin beneath the left breast was fluttering. Penitence pressed her hand over the heart to try to contain it. Fanny's eyes stared at Her Ladyship's face as if it could save her. 'There, pippin. There, my good little girl,' Her Ladyship was saying.

They were so far away, isolated from the struggle going on inside the poor body. They could be standing on a shore watching her drown.

The flutter beneath Penitence's hand went into salvoes, paused, burst into an artillery of thumps. And stopped.

'No,' said Penitence. 'Don't do that, Fanny.'

Her Ladyship put her hand on Fanny's eyes and drew the lids down.

They sat a while beside the body, as much from exhaustion as respect, then Penitence dragged herself upstairs to get a clean sheet from the press in what had been Mary's attic. For a moment she stood and looked out of the tiny back window over the misty configuration of roofs to where the Tottenham Court road wound its way into the countryside. The light blobs on the fields were sheep. A lone bird began to twitter. It was going to be another blistering day.

A rattle of hooves and wheels over setts announced that other presager of dawn, the burial cart. She went into her attic to wait for it.

The actor's room was empty. She stood at the side window, kneading the sheet in her hands. *Please God. Please God. Please God.*

His door opened and he came in. His eyes went immediately to her window. He looked dreadful. 'Fanny?'

She nodded.

'Tell the bearers to call here too. The baby orange is dead.'

'I'm s-ssorry.' The orange-seller's children had been the bane of his life, running in and out of his room, interrupting his writing, but he'd formed an attachment for the smallest and cheekiest.

'Boots.'

'Yes?'

'Take care.'

'You too.'

From her balcony she added her 'Here' to the chorused answer to the buryers' call, and started back downstairs to sew Fanny into her winding sheet. On the clerestory she heard Sabina's voice: 'Is it time?' She went into Phoebe's room where the two girls always slept together, despite the heat. Two pairs of eyes looked warily at her. They didn't want to hear. She didn't want to tell them.

'I'm s-sorry.'

Phoebe's arm went round Sabina's bare shoulder. 'We'll get up.'

'You've g-got an hour yet.' They divided work into shifts, but all four were becoming exhausted.

'We'll see her off.'

They'd been unprepared for the casualness of the buryers and their grappling hooks. They were ashamed that Kinyans and Francesca had been taken away like sacks of rubbish to a tip, no ceremony, no priest, and, they knew, at the end of the bouncing plague-cart's journey, no marker for the grave they shared with hundreds of other corpses.

As Penitence sewed the sheet round the body, Her Ladyship said: 'You're the Bible-pounder. I want something said over Fanny. A bit of a psalm. Only I don't want no God in it, and nothing to do with sin.'

'That's w-what the Psalms are ab-bout,' protested Penitence.

The four of them carried Fanny to the door and laid her down.

Adapting the first Psalm, Penitence said: 'And she shall be like a tree p-planted by the rivers of water, that b-bringeth forth its fruit in its season; its leaves also shall not wither; and whatsoever she doeth shall p-prosper.'

She'd won Her Ladyship's approval for once: 'That's nice. Like she's going to the country.'

A key turned, the door opened, letting in sunshine. In the foulness of the salon the incoming air from Dog Yard smelled as fresh as a summer river. Penitence lifted Job's head so that it could cool him and closed her eyes, letting it wash over her. A voice said: ''Morning, girls. Mind yourselves now.' She heard the clunk as the hooks were thrown expertly over Fanny's body, the rattle of the chains to which they were attached, the sound of dragging.

There was a sudden kerfuffle. Sabina screamed. The door slammed. She opened her eyes. Sabina was clawing at the door: 'Out. I've gotta get out.' She collapsed, sobbing. 'There's people living out there.'

Her Ladyship pulled the girl to her feet. 'No they ain't.'

'They are, they are.'

'They ain't. Listen.' The bells were starting on the day's toll. Today it was louder than ever, as if encircling steeples were bending over them. 'All London's got it now. There's thousands like us.'

Sabina sniffed, listened. 'All our clients?'

'Yes.'

'All the lords and ladies?'

'Yes.'

'Even the King?' Her Ladyship nodded. Sabina hadn't seen the gentry's mass exodus. Penitence watched her find comfort in the unexpected democracy of pestilence. The girl wiped her nose on her sleeve. She was magnanimous: 'Hope all them mistresses is taking care of the poor King.'

August came in with the temperature rising.

As manufacture stopped and the chimneys of dyers, brewers and soap-makers ceased smoking, London became sharp-etched. The Bridge stared down at a traffic-less river which reflected back its span of houses in upside-down exactitude.

If it hadn't been for the bells of 130 churches ringing the news that the Plague was now in each parish, the City would have been reminiscent of an Italian town in the afternoon where everybody slept.

In the church of St Giles-in-the-Fields, the Reverend Robert Boreman led his congregation in the litany prescribed for this special day of Fast and Humiliation.

'Deliver us, Lord ...' He was so afraid for the people massed before him that he couldn't meet their eyes. Where had they all come from? What marvellous expectation compelled them to take such a risk? Did they really think the Lord would deliver them?

'For there is wrath gone out against us, and the Plague is begun.'

Last week's Bill of Mortality had been such it had deluded him into thinking his entire parish was either shut up or dead. Only God knew what next week's would be like.

'That dreadful arrow of Thine sticks fast in our flesh.'

He felt a rise of irritation at Peter Simkin's absence. The clerk had begged leave to come in late so that he might stay in the vestry and finish the Bill that must be delivered tomorrow. But he should be here by now. It was the fault of that damned whorehouse Puritan he set so much store by, who'd let him down.

As he knelt for the Silence, the Reverend Boreman fought to overcome the surge of anger. *Cleanse me from all uncharitableness*. He had no right to condemn her. Peter said she had her hands full nursing her harlots. He must stop despising Puritans. And Anabaptists. And Presbyterians. Even Quakers.

There were churches round about where congregations would be facing empty pulpits this day if it hadn't been for these Nonconformers who'd come out of hiding to preach and tend to flocks deserted by their Church of England pastors. If the country survived the Plague and found Nonconformism popular, the established Church would have only itself to blame.

He'd already seen a fly-sheet which jeered 'Pulpits to let'.

A Day of Humiliation indeed.

But will it survive? There'd been one baptism this week; one child born against almost five hundred deaths. They were facing annihilation. At the font he'd found himself huddling over the baby as if protecting a tiny flame from the wind.

Peter Simkin had got writer's cramp entering dead names in the register. Where was Peter? Still in the vestry? Sometimes one didn't even know their names. Damn, damn, damned Holborn had found a woman and child dead from the Plague in one of its streets and grapple-hooked them both over the parish boundary into St Giles so that they shouldn't be a charge on it. To the burial of an unknown woman and child: 2s 3d.

He clenched his hands tighter to stop them trembling. *Cleanse me of anger. Help my fear.* Let Thy nostrils be appeased by this foul disinfectant concoction now burning in Thy church's nightlights. By order of the magistrates he'd had to outlay £20 on the stuff. Let it be useful for something other than to make the congregation cough.

He stood up for the Peace. 'Guard them, God,' he prayed. 'Guard these poor people whose faith in You has sent them to this, Your house, in this time of utmost peril.'

At the church door, he shook hands, patted shoulders, reassured. Old Mrs Harris asked: 'Is He placated now, Rector? I'd like to die quiet.'

'Pray,' he told her, and sent her out into a sunshine as remorseless as the God who made it.

The bells of London, which had ceased ringing so that God could hear the general supplication, began tolling again.

He stamped off to the vestry. It was not seemly for Peter Simkin, however busy he was, to absent himself on such a day. He began berating as he opened the door, 'It is not seemly—' and saw his clerk slumped over the tall desk on which the register lay open, the quill still in his hand, ink dripping from the overturned pot on to the floor.

'Peter!'

The eyes were open but the soul of the good little man had gone.

The gold mayoral carriage was collecting its Lord Mayor and the Duke of Albemarle from the crowd on the steps of St Paul's. Its padded interior was sweltering.

'Went well,' said the Duke, settling back. 'A lot of folk.'

The Lord Mayor snorted moodily out of the window. 'Where was the Dean?'

'Overcome by an urgent need to take the waters at Tunbridge Wells, so I'm told.'

The Lord Mayor snorted. 'Let's hope they drown him.'

He detached his kerchief from his sleeve and wiped his face

before holding it to his nose. He'd spent a fortune on brimstone, hops and pepper for the disinfectant fires that burned day and night in the streets, but as buryers collapsed from heat and plague into the pits they'd dug, the smell of rotting corpses joined the rising poison from refuse left lying even in the richer thoroughfares where there was no one left to clean them.

He might as well be burning old shoes, like the poor did.

He looked out at beautiful, still-whole buildings and saw ruins. Foreign buyers were refusing to accept goods manufactured in London. The Dutch were gaining confidence. One of their damned newspapers had said: 'The English Nation is now brought so low with the Plague that a man may run them down with his finger.'

Even provincial towns one hundred miles away turned back trade from London. He supposed he couldn't blame them. Despite everything he did to contain it, rivulets of Plague escaped the shut-up and wound their way to Kent, to Yarmouth, up the arterial highways to Northamptonshire and Cheshire, to the Isle of Wight, and became a flood.

A trickle of infection had even made its way to the willow-shaded meadows of Salisbury where the King was sheltering. One of the royal farriers had contracted it.

Charles had been charming, by all accounts, and called up to the farrier's window on his way back from a stag hunt to ask if there was anything he could do.

He wouldn't do it, of course, but the farrier would probably die cherishing the memory.

He looked across at General Monck. 'Have you heard from the King?'

'There were the Royal Proclamation disbanding officers and soldiers who served with the Parliamentary armies, forbidding them to come within twenty mile of London.' George smiled wryly. 'He were kind enough to send me a letter saying it weren't to apply to me.'

The Lord Mayor said: 'He's afraid of rebellion, of course.'

'Aye.'

Rebellion, thought the Lord Mayor; the one matter he

163

worries for and the one matter on which he can rest easy. Put half a million people in an oven with the Plague and you don't get rebellion, you get despair.

The carriage bumped through the porterless gateway of the Guildhall. Upstairs curtains had been drawn allowing one crack to send a roadway of sun over the mayoral desk. Sir John dispatched his nephew for wine. 'I've had a letter from Salisbury too. From its mayor. He's unhappy.' His voice displayed a relish it hadn't shown for weeks. 'He's had to evict half his townspeople to make room for the royal party.'

He picked the letter up. 'How big *is* the royal party, would you say?'

The General considered. 'Ooh, mistresses, maids, pastry-cooks, horse, grooms, bottle-washers. Four, five hundred?'

'At least. Hoo, hoo. Poor old Salisbury. It's sweating him.' Sir John wiped the sweat from his own eyes and read: '"In acknowledgement of the honour done to it, the Corporation did present His Majesty with a pair of silver flagons, having had to borrow £100 for these and other gifts." Hoo, hoo. *And* he'd forgot till I reminded him that there were fees of homage due to royal servants from every Corporation when the King visits for the first time. Where is it? Here it is. "£5 to the day waiters of the Gentleman Usher. £3 16s to the Serjeant Trumpet, 10s to each Page of the Presence and a sum to the King's Jester."'

He stopped being amused and flung the letter down. 'Jesus, London needed that money. Has the royal purse been opened in your direction yet?'

The General shook his big head. 'Nowt.'

'Nor mine.'

He walked to the window and pulled back the curtain another inch. Behind him he heard Old George pour himself more wine.

Why didn't the bells *stop*? All day, every day, jarring the marrow of his bones. Where did the sextons receive the energy to keep ringing? The stone of the mullion was hot against his hand. Below him the Guildhall lawn had turned yellow with nobody to water it. Why didn't it *rain*?

'They're beginning to starve, George.'

'I know it, John.'

There was a knock on the double doors. They'd been waiting for it.

'Come in.'

The clerk to the Parish Clerks was apologizing as he entered. 'Not all the returns is in, my lords, I fear. Manifestly, there's been mortality among the clerks . . . and, in course, there's the Quakers as won't have the bell rung for 'em, and we don't get no returns from the Jews . . .'

'Give me the damned thing.' But when the paper was put in his hand, he didn't want to look at it. It was warm and crackling from the disinfecting oven. An idiot's precaution. If heat could kill the Plague, his city would be the healthiest in Europe. 'Well then.'

Putting off the moment, he checked the date at the top of the columns of parishes and figures. 'From the 15 August to the 22. 1665.'

He turned the sheet over. 'The Diseases and Casualties this Week.' Reluctantly his eye scanned the list: 'Abortive: 4 . . . Chrisomes: 9 . . . Head-mould-shot: 1 . . .' What the hell was that? 'Lethargy: 1 . . . Palsie: 1 . . . Plague . . .' He dropped the paper. 'Oh my God.'

'Tell us, lad,' said General Monck.

'Five thousand, five hundred and sixty-eight.'

Chapter 9

JOB DIDN'T die. Alania did. The next day Phoebe and Sabina developed the symptoms. On the day after that Her Ladyship said: 'Penitence, go get a sheet from the attic. We're going to have to make up another bed.'

She was stupefied from tiredness: 'Who for?'

'Me.'

She didn't believe it, couldn't. By the time she'd fetched the sheet, Her Ladyship had got everything ready; a bucket, a candle, a bottle of water and a beaker stood by the couch Fanny had died on. They made up the bed together as they'd done with all the others.

'Are you sure?' Her Ladyship was thinner, but so was she.

Her Ladyship tutted and, with an oddly prudish gesture, pulled aside an inch of peignoir to show the tokens. 'I'm not having any of that old electuary,' she said. 'There's two guineas in a purse under my bed for housekeeping. And get that slut Dorinda on her feet. You'll need her.'

Penitence helped her on to the bed then ran for the stairs.

'Penitence.'

She paused. 'Yes, Ladyship?'

'Whatever I say in the ravings is not to be taken notice of.'

'Yes, Ladyship.'

Dorinda's eyes were closed. They'd checked on her every day, emptied her pot, put food and water by her bed and left her. Downstairs her name was not mentioned.

Penitence shook her with both hands. 'You've got to wake up. You've got to.' The girl's eyes stayed closed but her face was sulky. *She's ashamed. The bitch doesn't know how to face me.* She wanted nothing so much as to hit the girl till her teeth rattled. Instead, she said: 'Her Ladyship's got it. She's asking for you.'

For a moment the appeal seemed to fail, then Dorinda's lips blew a petulant sigh. 'All bloody right,' she said.

Phoebe began to cough. Her voice bubbled like somebody's under water, but she wouldn't stop talking. 'Haven't seen him since he were born, but I sent three shilling every week.' She turned towards Penitence. The skin of her face shone wet and grey, like clay. 'He's being brought up a gent.' She looked back to Dorinda. 'Turnstile Alley, Cheapside,' she said urgently. Her body arched and she cried out. 'Who'll look out for him now?'

'I will, Pheeb,' said Dorinda. 'Hold on, girl.'

'I'm trying.'

If she hadn't been so tired, Penitence would have been

appalled at her own naivety; it had never occurred to her that any of the girls might have had a baby.

'Has Sabby gone?'

'No,' lied Dorinda. 'She's holding on. And there's Her Ladyship, look. And Job. We'll beat it yet.'

Phoebe turned desperate, blind eyes towards the others. 'I'm trying.'

There was a moan from Her Ladyship's bed. Dorinda went to her. Penitence sat on as Phoebe's hand ground the bones of her own. She bent her head down to listen to Phoebe's whisper: 'Sabby's gone, ain't she?'

'Yes. A little while ago.' She'd died almost gratefully, as gratefully as she'd received the infection once she knew Phoebe had it.

Phoebe nodded. 'Ask 'em to put us in together.' There was another burst of agony: 'I know it was sin, Prinks, but He won't punish us, will He? He'll forgive us now, won't He?'

How could He punish this girl any more than He had? Like Dorinda, she lied. 'He's the G-God of love, Pheeb.'

Half an hour later a long moan of breath came out of Phoebe's throat. Gently, Penitence pulled down the lids. 'She's gone,' she said, crying.

'What you sorry for?' Dorinda's voice shook. 'She weren't your friend.'

'Be quiet. B-be quiet. She was nice to me.' Her own voice shook with hysteria, shocking her and Dorinda both. A groaned remonstrance came from Her Ladyship.

Penitence got up and went to the kitchen to draw water for washing the body. Shaking, she began winding, watching the empty bucket go down. A loved soul had just departed and they quarrelled like petulant children. There was no time, that was the trouble. They were too tired to assimilate what was happening or how deeply it affected them. They skated from one death to another with not enough pause to accord them the dignity of grief. They fumbled through perpetual darkness. They were thin. They'd spent the last of Her Ladyship's guineas on eggs and wine for their patients and ate scraps themselves.

Let me keep patience with her. She's new to seeing them die. Phoebe was the last of her sisterhood. And she's a help.

But she was a help only so long as Penitence confined her nursing to Job and the others and left the care of Her Ladyship to Dorinda.

'She's *my* aunt.' The words echoed back at her from the well, bringing her up short with their peevishness. What was happening? She had become numb to everything but irritability.

Penitence fetched two more sheets for Sabina and Phoebe, checked on Job, who was sleeping, and came back to sit opposite Dorinda on the other side of the comatose body. They quarrelled across it in hisses.

'Sew Pheeb and Sabina in the same sheet.'

'No. They'd tumble about.' There'd be little enough dignity as it was; the death-rate among bearers had left the job to the mercy of men who enjoyed it. They collected at night, like ghouls, and it was whispered that there were terrible practices at the burial pits.

'They got to go together.' The candlelight threw shadows wickedly upwards on to Dorinda's face. 'They were lovers.'

She didn't know what it meant at first. Her mind grasped a concept it hadn't known existed and found it had lost the ability to feel shock. Tears came into her eyes. 'They won't be p-parted in Heaven.' *Do I believe that?*

She sewed them separately. The effort of carrying them to the door left her and Dorinda gasping. They helped Job on to the pot, gave him a sip of water and settled him down again. They sponged Her Ladyship's hot, loose skin and smoothed back the grey-rooted gold hair. Sometimes she moaned. The suffocating night went on and on.

Somewhere there were the full hedges of August, banks of cow parsley, somewhere ferns curled in the cracks of wet rocks.

She'd abandoned her black dress which absorbed warmth and wore an old basque of Phoebe's, its lacing open to cool the sweat that trickled between her breasts. Dorinda had tried wearing nothing at all, but Her Ladyship had managed to say

'Not nice', so she'd put her shift back on. She sat collapsed in a chair on the other side of Her Ladyship, her knees wide apart, her face shining with sweat, asleep.

Penitence listened to her breathing, to Her Ladyship's, to her own. She became alert to a pain in her chest. *Here it is.* Time and again a cramp rang the alarm and she panicked. Dorinda, she knew, kept the same internal vigil; so far the alarms were merely symptoms of their lowering general health. Soon . . .

Her wrist ached with flapping the fan back and forth over Her Ladyship, but she kept on. *We're losing her.* The woman's endurance was extraordinary. Night after night the fever came back. Night after night, gasping and rocking, she fought it and was alive the next morning. Each breath bubbled, as had Phoebe's. Her eyes looked straight ahead, never beseeching for help; she waged her battle by herself.

Penitence's only hope for her lay in the recovery Job was making, painfully slowly. If they'd had more and better food, she thought, it would be quicker; he was so skeletal and weak that a rheum could snatch him away.

Penitence dozed and heard Dorinda say: 'She's here, Ladyship.'

The brothel-keeper's eyes were staring in her direction. 'Look after the girls. The papers is under the bed. I'm sorry.'

It was unbearable from a woman who'd apologized for nothing. 'P-please d-don't. You t-took me in.'

The face was settling, but at this it frowned. Understanding left, then came back. 'Your daddy stuttered.'

It was the first human link she'd felt with the worthy, indistinct figure of Ralph Hurd, the Roundhead who had died storming Papists at the Basing House siege in the Civil War. Except as an example of saintliness, he'd rarely been mentioned by her mother and grandparents. And Her Ladyship had known him.

'Tell me, p-please.'

An extraordinary relaxation came over Her Ladyship's clenched face, as if the stifling air had assumed the scent of hay. 'You've got his eyes,' she said. 'He would've married me.'

And there it all was, the old, old explanation, a man who'd chosen the wrong sister and left this one. Had he regretted it? Was her mother's bitterness because her husband had loved Margaret Hughes first? *Tell me.*

Gentleness became fixed on the thin mouth, the eyes stared.

Come back. But her hand automatically went out to close the lids.

Dorinda knocked it away. 'She ain't.'

'Don't I know? You've g-got to do it now.' *Come back.* Decorum was going with Her Ladyship. Disorder would take over the world. *Come back. I'm not safe without you.*

She tried to keep her aunt with her by obeying her rules. She went upstairs to get another sheet, and found there were none left in the press. Frantically she ran to the kitchen. The drying rack was empty. She began to sob. She ran back into the salon. 'There's no sheet. We'll have to wrap her in the one she's lying on.' It was the most terrible thing in the world.

Dorinda had closed Her Ladyship's eyes. She said dully: 'She ain't going dirty. She's going in my prunella cloak.'

She was on the water in the light birch-bark canoe Matoonas had built for her. It was just before dawn and the ducks hadn't come in yet. Over the other side of the river, pelicans floated asleep with their heads and beaks tucked back, like tiny, humped, white islands. Through a prickle of rushes she was watching the river turn from black to steel-grey. The air hadn't yet picked up scents from the land; it smelled of water, an immensity of clean, cold water . . .

'Stop it.' Dorinda was pinioning her arms. 'Stop it now.'

'I c-can't.'

'I know, but you've got to. You taught me that. She'd want you to.' Dorinda's sleeve gently wiped Penitence's nose and chin. 'Sit down a bit. I'll sew her.' Penitence sat.

'Ready now.'

She managed to stand up on legs that shook. Together, grunting, they carried the body over to where Phoebe's and Sabina's lay by the front door and Penitence said the words she had said over Fanny. From outside came the sounds of hooves and the heavy creak of the cart. 'Bring out your dead.'

The lock was being turned. Involuntarily, they moved forward to stand in the moonlight and look up at a sky that had stars in it.

'Get out 'a way.' Two bearers pushed past. They didn't bother with grappling hooks any more. A smell of sickness emanated from the sacking they wore over their heads and shoulders. Outside on the cart, the driver was standing on a pile of corpses. The lantern hanging on his whip-post lit the absorption on his face as he pressed down with his boot.

Each man took a foot end of the first two winding sheets. The white roll that was Phoebe was left crooked against the cart-wheel while the men swung Sabina to get the impetus to throw her up on the piled cart.

Harry Burford, the night-watchman, was chatting to the driver. They were coming back for Her Ladyship. Dorinda's rough stitching came apart as the body bumped over the threshold and her hair trailed across the cobbles.

Penitence ran forward, pushing the hair back, trying to hold the sheet together. One of the men kicked her out of the way.

'Let her alone, you bastards, you bastards.' Dorinda was sobbing and fighting. 'That's her mother.'

The driver on the cart grinned at the two women and picked up the body of a child by its leg. 'Faggots, five for sixpence,' he said.

The bearers threw Her Ladyship into the cart. One of them came back to the doorway. 'How's about rattling my ballocks afore I go?'

'That's enough.' Harry extended his halberd in front of the man and pushed him back. They heard the bearer say: 'They're whores, ain't they?' before the door closed.

It took concentration to go upstairs. She kept mounting one rise and forgetting how to step on to the next so that she stood bewildered before gathering enough wit to do it. There was a band of iron round her chest.

She'd reached the end of the clerestory and was considering the flight up to the attic when somebody called from its top. 'Boots?'

She thought for a long while. 'What?'

There was a moment's silence, then an outburst. 'Where the hell have you been? MacGregor said there were three bodies . . .' She stood where she was and he came downstairs, still put out. He had a lantern. 'It seems yours wasn't one of them.'

After a moment she said: 'What?'

He lifted the lantern to look at her face. 'Damn it.' She felt his hand press against her forehead, then he was helping her up the stairs. 'How did you get into this state?' At the top he lifted her up, slung her over his shoulder and carried her and the lantern into the attic. He stooped and slid her on to her bed. She felt the warmth of the lantern on her skin as he lowered it to examine her. She heard an exhalation of relief. 'But you've got to do better than this. Where's that bloody apothecary? Stay here.'

The injunction was needless; she couldn't do anything else. Time, people, ministrations came and went.

The house was the Cock and Pie but at the same time bigger, cavernous, its steps and corridors transformed here and there into uneven galleries of rock. Its darkness was total, though she could see through it. High up in the galleries, a cat was mewing. Men with guns were moving through the house in order to shoot it because it had the Plague; they were out of her sight, somewhere ahead of her, but the malevolence they radiated was so tangible she could track their progress by it.

They would shoot the cat thinking it was just an animal. Exactly who it was she couldn't be sure; someone enormously important to her, vulnerable, in need. She felt fear and love as she had never felt before; almost annihilated with terror, but loving the cat so desperately, she must get to it before they did. It impelled her through the silent house. She kept taking wrong turnings and ending up in empty caves while the creeping men closed in on the mewing. She screamed soundlessly as she ran. Her throat was raw, her breathing painful, but the only compulsion was to get to the cat.

During rises to consciousness she found she was being nagged: 'Do you hear me? I've worked hard on you, you miserable item of humanity. Until I came along you crawled in mud like the base clay you are. I took you up. I transmuted you into gold. For one moment I heard the authentic voice of Beatrice come out of the mouth of a stammering, tuppenny-halfpenny whore. One moment. My achievement out of my Gethsemane. Are you listening to me?'

She wasn't sure. The aggrieved argument held flaws she was too tired to put her finger on; she allowed it to become a lullaby, the only one she'd ever known, and slept to it.

The dream recurred. 'Never knew you had a beau, Prinks.' The voice was rallying but flat, as if its owner talked for the sake of talking and expected no answer. It came into the caverns in the form of light.

Reluctantly she lifted the weight of her eyelids and saw Dorinda's face. 'Who's this Benedick then, you dark horse you?'

'Cat,' said Penitence. She'd left it behind, so valuable, so hurt. Tears oozed out of her eyes and Dorinda dabbed them away. 'Cat, was it? Thought you'd got a secret beau.'

Apothecary Boghurst diagnosed pleurisy and recommended honeyed electuary, seethed red meat, eggs and rest.

It was from Dorinda she received these things, Dorinda who nursed her, washed her, potted her, spooned food into her mouth. Sometimes Job, very gaunt, sat by her bed through the hot nights, but most often it was Dorinda, encouraging her with good news. 'Ma Hicks's beat it, like Job. Henry and MacGregor and the rope-walker's got her through. Henry's going to win the war by sending her against the Dutch. Mistress Palmer still ain't got it. There's two dolly-mops left alive over Hubbard's. The parish Bill's down this week. And Sam and Molly Bryskett's third youngest's still going strong. An' we got a *plan*.'

'What plan?' She asked out of gratitude; she wasn't very interested.

During her illness, it appeared, matters had got both worse and better. In St Giles the mortality rate was slowing, though London as a whole was suffering a thousand Plague deaths a day. Services were breaking down; parish relief deliveries were intermittent; most serious of all, the water cart only came every four or five days.

Faced with thirst and starvation, the survivors of Dog Yard had organized. There had been rooftop meetings.

'See that?'

'That' was a ladder leading up to an unsuspected skylight in the attic-tiles above the beams. 'You get on to Mistress Crawford's, over a plank on to the Ship, then more planks round to the flat roof of the Stables. That ballocking Dogberry said it was agin promulgation to have gatherings, but 'Pothecary said as we was all shut up it didn't make no difference.'

The Yard was pooling rations. Mistress Palmer cooked stews in one of her iron wash-tubs. The pawnbroker's widow baked communal, though kosher, bread. The two remaining Tippin boys risked prison, this time in a noble cause, by making rooftop forays out of the Rookery to the countryside where they acquired chickens and any other edibles left unguarded for the Dog Yard pot.

Obediently, without enthusiasm, Penitence swallowed the proffered spoonful of stew. 'B-beef too?'

Dorinda looked shamefaced: 'Dogberry got that. He's kin to butchers.'

Wearily she remembered that a charitable Dogberry was a contradiction in terms. 'What with?' Her Ladyship's two guineas had long gone.

Dorinda worked herself up into aggression: 'Out your bag, acourse. You been hiding a fortune in there could've bought us Whitehall with some left over.' Seeing Penitence's incomprehension, she said: 'Funk. Fume. You know what it fetches? He's a fumer our Dogberry, do anything for a pipeful, and you got a mass on it.'

The tobacco the Indians had given her. She'd forgotten it. If she'd realized its value before she could have afforded better food for Her Ladyship and the others. Tears dripped down her face. Dorinda wiped them away. 'Wouldn't've made no difference,' she said. 'Get to sleep.'

By day her attic became a gathering place and thoroughfare. Unable to bear the salon, Job and Dorinda used it as a sitting-room and, since the Cock and Pie's well was supplying water to most of the Yard, the actor and his surviving male neighbours from Mistress Hicks's regularly crossed the plank that now served as a bridge over the alley to help wind up buckets and carry them via the ladder to those in need.

Then there was the Plan. Dorinda was full of it. Its aim was to save the Brysketts' last living child from further threat of the Plague. 'Sam Bryskett — Gawd, you ought to see him. Prinks, it's pitiful — he asked for help and it was our Henry came up with it.' The Cock and Pie was to produce a version of *Much Ado About Nothing*, on its balcony.

Originally, the idea had been to perform extracts, just the Beatrice and Benedick scenes, with the actor narrating the rest of the plot. Dorinda, however, had seen her chance. 'I'm going to act and all.' She had persuaded the actor to include both her and Job in the cast; it meant considerable complication, not least of which was that, due to their illiteracy, the two of them had to be taught their lines by word of mouth. On the other hand, as Dorinda pointed out, it would lengthen the duration of the play and thereby give the Plan a better chance.

Across the alley, the actor was now writing, rewriting and swearing as he turned a comedy intended for a *Dramatis personae* of eighteen, to say nothing of messengers, watch, attendants, etc., into a play for four, while in Penitence's attic MacGregor, the erstwhile Scottish piper, who could read, spent much of the day repeating Shakespeare's lines so that Dorinda and Job could learn them by heart.

The only one who had no response to the general animation was Penitence. She lay incuriously watching the comings and goings, finding the constant company tiring, too feeble even to experience embarrassment at this most public of convalescences, unsure that it *was* convalescence. The emotions from the dream, emotions she'd never felt in her waking life, oppressed her. She couldn't free herself of them. The thought of what waited for her in Her Ladyship's room flattened her on to her bed like a stone slab.

So, on an afternoon when nobody was around, she went and faced it.

There was a lining of dust in the frills of the satin valance of Her Ladyship's large bed. As Penitence's hand ran tentatively over the rough floorboards, it encountered furred rolls of more dust, then a knot-hole. With an effort, she pulled up a square section of board, groped in the cavity underneath and retrieved a box. She squatted back on her heels with it on her lap.

It was not the box she had fetched from Lawyer Patterson. It was small, with an arched lid striped by two brass bands. It was the twin of one her grandfather had made for her when she was ten years old, and which was now ashes blowing in the breeze from a Massachusetts river; perhaps it was from the same piece of cherrywood. Perhaps he had made it for his daughter, Margaret, when she, too, was ten years old. She had pokerworked her initials into the lid – M.H. – just as Penitence had.

She was shaken by sudden agony for that unknowing child Margaret Hughes and what had become of her. Still kneeling, she lifted the box on to the bed and opened it. Inside were scrolled papers tied with ribbon.

The first was a deed naming Margaret Hughes of St Giles as purchaser of 'the property called the Cock and Pie, heretofore known as Appleyard House'. It was dated 14 April 1651 and the vendor was a John Appleyard. The price was £186 16s.

The wages of sin must have been high, thought Penitence, for Her Ladyship to have been able to afford a sum like that.

The next roll showed that they hadn't been. It was a deed of mortgage, making the Cock and Pie security for the sum of £185 0s 0d. The interest to be paid on said sum was 45 per cent per annum.

Penitence felt her first reaction in days. She yelped. 'Forty-five per cent?' Her grandfather had only been charged 20 per cent when he'd borrowed for one of his trading ventures, and he'd grumbled enough about that.

Margaret Hughes had signed with a cross, and so had a gentleman called William Calf, described as 'Agent', though agent for whom was not set down. The witnesses were a doctor of divinity and a canon, presumably two of Her Ladyship's clients.

The parchment of the second scroll was less yellowed and its ink fresher than the first. It was the last will and testament of Margaret Hughes. Apart from some small personal items to Job, Kinyans and the girls, it bequeathed all her property and possessions 'to my daughter, Penitence Hoy, yclept Penitence Hurd, recently come from New England'.

She had not needed the proof; at the moment when Her Ladyship's body had been dragged to the burial cart and Dorinda had shouted, a hundred flakes of memory, whispers, looks, hurts, had drawn together into a core of certainty.

Nevertheless, to see the words written was shocking, an official command to remake herself. She rested her head on her mother's coverlet while the person she had thought herself to be disassembled.

Hoy?

Is that all you will tell me? She scrabbled in the nearly empty box and brought out a thin, flat package wrapped in silk. It was a letter. The superscription on its stained outside read: 'Mistress Margaret Hughes, to be found at the George Inn, Taunton'.

Penitence unfolded it carefully. It was coming apart along the heavier creases. It was dated Oxford, April 1646.

> Mistress, I must report to you the doleful news that Capt. James Hoy is dead of wounds gained in a skirmish. It is a grief to me to lose an officer as valiant in the field as he was merry in company. At the last he begged me write to you of his affection and send these enclosed pieces and recommend you to the kindness of his people. Would I could do more for the memory of a faithful friend but I and my brother are bid by Parliament to quit England and take ship for Calais.
>
> God keep you, mistress. Your servant, Rupert.

She had to read it twice to decipher the hasty scrawl and three times to absorb its significance.

Rupert? Only royalty signed with a Christian name. Prince Rupert of the Rhine and his brother, Maurice, had been banished by Cromwell at the end of the Civil War.

Remorselessly, her mind pursued the logic while the person she had always assumed herself to be unravelled further.

Capt. James Hoy. *My father*.

The exemplary Ralph Hurd, that martyred saint of the Puritan revolution, faded into smoke and in his place stood a stuttering blue-eyed man who turned her into as much of a stranger as himself.

He had fought on the wrong side. She was not Penitence Hurd, sprig of solid Puritan stock, she was a royalist's bastard. If she was now eighteen years old − if that was not a lie, like everything else she had been told about herself − he had impregnated her mother just in time to go and get himself killed in a last 'skirmish' against Cromwell's forces.

At that moment it was indignation she felt. *You stupid, Papist . . . Bartholomew*. Wrong side, wrong loyalty, wrong death, wrong time. A most perfect disordering of everyone's life, her mother's, hers, that of the woman who had passed herself off as a mother, his own most of all, a microcosm of upheaval in the upheaval going on around them.

Had Margaret Hughes been a harlot then? But even royalist captains did not make death-bed professions of love for prostitutes, nor recommend them to their families. Perhaps he felt guilt. Perhaps it had been rape. The expression on Her Ladyship's face as she'd died remembering Captain Hoy did not support that premise and Penitence was forced to abandon it.

Still she held on to her indignation for fear that she would be formless without it. Seduction, then; the blandishments of a be-plumed Cavalier from the squirearchy overcoming the scruples of an innocent country Puritan.

However it had happened, if poor, pregnant Margaret Hughes had thrown herself on the charity of the Hoys, she had been rebuffed. Penitence's lips thinned as jeering landed gentry in her mind directed the pleading young woman from their magnificent door.

She was on stronger ground of interpretation when it came to the reaction of her own family. How her grandmother would have shrunk back from the sullied flesh of her flesh, how that hard little mind would have rejected the path of compassion for the road of outraged righteousness. Margaret Hughes had been ostracized.

It must have been around this time, not earlier, that her grandparents had joined the ranks of other Puritan saints in the New Jerusalem of the Americas, leaving the shamed daughter behind, taking her bastard and the virtuous daughter with them. Did they wrench the baby from Margaret Hughes's sinful arms? Or had she, knowing she was to be abandoned and could not support it, begged her sister to bring it up as her own?

And what of the sister? Warily, Penitence's mind explored the loveless parenting she had received from the woman she now knew to have been her aunt, and found it less painful in understanding it better.

Unless Ralph Hurd had been a respectable fiction, his poor widow had had foisted on her, to bring up as her own, a child who had not only been conceived in sin, but fathered by one of her husband's enemies — for all she knew, the man who fired the shot that killed him. It was not a recipe for happy motherhood.

As for the real mother, left in England by her nearest and dearest to suffer the wages of sin ... there would have been no wages *but* sin's.

Penitence studied the dates on the documents. James Hoy had died in April '46, her birthday was four months later. Five years after that Margaret Hughes had bought the Cock and Pie and begun her career as Her Ladyship.

Knowing what she knew now, Penitence could imagine the poverty of those five years, the struggle to stay respectable, the inexorable sinking below the waves of corruption, the bleaching out of all virtues except that of survival. *You had no Her Ladyship to offer you a refuge.*

Penitence raised her head and her eyes encountered the black shapes of the manacles, chains and whips that hung on Her Ladyship's pink bedroom wall. *Couldn't you have stayed a victim? Did you have to survive so well?*

She rewrapped the letter in its silk, retied the ribbons

round the scrolls. The reconstructions and rehabilitations she must make to her own and others' past would take time. Oddly, her overriding emotion was still indignation, a child's anger at adult secrecy. How devious they had all been. She had been deterred from loving her mother/aunt and grandparents as she would have liked, but she had respected them for their ideals of plain-dealing and truth. It was they who had taught her to despise deception. She'd trusted them to be who they said they were.

They lined before her now in masks. *Why didn't they tell me?*

Dorinda was standing at the door, watching. Penitence turned on her: 'How d-did you know?'

Dorinda shrugged. 'Plain as Paddy's pig, it was.'

'Not to me. Why d-didn't she tell me?'

'Oh, Prinks.' Dorinda spoke with tired exasperation. 'What you expect? Your goggles stared at all of us like we was stale herring and you was still swimming. Was she going to look into goggles like that and say "Welcome home and I'm your ma"? Acourse she ballocking wasn't.'

It was a simplistic explanation and probably true, but Penitence had also seen in Her Ladyship a woman who had been leached of the ability to feel anything very much, not sorrow, nor happiness, not good, not evil, and certainly not mother-love. Whatever agony she had gone through when her baby had been taken away, it had been lived with and layered over too long. There had been discomfort when Penitence turned up on her doorstep, a memory that there had been pain, not the pain itself. *I was a nuisance.*

Her Ladyship had done her duty, given her child her protection, found it proper to pass on the Cock and Pie to her but, if there had been any sensation in the numbness in which she existed, it had brought with it resentment that she should feel anything at all. The affection between them, such as it was, was makeshift, not the love of mother and daughter. Penitence doubted if, on Her Ladyship's side, it was greater than for Dorinda and her other girls.

The only love that had warmed her daughter's life had

come from a wizened Indian called Awashonks, the truest mother of them all.

She was so tired. She put the papers back in the box and shut its lid. 'She's left me the Cock and Pie,' she said.

Dorinda's face sharpened with the old jealousy. 'I was a better daughter to her than you ever was.'

Through mental and physical exhaustion, Penitence wrong-footed her. 'I know you were.'

She suffered a relapse, really a form of lethargy in which she reluctantly transferred her identity from respectable child of respectable parents to the bastard of a royalist and a whore-mistress — moreover one who found herself the owner of a brothel.

It was a painful transition for one with a Puritan upbringing, though it was that same upbringing which brought her through it eventually with belief in her individual worth intact. The Church which had formed her might lean heavily towards group responsibility, but its glory lay in the value it put on personal salvation, and it was that which helped her now.

Irritatingly, so did the exchange of fathers. Devout Ralph Hurd, so long presiding over her from his position among the Lord's host, had been credited with many virtues, but merriment wasn't one of them. Now suddenly, perched up on his branch of her family tree, was a man who had been 'merry' in company. *Probably drunk*, she scolded him. *What right had thhe to be merry, seducer?* But as she frowned at him, he gave her a wink, one stammerer to another, and she very nearly winked back.

The apothecary pronounced her better.

'P-please inform P-Peter Simkin I can help him again with the Mortality B-Bill,' she requested, and found she was weaker than she'd thought when he told her the clerk had died many days before.

'B-but it's over now, isn't it?' she asked through tears. The vibrations of hope rising from Dog Yard had matched her own.

The apothecary looked at her out of his expressionless eyes. '*Sera nimis vita est crastina: vive hodie*,' he said. She didn't know what it meant, but it frightened her.

Whatever it was, he was right. The next evening Mistress Palmer called from her balcony to the Watch that there'd been no movement all day from within Mistress Fairley's room. 'And the door's locked.'

It was William Burrows on duty. He called his fellow-watchmen from the Cut, they wound mufflers over their mouths and entered the Buildings. The Yard heard them break down the door, listened to silence, and waited.

Mistress Fairley and both her babies had taken the Plague, but it was only Mistress Fairley had died of it; before doing so, she had smothered each of the children so that they should not be left to die without her.

That night, in pursuance of the plan to save Kitty Bryskett, the only child still alive in Dog Yard, the Cock and Pie went into rehearsal.

Chapter 10

BEATRICE and Benedick danced together in Leonato's pillared hall in Messina, ignoring the fact that their raised fingertips were separated by a five-foot width above the stinking alley in the Rookery and that the light was going. Most of the rehearsals took place at night; it was cooler, though not much.

'Will you not tell me who told you so?' asked Beatrice.

'No, you shall pardon me.'

'Nor will you not tell me who you are?'

'Not now.'

'That I was disdainful, and that I had my good wit out of the "Hundred Merry Tales"? Well, this was Signior Benedick that said so.'

'For God's sake, Beatrice.' The play-actor dropped his hand and hammered with it on his table. 'We've been through this. The first line's a question so put a bloody rise on it. Say it again.' She said it again . . .

'Hand *up*, woman. You're supposed to be dancing with

Benedick, not goosing him. Extend your fingers. Gracefully. That's good. Again.'

His attitude towards her had changed; such patience as he'd shown in enabling her to speak in the first place had gone now that she could.

The irony was that it was only as Beatrice that she could speak to him at all. When, as everyday Penitence, she talked to Dorinda or Job or exchanged news with the rest of the Yard she stammered very little now. If, as Penitence, she tried addressing herself to her mentor, the stammer became so appalling that she didn't say anything.

Nor did he notice. The play was the thing and only the play. It was Beatrice he was rehearsing, Beatrice's voice he listened for and corrected: the woman who played her needed no other purpose. He was a Pygmalion chipping away at his sculpture to produce his ideal woman and the ideal woman was not Galatea, but Beatrice.

Beatrice didn't mind. Shakespeare had given her a hundred revenges in his lines; the actor's strictures enabled her to deliver them better.

It was Penitence, still rocked by the revelation of an unsuspected identity, who minded. She minded that she was being treated like two people, one important, one insignificant. She minded that she was *becoming* two people: Penitence, the retiring identical twin of an outgoing and popular sister, Beatrice. Every time his nod of dismissal betokened the end of a rehearsal, she took off the vizard mask and, watching him, had the uncanny experience of seeing her unmasked self disappear.

Unmasked, she resented that she had not even been consulted on whether she would co-operate on the play. She went on with it because it was only as Beatrice that she regained visibility and – she accused herself of being fanciful, but it was true – because Beatrice willed it.

Beatrice lived for and in the hours at the window, falling in love with Benedick more deeply with each one.

A shuffle from the alley below told her that Dogberry had come on night duty. They paused while he settled himself on

183

the stool which was now his regular stall. 'Thought you were going to start the love bit.'

'We are,' said the actor, shortly.

'Good.'

The dance scene was brief. As usual, Beatrice wiped the floor with Benedick.

'Very well, then,' said the play-actor, 'Beatrice has been gulled into believing Benedick loves her, we know he does, etc., etc., he's been gulled into believing she loves him, we know she does, di-da-di-da, poor Hero's been wrongly accused of unchastity but Claudio believes it, tum-ti-tum, and now we get to it.' He peered across the alley which was lit fitfully from below by Dogberry's lantern and above by a harvest moon. 'We've finished the masked scene. Take it off.'

She shook her head.

'Take it *off*. It's served its turn. You can't go out on that balcony next week in a mask, for Lord's sake.'

Beatrice was the mask, the mask was Beatrice. Besides, Beatrice's love for Benedick was such that Penitence needed to stay free of it; there must be no confusion of roles.

'Don't you realize, we haven't got *time* for this.' His fury was partly from exhaustion. Dorinda thought he was a marvel to work so hard for the Plan, but from the unidentified source by which she understood him Penitence knew that the approaching end of shut-up was unnerving him. The forty-day period since Mistress Hicks had contracted the Plague would be over two days after the play's performance. The Cock and Pie's shut-up extended a week longer. They were all strung up on tenterhooks from the ever-present threat of another death shutting them up for a further forty days, or, if it was their own, for eternity. The gallantry with which he had borne his imprisonment, like his temper, was getting threadbare as his release came nearer.

He was rubbing the back of his neck. 'How can it stay so bloody hot, so bloody long?' He looked down at Dogberry to ask, as he always did: 'Why don't you go and get me a drink?' Dogberry gave his usual answer.

The actor took in a breath and let it out again. 'Look,

Boots ...' It was over a week since he'd called her that. '...
you don't need a piece of silk to be masked. Everybody wears
a mask. If I were to take you to court and tear the visages off
the lords and ladies who parade around it, you would be
astonished by the rogues, double-dealers and strumpets who
would then stand revealed. Who am I? You don't know. Who
are you? I don't know. For all I know Dogberry in the alley
down there is an Oxford scholar. What I do know is that I am
making you into the finest actress of your generation. You
have the ability to be anybody you wish, I swear it, anybody.
Now, please, take that damned bit of material off and show
me the face of Beatrice.'

You dear man, she thought. *As it happens I am of a line of
mask-wearers. If they could do it, I can.*

'Thank you. Now then. Lady Beatrice, have you wept all
this while?'

Through real tears, she said: 'Yea, and I will weep a while
longer.'

At last Benedick told Beatrice: 'I do love nothing in the
world so well as you — is not that strange?'

And Beatrice said truthfully: 'I love you with so much of
my heart that none is left to protest.'

'Come, bid me do anything for thee,' begged Benedick.

'Kill Claudio.'

'Not like that,' shouted the play-actor. 'You don't say it
quiet, like that. This is the great demand, the shock. It changes
the play. It takes the audience by the throat.'

'Took me,' said Dogberry from the alley. 'Fair took aback, I
was.'

'Shut up,' said the actor. 'Beatrice, even in this moment of
declaration you do not give all your heart to this man. He
gives all his to you, but you retain compassion for your
cousin's unhappiness and the need to avenge her honour. The
audience is thinking: hurray, now Benedick'll take her off to
bed, then comes "Kill Claudio" and it thinks: shit, it's all gone
wrong. You have them in your hand. Whisper it if you must,
but also shriek. Shriek for poor maligned Hero. Feel it.'

She was quiet for a moment. Beatrice was an amateur in the

insult stakes; it was Penitence who knew about insult to women. She gathered up the Reverend Block, encompassed the men who came to the Cock and Pie, took in the actor who thought Penitence was a whore.

She said: 'Kill Claudio.'

There was silence.

'Gawd 'elp,' said Dogberry.

'Not bad,' said the actor. 'Not bad at all.' He yawned. 'I'm tired. We'll finish the scene tomorrow.'

'What's the cat look like?' asked Dogberry in her dream.

'Not handsome,' she said, 'but its features are relevant.' The too-large nose, the long planes of cheek, chin and throat . . . she knew them as well as the bole of the tree she climbed down by the river. Uproot it, plant it in a forest and she could still pick it out from all other trees.

'Oh, him,' said Dogberry. 'That's Henry. Lives up there. Hey, Henry.'

She woke up at the shout. There was a rattle on the shutters opposite hers as someone threw stones at them. She got up and went to her own shutters to peer through the crack.

She heard the actor yawning and asking who the hell was there.

'Some nob wanting you, Henry,' called Dogberry.

'It's me, my lord,' said a different voice.

She saw the actor come to his window in his shirt. His eyes were on her shutters, but she doubted if he saw her, or the shutters. He looked down very slowly to the person who stood down in the alley out of her sight. 'And when did I become "my lord"?'

'Four days ago, my lord. Our deepest sympathy, my lord. He was a fine man. We've been looking for you ever since. The King has realized his obligation to you, my lord, and commands me—'

'Better say it in French, George.'

Blast you, Dogberry. The watchman would be sitting immovable on his stool, watching this as he did every other performance.

Whoever George was, he spoke French rapidly.

'I see,' said the actor. 'Well, one's heavily engaged just now, but another week, God willing.'

More French.

'No,' said the actor. 'Not too bad. Quite instructive, really. Amusing people. But one won't be sorry to leave. Where will the coach be?

'Then I'll see you there. Bring a change of clothes.'

And that was that.

'By popular demand,' roared Job from the balcony, 'brought all the way from France by our own His Majesty King Charles to personal perform at the Court of Whitehall, we give you tonight THE famous, THE inmit—THE only Lord Henry KING.'

Dogberry's account of the actor's night visitor had obviously lost nothing in the telling.

The play-actor stepped on to the balcony and bowed to the applause. Job pushed forward again. He was getting carried away. 'And pre-senting THAT well-known beauty, THAT moon of the Americas, all the way from her recent success among the Red Men, Princess PENITENCE.'

I'm not going to be able to do this. She felt sick. She had the Plague, worse than the Plague. She was dead, unable to feel her feet, her hands. Slouching, she nodded in the direction of the Buildings, and slunk back into the attic.

'How many Watch out there?' asked Dorinda.

'I d-didn't notice.'

'You pudden. That's why we're doing this.'

Was it? It had seemed a splendid cause while still a project, but while it was still a project she hadn't known she would feel like this.

Job was barking Dorinda now and the girl swept out for it. '. . . THAT mistress of the comic arts, THAT rose of the Rookery, OUR own Mademoiselle DORINDA.'

Where had Job learned all this? Dorinda, of course. Dorinda and the actor. He'd taken to it like a duck to water. Dorinda was a natural, Job was a natural, the actor was a professional – which left just her.

Reasonably, Penitence looked towards Dorinda as, preening, the girl climbed back down into the attic. 'I can't d-do this.'

'Stop thinking about yourself. Think about the Brysketts.'

Job clambered in. 'They're gatherin',' he reported. 'There's most of the Rookery Watch down there already and word's spreading.'

'We need the ones towards Tottenham Court,' said Dorinda.

'They'll come. Listen to Henry. He'll fetch 'em.'

The actor was explaining theatre, and this play in particular, in case there were those among the audience who'd never even seen a fairground performance. His voice permeated every cranny of the room behind him, just as it was carrying through Dog Yard without strain. If they were to succeed tonight it had to reach down far-away alleys to tickle the ears of bored watchmen and lure them from their posts.

'C-couldn't they smuggle her out through the b-back?' pleaded Penitence, as she'd pleaded times before. Perhaps, even now, this trial was avoidable.

Dorinda tutted. 'All the back windows is boarded fast. Knocking 'em out would make a racket. We been through this. Pull yourself together.'

She couldn't. In a moment she would have to go out on that balcony and begin speaking. *This is for the Brysketts. After all it's done we are going to beat the Plague this one time.* But it was no good, altruism was not enough. Her legs ended at her thighs; she was standing on stumps. How could she do it without the mask? How could she do it at all?

The actor was in front of her now. 'Breathe.' She breathed, her eyes fixed on his.

'Who are you?'

'I am Beatrice.'

'Are you rich? Beautiful? Witty?'

'Yes.'

'Who am I?'

'Benedick.'

'Do you love me?'

'Yes.'

He extended his hand, palm-upwards. She put her own on it and together they walked out on to the balcony.

They were welcomed by applause so loud it took her by surprise; word that there was to be an entertainment had been carefully filtered through the Rookery grapevine, but she had not expected so many to risk the journey across the roofs to see it. She had underestimated the desperate need for distraction. Not daring to look outwards, she kept her eyes on the actor, heard her cue coming with the same dread with which she'd awaited an inevitable plosive consonant. *I'm going to stutter.*

Then the actor turned to her in his disguise as Leonato and instead of bowing, as they'd rehearsed, he took her face between his hands. '. . . There are no faces truer than those that are so washed: how much better is it to weep at joy than to joy at weeping.' He looked her full in the eyes and kissed her.

How much better. Dorinda was right. Penitence was an irrelevance; Beatrice was waiting to dispel fear, pain, hers, everybody's. For one hour, just one hour, by God, there should be enchantment and Penitence could go hang herself. She heard Beatrice's voice float over the chimney-pots: 'I pray you, is Signior Mountanto returned from the wars or no?'

When Beatrice said that Benedick would hang upon Claudio like a disease, there was a laugh. A *laugh.* How long since the Yard had laughed? The actor had worried about this; would lines like 'He is sooner caught than the pestilence' go down well with a Plague-ridden audience? But she had done it. She could do anything.

That there'd had to be a false floor built on to the balcony to give them more height and that every time they moved it juddered like a drum, that when three of them appeared together their elbows jostled, that the audience was getting too involved – during the masked scene Mistress Hicks could be heard shouting from her roof 'It's her, you fucking pudden' – that they had to incline slightly backwards so that their costumes didn't singe against the lanterns ranged along the balcony edge, none of these inconveniences could dint the omnipotence that had come over them all.

With her hair pushed into a boy's cap, she sang Balthazar's song and for the first time looked at her audience. It was dark but the moon was up and the watchmen gathered below carried cressets. It wasn't the watchmen she saw, it was Mistress Palmer sitting on her balcony, Mistress Hicks leaning perilously over her eaves, the empty darkness of Mistress Fairley's window, the two lonely figures in Mother Hubbard's, a child brought from somewhere in the houses behind tied to a chimney-pot so that he wouldn't fall off, the faces ranged along the roof-poles intent on hers, some of them with still-healing plague spots, all white, all thin.

'Sigh no more, ladies, sigh no more,' she sang to them, and heard Balthazar's voice quaver before she pulled herself together; tears would be self-indulgence; these people deserved the best.

> 'Men were deceivers ever;
> One foot in sea, and one on shore,
> To one thing constant never . . .'

The melody was the actor's and as potent as the words. More watchmen coming into the Yard stood still under its spell.

> 'Sing no more ditties, sing no mo'
> Of dumps so dull and heavy . . .'

There was a shift on the cobbles below; two figures, a man and a woman, were quietly passing behind the crowd of watchmen in the direction of the Ship. They'd come then. How brave. She'd almost forgotten the *raison d'être* of the entire performance. She saw some of the faces in the windows glance down and sang as she'd never sung before to get their attention back. The Dog Yarders were privy to the secret, but the watchmen must not be distracted, it was vital to keep their gaze riveted on the Cock and Pie's balcony, away from the Ship.

> 'Then sigh not so,
> But let them go . . .'

She had the Dog Yarders back now, conspiring with her, knowing what she knew, knowing she knew they knew, part of the mystery in which the group became greater than its constituents. She smiled at them and poured out her blessing:

> 'And be you blithe and bonny,
> Converting all your sounds of woe
> Into Hey nonny nonny.'

She backed into the attic where Dorinda and Job were wiping their eyes. The play-actor took over in his evil guise as Don John, soliloquizing over the hisses his plot to make Claudio believe that Hero was unfaithful, then whipping back into the attic to pull a ridiculous hat over his eyes. The next scene was his and Job's. They'd worried about this one too; it was all very well for Shakespeare to portray his Watch as clownish dolts, *he* hadn't had to present it to an audience of watchmen.

She listened while she changed. Job's delivery was leaden, not unfitting the part of Verges; the actor was playing Dogberry with a perfect East Anglian accent. He'd studied his fellow-lodgers, the pipe-makers, who came from Suffolk. He was very funny. She heard whoops from the rooftops, but it was drowned by the delight from the cobbles.

'They don't think it's them,' Dorinda said.

They snatched the hats and wigs off the two men as they came in through the window, and replaced them with Claudio's and Leonato's. Job was almost drunk with his success, but the play-actor was groaning for the interval they didn't dare allow themselves. The watchmen could not be permitted time to do a patrol. Her next scene was the crucial one.

Listening at the window she heard Job miss his line. He was beginning to think of their purpose rather than the play. She prompted him. Even Dorinda wavered; it was the actor who held the scene together. As the men came in she swept out to comfort the slandered Hero.

Now it was the love scene, the crux of Master Shakespeare's

play and of the Dog Yard plot. She stood at the far end of the balcony looking down along the alley that ran past Mistress Hicks's which tonight was the nave of a church with moonlight falling in splashes on its marble flagstones. The floor resonated as the actor stepped out behind her. 'Lady Beatrice, have you wept all this while?'

Without turning round she said: 'Yea, and I will weep a while longer.'

Question. Answer. Benedick's voice held surprise as well as compassion, a man amazed at himself. Question. Answer. Their awareness of each other gathered up the magic of the night.

'Tell her, for Gawd's sake.' Mistress Palmer's whisper crossed the church, 'tell her you bloody love her', and turned into a puff of relief as Benedick said: 'I do love nothing in the world so well as you — is that not strange?'

It was coming. Below them, round about them, nothing moved, nobody breathed.

'Come, bid me do anything for thee.'

Then she turned, every eye in the world on her, her own registering for one second the scene being enacted at the Ship.

She put out her hand with the Rookery in it. 'Kill Claudio.'

Dog Yard dragged in its breath. Mistress Palmer was peering through her fingers. The child attached to the chimney began to cry. A halberd fell from nerveless fingers on to the cobbles. Nobody stopped watching. Only Beatrice and Benedick were aware, in another life, that a man and a woman were tiptoeing down an alley on their fraught, maze-like route towards Tottenham Court and the country, with a bundle in their arms.

She left the stage. Dogberry and Verges were on again. She fell on to her bed. Dorinda was shaking her. 'Did they do it?'

'They did it.' The second's glimpse was on the retina of her eyes; she could see, would always see, the naked body of a little girl being lowered by its parents to a couple standing in the street below. She began to sob; the emotions she had called up had opened her to the pity and terror of the world.

'Don't you bloody give way,' said Dorinda, snivelling. 'They ain't out the wood yet. They got a long way to go.'

'They'll get there.' The Brysketts' friends, whoever they were, *had* to get there, wherever it was, with the one tiny brand they had plucked from the burning. Thought of them stayed in her mind as Beatrice and Benedick teased each other to the last.

'They swore that you were almost sick for me.'

'They swore that you were well-nigh dead for me.'

There was still no hue and cry. They must have reached the outskirts by now. There would be a wagon filled with straw, Sam Bryskett had said.

'Come,' said Benedick, 'I will have thee; but, by this light, I take thee for pity.'

She spoke her last lines: 'I would not deny you; but, by this last day, I yield upon great persuasion, and partly to save your life, for I was told you were in a consumption.'

'Peace! I will stop your mouth.' They kissed.

Dog Yard gave a sigh of utter satisfaction. The applause began as, joined hands held high, they backed into the attic. Stamping feet dislodged tiles from the Buildings' roof, roars came up from the Yard where over thirty watchmen pounded halberd hilts on to cobbles; bandages, kettles, chamber pots waved from the windows in lieu of programmes. A voice from the crowd demanded: 'Encore, encore.' Mistress Hicks was heard to answer: 'Never mind about "encore", make the buggers do it again.'

They went out again to bow and bow. Dorinda and Job drew more applause as they squeezed in beside them. Adoration poured at them, between them, and was poured back by them into the shared experience. She had never known love like this, never known love at all until now. If she leaped high the wheat would grow; she had all that was glorious here, in her fingers.

Back in the attic at last she hugged Dorinda and Job as they hugged each other. In the mutual congratulations one voice was silent, Benedick's.

Instead, a haggard and displeased actor was looking at her.

'You lost concentration,' he said. 'After "Kill Claudio" Beatrice was gone.'

He was ruining something as near perfection as she would ever reach. 'She w-wasn't.'

'Oh yes she was.'

She said: 'Th-thumm-they liked it anyw-way.'

'Th-they liked it anyway,' he mimicked. 'They like anything. They don't know acting from their arse. You gave them short change.'

Surprisingly, Dorinda came to her aid: 'I thought she was ballocking good', and got turned on for her pains.

'One performance and you're an expert? She was good to "Kill Claudio", then she was bad.'

'We got the job done anyhow,' sulked Dorinda.

He spoke very clearly. 'The job, my dear girl, is the play. If those people had been discovered, if the child had been put back into the pest-house, we'd still have given the best we know.' He swung round to Penitence. 'Understand that or you are no actress.'

The palace of Messina had been broken into shards. She wanted to hurt him back so badly that she managed: 'I d-don't want to be a b-bl-bloody actress. P-pretending to be s-some-body else. It's no job for a g-g-grown woman. N-nor a g-g-grown man neither.'

'It's a step up from being a whore.' He nodded to his cast, jumped up on her side sill and swung himself back into his room.

Chapter 11

THE FIRES burning in the streets outside every twelfth house were adding to the heat and overriding with disinfectant the smells of summer from St Giles's rectory garden.

'You mean to tell me, Master Boreman, that you know nothing of this?'

'I know now, Master Flesher,' said the Reverend Boreman, tiredly, 'because you have been so good as to tell me. At length. I did not know before.'

The inquisition turned its attention on the other occupant of the rectory drawing-room. 'Nor you, Master Boghurst?'

'It is hardly likely that Sam Bryskett would have informed me of an intention to break the law, if indeed such was his intention.' The apothecary spoke with his usual precision, but Flogger Flesher detected evasion.

'Your disapproval of the shutting-up law is well known, sir.'

'Murder I called it and murder it has proved to be, but it *is* the law and I would not flout it.'

'Then perhaps, sir, you will tell me whether there are any children remaining at the Ship Inn this morning?'

'There are none.'

'Though when you visited last week there was a child yet alive?'

'There was.'

'And Bryskett told you today it had died in the interim?'

'He did.'

'Ah ha.' Magistrate Flesher had dug up his bone. 'Then the good rector here will be able to prove whether or not he buried it.'

The Reverend Boreman waited to be overcome by enough anger to inject a flea into the ear of this horrid little man, but it didn't arrive; there was no energy left in him for it to feed on.

He had held services pleading with God at least to bring back rain and wind from the exile to which He had banished them.

And, in the week when London's Bill of Mortality for September recorded 8,252 deaths, it had duly rained. For two days fires were put out by a downpour which allowed the clogged sewers to run free, brought down the temperature and the next Bill to 562. There had been other good omens. People said the jackdaws had returned to the Tower. The clapper had fallen out of the Great Bell of Westminster, a portent which had marked the end of the 1625 Plague. Like everybody else, he had allowed himself to hope.

Then the rain had stopped, the heat had come back and the latest Bill recorded the biggest total yet: 8,297 of London's men, women and children had died. So had hope.

He got up and took himself towards the door. 'Master Flesher, I now bury wholesale. I say the service, the bodies go in the ground and their only name is Legion. My clerk died as he wrote up the register, since when there has been nobody to keep it except as and when I have had the time.'

'It is an offence not to keep up the parish register.'

He is almost cherishable, thought the Reverend Boreman. Men practise necrophilia with the naked corpses of young girls in the burying pits, the dying so hate the living that they throw their infected bandages on to them from their windows, corpses stack the streets awaiting burial, a population is swept away, and Magistrate Flesher remains exactly as he was before it all began.

He said: 'If you wish to exhume the bodies in my churchyard you are at liberty to do so. In the meantime I wish you good-day.'

At the doorway, the magistrate paused for the last word. 'Harlots and pimps connived at this transgression. They and the Brysketts shall be brought to book for it. I shall report the matter personally to His Grace of Albemarle.'

Before he'd got into his carriage, the rector had shut the door. He slumped into a chair opposite the apothecary. 'What harlots? What pimps?'

'The Cock and Pie put on a performance of *Much Ado About Nothing* from its balcony last night. There can be little doubt it was a conspiracy to beguile every watchman in the Rookery away from his duty.'

The Reverend Boreman shook his head slowly. 'Lamentable.'

The apothecary shook his. 'An outrage.'

The rector leaned forward and poured them both a glass of malmsey from the bottle which he had not offered to Master Flesher. 'Only one hundred and twenty-five in the parish this week, William. Is it passing?' He heard his own words. 'Only', he thought. Nevertheless the number was just over a third of what it had been during the worst week of August.

'It is passing St Giles, perhaps, but don't raise your hopes too high. It is still capable of return.'

Hope. He had lost one and a half thousand parishioners, his parish was a desert of empty houses around a stinking, over-spilling churchyard. He had prayed beside hundreds of beds for the deliverance of their occupants, and seen only a handful survive. Every moment of his waking life had presented him with suffering or with obscenities of human behaviour he had previously thought impossible. Hope had long gone. And with it, God help him, faith. But charity clung on, it seemed. It had flickered in Dog Yard last night when a collection of harlots and pimps had braved the law in an attempt to save a child.

Shakespeare. His wife had been fond of that vagabond's plays. 'We have heard the chimes at midnight, Master Shallow,' he said. They had been death knells for too long, too long. Oddly, he felt himself cheered. He squinted across his glass at his friend. 'And how did they perform, these pimps and har-lots?'

Apothecary Boghurst measured out his smile with his usual care. 'I rather think I have never enjoyed a play so well,' he said.

The day after the play was the first of leisure the Cock and Pie had known for some time.

Job, overtired with excitement, kept to his room. The actor kept to his, with his shutters closed.

Dorinda wanted to pick over last night's triumphs but Penitence was too angry. Reflection made her acknowledge the actor's criticism of her performance as justified, but the viciousness of his last thrust had gone deep. As much as anything her anger was disappointment, not only at his lack of insight, but at his rudeness. 'How d-dare he.'

'He didn't mean it, Prinks,' comforted Dorinda. 'It was all that acting. Makes you raw. He's begun to admire you, that's what it is. I saw his face as you was singing.' Penitence could hear how much it cost her to say it. 'I'll tell him. It's only fair.'

'You w-won't.' She would not be explained or pleaded for; he should know already. 'I d-don't care what he thinks.'

'Then stop bloody brooding.'

Freedom from the real tragedy and the theatrical comedy which had dominated their lives these past weeks brought a silence over the house allowing those it had lost to make their absence felt. Every so often banter from the empty clerestory would reach the two living women with the soundless clarity which memory gives to the voices of the dead.

Her Ladyship's presence was everywhere but unmentioned, both girls conscious that the other had a better right to mourn her. They were aware of their mutual dependence on each other and afraid that, without her, there was no last court of appeal if they fell to quarrelling.

Despite the heat, they spent most of the day on the balcony. The rain which had fallen almost unnoticed during the hectic days of rehearsal might never have been. Far off, the Thames was a gleam that made the eyes water while the towers of churches and houses seemed to be wriggling on their roofs.

The Yard shrank under the sun's onslaught, its thatch and wood bleached, new cracks opened in its walls. There was dust in the bottom of the horse-trough.

'Wonder how Footloose never got it?' mused Dorinda idly, watching the beggar's stumps twitch in the mouth of his barrel as flies landed on them while he dozed away the afternoon.

'D-don't.' Madness lay in attempting to make sense of the Plague's arbitrariness; why this one, not that one. It wasn't mentioned during the survivors' rooftop gatherings in the cool of the evening. Who dared claim special dispensation from God when He had killed innocent children wholesale? It was better to find reason in utter reasonlessness.

They watched a long shadow preceding the tidy figure of Master Boghurst sprawl over the Yard as he crossed it. Dogberry heaved himself out from the shade to go and unlock the door of Mistress Hicks's. The apothecary had come to give her and her remaining tenants an official bill of health before their shut-up ended tomorrow.

'One thing's for sure,' said Dorinda, 'it bit off more than it could chew when it took on Ma Hicks. What we going to do, Prinks?'

Off her guard, Penitence said: 'We managed before he came, we can manage when he g-goes.'

'I *meant*,' said Dorinda, sternly, 'what we going to do when we get let out next week? What we going to do with the rest of our lives? I don't want to go back to the game.'

Startled, Penitence realized she had acquired responsibility for Dorinda. The girl was Her Ladyship's bequest to her as much as the Cock and Pie itself. 'You won't,' she promised. 'I'll th-think of something.'

'First thing we'll do,' said Dorinda, 'we'll go and look for Pheeb's little 'un.'

Your friends, it seemed, were those you got landed with. She wouldn't have chosen her, but if she must explore the featureless plain that was the future, there could be worse companions to take along than Dorinda with her hidden reservoirs of affection and loyalty. And she was right; if Phoebe's child was alive, they must find it.

'And we could try the acting game,' went on Dorinda. 'Henry says I'd make a good comedienne.'

Penitence wouldn't join in the speculation because she couldn't think beyond the next day. She was, she suddenly knew, waiting for the actor to go. His departure took on the depth of an abyss she must descend into and climb out of before she found out what of herself was left and usable.

What was she doing, being angry with him? He was blind, but his blindness merely increased the debt she owed him for his care in rescuing her not just from Rookery attackers but from a lifelong strangulation.

The freedom when Dogberry unlocked the Cock and Pie's door next week was as nothing to the freedom she had been given through a window that had opened on to poetry and enabled her to speak it.

'I'm hungry,' said Dorinda. 'What's for dinner?'

Penitence went down to the kitchens to begin preparing it and heard Dorinda shout, then shout again. She scrambled back up the stairs to the clerestory. Dorinda was rattling the latch of Job's room: 'He don't answer.'

Ridiculously, she pushed the girl out of the way and jiggled the latch herself. 'He's bolted himself in.'

'Get an axe. I'll call 'pothecary. Maybe he's still with Ma Hicks.'

It was a solid door and by the time she'd made enough of a hole in it to put in her hand and draw back the bolt, Dogberry had let in Master Boghurst. She kept calling 'Job, Job', but already they knew. The silence on the other side of the door was terminal.

He was lying on his bed with his mouth open, as if snoring. His face had the familiar shocking whiteness of the dead.

Dorinda sobbed: 'How could you, Job, how could you?'

Penitence felt it too; lonely and grief-stricken. How hurtful of Job to choose to die without benefit of their company. And how brave.

Dorinda was grabbing the apothecary's arm. 'But he got over it.'

The apothecary shook his head. 'It has changed its form and come back.' Fastidiously, he brushed the girl's hand off his sleeve. 'Tell me, Penitence, did he have any communication with Mistress Hicks?'

'He took water over there last night. B-before the play.'

Master Boghurst lifted one of Job's eyelids. 'The one infected the other. This time, I think, it is carried on the breath. It is as well he locked you out. Mistress Hicks is still alive, but not, I fear, for much longer. Where patients would linger four or five days with the old plague, they now live not forty-eight hours.' He turned to the two girls. 'Wrap him up. I shall help you carry him down.'

Penitence backed away. Then she was running. It was dark along the clerestory and darker still on the stairs leading to the attics. She ran through the cat nightmare while the Plague stalked ahead of her through the black house intent on killing the most beloved thing. She wouldn't get to it in time. Her foot slipped on one of the stairs and she fell, scraping her shin. She clawed herself up and into her attic.

There was no light in the actor's room but her window was an oblong of paler darkness. The plank. Where was the plank? She tore her nails as she scrabbled for it, found it and shoved it across the gap between the two windows, and was crawling across, feeling it bend beneath her weight. Her throat was rasping warnings that came out in gasps. The killer was ahead of her, already in the actor's room. Papers fell to the floor as she slithered over his table. She felt her way to the door and groped her way along an unfamiliar landing, to a space, a banister. She went down and came up against a door, wasting minutes searching for its latch.

A candle on a table, a bed, a figure on it, a figure bending over it.

She screamed: 'Don't touch her.'

The actor looked up, bewildered, and then back to Mistress Hicks. 'She's dead. I didn't think she'd die.'

'Don't touch her, don't touch her.' She ran round the bed. 'It's come back.' She threw herself at him, putting her body between his and the corpse. 'It's come back.'

She was against him, his arms round her. Her body and his. That's why she knew him. Not through the spirit, not through words. Her body for his, his for hers. Clapped together, squirming to get closer.

'God, I wanted you,' he said.

As he carried her up to his bed, kissing her all the way, there was time for a hundred Puritan voices to squeak protests and censure. Dead voices. Corpses. Her body and his, the only living, pulsing, beautiful imperatives in the cemetery of the world around them. Whatever damnation she was condemned to after, she had to have him first. She was centred into a vibrating hole waiting for him to fill it.

They were on his bed, which smelled of him. She struggled out of the clothes which kept her skin away from his. It wasn't shamelessness, it was necessity. Lord, how she knew him. Through his body she could sense his surprise at his need for her, hear the admonishments which tried to keep him away from her, reproving him like her own Puritan voices and as uselessly.

Is this what happened? To nipples? Between the legs? How juicily, slidingly, painfully, pervadingly miraculous. They were riding the Pocumscut rapids together, swivelling up waves, down, up, higher, higher, definitely, most definitely, up until she went over the edge of the great fall . . .

When she woke up he was already awake. She rubbed her nose against his chest, then stopped. He'd been thinking, lying there and thinking.

'Boots.'

'Yes?'

'I am sorry, so sorry. It shouldn't have happened.'

'Oh?'

'I've turned out as bad as the rest of them, haven't I?'

The rest of who?

'I was in a bad way, you see. And you've become precious to me.'

'Oh.'

'Forgive me and don't remember it. Put it down to the Plague.' He became self-consciously brisk, and got out of bed, fumbling for his clothes. 'I must go, before they shut me up again.' His shirt was on. 'I'm going to get out over the roofs. If I can reach the end of the Cut . . .' He was struggling into his breeches. '. . . there's a coach waiting for me in the High Street.' Jerkin, hat were being folded into his cloak. He was tying it into a bundle, still trying to think of things to say.

The bed bumped as he sat down on it to pull on his boots. One, two.

He turned to look down at her. She could see the shape of his head. 'Now you listen to me, Boots. You're too good for this life. When they let you out next week, you're to start a new one. I want your promise. I'm writing to Killigrew — Dorinda knows who I mean — telling him that if he doesn't take you on he's a fool.'

She heard the rustle of papers as he stuffed his play into the bundle of clothes.

'One of these days,' he said, 'if and when I get back, I'm going to walk into the King's Theatre and the voice I'll hear speaking from the stage will be the most beautiful and admired of all voices. And I'll think: "That's my voice. If I've done nothing else with my life, I gave that sound to the world." Promise me now, Boots.'

He wasn't expecting an answer. He never had.

He was suddenly fretful. 'I wish I had something for you . . . there's only this.'

Leave it on the mantelshelf. Like the other clients.

He was back by the bed, groping for her hands.

Kiss them and I'll kill you. He laid something heavy across them. It was his sword.

'God keep you, Boots.'

He stood for another moment and she knew he wanted help with his exit, stage left.

Just go.

And he just went. Climbed out of the window, reached up to the guttering and heaved himself up. There was some scrabbling, and his face appeared upside-down.

'Keep breathing,' he said, and disappeared.

After a while she got up and searched for her clothes among the tangle of bed-linen, dressed, and crawled back to her attic, carrying her fee with her.

They never found Phoebe's child. On their first day of freedom they went looking for him, stepping delicately, like cats, aware there was no level above their heads. Mistress Palmer gave them a cheer. Dogberry nodded as if they'd passed a test he'd set.

There was nobody else around. The absence was a positive presence, a suspension. Any moment now a door would slam, there'd be a rush of footsteps and the hiders would come running to say peep-bo. It didn't. There wasn't. They never would. The two girls tiptoed, hunched for a surprise that didn't come. The open doors showed overturned cups, beds with ragged blankets thrown back, a pull-along, roughly carved rabbit on wheels.

For the first time they took in how big was the disaster of which only a ten-thousandth fraction had been played out in the Cock and Pie.

The address Phoebe had given Dorinda was another empty building. The only person in the street, an old man, said: 'They're all dead.' Other enquiries brought them the same answer.

On their way back, they went by Goat Alley. Penitence stopped at the door leading to the printer's. 'What you want here?' asked Dorinda. 'He's dead. The whole family's dead.'

Their footsteps left prints in the dust on the stairs. Cobwebs were strung across the open door to the loft. 'It's still here,' said Penitence. The press was as she'd last seen it. Some unfinished text was in the forme, a few letters scattered on the floor.

'Lovely,' said Dorinda. 'Now let's go. I'm breaded.'

The typeface of the print was worn, but still sharp. Holland-ish from the look of it, like her grandfather's. *Smuggled in.* Only the Dutch could cast good type; English type was rub-bish.

'Will you ballocking leave it?' Dorinda's voice was sharp. Not finding Phoebe's child had added to her loss. 'The parish'll come and collect all this stuff sooner or later.' The goods of those who had died intestate – and since the Plague had taken whole families there were no heirs for most goods to be passed on to – were sold by the parish to defray the cost of relief.

'It won't.' She might as well add theft to her sins. 'I'm going to get the Tippin boys to carry it over to the Cock and Pie.'

'What for? Prinks, what do we want a ballocking great machine like that for?'

'Our livelihood.'

Within the month the Cock and Pie publishing house had gained its first commission – some handbills for Dogberry, the former watchman, who had returned to the butchery trade.

By then Penitence knew she was pregnant.

The baby was born in the spring.

Three months later Penitence was arrested for debt.

BOOK II

Chapter 1

FOR NEARLY as long as there had been a London there had been a Newgate, one of the seven portals into the city. And for nearly as long as there had been a Newgate it had been a prison. Also known as the Whittington, or Whitt, in honour of the Lord Mayor whose bequest had rebuilt it in the fifteenth century, it was an impressive gateway, providing an equally impressive bottleneck for traffic. Its castellated turrets were five storeys high and over the archway between them were pilasters with statues symbolizing Peace, Security, Plenty and Liberty. Originally, Liberty had a cat at her feet, in memory of Dick Whittington's cat, but this had fallen off. Still, it was a fine gate and had cost considerably more than the prison that lay behind it.

Penitence Hurd entered it in the company of a boy who'd been fined forty shillings for not paying a penny bridge toll, a female Quaker, a highwayman, and a woman who'd stolen a kerchief worth sixpence.

They were taken under the archway into the Lodge where their particulars were taken down by a male keeper, and the Quaker's and Penitence's cloaks dragged off them by a squat lady who said they wouldn't be needing them, but that she would.

Their next stop was the Hold, a room twenty foot by fourteen, with iron bars over a tiny window that looked out on to Newgate Street. Part of the floor was boarded over as a sleeping area, the rest of it decorated with chains, hooks, iron staples and dried excreta.

The keeper pointed to the spiked aperture over the door and gave them the prison rules in a fast monotone: 'Speaking through that to friends eighteen pence, said friend's visit sixpence, room of your own twenty guineas down and eleven shilling a week, cleaning woman one shilling a week, furniture ten shilling and twelve pence a night for a whore. Any of you lot got the garnish?'

The highwayman said he had at which the keeper perked up and took him off to share it with him. The woman felon and the boy who hadn't paid his toll both cried, the Quaker didn't.

Nor did Penitence. Neither did she pray, as the Quaker was doing. Somewhere within her was fear at her plight, but her mind couldn't quite make contact with it. It hadn't been able to experience anything as vivid as fear, or happiness, or even boredom, since her baby was born. Dorinda and Mistress Palmer had delivered the child and laid it in her arms, telling her what a beautiful boy it was, and although she could see for herself that it was the truth she had felt no emotion. She had been quite surprised, when her breasts produced milk, that her body should respond like a mother's.

Dorinda was the one who called the baby Benedick, rocked him and crooned to him and, when Penitence's milk dried up, found a wet-nurse and toted him back and forth for his feeds, though it was thanks to Penitence's enterprise that the wet-nurse could be paid and the two of them have enough to live on.

The Plague's toll on licensed and unlicensed printers had been high and as yet there was no influx of printers from the provinces sufficiently daring to take their place. It had been surprisingly easy to find work for the stolen press she had set up in the Cock and Pie's kitchen – Apothecary Boghurst wanted bills printed, so did the late Mistress Hicks's rope-dancer, the Reverend Boreman had hired her to print his polemic against the cowardice of his fellow-priests who had deserted their posts at the first whiff of Plague. Their word of mouth brought in more work until Penitence had as much as she could cope with and had to employ MacGregor, the ex-piper, as a printer's devil.

She laboured ten hours a day in a lead-heated, paper-filled kitchen, doing the work because it was there to be done, taking no joy from it, not minding it, just filling the limbo in which she existed.

When the bailiff came to take her off to debtors' prison because she hadn't paid her mortgage, it was Dorinda who protested: 'But nobody asked us for it.'

'Don't matter anyway,' explained the bailiff. 'Debt's been sold.'

'How can you sell a ballocking debt?'

The bailiff was surprised by her ignorance. There were agencies which bought debts and then enforced them and would the decoct come along please and make no trouble for a man as was only doing his duty.

Penitence went.

Dog Yard turned out, prepared to lynch the bailiff if she gave the word, but she refused to give it. 'It d-doesn't matter.' Nothing mattered, not the sound of Benedick crying as she was led away, not the young Tippins running along beside her bellowing out expert instructions on Newgate survival, not Dorinda promising to somehow, anyhow, pay the money. It was as if it was happening to somebody else.

It went on being something happening to somebody else. The Quaker was taken off to the dungeon, the boy to the men's quarters, the woman felon produced some cash and was allowed to go to the dining-hall before her incarceration in the women's ward. Penitence, with not a halfpenny to bless herself with, was left alone for the night without food, water, or light.

In the early hours the lock turned and a man with a large number of keys on his belt came in carrying a lantern and a jug of ale. He held it out to her and Penitence drank it.

'You don't like me, do you?' he asked.

She was unaware of having seen him before. In this light she could barely see him now until, obligingly, he held up the lantern. Incuriously, she considered the pockmarked face of a man in late middle age, whose eyes would have been nondescript if it hadn't been for an almost ferocious intensity. The hand holding the lantern had a bad state of shakes.

She shrugged.

'Haughty,' he said. 'You look down on me, don't you? They told me as there was a lady-in. You're a lady-in, ain't you?'

She had no idea.

He came closer, nodding. 'Lady of three ins. *In* debt. *In* gaol. And *in* danger of staying there. I like lady-ins as is high-nosed. I won't sard with trollops. I'm particular. I like 'em when they don't like me. Lady-ins ought to have a room of their own, and a soft bed to snuggle in and have some meat in their gravy.' He was shaking so that the lantern vibrated frenetic shadows around the walls. 'Your guts is chiming twelve, ain't they? Want George to fill 'em? George'll do it, George'll put meat in your gravy. There's other ways of garnishing George than crossing George's palm with gelt.'

She'd guessed that there were. She said: 'No.'

Oddly, he was gratified. 'Lady-in says no, does she? Too good for old George, is she? Then George'll escort her to her quarters. He can wait, can George. He's waited before.'

He bowed her out, and accompanied her down a stone passage which was punctuated by snores or moans emerging out of the grilles in its doors on puffs of foul air. The large and insalubrious courtyard it led into smelled fresh in comparison.

George's lantern swung to show her the windows looking over the courtyard. Some of them were lit and from one of them came the sound of a mandolin. 'Press Yard. Private rooms,' he said. 'You garnish George, he'll garnish you. You don't like me, though, do you?'

More passages, more smell, a large door requiring an enormous key for its lock. As George opened it fetor came rushing out at the two of them like escaping gas.

At that particular moment Newgate's common female ward, known to its familiars as Flap Alley, was at its best, which is to say dark and quiet. Down one end of its narrow thirty-foot length some women were gathered on their knees in front of what appeared to be a box on the wall with candlelight from inside it concentrated on their faces and necks. It looked like a painting in which the artist had depicted a nativity scene with female shepherds staring into the illuminated crib. The grime on the canvas darkened the intervening area but George's lantern showed that the box was a bed, one of a series of barrack beds formed by planking which ran in two tiers the length of the side walls partitioned by wooden uprights.

Penitence saw that each bed within her vision, and presumably those out of it, was occupied not by one woman but two or more. The lower one by her elbow had two women sleeping at different ends with three children tucked in at angles around them. It was, in fact, a room, three feet wide, four high and five long.

'Looks bad,' said George at her side. 'Whitt fever.' He nudged Penitence. 'You want to remember that. Four go off of Whitt fever for every one as we hang. You want to remember that when George comes for his garnish.'

One of the women at the far end hauled herself to her feet and came towards them. 'Get the carriers, George,' she said.

'Gone off, has it?' enquired George, not unsympathetically.

'And her. Where's that bloody leech? We asked for him yester morning.'

George shrugged. 'You know *him*,' he said. He went off and the woman returned to the group. Penitence followed her and looked into the oblong where a rushlight cast a glow on to two yellow-white dead faces, a woman's and a baby's. From the amount of blood on the sacking beneath the woman's legs she had haemorrhaged to death.

Penitence turned away and went to sit in the shadows next to the empty grate in the end wall. Some part of her was connecting with what she'd just seen; the other part considered the ineffectualness of women. Women cast out, women shut up, women dying, women watching other women die. In the clarity of her depression she saw that the beds were hutches to contain creatures who'd no more control over their own lives than small animals at the mercy of weather and predators; powerless because they were ignorant, ignorant through powerlessness.

There was quiet until George came back with some keepers carrying a hurdle. Their boots made sharp, authoritative sounds on the stone floor and they were teasing each other about a

211

card game they'd been interrupted in. Whether or not she resented the masculinity of this intrusion, one of the women by the bed suddenly screamed and threw herself at them, clawing. Within seconds the room was in pandemonium, women with children clinging to their skirts emerging from their beds to join in the attack on the men, and in some cases each other, yelling and swearing.

At the door, George pulled on a bell rope, adding clangour to the general howl. Other keepers came rushing in, carrying buckets of water which they threw indiscriminately over rioters and children alike. The speed with which the scene quietened down with no apparent ill-will on either side indicated that it was a regular occurrence. The bodies were taken away; women, wringing water from their hair and dresses, gathered up their children, went back into their hutches and once more allowed peace to descend on Flap Alley.

Penitence hauled herself out of the fireplace in which she'd taken shelter and squelched a puddled way along the beds, trying to find one that was empty, knowing it was a hopeless search, that hopelessness was all she would ever feel again, that the women prisoners' rage had come from their own hopelessness, an expression of despair so deep that it could only be expressed in hysteria.

Eventually, she went back to her spot by the fireplace, took off her wet shoes, tucked her feet under her skirt and went to sleep.

She was woken by a boot nudging her hip and a voice saying: 'What you in for?'

One of the women who'd attended the dying mother was looking down at her with the hostility of an old hand for a new recruit, a tall woman whose facial skin seemed to have been soaked too long in water before being squeezed out.

'Hundred and eight p-pounds,' Penitence told her. Her Ladyship hadn't bothered to pay off much of the mortgage, content to keep her creditor at bay with the appalling rate of interest.

'Any garnish?'

Penitence shook her head.

'You ain't having Colley's bed,' the woman told her fiercely, 'I'm in it now.' She was overtaken by a fit of coughing.

Penitence nodded wearily. She could die on the floor; it wouldn't be long in any case. Not here.

'Hungry?'

Penitence nodded again.

'Yes,' said the woman, 'and if you ain't got no garnish you'll stay hungry lessen you want to eat Whitt stew what's already gone over a goodish piece o' grass and that don't come 'til noon. You'd better take your turn at the windy.' Coughing, she pointed to where a line of women and children waited in a queue behind a grille set in the side of the fireplace wall through which came the uncertain light of dawn and the sounds of traffic. One of their number had her arms through the bars and was shouting: 'Have pity, good people. Have pity on a poor debtor and her childer.'

'Debtor,' scoffed Penitence's new acquaintance, 'only ones she's in debt to is glaziers for breaking in through too many of their windies.' She had been mollified by Penitence's compliance over the matter of the bed and now indicated that Penitence could get in it. 'A couple hours is all. Don't think you'll have it for regular.'

The palliasse on the bed's base was soaked with blood. Penitence removed it, clambered in and fell instantly asleep. She had an infinite capacity for sleep these days, dreaming dreary dreams but finding them preferable to waking life.

She was woken by hearing her name shouted. 'Hurd. Anyone here called Hurd?' She was summoned to the begging window by the queue which bad-temperedly allowed her to go to its head: 'You're asked for, and don't take all bloody day. It ain't your turn.'

A warm sun shone on Newgate Street which was already busy with be-wigged men on their way to city businesses, vendors on their way to St Paul's and the markets and wains coming in from the country blocking the egress of coaches, but all days were grey to Penitence.

Dorinda stood in the road with Benedick in her arms, swaying back and forth as people pushed past her. Seeing Penitence, she came close to the bars. 'You all right?'

'Yes.'

'Don't look it. We got another printing order – Fifth Monarchist crackpot, but his money's good and MacGregor says he can cope but we need more ink.' Her voice sank to a whisper. 'I pawned the sword.'

Penitence nodded. A woman behind her was already trying to pull her away from the window, but she held on to the bars. Dorinda looked her straight in the eye and then down at Benedick. 'See his dear little shawl?' she said. 'Ma Palmer knitted it.' Mistress Palmer had knitted it weeks ago. 'Lovely, ain't it? Rich. Feel it.' She held Benedick up to the window and Penitence's hands, apparently stroking the shawl, felt the shape of a purse and curled over it. As she did it her son's fingers gently went round one of her own and she had to shake them off so that she could transfer the purse to her sleeve. The baby's eyes widened and his mouth opened to give out a tiny mew of sound.

Sensation rushed in on Penitence then. It was as if she was seeing her son for the first time, not as something foisted on her, but a personality she had just badly hurt. Her hands went out to clutch him, but Dorinda had taken him back. 'Say bye-bye to Mumma. Say see you tomorrow.' She was bobbing Benedick's fist up and down in a farewell. The baby was still looking at his mother and as Dorinda carried him away he turned his head to keep watching her.

Oh God. The bars indented Penitence's face as she pressed against them to keep the round little head over Dorinda's shoulder in sight as the two of them dwindled into the press of the street. Every step away from her was a reproach. How could she have overlooked him all this time? How could she have spurned her son's touch for a damned purse? Where was he? She couldn't see him. Then she glimpsed Dorinda as she paused at the gate, waiting for a cart carrying planking to come through. As it jolted past a plank slid off its load and Dorinda had to skip out of its way.

But if she hadn't. Penitence's nerve-endings were no longer the exclusive property of her own body but connected to those of the morsel of humanity being taken away from her towards the Rookery, its pain now her pain magnified. A carelessly loaded plank of wood would obliterate her at the precise moment it crushed in that small skull. Love for her baby shrieked through her like a typhoon. They had to batter her hands before she would let go of the bars.

I shook him off. She felt the softness of the boneless little fingers still. Until that rejection it was as if she hadn't been aware of him, the most important thing in the world, hadn't known the diseases that could kill him or the need to stay alive so that she could protect him. This was the cat nightmare brought into the everyday; she would never be free of it.

Dorinda's chatter screamed into her ears. *Fifth Monarchist crackpot.* She cried out: 'Oh Jesus.' Fifth Monarchists were illegal, and so were the people who printed their sedition or blasphemy or whatever it was. They got hanged. If they caught this one, he'd be forced into revealing who'd printed his pamphlets, and then Dorinda would be arrested, and Benedick left alone. She was lacerated by the sound of weak cries from the crib where he was starving to death. Men with guns were advancing through the nightmare to shoot him and she couldn't get to him in time.

'No good giving way, duck.' The bed-owner put an arm round her shoulders. 'Nice little fella like that, he's better off out there. I know. My last died in here.'

Penitence stared at her. In this new state she'd woken to, it amazed her that a woman could say such a thing without screaming. 'What's your name?'

'Bet.'

'I've got to get out of here, Bet.'

What might have been a laugh turned into a fit of coughing. Ineffectually, Penitence patted the woman on the back, then guided her to her bed and helped her in. She sat down on the edge: 'Help me, Bet. I've got to get out of here.' Now that her brain was working, a new horror had manifested itself. Her creditor was entitled to repossess the Cock and Pie in lieu of payments. The spectre of Dorinda walking the streets with Benedick in her arms and nowhere to shelter flashed in a vivid image before her mind's eye. 'I've *got* to get out.'

'Ain't we all,' said Bet, flatly. 'Well, there's the silver bridge to the outside for them as can afford the toll.'

'P-pay the debt, you mean.'

'Ain't just the debt,' Bet told her. 'There's exit money. Them bastard keepers need garnishing afore they'll let you out, debt paid or no. Ain't you got nobody to hark-ye?'

Perhaps she could borrow from the Reverend Boreman or the apothecary. If they'd let her develop the printing business she could pay them back in time. Or she could throw in with the Tippins and steal it. She'd do *anything*. But to do it she needed to be outside.

No, Bet told her, nobody from Flap Alley was allowed out on parole. 'You want to get yourself a place in Press Yard. Them hoi polloi get privileges if they garnish. Let out on day passes, them. Only way out for us is when we done our time, or if we get turned off.'

Bet's husband, it appeared, had been 'turned off', hanged, for theft. She herself was serving a four-year sentence for assaulting the neighbour who'd informed on him. Apart from wondering how a woman could risk such consequences for herself and her children — Bet had three left from the Plague, all of them struggling to survive on the outside — merely to avenge a husband, Penitence paid her little attention. She was looking around her with eyes suddenly sharpened to danger, taking in the slopping chamber pots under every bed, the sores on the children's mouths, the coughing, the woman who was vomiting, the old woman in the next bed gasping for breath. Even life in Dog Yard had not prepared her for this place. It would kill her. Just breathing its air was a death sentence. More important, it would kill Benedick by extension. She could trust nobody, not even Dorinda, with his survival without her. *I've got to get out.*

'How do I get a room in P-Press Yard?' she asked. If Press Yard was the only starting place for her release, then to Press Yard she must go.

'I'm due at the windy.' Bet was scrambling out of the bed to get to the queue at the window. 'Midday's 'a best time.'

Penitence clutched her arm. 'How do I get into P-Press Yard?'

'You aren't half green,' said Bet, impatiently. 'Did George do his you-don't-like-me?'

'Yes.'

'There y'are then. Get out my way.'

Penitence followed her as she barged to the head of the queue. 'What d-do you mean?'

Bet put her arms through the bars of the window. 'Of your charity, lady,' she whined, 'remember the poor debtors. I got six childer starving, my lord. George is all right, is George. Remember a poor debtor, lady. I wish as he'd ask me for garnish but I ain't high-sniffing enough for him. In debt for sixpence, my lord, that's all. Remember a poor debtor.'

The woman behind Bet, who'd allowed her precedence at the window, chimed in: 'George offered for you? That's luck, that is. No harm in George.'

There was approval from the rest of the queue. As a purchaser in the sexual favours market, George apparently ranked high. Penitence was regarded as fortunate. 'He's more one for the lady-ins.'

'Just lay back and tell him you hate him and he's happy.'

'An' he delivers. Not like that bloody Pudsey.'

The conversation became a discussion on which keeper liked to do what to whom and for how much. Using their bodies to gain privileges from the keepers was as normal in Flap Alley as begging from passers-by. They might have been discussing fat-stock prices. Penitence left them and climbed back into Bet's bed while it was empty.

I've got to get out. Cautiously, huddling against the wall, she manoeuvred Dorinda's purse from her sleeve and opened its string. Two crown-pieces. Not even enough to rent a Press Yard room for a week. She'd have to beg, borrow, or steal the rest. Where was the crime in theft? Newgate was a royal prison; the King and his authorities were prepared to let it be run by thieves more rapacious than any the Rookery had ever turned out.

She flopped back on to the bed, allowing her thoughts to run on highway robbery and associated crimes, unaware of a hand sidling from the bed behind her until it snatched the purse away from her side. Yelling, she scrambled after it but the thief, a skinny little girl, had run with it to a group of women. In the centre of it was Bet. She faced Penitence with a sly hostility. 'Forgot to tell Your Ladyship, didn't I,' she said, 'but the rule is if one of us's got gorse, we all got gorse.' The group sniggered.

Penitence charged. 'Give it back. It's mine.' Two of the bigger women grabbed her arms and held her while she struggled.

'Ours,' corrected Bet. 'Orders of women prisoners' tribunal. Let's see what the Lord sent.' Her spiny fingers delved into the purse and came out with the crown-pieces. 'Two coach-wheels.'

'Flanders fucking fortune,' said one of the group, appreciatively.

Without taking her eyes off Penitence, Bet handed the silver pieces to the thin young thief. 'Sary, you take these to the tap room and you tell 'em as Bet wants enough pints of Geneva for all Flap Alley. No rag-water, neither. Best Geneva. Order of a tribunal. On our Ladyship here. Off you go.'

Penitence stopped struggling as she watched the child run off. That they were going to spend money on gin which might have bought food or medicine was almost as bad as the theft itself. Almost. She took up her old position by the fireplace and watched Sary run back and forth with relays of blackjacks, watched the women gulp the spirit and pour it down their children – even babies were given sips – watched as it sent them silly or quarrelsome or comatose. She watched little girls and boys stagger in circles, giggling, until they fell down.

Bet wavered up to the fireplace holding out a blackjack by its neck. 'Put some of that where the flies won't get it. No hard feelings, eh?'

Penitence took it. 'No.' She hadn't. As well to have hard feelings for rain or cold. These women were elemental, too random in their cruelty to be resented.

'Got to have a bit of fun now and then, eh?'

'Yes.'

'Everyone for themself in this life, ain't it?'

Penitence drank to the woman who had just voiced the only principle to life which had any validity. 'Yes.' Bet, if you only knew it, you're my midwife. A new Penitence was being born.

Bet stretched out a skinny hand. 'My turn.'

Penitence held the bottle out of her reach. 'Oh no you don't. I paid for this. And I need to be d-drunk to do what I'm going to do.'

Bet squinted at her. 'What you going to do?'

'I'm going to get out of here, Bet. By Christ, I'm going to rise above this rat-hole, *all* rat-holes and the stupid bitches in them. And I'm going to take my son with me.'

When the keeper George came on duty that night, Penitence was waiting by the door for him.

Chapter 2

FOR HER first venture into harlotry, Penitence Hurd could have chosen worse clients than Keeper George. The turnkey aspired both above his station and his performance – the Cock and Pie would have put him in the fumbler category. Also, as far as honesty went in Newgate – which wasn't far – he kept his word. Dorinda would have told her she was lucky (and later did).

That first night, however, as Penitence followed him and his shaking lantern into the bowels of the prison, such blessings were not apparent. He dithered with excitement, touching her, insisting that she didn't like him.

She could not, *could* not have survived the Plague for this; any moment there would be a miraculous intervention. She'd made a mistake; there were other ways out of Newgate, must be. Oh God, she could get *pregnant*. She'd tell him, sorry, but she must return to Flap Alley. At that she kept walking. Flap Alley was death. Criminals had a defined sentence: debtors were imprisoned until they paid. She wished she'd drunk more gin.

'P-PP-PPress Yard?' she asked him. 'You p-promise?'

He looked at her suspiciously: 'You got a stutter?'

Mustn't stutter, mustn't stutter. Must stay alive. Why didn't I bring the mask? He had no use for vulnerability; she had to play up to this grotesque fantasy of his. 'No,' she told him clearly. 'Ladies like myself do not stutter.'

Gratified, he opened a small, iron-studded door and ushered her into a cell and put his lantern down on a table. 'This is where we keeps them as is going to be turned off.' The place was tiny and windowless. From its smell and the wet walls, it seemed to be drying out from inundation by a river carrying corpses. The bed had been made up with blankets.

She felt the area round her mouth go cold and press against her teeth as her blood retracted.

'You going to faint?' asked George, admiringly. 'Ain't used to this, lady-in like you.' He sat down on the bed, indicating that she should undress and holding up the lantern to watch her better. 'Tell us what you *are* used to.'

It can't be happening. It won't happen. She knelt down and forced her hand to touch his knee. 'P-please, Master George,' she said, reasonably. 'P-perhaps you have children. I have a s-son.' She had difficulty emitting the lovely word, but she was sure he could not withstand it. 'For their sake let us live in decency. Allow me a room of my own, and I promise you in time you shall be paid very well. I have a p-printing—'

She had timed it wrong; his expectation had grown too high for his better nature, such as it was, to respond to appeal. His mouth stretched like a baby's about to cry and he yelled: 'You're spoiling it.'

He picked up his lantern and began pushing her to the door. 'You've spoiled it. You ain't a lady-in at all. I'm taking you back to the Alley.'

'NO.' Somewhere, at some time, someone had taught her to act. *Act.* She stepped away from him. 'You horrid rogue. I shan't go back.'

He looked sullen. 'I'm not having you spoil it with childer and such.'

'It was a lie,' she told him.

He sat down, mollified but still suspicious. 'What then?'

She took the vizard mask out of a mental drawer and put it on. It wouldn't be her it happened to; it would be someone else. The voice of a high-born lady said: 'How should I submit to this life? Heretofore I have lived in mansions.'

'Lovely,' he said. 'Go on.'

She heard her mother's ... aunt's ... voice: 'All actresses are harlots.' *Wrong again. All harlots are actresses.* She began unbuttoning her basque with fingers she couldn't feel. 'Were I to tell you the name of my father, you would recognize it as among the highest in the land, but it shall remain unspoken, to save his shame and mine.' *This is ridiculous.*

'Lovely.' The lantern was vibrating so hard its flame was in danger of going out. 'More.'

Did survival rest on a hideous farce like this? She couldn't remember why she was here, didn't want to, only that it was necessary. Eventually, chattering nonsense, she was naked except for the mask he couldn't see. It wasn't her face, in any case, he was interested in.

'Ooh, them little lily bubbies.' He stood up and fingered them for a while, muttering to himself: 'You lady-ins. You ladies.'

She closed her eyes. *I'm not here. I'm somewhere else.*

'You lady, get on that bed.'

She got on it, staring at the wall. Her fists were clenched tight. She heard the keys rattle as he unbuckled his belt and threw it on the floor. He was struggling out of his breeches. *God save me. Oh God.* She panicked as she felt the heat of his body press down on hers.

'You look at me, lady. You look at old George.' His breath was awful. 'You don't like me, do you?'

With perfect honesty, she said: 'I hate you.'

'Oooooooh.' He was shrieking. 'Lovely.' It was over. His weight went slack on top of her. There was liquid on the top of her thighs. He lay, panting into her neck. 'Too quick.'

She felt a moment of gratitude that he hadn't penetrated her, and then she was sick.

He was good about it, bustling cheerfully to help her dress; the vomit was an indication of her disgust and, therefore, her nobility. He'd clear it up later.

She was never able to remember the walk to the room she'd just bought in Press Yard. It had a window. 'Water,' she said. 'Get me lots of water.'

'You lady-ins.' He was roguish, but he brought her some in a bucket, a sliver of soap, and a stub of lit candle stuck in a square of clay.

When he'd gone she stripped and washed herself all over, put her clothes back on, took them off and washed herself again. She was very cold as she dressed herself once more. She lay down on the bed, shivering, afraid to think. If she thought, disgust would destroy her.

It's so cold. Like winter. Winter. The Pocumscut winter. In winter she always went out to watch the tree swallows ... and she didn't want to miss them. She made herself float down to the stream where they congregated on the last of the bayberries. They were the only birds she knew that played, dropping a feather to float in the air, twittering cheerfully as they skimmed down to pick it up again, the sun catching their metallic blue wings. Matoonas was fishing along the river bank; she didn't want to face him, so, cold as it was, she stepped into the stream and lay down, letting it carry her into the river which swirled her along to where her stains could be pounded clean by the rocks of the rapids.

Somebody was dragging her back, which made her irritable. She wanted to be pounded clean.

'There,' said a voice. 'We're warmer now.'

They might be. She wasn't. She was turned to stone. Galatea in reverse. She opened her eyes. A heated brick warmed her feet, a spoon was hovering near her mouth and, above it, a face.

'I heard your arrival and thought, God's dines, a neighbour of one's own gender and station at last. Then, nothing. So I ventured in, and just as well. How did you get so cold, you poor creature?'

222

The woman's affected drawl suggested falseness, an attempt at the languid assonance of the upper classes, so did the elaborately untidy hair, the clothes that were not so much worn as draped, but Penitence noticed none of these things at that moment. She saw only the interested yet vague large blue eyes and great kindness.

'We must eat some of this calves-foot jelly, mustn't we?' The woman sniffed at the spoon. 'One *asked* for calves-foot jelly, but . . . My name is Aphra Behn, by the way.'

'Penitence Hurd,' whispered Penitence.

'How very . . . biblical. Now then, whatever this mess is it's nourishing. We must eat it up or nasty Noll will come and get you. That's what they used to tell us, didn't they? Nasty Noll Cromwell will come and get you.'

They'd told Penitence no such thing. This woman was a royalist, then. But she was right about the soup; it was nourishing and Penitence felt better after some spoonfuls. Even more nourishing, after Flap Alley, was the friendship on offer from a woman of about her own age.

Aphra Behn dabbed her patient's mouth. 'There, dear. Oh, the vicissitudes of life, that women like us should be so reduced . . . and for such small matters as a hundred and fifty pounds.'

So Aphra was a fellow-debtor. 'Mine's a hundred and eight.'

'We shall not despair,' said Aphra, patting her shoulder. 'We shall arise from this darkness and our banners shall yet stream in a new dawn. "Stone walls do not a prison make, nor iron bars a cage; minds innocent and quiet take that for an hermitage." Dear Lovelace, also in prison when he wrote that to lift our hearts.'

There was only one person to lift Penitence's heart and it wasn't Lovelace, whoever he was, nor this prattling woman. Kind as she was, Aphra Behn was a reproach; her mild clear eyes showed no experience of a world where to inhabit a room in Press Yard at all was a step up from somewhere more terrible. For her, it was a step down.

At that moment Penitence would have cowered from the gaze of her son; it was for him she had prostituted herself, but by that same prostitution she had made herself unworthy of him. It was Dorinda she wanted, the only person to understand and not condemn. Until this moment she hadn't valued enough a relationship that went deeper than friendship and liking — there were times when she actively disliked Dorinda — but existed in the bone, uncosseted and unremarked.

'Perhaps I should mention at this stage,' said Aphra, 'that one is a playwright and a widow. In that order.'

'A playwright?' She'd never heard of such a thing as a woman playwright. Penitence asked the one defining question: 'Have you children?'

'Alas, my lord and I were not blessed with offspring.'

Penitence lay back on her wooden pillow. This woman was a calves-foot jelly supplier, of no use to desperate states of mind.

She was wrong, but it took time to know it. As it was, she found the instant, intimate friendship being thrust upon her both warming and surprising. Without being asked, she gave a few details about herself. Recently arrived from the Americas. Trapped by the Plague. In debt.

There was a squeal from the next room: 'Where's my Aphra? Them bastards taken my Aphra. Aphra-a-a.'

'Visitors. Excuse me, dear.' Aphra Behn stuck the spoon in Penitence's mouth and left it there while she hurried next door.

She came back accompanied. 'This is my mother, Penitence. Mistress Johnson. And this my brother. Brother dear, fetch stools from my room. Mistress Hurd should not be alone.'

Penitence was surprised by the sensitivity, and grateful. The Johnsons looked a mixed blessing; young Master Johnson being languid to the point of vapidity, and old Mistress Johnson undeniably drunk. But Penitence was so frightened of being left alone with the memory of George — even worse, with George himself — that she would have welcomed the company of the undead.

Slouching, Master Johnson brought the stools, nudged his mother on to one and slumped on to the other. Aphra, begging Penitence's indulgence at discussing personal matters, asked him: 'Did my letters reach the King? What did Sir Thomas say?'

'The King ain't a goer.' Master Johnson dispensed words as if they might fall into enemy hands. He handed over some letters. 'His foot-licker gave 'em back. Killigrew's another'n. Only stumped up ten decus, which won't keep Ma and me, let alone you.'

'But he promised,' wailed Aphra.

Mrs Johnson lurched forward, took the letters and shoved them at Penitence with a blast of alcoholic triumph. 'My Aphra spied for the King.'

Penitence gave her an indulgent nod.

'Spied for the King. My Aphra.'

'Mother!' said Aphra.

Mistress Johnson winked. Her mouth made shapes that eventually produced more words: 'Spied on the Dutch. And Dissenters. My Aphra.'

'Mother!'

'Now she's written to him for to ask why he ain't paid her.'

'Mother!' Distraught, Aphra held her mother back and explained in a whisper, 'Poor Mother never fitted into England after Papa's tragic death. She has never recovered from that. And now we have fallen on bad times. So insalubrious. So shaming. You must forgive her.'

Mistress Johnson nudged Penitence in the ribs, shoving the letters under her nose. 'Letter to the King,' she said. 'My Aphra.'

A dispirited nod from Aphra gave Penitence permission to read them, which she did while the family talked.

Bartholomew. She really did spy for the King. Either this was an extraordinary charade for which Penitence could divine no purpose, or Aphra Behn had indeed gone to the Netherlands as a spy. Without hiding her light under a bushel, Aphra's letters dwelled on her services as the King's agent in Holland in the previous months. She had extracted secrets from this one, passed on intelligence from that one. But it had been an expensive business and her appeals for money had been ignored by her English spymasters, despite her petition after petition to the King, so that she had sold her jewellery in his royal cause, at last being forced to borrow £150 from an acquaintance in order to purchase her and her family's passage back home.

Penitence kept glancing up from the letters to study Aphra, finding the story they told and the fluent raciness with which they told it irreconcilable with the woman who'd written them.

Nothing in Aphra's style of dress complemented anything else; her grubby, low-necked, light-blue gown was of rich taffeta draped with scarves, some silk, some wool woven in barbaric colours, and to Penitence's untutored eye, owed more to the time of Charles I than Charles II. On top of her hair was a red taffeta cap of unknown origin with black feathers, one of them broken and dangling. She wore it with composure, apparently sure that if it wasn't the fashion now it soon would be. Without her youth she would have been merely eccentric, as it was she looked extraordinary, but not extraordinary in the right way; the limp attitudes she affected gave no hint of the recklessness which had sent her traipsing off to the Netherlands to become a spy. Penitence, having never met a woman spy, nor having imagined there could be any such animal, might have expected one to be bold-faced, sharp, something of a hussy. Yet, while the letters denoted their author to be an adventuress, a female with no margin of safety, somebody Penitence's grandmother would have described as 'having no hem to her garments', sitting on Penitence's bed was a woman whose appearance merely revealed amiable oddity.

Penitence returned to her reading. Even on her return to England, Aphra's pay had been withheld. The acquaintance demanded the return of his loan, she didn't have it, he took out a writ.

'Sir,' read Aphra's last letter to Killigrew:

> if you could guess at the affliction of my soul, you would, I am sure, pity me. 'Tis tomorrow that I must submit myself to prison. I have cried myself dead, and

could find it in my heart to break through all and get to
the King and never rise till he were pleased to pay this;
but I am sick and weak and unfit for it, or a prison.

'Killigrew?' asked Penitence, allowing herself to remember
the name.

'He recruited me in the first place,' complained Aphra. 'He is
head of the King's Company of Players and a powerful friend
of the dear King's.'

An actor. Faithless, like all actors.

'He's a powerful welcher,' said Master Johnson, 'nor the
dear King ain't much better.'

'He is our king.' For the first time Aphra was sharp.
'Parliament keeps him short, poor man. Sir Thomas, too, has
troubles, the Plague having interrupted the theatre.'

'He ain't in the Whitt,' pointed out Master Johnson, gloomily.

Neither are you. Despite her own misery, Penitence was
being drawn to the suspicion that this woman, little older than
her brother, carried him and their mother as if they were baby
apes clinging to her back.

'My guts is gnawing,' grumbled Master Johnson.

'Of course,' said Aphra, rising. 'We must dine. Mistress
Hurd, you will accompany us?'

Mistress Hurd was not hungry; she was also reluctant to
face anybody else. She felt as if P for Prostitute burned on the
skin of her forehead. Aphra insisted – 'One begs you, be our
guest' – and in minutes Penitence was being towed along a
passageway arm in arm with Master Johnson and an unsteady
Mrs Johnson while Aphra brought up the rear as if ushering
them to her own dining-hall.

By day Newgate became what it in fact was, a town locked
within a town. It shed some nightmares, gained others, while
its corridors assumed the bustle of streets of which cells were
the shops and meeting-places.

Twice Aphra called a halt while she stopped off, first at one
cell to collect a pair of shoes from the cobbler who inhabited
it, and then at another to hand in a tattered pair of gloves for

mending to the tailor who sat cross-legged on his bed, his cell crowded with suits of clothes on hangers. Further along, a wig-maker was fitting a customer with a periwig while three others passed the time in a game of cards.

Every cell door stood open, whatever the activity going on inside. A man enveloped in steam and a slipper bath, whose only item of clothing was his hat, cheerfully raised it to Penitence and Mrs Johnson as they passed.

'Is no one shut up?' asked Penitence over her shoulder.

'Not on this wing,' Aphra told her. 'The limbos are elsewhere. That's where they keep those to be transported or executed. And Quakers, of course.'

What struck Penitence about the prisoners in this part of Newgate was the normality of their demeanour. In one cell, which had curtains at its window, a husband read *The Intelligencer* while his visiting wife laid a table with provisions from a hamper — Penitence saw her add a sprig of parsley to his plate of chops — as their children played marbles in the corridor outside. Two gentlemen discussing the international situation swept off their hats to Mrs Johnson, Aphra and herself as if they were passing in a street.

There was no trace on the faces here of the desperation that existed in Flap Alley, no joy either, but few showed outward distress, merely the assurance of people going about their everyday concerns. The debtors and minor felons here had enough resources, or friends, to maintain life at a just-bearable level. They've got used to it, thought Penitence, incredulous.

The noise as they neared the dining-hall had the echoing resonance of any large gathering in any large, enclosed space. The smell of cabbage struggled for supremacy with the stink of bad health and poverty. The hall itself was beautiful, with the dimensions of a small cathedral nave, hammer-beam roof and high, arched windows, but religiosity ended with them and the huge refectory table down most of the room's length around which some three hundred men, women, children and dogs were eating — the animals making disconcerting pounces into the floor rushes as Newgate's more desperate rats tried to intrude on the feast.

Flap Alley was well represented. Penitence saw the tall figure of Bet crouching so far over her trencher to protect it from the fingers of the women around her that she was almost kneeling on the table. A mixed crowd of men and women by a wide hatch in the wall shoved and quarrelled for positions in the queue as they lined up for their ration, carrying a variety of dishes on which to receive it; some only a slice of bread, in one case a chamber pot. The sparse, grey substance splattered on to them by the servers' ladles was, presumably, Whitt stew.

As Aphra ushered them up the hall, they passed a frail, elderly man urinating against the side wall. Nobody was taking much notice of him, though one diner stopped eating long enough to shout: 'Not in here, Piddler, for Gawd's sake.'

A long trestle set crossways at the top of the room, like a baronial high table, kept off those prisoners in the body of the hall who subsisted on staple Newgate diet from those who could afford to pay for something better. Not much better – Newgate cooks were skilled at rendering meat, vegetables and gravy into a uniform shade of grey – but brought to its customers on platters by a serving man, though his manner and the keys at his belt showed he was a turnkey only doubling as waiter, while the condition of the napkin tucked under his armpit suggested he should have stayed with the day job.

Manners were better here. Three or four of the men actually rose as the Johnsons and Penitence took their seats, though one of them clanked noisily in doing so, having a ball and chain attached to one foot and manacles joining his wrists.

The courtesy was directed mainly at Aphra, obviously a favourite. She introduced Penitence: 'My dear friend, Mistress Hurd, recently arrived from the Americas.'

There was a general welcome, except from the waiter who grunted: 'Transported, was she? What you want eat, I ain't got all day.'

'I advise against the pork,' said a small man.

'And the beef,' said the man in fetters, 'and tell 'em to pour the ale back into the horse that pissed it. 'Morning, Aphra.'

Apart from Aphra, her brother and Penitence, he was the youngest of the diners, with sharp good looks and over-bright clothes.

'My poor Swaveley,' said Aphra. 'A very good day to you.'

Her brother showed his first animation: '*The* Swaveley?'

A woman at the far end of the table said clearly: 'And that such rogues should dine at our table is beyond belief. I shall complain to the Keeper.'

The waiter turned on her. 'Keeper's orders, so blurt to you, missus. Ordinary wants to talk to him.'

'The Ordinary can talk to him in his cell,' complained the woman.

'Can't then,' said Swaveley. 'I'm partickler who I talk to.'

Even Penitence had heard of Swaveley, a highwayman whose exploits, while committed mainly south of the river, had been widely publicized and gained the Rookery's hard-won admiration. To judge from the nudges and looks accorded him from the body of the hall, in Newgate he had achieved hero status. Even the waiter treated him with respect.

To Penitence he was merely part of the horrific kaleidoscope that flickered around the edges of her misery. *I must get out.*

Aphra was choosing her meat for her, she was aware that Mrs Johnson was agitating for something stronger than ale to go with it and that Swaveley, against Aphra's wishes, was ordering it, that Aphra and her brother were arguing as to which of them should keep the larger share of Killigrew's ten crowns, but these sounds and movements were removed from her. *Get out. I must get out.* When the food came she forced some down, uncaring as to what it was or how bad, so long as it sustained her strength to plot deliverance. It wasn't until Aphra began pestering Swaveley that she became conscious of another's reality.

'One begs you to plead,' Aphra was saying, earnestly. 'I beg you. It's a terrible death.'

'Ain't none of 'em congenial,' said Swaveley. 'Least with this one, me old gaffer gets me horse.'

Master Johnson nudged Penitence enthusiastically: 'He won't plead. Chosen to be pressed. Ain't been a pressing in years.'

'What's pressing?'

Swaveley put his manacled hands behind his head and leaned back, regarding her with amusement: 'Ain't they got pressing in the colonies?'

'I d-don't think so.'

'Backward, ain't they?'

The diners enlightened her. By 'standing mute', refusing to plead either innocent or guilty, a malefactor earned the right to be pressed to death rather than hanged. '*Peine forte et dure,*' moaned Aphra. The procedure's advantage, from the malefactor's point of view, was that it allowed his estate, goods and chattels to be passed on to his heirs instead of forfeited to the crown, as they would be if he went to the gallows.

'Old Rowley ain't getting my Bess,' said Swaveley, firmly. 'Too good for him, she is. Sweet little Doncaster-cut like that, he'd have her pulling a coach, or give her to one of his wenches.'

'I'm wagering you won't bear three hundred pounds' weight,' blurted out Master Johnson.

Swaveley grinned. 'Put a dozen more decus on for me, and send the winnings to Bess.'

He reminded Penitence of the Tippin boys. He was little more than a boy himself, made old, like the Tippins, by enforced cunning. His exaltation from attention and terror made him more alive than anyone in the whole room. His pale nostrils twitched at every movement, his own or anybody else's, like an animal aware of scent imperceptible to humans.

Benedick could grow up like him. Here was the child of another Rookery who'd opted for the criminal life with its built-in early death. Now it was nearly on him. She wondered whether, if the choice could be offered again, he'd make a different one. Perhaps not. By his lights, he was going out with glory.

I'll save Benedick. I can't save this lad but I'll save Benedick.

A large shape exuding the smell of alcohol and sweetish sweat took a seat opposite. 'Tut, tut,' said Newgate's Ordinary, 'eating without benefit of grace? Doubtless you would still wish me to say it?'

'No,' said everybody, but the Ordinary insisted on intoning some Latin to which nobody paid attention.

Being among the last things men and women on the scaffold saw before the noose tightened, it was regrettable that the prison chaplain's nose showed signs of having been directed into more ale cups than prayer books. His knobbled and alarmingly puce face shone with perspiration and seemed about to burst. From the stains on his velvet coat and from his aggressive bonhomie, he had dined already, better, and elsewhere.

'Now, my son,' he said, focusing on Swaveley, 'About your confession . . .'

'I ain't making one,' said Swaveley, wiping his platter with a piece of bread held in both hands. 'And I ain't having you sing the dismal ditty while I'm being ironed, so stick that in your ribs, old giblets.'

The Ordinary's forefinger was as brown as his teeth, shading to black at the tip from tamping tobacco. He wagged it at Swaveley, to indicate that he took the insult as jovial raillery. 'If you won't consider your soul, my son, think of your fame. See how I have reconciled our next unfortunates to the public . . .' He fetched a sheaf of bills from his pocket and distributed them round the table.

Swaveley crumpled his between his cuffed hands and flicked it at the Ordinary's stomach. 'I got fame already.'

Swaveley's generosity in the matter of gin had gained him an ally in Mrs Johnson who toppled affectionately on to his shoulder. 'Knock his hat off,' she said.

'Mother.'

Master Johnson was scanning a bill. 'Our Affie could write a better'n 'n this.'

Aphra, restraining her mother with one hand, scanned hers. 'As a matter of fact, one could.'

Mrs Johnson toppled again, belligerently: 'My Aphra writes, so there,' she told the Ordinary. 'Wrote to the King.'

Her professional interest aroused, Penitence glanced at the bill. It was the last, and lurid, confession of a James Spiggot and a Mary Moders before being executed, he for blackmail and theft, she for fraud and prostitution, and as vile a piece of printing as she'd seen.

'They ain't being turned off 'til Monday,' said the small man. 'Supposing they get reprieved?'

'Reprieved?' bellowed the Ordinary. 'With a confession as sweet as this? They'd better not.'

The small man was still considering the bill. 'It could do with a nice woodcut,' he said. 'I could do you a nice woodcut.'

A turnkey approached the highwayman. 'Couple of wagtails asking for you, Swaveley. Shall I show 'em to your cell?'

'Pretty?' asked Swaveley.

'Young anyways,' said the turnkey.

The highwayman turned to the table and rose. 'My public,' he said. 'Time for me greens, ladies and gents. So farewell.'

The Ordinary grabbed at his sleeve. 'Spend not thy last days in uncleanness, my son, but go shriven to the feet of God.'

'Oh, make it up,' Swaveley told him, 'you will anyways.' He shuffled out of the hall to applause, the Ordinary still talking in his wake.

Mrs Johnson was so overcome that Aphra told her brother to take her home. She and Penitence accompanied them to the guardroom at the prison's entrance where Mrs Johnson took against the hat of the turnkey who insisted on charging Master Johnson sixpence for the privilege of letting them out.

'My poor mother,' said Aphra, standing at the gate to wave them off. 'Had my father not died when he did, she would have graced her position as Governor-General's wife of Surinam. Alas, his death aboard ship whilst we were yet on our way out there quite o'erwhelmed her.'

Penitence didn't know where Surinam was, but, watching Mrs Johnson overwhelmed by the desire to sit down in the road, she found it difficult to imagine her, even sober, gracing it in any high capacity. Unless the late Mr Johnson had married beneath him, the Johnsons just weren't the sort of family from whom colonial administrators were chosen. Their accents weren't right, Aphra's being spurious and Mrs Johnson's downright common.

She didn't want to doubt her new-found friend, but she was inclined to think that Aphra Behn had invented the story.

By day two in Newgate, all of it spent in Aphra's company, Penitence was inclined to think that she had also invented Mr Behn. Aphra's accounts of him were inconsistent; one moment he'd been a Dutch merchant, the next a City business man. He'd died of old age, he'd died of the Plague. The only definite fact to be ascertained of the late Mr Behn was that he was dead.

By day three in Newgate, Penitence was inclined to think that Aphra had even invented herself, but by then she didn't care.

This was an advance for Penitence who, Puritan-like, was irritated by elusiveness. But she had come to recognize Aphra not as a liar but as someone whose imagination created its own truths. She had been born in Kent, that much she acknowledged. Pretty, precocious and, most likely, poor, she had pursued the life of the country gentry whose homes dominated her vision, somehow persuading her family to provide her with an education. The world as young Aphra had wished it to be was exciting and romantic, and her imagination, not to mention her ambition, was so powerful that it had bounced over all unpleasantnesses into adulthood with the excitement and romance still intact. Considering her present position, her refusal to abandon that belief made the woman ridiculous but it also made her generous and formidable. The manicured creation she had become radiated such wish-fulfilling optimism into the darkness of Newgate that it was survivable, not just for herself, but for Penitence who was commandeered into the fiction Aphra made of it.

'Sister Penitence,' she said, coming into Penitence's cell on Sunday morning, 'did you not hear the bell for Mass?'

'Aphra,' said Penitence, warningly, 'I am *not* turning Papist.' Aphra's sojourn in the Netherlands had given her what Penitence considered to be an overly rosy and affectionate view of Flemish convent life and Roman Catholicism in general.

'Would that we were not forced to,' said Aphra, whose hands were clasped round her Bible, 'but walled up in these cloisters as we are, we must conform or be punished. And think, Sister, perhaps our lovers will find an opportunity to procure our freedom while we are at our devotions.'

They had two mythical lovers, Castor and Amphion, who spent their days lurking outside the walls plotting their ladies' escape from whatever bondage they happened to be in that day.

Penitence picked up her Bible; it was easier to swim with Aphra's tide of invention than resist it, and more fun. Besides, she had not yet been to the prison chapel.

They glided along the corridor, disconcerting the cell inmates by returning their greetings with a 'Pax vobiscum'.

'How did we get into a convent?' asked Penitence.

'Sister, Sister,' chided Aphra. 'Can you forget so soon our father's insistence that we marry those rich elderly suitors? Our brave refusal? Do not despair, Castor and Amphion will rescue us.'

'They didn't rescue us yesterday,' Penitence pointed out.

Yesterday she and Aphra had been immured in a harem ruled by a cruel Turk who had captured them in a pirate raid on their ship.

'They will today,' said Aphra.

From the regularity in which the two of them were in danger of being forced into marriage with rich and uncongenial suitors, Penitence had come to the conclusion that Aphra had, after all, made a real marriage, that it had been horrible enough to leave her with an aversion to husbands in general and that she had only kept Mr Behn's name because it was more unusual than Johnson and added a foreign shimmer to the haze that was Aphra's past.

At the bottom of the stairs their way was blocked by Sumner, a debtor who was enjoying more power in his position as head of the prisoners' tribunal than he had as a grocer. Two of his cronies stood at his back. 'I'm sorry to say as the tribunal's been complained to about you, Mistress Behn,' he said, ponderously. 'And your friend here.'

In her role as a novitiate Aphra genuflected, making him blink. 'Mea culpa, Father. In what have we offended?'

'You been playing rackets. I'm sorry to say as ladies can't play rackets.'

A beaten piece of ground with a wall behind Press Yard had been turned into a rackets court. It would never have occurred to Penitence that it was available to women, but it hadn't occurred to Aphra that it was not: 'One was initiated into the game during one's attendance on the Duke of York.' It was a long time since Penitence had done anything athletic, and her dismay at finding herself out of condition, as well as her enjoyment of the game, had made her vow to play regularly. Now, she supposed, she could not. To her surprise, Aphra's sharp 'But we played it' supposed nothing of the sort.

'Yes, well.' Sumner had been expecting an apology or excuses, but he soldiered on bravely. 'There's been complaints as it ain't ladylike, and Master Giltspur said as he was kept waiting for his game acause you was playing.'

'Master Giltspur, friend of Dick Cromwell?' asked Aphra.

'Yes, well, I don't know nothing about that, but he always—'

'So, if one may sum up,' went on an Aphra in whom all conventual submissiveness had disappeared, 'it comes to this, that women are not to be allowed to exercise for their health *in the King's own prison* because it interferes with the sport of regicides.'

'Yes, well. Well, no . . .'

'Mistress Hurd and myself will be on the court tomorrow, Master Sumner, and one is sure that His Majesty, *with whom I am in correspondence*, will be interested to hear of the politics of those who try to bar us.'

She swept on, followed by an admiring Penitence. 'Aphra, that was colossal.'

'They shall not play because they are women,' fumed Aphra. 'Did one serve one's king for *this*?'

The chapel was full, not because of the drawing power of the Ordinary's sermons, but because Newgate's latest batch of those condemned to death were on show to visitors – tomorrow being their day for hanging. They had been crowded into a pen erected in the middle of the nave, some swearing and shouting at the congress of people who had come to stare at them. In the pulpit the Ordinary was trying to preach a sermon which could barely be heard over the noise. The Piddler, having just added his contribution to the chaos, was being ejected by an outraged member of the congregation.

It was two of the visitors who caught Penitence's eye, both men, both exquisitely dressed and both holding pomanders to their noses. They were pleased to be indulging in the fancy that the prisoners were horses in a parade ring.

'Look ye here, Wilmot, here's a winner.' One of them poked his ivory staff bedecked with ribbons into the thick neck of one of the condemned's better male specimens, who spat on it. 'Regard the muscles. I'll wager a hundred guineas he'll go all of fifteen minutes.'

'You *are* a Dutchman, Charles, did your mother never confess? He'll be weighted.' The man called Wilmot lightly struck the prisoner on the shoulder with his own, also be-ribboned, staff. 'Neigh to me, my fine stallion, you've a sweetheart who'll hang on your prick and so pull you out of the race. Not so? It's the light ones who last the course. I won five hundred once on a bare-ribbed mare who lasted seventeen and a half. I pick this one.' He prodded a thin, pale woman who was sitting on the floor, cuddling an equally thin, pale girl of about ten years old. 'Win for me tomorrow, Rosinante, and I'll see your filly gets the stake money.'

So these are rakes. Although Puritan hagiography had vented most of its spleen on the evil-living and effeminacy of the high-born young men who had attached themselves to the court of Charles II, Penitence was unprepared for the impact of the reality. Their long wigs curled over silk, embroidered coats that were waisted and fell below their knees to show the bottom of frilled breeches and high-heeled shoes. Everything that could bear lace or ribbon was laced and be-ribboned, from the bunches on their shoulders to their insteps. They were a deliberate outrage, in their costume, the strut of their walk and the high flute of their drawl. But what Penitence had not expected was their aggression, a radiation of power without rules; she was in the presence of tigers.

Because she couldn't cope with the thought of men who could bet on the length of time it would take for human beings to be strangled, she dismissed them. More important was the woman one of them had prodded, and her child. The mother and daughter formed a tableau of stillness in the turbulence of the chapel, noticing nobody, clinging together in their own pen of desperation where their minutes together ticked away in its silence.

Penitence could hardly bear to look at them, but she couldn't bear to look anywhere else. 'Who's that?'

'The fair one is Sir Charles Sedley,' said Aphra, excitedly, 'and I think, I'm not sure, but I *think* the other is the Earl of Rochester.'

'Not them,' said Penitence. 'The mother with the little girl.'

'That? That's Mary Moders.'

The prostitute. And nearer to the meaning of the crucifix on the altar than anyone else in the chapel.

The rakes had tired of their game. The fair one was clambering up into the pulpit and was heard to say in the sudden silence: 'Reverend, I should like to address a few words of comfort to these unfortunates.'

The Ordinary sweated ingratiatingly as he vacated his position. 'Of course, Sir Charles, I am sure we shall all be edified.'

'You will, indeed.' Sir Charles folded his hands, raised his eyes to Heaven and spoke in an unctuous sing-song. 'Brethren, our lesson today comes from the Sedley book of epigrams, Chapter 2, verse 1:

'If death must come as oft as breath departs,
Then he must often die who often farts;
And if to die be but to lose one's breath,
Then death's a fart . . .'

He turned his back, wriggled his breeches down, exposed a plump, pink bottom over the edge of the pulpit and broke wind:

'. . . And so a fart for death.'

Pulling up his breeches, he turned round. 'So endeth the lesson.' An astounded silence was broken by a slow handclap from the Earl of Rochester to which Sir Charles, doffing his hat, left the pulpit, bowed to a sickly-smiling Ordinary and rejoined his friend on his way out.

Aphra pushed forward: 'You may not remember, Sir Charles, but we met at His Grace the Duke of York's a while ago ... Aphra Behn.'

She was spoiling his exit but he took the new opportunity. 'Mistress Behn. Wilmot, it's our old friend Mistress Behn. And looking so well. The Duke talks of you constantly. Wilmot, wasn't the Duke talking of Mistress Behn to the King but yesterday?'

'Never off his lips,' said the Earl of Rochester, yawning.

To Penitence's fury, Aphra pulled her forward. 'Permit me to present my friend, Mistress Hurd.'

Sir Charles bowed. 'Mistress Hurd's name is also the toast of court. Ah, how pleasant to stroll through this orangery and find such fruit. Shall we move on out of the sun and sup a dish of tay?'

Penitence dragged her eyes away from the mother and child. 'Thank you,' she said, 'I prefer the present company.'

It was a mistake. They couldn't bear contempt. Two pairs of eyes focused on hers, one pair suddenly vicious, the other interested. 'One can see it would be more congenial to you,' said the Earl of Rochester.

'I believe we have offended Mistress Hurd,' said Sir Charles Sedley.

Had she cared enough to bother, she would have told them they were a sacrilege, not in their shamelessness nor their schoolboy shocks, but in their inability to feel pity. However, she didn't care enough, and if she stayed in the same place as Mary Moders and her child any longer, her heart was going to break. She turned on her heel and went back to her cell.

'Just high-spirited,' said Aphra, when she came back later.

'Just high decadence,' said Penitence. 'Nor they didn't know you from Adam.'

'They will,' said Aphra, comfortably. 'And one had to admire the epigram, however indelicate. A nice turn of phrase, our rakes.'

'Give me Castor and Pollux any day.'

'Amphion, dear,' said Aphra, 'Castor and Amphion. Ah, those dear gallants. May Neptune preserve their ship from storm as they plough through the seas towards this desert isle on which we've been cast up while escaping from—'

'What happened to the convent?' asked Penitence.

'It got dissolved,' said Aphra, 'after a visit from Sir Charles Sedley and the Earl of Rochester.'

Chapter 3

AT FIRST Aphra merely provided the flimsy blossoms decorating what Penitence saw as her life, a plant whose centre was rotten. If, in the course of their games, she forgot for a few minutes that she had pleasured and would have to go on pleasuring George or be thrown back into Flap Alley, some word, a glimpse of a bed, would spit her like a spear through the stomach.

Disgust at herself coloured everything. George she regarded not so much a person as a phenomenon, like Newgate, which was happening to her. Her mind screamed 'Whore' at her by day and the Reverend Block came into her dreams thundering exultant damnation. 'I could have said yes to you and avoided the whole bloody business,' she told him wearily. She felt physically and continually nauseated.

When Dorinda brought Benedick on a visit after Penitence's first encounter with George, she was reluctant to hold him. 'I feel so dirty,' she said, 'I feel dirty all the time. Didn't you?'

'Not after that old bastard,' said Dorinda of her grandfather. 'You'll get used to it, Prinks. I never had a choice and you ain't neither if you don't want to go back to the Alley. And you don't. My ma died there.'

'Did she?' Penitence had never heard Dorinda mention her mother.

'I *think* it was my ma,' said Dorinda, doubtfully.

Penitence knew she would never get used to it, and didn't. On the second, third and fourth nights when the turnkey came for his rent, she was vomiting even as he led her to the empty cell which, for some reason, he felt to be appropriate for their assignations. She was grateful he didn't insist on using the room she lived in and equally found the condemned cell appropriate in that what went on between them there was in itself a form of death. But a better form of death in that she passed through it and was alive again.

She had the choice of going mad or rationalizing her harlotry. 'Better than death,' she kept telling herself. 'Better than Flap Alley.' It was a form of professionalism; she couldn't do as Dorinda and the others at the Cock and Pie had done and regard whoring as a job like any other and forget about it when she was off duty, but the knowledge that it was essential if she was to stay alive stopped it overwhelming her.

Dorinda was helpful on procedure. 'Oh, a fumbler,' she said as Penitence reluctantly described George's sexual proclivities. 'That's easy. Brim him early.'

It added to her self-contempt to employ the art of early-brimming – playing more elaborately to his fantasy, embroidering to absurdity the character of the despising aristocrat, allowing her disgust to display as he fumbled and sucked at her breasts – but it was so effective that sometimes his ejaculation occurred before they reached the bed, and he was too old and usually too busy to insist on another turn.

She became skilled at it. It took on the aspect of work, a filthy job which could be ameliorated by expertise. 'Better than Flap Alley' became an incantation.

She had discovered the truth women in her position had known through the ages: there is no fate worse than death when you have a child to live for and when death is the only alternative.

She refused to allow the gaoler humanity since he had shown her none, but she had to admit he played by the rules.

His power over her was absolute; he could have summoned her to the condemned cell every time he came on duty, but he'd reckoned the cost of her room over Press Yard to be worth £20 a week to her and the price of her service to him at £10 and, on this accounting, only called her out twice in every seven days.

Since he was a permanent night gaoler, they rarely ran into each other during the day, but on the one occasion when they did, his thumbs-up and winks sent her into a frenzy of fear that everybody would guess their relationship. Sensitized, she read into the other gaolers' every smirk that they were aware of what was going on. She was sure that Aphra did, although her friend never mentioned it; the woman's especial kindness on days after the nights in the condemned cell suggested she had heard Penitence's dragging footsteps follow George's excitedly pattering boots past her cell door.

She was paying for her room not just with her body, but with her youth. Her face took on the expression of one who in the extremes of need had asked for God's intervention and, receiving none, would never ask for it again.

The Assizes were still trying to catch up on lists interrupted by the Plague, so that the numbers hanged on execution days tended to be large, while spectators, deprived of their amusement for so long, turned up in their thousands. Aphra's mother and brother followed the carts to Tyburn and on their next visit were full of detail which Penitence refused to hear. She didn't want to know how long it had taken Mary Moders to die. What interested her was Peter Johnson's account of how the Ordinary's 'confessions' had sold. 'He'd got six or more barkers shouting 'em at thruppence a sheet and they went like hot cakes.'

'He ordered eight reams p-printed,' said Penitence, who'd taken the trouble to find out.

'And they all sold,' said Master Johnson. 'You never seen such a crowd. There was more died in the crush than on the gallows. Gawd knows how much he'll make from Swaveley's confession if he gets it. That'll fetch 'em. There ain't been a pressing in years. He could sell that at fi'pence.'

'Sixpence with a nice woodcut,' said Penitence, thoughtfully.

When Mrs and Master Johnson had gone, she said: 'Aphra, you know my printing press . . . and you know Swaveley . . .'

Aphra was ahead of her: 'How many sheets in a ream?'

Penitence smiled. 'Five hundred and sixteen.'

'So he sold . . . what's eight times five hundred and sixteen?'

With difficulty they worked out that the Ordinary had, not counting the cost of paper and barkers, raked in an astonishing £51 14s 4d in the course of one afternoon. They got carried away with calculation: if they printed ten reams . . . if they sold at sixpence a copy . . . if they had a nice woodcut . . . if Swaveley would agree.

'Will he?'

'It would be base for us to do it if he will not,' said Aphra, firmly. 'On the other hand, he is intent on his course, one is favourable to him, and one can wipe the floor with the Ordinary when it comes to syntax. Did I tell you I was writing a play?'

'Yes,' said Penitence. She still didn't believe it. 'Aphra, what we'd want is not so much literature as sprightliness.'

'One can certainly be sprightlier than the Ordinary.'

Penitence sat back. This unsuspected business sense of Aphra's, while most welcome, was still surprising in such a fantastical woman. 'I thought you'd despise the enterprise.'

'Dear one,' said Aphra, 'one does not intend to pass one's life in Newgate. One intends to *get on*. Ah, if one could live on love *for* love. But the world is against it, alas.' She patted Penitence's knee. 'There are occasions when we poor women must stoop, however against our nature, if we are to win our freedom.'

Penitence felt tears come into her eyes. 'Thank you,' she said.

In a way it was as much a fantasy as one of Aphra's. She didn't really think it would succeed. It was men who thought up schemes to make money. Women didn't initiate things: they reacted. Everything that had happened to her had been in response to an act of God or man. Her enterprise in liberating the printing press had only come about because it had been going begging ... it was hopeless, They would foil the plan, whoever They were, it wouldn't succeed.

But it began to. Swaveley said he'd be damned if he confessed, but he'd tell Mrs Behn his life story if she wanted to publish it, and proceeded to do so with a frankness, especially on the subject of his sexual prowess, which raised a flush on even Aphra's cheeks.

'On horseback?' repeated Penitence incredulously. 'You can't.'

'He assured me that he did,' said Aphra. 'And performed the same exploit with the lady in the next coach he robbed. He tells me both were willing. And enjoyed it.'

'B-Bartholomew me.'

'Exactly,' said Aphra. 'Master Swaveley's life may be short but it has most certainly been full. And, one imagines, will sell.'

'It'll burn the paper,' said Penitence. 'We'd better print on tin.'

While Penitence visited the cell of the little man who had complained of the pork in the dining-hall and turned out to be an engraver, Aphra demanded, and got, an interview with Newgate's Keeper for permission to attend Swaveley's hearing at the Old Bailey the next day.

She came back fuming. 'The nauseous old fool said i'faith and diddums a delicate young thing like oneself would faint at such things as I should see there.'

'So you said . . .?'

'One told him the late Mr Behn had fought for the return of English justice and it was a poor thing if his widow was to be denied the chance of seeing it in action.'

Aphra, Penitence noticed, used the late Mr Behn like an umbrella, wielding him when necessary, raising him to protect herself from charges against her respectability, and forgetting him when he wasn't of use.

'*Did* he fight for the return of English justice?'

'That's neither here nor there,' said Aphra. 'That they shall not see it because they are women is the point.'

'But the Keeper refused permission.'

'Oh, he gave it,' said Aphra. 'Eventually. It's the obturation one had to fight through to get it that puts one out of countenance.'

She came back from the Old Bailey pale and feebly flapping. 'The flies, my dear, and the *people*.' Penitence had to fetch her a restorative from the tap room before she could give her account.

Swaveley had persisted in his refusal to plead and the judge had passed his sentence. 'You, Richard Swaveley, shall be sent back to the prison from whence you come and lie naked on the earth, without litter, rushes or raiment save that for decency, and one arm shall be drawn with a cord to one quarter, the other arm to another quarter and in the same manner let it be done with your legs, and let there be laid upon your body iron and stone as much as you can bear or more, till you die.'

'Should we be doing this?'

But the Ordinary was going to, even if they didn't. Unaware of competition, the man was boasting that he was preparing for publication an Awful Warning as Evinced by the Wicked Life of John Swaveley, Highwayman.

'He'll make his up,' said Aphra. 'Ours will be the real thing. And Awfuller.'

The anti-pork engraver, whose name turned out to be Clarins, agreed to wait for his fee until the bills should be sold, but they couldn't expect the same patience from the paper suppliers who would want cash on delivery.

MacGregor and Dorinda came in for a consultation, leaving Benedick in the care of Mistress Palmer. 'We made a wee profit from the Fifth Monarchist madman,' MacGregor said, 'but not enough to buy ten reams, leave alone the ink. Have ye no more assets to sell, Penitence? I'd pawn my pipes, but the dear things are long gone, long gone.'

'While we're on the subject,' said Penitence, 'there's to be no more p-printing for Fifth Monarchist or any other madmen. We don't want trouble from the authorities.'

'We'll maybe get it anyway,' said MacGregor, examining the confessions of James Spiggot and Mary Moders. 'This was set by Catnatch of Seven Dials. He's a licensed printer. We're not.'

'Our bills won't carry our name.'

'Aye, maybe, but we'll be needing barkers with a good turn of speed not to be caught.'

Penitence's eye met Dorinda's. Together they said: 'Tippins.'

MacGregor nodded. 'Ye'll no' catch the Tippin lads. But there'll be precious little *to* catch if we don't get the siller.'

There was silence as they racked their brains.

'Oh, that one hadn't been forced to sell one's rings,' said Aphra.

'Oh, if one had kept one's ballocking diadem.' Dorinda was jealous of Penitence's friendship with Aphra Behn and mocked her continually, though Aphra herself took no notice. 'Here,' she said, throwing something into Penitence's lap, 'why not sell that? You paid enough for it.'

It was a silver oval. A gentleman's embossed travelling mirror.

Damn.

She had put it away in the attic and tried to forget it, like everything else about him. The hurt and anger at his manner of leaving had redoubled, tripled, at finding herself carrying his baby, to say nothing of the realization that, by the act of bearing the child, she was, in the eyes of the world at least, the whore he thought her to be.

She'd railed against it over and over. 'It's unfair.'

Dorinda had shrugged. 'Fairness ain't life's speciality.'

They had tried to abort the baby by every way Dorinda knew. On her instructions, Penitence had drunk gin, taken hot baths and jumped from the clerestory – ending up with a hangover, a sprained ankle and still pregnant.

'Old Ma Perkins over in the Cut used to do it for us with a knitting needle,' Dorinda said, 'but the Plague got her.'

It was as well this option was closed to Penitence because otherwise she would have taken it. She was desperate; she didn't know how to support herself, let alone a child. She was ashamed and frightened. Badly she wanted Her Ladyship, except that the thought that she was following her mother's path down to Hell loaded her with such depression that she had moved into the fog which was only now beginning to disperse.

Her one advantage had been that she was among the sinners of the Old World rather than the saints of the New who would have cast her out, as they had her mother. The Rookery didn't give a damn that she was unmarried; most of its mothers were unmarried. Indeed, it made her more one of their own, and, with the occasional nudge and wink, it supported her in a way for which she was to be grateful to the end of her days.

Now, regarding the mirror in her lap, she found that she could tolerate the memory of the actor. She could hardly blame him for giving way that night to a passion against which she herself had been helpless, and of which she had been as much an instigator as he was. And as for his persistence in thinking her a prostitute . . . well, he'd had plenty to go on, and she'd never been able to tell him she wasn't. *And I am now, anyway.*

She remained still for so long that MacGregor took up the looking-glass and opened it. 'Ah, Master King,' he said, to the portrait inside, 'I wonder what's happened to you, laddie. I liked ye fine. You gave us joy.'

'Some of us more than others,' said Dorinda, tartly.

Joy. But perhaps MacGregor was right to use the word. Her very speech was the actor's gift. Like her son.

One day she might even forgive him.

MacGregor bit the edge. 'Fine siller,' he said. 'Aye, the bauble will fetch a good penny or two.'

Aphra Behn stretched out a limp hand. 'May I?' She looked at the portrait and her eyes widened. 'Did you say "King"?'

She knows him. Suddenly Penitence could bear no more discussion of the man. She hadn't got over him that much. *Find out later.*

She took the mirror and handed it across to Dorinda. 'Sell

it.' She could trust Dorry to get the best price, whereas though MacGregor was better than he used to be and turning out to be a good printer, his money still tended to transmute itself into ale.

Later, as usual on fine evenings, Aphra and Penitence strolled together round Press Yard to avail themselves of what little air there was. Press Yard was deep, like a lidless box, and the attentions of the Piddler and several cats had not enhanced its atmosphere, but the sky above it was turning gold, while a lilac straggling over the wall from the Keeper's private garden attracted peacock butterflies.

It was the prison's quiet time. The habitués of the tap room who made the place a tumult by day and dangerous by night were sleeping off the afternoon session in preparation for the evening's, and Press Yard was left to the sober and harmlessly eccentric. An elderly debtor who had computed how many turns of the Yard made up the distance to Hampstead was religiously walking them as if he were taking a constitutional, as he had in the days before debt took away his freedom.

He swept off his hat. 'Good evening, ladies, a pleasant evening. Forgive me not pausing, but I must save my breath for the hill.'

'Good evening, Master Salter.'

'Aphra.'

'My dear?'

'Aphra, that portrait this afternoon. You recognized it, didn't you?'

'I wasn't sure and didn't pursue it since you seemed bent on not having the matter mentioned, but . . . and, of course, he was younger then though the likeness was remarkable, but again . . .'

'For God's sake, Aphra, who was it?'

'Sir Anthony Torrington.'

Anthony Torrington? She tried squeezing her memory of Henry King into the new name. It didn't fit. Neither did the 'Sir'. Too respectable, too reminiscent of the squirearchy. 'Are you sure?'

'One wouldn't wager one's life, but it's not a face to forget.'

'Where had you seen it before?'

'In the chambers of Sir George Downing. Somewhat fleetingly, but I made enquiries . . .' Aphra fluttered her eyelashes. '. . . to discover that he was the King's secret emissary to Prince William of Orange.'

'When was this?'

'When I was in the Netherlands. Sir George is officially our ambassador to Holland, less officially the King's Scoutmaster-General.'

'A spymaster.'

'Certainly Downing sees it as part of his duties to gather intelligence. There were those of us out there who knew that keys were removed from the pockets of the De Witt brothers while they were asleep, papers taken from their closet, left in Downing's hands for an hour, and returned without anyone knowing they'd gone.'

'Ah, ladies, how beautiful the Heath is on a June evening.'

'Indeed it is, Master Salter.'

'One was of considerable assistance to Sir George,' continued Aphra as they strolled on, 'and warned him that the Dutch were impudent enough to consider invading my own dear Surinam and even had plans to sail up the Thames. He was good enough to congratulate me most handsomely, though without the financial reward one could have wished. "Madam," he said, "we'll pass it on, but our royal master knows better how to use what comes out of his arse than his agents." A forceful speaker, Sir George.'

Penitence persisted. 'So this Torrington was a royal spy?'

Aphra shrugged. 'How you do use the word. It was rumoured that Sir Anthony was received into every court in Europe and spoke the language of most.'

'But if he was in the Netherlands when you were, he can't be the Henry King who was in the Rookery during the Plague.'

'Ah,' said Aphra, 'but he could. He left shortly after I arrived. A little bird told me that the dear King and Sir Anthony had a falling-out. Something to do with the French. He was recalled in disgrace.'

In a winter's alley in the Rookery a drunken voice had once suggested they sit upon the ground and tell sad stories of the death of kings. 'And how you can't trust any of the buggers.'

And she thought she'd known him.

'One doesn't wish to pry,' said Aphra, delicately, 'but do I gather there was an understanding between you and this Henry King?'

'No understanding at all.' And because Penitence was weary of people who pretended to be one thing while being another, she told Aphra her whole story. The butterflies retired to wherever butterflies retire to, Master Salter returned from Hampstead Heath, sounds of roistering grew from the tap room, a star appeared in the darkening square of sky, and strollers in Press Yard were encouraged back to their cells by turnkeys' shouts of 'All in, all in'.

Excitedly, Aphra clasped Penitence's hands. 'What *romance*. My dear, my dear, such star-crossed drama. And all enacted from balconies while the Plague raged. The Muses couldn't do it justice.'

'Don't tell 'em then.' Penitence was alarmed. She had expected some reaction, but not this rapturous twittering.

'All in, I said.' The turnkey was becoming agitated. 'Didn't you bloody women hear me say All in?'

'They heard you, fellow,' said Aphra, 'down in Cheapside. One will go when one's *ready*.' She took Penitence's arm to saunter to the steps to their room. 'What a play it would make.'

The gush of her enthusiasm took hours to subside. 'Romeo and Juliet, Pyramus and Thisbe, King Cophetua and Zenelophon. In faith, my dear, if I had a lyre I'd sing the lay of Sir Anthony and Penitence.'

'It wasn't like that,' said Penitence, wearily.

'But it was, my dear. It is. He'll come back, don't you see? He'll find the truth of it and return to you, swim across the Hellespont, like Leander.'

'I hope he drowns. I don't want him back.'

'Of course you do.' Aphra brushed aside detail. 'The Torringtons are wealthy, or were. An old Cavalier family with

250

acres and acres in Somerset. I believe Augustus, the father, was even sheriff at one time, but they lost everything under the Protectorate when they went into exile with the dear King. I think they have it back now.'

'Cavaliers,' disapproved Penitence.

'Of course Cavaliers,' said Aphra. 'Would you have your lover a damned Roundhead? Oh, forgive me, dear. One forgets your provenance.'

'Henry King hadn't a penny to bless himself with.'

Aphra pressed her fingertips against her forehead. 'There was a quarrel. Some disagreement over politics. I seem to remember his father disapproved of his ma— Oh dear.'

'His marriage?'

'Well, yes.' Aphra was crestfallen, then perked up. 'But it was a long time ago, and I seem to remember she died, or there was a scandal, *something*.'

'This Sir Anthony seems unfortunate in his relations,' said Penitence. 'A quarrelsome fellow.'

'High-spirited,' said Aphra, automatically. 'But think, should his father die he will come and claim you, and little Benedick will be heir to a fortune.'

'Should his wife die, and his legitimate children die, and if I don't spit in his eye. Look at me, Aphra, I want you to p-p-promise that you will never, ever, repeat what I told you tonight.'

Aphra sobered. 'Has it been so terrible?'

'Yes, it has. Benedick and I will manage without him.'

'But . . .'

'If, *if* we get the Swaveley bill printed before the poor man's buried.'

'As good as done,' said Aphra. 'It only remains to be written.'

'Then write it.'

Left alone, Penitence stayed at her window. The warmth of the June night managed to overlay the staleness of Press Yard with the scent of lilac. Aphra had taken Henry King away and replaced him with an unrecognizable person from a world for which Penitence had only contempt. The funny, gangling, attractive man had gone, had never existed. He'd worn a mask and been somebody else underneath it. *Well and good. All the easier to dismiss him.*

She could almost smile at the romance Aphra had made out of their pitiful affair. If Aphra Behn had charge of the world it would be more entertaining than the squalid feculence it was. Tomorrow was the night George came for his rent. A week after that a young man would be lain on the cobbles below and crushed to death.

And not a Leander to save either of us. Whoever *he* was.

There hadn't been a pressing at Newgate since the execution of a Major Strangeways for the murder of his brother-in-law eleven years previously, so the prison went *en fête* for Swaveley's. All those with rooms overlooking Press Yard were turned out of them for the day to accommodate the Quality, who were paying high prices for a good view. A grandstand was erected in the Yard itself for judges, aldermen and other dignitaries. It was rumoured the King might attend, or at least send one of his mistresses.

Quakers and hard-core criminals kept in the limbos were transferred to a deeper dungeon where their cries would not disturb the occasion.

There was even an attempt to clean Newgate in the unlikely event that the authorities might wish to inspect it, but that petered out after the Yard had been scrubbed.

'I wonder they don't put up bunting,' said Engraver Clarins, bitter at having to vacate his room on the men's side.

Aphra's complaints at having to vacate her room included several references to the patriotism of the late Mr Behn and her own services to the King and secured her, Penitence, Mrs and Master Johnson a place in one of the attics high under the roof of the Keeper's own apartments, the servants whose room it was having been impressed to wait on visitors for the day.

Aphra had attended the early morning service to which Swaveley was dragged for his last communion. 'Poor boy, he looks so pale and that poxy Ordinary continually dunning him to repent. As they took him out I managed to tell him where we'd be. One said we'd wave.'

'That should keep his spirits up,' said Penitence. There had to be executions – her grandfather had taken her to a few in Springfield in order to impress on her the fate which awaited sinners – but this air of holiday was getting on her nerves. The colours of the scarlet-robed judges, the gold chains of the aldermen, servants' liveries, the ladies' hats made the stand into a tapestry depicting knights and ladies watching a tourney.

On a trestle gallery the small band of musicians had exhausted all the sacred music it knew and fallen back on the profane played slow.

She noticed that everyone was carrying one of the Ordinary's bills. 'Complimentary copies,' said Aphra. 'That should cost the swine.'

Their own had been on sale all over London for two days and, such was the interest, the Tippins were reporting a good response. At this moment Dorinda, MacGregor and other Dog Yarders were selling them to the large crowd at the prison gates. They were ready to run another reprint which would include Swaveley's last exclamations. The Ordinary hadn't bothered to wait to see what they were, and his carried Swaveley's supposed, suitably penitent, final words.

Swaveley had done them proud, but Aphra had done them prouder, drawing a nice line between the racy and the improving. 'You can head others off following my example,' Swaveley had told her, and then smirked, 'always supposing they could.' She had put his seduction of his employer's wife while he was yet an apprentice into the first paragraph. For his woodcut Clarins had enquired of old turnkeys the procedure followed in a pressing and his picture of a prone man with a heavy weight being placed on his chest gave their bill a graphic drama lacking in the Ordinary's.

Voices, two of which Penitence recognized, carried up to their attic from the Keeper's apartments below, complaining at the wait.

'Where is the rogue?' asked a woman's voice. 'He's damned late.'

'And him with a pressing engagement,' answered a male's. The court rakes had arrived, with female companions, and were employing their wit.

'Rochester and Sedley,' said Aphra, 'and, if I'm not mistaken, the Duke of Buckingham.'

The door to the cells opened. There was silence. Swaveley appeared, naked except for breeches, a turnkey on one side, the executioner in his mask on the other. The Ordinary followed, intoning.

'He's so frightened,' said Penitence. The boy was having to be supported. *That's enough. He's learned his lesson. Let's all go home.*

'Whoo hoo.' Mrs Johnson was leaning out of the window and had to be dragged back by her daughter. 'Mother!'

The band began playing Blow's requiem as Swaveley was led to the middle of the Yard and laid down, and the irons on his legs and wrists attached to stakes.

Executioner and turnkey stood back to attention while another turnkey came into the Yard pulling a low trolley containing a large piece of stone. *They've rehearsed this.*

The executioner looked towards the stand, a judge stood up and nodded. There was a drum roll. The three men around the spreadeagled figure stooped and, with an effort, lifted the stone off the trolley and on to Swaveley's chest.

Air left the boy's lungs in a whoomph heard all over Press Yard.

The executioner regarded the stone critically, like a bricklayer, then straightened his back. 'Three hundred pounds,' he called. The Ordinary was on his knees, hands steepled in prayer.

It's a stone specially made for this. What was the matter with the mind of man that it could put such care into cruelty?

'I can't bear it,' she said quietly to Aphra, 'I'm going.'

Aphra took her arm in a surprisingly strong grip. 'He's bearing it, and we're profiting from it,' she said. 'We stay.'

She stayed. Master Johnson was bemoaning his lost bet. Below, other wagers were being laid: 'Three and twenty-five.' 'Three and fifty.'

Aphra quoted:

'At Golgotha, they glut their insatiate eyes
With scenes of blood, and human sacrifice.'

'Who wrote that?' asked Penitence.

'I did. In Surinam. There was a slave there, a negro they'd shipped from Africa. He became our friend. His name was Caesar.'

Penitence stared at her. Aphra was astonishing; the memory of the slave was causing her pain. All artificiality had dropped away. 'What happened?'

'They killed him. They took his wife from him. Sold her to another plantation. He set up a revolt with other slaves.' She shrugged. 'He was defeated, of course. They tied him to a stake and hacked him to pieces.'

'Oh.'

'He was my friend,' said Aphra.

Yawns issued from the window below where the rakes and their women were becoming bored. 'He's just lying there,' complained a female voice.

'True, he's very flat.'

Penitence had hoped for Swaveley that the stone would be dropped on him, killing him instantly; instead he was slowly being asphyxiated as it crushed his lungs. Head arched back, his mouth opened and shut like a fish's to snatch shallow, panting breaths.

'Tell them to hasten the matter, my lord, I beg you,' said a voice, whether from humanity or impatience.

Some signal passed from the Keeper's window to one of the judges on the stand, who nodded, and raised a hand to the executioner. The trolley was taken to fetch two smaller stones. 'Three hundred and twenty-five pounds,' announced the executioner.

Swaveley's mouth opened wider. The judge signalled again.

'Three hundred and fifty.'

Stop it. Get it over with. Stop it.

Swaveley's left hand struggled against its manacle. He was

255

trying to speak. The Ordinary was alarmed and shaking his head, but the executioner bent down to Swaveley's mouth and looked to the judge. 'He wants to plead guilty, my lord.'

The Ordinary was protesting; his Awful Warning was being spoiled. But the judge – after a glance at the Keeper's window – signalled that the stones be lifted. Swaveley's feet trailed on the ground as he was dragged away to face trial and hanging.

On their way down the backstairs, the party from the attic encountered Sir Charles Sedley. 'Mistress Aphra, Mistress Penitence,' he said, 'one was hoping the occasion would ferret you out. We are downcast by its dullness and beg you to enliven us. Your friends too.' He bowed to Mrs Johnson.

Penitence was surprised he had remembered their names, but was in no mood to make sport for the likes of him. 'Forgive me,' she said, and hurried on, hearing Aphra make introductions.

Gaining her room, she shut the door. She wanted quiet.

An hour later there was a tap on the door. 'Beg your indulgence, madam,' said Sir Charles Sedley.

Since Penitence didn't ask him to sit down, he lounged against the dirty wall, the sun from the window shimmering on his silk coat and the gloss of his wig, intensifying the perfume he was wearing, glancing off his rings as he flapped his hands and commented on the heat and went through the procedure of taking snuff. If she hadn't been sure he had been sent as the result of some bet, Penitence would have thought him unsettled. He unsettled her; she wanted rid of him. 'What is your b-business, sir?'

'My b-business, ma'am. My b-business is with your eyes. I wished to assure myself they were as astonishing as I remembered and, behold, they are.' As Penitence's lips tightened, he added: 'Though one has seen kinder over a duelling pistol.'

His own, which watched her carefully, were bloodshot. He wasn't much older than herself and had excellent baby skin with a bloom on it. It oozed perspiration in tiny bubbles of the fat which would one day overwhelm him.

'Since that's settled,' she said, 'I wish you good-day.'

'Cruel charmer, would you banish me so soon?' He had a slow delivery; words drooped out of his mouth to make everything he said sound like a jeer. 'I await Rochester and Buckingham who are much taken with Mistress Behn. At this moment the three of them discuss the art of writing and the beginning of her play. It seems we have another Matchless Orinda on our hands.'

Refusing him the satisfaction, Penitence didn't ask who the Matchless Orinda was.

'But you, mistress, are more intriguing than she – of Puritan persuasion, I gather, with leanings towards the stage. One has one's own connections with the theatre, and it might be that one could assist the latter aspiration.' His eyelids drooped. 'Though certainly not the former.'

DAMN Aphra. Must the woman blab everything? 'I have no aspiration, sir, except to be left alone.'

'You should, you should. Those eyes could conquer an audience as they have conquered me. But give me a kiss and I shall wing to the errand.'

The only winging he'd do would be back to his friends to tell them he'd seduced the poor slut in the cell. There was too much silk here, an overwhelming plumpness like an eiderdown filling the room; she wanted to claw her way out.

The door opened. 'I say, Penitence, do you want a woodcut done of the hanging?' Clarins, lovely, unprepossessing and cloth-coated, had come to discuss important things in plain language.

Sir Charles bowed and withdrew.

The next day, returning from the dining-hall with Aphra, she found her cell full of roses, pots of them, so many she couldn't reach her bed. 'My dear, how charming,' said Aphra, regarding the petalled sea, 'I knew he was much taken with you.'

Penitence was furious. 'Do you realize the money these cost could nearly pay off my debt?'

And then *she* realized. Sir Charles was offering to get her out, had offered, and she'd snubbed him. She'd had no idea. *Penitence Hurd, you'll never make a whore.*

She considered it. After all, having put her foot on the ladder of harlotry, she'd be a fool not to climb to its higher rungs. Satin sheets instead of dirty blankets. Mistress to a rich young man about court rather than the twice-weekly drab of a prison turnkey. She'd acquire connections, enter Benedick into a good school when he was old enough.

Logically, her next move was to send a note to Sedley. It only needed to say 'Yes'. She couldn't hate bedding with Sedley more than she loathed those moments in the condemned cell with George. *But I can control George.*

Illogically, she didn't do it. For one thing, when it came to the point of asking Aphra for ink, quill and paper, she was overcome with a fit of gasping as if, like Swaveley, she was being asphyxiated by a great weight. For another, she was optimistic about her chances of paying off her debt by herself.

No more flowers arrived either, so that was that.

The profit to Aphra and Penitence from Swaveley's Last Exclamations, combined with that from his Positively Last Exclamations, which went on sale at his hanging in August, came to £94 6s 10d, nearly fifty pounds each.

They couldn't believe it. 'Is that with all paid?' asked Aphra.

'Aye,' said MacGregor. 'All paid. We had to rush a reprint of the reprint for Tyburn.'

'The Tippins reckoned the crowd above six thousand,' Dorinda told them, 'and I hope Swaveley was grateful for all we done to get 'em there, though he didn't look it. All the stuffing gone out of the poor ballocker. The Tippins lifted so much blunt out of the crowd's pockets as they refused to take wages.'

'All we need now is more executions,' said MacGregor.

Penitence winced. 'We'd better call ourselves the Vulture Press.'

'That's a terrible bad name,' said MacGregor, 'but as we're not likely to display it, it'll do for the now.'

'What'll we do with your share, Prinks?' asked Dorinda.

'Pay the b-bills. Buy B-Benedick what he needs. Keep some for housekeeping and pay the rest towards the debt. Deposit it with a lawyer called P-Patterson in Leadenhall Street. He was Her Ladyship's man and he can pay the debtor when we've got enough.' She winked at MacGregor. 'Another Scotsman, but I trust him.'

The load was lifting. She was going to get out of Newgate. By her own enterprise.

Newgate's Ordinary went to the Stationers' Company to complain about the emergence of the mysterious and illegal press which had taken away his business. The Stationers promised to try to track it down, but in view of the number of unlicensed presses in operation they weren't sanguine of success.

However, the Vulture Press laid low for a while. There would be no more hangings until the authorities had accumulated enough death sentences to make the spectacle at Tyburn worthwhile.

There was nothing for the two young women to do and Aphra, who had been in prison the longer, began to decline. The staple food given to those who couldn't afford to pay proved unfit to eat more often that not, and Aphra, always fastidious, was unable to keep it down.

Penitence begged her to draw on the money lodged against their debts, but Aphra refused to eat, literally, into it. 'One will never get out if one does.' Penitence began to be frightened that one would die if one didn't. She suspected Aphra's lassitude to be the first stage of Whitt fever which carried off so many in Newgate. 'You can't give way now.'

Aphra closed her eyes. 'Send *The Young King* to Rochester and Buckingham,' she murmured. 'Perhaps they will find it worthy to finish it for me.'

'*You'll* finish it. And what about that slave? Weren't you going to write his story?'

Tears oozed out of Aphra's eyes. 'Ah, poor Caesar, both of us doomed to oblivion.'

'Damned if you are,' said Penitence, irritably. She didn't send the play, but she wrote notes to Buckingham and Rochester informing them of the situation. If Sedley had told her the truth, they might be interested enough in Aphra to save her life. *What they pay for blasted ribbon in a day would keep her alive for a month.*

That night, in the condemned cell, she asked George to bring in some decent food. She knew enough not to plead for it. 'I want cheese, good bread, fresh milk and I want it tomorrow,' she commanded, as she stripped. 'And some wine.'

'You lady-ins,' admired George, 'Whitt fare not good enough, eh? Tell us what you eat in that mansion of yours.'

What do the rich eat? She could only think of the meals her grandmother had served up in her forest kitchen, and hoped their unfamiliarity would sound sufficiently exotic. 'Pumpkin pie,' she said.

'Oooh. Pumpkin pie.' He was snuffling at her thighs. 'Oozing gravy.'

'Lots of gravy. Wild turkey stuffed with blueberries. Chowder . . .'

It was gastronomic pornography, and effective. George brimmed earlier than ever. But there was a price. As he left her, he said: 'Ready yourself for tomorrow night. Good food's extra.'

Aphra was too poorly to ask where the provisions came from, but they improved her slightly. Since she wasn't well enough to leave her bed, Penitence sat and read to her: 'Me, too, the Pierian sisters have made a singer; I too have songs; ay, and the shepherds dub me poet, but I trust them not. For as yet, methinks, gooselike I cackle amid quiring swans.'

'Oh Virgil,' sighed Aphra, 'if one could but cackle like you.'

Aphra's hunger for literature was greater than for food. Through reading to her the library she had brought into Newgate with her, Penitence was acquiring a culture she hadn't dreamed of. It still wasn't enough for Aphra: 'Alas, that our sex is denied the teaching of Latin and Greek so that we are barred from the originals. That my eyes could drink in the Greek of Homer.'

Penitence found some of the English translations hard enough, but she would read on long after Aphra slept, fascinated by Socratic argument, or listening as the bronze trumpets blared their challenge over the walls of Troy, or softly repeating again and again a honeyed Virgilian phrase. If Newgate took her to the depths of human abasement, it also, thanks to Aphra, showed her the heights of human achievement.

And woman's. She had never heard of the poetess Aphra always referred to as 'Sacred Sappho' – she understood, when she read her, why the Puritans had ignored her existence, nor did the Lesbian's sexual proclivities agree with her own, but she was spellbound by the lovely, feminine fragments of verse that sang themselves into a prison cell with such immediacy from another country twenty centuries away.

She still doubted whether Aphra's ambition to put her play on in a public theatre was feasible. But at least there was a precedent for a woman to be something more than a writer for purely domestic consumption.

'Who's the Matchless Orinda?' she asked, remembering Sedley.

Aphra's stricken eyes gained a touch of frost. 'Ugh.'

'Who?'

'Mention the fact that one aspires to write,' said Aphra, 'and that's all one hears. "Another Matchless Orinda." If I thought I was to be bracketed with that vapid, watery, flatulent female, I would cut my wrists here and now. Ugh one said, and Ugh one meant.'

Little wiser, Penitence was not sorry she'd asked; Aphra's flash of spirit had been her first in days.

But the real panacea was delivered to Newgate late in the evening on the first day of September in the shape of a young man whose eyes seemed too lively for his sober, elegant, clergyman's cloth.

Penitence collided with him as she ran into Aphra's cell, hearing the screams. She nearly punched him. He held her off, apologizing. 'I assure you, madam, Mistress Behn's cries are of a rapturous nature.'

Aphra lifted her head. 'Penitence. Oh my dear, we're free.'

'Ah well . . .' said the young clergyman.

'Two hundred guineas. We can leave this minute. This beautiful deliverer, this Mercury—'

'Sprat,' smirked the young man, 'Thomas Sprat.'

'— our benefactors, His Grace of Buckingham—'

'An anonymous gift,' said the Reverend Sprat.

'— and the Earl of Rochester. How can words—'

'I was to say it was an appreciation from the Muses,' said the Reverend Sprat, delicately, 'and while I am sure that, were the *anonymous* donors aware of this lady's plight, they would be only too happy ... but the gift is to liberate *you*, Mistress Behn.'

Through tears and tangled hair, Aphra looked at him straight. 'If Penitence isn't freed, neither am I. There's enough now to pay both our debts.'

So it was arranged. There were comings and goings. A disgruntled Lawyer Patterson was called out from a musical evening at his home to sign notes and swear oaths. Warrants were withdrawn, creditors paid, and in the early hours of the morning a bemused and still-unbelieving Penitence had settled herself alongside Aphra in a carriage which carried a crest it was too dark to see, and was driven to Aldersgate where the young Reverend Sprat, his duty done, delivered them to the cheap lodgings of Mrs and Master Johnson, which, cheap as they were, beat seven bells out of Newgate.

And half a mile away, a spark from a carelessly left baker's oven in Pudding Lane ignited a pile of faggots lying too near it.

A red cinder from the burning shop fell on to a pile of hay in a nearby inn yard. The inn caught and the flames ran into Thames Street lined by warehouses stacked with tallow, oil and spirits.

The new Lord Mayor, Sir Thomas Bludworth, was woken up and chose to ignore the fire as just another outbreak; the City had them all the time. This one, however, coincided with a dry spell and a strong east wind. Pitch-coated, thatched, closely packed timber buildings fired up like torches.

The usual teams of men with buckets of water, long-handled fire-hooks and hand-squirts tried dealing with outbreaks as they occurred and then gave up. The only way to fight a fire of these proportions was by wholesale demolition of the houses in its path, and Sir Thomas Bludworth was too concerned about the compensation which would have to be paid to give the order which would have saved London.

By the sunny, blowy, Sunday morning, crowds of frightened Londoners were evacuating their homes, flinging their goods into boats moored along the north bank, clambering down the steps to the waterside. Some people stayed in their houses until those, too, caught fire, and then ran in panic. Bewildered pigeons remaining overlong on the rooftops before taking flight fell with singed wings as the flames whipped a hundred feet into the air.

Refugees, Aphra Behn and her family among them, abandoned the City in terror. Some swam the river, others silted up at the gates or queued to cross the mercifully unburned Bridge. The price of a cart went up to £40.

Not until Monday, when the King and his brother James, Duke of York, took charge, was there any decisive action.

By then Aphra and the Johnsons were safely ensconced at the Cock and Pie and, like the rest of the Rookery, had a grandstand view of London as it burned to death.

Smuts stung their eyes, but they couldn't look away from the corona of near-invisible flame that shimmered above the City. Smoke streamed from it over the countryside like the hair of a giant hag. More appalling even than the sight was the noise, the huge, self-satisfied roar of fire punctuated by the crash of avalanching buildings, the percussion of explosions that shook the balcony they stood on as seamen, drafted in from the dockyards, began the systematic destruction of whole streets with gunpowder.

'The history, oh, the history,' cried Aphra.

Penitence was remembering her walks with Peter Simkin through the carved gateways into the Middle Ages. His ghost, like Aphra, would weep for the streets that had seen Chaucer's pilgrims set off for Canterbury, and cheered Elizabeth's coronation procession.

There were no tears in her eyes. Aphra's brother, like some of the Rookery men, had gone to help the evacuation and came back with the news that, though five-sixths of the City was lost, nobody had yet reported a death.

'And Newgate?' she asked him.

'Gutted.'

Cleansed. The past of a city was burning, much of it as filthy as her own in it had been. The condemned cell was cauterized by flame. She and London, the two of them, could start again.

She put her arm round the weeping Aphra and went on watching the holocaust.

'Good,' she whispered.

Chapter 4

RIDING YARD ALLEY led from the Strand end of Catherine Street and was surprisingly narrow. 'Is this it?' asked Penitence, dubiously.

'I know, don't I?' said Dorinda. 'It's the back way in. The front's off Drury Lane, though it ain't much wider. But wait 'til you get inside.'

She led the way, picking up her skirts to avoid a dead cat just visible in the shadows cast by a thin, wintry sun. They followed. 'One went to the old Cockpit, of course,' said Aphra, stung by Dorinda's familiarity with the surroundings, 'but one's been too occupied since they built this one.'

'You tell him that,' sneered Dorinda, over her shoulder. '"One's so sorry, Sir Tom, but prison's kept one *so* busy."'

'Stop it,' said Penitence, automatically. Dorinda's persistent carping at Aphra Behn made home life wearing, and life at the Cock and Pie was wearing enough. The place was nearly as full as it had been in the days of Her Ladyship. The attics were the home of the Johnsons, MacGregor had moved into Job's old room to be near his press, which was in the kitchen, and Mistress Palmer now carried on her laundry business from the scullery, because of the proximity of the well.

It was paradise compared with Newgate, but on the days

when Benedick was teething, and the press was thumping, and MacGregor was shouting at Peter Johnson because he wouldn't help when there was printing work to be done — not that there was much — and Dorinda was tormenting Aphra who was trying to write, and Mrs Johnson had eluded their vigilance and slipped down to the Ship for a bottle, and she didn't know where the next meal for them all was to come from . . .

'He is already aware of it,' said Aphra, with dignity. 'I wrote to him at the time. One is well acquainted with Sir Thomas.'

She's nervous or she wouldn't be answering back. Usually Aphra was patient with Dorinda.

Penitence was herself nervous. She had been subjected to Puritan teaching for too long to feel easy about entering the temple of sin which they were now approaching.

'Didn't get you out, though, did he?' Dorinda stopped before a dusty green doorway and addressed the hulking figure lounging in it: 'These are friends of mine, Jacko.'

'How's the orange business, Dorry?' By borrowing the necessary money from Sam Bryskett and employing the Tippins to put the fear of God into the then incumbent, Dorinda had bought the orange concession at the King's Theatre and was doing well with it. Such food as appeared on the table at the Cock and Pie came mainly from her small profits.

'Shockin'. Let us pass, then.'

'Can't be did,' said Jacko. 'You're all right, but Sir Tom's give orders. Your friends stay outside. They're rehearsing in there.'

Dorinda's tone sweetened: 'Jacko, my little quiffer, if you don't let us in I'll have to tell Sir Tom as I saw you scratch your neck three times when you was admitting yesterday.'

'You wouldn't.'

'I ballocking would.'

The doorman sighed. 'Pass, friends.'

Inside the theatre they were in a dark corridor with many doors. Aphra was curious: 'Why shouldn't he scratch?'

'He's paid to take admittance money,' said Dorinda. 'Every time he scratches his neck he slips a sixpence down the back of his jacket.'

Penitence's nose was twitching. If she'd been a dog she would have been casting about. She stumbled through the gloom after Dorinda, almost stepping on the girl's heels. Overriding prejudice, turning it into excitement, was this vibration, this wonderful smell, at once strange and at the same time wooing her.

And then she was there. She stood in the doorway to the pit. To her right, rows of empty benches, raked at an angle of fifteen degrees, led in darkness to the steeper rake of the amphitheatre. Above that were the boxes — she got the impression of gilt leather.

Dorinda guided Aphra towards Sir Thomas Killigrew's office, but Penitence fell on to a bench and stayed there, her hands gripping it.

Ahead and slightly above there was light and men's voices, figures moving. She was enveloped in a smell compounded of orange peel, baize, fish-glue, old scent, tobacco and dust. She fixed her eyes on the light and the stage came into focus.

The front of it made an apron. On that, further back, was the proscenium arch formed by two great golden statues of Neptune on marble pedestals. Its top was a frieze of clouds and nymphs and cherubs that seemed to hold up swathes of red velvet curtain, the tasselled ends of which hung down behind the sea-gods. In the centre of the frieze the royal arms blazed in gold and silver.

Her eye was drawn further into the square of light. It was a forest. Not a forest with wolverines or elk or undergrowth. Here all was clear and sharp. It was a dryads' forest; she couldn't see them but she knew they were there, hiding among the flat, painted trees which stretched back in cunning perspective to a far-off grove. It didn't seem odd that its sunlight came from banks of chandeliers. From that moment she was lost. The god of this temple asked for her soul and she gave it. A thousand whispered screams reminded her that this was the Devil's chapel, the pit of artifice. But it was the artifice that transfixed her. The light which fell so lovingly on these glades had never fallen on sea or land, but it had coloured the most beautiful of her dreams. Outside, a million miles away, it was grey winter; here, encapsulated in a frame, was summer, and it always would be.

The hair stood on her neck. She knew this place as she had known Henry King. The essence of the man was here, or he had carried the essence of theatre in himself. She'd been in exile from this sumptuousness, this unbearable delight of childhood. Like a turtle sensing the sea, she yearned towards it.

Here and there a few people on the benches read by tapers. Above the stage a man was knocking at the curtain mechanism with a hammer while below, in a fenced-off part of the pit, a violin tuned up.

Voices came and went from the flats at the side of the stage, somebody was swearing. Penitence didn't notice them any more than birdcalls or a breeze rustling in the leaves of a true forest; they fitted. She wasn't even surprised that an actor on stage was speaking dearly familiar lines: 'Signior Leonato, let the friar advise you . . .'

Penitence's lips moved in synchronization. '. . . And though you know my inwardness and love is very much unto the prince and Claudio, yet, by mine honour . . . is that bloody woman here yet?'

A head popped out from behind a flat. 'No she ain't.'

Happily, Penitence settled herself to watch this new play.

The actor flung out his arms. 'Where is the Athanasian slut? How can I make love to a bloody vacuum? You read it, John.'

'I haven't got time,' said John's head, crossly, 'I've got—'

'Then find somebody who has. Why should I waste my breath if the harlots who pose as actresses in this ballum rancum can't be bothered—'

'All right, all right,' grumbled John's head. Its body joined it as it limped to the front, peering, and called to the prone figure of a woman on the bench behind Penitence: 'Knipp, you wouldn't . . .?'

'No, I bloody wouldn't.' Knipp didn't look up from her script. 'I've got to learn Sabina by this afternoon, so cock off.'

John raised his eyes to Heaven, then cast them hopelessly round the silent figures on the other benches, finally coming to rest on Penitence. 'Here, you.'

Penitence looked around her.

'You. In the cap. Can you read?'

'Me?'

'Oh, for God's sake. You. Can you read? Then come up here.'

It was inevitable; fitting. She was going up the steps. She was under the lights. John grabbed her arm and led her to where the actor had sat himself down, his head on his knees, his arms over his head. 'Now then, dear,' John said, as if she were a baby but directing his look, which was venomous, at the hunched figure on the floor. 'That gentleman there is an actor, believe it or not.' A book was pushed into her hands. 'If he ever stands up I want you to read to him all the little words that come after the name Beat. See here? Beat. When it comes to the name Bene, he'll talk. All right, dear? All right, Kynaston?' He went away.

Kynaston sighed and stood up. He was tall with fine-boned head and hands. His hair, which was his own, hung in a beautiful wave over his eyes and he pushed it back. 'Lady Beatrice, have you wept all this while?'

By the mercy of God nobody was looking at her. Even so she stuttered. 'Yea, and I w-w-will w-weep a w-while longer.'

Kynaston covered his eyes. 'Why?' he asked. 'Why me?' But he kept on. 'I will not desire that . . .'

Put the mask on. You can join the cavalry. 'You have no reason. I do it f-freely.'

Kynaston was concentrating on his moves and not looking at her, so gradually she improved. *I can do this.* There was a 'p' coming up in a couple of lines. *Breathe.* 'It were as possible for me to say . . .' *Did it.* '. . . but believe me not; I confess nothing, nor I deny nothing. I am sorry for my cousin.'

Her voice became stronger as it hit the stride Henry King had taught her; she could hear it issue out into the auditorium and thought how nice it sounded.

Kynaston, too, was gathering momentum. 'Come, bid me do anything for thee.'

She gave it what she'd given it on the balcony of the Cock and Pie. 'Kill Claudio.'

'Ha, not for the wide world.' He was a very different Benedick from Henry King, but he was feeding the same anger.

'O! that I were a man,' hissed Beatrice. 'O God, that I were a man! I would eat his heart in the market-place.'

'Hear me, Beatrice . . .'

She rampaged into the 'Princes and counties!' speech without a single misplaced 'p', then Benedick had turned back into Kynaston who was kissing her hand, bidding her farewell and saying: 'Very nice, my dear, thank you. You can go back now.'

As she shambled back into exile, she heard him tell John: 'Get her to do something about that walk. She moves like a bloody horse.'

The man above the stage was still hammering, the violin still tuning up. But it had all changed. Taking her seat again, she thought she heard Knipp hiss: 'He wanted a read-through, dear, not a bloody audition', but when she looked round the actress's eyes were fixed on her book.

Then Dogberry, Verges and Sexton came on for the discovery scene and the Dogberry was so funny she gave a yelp before she could clap her hands over her mouth. From then on he played to her, until Dorinda tapped her on the shoulder and she had to follow, still looking back, out into the corridor. 'It's not what I expected,' she babbled, 'and yet it is. Oh, Dorry, I've had such a lovely time.'

To her surprise, Dorinda kissed her. 'Ain't been able to say that in a bit, have you?'

No. In the minutes, hours, she'd been here she'd been given a childhood, somebody else's childhood, full of presents and wonder.

'Aphra ain't though.'

She came back to earth. 'Won't he take her play?'

'Won't even read it. The old gut-fucker's pretending he's never met her before. I reckon he's ashamed he got her into the spying business and then wouldn't help her.' Aphra in trouble had become one of Dorinda's own.

A rich, deep voice rolled out of an open door. 'Madam, plays I have got. What I lack are audiences. D'ye know how many attended *The Slighted Maid* yesterday, even with the damned masque?'

A large fat man with a brutal jaw was sweeping a twittering Aphra out into the corridor. 'Two hundred and four. Two paltry hundred – most of those with their knuckles brushing the ground – and four. Twenty-one pounds and ninepence, madam. From which rent will take five pounds fourteen shillings leaving fifteen pounds six shillings and ninepence for running costs, not to mention actors who insist on being paid even though they couldn't make a goose hiss. Don't talk to me of new plays, madam. We're having to recoup with *Much Ado* tomorrow. Thank God for Shakespeare, I say.'

His voice brushed all three women before him, like a broom, and piled them up at the exit where Jacko held open the door. Sir Thomas pushed up Aphra's sleeve and ran his moustache along her forearm, making pecking noises. 'Your play may be worthy of you, madam, but the last we had by a damned woman ran one night. Too damned virtuous. A play needs balls, madam, balls, and women don't have 'em, thank God. Return to your husband, madam. I wish you good-day.'

The door slammed behind them and they trudged back up the alley. Penitence put her arm round Aphra's shoulders and found Dorinda's arm already there. 'Did you tell him Buckingham and Rochester were your patrons?' It was stretching things a bit; since the gift of money that had liberated them from Newgate, they had heard nothing from the noble lords. The aristocracy had mostly retreated to the country away from the dismal ruin of London where detritus still lay so thick it had raised the ground level by four feet.

'Yes,' said Aphra, miserably.

'I'll give him balls,' said Dorinda. The entire Cock and Pie had been depending on Aphra's play. 'Wish I'd twisted his off when I had the chance.'

Penitence shot her a look over Aphra's head. 'You *didn't*.'

'Had to,' said Dorinda, 'or it was goodbye oranges. He's got droit . . . droit something over every quim in the house. King's warrant, he calls it.'

They were back in winter with a dead cat in a dirty alley

and worry gnawing their stomachs, to say nothing of hunger. *If I shave the remains off the lamb bone and boil it with the last of the carrots we can have soup.*

Aphra stopped. 'Dorinda.'

'Yes, Affie?'

'Can you smuggle me into the play this afternoon?'

'You're not going back?'

'One is not living off Penitence's charity for ever . . .'

'I took yours quick enough.'

Aphra was trembling with desperation. 'I don't know what else to do.' She straightened herself up. 'One's talent lies with the pen, that I know. It's the only recourse one has. I shall go back today. I shall go back tomorrow. I shall go back the day after. Whenever there is a play, one will be there watching it. I'm going to see what the public wants and what it doesn't. And if testicles are the order of the day, testicles it shall be.' She dashed tears from her eyes. 'With knobs on.'

'Hey you.' The shout came from behind them where John had emerged from the theatre door. 'You. Where you going?'

'Home,' shouted back Penitence coldly.

'Back here on the chap of two and we'll practise moving. I'm not having my walkers tramping the stage like woodcutters.' The door slammed. He'd gone.

'Walkers?'

'Spear-carriers.' Dorinda was torn between pleasure and envy. 'Ladies-in-waiting. Them as don't speak. Divers attendants.'

'Oh.'

'*There's* a turnaround,' said Dorinda. 'We come here to sell Aphra's play and you get the ballocking work.'

'Oh.'

They hurried to catch up with Aphra who, deaf to everything but her own misery, had reached the mouth of the alley and was turning in the wrong direction. They took her arms and piloted her north. She looked up at them ferociously. 'With knobs on,' she said.

The ill wind which had fanned flames across the City brought prosperity to the untouched West End. Masons, bricklayers, wagoners, carpenters, architects came in from the four quarters of England needing accommodation and provisioning.

Even the Rookery profited from the boom; there was work for those prepared to do it, and plentiful pockets to be picked by those who weren't. Houses which had been empty of humans and rats filled up again.

Penitence was tempted to turf MacGregor out of Job's and Kinyans's room, put him in what had been Phoebe's, and rent the vacated space. She was stopped by a warning from the Reverend Boreman on one of her visits to St Giles's to pick up a text for printing. She had fallen into the habit of asking his advice, though not necessarily taking it.

'Bring strangers into the Cock and Pie? Are you mad, girl?'

'Sam Bryskett's renting to a pair of tilers from Bedford,' she said, 'at a guinea a week. What's mad in a guinea a week?'

'Sam Bryskett hasn't got an illegal press in his kitchen.'

She still found it difficult to grasp the concept of censorship. 'If I may point out, sir, you use it.'

'You're cheaper than the others.'

'Nobody's b-bothered me yet.'

The Reverend Boreman shook his finger at her. 'They haven't bothered you, my girl, because the country's at peace and you're printing nothing inflammatory. But times change. And they change fast.'

Penitence scanned the scrawled sheet he'd given her, a blast against the authorities for still ignoring conditions in suburbs like St Giles which had given rise to the Plague. '"... The debauched who build their piazzas while the poor have not even clean water to drink."' She looked up. 'And this isn't inflammatory, I suppose?'

The rector was pleased. 'Pray God it is. Pray God they put me on trial that I may denounce them to their faces.' He frowned. 'You have my assurance, Penitence, that they would never learn from me who printed it.'

She knew they wouldn't. They wouldn't put him on trial either. Who among the powerful cared for a poor rector's tantrums over clean water?

'You look tired, child. Is it too much cavorting at the theatre?'

Cavorting. This idea of the public's that theatre life was an endless Lucullan banquet. She got up to go and changed the subject: 'Do you think it was the Papists who set the Great Fire? Everyone says so.'

'I wouldn't put anything past those idolators,' said the Reverend Boreman, 'but I don't think so. Not the Papists, nor the Dutch.' He smiled at her. 'Not even the Puritans.'

He's changed. In the old days he would have said it was God's punishment. *He's lost certainty.* The Plague had taken everyone's certainty.

Waving goodbye to her from his gate, the Reverend Boreman remembered the dumb creature who had challenged him at this very gate two years before. Such a change. For the better? She would think so, he thought; she had gained comeliness, she walked and talked with elegance. Yet at what cost. No face as young as hers should have eyes so old.

She had returned to prostitution. Having taken the first step down the slippery slope in Newgate, it had been easier to take the second, though it had left her even more burdened with guilt because this time she hadn't *had* to take it.

Mrs Compton, one of the walkers, had come into the ladies' back foyer where Penitence was changing into her attendant's costume for *Secret Love*. 'He's asking for you, dear.'

There was only one 'He' at the King's Theatre. The other women looked at her in commiseration as she finished dressing and left the room with resolve and good intentions. *I shan't. It stopped with George. I won't. If he dismisses me, so much the worse, but I won't go back to that.*

She paused outside the door to Killigrew's office. *Damn the man. It's not as if he's paying me.* Walkers, she'd found to her dismay, were expected to do their stage work for the experience and the meal they were given after the performance. She knocked.

Sir Thomas was sitting at his desk in a loose robe, what looked like a furry nightcap with earflaps, and a temper. 'And what is this, miss?' He had a playbill in his hand.

Oh God. 'A friend of mine p-prints them, sir. A good printer and cheap.'

'And licensed, I have no doubt?'

'Not entirely, sir. But they are only handbills, not p-posters.' She gave him the same persuasion she had given John the prompter, who in turn had persuaded the actor Hart, who, as one of the theatre's shareholders, had commissioned them: 'Ten shillings a ream and a well-written text. Master Hart was pleased to say they have put up attendances.'

'Master Hart was, was he? And should His Majesty find out that his own theatre is using an unlicensed press, will Master Hart be equally pleased to be sent to the Tower?'

She hung her head. Damn. *Damn.* It had been a nice little commission and the only one they had at the moment. That and Dorinda's oranges were keeping the Cock and Pie eating, but only just.

'What's your name?'

'Penitence Hurd, sir. I'm a walker.'

'And a pretty little walker, too.'

She looked up, alarmed. Killigrew's eyes were on the bill, but she wished she were wearing her old high-necked dress. She'd had to shut her ears to the Puritan voices that shrieked in her mind the first time she had tottered on stage in high heels and trailing décolleté best silk – one thing, Sir Tom insisted that even his walkers be finely robed. The thrill of being on stage at all, part of that entrancing charade, the startling seduction of seeing herself in the looking-glass, painted, large-eyed, foreign, the applause, all these things had drowned out the mental chorus of disapproval – after all she was supposed to be a Persian lady and perhaps Persian ladies displayed the swell of their bosoms – but it still made her uncomfortable to be in costume offstage, and Killigrew's tone just then had plunged the low cut of her basque several inches lower.

'It's well done, I admit,' said Killigrew. 'Who wrote it?'

The purpose of handbills was to extol the forthcoming production and Aphra made hers so mouth-watering they were frequently better than the plays themselves. Would it profit Aphra if she told him, or not? 'I'm not sure, sir.'

'You little minx.' Killigrew had become skittish. 'Is this printer your lover?'

'I have no lover, sir.'

'But you would wish him to keep his commission?'

'Yes, sir.' He was wandering the room, fingering his chin. Penitence became uneasily aware of the couch on the other side of the room. Its velvet was rubbed and well used.

'The question is, how could I persuade His Majesty to overlook this matter, should it come to his attention.'

'It's unlikely to, sir, unless you tell him.' *You pig.* Killigrew wasn't afraid of the King. He'd supplied women to Charles in exile. His rudeness in the royal presence was legendary. He'd once threatened the King that he'd dig up Cromwell's bones 'because no one else is taking care of the kingdom'.

'Then perhaps it is myself who should be persuaded.' He sat down on the couch, as she'd dreaded his doing. He even patted it. 'Come here, little maid, and give old Sir Tom a kiss.'

He *was* old, over fifty, and fat. She could see a roll of his belly protruding from the bottom of his shirt and overhanging the band of his breeches. *I can't.* On the other hand, she'd had to pay half a crown to Apothecary Boghurst to treat Benedick's croup, which still wasn't better. 'Keep him warm,' the apothecary had said, disregarding the fact that the tax on coal had gone up to pay for the rebuilding of London. 'Give him honey mixed in white wine. Build up his appetite.' As it was, the meals she ate four times a week at the theatre had to last her seven days.

Killigrew's jowls tightened. 'Do you want to keep the damned commission or don't you?'

'Yes.' But still she held back. This wouldn't be like the last time, with George. She didn't have to. Somehow they could survive if she didn't. But it would mean leaving this wonderful place she had discovered, permanent exile in the grind of every day. She made her decision. *What does it matter? I'm spoiled goods anyway.*

She went and sat down beside him and he flung her backwards.

'He was like a dog,' she told Dorinda dully, as they walked

home through the freezing fog after the performance. 'I didn't have to do anything or say anything. He just . . . rutted.'

'He *is* a dog,' said Dorinda. 'He's marking out his ballocking territory. Most like he won't trouble you again. He'll find another tree to cock his leg against. Did it take long?'

'It seemed like it.' Afterwards, he'd told her to hurry and straighten herself or she'd miss curtain-up. 'It probably wasn't.'

'That's the best sort,' said Dorinda, 'the quick ones. The times I've laid there saying "Ooh" and "Ah" and "You're a stallion, my lord" and wondering what the hour is.' She patted Penitence's arm. 'Look on the bright side. You got your flowers, so he ain't planted any little Killigrews. And you kept the commission. That's good, in't it?'

'Oh yes,' said Penitence, 'I'm getting to be a good whore.'

Penitence had slept with Keeper George because she needed to survive Newgate and get out. She slept with Killigrew because she needed to stay in the theatre in order to act.

How long she had wanted to become an actress she couldn't say; possibly always. Perhaps that was what had first attracted her to the Indians to whom acting was second nature; desire to transcend herself had given her the imagination to turn into an eagle, anything she wanted.

Distorted by Puritan teaching, suppressed, the seed germinated when Henry King had tossed her the vizard mask, sprouted into life when she'd set foot on the balcony of the Cock and Pie as Beatrice. Now only Benedick was more important.

At King's she found herself in an environment as natural to her as the Massachusetts forest and if that made her a creature of the Devil, then she was sorry, but she couldn't help it.

Besides, the summonses to Killigrew's room were mercifully infrequent. It was only if she happened to attract his attention that Sir Thomas remembered his *droit de seigneur* and exercised it. Mostly he forgot her. He was rarely around in any case, being much at court indulging in political and sexual activity and pursuing his vendetta against his great rival, Davenant, who managed the only other playhouse in London, the Duke of York's. The day-to-day running of the King's Theatre was left to its greatest male actors, Lacy, Kynaston and Hart.

And George had tempered the wind to the shorn lamb by making its breath so terrible in her encounters with him that no blast would ever be so chill again. By contrast, the few minutes on the couch with Killigrew were easy – disgusting, debasing, but easy.

Her grip on moral certainty was weakening. She had been assured the theatre was a sink of iniquity and found it wasn't. True, the players' lives, with only a few exceptions, were immoral by Puritan standards but there was none of the hypocrisy that Puritan standards inevitably entailed. Above all, they were *players*; they laughed at what was serious, they turned things upside-down, they made a game out of hardship, they were brave, they had *style*, they reminded her of Henry King. As she had known him, she knew them. Even though they ignored her, in some other existence she had breathed the air they breathed.

And refusing Killigrew meant dismissal from this Eden. Already he'd spoiled it; when he was around she hid herself as well as she could among the other walkers, full of tension until he'd gone. But she still turned up because she couldn't stay away. She raged against the vulnerability which put women like her at the mercy of men like George and Killigrew. But if her body was the only asset she had, why not use it? So the Serpent whispered to Penitence Hurd, and she listened.

The gloss would have tarnished anyway; behind the stage there was overcrowding and frequent ill-temper. Gods and goddesses materializing so wondrously into the light looked ridiculous when seen from under the stage wobbling upwards towards the traps with Percy and Hobbs, the stagehands, sweating and swearing as they pulled the ropes.

However, Penitence's was a true marriage; romance went but love and respect took its place. It satisfied the final remnants of her Puritanism that the illusions against which the likes of the Reverend Block had railed were born out of professionalism and sheer hard work.

And talent. Offstage the King's players exemplified all the

petty sins – and some not so petty – that human flesh was heir to. On stage they joined the immortals. When she wasn't 'walking', Penitence spent her time in the wings, watching Kynaston, who had been standing beside her seconds before complaining querulously of a draught, transform to greatness, or Lacy bring magnificence to a weakly written speech, or foul-mouthed Knipp reduce an audience to tears with her pathos, or 'Scum' Goodman – a comedian who hadn't earned his nickname lightly – time a line and a wink with the accuracy of a champion archer.

She forgave them their sins and sillinesses offstage for what they did on it. Hart's vanity, for instance, made him ridiculous – Hart thought nobody was greater than Hart – yet watching him as Cyrus, displaying a majesty that could have taught emperors how to behave, she believed him.

She studied him and the other chief players during a performance, listening to inflection and timing, increasing a knowledge she seemed to have been born with – and longed to apply.

Every night she prayed to Thespis, her new Almighty, to give her a part, but *Much Ado*, always a crowd-puller, was put on three times in the course of three months without any of the actresses in it breaking a leg, or even catching a cold. Only John Downes, the prompter, in his surly way, was helping her dramatic education. He insisted she turn up an hour before each performance so that he could teach her to walk, sit, pick up a glass, wield a fan, project her voice to the gallery, sing. He'd even begun giving her fencing lessons, which mystified her.

'Balance,' he told her, curtly, when she asked why. 'And you'll never play Penthesilea if you can't use a sword.'

'I'll never play Penthesilea anyway,' she said, fishing. 'Nobody here notices me, except you.'

'I'm not bloody surprised,' he said, 'the way you lunge. You're not casting for trout. Now lunge.' She got nothing out of him. He'd been an actor in the days of Charles I. He was as old as Killigrew, but leaner and without the lust. In a rare confidence, he told her he'd once met Shakespeare's brother.

'What was he like? What did he say Shakespeare was like?'

'Couldn't remember much, witless old fart.'

Like all actors in the Civil War, Hart among them, he'd fought for the King, receiving a wound that had finished his stage career. But the theatre took care of its own. No actor, however old or decrepit, wandered the streets begging his bread. John more than earned his: he was prompter, he copied out parts, hired walkers, and stagehands, trained them, ordered the meals, and made sure before he went home that the candle-snuffer had put out every flame in the building — including the stove which warmed the back of the auditorium in winter. Penitence doubted if the theatre would have stayed vertical without him. Since his efforts went unremarked, she also doubted whether the pains he was taking to fit her for the stage would bear fruit.

She was wrong. After a performance in May of *Flora's Vagaries* she came offstage with the other walkers and John put a scrap of paper in her hand: 'All right,' he said, 'I got you to walk like a human being, let's see if you can talk like one.'

'It's a part?'

'It's a line.'

'Oh, John. Thank you.' She read it. '"Pray spare her, Your Majesty."' She read the cue. 'I speak this to . . . *King Lear*?'

'It ain't Shakespeare's,' said John bitterly. 'Some scribbler's adapted his into a comedy.' He had no high opinion of authors. 'Said he was rescuing the spars of *Lear*. I didn't know it was shipwrecked.'

In her excitement, Penitence didn't care if the author had put in song and dance — actually, he had. That night the Cock and Pie turned critic as Penitence practised in its salon: 'P-pray spare her, Your Majesty. P-pray *spare* her, Your Majesty. P-pray spare *her*, Your Majesty.'

'I'd leave out the praying bit,' said Dorinda. 'Just spare her.'

'Why does it begin with a "p"?' moaned Penitence. 'Why? Why?' Benedick, tottering over the floor towards her, fell over and she picked him up. 'Your mama wanted to earn you some money, yes she did, and she can't say the first word right, no she can't.'

279

'You said all them words lovely that night on the balcony,' said Mistress Palmer.

'And will again,' said Aphra. They all looked at her, unused to hearing her stern. 'You were rescuing the Brysketts' child that night, Penitence. Next week you will be rescuing your own.'

Breathe. 'Pray spare her, Your Majesty,' said Penitence.

The Cock and Pie applauded.

For the first two acts of *The English King* – her line came in the third – Penitence was more aware of the audience than at any time so far; walkers were generally kept at a distance from it at the back of the set. She had, in any case, been too occupied with her own moves and in watching the actors, to concern herself with how they were being received, relying on John's dictum: 'If they don't throw things, it's a success.'

Now, because for the space of five words its attention would be on her, she became alive to the creature beyond the chandeliers and footlights.

Dr Rhodes, the author who had been good enough to rescue Shakespeare and his *Lear*, had paid Killigrew to put the play on and packed the benches with friends and admirers, most of them new to the theatre. Penitence, peering through the curtain before it went up, saw the pit full of citizens dressed in Sunday best, gaping at the prostitutes in their vizard masks who hoped to be mistaken for young ladies, and the young ladies in *their* masks giggling with their beaux and hoping they wouldn't be.

The musicians behind their spiked rail were tuning up just below the stage. Dorinda strolled the benches, selling her oranges. The lemonade girl had lit the chandelier in her kiosk beside the entrance door and was doing brisk business, though not as brisk as her rival selling hot Burgundian. Servants who were saving seats for their masters were romping and quarrelling. Aphra was in one of the boxes, now such an accepted part of theatre furniture she no longer had to hide.

A hand pulled Penitence away. 'Get off,' said John Downes, wrathfully, 'that's unprofessional.'

'It looks a good quiet house.'

He was gloomy. 'Don't wager on it. The court's back at Whitehall.'

'Do you think the King will come?'

'Not for this hocus. But the young buggers who attend him might. Your friend's bill could fetch 'em.' Aphra, with gritted teeth, had written a description of the play that could have dragged in a Puritan.

Waiting behind the prompt door with her fellow-walkers and Nelly Gwynn, who was playing Cordelia, Penitence practised her breathing and the technique of metamorphosis she had used as a child to escape from the restrictions of home and fly as an eagle upriver to the Indian camp.

The chatter from the auditorium fell away, the violins and trumpets muted to a hum. She altered herself to her part, thinking herself smaller, a little thing, admiring, adoring the mistress whose sisters treated her so wickedly. It didn't work as effectively as usual; that she was to speak into that maw out front obtruded itself around the edges. It came to her that, if she was to be an actress at all, part of her would have to be in touch with that space and respond to it.

Lacy, who was playing the King, finished the prologue.

'Here we go, my cockies, Decus et Dolor,' said Gwynn and they were on.

The author's claque was polite, enjoying Gwynn's pert performance, and the juggler, and the spirits rising through the traps, and the thunder. Penitence silently emoted for all she was worth.

It wasn't until Act II, Scene ii that noise from the pit obtruded itself on her notice. Loud, careless voices were asking where they should sit, demanding that citizens move up, shouting whoo-hoo at Dorinda and the masks. 'They're here,' breathed Mrs Warner, next to Penitence. 'Damn 'em.'

It was one of Lacy's big scenes — bravely he ranted on as protests came up from the musicians' pit and a heavily powdered face adorned with patches appeared between two foot-lights, its periwig raised at the front in a pile of curls like a hat. 'Peep-bo.' Cheered by his friends, the fop heaved his thin, be-ribboned body on to the apron, arranged himself and took snuff. 'Can see now.'

'Well, we can't,' shouted a stout citizen.

'Then blurt to you, sirrah.' Wavering, the fop turned to the cast: 'Continue. Oop, no, wait. Got to get the others up.' Things went downhill from there. More beautifully clad drunks joined their friend. They dragged King Lear's throne to the side of the stage and sat on it. They shouted for 'Nelly, give us a song', and took against Goneril and Regan. When Becky Marshall, in villainess's make-up as Goneril, came on, they booed. She was joined by Regan (Anne Marshall), also heavily browed. 'Oh Gawd,' said a fop, 'there's two of 'em.'

Gwynn had her bottom pinched, and kicked backwards at the offender without faltering in her line. One of the fops was sick and a fight broke out as a citizen tried to drag him off the stage.

Heroically, the King's cast continued to play as if their audience was hanging on every word.

Her line was coming up. 'The job, my dear girl,' said a voice from long ago, 'is the play.' *Breathe*. There were people out there who'd paid for their seats and deserved the best.

Lear was castigating Cordelia. It was time to save her. She ran forward on cue . . . a fop put out his foot and tripped her. She slid along on her front to King Lear and ended up with her head on his toes.

Amid the laughter in which even the author's claque joined, she lifted up her face to Lacy's glare. 'Pray save her, Your Majesty,' she said. It had been a short theatrical career. As the King spurned her entreaty she limped back to her place, resisting the temptation to kill the fop and then herself.

Understandings were cleared up, Edgar and Cordelia were paired off. King Lear and his daughter, reunited, pirouetted happily forward to face the jeers of the fops and the counter-cheers of the citizens.

Gwynn, perhaps the only one capable of quietening the house, was sent out to give the epilogue.

Behind the curtain Lacy's eyes scanned the assembled walkers and stopped on Penitence. He looked grim. 'Is she one of yours, John?'

John Downes came on stage. 'Yes.'

'I won't be fallen on. Forfeit her.'

'She's not on salary, Lacy.'

'No? Well, she is now. Put her down for ten shillings a week. And forfeit her five.'

In June she had a small speaking part in an adaptation of Beaumont and Fletcher's *Valentinian*, an even smaller one three nights later as another Persian lady in *Cambyses*. She was a page in *The Death of Richard II*, and Ursula in yet another *Much Ado*.

In the kitchen printing works at the Cock and Pie, while MacGregor set the type – Penitence didn't do it any longer in case it stained her fingers, confining herself to the guillotine – and Aphra rolled the ink and Dorinda operated the press's lever and Mistress Palmer sang in toneless song to her washboard in the scullery next door, each tiny role was analysed until it squeaked.

'I detect malice in Ursula. Do you think I should give her malice?'

'You should give her some peace,' said Dorinda, 'I'm sick of the cow.'

'She's only there to get sent on errands, Penitence,' said Aphra.

'She's still a person. What do you think, MacGregor?'

'I like her fine. I wonder, now, should we have some italics here?' Aphra joined him to ponder it. Her handbills were the only work the Vulture Press had. Other unlicensed presses had come in from the provinces to fill the vacuum left by the Plague. And even the handbill business was diminishing as Killigrew cut more and more of his theatre's costs.

Penitence slammed the guillotine handle down, and the knife cut a badly angled line into the sheets, sending strips on to the floor where Benedick was playing, tethered by a washing-line because of the well's proximity. 'I'm sorry to bore you,' she said, pettishly, 'but somebody's got to tell me if I'm doing it right.'

There were plenty of people to tell her if she did it wrong.

Knipp, the Marshalls and the others were quick with their disapproval if she didn't cue them exactly right or if she put more into her part than was necessary, thereby distracting from their own. Even the good-tempered Gwynn was forced to reprimand her: 'Don't overdo it, ducky. They come to see me, not you.'

The rest of the time she acted into what seemed a vacuum. She tried to tell herself and the others that her eye was on the £1 a week a top actress earned, and to an extent it was, but the spur that goaded her was the frenzy to express something within her which had woken on the balcony of the Cock and Pie when the people on the rooftops had been moved by one impulse – hers.

That night she had experienced control; she had used magic as a projectile, she had been the gyrating stoat bringing the birds closer. She had tasted power after a lifetime of powerlessness and she wanted, she lusted, to taste it again.

Then Hart told her she was to play Desdemona. She was so astounded she almost argued him out of it. 'But she's the *heroine*.' They had just come offstage after the last curtain of *The Indian Emperor* and Hart's large painted eyes were tired. 'Thank you for telling me, dear. Of *course* she's the heroine, or she was when I played her in the old days. What you do with her remains to be seen. Now run away and learn the words. We go on in a month.'

Penitence floated home, babbling. 'It's the first time she's ever been played by an actress. The first time. *Othello* hasn't been put on since only men played women's parts. Hart's been watching me, he says, and he thinks I can do it.'

The Cock and Pie was sure of it and MacGregor insisted they have a night out with ale all round at the Ship to spread the news.

The Ship was the same fine inn it had always been but much of its atmosphere had gone with its children. Mistress Bryskett was a broken woman and rarely put in an appearance. Her remaining child had never come back; the friends who'd taken her to the country had begged to keep her, and since the little girl was thriving in the good air, she had been allowed to remain. Sam was quieter and sterner, but that night he insisted on treating everybody. 'Playing the heroine? Make her jolly then eh, Prinks? Need a bit of jolly nowadays.'

'I'll do my best, Sam.' Penitence couldn't bear to mention the word 'tragedy' in the presence of the Brysketts, and Sam, who never left his inn, was unlikely ever to find out that *Othello* lacked jollity. She doubted if any of the Rookery would; the theatre may have had common appeal in Shakespeare's day but now it was almost exclusively the resort of the upper class.

She reckoned without Dogberry. The ex-watchman had made the Ship his local, though he now had a thriving butchery business in Drury Lane. He put a proprietorial arm round her waist and hoisted her on to a table: 'We're drinking tonight to my progeny,' he announced, 'as I taught everything I know to. The hours I spent in the alley listening to this girl go through her lines was ... hours. The toast is Mistress. Penitence. Hurd. My progeny. May she bring the house down and the butchery trade be there to watch it.' As he lifted her down among cheers, he was troubled. 'Penitence Hurd,' he said. 'It don't sound right, Prinks. All right for pummelling pulpits, but not for bringing houses down.'

Hart said much the same thing. 'You'll have to change it, dear. It won't look good on the programme. We're trying to entertain them, not save their souls.'

'Can't it be just Pen Hurd?'

Hart shuddered. 'We're not in the cattle business, either.'

She was not averse to a change of name. The Indians, who regarded names as magic, had always changed theirs when they wanted to make a new start in life. Matoonas, when she'd first known him, had been Manitowwock and only became Matoonas after passing the test of his initiation ceremony. In this, her great departure, she would be not unhappy to leave behind the detritus carried by her old name. 'Penitence', after all, had been foisted on her as an atonement for her mother's sin, and strictly speaking, she was a Hoy, like her putative father, a FitzHoy, rather than a Hurd.

Aphra suggested 'Miranda' and Dorinda 'Roxolana'. Oddly

enough, it was Mistress Palmer who said: 'Her Ladyship'd been so proud of you. Why not do her proud, eh? Take her name.'

'Margaret Hughes,' Penitence told Hart, firmly.

He raised his eyes. '*Most* exciting, dear, I'm sure. Very well, if you must, you must. Only I think we'll give it a *teeny* bit more verve and make it Peg Hughes.'

So Peg Hughes was what went on the posters.

It was only because Hart, having played Desdemona as a young man, had always coveted the part of the Moor that King's was putting on *Othello* at all. Nobody else was sanguine about its chances of running more than one night; tragedy was out of date: heroic drama was what the public wanted nowadays, while Charles II was well known for his preference for comedy. 'I don't care, it's a great play,' Hart said stubbornly.

What he really meant, Penitence discovered when they began rehearsals, was that it was a great part and he intended Desdemona to be merely a sounding board to his playing of it. He had picked Penitence, an unknown, *because* she was unknown.

'She's the epitome of innocence,' he told Penitence in their first coaching session. 'And, while one wouldn't wish to cast aspersions on the other ladies of this company, to represent any of them as lily chaste would make a cat laugh, let alone an audience.'

Penitence was used to the double standard of morality as it applied to Puritan men and women, but was surprised to discover it in the free and easy atmosphere of the theatre. Hart, for all his elaborate effeminacy, was no lily maid himself. Some women, though not Penitence, found his slim, well-preserved body and languid air irresistible; his affairs were legion. It was rumoured in the walkers' foyer that his present one was with the seventeen-year-old Nell Gwynn. But she was forced to admit he knew his public. The fops could jeer at anything. Hart was afraid of casting Gwynn or Knipp or either of the Marshalls in case Othello's demand of Desdemona, '*Are you not a strumpet?*', was answered by a roar of 'Yes' from the pit.

'Whereas you, dear,' he said, 'look like a primrose nobody's picked yet.' He raised an eyebrow. 'Though, does one gather there's a little fatherless bud?'

'My son, yes.' She was too proud of Benedick to conceal him and had even brought him to the theatre once or twice.

He nodded. 'Well, don't worry. The audience won't know. Married or unmarried, all our lady Thespians are "Mrs". Since our dear King was restored, the title "Mistress" has acquired unfortunate connotations. But we digress. Now then . . .'

Penitence reported back to the Cock and Pie in discontent. 'He wants me to play her all insipid. He keeps referring to her in terms of little white flowers.'

''Course he does,' said Dorinda. 'He's the cock. He don't want no hen sharing his ballocking applause.'

'One's never seen the play,' said Aphra, 'but, reading it, I am forced to say that Desdemona *appears* insipid. A Venetian Matchless Orinda.'

Together in the attic she and Penitence scoured the text for clues to Desdemona until they practically knew her shoe size. 'The poor, poor soul,' said Aphra, wiping her eyes. 'To be as innocent as she was, and yet suspected of being a whore by the man she loves.'

'I can play that,' said Penitence, quietly.

But Aphra decided there was more. 'Not so insipid after all,' she said. 'The dear girl doesn't know it, but she has *appetites*. She positively *lusts* after Othello. She is a creature of nature, like my poor, dear Caesar's wife. She makes "the beast with two backs" — *what* a powerful phrase, how *did* the man do it? — with that lovely black Othello in the artless joy of love.' Aphra picked up her fan to cool herself. 'The thing is, Penitence, she radiates animality. She can't help it. It's directed at her husband, but other men pick up its scent. Cassio does. That horrid rogue Iago does. It is why he sets out to destroy her. It's the old, old story. Men want us, and hate us for making them want us. Desdemona is Eve.'

Penitence was floundered. 'You are clever, Aphra.'

'If you ever felt lust,' said Aphra, 'prepare to play it now.'

Penitence's eyes went to the attic window; she *had* felt it. Once.

*

'No, *no*,' shouted Hart. 'Would you make the girl into a wanton?'

Rebecca Marshall and Kynaston were in the pit, learning the parts of Emilia and Cassio. Knipp, with the smaller part of Bianca, was watching. 'I don't know, Charlie,' she said, slowly. 'Her playing of it makes sense.'

'When I want the interpretation of someone who's never seen the damned play, I'll ask for it, thank you *very* much,' said Hart.

Penitence felt a fool. She also felt relieved. Taking the memory of the passion that had possessed her for Henry King on the night nearly two years before, distancing herself enough to control and direct it towards somebody else, even a fictional somebody else, had given new meaning to the dictum 'All actresses are whores'.

But Kynaston joined in. 'I agree with Knipp, Charlie. It gives an explanation for Othello's jealousy. I always wondered why the silly bugger was so quick to believe Iago's lies. But if Desdemona's a bit of a wagtail, even if she's only wagging it for him, Iago's just confirming Othello's fears.' In an aside to Knipp, he added: 'It makes sense of Iago, too. The sod's jealous.'

Hart raised his eyes. 'If only Shakespeare'd had your command of language.' He came to the unlit footlights. '*Othello* isn't about *sense*, my dears. It's about chaos. The destruction of a great man. They're not coming to hear *sense*. They're coming to hear me reduce them to terror and pity. I shall be wonderful.'

'Good. Good.' Kynaston held up his beautiful hands. 'Sorry I spoke.'

'You do see, though . . .'

'Please,' said Kynaston. 'Continue. Lay on being wonderful. Turn the girl into a dairymaid. If the audience wonders what Othello ever saw in her, it's no skin off my nose.'

'No, it isn't. But you do see . . .'

Kynaston returned to his script. 'Go ahead.'

Lacy, who was playing Iago, was called in for his opinion. Penitence, not called for hers, settled herself on a couch set for the afternoon's production of *The English Monsieur*, while the argument continued.

To her surprise, Knipp came up from the pit and joined her. 'Reminds me of my husband,' she said.

'Hart?'

'Othello. Wants a woman attractive, but only attractive to him.' More than once Penitence had noticed that Knipp's delicate small face sported a black eye. It had one now. Close to, the wrists of her stylish sleeves were worn and there was a hole in her stocking. 'Did you hear Gwynn's sent in her scripts?'

It was promotion for Penitence that, for the first time, Knipp was prepared to gossip with her. In King's hierarchy, the top-rank actresses rarely addressed their inferiors unless in the course of work, and when they did they referred to each other – and insisted on being referred to – by the title 'Mrs'.

Nevertheless, she was sorry that Nell Gwynn was leaving, and said so. 'Where is she going to?' It seemed incredible that someone who already possessed the moon Penitence was reaching for should surrender it.

'Higher things. The King's setting her up. Didn't you know?'

'I'm sorry to hear it.' For all her rejection of Puritanism, two generations of free thinking had inoculated Penitence against monarchy. Nor had her glimpses of the King during his attendances at the theatre changed her conviction that it was wrong to set up a man and worship him. On her very first day in England, when she'd seen Charles II pass by in his coach, she'd decided he was a bad thing and nothing had since changed her mind.

Knipp glanced at her. 'And why be sorry, miss? It ain't every day a child who had to serve drink in a brothel becomes a royal mistress.'

Penitence shook her head. 'I like Mrs Gwynn.' It had been a pleasure to watch her. Penitence knew that when it came to acting she was already the comedienne's superior, but that if she remained a player until Doomsday she'd never be able to pick up an audience and bounce it like a ball as Gwynn did. 'I hope she will not become another Mrs Farley.' Elizabeth Farley's story was still bandied about the walkers' foyer as an Awful Warning of what could happen if an actress gave in too easily to the King's priapism. She'd been Charles's fancy for a night or two, was discarded to one of the courtiers, discarded again, became pregnant, was put in a debtors' prison and now, so legend went, walked the streets of Cheapside.

'Oh Lord,' said Knipp, 'a bloody sermon-sniffer. Farley was a fool. As to that, we were to talk to you later, but it might as well be now.' She looked to where the actors were still in discussion and shifted round so that she was facing Penitence. 'Look, Hughes, you can end up set comfortable for the rest of your life, or you can end up like Farley. Which do you want?'

'I want to act.'

'We all want to act, dearie,' Knipp was impatient, 'always supposing they let us. But what happens is, the moment you step out as Desdemona on that stage in front of that audience, you're prey. You're hunted. You're the hind and they're the stag-hounds. This theatre's a pudding and actresses are the plums. It's all a matter of which hand you let grab you.' She wagged a finger under Penitence's nose. 'Make sure you pick the one with the best rings on. And get guarantees. Put away a nest-egg for when your looks go. Believe me, that's soon enough.'

A figure squatted down beside them and Knipp looked at it for confirmation. 'I'm telling her Farley was a fool as didn't get guarantees before she got the pox, ain't that right, Becky?'

The younger Marshall's face remained beautifully remote. 'I'm afraid it is.'

'Nelly never made Farley's mistake,' continued Knipp. 'No more did Moll Davis over at the Duke's. They got Old Rowley to cough up before he lost interest. He's given Moll a baby, but he's given her a house and a thousand a year to go with it. And our Nelly's got that out of him already.'

'And not even pregnant yet,' said Becky Marshall.

Penitence was warmed by their concern – there was no doubt these two lovely women were very much in earnest – but she was repelled by their assumption that an actress

290

should pick a protector on the basis of his income. She thanked them with the complacence of one about to receive the heady sum of £52 a year.

Knipp shook her head at her and went off to the tiring-room.

'You'll learn,' said Becky Marshall.

'Mrs Knipp doesn't seem to have profited from being a plum,' Penitence said, defensively.

Marshall yawned. 'Ah well, you see, she married for love, poor thing.'

Hart was beckoning her over. Penitence went, prepared to feel sympathy for him. If what she'd heard were true, he'd just lost his beloved to a king. But the actor was insouciant. 'Now then, dear,' he said, 'we're going to try an experiment. We're going to make Desdemona a woman for these lusty times. I want you to give her *passion*. She doesn't just dote on Othello, she's *on heat* for him . . .'

Frangipani was the in perfume that month, and the actresses had splashed it on. Warmed by bare necks and bosoms and the heat trapped within the tiring-room's baize-hung walls, it reached a level that interacted with the noise of female voices crescendoing as the time came for curtain-up and actresses and their dressers jostled for places in front of the looking-glasses.

Outside the door, Jacko and the property boy, Cully, seventy if he was a day, were arguing with Sir Hugh Middleton, who was enamoured of Rebecca Marshall and wanted to enter. Further off the audience's chatter had become a one-pitch note interspersed with the thump of tabors, and the 'Penny-a-pipeful' call of the tobacco-sellers.

Mrs Coney stepped back and looked at Penitence with her head on one side. 'Does she need more powder, Marshy?'

Rebecca Marshall put down her own powder-puff. 'Lord, no. Here, put some of this on her cheeks.' She passed over a leaf of Spanish rouge.

'Hart said "a lily".'

'He didn't say Hamlet's ghost. Watch out.' Penitence was gulping.

'Sick bowl,' called Mrs Coney.'Quick.'

A bowl was brought. Penitence vomited into it. Sighing, Coney wiped her face and began again. 'There, pigeon. You're not the first.'

The argument outside grew louder. Sir Hugh Middleton was refusing to accept the ruling that no male except the property boy was allowed in the tiring-room on first afternoons. 'Becky,' he was shouting, 'Becky, my little bone-ache.'

Marshall covered her ears. 'Why do we have to put up with this? I'm going to complain to the King. I never encouraged the stinkard.'

'Cully's called for Sir Tom to take him away.' Coney patted Penitence's hair and put on its wreath of flowers. 'There now, pigeon, you look lovely. Don't she look lovely, Marshy?'

'She does indeed.' Rebecca gave her own hair a final pat, and stood up. Carefully, one by one, she uncurled Penitence's fingers from around the posy of roses Dorinda and Aphra had given her before she left home. 'Let go now, there's a good girl.'

Freed, Penitence's hands fastened desperately on the front of Rebecca's robe. 'I c-can't remember the first line.'

'I know. Stand up now.'

Outside Sir Hugh's shouts were diminishing as Killigrew persuaded him back to the auditorium. Anne Marshall was panicking as usual. 'Oh hell, oh hell, I can't find my ... oh there they are.' She gave Penitence's cold cheek a kiss. 'You look lovely, dear. Good luck.'

Coney put her head out of the door: 'Mrs Hughes's cloak.'

'Mrs Hughes's cloak coming up.' Theatre costumes were guarded like gold, which generally was what they were worth, being mostly royal cast-offs. On performance days the floors on stage and backstage were laid with calico sheets to protect them. Cully, the property boy, hobbled in with the shoulders of the blue silk cloak laid over his rheumatic hands, his assistant holding its train.

Coney draped it around Penitence's shoulders and fastened it.

The callboy knocked on the door. 'Act I. Scene iii. Mrs Hughes, please.'

Penitence clutched Rebecca Marshall again. 'P-p-pplease. I can't remember anything. Not a line.'

'I know.'

'Bb-bb-bbut it's gone. I want to g-g-go home.'

'I know.'

Between them, the Marshall sisters walked the sagging Penitence to the wings where they stood crammed between John Downes and the cut-out of Othello's ship which had been dragged offstage along the groove that held it. John switched his eyes from his prompter's script for a second and gave her a thumbs-up sign.

Penitence stared ahead. Through the unglazed window of the prompt-side door the actors on stage appeared unreal and far-away in their brightly lit frame. Hart, black-faced and opulent in green and gold, was declaiming, a puppet facing the unseen monster she could hear breathing in the cavern beyond the footlights. It was an animal. She could smell it. Aphra was out there, and Dorinda and MacGregor, Dogberry and his friends, and it had eaten them, absorbed them into its maw.

She was limp. She'd reached the stage of terror beyond terror. *I'll stutter. I'm going to stutter. I can't even stutter. I'll stand there and they can send me home. I'll die. This can't be happening. It doesn't matter. It's all silly. No job for a grown woman.*

'*It's a step up from being a whore. The job, my dear girl, is the play. We give them the best we know. Now* breathe.'

Hart's great voice throbbed out:

> 'She loved me for the dangers I had passed,
> And I loved her that she did pity them,
> This only is the witchcraft I have used.'

Rebecca Marshall saw Penitence's hands go up to her face as if adjusting a mask. She touched her on the shoulder: 'Decus et Dolor,' she said.

'Decus et Dolor,' said Penitence.

'Here comes the lady; let her witness it,' said Othello and held out his arms.

Desdemona ran on to the stage . . .

She used everything she'd ever known, emitting it out of skin and mouth to the huge shape in green and gold that dominated the stage. The audience was small and had a respectable feel, mostly citizens who hadn't fancied the risqué play at the Duke's. She felt their hostility; they wanted a Desdemona they knew, sexually naive. There was a wave of shocked disapproval as she kissed and stroked the black face.

Hart amazed her; even in rehearsal he'd never responded like this. It wasn't Desdemona's play, it was Othello's, but her rendering was allowing the Moor subtleties that hadn't been explored; he grew as she fed him and fed her back so that she grew alongside, taking the audience with her.

Then it was the interval before Act II. Marshall came groaning into the tiring-room where Mrs Coney was repowdering Penitence. 'There's stinkards arrived,' she said, 'Sedley and some others. They're with Middleton up on the apron already.'

I'll stutter. Now I'll stutter.

'Sick bowl,' called Coney.

But Becky Marshall had taken Penitence by her shoulders and was shaking her. 'Look at me. It doesn't matter what they do. You and Hart are . . . well, it's like sharing the stage with tigers. You've conquered the cits to the point where they'd cut their throats if you told them to do it. You're not to let them down. Whatever the other bastards do, ignore them. Do you hear me?'

It was a generous speech; Becky Marshall had wanted to play Desdemona herself.

'Yes, Becky. Thank you.' *Breathe.*

But it was still terrible to stand at the prompt door listening to fops' chatter, rebuilding Desdemona's energy to go out and face it.

On stage, Kynaston as Cassio was too old a hand to be distracted, but the others with him were being put off their stroke. As John Downes in the wings called out: 'A sail! a sail! a sail!' to signal the arrival of Othello's ship into Cyprus, one of the fops got up and did a hornpipe to the applause of his friends. The citizens in the pit were getting restless at the interruptions. Another moment and the theatre would be in uproar.

Beside her, Lacy took her hand. 'Last time I played Iago,' he said, 'we got raided by Cromwell's troopers. Rough? You think those lily-pinks out there are rough? Wait 'til you've been on the end of a Puritan pike.' He crossed himself. 'Decus et Dolor.'

'Decus et Dolor.' Radiating happiness, she swept out.

The scene quelled some of the hoots with which the fops and rakes always accorded a new actress in a leading role and, though they rose again at the passion of her greeting to Othello, she felt the aggression waver. It was a matter of mastery, hers or theirs. Power was leaving them as she and Hart sucked it out of them, transmuted it, and turned it into indomitable tragedy.

She forgot them; she wasn't playing to Othello, but to another man who had believed her to be a whore. She cried Desdemona's cry, 'I have not deserved this', to Henry King.

In the Willow Song she glimpsed Sir Hugh weeping like a baby and Sedley leaning forward, his hand cupped on his chin. She allowed her voice to break on the last line and felt the anguish of the pit rush forward out of the darkness to comfort her. She begged Othello not to kill her.

'It is too late.' Hart's voice was begging himself not to kill her.

She felt the pillow over her face and almost panicked. *Suppose he gets carried away.* Her last lines were the trickiest; the not-quite-dead-yet was, she felt, Shakespeare overdoing it. 'O! Farewell,' but in the audience somebody sobbed as her hand went limp over the side of the bed.

At last Othello's body fell on hers: '... to die upon a kiss,' enveloping her in a smell of stove-blacking. She heard the sigh of the curtain come down on a house that was totally silent.

'Oh God,' she muttered. 'They didn't like it.'

'Stay still.' Hart's white eye glared at her, like a shark's. 'Anyone can rouse a house. To subdue it is the true artistry. And we've done it.'

The curtain rose with the bodies still lying on the bed, the dead Emilia (Rebecca Marshall) artistically draped on the floor.

It wasn't until Hart handed her up that the applause came at her. She stood in it, Hart's hand holding hers high. She loved him. She loved the fops now standing in ovation, loved the beast out there she had conquered, the unicorn that was laying its head in her lap. A fountain of eternal youth played about her.

I wish Benedick were here. They'd left him with Mistress Palmer, in case the sight of his mother being smothered was too much for him.

The triumph wasn't complete. It was missing somebody.

Kynaston and Marshall came on to be washed in their turn, as they deserved. Appreciation gained solid form; flowers, ribbons, coins landed at their feet. Somebody threw a gold watch.

Anne Marshall was due to speak the prologue and whet appetites for the next day's performance of *The Humorous Lieutenant*, but Killigrew took her place to say that in view of the reception 'the King's Servants will oblige with yet another rendering of *Othello* on the morrow'.

Having received a heart-warming 'Not bad, not bad at all' from John Downes, Penitence made her way to the tiring-room and chaos. The place had been invaded by a dozen or so stinkards dodging Jacko's efforts to eject them, drinking, tweaking the dressers' bottoms, staring down Becky Marshall's cleavage, experimenting with the powders and patches before the looking-glasses.

A cheer went up at Penitence's entrance and Sir Hugh Middleton threw himself, literally, at her feet. 'You wonderful creature, you moved me. I adore you. Be mine.'

Sir Charles Sedley bowed before her, for once only in half-mockery. 'Well, well,' he said.

Penitence hobbled towards her stool with Sir Hugh attached to one of her ankles. She was drained; she'd been hoping for a reflective post-mortem with her fellow-players. As always, the rakes were drunk and, as such, alarming; she felt vulnerable and exposed. Adulation was preferable coming from beyond the footlights.

She tried to smile and thank them, but became irritable with fatigue. Sir Hugh's hands kept leaving her ankle and going higher up her leg. 'You move me, you splendid creature.'

She kicked but he hung on. 'I wish somebody would move *you*.' She appealed to Sedley. 'Can't you get him off?' But he made no attempt, just watched her as if she were a game retriever puppy and he was assessing her reaction to the sound of guns.

Cully came in, demanding her costume.

'Let me keep it on, just for tonight,' she begged. Becky Marshall was trying to change behind a screen which, despite the combined efforts of Jacko and Mrs Coney, who was wielding the sick bowl, was rocking as the rakes peeked over it.

'"Any actress wearing costume for other than theatre purposes to forfeit a week's wages",' Cully quoted, unmoved.

'Then go and ask Master Hart and Master Lacy to come and remove these people.'

'Gone home,' said Cully.

'Sir Tom, then.' It had come to something that she must ask Killigrew for help.

'Gone home.'

She had to join Marshall behind the screen in the awkward business of putting her old dress over her head and struggling out of her costume beneath it, with Sir Hugh Middleton crawling round and shouting the colour of her stockings and garters to the others, until Coney brought the sick bowl down on his head.

'Why is this allowed?' she asked furiously of Marshall.

Becky shrugged. 'They're the King's friends. This is the King's theatre. We're the theatre's playthings.' She grinned. 'I see Sir Hugh has changed his allegiance, faithless fellow. You're welcome to him.'

They had to charge for the door, turning down invitations to supper, weekends in the country, carriage rides home. Outside in the corridor Penitence was waylaid by a soberly dressed, round-faced man who offered her a thick manuscript: 'Mrs Hughes, would you do me the honour of reading this play?'

Some of the rakes were trying to lift her. 'What? Oh, put me *down*.'

'It's my play,' the man was running alongside as she was carried through the corridor, shoulder-high, 'I want you for the heroine.'

As she was carried into Riding Yard Alley, Sir Charles Sedley finally came to her rescue: 'Put her down, my buckos, the lady is out of humour.' He picked the manuscript out of Penitence's hand and read the cover by the light of the stage-door flare. '*The Indian Queen*. Full of bombast and rant, I have no doubt. Still, the fellow has a felicity with words and panders to popular taste.'

Penitence straightened her skirt. 'Who is he?'

'Dryden? A useful enough scribbler, though not in the same class as myself, in more ways than one.' He eyed her dishevelment and the fawning Sir Hugh, whom she was still trying to bat away. 'I really think, my dear, you should find yourself a protector.'

But for one night at least she had one, many. As she emerged from Riding Yard Alley, there was a cheer from a crowd of very different men.

That night Penitence was carried home to the Cock and Pie on the shoulders of Drury Lane butchers.

Chapter 5

PENITENCE was sworn in as one of His Majesty's Servants on a fine non-performance day at the beginning of June at the Lord Chamberlain's house in Whitehall. She was dressed in latest 'shepherdess' fashion: a straw hat as big as a coachwheel with blue satin ribbons tied under her chin matching the bows on her silver-kid shoes, a dress of sprigged cream muslin over silk petticoats and a hidden whalebone bodice which cupped her bosom into globes. An inch of lace saved her nipples from exposure – as long as she didn't bend too far forwards.

She copied Knipp and Marshall in using a walking-cane more as an accessory than an aid, arm extended, fingers quirked, but whereas Knipp's and Marshall's were the usual mock-ivory affairs smuggled out of the property cupboard, hers was gilded and carved in the shape of a shepherd's crook, a token of esteem from the Drury Lane butchers.

The ceremony, like the Lord Chamberlain himself, was dignified and short. Hart, Kynaston and Lacy stood beside her in the scarlet and gold livery of royal players; Penitence was disappointed to find that the King's actresses weren't presented with a suit of clothes when they were sworn in, only a gold medallion with Charles's head on it.

As they stepped out into the sunshine and St James's Park, Hart said: 'How do you feel now, young Peg?'

'Official.' It was a delicious sensation, as if she'd been a thing of two dimensions and, pop, expanded into three.

Two pubescent girls spied her from under the limes and came rushing up, dragging their father with them. 'Oh Mrs Hughes, we saw you ... indeed, we did, but yesterday. In *The Great Favourite*.'

Their father swept off his hat: 'These chits of mine try to say, ma'am, that at last we have seen nobility tread England's boards again. We thank you.'

Penitence bowed.

'Bribed,' said Lacy as they walked on. The others nodded sadly.

Penitence examined her fingernails. 'Nobility,' she sighed. 'What a shame more of us don't have it.'

Kynaston stared around him: 'And this whippersnapper, this ungrateful weanling, this serpent's tooth, now expects us to treat her.'

'Let's go to Potiphar's for one,' said Becky Marshall.

'Let's stay in the park,' said Lacy, careful with his money, 'I'll stand her a milk.'

'Let's go to Gwynn's house,' said Knipp, 'and the King can stand us all a wine.'

It was a little early. As Lacy pointed out: 'Better not catch him with his breeches down.'

It was no hardship to saunter along the lake edge and watch the ducks and pelicans. Penitence had a moment of guilt that she was not spending this free time with Benedick — she was kept so hard at it nowadays learning scripts for productions which frequently only lasted a night before being replaced by another that the words she most often addressed to him were 'Run away and play, darling. Mother's busy.' As for the others at the Cock and Pie, virtually her only intercourse with them took place if they came backstage after the performance and walked her home.

Why shouldn't I have some pleasure? This had become another standard phrase. For all its work and tensions, King's was like some marvellous pantry to which she had been given the freedom after a lifetime of starvation. Moments like this, relaxed in lovely surroundings among peers whose creativity she respected as they respected hers, whose shop talk was of consuming interest, were addictive candied cherries.

They were in their playground. In the City, among *nouveau riche* financiers and merchants, they were less inclined to display themselves, especially the actors when identifiable in livery. There the old Puritan ethic was still in evidence and they could be subject to abuse from citizens who objected to the more risqué plays, or even the occasional handful of horse manure thrown by a prudish apprentice. Here, among the parks, palaces and gardens of the old money, they were surrounded by their audience.

Though even here, she noticed, her companions were keeping a look-out and not just in order to acknowledge the salutes of their adorers. They were still vulnerable to the fury of a wronged husband or wife, or even some rake who had been pilloried by one of the wits' plays or prologues, and who blamed the actor who spoke the offence rather than the author. Last week Hart had been nearly run through by an inflamed fop who'd recognized his own posturing in a prologue written by Howard.

They wandered on to where the milkmaid was calling as her cows grazed around her. 'Ah,' Lacy said to her, 'sweet child, whose breath is your own and scents all year long of June, like a new-mown haycock.'

'Just tell us how many you want,' said the milkmaid, wearily.

'Seven,' said Lacy.

They sat down on a bench while the maid squatted, put her large, red hands round an udder's teats and squirted them towards the pail.

'I'm sorry the King didn't attend the inauguration, Peg,' said Kynaston. 'He was there for mine.'

'Ah,' said Becky Marshall, 'but *you* didn't refuse the King's invitation to bed beforehand.'

'He never asked.' Kynaston fluttered his eyelashes, and turned on Penitence. 'You didn't. *Did* you?'

'She cocking well did,' said Knipp. 'Chiffinch came into the green room yesterday and put it to her.'

'I didn't know who he was,' explained Penitence. At first he'd been just another among the hot-eyed, well-dressed men who crowded into the actresses' tiring-room after a performance. 'I didn't know he was the King's pimp. It was so . . . oblique.' Her voice became lofty: 'His Majesty had enjoyed my interpretation, and should I wish to avail myself of the Privy Stair at any time, His Majesty would be graciously pleased.'

'Stupid colonial, she didn't know what the Privy Stair was,' crowed Anne Marshall, kicking her legs in the air at her amusement. 'She thought she was being given the freedom of the royal water closet next time she was in Whitehall.'

Kynaston clapped his hands over his mouth.

'What did you say?' breathed Hart.

Penitence grimaced. 'I said, thank you, but I usually went before I left home.'

Amid whoops of joy, the milkmaid shoved a tray holding seven beakers at Lacy. 'Tenpence ha'penny,' she said. 'And I ain't got change.'

Wiping his eyes, Lacy counted out the coins. 'Whatever became of the Arcadian spirit?' he asked.

'Never touch it,' said the milkmaid, and whacked the leader of her herd on its rump to discourage its interest in Knipp's flowered hat.

'Will Old Rowley be cross?' asked Penitence. It worried her slightly. She was making a good story out of the incident, but she'd quickly realized who Chiffinch was that evening, and what he was asking. Appearing to misunderstand had seemed the best way of avoiding a situation she had no intention of getting into. She wanted to make a career from acting, not whoring.

'Nah,' said Knipp. 'He's been turned down before. Frances Stewart insisted on keeping her cherry and turned him down in public.'

'I don't know, Peg,' said Lacy, 'he's my king and I love him and-he-died-and-then-she-died, but odd things happen when he's insulted. Look at poor Coventry's nose.'

A shudder ran round the group; mutilation of their looks was the players' nightmare. Coventry's had come about from a debate in the House of Commons when a member, trying to avert a tax on playhouses, had pointed out what pleasure the King derived from the theatre. 'From the actors? Or the actresses?' Sir John Coventry had asked. Next day, walking in the park, he'd been waylaid by ruffians and had his nose slit.

'Come along, my little republican,' said Kynaston. Wiping off their milky moustaches, the King's servants strolled on, twitting Penitence for her lack of patriotism. 'Would *you* have gone up the Privy Stair?' she enquired of Becky Marshall.

'I wasn't asked.'

'But *would* you have?' She didn't regret turning down the King's offer — she'd have felt more of a whore in the King's bed than on the blankets of Newgate's condemned cell or even than she did on Killigrew's couch — but until Chiffinch had bowed and gone she hadn't realized the enormity of what she'd done and its possible consequences. And though the actors were teasing, she sensed surprise that she priced her tarnished virtue so high.

'No,' said Marshall.

'Why?' Penitence was comforted but curious. Unlike her

sister, Becky had gravitas. While Anne took lovers, all of them rich and generous, the younger Marshall accepted gifts without giving more than her company at dinner in return and made it clear that only those prepared to make an honourable offer need apply.

Marshall slowed her walk so that the two of them fell behind. 'Like you, I don't believe in absolute monarchy – in bed or out.' She dropped her voice. 'One doesn't bruit it about, but Stephen Marshall was our father's cousin.'

'Presbyterian Stephen Marshall?' Penitence was impressed. In Massachusetts the Reverend Marshall's reputation for saintliness was high. Under the Commonwealth his bones had been interred with honour in Westminster Abbey. They'd been thrown out after Charles's restoration. It was strange to discover an actress related to such a Nonconformist divine.

Stranger still, Becky said: 'My father followed him into the Presbyterian Church, but, of course, the Conventicles Act has stopped him preaching.' She smiled. 'He has no high regard for his daughters' honour, but he might be comforted to hear we both draw the line at sleeping with a Papist like Rowley.'

'Is the King a *Papist*?' The word still vibrated with Puritan abhorrence.

'Oh yes,' said Becky Marshall, calmly. She nodded to the others ahead. 'Though you wouldn't get our friends there to believe it.'

They were walking along a narrow path edged by the canal on one side and pollarded willows on the other. A little way beyond the trees a coach had drawn up. As they passed it they saw its driver's seat was empty and its curtains drawn. Marshall was saying how dangerous it was to leave horses unattended when the coach door opened and two men jumped down. Penitence just had time to recognize Sir Hugh Middleton before both men grabbed her and began dragging her towards the coach where a third man was holding open the door. She screamed.

Marshall was running after them, shouting for help. One of the captors had to release his hold to fend her off, and Penitence managed to get her arm round a tree trunk. Her face scraped against bark as they pulled her away, wrenching her arm, but the delay had given the players time to reach her. She had a confused impression of the actors, swords drawn, in approved fencing positions encircling her and Middleton, who was clutching the back of her dress, shouting: 'The slut's mine. I adore her.'

'Let her go.'

The other man released her and ran back to the coach. Penitence kicked backwards, connecting her brand-new high heel with Middleton's shin. His hand tore her dress as he let it go and began hopping, rubbing his leg. 'She's mine. I want her.'

Lacy, recognizing farce when he saw it, sheathed his sword. 'Get back in the coach, Sir Hugh, there's a good lad.'

Middleton's face crumpled and he dithered his hands, like a frustrated baby. 'But I want her.'

'Not today.' Kynaston and Hart marched him back to his coach, watched it pull away, then bowed gracefully to a crowd that had hurried up to watch.

It had turned into a performance and Penitence, shaking, responded to it by bewailing her torn dress and ruined hat as if they were her grievance. In a way they were; she still owed dressmaker and milliner £20. But the true shock was not so much the assault as the words Middleton had been hissing at her as he'd dragged her away, protesting his adoration with vituperation so violent it had been like the snarls of a predator with a rabbit in its jaws. Knipp had been right. *We are prey*.

Knipp and Anne Marshall exclaimed over her grazed face. It was Becky who insisted that something be done. She was furious. 'What are we? Animals?' she raved. 'All we do is try to earn a living, and they think they can snatch us up like stray dogs. This isn't the first time. And what about that fop who nearly *raped* Knipp in the tiring-room the other night? Where's the King? I'm going to give him a piece of my mind.'

'It's not his fault Middleton's a lunatic,' said Kynaston, reasonably.

'We're under his protection, he can damned well protect us. Where is he?'

It was easy enough to find him; Charles II was the most accessible of kings. The first person they asked directed them to Pall Mall. A crowd hid him, but as they came up it emitted an admiring 'ooh' at a ball which curved into the air above its heads and through one of the loops hanging from the gibbet-like poles along the course that was out of the actors' view. Suddenly it scattered as a less well-directed ball went skywards. Determinedly, Marshall led her force into the gap.

Penitence held back; reaction was making her feel sick. She could hear Marshall's voice expostulating and the news being passed around the spectators. Becky meant well, but she wished she wouldn't *fuss*. She didn't want to be drawn to the King's attention.

A very tall shadow blocked out the sun. 'Mrs Hughes. Allow me.' A hand under her elbow led her to the shade of an oak tree. The figure beside her took off its coat, folded it neatly and put it on the ground. Gratefully, Penitence sank on to it.

'You're hurt, ma'am. Allow me to fetch a doctor.'

The voice was deep and prim. The face high above her was unmistakably a Stuart's, the same swarthiness, same jawline, cleft chin and dark eyes. Only the mouth was distinctive, being thinner and less sensuous than the King's and more intelligent than James's. Below the hairline of his periwig an old scar formed an ugly dent of puckered skin. This man was even taller than the royal brothers, about six foot four, had seen more years and, from the look of him, had liked them less, but at the moment he was registering an almost nervous concern. 'A restorative, ma'am. At least permit me to fetch a restorative.'

'Thank you, sir. It's nothing.'

'It was a foul assault so I have just heard. But give the word, ma'am, and I'll horsewhip the varlet into the next country.' It was said with an energy which sent a thrush in the branches above his head flying to a quieter perch.

'You are kind, sir.' She smiled in real appreciation. 'But I think His Majesty is being asked to take action. I'm one of his players.'

'Indeed. I had the privilege to see your Desdemona but last week.'

That's who he was. It had been an occasion when the house was exceptionally well ordered and Hart had explained: 'Prince Rupert's in the audience. The stinkards daren't misbehave while Rupert's around.' The romance still attached to the name of Charles I's great cavalry general had sent twitters of expectation round the tiring-room, but the Prince had disappointed them by merely sending his compliments. Penitence, too, had been curious to see the commander who'd written the news of her father's death to her mother with such courtesy.

Now here he was, an ageing, embittered-looking hawk of a man and, at the moment, ill-at-ease. There was a silence.

'I prefer Shakespeare to the taradiddle they put on nowadays,' said Prince Rupert.

'We're performing *Hamlet* next week,' she told him.

'With yourself as Ophelia?'

'Yes.'

'I shall be in attendance.'

There was another silence and they both studied a herd of deer grazing nearby. It was a relief when the crowd by the pell-mell course opened to let a group of courtiers, led by the King, walk in her direction.

Prince Rupert assisted Penitence to her feet and bowed. 'I shall instruct the troopers to keep back the rabble. Farewell, ma'am.'

'Thank you, Your Highness.'

Sedley and Rochester had been among those pell-melling with the King and all three were in their waistcoats. Charles II expressed a lazy concern as Penitence raised herself from her curtsey. He cupped her under her chin: 'Oddsfish, did the villain scrape this peach? He shall die, what do you say, Rochester?' His eyes were amused and gently malicious.

Did he set Middleton on? She dismissed the thought as unworthy. *But he's not displeased that it happened.*

The Earl of Rochester said: 'Chop his head off, sire. We need a new pell ball.'

'More than one,' said Sir Charles Sedley. 'Let's detach him from another part of his anatomy.'

Poor Becky Marshall was still trying to instil some of her outrage into the royal ears but she had been wrong-footed and merely sounded shrill.

There was a piercing whistle from the wall which marked the garden end of the houses flanking the pell-mell court and where, to the delight of the crowd, Nell Gwynn had climbed up from the far side of hers and was leaning over to find out what had happened.

Some two hundred people now pressed against the restraining troopers to listen to their king explain the situation to his mistress.

'You all right, Peg?'

'Yes, thank you, Nelly.'

'Now you listen to me, Charlie,' said Gwynn. 'Your Majesty, I mean. There's too much of it. We get it all the time, in the tiring-room, outside. You got to put a stop to it.'

'Get what, Mrs Gwynn?' asked Rochester, slyly.

'Too much of you. Treating us like we was common as hedges,' said Gwynn. She flirted as she scolded, playing the jester-mistress. The crowd was loving it.

Charles staggered back in mock surrender. 'Pax, O fair one. It shall be done. Laws shall be passed. Edicts issued.'

This game was obviously going to go on for some time. Penitence wondered if she could go home.

The only one paying her attention was Sir Charles Sedley. She felt his shirt-sleeved arm slip under hers. 'I told you you'd need a protector,' he said.

In the end nothing came of it. A sulky Sir Hugh was reprimanded by the Lord Chamberlain. The King ordered members of the audience banned from the actresses' tiring-room, but nobody took any notice.

Neither did Prince Rupert attend the performance of *Hamlet*. On that same day, 10 June, the Dutch fleet appeared at the mouth of the Medway and bombarded the fort commanding it into surrender before sailing upriver, burning three of the biggest vessels in the Royal Navy and towing off its flagship as a prize.

The news reached Whitehall the next morning.

Charles and James reacted with the energy they had shown during the Great Fire and immediately took horse to supervise personally the sinking of ships in the Thames so that the enemy should be blocked from further advance. The militia was called out in every county and a large field army raised with commendable speed. But although they limited the harm, this time they got no praise. This time, the reverberation of cannon that travelled up the Thames to the ears of Londoners came only from enemy guns.

The Royal Navy had been caught napping, and the greatest damage was political.

Penitence heard the news in Dog Yard as she set out for the theatre. Even in the Rookery, usually unconcerned with anything happening outside a half-mile radius, angry knots of people gathered in Dog Yard to ask the pleasant June air what things were coming to. By Holborn the knots had become crowds. Drury Lane was almost impassable. She detected little panic, only rage. The country had suffered the worst humiliation in its naval history and the howl wasn't directed so much against the Dutch who'd committed the offence, as at those who should have prevented it. She struggled through crowds surrounding upturned tubs on which furious men ranted against the government, Lord Chancellor Clarendon, even against Charles II.

On one tub a man with clerical tippets on his ragged collar was whipping up the anti-Catholicism that seethed just under the surface of any English Protestant crowd. 'Punish the Papists who wind their heresies around our king and make him weak. The Whore of Babylon is loose in the court.' One of his listeners took the opportunity to shout: 'She ain't the only one.'

Further on another tub-thumper was calling up an equally powerful genie: 'And what I say is: Where's our taxes gone? Eh? What they doing with our money if they ain't spending it on our defence. Eh?' He was supplied with the answer he wanted. 'On the back of that Papist bitch, Castlemaine.' The jewels and palaces with which the King had loaded Barbara Villiers, now the Duchess of Cleveland, for keeping his bed warm were resented by the Drury Laners in a way that his conspicuous spending on the latest favourite, Nell Gwynn, was not. Nelly was one of their own and a good Protestant; Castlemaine was haughty and a Roman Catholic and a useful scapegoat.

Passing the butchers' stalls, Penitence was called over to a Dogberry surrounded by fellow-traders, flies and hanging halves of beef. 'She'll know,' he said. 'Here, Pen, is it right last night while the Dutch was attacking, the King was careering around with his women hunting a bloody moth?'

She was glad to dissociate herself from the doings of the court. 'I'm just a poor actress, William. I'm not in that circle.'

'It's bad though, Pen. Iffen you see him, you tell him. We didn't survive the bloody Plague so's we could be murdered in our beds. It wouldn't have happened in good Queen Bess's time. Nor Cromwell's neither.'

It was the first time since arriving in England she'd heard the late Lord Protector's name mentioned with approbation. It seemed that King Charles II's honeymoon with his common people was over.

Her fellow-players were gloomily gathered on stage for rehearsal. She made her apologies for being late. 'Everybody's blaming the King more than the Dutch. They don't seem to be blaming the Dutch at all.'

'Well, it shouldn't have happened, Peg,' said Lacy. 'The Medway fort was only half built, ran out of money. And they say the navy's sinking for lack of supplies.'

'He'll have to treat with the Dutch now,' said Kynaston, 'The war's ruining us.'

'We should never have fought them in the first place.' Becky Marshall was betraying her Presbyterian sympathies. 'I don't mind the Dutch. It's the French who worry me.'

John Downes called Penitence to the wings. 'Letter for you.'

She broke the seal and read neat, but hurried, writing.

I go to plant cannon at Woolwich and down the Medway. Pities be that I was not allowed to do so before, as I urged, and that I shall not have the pleasure in watching perform the lady whom I regard as England's noblest actress. May you be in God's keeping and excuse your devoted servant, Rupert.

'Interesting?' asked John.

'From Prince Rupert,' she told him, 'he's gone to war.'

'God love him. He was on our wing at Edgehill, the mad sod. Pity there aren't more like him nowadays.'

Hart's complaint reached them: 'No doubt our audience today, if we have one at all, will be meagre, but do you think it might just *possibly* notice if Ophelia isn't in it . . .?'

The audience that afternoon was meagre indeed; for once there were more 'vizards', as the players called the pit prostitutes, than customers, and even they kept clustering in irritating groups to whisper the latest news of the blockade. Hart did his best, but as the four captains bearing Hamlet offstage reached the wings, the corpse was heard to remark: 'Bugger Shakespeare. We're doing Dryden from here on.'

Penitence didn't like Dryden's heroic drama. His rhyming couplets were more difficult to speak than Shakespeare's blank verse – good as far as rhyming couplets went, sometimes even sublime, but needing a lot of work if they weren't to sound banal – and she found his female characters flat; for all their bravura speeches on love and sacrifice, they were empty of humanity.

She didn't like Dryden much either. The genius was there and the poet's country-dumpling head was packed with more learning than any head had a right to be, but she found him curiously lacking in conviction. He had a chameleon quality, a theatre man when among actors, a watchful rake when among rakes, the complete courtier in the presence of the King.

One day, when he was rehearsing them for *The Rival Ladies*, she placed him. There'd been a quarrel between Anne Marshall and Knipp over who was upstaging whom and Dryden had to separate them. 'Come, come, ladies, a theatre is as it were a little commonwealth, by the good government whereof God's glory may be advanced.'

'A Puritan,' exclaimed Penitence, recognizing a misquotation from the book of management that had dictated her childhood, '"an *household* is as it were a little commonwealth" . . . how do you know Dod and Cleaver, Master Dryden?'

She was taken aback by his fury: 'And how do *you* know it, madam? Were you of the Levelling rabble?'

'Neither Levellers nor rabble,' she said. She didn't let insults pass nowadays. 'But people who used their tongues with courtesy.'

Later he sought her out and apologized. 'Though it does no good, Mrs Hughes, to insist on an upbringing hateful both to us and our royal master.'

She shrugged. 'I neither insist on it nor conceal it.'

Discussing the incident with Aphra, she said: 'He's a trimmer. He wrote fulsome praise of Cromwell during the Protectorate. Now he's the complete royalist. I hate trimmers.'

'You're not a playwright dependent on patronage,' said Aphra, who was still unsuccessfully hawking her writing around town. 'But you're happy enough to speak the words he writes. I don't blame the poor man. I'd praise the Devil if I thought he'd put my play on.'

Chastened, Penitence had to admit that Dryden knew what the public wanted. England's pride had been hurt; its people had to look backwards to find heroism and principle, aware their own age had none.

Dryden provided both qualities with grandeur. He also provided spectacle. Killigrew groaned at the expense of exotic costumes, the dancers, the equipment to enable gods and goddesses to descend from the heavens in cars and spirits to rise from the underworld, the storms, the dungeons, the magical effects. But audiences loved it. Crowds flocked in. The carriage trade blocked Drury Lane in both directions.

And it was Peg Hughes it saw. Her blonde hair and height advantage over the other actresses, nearly all of whom were shorter and dark, the stateliness of her walk, thanks to John Downes's training, and the careful diction with which she still had to control her stutter made her Dryden's ideal heroine. 'The perfect Englishwoman,' he said.

That she played an Inca maiden in *The Indian Queen* and a Spanish girl dressed as a boy in *The Rival Ladies* didn't matter; Englishness set in exotic climes was what Dryden gave them.

And rant.

'Die, sorceress, die! And all my wrongs die with thee,' shrieked Penitence as she plunged home a stage dagger during the first performance of *The Rival Ladies*, wondering whether the audience would laugh, and instead hearing it drag in its breath with horror.

She became expert at tortuous lines:

> Oh, my dear father! Oh, why may not I,
> Since you gave life to me, for you now die?

and made them, if not natural, at least thrilling.

> O Lust! O horror! O perfidy!

It seemed to her she emitted more 'O!s' than verse. But Dryden's O!s were turning her from a promising actress into the toast of London.

What she said became less important than the way she said it. She was gaining power in more ways than one. It only needed her name to figure in large type on a Dryden playbill for the Theatre Royal to be so packed as to be dangerous. Wits, rakes, fops no longer dared interrupt a Hughes–Dryden play for fear of being lynched by the pit. In any case, Penitence could now quell their hesitant jeers with a single 'O!'

Power. She knew what it was on the day Killigrew called her into his office before another performance of *The Rival Ladies*.

He was sitting on his couch, and patting it. 'Well, my dear girl,' he said, 'it's been a long time.'

She smiled at him and didn't move from the doorway. 'It has indeed, Sir Tom.'

He continued to pat. 'I knew,' he said, tilting his head at her, 'I knew when you were just a little walker you'd have London at your feet one day, and now you have.'

'Yes, Sir Tom.'

'All due to me, you know.'

'Thank you, Sir Tom.'

'Come and give us a kiss then.'

She planted one of her feet on the chair by his desk — she was in boy's costume. 'Davenant sent me round a note of congratulation the other day, Sir Tom. After he'd come to see *The Indian Emperor*.'

Killigrew had been confidently lounging. Now he sat up. 'Don't believe it. Whatever that street-juggling coxcomb promised you, don't you believe it.'

'I *believe*,' said Penitence, 'that he thinks I'm even better than Mrs Sanderson. I *believe* he pays Mrs Sanderson thirty-five shillings a week.'

'Nonsense. There's no actress in the world worth thirty-five shillings a week. *Hart* only gets two pounds a week. And don't you start blackmailing me, Miss Majesty. For one thing, the King wouldn't let you go.'

'I *believe*,' said Penitence, 'that Davenant will persuade the Duke to play his brother at cards for me. If I give the word. I *believe* that the King's been losing heavily lately.'

Sir Tom stood up, took off his wig and flung it to the floor. 'God damn all women. This is my reward for employing the bitches. I should have listened to the Puritans. I should have stuck to boys. I could have trained orang-utans better and cheaper, but no, in the goodness of my heart, I take a gaggle of bare-arsed geese out of the stews, turn them into swans and what happens?' He thrust his face close to Penitence's. 'Eh? They bite the bloody hand that feeds them.'

Penitence forced herself not to recoil. 'But is it going to feed me thirty-five shillings a week?'

Sir Tom jerked his chair from under her foot. 'You've got too big for your boots, madam.'

She looked down at her boots, a pair of gilded kid, cast-offs from one of Castlemaine's young royal bastards; they fitted perfectly. 'It's nearly curtain-up time,' she said. 'Do I go on today or don't I?' Even with the door closed, they could hear the subdued roar of a packed house coming from the auditorium. 'What?' Sir Tom had mumbled something.

'I *said*,' he said nastily, 'I suppose you'll have to go on. And don't blame me if the whole company goes bankrupt.'

'There's just one more thing,' she said. *Might as well go the whole hog.* 'I should like Dorinda to become a walker.'

'Who the hell's Dorinda?'

'The orange-girl.' *Doesn't he remember* anybody *he leches?*

'*That* Dorinda.' Sir Tom became reflective. 'Amazing girl. Twat like a corkscrew. Certainly, certainly.' He sighed. 'What's another harlot? Anything else, madam? No husband you want a dukedom for?'

'No thank you, Sir Tom. I have no husband.'

'That's a mercy for some poor devil. Now get out on that stage. And I tell you this, madam, I'm regretting the day—'

'There is one last thing. I wish you would reconsider Aphra Behn's play.'

Killigrew got up, pushed past her, opened the door and pointed. 'Out. It's bad enough being blackmailed by sluts of actresses, but ruin myself with some female's scribble I shall not. Out.'

Penitence outed. Becky Marshall, also in boy's costume, was waiting for her in the corridor. 'Did it work?'

Penitence took her hands and swung her round. 'It worked. I avoided the couch *and* I got a rise.'

Her ambition leaped like a mountain goat into higher, greener pasture. It was true Hart received only a £2 a week salary, but as a shareholder in the company he also got £1,000 a year. *Why shouldn't a woman become a shareholder?*

Telling Dorinda that she had procured her at least a start in the theatre was another ferocious joy. As they walked home together that night, their plans ran into fantasy.

'I'll put Benedick's name down for Westminster School.'

'We can do up the Cock and Pie.'

'We could leave the Rookery altogether. We could move into Westminster.'

'Pity about Aphra's play.'

'We'll put it on ourselves. We'll have our own theatre.'

Drury Laners stared at them as they twirled along, their voices calling out into the summer evening.

At the entrance to Dog Yard Dorinda, at least, calmed down. 'I'll lease out the orange business. Can't afford to lose them profits.'

'Oranges,' scoffed Penitence. 'We won't need them for long. We're professional women now.'

'I always was,' said Dorinda.

'A real profession. Respectable. Well, respectable-ish. Oh, Dorry, we're independent. We can survive. We don't have to sleep with any man ever again.'

They stood in the middle of the Yard so long, transfixed by the thought, that Footloose came trundling over to see what was the matter. From the window of Mother Hubbard's where a new generation of girls had taken over from the old, a voice asked a passer-by: 'Want some fickytoodle, dearie?'

Penitence snatched Footloose's cap from his head and threw it in the air. 'We don't have to sleep with anybody ever again.'

'Lessen we want to,' said Dorinda, catching the cap and kissing the scabby head before replacing its covering.

Hearing their voices, Benedick came toddling out of the Cock and Pie's door. Penitence ran up the steps and lifted him before he fell down them. She put him on her shoulder and turned so that he could survey the empires of the earth.

Dog Yard was in the shadow cast by the tall wooden frame of Mother Hubbard's, but the sunset was gilding the tattered rooftops and the view beyond. 'We're rising, my son,' she said.

As Penitence rose so did the City of London. In place of the destroyed ancient forest of buildings sprang up an elegant plantation.

It wasn't as elegant as it might have been; Christopher Wren's visionary plan as Surveyor-General which would, if built, have rivalled Rome or the Paris redesigned by Henri IV, was rejected as too expensive. Obstruction, procrastination

315

and corruption inevitably took the fine edge off even the compromise.

But if Wren wasn't allowed to design Utopia, he designed practically everything else. Under his supervision fifty-one churches began to raise their differing and beautiful steeples into the empty sky, some like pagodas, some tiered, or with columns, consoles and obelisks, some Flemish, others Gothic.

The labour to rebuild houses and shops, big or small, went on every day and sometimes into the night by the light of flares. Timber was brought not only from all over the country but from as far away as Norway. Brick kilns ringed the city with smoke, the one at Moorgate alone turning out over a million bricks a year.

Anguish for the past was replaced by pride in the new as a modern, wider-thoroughfared city of brick, stone and tile emerged from the ruins.

Yet for all the growth, there was a sense of incompleteness. Londoners up to their elbows in plaster would pause as they looked towards the uncrowned rise on which had floated the great whale to which their homes and churches had been the accompanying school of porpoises. It would take years, perhaps they would never live to see it; until St Paul's was resurrected London could not be London.

But up on the hill, a foundation stone was being laid without ceremony. 'Here,' Christopher Wren said. 'We'll start here. Get a flat stone and put it here.'

His workmen looked around the scree of fire-scarred rubble. 'Which one?'

'Any one.'

The nearest and flattest was part of an old gravestone; as they tipped it down on to the spot that Wren indicated they saw what word was on it.

'*Resurgam.*'

Entering his mother's bedroom for a morning kiss, Benedick took one look and yelled. Mistress Palmer came running. 'Gawdelpus, what you wearing that bloody thing for? You look like the Devil crapped hisself flying.'

316

Penitence was struggling to undo the mask strings that had got tied up with her back hair. 'I slept in it. It's got ... blast the thing, don't fret, darling, it's only Mama ... cream on the inside. It's to feed the skin. There, now give us a kiss.'

'You got bloody gloves on an' all.'

'Same thing. And I wish you'd watch your language in front of the boy.'

'I don't fright him shitless, that's one thing', and muttering that in her day they used soap and water, Mrs Palmer took herself off.

'We'll have to get you a tutor,' Penitence told her son.

'Don't want a tutor. You said MacGregor was my tutor. He's learning me—'

'Teaching.'

'—teaching me ever so well. You ain't heard me read my new horn book.' Benedick's small forefinger traced a 'B' in the grease on his mother's face. 'Will I read it to you now?'

'I've got to get up and make pretty.'

Benedick bounced up and down on her stomach. 'Why? Why do you? You said you was resting today. You said we'd go to the park.'

He was a dark-haired child with fine, sallow skin. As he glowered at Penitence just then she saw his father and shut her eyes to get rid of the image. So far the boy hadn't questioned his one-parent state – so many of his contemporaries in the Rookery lacked a father that it seemed a natural condition to him.

She was prepared for when he did. 'Your father is dead, Benedick.' She wanted Henry King dead. Every day she wanted him deader. The nights were a different matter, but by day she obliterated the man's personality. Each year increased her resentment at the ease with which he'd gone away and stayed away, until her memory of the man deliberately diminished him into the caricature of a seducer. She'd forbidden Dorinda and MacGregor to mention him.

The first time she heard his name at the theatre, when Hart and Lacy were discussing the possibility of putting on a translation of *Tartuffe*, it was a shock. 'I wish Henry

King were still with us,' Hart said. 'He was the Molière expert.'

'Ah, Henry,' sighed Knipp, 'I miss him.'

It was like hearing that a centaur, some mythical creature, had once dropped in for tea. It was against her pride to seek more information, though she would have welcomed it unsought. There were other mentions, but none seemed to know where he had come from or gone to and, typical players that they were, concerned themselves with him only as he had affected their theatrical lives.

The momentary resemblance hardened her heart against the boy. 'I must shop for when I go to the races with the King,' she told him. 'You want Mama to look nice, don't you?'

'I wish he'd fight battles, then I could go. I want to go to war.'

She rinsed her face and began sorting through the silver-gilt boxes, tweezers and bowls that Sir Hugh Middleton had given her as a peace offering. 'Your Auntie Aphra should never have taken you to see *Henry the Fifth.*'

'Wasn't it grand when they killed all those Frenchies?'

'It wasn't very grand when the Frenchies killed the little boys in the baggage train.' Lemon juice on Spanish wool cleared the last of the grease from her face. A little cochineal went on the cheekbone as her son dispatched the nobility of France with her long-handled powder-puff.

'I wish I had a sword.'

You should have. We had to sell it. 'Sir Charles says he'll give you one he had as a boy.'

'Will he?' His face went sullen. 'Don't like Sir Charles Sedley-pedley-wedley. Why do you like him? He makes fun of me.'

'He makes fun of everybody. Powder-puff please.'

'*Can't* we go to the park?'

'Come here.' As he stood between her knees they looked at each other with mutual incomprehension. They spent so little time together that she was self-conscious when she talked to him. 'Benedick, you know when we went to Auntie Knipp's house?'

He nodded.

'And there wasn't much furniture in it?'

'It was cold.'

'It *was* cold. That's because she doesn't earn as much money as I do and can't buy coal. And that's because her husband doesn't let her go out and make friends. And if you don't make friends you don't get good parts to play and people don't give you presents.'

'Auntie Dorry's got lots of friends. She gets *very* good parts. Wasn't she bloody funny yesterday?'

'*Very* funny. I've told you not to swear.' Dorinda had now adopted the stage-name Roxolana she'd once suggested for Penitence, and her success on the boards had taken Penitence aback; having taught her friend everything she knew, it had been disconcerting to discover that, as far as comic timing went, Dorinda had a thing or two to teach her. 'But you do see, Benedick, that if you're to learn Latin and Greek and how to use a sword and—'

'And he died and then she died.'

She couldn't help grinning; he'd picked up theatre slang quickly. 'But you do see. We've got to have money if you're to go to school. And so I've got to go out and about.'

He'd lost concentration. 'I've got a lot of friends, haven't I? I've got the Tippins and—'

'Exactly,' she said grimly. 'Now then. Shall I put a patch here? Or here?'

She gave the day's instructions to MacGregor and Mistress Palmer and stepped out into Dog Yard, the scent of 'Hughes' chypre which Charles Lillie of Lillie's-in-the-Strand had created especially for her battling against the Yard's stinks, and losing.

She kept to the terrace past the Ship in order to avoid the mud and ordure below the steps. *Here I am* – she always glissaded into this thought at this point – *most popular actress in England and still living in this hell-hole.*

''Morning, Pen.'

'Good morning, Sam.'

From the pawnbroker's across the way, Mistress Fulker, who was carrying on her dead husband's business, yelled: 'Time's up on that ticker, Pen. You going to redeem it or not?'

Everywhere else they treat me with respect. Should she redeem the watch or sell it? It was gold, a tribute from an unknown admirer. Unlikely that Mistress Fulker would pay anything near its true value. 'I'll speak to you tomorrow.' Damned if she was going to haggle in public.

She had to back away as a young Tippin ran up and seemed about to clutch her skirt. 'Here, Pen, can Benny come out to play?'

'No,' she told him, coldly. 'Benedick is at his lessons.'

I've got to get us out of here. Merely to emerge out of the Rookery with one's shoes and petticoat unstained was a problem. She had to refuse Sedley's offers to send a carriage for her because she dared not let his servants see the sort of place she lived in. She certainly couldn't afford a carriage of her own. Yet to rent a house in an area which sported pavements or even duckboards would take up too much of the money she was saving for Benedick's education.

She was less worried about the boy's health than she had been – anybody who could survive babyhood in the Rookery usually survived the rest. But unless she made a move soon, his language, let alone the bad habits he was picking up from the Tippins and their ilk, would debar him from a school like Westminster.

She'd thought a salary of £91 a year plus the money from her benefit performances plus the gifts, most of which she turned into cash, would be enough to maintain a decent life-style and, more importantly, her independence.

She'd reckoned without the necessity of appearing affluent. This was Restoration England. You were what you wore and how you wore it. She'd told Benedick the stark truth; Knipp was getting fewer and fewer parts, not because she was a bad actress, but because she had a jealous husband who suspected every present and who refused to allow her to make the social round of the coffee-shops where the playwrights – and it was playwrights who did the casting – hung out, or to appear in the park where the public appetite was whetted by the sight of its heroines. Knipp was disappearing.

If Peg Hughes was to stay visible, she had to buy silk stockings at 15s, scented gloves at 12s a pair, have her mantuas made in Italy, her shoes at St James's and her cosmetics in the Strand. The lace adorning her handkerchief alone cost 5s a yard. By rights she should have employed a personal hairdresser, but had managed to come to an arrangement with Nell Gwynn's, who moonlighted.

Holding her skirts high and lurching from one clean piece of ground to another she reached Holborn where the traffic had left so much manure that she had to pause and make a calculation, not only whether she should sacrifice a florin and hire a hackney to take her to the Royal Exchange but whether, by doing so, she would commit that gravest of social sins and arrive on time. 'Always keep 'em waiting,' Gwynn had advised her in a tutorial on how to treat men. Easy enough for Nelly, who never rose before midday, but an effort for Penitence, who had punctuality engraved on her soul. In the interest of her shoes, however, she hailed a hackney which, luckily, was delayed by the usual jam at the Poultry.

She loved the new Exchange. The grandeur of its piazza was made friendly by the arcades of shops around it. It was like standing at the ancient crossroad of the world watching the caravans go by to see the foreign merchants, Russians in furs, robed Arabs, Jews in their gaberdines, bargaining over sables, tea, coffee, tobacco, spices in this international Babel.

She posed herself in the great doorway and waited for attention, knowing she was worthy of it. Unable to afford the fashionable dressmakers, she employed one of the Huguenot women who'd settled in exile in the Rookery as seamstress. Her costume today was designed to wrong-foot the fripperiness that was getting out of hand. It was plain, dark blue broadcloth cut close-fitting to the waist and flowing out into a divided skirt, relieved only by white lawn collar and cuffs. Her hat, of the same dark blue, was like a cavalier's curled round by a white ostrich feather. The severity of the outfit would, she hoped, make a virtue of her lack of jewellery. Judging by the admiration she was attracting, it did.

She saw Rochester and Sedley start to cross the floor, then veer away as the six foot, four inches of Prince Rupert cut them off: 'Well met, Mrs Hughes. Will you take chocolate with me? One of my ships has brought in some particularly fine beans.'

'Thank you, sir. Unfortunately, I am committed elsewhere.' She curtseyed. 'I hope you are pleased with the use I've made of the feather you gave me.'

He regarded her hat gravely. 'Even the ostrich would approve.' For Rupert that was a joke. She smiled as they stood together in one of their silences.

Abruptly he said: 'Will you do me the goodness of dining with me next Saturday? The invitation, of course, extends to your chaperone.'

Bless him. Only Rupert could think that modern society demanded chaperones. 'Thank you, sir, I shall be honoured.' The King had teased her: 'Take care that my besotted cousin doesn't storm your citadel as he stormed Lichfield, Mrs Hughes. He wasn't known as Hot Rupert for nothing.' But she'd be as safe with him as she was with MacGregor. His letters to her were a combination of studied, old-fashioned compliments and military communiqués. She hoped very much that they could be friends, and nothing more.

The rakes came up, mocking, when he left her. 'What, Mrs Hughes?' asked Sedley, adopting a deep voice and a limp. 'You've never been drowned? You haven't lived. Do me the goodness to sail with me in my yacht. Coxswain, wheel to the right.'

Rochester limped on her left. 'Why you young whippersnapper, you should have been with us when we ate all Cromwell's babies in '42. That'd have made a man of you.'

'You're jealous,' said Penitence. They were even nastier about Rupert than about their female conquests once they'd slept with them, and with the same touch of self-disgust. It ate at them that they had never tempered their courage in war like Rupert and were reduced to showing it in idiotic duels. They were destroying themselves with debauchery because they couldn't die gloriously in battle.

'And you're late,' said Sedley, proffering his arm. 'We're meeting the King and Nelly for dinner at the Bear later. His Majesty is pleased to be coming in disguise.'

322

'Which means everybody will recognize him,' said Rochester, 'but the bill will be presented to us. Shops?'

'Shops,' said Penitence.

'It's like watching an apothecary attempting to keep the flies off his treacle,' said Sir Charles, as she agonized over the price of ribbon.

'What is?'

'Watching a pretty actress trying to keep her independence.'

'I'm going to, Charles,' she said, warningly. She was keeping him at arm's length, refusing his blandishments and his elaborate presents; he persisted with the assurance of one who knew she'd given in eventually. He alarmed her; she was frightened he might be right.

'Of course you are, of course you are. But pray permit me to buy the ribbon. It's nearly the blue of your eyes.'

'No, thank you.'

'My dear, this particular fly doesn't think a few shillings is the admission price to your honey pot. It merely gives him consequence to wear such a pretty creature on his arm.'

Rochester nuzzled her neck. 'Don't listen to him. He's a flesh-loving insect. He'll lay such a maggot in your cunt as all the medicine in the kingdom won't keep your reputation from stinking.'

She jerked away from him. Every so often the game they played turned into verbal violence. When they saw they'd perturbed her they'd woo her back with a line of verse that sang. She was being tenderized, bashed like a piece of meat to make her fit for their palate. They used their sophistication like a weapon. Already they'd beaten her into being more afraid of looking 'virtuous' – they made it a dirty word – than of protesting. She coped with them by appearing lazily unshockable. 'Be easy, my lord,' she said, 'my price comes higher than a few yards of ribbon.'

But Sedley bought them anyway. And later on in the morning, as they turned into Will's Coffee-House, he tucked them into the front of her costume and, because the dress she was planning to wear at the races really needed ribbon, she pretended not to notice and left them there.

Dryden was in his usual place by the fire, celebrating his new status as Poet Laureate with his fellow-writers, and was put out by losing the attention of his audience to Penitence.

'Mrs Hughes, Mrs Hughes, have you read my play?'

'Mrs Hughes, I've a part for you will make your mouth water.'

'Mrs Hughes,' said Dryden, 'like the percipient artist she is, will concern herself only with plays that adhere to the unities.'

But Penitence had spotted an outlandishly dressed figure across the room and was running to it. 'Aphra. What are you doing here?'

They hugged. Though they lived in the same house, Penitence's hours and Aphra Behn's no longer coincided. It had been weeks since they'd had time to do more than greet each other on the stairs.

Aphra tipped her barbarously coloured cap to the back of her head. 'One has done it. I heard today.'

'Heard what?'

'Davenant's taking my play.'

'Oh, Aphra.' It was impossible. It was joyous. She had to blink back tears. 'I'm so *glad*. Which one?'

They dragged two stools to the back of the room and sat down to chat. '*The Forced Marriage*.' Aphra's mouth gave a moue of pretended disapproval. 'Not one's best, but it's a start.'

'It'll run for a week. I'm so *proud* of you.'

'How ironic it will be at Duke's. I so wanted you for the lead.'

'My dear girl,' Penitence jerked her head towards the fireplace where Dryden still pontificated, 'unless it preserved the unities I couldn't possibly. What *are* the unities?'

'Lunacies,' said Aphra promptly. 'As if one could write to rule. But, my dear' — she took Penitence's hand — 'should it be a success, well, my brother has found us a little house . . .'

'You're not leaving the Cock and Pie?'

'We cannot batten on you for ever.'

'You haven't battened, you haven't.' Penitence's alarm lifted

324

her voice so that Sedley, always aware of her, turned round to look. 'Don't go, Aphra.' It would be a relief to see the back of Mrs Johnson, but Aphra had brought poetry and intellectual enquiry into the Cock and Pie. 'What will Benedick do without you?' MacGregor had taught her son to read, but it was Aphra who'd taught him to love reading.

'He will visit his honorary aunt every day. As will you. But we are the new women, my dear, and must try for independence.'

Penitence shook her head. 'It's hard. You'll find it so hard.'

Sedley's scent enveloped them as he leaned over, rolling his eyes. 'Whose is hard? Don't quarrel over it, ladies. I can be hard enough for both of you.'

'Oh, shut up,' said Penitence wearily.

Immediately he became vitriolic, turning on Aphra. 'I hear you've been brought to bed of a play, mistress. Surely the infant is not all your own. Who is the father?'

God protect her. Penitence blew a kiss to Aphra and ushered him out, frightened for her friend. Spying for the King and a debtors' prison had been ease and comfort compared with what faced a woman who was preparing to compete in a world in which every wit and half-wit fancied himself a playwright. *God, protect her.*

Chapter 6

THE TRIP to the races had been planned as part of a relaxation for the King's nephew, Prince William of Orange, towards the end of the young Dutch prince's state visit to England to cement the new alliance between the two countries. After all the formality, Charles thought William would be glad of entertainment, and knew that *he* would, so actresses had been included in the invitation.

'And if one of you ladies should relieve the lad of his virginity while you're about it, the King will not be displeased,' the Earl of Rochester told the tiring-room, two nights before they were due to go.

Anne Marshall pulled her dress over her head. 'How old is he?'

'Nineteen, twenty.'

'And still a ballocking virgin?' Dorinda paused in the act of untying her basque strings.

'My dear Roxolana,' said Sedley, trying to balance his staff on his nose, 'the Dutch court does things differently. For one thing — damn it, I'll never get the trick of it — it's not a court at all. The Netherlands are a republic, poor flatlanders that they are. Our William may be a prince of the blood, but in that benighted country he's only a councillor or stadtholder, or whatever dreary titles they give themselves, of one little state. There, I've done it. Look at me.'

'He's more than that,' said Becky Marshall, quietly.

Rochester shot her a glance. 'Sometimes, my dear Becky, I wonder where you get your political knowledge. Anyway, our royal young lumpkin's been a prisoner of the De Witts for years, locked up on a diet of cheese and sermons. Soured his disposition.'

Penitence rolled down her stage stockings carefully, sequinned cast-offs from Gwynn. 'He must have some importance. Old Rowley's making a rare fuss of him. I suppose it's all to celebrate the new alliance.' She smoothed on her own stockings, slapping Sir George Etherege's hand as he tried to snap her garter. 'Stop that.'

'He's put your lover's nose out of joint, I'm afraid,' said Sedley. 'The revered royal Rupert was so offended at the state dinner the other night to find his nephew given precedence over him at the table that he stalked out. Positively *stalked*, my dear. He looked like an offended walking-stick.' He adjusted the lace of his cuffs. 'And talking of offence, my dears, I hear that Kynaston gave the epilogue yesterday dressed up as *me*.'

The actresses busied themselves in finishing their toilet. 'Only a bit of fun, Sedley dear,' said Anne Marshall.

'Of course it was. Of *course* it was. Did the audience enjoy it?'

'Oh, he died and then she died,' said Dorinda, vaguely. She turned the conversation back to the Prince of Orange. 'Well, I ain't fucking the young squib,' she said, 'I got other fish to fry.'

'Would that be the noble fish of Oxford, Roxolana my dear?' asked Rochester, slyly. '*Twentieth* fish of that ilk?' Dorinda was being strongly courted by Aubrey de Vere, Earl of Oxford.

'It would. *And* his intentions is honourable, *and* he's coming with us to Newmarket. Somebody else can swive the Dutcher.'

'Orange-girl turns down Prince of Orange,' sighed Rochester. 'But think on't. You *may* be rejecting the future King of England.'

Dorinda stared at him. 'How'd you make that out?'

'Well, our own dear Queen, poor Portuguese bat, seems to be the one woman in England whom the King *can't* impregnate, and brother James has only daughters, the elder of whom may be given to our little Dutchman – I don't say she will, but she may.' He shuddered. 'So, in the natural course of things, we might end up with that constipated young Hollander on the throne, God save us all.'

'And he died and then she died,' said Dorinda, again. 'I'm bored of politics. Let's go out to dinner.'

'We had our differences, ma'am,' said Prince Rupert of the Earl of Clarendon. 'Hyde was never my friend, but he was an honest enemy, and a faithful servant of the King. I regret his scapegoating for the mismanagement of the war. No, ma'am, I regret his exile.'

Penitence nodded sagely. 'But at least we have peace once more.' *Keep the conversation neutral.* She had expected there to be a large party, that he'd invited her as part of a quota of pretty women to flaunt at his table, like other courtiers did. But they were ominously alone, facing each other from opposite ends of a long, polished table. She wondered if he would mention his offended departure from the state dinner over the precedence given to the young Prince of Orange, but he didn't.

'The Triple Alliance? Long may it last. I fought the Dutch fleet more from duty than conviction. Another honest enemy, Mrs Hughes, and glad I am to have them as ally. The true enemy of England, ma'am, is France. Louis and his Popery. Popery above all. Did I ever recount to you my imprisonment at the hands of Ferdinand III when I was offered my freedom if I would but convert to Rome?'

This was better. She was ignorant of so much of the European past, and Rupert, who had figured in a great deal of it, linked up history for her. She listened warily as she ate, the slight and occasional Bohemian accent giving his pedantic English a trace of the Oriental. *Perhaps he only wants someone to talk to.* It would be upsetting to find that he was like all the others and she ended the evening fending off a sexual attack. *I should have brought a chaperone after all.* He might interpret her lack of one as an invitation. *But who could I bring? Dorinda? Mistress Palmer?*

The apartments were dark, tucked away in a corner of Whitehall's vastness overlooking a private garden, and smelled of hounds. A half dozen of them had greeted her entrance and he'd watched her reaction before he commanded them away. 'You are not frightened, Mrs Hughes,' he said. 'That's good. That's good.'

He seemed to imagine her the epitome of delicate woman-hood. She spared him the knowledge that if you could stand up to an Indian dog pack, you could stand up to anything.

It was the most masculine room she'd ever been in; the space on the walls above the looming furniture was hung with spears, swords and armour. Books were everywhere else. The table was set with exquisite napery, silver and crystal. The food, however, was cold. He apologized. 'I make them run with it from the kitchens, but they never run fast enough.'

She became apprehensive as the servants cleared the table and left. *I liked him. What a pity.* He got up to peer out of the casement behind him through which issued the smell of wet autumn leaves. 'I had hoped we could walk in the garden, but it is too damp.'

Here it comes. She looked around for the inevitable couch, but failed to see one.

He took his place back at the table, the evening sun outlining his wig and the still-athletic spread of his shoulders. 'Do you know that I have a son, Mrs Hughes?' he asked.

She did. Charles Sedley had apprised her of the fact as soon as he became aware of the Prince's interest in her. 'Wouldn't think the old boy could still raise his banner, would you,' Sedley had said. 'But he did. Got the little bastard on some poor Irish chit whose father fought with our Rupert in the war. Tricked the girl into thinking she was marrying him, dirty old devil, and chucked her over once he'd had his way with her.'

Neither the trickery nor the chucking over sounded like the Rupert she knew. But perhaps she didn't know him. She waited.

He coughed. 'The boy's mother had and still has a claim on me. There was a ceremony, which I somewhat foolishly regarded as merely the blessing of an alliance and she as a wedding.'

He leaned forward 'She was a Catholic, you see.'

Penitence nodded, not seeing at all.

'She has no complaint of me, and were she here she would tell you so. She has found accommodation that suits her better with my sister, the Electress of Hanover. Our son she has been good enough to leave in my care.' He paused. 'I've put him down for Eton.'

She had to stop herself smiling.

He was speaking so stiffly now he might have been angry with her. 'I tell you this so that you will understand, madam, why I am unable to offer you marriage. Had my circumstances been simpler, you would now be receiving such a proposal. You must believe that in all other respects my offer is honourable. Safeguards, permanence, a home I hope you will find not unworthy of you, these things I lay at your feet with all the affection of which my soul is capable.'

Whatever she had been expecting, it wasn't this.

'You have a son, I believe?' They'd been as quick to pass on the gossip about her as to tell her about him. She nodded. 'You have my assurance that, should you take me, he would be raised with all the consequence of my own.'

She was silent for so long he said: 'Is it my age, madam? Am I too old for you?' It was the first time he'd shown agitation.

'No. Oh no. Your Highness . . .' This formality was ridiculous. She sounded like a Dryden heroine. '. . . I am overwhelmed. And muddled.'

'I beg you not to answer now,' he said. 'For all they think I should be put out to grass, I am a man of the world and did not expect your life to be any less complicated than my own has been. Sir Charles Sedley has been making free with your name, perhaps with your permission, perhaps not. I ask no questions.'

'Why?' Somebody had to break through this courtesy and say something real. 'Why don't you? You don't know anything about me.'

'It is your future that exercises me, not your past.' He became brisk and rang the small silver bell on the table by his hand for a servant to fetch her cloak. 'You will need time to consider the matter. I shall not take up any more of it.'

He rose and stalked down the table to hold the great oak chair so that she could get up. He smelled of cologne and camphor. As he kissed her hand, he stayed bending so that he could look into her face. 'I know by your eyes, madam,' he said, 'that should you agree, my honour would be as protected by you as yours by me.'

She saw *his* eyes and, for the first time, the passion in them. This calculated reserve wasn't natural to him; he was an impetuous and hot-blooded man. His hand under hers was vibrating. *I couldn't. I wish I could, but I couldn't.*

'Yes,' she said, 'it would. That's why I'm not going to do it. Believe me, you have paid me the greatest compliment of my life, sir. But you deserve to be loved. I'm sorry, so sorry, but I don't love you.' She wasn't going to act for him. He deserved the truth.

For the first time he smiled, and she saw the man who'd fought for a lost cause before. 'An honest woman,' he said, 'and worth waiting for.'

As he took her through the maze of corridors and courtyards

to his coach – odd that she hadn't minded him knowing her address when she'd kept it from Sedley – she babbled mollifications. 'I am enjoying earning my own living, you see. I value my independence.'

He had no idea what she meant. An independent woman was a contradiction in terms. 'I shall wait to hear from you. God bless you.'

She waved, then flopped back on to the buttoned leather seat. *Well, well, Penitence Hurd. You have come up in the world.* Instantly, she was ashamed at her gratification. She must guard against being impressed by titles. It didn't matter that he was a prince of the blood; what mattered was that he was a good man.

A good man? Prince Robber? Devil Rupert? Scourge of the Puritan cause? If she'd accepted him the shades of her grandparents wouldn't know which to bewail the more – her living-in-sin, or her living-in-sin with the most feared royalist general of the Civil War.

Speak as you find, she told them, cheerfully. *My mother would approve.*

When Charles Sedley had offered to set her up he'd made no mention of Benedick. His proposal was a transaction: 'And a thousand pound cash when we tire of each other.' It wasn't her Sedley wanted in any case. He merely liked the idea of a trophy, a pretty head on the wall of his vanity. 'Actress, Drury Lane, *c.* 1670.'

Rupert had offered her his life.

Bless him, she thought, and yawned. It had been an emotional day. *But Benedick's going to Westminster, not Eton.*

To get to Newmarket in good time meant leaving London at three in the morning. Penitence and Dorinda spent the night with the Marshalls in their small house near Temple Bar so that the coach coming to collect them all need make only one stop. Knipp's husband had refused to let her come.

Dorinda was wild with excitement and nerves – it was her first inclusion in a royal party – and varied between If-only-Her-Ladyship-could-see-me-now and Suppose-they-know-I-was-on-the-game.

'They think we're all on the game,' Becky Marshall told her, and repeated the Awful Warning of Elizabeth Farley.

'I know, don't I?' Dorinda said. 'Knipp's already told me. "Don't sell yourself cheap." An' I won't. Trust me, them days is over. Asides, Aubrey's intentions is honourable.'

To find any friend of Charles's capable of honourable intentions was a novelty, and the sight of the Earl's beery face as he hauled Dorinda into his own coach when they joined the royal cavalcade at Whitehall made Penitence doubt it. In the general redistribution she found herself in another coach, alone with Sedley, who had a hangover. She went straight to the attack. 'You've been making free with my name, it appears,' she said. 'You know we're not on those terms, and I'll not have it said that we are.'

'Oh God,' he moaned, 'wait 'til my head's smaller. I can't stomach Puritans at this hour of the morning.'

'And you're not coupling with them at nights either,' she said, but he'd already fallen asleep.

As the mother of a child she didn't keep secret, she was in no position to go around posing as a virgin. But neither would she have it bruited about that she was anybody's for the asking. So far she'd been spared but if once her reputation went she'd be carrion. The court wits would tear her apart.

They hymned faithlessness in wonderful live-for-the-moment sonnets to their beloveds, but woe to the girl they persuaded, then tired of. Within days, details of how she performed in bed were distributed round town with exact descriptions of her pudenda.

If she tired of them first the savagery was frightening. Rochester had hounded a mistress who'd thrown him over with:

> While she whines like a dog-drawn bitch;
> Loathed and despised, kicked out of town,
> Into some dirty hole alone,
> To chew her cud of misery
> And know she owes it all to me.
> And may no woman better thrive,
> That dares profane the cunt I swive.

For an actress to be out of their company meant professional oblivion; to be in it was dangerous. Every minute she was with the court, Penitence was aware of the depth beneath the high wire she balanced on. But if it was frightening, it was exhilarating. With their style, their careless erudition and their wealth they made life a brilliant feast at which the trick, for their guests, was to avoid the poisoned chalice.

She studied Sedley's chubby face, one side of his wig pulled up against the seat-back, like a spaniel's ear, the mouth whistling alcoholic snores. *I don't trust you*. But in that case, what was she doing here? Partly because he wanted her to be. But the honest answer was that she was sick of penury, sick of living in a house with the ghosts of the Plague, sick of worrying about Benedick, sick of thinking of a future when her looks went and with them her career.

> At twenty-five in women's eyes,
> Beauty does fade, at thirty dies . . .

Sedley had written that to her. And she was already twenty-four, going on twenty-five. And she hadn't been out of London since she arrived in it from the Americas. And travelling in upholstered comfort to a new experience in a cavalcade which included a king, a prince, a duke or two, not to mention several earls, had to be good going.

Just before Baldock there was a stop for a change of horses and relief of bladders, the men of the party wandering off like hungover ghosts into the woods while the ladies were accommodated by hastily erected little tents. Back in the coach, Sedley fell asleep again but Penitence, hanging out of the window, saw the dawn come up over the frosted chalk downs of the Icknield Way and watched the sun bring out the reds of haws and hips in the hedgerows. She switched to the left-hand side after Royston to see the land go flat to the horizon in common fields where vegetable plots alternated with strips of sooty tilled earth in a black and emerald chessboard. In the distance the spires of Cambridge floated on a cushion of mist.

She was entranced by the variety of landscape England could pack into a distance of sixty miles. Now they were going through tiny villages where even the meanest cottage was pargeted and the thatching put little wolf's ears at either end of each roof. She would have woken up Sedley to ask him why that was, but she dreaded his jeer at her excitement, and thought that in any case he wouldn't know.

'And that, my dear,' said the Earl of Rochester, pointing at a black stallion being paraded round the stableyard, 'is the original Old Rowley. He's sired nearly as many progeny as our own dear king.'

'Who is known,' added Sir Charles Sedley, 'as the Father of his People because he's fathered most of 'em.'

> 'Nor are his desires above his strength,
> His sceptre and his prick are of a length,'

sang Rochester. Penitence glanced towards the King only a few feet away, and saw his lips twitch. *Well, if he thinks it isn't lèse majesté, it isn't.*

And the wits had a point. Royal bastards were well represented at Newmarket, not to mention their mothers. The mother of the Duke of Monmouth, the handsome young man who was showing off by doing steed leaps over Old Rowley, was safely obliterated in the King's past. But the fecund Castlemaine was here with her children, so was Nell Gwynn, and both were pregnant.

Penitence winced for the barren Queen, though she seemed to be on fairly good terms with the mistresses. 'Has to be,' Sedley had told her, 'ever since she lost the fight over Castlemaine when the King insisted on making the whore a Lady of the Queen's Bedchamber.'

The only one, apart from herself, who seemed to find the situation bizarre was the Prince of Orange. He looked like a boy who had been transported to an Arabian harem and kept blinking as he glanced from the plain little Queen to the lovely, rounded women, one tall and dark, the other small and fair, who were her rivals.

Unusually for him, Charles patronized the boy. 'Come over here, nephew. You'll not have seen horseflesh like this before.' As William obediently crossed the stableyard, Penitence studied him. The Stuart genes were apparent in his face, though he was shorter than his uncles and had the rounded shoulders of an asthmatic.

'You should build as good a stables as these at Dieren. I shall send you a brood mare carrying Rowley's foal. Gelderland could provide a fine racecourse.'

'Over the flats, of course,' drawled Rochester. The wits found the Netherlands' flatness inexhaustibly funny.

'Thank you, Your Majesty,' said the Prince of Orange. He spoke English well, with a slightly sing-song accent. 'But should France advance on us further, there will be neither time nor land for a racecourse.'

Sedley and Rochester put languid hands over their mouths and patted away feigned yawns. Charles was irritated. 'Make a friend of France, nephew. You will find Louis a better one than all your Dutch blockheads. Now, let us see if they have taught you to ride.'

The ladies queued at a mounting block to be hoisted up on horses behind the men for the journey out on to the heath. Dorinda, who was afraid of horses, made the King laugh by shrieking: 'I ain't getting up on a ballocker that big. I'll get the vertigoes.' Eventually she was persuaded, and with her arms around the Earl of Oxford's considerable waist, bumped out of the yard alongside Penitence, who had her arms round Sedley's, followed by the jockeys in their surcoats and tapestried caps.

It was a glorious day. Gorse and bracken edged the swathes of sheep-nibbled grass that looked as if it had been smoothed on to the hillocks. Rooks, disturbed by the noisy cavalcade, circled over elm and beech hangars which were just beginning to turn into the yellows and copper of autumn.

'See that lady-in-waiting there, the one up behind Buckingham?' shouted Sedley over his shoulder, pointing at a graceful figure jolting along in front. 'That's Winifred Wells, Charles's latest. Figure of a goddess. Physiognomy of a dreamy sheep.'

Penitence felt a sudden nausea for herself and her companions.

335

The landscape's freshness was a reproach. She wanted to wander off into it alone and read a book by a stream. Homesickness for the innocent forests of Massachusetts brought tears to her eyes.

'And that one there? Face like a gargoyle and smells? That's one of James's. Where does he find 'em? She'd better watch out. Lord Carnegie doesn't like his wife sleeping with James as well and is trying to contract the pox so that he can pass it on to them both.'

She shut her ears to everything but the larksong.

They watched the racing from a pavilion set on a rise, though the male court was unable to resist joining in the last race which ended with the King passing the winning post to the sound of drums, huzzas and trumpets. *He's even brought a band.*

She couldn't help feeling that if as much money and care had been spent on the country's defences as was being lavished on this outing, the Prince of Orange's countrymen would never have forced their way up the Thames. The organization that had gone into arranging the large apiary of tents from which liveried servants buzzed back and forth with refreshments was extraordinary. So was the picnic that came later. Pretty wenches had been hired to waft bracken fronds over the trestles to keep the flies off every kind of meat, fowl and fish in every form known to the royal kitchens, roast, pied, tarted, ragouted, boiled, with pistachio cream, sauces of artichokes, peas and saffron, morelles, truffles.

To foster the back-to-nature spirit, the company sat on silk cushions and, much to Dorinda's relief, ate with their fingers.

Having helped Penitence to sweetbreads and asparagus, Sedley disappeared behind a small hill of chops. 'What will you drink? Beer, Lambeth ale, mead, claret, champagne, Spanish or Rhenish?'

What she wanted most was cold water. Taking a fine pewter tankard with her, she went looking for a brook and found a stream running along the edge of a wood. She knelt beside it and drank, enjoying the rustle of leaf and water, examining paw prints and remembering her tracking days.

'Another water-drinker,' said a voice. It was the Prince of Orange. He had no receptacle and after she'd curtseyed she offered him her tankard. 'They try to make me drunk, I think,' he said.

She nodded. 'They would.' As he drank she remembered Becky had said the boy was special, something like that, and thought Becky was probably right. Somebody'd said he was younger than the Duke of Monmouth, but his fewer years had given him a caution the King's son would never know. She decided she liked him.

'Lovely lady,' he said, 'I am bewildered by so many lovely ladies. Who do you belong to?' When she raised her eyebrows he apologized: 'Forgive me. My English.'

'I'm an actress. And, thank God, I don't belong to anybody.'

'So?' He had a nice smile when he was animated. 'An actress? Do you know Molière? I have a friend has introduced me to Molière. I like him very much.'

'So do I.' They strolled back over the heath, talking theatre. He had recently produced a ballet, he told her. As if he were becoming too informal, he put his hands behind his back and asked conscientiously: 'Have you always been an actress?'

'No, before that I was a printer.'

They had to stop then while he questioned her, and if he'd been knowledgeable about the theatre, he was twice so on the printing trade. 'My country makes the finest type, I think.'

'So do I.' She found herself telling him about the Cock and Pie Press, then remembered and looked suspiciously around at the bushes. 'But please don't mention it to the King. I'm not licensed.'

'You have no free press in England?' He was horrified.

'I must go,' she said. Sedley was coming towards them, chewing a capon.

He insisted on shaking hands. 'Goodbye, madame.'

'Goodbye.'

Sedley put an arm round her waist to draw her back to the picnic. 'It's not safe to let you near princes,' he said, 'young or old.'

Dorinda and her earl had also been for a walk. Dorinda

floated to where Penitence was sitting with Sedley and the Marshalls. 'He's done it,' she whispered. 'He's only gone and done it. Asked me to marry him.'

'Congratulations,' said Sedley, while the girls fell on her.

'I'm so *happy* for you,' said Penitence, 'if you're sure.'

'If I'm sure?' Dorinda was still whispering. 'If I'm sure? What do you think? But it's got to be hush until the dirty deed's done. Acause of his family. We're creeping off soon. He's found a priest as'll tie the knot. Wish me luck.'

When she'd gone to rejoin her beloved, Penitence and Rebecca looked at each other, doubting the ease of the fairy-tale. Becky asked Sedley quietly: 'The Earl's not married already, is he?'

'Quiet your virginal suspicion, my dear,' he said, 'the noble de Vere is between wives at the minute.' The way he said it did nothing to lessen Penitence's unease for her friend, but when she went to look for her to offer herself as bridesmaid, the Earl and his future Countess were nowhere to be seen.

There was a diversion as the Queen and some of her ladies borrowed red petticoats and waistcoats from the servants' tents and, amidst a lot of giggling, set off on cart-horses, accompanied by guards dressed as peasants, to visit a nearby fair in what they hoped was bucolic incognito.

'Incognito,' scoffed Sedley. 'They look about as countrified as the Old Bailey.'

There was the night's jollification still to come, but Penitence was beginning to look forward to the whole thing being over. The reality of court life, though dazzling and magnetic, was also full of tension. And with the departure of the Queen on her country-fair adventure, what little restraint there'd been on those who remained behind was lifted.

Penitence and Becky were constantly harassed for sexual favours by courtiers who assumed, probably rightly, that was why actresses had been invited. Anne early deserted them and disappeared with the Earl of Dorset. The drinking became frenetic; Rochester got pale and vague as he grew drunker, Sedley got redder and a foul-mouthed nuisance. She had to keep batting him off, like a hornet.

Day turned to night, the pastel silks and muslins of afternoon costume were laid aside for deeper colours and richer cloth. The venue became the lovely gallery of the Earl of Suffolk's palace at Audley End. Cards replaced horses, dalliance was transferred from behind bushes to couches in discreet niches. Everybody became drunker. She and Becky sang for their supper, but got booed for not singing bawdy enough songs, though they'd seemed bawdy when they'd rehearsed them. Sir George Etherege took their place and, wavering, plaintively sang:

> 'Love's chiefest magic lies
> In women's cunts, not in their eyes . . .'

Penitence saw William of Orange trying to take his leave of the King and go to bed, but being impeded by the Duke of Buckingham who lectured him on incivility.

Fatigue, the noise, tobacco smoke and fumes from the brandy glasses gave her the sensation of drunkenness from which she kept waking up to vignettes of awful clarity, Sedley pawing at her breasts, the King pawing at Castlemaine's, Buckingham repeating his lecture, this time to a legal-looking gentleman who seemed to have wandered in by mistake . . . 'and I advise you, my lord, to keep a whore, for it is politically ill-advised in this court to be faithful to your wife.'

Everything's upside-down. She'd stepped into a distorting mirror where immorality was as rigid as the Puritans' adherence to piety. If she half-closed her eyes the impact of the candle-light on the costumes and jewels created a rainbow shimmer-ing. *They're so beautiful. These are the cleverest people in England. They must be right.* The room was whirling. She was very thirsty. The orange-water in her glass tasted strange.

There were a lot of dogs around. A bitch was suckling some whelps on a satin-covered couch to the discomfiture of a couple who had other uses for it. The man tried to push the bitch off, there was a snarl. The King lurched to his feet: 'Leave my dog alone, varlet.'

The courtier held out a bleeding finger. 'God save Your Majesty, but God damn your dogs.'

'That's funny,' Penitence said and laughed. 'That's so funny.'

'And you're so desirable,' said Sedley. They were in a dark corridor, which struck cold after the heat of the gallery.

'Where's Becky?'

'She'll be along in a minute. You're so lovely, so desirable.'

'Where's the Prince of Orange? Orange-water. Something in my orange-water.'

'Quiet now. Buckingham's putting something in his. In here, you beauty, you lovely baggage.'

'Can't see.'

'Over here. Ups-a-daisy.'

'It's cold,' she said. The silk bedcover was chill against the back of her shoulders.

'Here's something'll warm you.'

Part of her mind was aware of what was happening, but it was stuck high up in the corner of the bed's tester which she could just see in the moonlight, and she couldn't reach it. Her body was crying: Why not? Why assume the mask of lust and not experience it?

> Tell me no more of constancy,
> The frivolous pretence
> Of cold age, narrow jealousy,
> Disease and want of sense.

Constancy was withering her, and for whom? He'd left her, paid her and left. 'You're right,' she sobbed, 'I've grown old for him.'

'You're beautiful, you Puritan bitch. Stay still.'

She wished he wouldn't talk. So long since he'd lit the heat between her legs to warm her. Rub me, rub me back to life.

He was rubbing hard; her head was knocking against the bedhead. Why did he spoil it with swearing? Not nice.

'God damn it.' She woke up. 'No you don't. Get away from me.'

'Stay still, you whore. I'm coming.'

'NO.' With all her strength she jackknifed, jerking Sedley out of and off her. He lay screaming and bucking, then collapsed.

'You got me drunk ... you, you,' she couldn't think of a word bad enough for him, or for her, 'you vile *thing*.' She stumbled against a wall, feeling for the door, traced the shape of a panel to a doorknob and turned it, shook it. It was locked. No key.

She was in fuming control now. She marched back to the bed and slapped the shape on it. 'When I say so, do you hear me? When *I* say so. Me. Not you.' He mumbled something. She pulled the bed-curtains back further and saw the gleam of the key that was still in his hand. She found later that it had scored her skin.

Out in the deeper darkness of the corridor, she stopped and ran her hands down her body. Her breasts were hanging out of her basque. She pulled it up. *Where's my damn room? Don't they keep servants in this damn house?* There was a hullabaloo going on somewhere to her right. Staggering, she moved towards it, slowing down as it resolved into the sound of shouts, drunken laughter and, in a recessed echo, high-pitched screams. There was a draught curtain between her corridor and the next. Carefully, she peeped round it.

A group of men — she recognized Buckhurst and Rochester — were standing around a wild figure, cheering it on as it hammered on a door. 'Go to it, Your Highness.' It was Buckingham's voice. 'What are maids of honour for but to lose their honour to princes?'

The feminine screams were coming from behind the door, but it looked strong enough, and was obviously locked.

Poor little devil. They've done it to him too. Keeping the curtain across her, she edged forward to lift a flambeau out of its sconce. Nobody noticed. As she scurried back, her eye's retina retained the image of the Prince of Orange's face, distorted and streaked with tears.

She tried every door except to the room Sedley was in, and at last found one that opened. Inside it was empty, the bed's curtains open and its coverlet neatly laid back. Women's clothes lay over the chairs, but their owners had presumably found other beds. She shut the door and locked it, put the flambeau in a Chinese vase and sat in a chair by the open window, welcoming the cold on her skin.

No good searching for her own room in this enormous house until things had quietened down. Then she'd find it — once the drunks had retired they'd sleep like the dead — put on walking shoes and her cloak and set off home. Highwaymen, dogs, distance, what were they to her after a royal recreation?

Out of her self-disgust had come at least negative knowledge of who she was. Not them. Never them. A deluded, prating, one-time whore of an actress she might be, but when St Peter asked her on the Day of Judgement where she belonged she knew enough now to say: 'Not with them.'

Occasionally she tensed as the courtiers staggered back to their rooms. Twice somebody lurched against her door, and once someone else rattled at its knob, then shouted 'Swive well, *mes braves*', and passed on.

The house fell asleep and so did she.

It was still dark when she woke up to the sound of sobbing. There was a scraping noise, more sobbing, then retching. Quietly she unlocked the door and peered out, reached for the flambeau and held it up. Two doors along a creature was crawling away from her on its hands and knees. From her viewpoint it looked like a monstrous poodle with its hindquarters shaved. It had lost its breeches while, ludicrously, retaining its wig and waistcoat. A trail of vomit marked its progress.

'Prince,' called Penitence, quietly. 'Your Highness, in here.'

The poodle looked back at her, crying. 'Daar is geen Prins in den lande,' it said. 'There is no more prince.'

'Oh, get in here.' She was tired of men. Her head ached. She had to venture out and help support him back, a process he hindered by doubling forward so that his waistcoat could cover his naked private parts. 'Get bending. Don't look at me,' he kept saying in his funny accent. 'Don't look at me. Get bending.'

'Be quiet.'

They staggered together into the room, and he struggled for the bed, covering himself to the waist with the coverlet, then sitting bolt upright, like an indignant maiden. 'I'm sick. Get bending.'

She held the Chinese vase while he vomited into it. In between spasms he insisted she bend. 'I'm not bending to any of you,' she lectured him, 'not ever again.'

He stared at her. 'Bent-inck,' he said clearly, before his mouth filled, 'get Bentinck.'

'Who's Bentinck?'

'Get him.'

'I don't know where he is, where anything is and I'm not stumbling around in the dark. Wait till dawn. I'll get him then.'

He was sick again. She didn't know how his slight frame could have held so much, and wondered if they'd poisoned him, but perhaps alcohol was a poison to him. There was a silver ewer of water and a basin on a chest. She helped him drink and bathed his face with a scarf she took from a chair.

His eyes began to focus. 'The water-giver,' he said. 'Twice in one day. I am ashamed before you.'

'Don't be. They made me drunk as well.'

'I am ashamed.' He was lost in his own misery.

They never listen. She sat on the bed so that their heads were level. 'Do you hear me? They made me drunk too. They got me into bed with a man I don't like.'

'You say this to ease my shame.'

'So that we're shamed together.' He was so young. 'Now go to sleep. I won't let anyone in. When it's dawn I'll find Bentinck.'

'What sort of people?' he asked. 'What sort of people do this?'

She didn't know the answer to that. As he closed his eyes, she went back to the window to watch for the morning. She must have dozed again, because rustling movement woke her up. The boy was holding on to the bedpost, fighting nausea, but impelled by God knew what sense of form to be on his feet. He'd taken a woman's petticoat off a chair and put it on, knowing he looked ridiculous, trusting her, courteously insisting on joining her vigil. He pattered over to the window and took the seat opposite her.

What a nice thing to do. She said easily: 'Is it a pretty part of the Lowlands, Orange?' He might forget to be sick if he talked.

343

'It is nowhere near the Netherlands. It is in southern France. Once it was an independent principality. There was a William of Orange among the knights of Charlemagne. Now Louis has gobbled it up and kills its Protestant children.' He wiped his forehead with the back of his hand. 'This I don't understand. I tell my Uncle Charles: "Beware of Louis. He intends to gobble up all Europe. England, too, perhaps."' He gave a shrug, just like Rowley's, and deepened his voice: '"Be easy, nephew. Louis is one of us."' He leaned forward. 'But if he is one of us, why has England joined my country and Sweden in the Triple Alliance against him?'

She gave him a shrug back. Politics were beyond her. 'Aren't you a Dutchman, then?'

'What is it you call a dog of many breeds?'

'A mongrel.'

'I am a mongrel. Of my great-grandparents three were Germanic, two French, one Italian, a Scot — your James the First — one Scandinavian. But, yes, I am a Dutchman.' His adam's apple bobbed as he swallowed. 'I wish I were home.'

Oh, bless him. He was only little. 'Tell me about home.'

The scent of late roses and honeysuckle came through the window from the garden, but his longing was so intense he replaced it with a sea breeze that blew without impediment across illimited skies and dykes and sand-piled dunes and tough, salt-stained people. She heard carillons ring out across canals and markets where countrywomen brought their produce in boats, a land of painters and thinkers and poets. 'It is very clean,' he kept saying, then he apologized. 'But, of course, you love your country too.'

'I don't know where it is.' And it was her turn to tell him about the forests of Massachusetts and their Indians, and the Pocumscut and the Puritans.

She could see him, as she had done, contrasting it with the cloying, tarnished sensuality that enmired them both. 'I ran away from the Puritans, or, rather, their hypocrisy,' she said, 'but from here they look . . . worthy.'

He nodded. 'They have a cause, at least,' he said, 'an ideal. Here there is no cause. Those men tonight believe nothing.'

He got up and paced, ignoring the swish of his petticoat. 'Do you know what my uncle said to me? He said' — again the voice went unconsciously deeper — ' "Nephew, if France should annexe the Netherlands, Louis would ensure you were given part of them for your kingdom. He is your relative. He will see you right. Listen less to your Dutch blockheads." '

He collapsed back in the chair. 'But they are not blockheads. The Dutch are my people. It is difficult to think I heard him say that.'

I expect he did. Charles was clever and in many ways amiable, but he horrified her. She couldn't rid herself of the sense that under the elaborate, many-layered complexities of his soul there yawned a vacuum. Empty, still, cold, nothing. There could be no understanding between this young man and the gilded King. That William might cherish above himself his religion, his people and the flat lands they lived on, was outside his uncle's comprehension.

'He thinks I am a prig,' said the Prince of Orange.

'You are,' she said. 'And so, I find, am I.'

They shook hands.

They heard the bang of a door, then another, hammering, protests from sleepy throats, more banging. The noise got closer and under it was a deep note, a growling, as if a she-bear was lurching up the corridor, searching for its cub. 'Bentinck,' said William.

Penitence unlocked the door, noticing for the first time that it was full morning. The figure just barging out of a room it had been investigating was as ursine as *Homo sapiens* could be, huge-shouldered, outheld menacing arms, squat-legged — and very angry. She gestured it into the room and shrank back as it lumbered furiously past her.

The Prince smiled at it. 'Mrs Hughes, may I present my faithful friend, Hans William Bentinck. Bentinck, your breeches.'

There was a grunt of surprise, but the young man's enormous hands went immediately to the ties at his waist. Thoughtfully, Penitence turned her back. When she faced them again, William wore a pair of breeches he had to hold up, and the bear was in a petticoat.

The Prince of Orange bowed. 'You are for ever my good friend, Mrs Hughes.'

Penitence curtseyed. 'Always yours to command, Your Highness.'

And both of them meant it.

'He'll be furious,' said Becky. 'There's three more days of royal relaxation still to go. You'll have to get his dispensation to leave. You're one of his servants, after all.'

'It's me who's furious,' Penitence pointed out. 'As you once said, if we're under his protection, why doesn't he protect us? Anyway, I found the house major-domo or whatever he is, and told him I need a coach to go home at once because I'm ill.' She held her head. 'And it's true. What did they *put* in that orange-water?'

Becky's face cleared. 'If you're ill, then you can't go back by yourself. You're not leaving me here alone.'

A passing maid helped them downstairs with their luggage and hat-boxes. But as they tiptoed across the hall, they were glimpsed through the open door of the card room.

The two women faced the men who came crowding out, Buckingham, Sedley, Rochester, Harry Jermyn, Lord Chesterfield, and the others, some unshaven, most of them pale from lack of sleep, and all vindictive from a night's drinking and gossip. Sedley looked triumphant.

'Going, ladies?' asked Buckingham. 'But surely, my dears, not after last night. Was it not the occasion when the great Sedley prick finally conquered the shy Hughes clitoris?'

She'd known. And she'd prepared. She opened her eyes wide. 'Did it?' she asked. 'I beg you next time, Sir Charles, to make it greater. I fear I didn't notice.'

She saw Sedley's face change before she swept on and the guffaws started.

As she settled in the carriage, she said: 'I'm not an actress for nothing.'

Becky was still gasping. 'Let's hope you can go on being one.'

*

'How is he?'

The light from a candle played on her face while Kynaston's landlady examined Penitence with suspicion. 'Better than his enemies'd have him,' she said, 'but bad enough.' She led the way up a creaking cupboard-staircase and unlatched a door. 'In here.'

Kynaston's apartment belied the appearance of both its entrance and its landlady. A fire in the grate threw reflections on the beeswax shine of the spare, fine pieces of furniture, his portrait had pride of place on one wall and a nice Oriental rug on the other. The bed-hangings were fresh, sprigged cotton. Yet the figure on the bed, bandaged and hideously bruised, altered it into a battle-ground. Knipp, sitting beside it, put a finger to her lips.

Tiptoeing, Penitence whispered again: 'How is he?'

'They broke both his arms. They were trying for his face, but he managed to cover it for the most part. He saved his teeth at least.'

'Did he say who they were?'

Knipp shrugged and avoided her eyes. 'Two men with cudgels, he said; he'd never seen them before.'

'What does the doctor say?'

'He's splinted the arms and given him a medicine. He should mend. But he's very feverish.'

Penitence sat down on the other side of the bed and, so as not to feel helpless, put out her hand to smooth Kynaston's wet hair, then drew back for fear of hurting him more; there was nowhere on the forehead that wasn't bruised. The message telling her Kynaston had been attacked had arrived at the Cock and Pie that morning while she was still trying to recover from her late arrival back from Newmarket. She looked across at Knipp who was radiating a proprietorial hostility. 'I came as soon as I could,' she said, 'but I was on stage this afternoon.'

'I'm sure you're mighty busy.'

Penitence ignored the tone. 'What did they take?'

'Who?'

'The robbers.'

'Nothing. They weren't after his purse.'

She didn't understand. 'What then?'

Knipp shrugged. 'Perhaps you'll sit with him a while. I've got to get home. My husband'll never believe I'm not cavorting.' She blew a kiss on to her fingers and very gently touched one of the splinted arms. 'Poor Kynaston, it'll be a long time before he cavorts again.' As she got up, she said: 'How was the King? How was Newmarket?' But as Penitence started to tell her she interrupted with instructions. 'And this is his posset. He's to drink it as soon as he wakes. The gozunda is in the usual place, he'll need your help to piss in it.' At the door she turned. 'If you're not too grand, that is.'

Penitence tidied the medicine table, tucked the bedclothes more neatly around the twitching patient, and sat down for her vigil.

Knipp's attitude hurt her. She supposed it was a natural enough jealousy, Knipp's career being on the decline and her own in full flower, but the little comedienne hadn't shown such resentment before. Perhaps it hadn't helped that when the attack on Kynaston had taken place, she and the others had been apparently enjoying themselves with the court.

Enjoying ourselves. Knipp, if you only knew.

It was very quiet. She got out her script for the *Tyrannick Love* they were doing in three weeks' time, and began rereading her part. Through the half-open casement came the alarm call of a thrush as it flew from whatever had disturbed its rest outside. She went to the window, hoping to see an owl. She liked owls.

The house was one of a terrace overlooking a square just off Hatton Garden. It was a damp still night, but one of the branches of an oak tree opposite was shaking from something more weighty than an owl. A cat? Weightier than a cat.

Squinting into the shadow of the branches she thought she discerned a human shape. She blinked, and it became a distortion of the tree trunk. Nevertheless, she barred Kynaston's door. Perhaps the disgruntled husband, the creditor, or whoever it was who'd beaten him, was out for more blood than had been shed already. She'd tell the Watch to keep a guard on him.

A pretty clock, a gift from one of Kynaston's admirers, chimed once and woke the patient up. She helped him to the pot, then held the posset glass while he drank. 'How do you feel, poor lamb?'

He groaned. 'I want the truth, Peg. Don't spare me. Am I marked for life?'

Bless him. A true actor. 'You'll mend as good as new.' But he wouldn't content himself until she fetched a looking-glass.

'Oh, my God. Banquo after the murder.' He fell back on his pillow, and if he'd been able to lift his hand he'd have draped it over his eyes.

'Who was it? What were they after?'

He looked painfully towards her, then away. 'Don't you know?'

Suddenly she did. 'Not Sedley?'

'Win a pair of gloves. I heard one of them say it would teach me to ape my betters.' A spasm of pain caught him as he shifted. 'And it will. Believe me, Peg, it will. I'm sorry. I know he's a friend of yours. But you can't offend the court and get away with it.'

'No friend of mine,' she said. She should have guessed. Sir John Coventry had sneered at the King's morals and had his nose slit. Kynaston had made fun of Sedley's pretentious dress. Retaliation on both had been swift and horrible. She heard the Prince of Orange's question: 'What sort of people do this?' People with whom, until two days ago, she had been pleased to consort. No wonder Knipp had shown her disdain.

'No friend of mine,' she said again, but the actor was asleep.

What sort of people? Men who had lost touch with the ordinary and the decent. Self-styled gods who sent thunder-bolts against mortals that dared challenge them.

Oddly, it wasn't Sedley she blamed but the man who led him and others in their wild tarantella, thickening the poison in their blood rather than dislodging it, a king who saw his sailors starving from lack of pay and gave his mistress £25,000 to gamble away in one night. He invited them into his dance, the clever, beautiful men and women whose talent, under a better monarch, could have been directed towards something more useful than debauchery. He had infected them all, Sedley, Rochester, Castlemaine, Gwynn, with his contempt for decency. *He nearly infected me.* For she, too, had felt the centrifugal pull of the whirling circle, and let go just in time.

But you can't offend the court and get away with it.

Disturbed, she went to the window again. There was nothing there. Yes, there was. Dragging footsteps were coming down the road.

She ran down to the front door and opened it. 'Dorry, what's happened?' She helped the girl up the stairs and sat her by the fire to get her warm.

Dorinda looked towards the bed. 'How is he?'

'Bad, but he'll survive. Tell me. Was the Earl married already?'

'No,' said Dorinda lightly. 'He wasn't married. Lovely ceremony it was. You ought to've been there. Bought me a beautiful dress, he did. Priest all prinked in black, coronet of flowers, stocking thrown, friends there to catch it, kisses, champagne for afters, bed sprinkled with holy water. Lovely, it was. Proper Haymarket.'

Penitence stroked her hands and waited.

Dorinda took in a breath. 'Only thing was, the priest turns up again next morning along of the rest. But he wasn't in black. Wasn't a priest at all, just another friend of his. I'd been goose-capped, doodled, coneyed. Gawd, how they laughed.'

Penitence rested her head on her friend's shoulder.

'Thing is, Prinks,' Dorinda's tone was remorselessly unconcerned, 'I don't know why he done it. We'd been to bed. He knew I wasn't no lily-white holding out for a ring. Thing is' — for the first time her voice shook — 'I loved the ballocker. I thought I did. So why all the flash?'

Because it amused him. 'What did you do?'

'Come home. Nothing else *to* do.' Her shoes were soaking and in tatters. She must have walked miles. Penitence took them off and rubbed the poor feet. 'Ma Palmer told me about Kynaston, so I come on here.' She got up and went to the bed. 'Who done it? Sedley?'

'Two of his bullies.'

Dorinda shook her head, almost admiringly. 'Them courtiers,' she said. 'Done us both in.'

'You'll bounce back, the two of you.'

She looked down at the body on the bed. '*He* might. I won't.'

'You will.'

Dorinda looked up. 'Oh yes,' she said, 'I'll be a ballocking sensation, won't I? Our Sedley'll write a play about it. *Roxolana, or the Fooled Bride*. The stinkards'll laugh me off the stage, and I can't blame 'em. No, I'm finished.'

Even as she protested, Penitence knew it was probably true. She felt a surge of hatred at the pitilessness of men. 'I'll go and get you a hot drink,' she said. 'Becky's to take over at dawn. Then I'll take you home.'

But Dorinda wanted to be alone. 'You go. You done your turn. Get back to Benedick, he ain't seen much of you lately. I want to think a bit. I'll see Kynny's all right.' She tried to smile. 'I'm good at men in bed.'

Nothing would move her. 'For fuck's sake, leave me *alone*.'

Reluctantly, Penitence left her.

Outside she stood in the doorway to accustom her eyes to the darkness. The trees and hedges of the square were still. High clouds moved at their own volition, suffusing the air with a mist of rain and allowing glimpses of a moon that put a soft shine on leaves and roofs. Her footsteps repeated a rhythm on the damp surface of the road: What sort of people? What sort of people?

What sort of man went to expense and trouble to humiliate a woman who'd done him no harm?

As she reconstructed the image of the Earl of Oxford in her mind, fat, laughing, at ease, she set him in the context of a court which – she saw it now – devoted itself to the humiliation of women. Castlemaine and Gwynn and all the other mistresses, parading their clothes and their tempers in their ceaseless battle to outdo each other, were pet monkeys kept for tricks, goaded by their masters to perform more and more outlandish antics. The poor little woman with the dark-haired top lip, the Queen of England, was forced not only to accept the attendance of her husband's bed-fellows, but to seem to enjoy it.

What sort of people? What sort of men?

No sort at all? Perhaps, just men? It worried her. Suppose there was a civil war in progress of which one side, women, was in ignorance, but which the other, the male army, knew about and waged. *I'm getting fanciful.*

Her imagination had released monsters into the sleeping streets; they were padding behind her. She looked round but saw nothing.

She was right, then, to have stood up to them. She grinned as her jeer at his potency wiped the victory off Sedley's remembered face. *A strike for our side.*

The grin faded. She *was* being followed. Somewhere in the darkness to her rear there'd been a splash as a foot went into a puddle. Reluctance to look round again froze her neck and shoulders. She was half-way up Holborn and on both sides the shuttered shopfronts with tall, gable-ended storeys above them contained empty road straight ahead for as far as she could see. She had grown careless with carriages, or chairs, or link-boys to bring her home and forgotten that gangs padded the streets at night.

But it was, what, four in the morning? The whole world was asleep. What gang would hang around when there was nobody to prey on?

She quickened her pace. If she could reach the High, she knew a dozen back alleys through to the Rookery and safety. They wouldn't be able to follow her there.

Ridiculous. It was someone going home as innocently as herself. She forced herself to turn around, but the buildings threw impenetrable shadows on to both sides of the road, leaving a paler path between them.

There was somebody there, though. Instinct bred in the forest was panicking her breath and legs to escape danger. She began to trot. Knock on a door and ask for shelter? But nobody here lived on the ground floor; if she could waken an occupant it would be minutes before they let her in, if they let her in at all. Too long.

A soft drumming out of synchronization with the falls of her own feet confirmed her into picking up her skirts and running. The drumming quickened. *Where's my knife? Why didn't I wear my knife? Oh, Matoonas, I've gone soft.*

The Vine, she'd turn off north at the Vine. If she got into Kingsgate and turned left she'd be bound to strike a cut-through to the Rookery.

Somebody ahead. Thank God, thank God. A large male shape. Another soul.

As she raced towards it, she recognized something wrong. The man faced her not with enquiry but expectation. She saw the white of teeth. He was smiling. The link between him and her pursuer flashed over her like a whip. *They've been sent.*

There was an opening on her right between her and the man ahead. Blindly, she ran into it, slipped in a puddle, got up and ran on into deeper darkness. She heard the call of greeting between the two behind and the squelch of their boots.

Scream? But screams meant nothing around here. It would make horror official, encourage the tiger to hear the bleat of the goat.

Left. Go left. The Rookery would gather her in, resort of coiners, whores and thieves, outcasts, her true home. She didn't know this alley, she was terrified it would end in a wall. Leprous wood, overhanging washing, silence except for her own running.

What would they do? Rape her? Disfigure her? Whatever it was, they'd won. She was broken. A rat squeaking with panic. Who were they? Sedley's men? Sir Hugh Middleton's? The King's? It didn't matter. You can't offend the court and get away with it. *Fool. What a fool.* Behind her was the executive of the world's power come to punish her puny defiance. *I'm sorry. I'll join. I can't take you on. There's no independence for us. Let me join. Don't hurt me.*

Ahead was a broken drainpipe outlined against space, like a hook, with moonlight catching the drip from its mouth. She'd seen it before. Another fifty yards and she would be in the mouth of Dog Yard, near the blessed, blessed Ship. Some steps.

She didn't make them. They caught her. She felt a hand drag her skirt. More hands wiping against her face. Not a sound from them but panting. Flesh on hers, fingers on her breasts, clawing through her hair. Their smell. Another, fetid and alien.

That was when she began screaming until one of the hands went into her mouth and smeared her teeth.

Then they went.

Three minutes later, woken by a hand hitting and hitting the Cock and Pie door, Mistress Palmer opened it to a creature that squirmed as if trying to shrink from its own flesh, a gagging, whispering woman whose eyes stared at her through a mask of dog excreta.

Next morning Penitence wrote a letter to Prince Rupert agreeing to be his mistress.

BOOK III

Chapter 1

WITHOUT warning, the English fleet fired on a convoy of
Dutch merchantmen, and the country found, somewhat to its
surprise and despite the alliance between them, that it was
once again at war with the Netherlands. It didn't mind particularly. The Dutch had too much of the world's trade for their
own good — and England's. But when a season of naval
warfare passed without a palpable English victory, even a
Cavalier Parliament decided enough was enough and refused
to vote the King sufficient money to go on with it.

Had it been coincidence that war was declared on the Low
Countries just as Louis XIV's gigantic army, outnumbering the
Dutch nine to one, invaded them? If it hadn't, if Charles had
meant to show that it was wiser to throw in with the French
than the Dutch, it was a mistake because English perception
changed. Suddenly the Netherlands were no longer a pain in
England's commercial backside; they were being overrun,
starved and tortured by a people more congenial as an enemy
than they had ever been — the French. What's more, the
remnant of their pitiful army was fighting — and fighting
bravely — against the invader under their new, young general,
Prince William of Orange.

People remembered the Armada, when another small and
gallant Protestant nation had stood up to the might of a
Catholic oppressor.

Who did the King and his advisers favour? Young William,
cutting his country's dykes to flood the enemy's advance, like
Good Queen Bess facing the hostile sea at Tilbury? Or Louis
XIV's army, so reminiscent of the menacing crescent of Philip
of Spain's galleons?

Protestant or Catholic? The question hung in the air.

Then the King took a new mistress, Louise de Kéroualle, a French Catholic, as, almost in the same breath, he brought in a Declaration of Indulgence suspending laws against those who dissented from the established Church. It was his right, he said, his 'supreme power in ecclesiastical matters'.

It wouldn't have mattered much that Nonconformists, Puritans, even damned Quakers and the like, were given the right to worship legally, but the Indulgence also included Catholics.

This might be good Old Rowley showing his usual tolerance, but with everything that had gone before, it looked a good deal more like the thin end of the Catholic wedge.

Who said the King had 'supreme power in ecclesiastical matters' anyway? Was Charles going the way of his father and trying to impose absolute monarchy? Was England secretly in the hands of Jesuits?

There was an outcry. Even the House of Lords refused to support the King. Charles was not only forced to withdraw his Indulgence, but a new and less compliant Parliament countered with the Test Act requiring anyone holding public office to pass a test which included Church of England communion, oaths of allegiance and a denial of the doctrine of transubstantiation – in other words, a hurdle no true Catholic could jump.

And the first person to balk at it was James, Duke of York. Honourably, he came out of the closet and admitted his adherence to the Church of Rome, resigning as Lord High Admiral – a post then given to his Protestant cousin, Prince Rupert.

It alarmed the country to discover the King's own brother a Catholic; he was, after all, heir to the throne. The Queen had still not borne a child and hope was fading that she ever would. If Charles should die, England would have its first Roman Catholic monarch since Bloody Mary of unpleasant memory.

True, James's two daughters, Mary and Anne, were being brought up as good Protestants, and a marriage was being arranged between Mary and the Prince of Orange, but . . .

At this point there were two ominous happenings. The King, renowned for his superb health, fell violently ill. And

James, now widowed, cast about for a new wife and chose a beautiful Italian princess, Mary of Modena, a Catholic.

The certainties on which the reign had begun were splintering. The King recovered, but he had shown he could not be relied on to outlive his brother. He couldn't even be relied on to defend his realm against Papists. Having turned morality upside-down, corrupted an entire aristocracy, created a theatre which extolled adultery as a virtue, he might very well die and leave an even worse mess behind him. The country was going to the dogs.

Good God, there was even a woman making a success of playwrighting.

The door of Hammersmith parish church stood open to let in the late October sun, the scent of leaves and cowpats and singeing horn from the forge down the lane where Coppy was defying Sunday and getting horses shod for the hunt tomorrow.

Inside it smelled of incense and Sunday best.

'And what is this thing, the Whig?' demanded Parson Fowler, lifting his hands to Heaven and thereby displaying the hole in the armpit of his cassock. 'I tell you it is an old enemy under a new name, a creature hateful to God, a latitu ... a latidinarian which is, *parentis mutandis*, an abomination in the sight of God ...'

Penitence, sitting in the front pew, heard the Reverend Boreman, her new chaplain, shift in the pew behind her, and smiled. The parson's sermons got on his nerves at the best of times, but the man's misuse of Latin put him out of temper, mainly because he was one of the few in the congregation to know it *was* misuse.

She wouldn't have minded learning what a Whig was – the term was being bandied about – but she was unlikely to be enlightened by Parson Fowler who probably wasn't sure himself. She let his thick Middlesex-accented harangue rattle past her, much as she had let the politics of the last years go by, unheeded. Politics were the court, and court life was now only peripheral to her own.

She put her hand over Rupert's and squeezed it to wake him up. Rupert's own form of criticism of the vicar was to fall asleep during his sermons. 'Blwah?' he said.

The parson hunched his shoulders and beamed uncertainly: 'Would Your Royal Highness be so good?'

Rupert stood up and marched across to the side aisle, to the effigy bearing a plaque, 'The Glorious Martyr King Charles the First of blessed Memory', and fetched the silver casket beneath it to the altar rail.

He still looks pale. He'd given her the fright of her life when his old head wound reopened after a strenuous game of tennis. He'd refused a doctor – he had a horror of doctors – and hadn't even wanted her to dress it; 'Too unsightly. Leave it to Peter.'

'I certainly won't,' she'd said. 'It's *my* job.' He loathed showing weakness in front of her for fear of accentuating their age-difference, but his gratitude for her nursing had been pathetic. *He's growing old too quickly.* He said he was more content than he'd ever been, and probably he was – his famous anger came rarely nowadays, and had never shown itself to her in any case. But his wars had caught up with him.

He's like me. He's retired hurt.

Rupert lifted the lid of the casket and the vicar poured wine and prayer on to the pickled heart of Sir Nicholas Crispe, Bart, contained within it. She heard the Reverend Boreman muttering. This was too heathenish for him. But Sir Nicholas had written in his will that he wished his heart refreshed with wine on every anniversary of his death, and as he'd been a friend of Rupert's and the builder of the home they lived in, the household was bound to attend. '*Noblesse oblige*', Rupert said it was.

'Good vintage is it, Sir Nick?' shouted somebody. It sounded like the Brewster son. Rupert returned to their pew, erect and glowering at the daring. Everybody else called a more decorous 'God bless Sir Nicholas', and they all knelt for final prayers.

It was a spacious church – Sir Nick had built this too – with a pretty ceiling of painted compartments. Into its quiet came the sound of birdsong and Coppy's hammering.

Tranquillity, thought Penitence. But *unearned* tranquillity. In escaping to the safety of Rupert's protection, she had not imagined how very much it would feel like desertion and how undeserved its peace.

There was a rustle of cassock past her as the vicar sprinted to the door to be ready to shake hands with his congregation; not that anybody would move until Rupert did. With great deliberation the Prince got to his feet and offered her his arm; together, with their household behind, they walked down the nave, every eye upon them. Royalle, Rupert's giant black poodle, followed them out.

Outside in the churchyard they had to pause for more *noblesse oblige*, nodding kindly to the villagers, enquiring after Mistress Cole's rheumatism and Jem Harper's youngest. Rupert was punctilious about this, though he was held in too much awe to get more than a 'Going on well, sir, thank 'ee kindly'. If she'd been alone, they'd have answered with more enthusiasm and anatomical detail. Jem added, with a nod at Penitence: 'That poultice of Mistress's eased his little cough something wonderful, sir.'

Rupert was gratified. 'Her Ladyship is skilled in these matters.'

Now it was the turn of the local gentry. They were surrounded by men and women like bullocks; the Brewsters bred large. 'Fine morning, Your Royal Highness and mmm . . .'

'Your Ladyship,' prompted Rupert.

'Your Ladyship,' said Squire Brewster, deliberately having trouble getting his tongue round it. 'Hunting tomorrow, Your Highness? Us could be doing with that lymerer of yours.'

Rupert looked at Penitence, who looked stolidly back. 'You may have the lymerer, Sir John, but not me, I fear. Her Ladyship still over-cossets me.' He loved the idea that he was henpecked. 'These women, you know.'

'You want to get her trained, Highness. A *wife* like Lady Brewster, now, she do know her place. Don't 'ee, Betty?'

'Ah well,' said Lady Brewster, managing to invest her sigh with a distinction between a wife and a mistress. 'There 'tis.'

They couldn't get over it. At first they'd watched her in

church with fascinated horror, as if at any moment she might strip and dance on the altar, on the principle that actresses would be actresses. And once, when Rupert had been away, the elder Brewster boy tried to kiss her on the principle that mistresses would be mistresses. Now they merely larded their conversation with heavy subtleties. But Lady Brewster, Penitence noticed, was wearing a fair copy of the striped gown which she herself had worn last Easter Sunday, though the short sleeves tended to show the woman's muscles somewhat blue in the October nip and the panniers to emphasize her hips.

At the lych-gate the Brewsters piled into a spanking new open carriage, a replica of the one Rupert had bought in the spring. Bob, their coachman, was raising his eyes at the trouble he'd been put to for a quarter-of-a-mile drive. Penitence helped Mistress Palmer into Rupert's with the other servants and smiled at Lady Brewster: 'It's such a fine day, His Royal Highness and I thought we'd walk home.' It was petty, but wrong-footing the Brewsters was one of life's little triumphs.

'With your permission,' said the Reverend Boreman, grimly, 'I shall go and give that bumpkin parson another lesson in Latin.'

'Don't you go hoeing his cabbages again,' warned Penitence. 'It put your back out last time.' They watched him hobble off across the churchyard to the decrepit parsonage.

'He was a good choice, my dear.' She'd been surprised when Rupert had suggested she have a chaplain. Since Rupert had been made Constable of Windsor Castle, his own chaplain was now installed there.

'Do I need one?' she'd asked.

'It is usual for one of your position.'

'I can't get used to being positioned so high.' She hadn't thought her old friend from St Giles would agree, but a heart attack had prompted his retirement away from his old parish and into this less onerous post in the country. It had worked out well. The air was doing him good, and London was near enough for his friends to come and stay at the pleasant little house Rupert had given him on the estate.

Mistress Palmer, too, had fitted in well, assuming a position in the household as Benedick's old nurse, and having her washing done for her.

It had been a dry autumn and their shoes puffed up dust as they walked down the village street, Rupert's hat more often off his head than on it as he doffed to curtseying women and the forelock tugs of the men.

With Royalle trotting beside them, they turned left down Upper Mall where fishing nets made a canopy over their heads along the quay, crossing the creek at High Bridge. Immediately they were in the meadowland that hemmed the Thames.

Four miles away was Charing Cross, but here cows stood up to their hocks in grass and kingcups, warblers sang in the reeds and willows bent over their own reflection in the river. *Compleat Angler* country. She'd bought a gold-embossed, calfskin-covered copy of the book for Rupert on his last birthday, hoping it would encourage him to do more fishing rather than risk his neck on the hunting field. He'd been delighted with it.

She liked to give him unusual birthday presents; this year's was extra special. She was waiting for the right moment to tell him about it.

The lane turned into enormous wrought-iron gates and became a drive lined with chestnut trees still to reach full maturity. Beyond, in the distance glowed the rose-brick turrets of Awdes with its cupola and winking, oriel windows.

Awdes.

When he'd said he would provide her with a house not unworthy of her, she'd had no idea of the value he put on her. Penitence had expected perhaps a smart little town-house, something like the one Charles had given Nell Gwynn. What she'd got was magnificence; sixty rooms, including one for billiards, an armoury, a tennis court, a dairy, a lake, and an ornamental garden laid out by a Dutch landscaper who'd managed to give it a prospect which included the River Thames.

Awdes was worthy of a queen; Catherine of Braganza had

offered for it as her country home and, thwarted, was now building one of her own nearby.

Unasked, the King had driven down from Whitehall to inspect his uncle's love-nest, bringing with him the usual courtiers, among them Sir Charles Sedley who'd been venomous: 'My, my, we *must* be good in bed to have earned all this.'

'On the contrary, my dear Charles,' she'd hissed back, 'to earn all this we had to be positively *wicked* in bed.' *Take that, you bastard.* She'd watched the thrust go home. He tried to smile but she could almost hear his teeth grinding. She'd never prove it but she knew he'd sent the men who'd smeared her with ordure that night as surely as she knew he'd sent the bullies who'd beaten Kynaston. It would make him writhe to reflect that in punishing her he had been the instrument of what must seem to be her great good fortune. That she and Rupert might be happy together would be gall and wormwood to him – not necessarily from sexual jealousy but because he hated and feared others' happiness.

Actually, of course, he'd won; he'd deprived her of something she valued higher than the luxury she now enjoyed – her independence. Though she'd rather be stretched on the rack than let him know it, Sir Charles and his thugs had pushed the price of independence so high that she'd been forced to abandon it. Thanks to him, she was back on the game – what else was being the mistress of a man you didn't love but prostitution? That the man was rich and noble just made it more successful whoring, the height of harlotry. From sleeping with a Newgate gaoler to sleeping with a prince of the realm – what success. In the eyes of the world she'd reached the pinnacle of prostitution, only second to the great Castlemaine and Gwynn. Even now brothel-keepers might be pointing her out as an example to their young, ambitious whores: 'You too can become a Peg Hughes.'

I tried, my dears, she told them, *I tried to earn an honest living. They wouldn't let me. They smeared dog-shit on my teeth.*

'You're very pale, my dear. You're not too tired?' Rupert was looking down at her with concern.

She stood on tiptoe and kissed him. 'Rupert, you're the only one who doesn't make me feel like a trollop.'

'Those damned Brewsters.' He hated the reminder that the two of them weren't married.

'It wasn't the Brewsters. And I don't mind, you know I don't.' The wedding ceremony was mostly hypocrisy, anyway; society's seal on a trade agreement. *That's what Aphra Behn's been saying all these years in her plays.* An heiress sold into a loveless marriage by her parents was no less a hapless whore than one forced into an alliance with a protector through harsh circumstance. For the thousandth time Penitence felt a rush of admiration for Aphra, still fighting out in the world where they rolled women in crap, still refusing to surrender.

Arm in arm, she and Rupert turned to skirt the parkland where red deer stood beneath the palisaded oaks. 'You're sure *you're* not too tired?'

'I'm not decrepit yet, my dear.'

She was glad to take her opportunity. 'Indeed you're not. I have proof that you are not. I'm pregnant.'

He went white with pleasure. 'My dear, oh my dear, my dear.'

When they got to the river path she made him sit down on the bench. He looked quite shaky. He made her sit down, too. 'We should not have walked so far. I hoped for this.'

She'd known he had. 'You didn't say.'

'It would not have been gentlemanly.'

She kissed him. 'Happy birthday for December.'

'Is that when he'll be born?'

'No, not until the spring. But it's this year's present.'

'By God, I'm not that old, am I? Let's run. No, not run. Let's drive to Eton this afternoon and tell the boys they're to have a brother. The world must be informed.'

'Or a sister.'

He turned that idea over as they walked on; it was new to him. 'A girl, by God. Let's hope she takes after her mother.'

It was a pleasure to give him such intense pleasure, but underneath the velvet contentment he'd wrapped her in remained the old discomfort: *unearned, unearned.* Once she'd tried to tell him how she felt: 'I wish you wouldn't give me so much, Rupert. I'm just as happy with less.'

They were in bed at the time and he was playful: 'Would I were richer and could give you more.'

She'd held him off. 'You see, I earned my own living. It wasn't a good living, but I earned it by my own effort. All this . . .' She waved her hand around at the lovely Jacobean bedroom. '. . . I haven't *earned* it.'

'You make me happy.'

She knew she did, but that was almost fortuitous, none of her doing; an accident that her particular blend of looks and personality magnetized him. For the security he'd given her, making him happy was the least she could do.

But never to know again the satisfaction of earning money for herself and Benedick through printing, or through her skill as an actress . . . to be *kept* instead of keeping . . . there were times when she felt the panic of claustrophobia. If she tried to explain this to him he would become distressed and say she'd feel differently if they were married. Which she wouldn't. Marriage, with its loss of individual legal identity for women, would be worse.

So she'd left the subject and kissed him and let him get on with making love to her, delighting his man-of-the-world sense of chivalry by simulating a climax – as Dorinda had told her how to do – just as he came to his.

And there lay her deepest guilt: she couldn't love him like a lover. She had to grit her teeth to respond to his advances, and got through them on gratitude alone. She was cheating him, although he didn't know it, and the fact that he didn't know it made her an even greater cheat. When her periods stopped and she'd realized she was pregnant, she didn't feel she was carrying a child so much as a recompense.

Driving down to Windsor in the carriage that afternoon, Rupert said: 'Will you still go to the theatre next week?'

'Of course I will. There are the rehearsals. I'll stay with Aphra until you come up for the last performance, then we can either spend the night at Spring Gardens or come straight back.'

'I meant, will you perform? There is the child to consider.'

He didn't really like her acting at all now but, as he was

careful not to forbid her, she insisted on appearing at least twice a year. For one thing, it meant she wasn't totally dependent. She'd bought *The Compleat Angler* with her own money.

'Rupert, I'm as strong as a horse. Anyway, it's Hart's benefit and I can't let him down. *Othello* was his triumph, and he says I was the best Desdemona he ever had.'

'So you were, so you were. But . . . very well, if you wish, my dear. As a matter of fact, I shall probably be bringing a friend to see it, Viscount Severn and Thames. With your permission, I shall invite him down to Awdes to stay for a night or two afterwards.'

'Of course.' His friends became fewer as more and more of them dropped off the perches; this would be another aristocrat who had outlived his time, like the Earl of Craven or Colonel William Legge; Cavaliers who had fought for Charles 1 and who were derided by his son's court because they still believed in honour. Their opinion of democracy made her hair stand on end – they were against it – and after dinner she usually left them to their pipes, brandy and talk of horsewhipping, but they treated her with a bluff and unfailing chivalry. *Speak as you find.* What did politics matter? If it came to that, Rupert's didn't bear thinking about, which was why they rarely discussed other than domestic matters.

A couple of pensioners were sitting on the plinth of Henry VI's statue, their sticks between their knees, as the carriage swept into Eton's beautiful schoolyard. They stared, not at Penitence nor Rupert, but at Peter sitting on the footman's seat behind them. Black men were a novelty this far out in the sticks.

The college was still at its lessons, but the Provost came waddling up to greet the illustrious parents, trailing his velvet gown and the smell of a rich dinner which, to judge from his girth, had been superfluous to requirements.

As usual Rupert prayed a half-holiday for all the boys and gained a cheer from the faces at the windows as the Provost signalled his acquiescence. Penitence didn't like the Provost; his expensive robes and obesity contrasted horribly with the condition of the seventy, skinny young Collegers in his charge who, according to Benedick and Dudley, subsisted on an unvarying diet of mutton, bread and beer. The mutton bones were used as bait for the rats which infested the Long Chamber in which the Collegers lived and slept. 'They catch the rats in their stockings and whack 'em to death.'

As Oppidans – fee-paying students – Benedick and Dudley were permitted to live out. Since their rooms were in the great castle which loomed over college and town, and their father was its Constable, the Provost spared them the frenzied application of the birch with which he corrected the grammar of less favoured boys.

Penitence's cup of gratitude overflowed for Rupert's treatment of Benedick. He'd kept his promise to give her son the consequence he accorded his own; sometimes she thought he gave him more.

Prince and boy had taken to each other from the first. Benedick openly hero-worshipped the man whose shock tactics had swept away the Roundhead cavalry at Worcester, who'd ridden into battle with his dog at his side, who'd activated England's first mine, who could still send a horse-pistol bullet through the tail of the weathercock on Awdes' roof. He listened to Rupert's stories till the cows came home and at play-time charged the box topiary of the ornamental garden with the Cavalier battle-cry 'For a king!', wielding the sword Rupert had insisted on having made for him.

When Penitence, worried by her son's monarchical tendency, had privately suggested to him that there'd been some justice in the Roundheads' cause, he'd disposed of the idea with a 'Pooh to the lobsterbacks. They were dreary.'

It was Dudley who listened to her; but Dudley was a listener. He was about the same age as Benedick, even taller, and fair where Benedick was dark. From studying him, Penitence guessed that his mother had been willowy, freckled and timid. She'd gone into her new relationship with a determination to love the boy as her own, and found she didn't have to try. He tugged at her heart; he was afraid of his father's disapproval, thereby bringing it down on himself; more bookish than athletic, he had to rouse himself to show an interest in Rupert's scientific experiments and talk of war which held such fascination for Benedick.

They spent the afternoon by the river at Cuckoo Weir so that Rupert could fish and the boys bathe. Peter laid linen tablecloths on the grass and set out a picnic of tartlets, quince comfits, toffee apples and gooseberry pasties to cater for the boys' sweet teeth.

'This is high eating, Peter, thank 'ee,' Benedick called through crumbs. Dudley was a good influence on his manners.

Peter stood in dignified isolation three yards away, watching the river, and didn't turn round. 'Your ma chose it,' he said. Over the years Penitence had managed to break down all the household's coldly courteous hostility towards herself, except Peter's. He was a relic from Rupert's buccaneering days, a child who'd been left behind in his village's flight when Rupert's ship anchored off the coast of Guinea. Rupert had brought him home as a souvenir, just as he'd brought a parrot and a monkey. Despite the agony of loss and isolation the boy must have suffered, perhaps because of it, he became an enthusiastic convert to the Church of England, though, Penitence suspected, he tended to confuse Rupert with God.

With education, he'd grown into the post of Rupert's major-domo, and he resented the advent of a woman he regarded as an adventuress into his master's life with a dislike Penitence might have expected from a disapproving mother-in-law.

Benedick joined Rupert in his fishing while Dudley and Penitence settled down to books.

'What are you reading?' asked Dudley.

'*Othello*. To be ready for the performance at King's.'

'What's it about?'

She outlined the plot and then put out a hand to him. 'Desdemona didn't have anybody to fight her Iago, like you and Benedick fought mine.' On the first occasion that she and Rupert had visited the boys at the college, it had been to find both of them with black eyes and plummy mouths. Dudley had refused to say why he'd been fighting, but Benedick, still angry, had blurted it out: 'They called you a whore.'

'Who did?'

'Some of the Oppidans, and some of the Collegers. They said you were a whore because you were an actress and weren't married.'

Rupert had wanted to horsewhip the entire school, not excluding the Provost. Penitence dissuaded him on the grounds that while it might procure her detractors' silence it wouldn't change their opinion.

The incident coincided with King's production of *A Merchant of Venice* in which she was enjoying a success as Portia. At the end of the season she persuaded Killigrew to bring the play down to Windsor Castle and asked Rupert to invite the entire college. 'There's nobody more respectable than Portia,' she said, 'and the tights will woo them.'

They did. Next term Benedick had reported back, somewhat disgustedly, that the entire school was in love with her. She feared she'd overdone it, because Dudley was too.

She could see that Rupert's announcement that the family was to be increased had disturbed the boy. Perhaps he was jealous, or felt the young's disgust at a parent still indulging in sex. But it wasn't that. Watching a dragonfly skimming between the reeds, he said: 'Is it dangerous, having a baby?'

'Not for me. I'm strong.'

'But it hurts, doesn't it?'

'A bit. Don't worry. You worry too much.'

'I hope it's a girl.'

She said: 'I like sons. If it turns out as well as the two I have now, I shall be a happy mother.' That would be enough of personal matters for him. She put them both back on neutral ground: 'Dudley, I've been meaning to ask. What *is* a Whig?'

Happily he said: 'I think originally it was some awful Scotsman, a renegade or Covenanter or something like that. But it's coming to mean people who don't want James to succeed to the throne if the King dies.'

'Ah. So what's a Tory?'

'Well, originally, Tories were equally awful Irishmen but now it's being applied to people who don't mind if James succeeds to the throne. I think that's what it means.'

'Thank you, Dudley.'

It was always a relief that, though they were sorry when their outings were over, neither boy dreaded going back to school. They were, after all, doing so on the best possible terms as privileged students, with a dame and staff to look after them in one of the finest castles in the country, doting parents living nearby.

But she had an attack of a recurrent fear as she and Rupert were driven home that evening. *God's got something up His sleeve.* The prodigality of the cornucopia from which He was pouring life's riches on her and her son was against the Puritan law. There would be an accounting. She hadn't earned it.

Chapter 2

THE LAST time Penitence had been in London, Titus Oates had just emerged as the uncoverer of a Popish Plot to hand England over to the Jesuits. With some of the King's players she had gone to see him on his soapbox in Hyde Park, declaiming to listening crowds the same story that he was telling the Privy Council: there was a plot between Louis XIV, the Jesuits and English Catholics to kill the King and conquer England for France.

It had been an exceptionally hot day in an exceptionally hot summer; she'd been surprised by the size of the crowd prepared to stand crushed together to hear the man.

'Isn't he a picture?' Lacy said. 'Listen to him.'

Her view obscured by the press in front of her, to listen was all Penitence could do at first. The voice was more a wail than speech, like a bad actor depicting the throes of grief.

'Brethren,' it sobbed, 'they have burned down our city once, are we to stand by while they do it again? For they will. Oh yes, in their malignity, they will. I have heard their plans.'

She had looked at the people hemming her in, surprised that they tolerated the artificiality of the performance. London crowds weren't known for their patience towards the absurd. Not only were they not jeering, they were rapt. The crowd's composition was equally unexpected; well-dressed men and women, usually conscious of distinctions, crushed against flat-capped artisans, careless that they were literally rubbing shoulders with the working class.

'Take warning, take warning, my brethren,' the voice throbbed on. 'To my shame I know them. I have heard their plans. They scheme to rise at the Pope's signal and massacre us, their Protestant neighbours, in our beds.'

'Why is it,' said Lacy, beside her, 'that nobody ever gets massacred *out* of bed?'

Hart and Kynaston had burrowed a path through to the front and at last Penitence set her eyes on Titus Oates. She blinked to make sure it wasn't a trick of the light. It wasn't. The man who was mesmerizing something like three hundred people was ugly — incredibly, memorably ugly. The low forehead, tiny nose, almost invisible eyes and vast, wobbling chins were irresistibly reminiscent of a pig.

'Who is he?' she whispered to Kynaston. 'Where did he come from?'

'An ex-Jesuit,' said Kynaston, 'who's seen the error of his ways. Seen every other damn thing as well.'

'As I speak to you, my brethren,' went on Oates, 'the army of that arch-idolator, Louis, is planning to land his army in Ireland. Our King, our statesmen, our divines of England who protect our Church, all are to be put to the sword.' He dashed the spit from his lips and raised his voice to a howl: 'Beware, my friends, beware the hordes of Babylon.'

The man was a mimic's dream. The actors had stood, enchanted, moving their mouths in time to his. Hart kept humming to get the pitch right.

As they walked away, Kynaston was making notes. 'Such bliss, my dears,' he said, 'I'll do an epilogue as Titus Oafs. The difficulty will be out-lampooning the lampoon.'

Becky Marshall was doubtful. 'I think you'll have to be careful, Kynny. The crowd were listening to him.'

'The man's a mountebank,' said Lacy. 'You don't mean to

tell me, Becky my love, that if there *were* all these plots, our Titus was standing behind the door each time, listening in. There aren't that many Papists in England. God damn it, there aren't that many *doors*.'

Becky shook her head. 'No smoke without fire.'

'Blurt to that,' said Hart. 'Granted, our revered King has been a teeny bit careless in allowing so many Catholics in his court, not to mention his bed, but I can't believe they'd plot to kill him. Rid the throne of Rowley and you get James.' He shuddered. 'Even the *Pope* wouldn't want James. What do you think, Peg?'

Penitence had shrugged. 'I don't understand politics,' she said, 'but I wouldn't underestimate him.' She'd seen preachers like Oates in Massachusetts. 'Lying or not, those people back there believed him.'

That had been in the summer.

When she returned for the *Othello* at the beginning of November, Penitence entered a London that had gone mad with hysteria. Two days before, the body of Sir Edmund Berry Godfrey, a Protestant magistrate, had been found murdered on Primrose Hill. And it was to Sir Edmund that Titus Oates had just made a deposition on oath that the Queen's physician and the Duchess of York's secretary had been plotting to poison the King. The assumption was that Sir Edmund had been killed by Papists because he knew too much.

The coach was rocking. Penitence, who'd been dozing since Hammersmith, woke up as she was tipped from one side of the seat to the other. Automatically, she put her arms round her stomach to protect the child within it. She could hear Boller, the driver, protesting: 'I tell you this is Prince Rupert's coach. It's his lady inside.'

The curtains were ripped open and she found herself staring into angry faces. 'That right?' asked one of them. The man was tapping the side of her coach. 'These Rupert's arms?'

'Yes. What's the meaning of this?'

'An' you his whore?'

A woman pressed forward and peered in. 'Yeah,' she said, showing the gaps in her teeth. 'That's Peg Hughes right enough. I seen her at the theatre. You can let her go.'

The man was unconvinced: 'Not a bloody Papist whore?'

'Nah,' said the woman. 'He's a good Protestant, Rupert.'

Penitence heard her relaying the information to the crowd as the coach jolted forward. 'That's Rupert's trollop. She's all right.'

It was getting dark, but she could see a great triple tree of a gallows with bodies still hanging on it like untidy washing outlined against the mauve sky. *Tyburn.* She rapped on the coach roof. The face of Geoffrey, the footman, appeared upside-down in the window. 'Sorry about that, Ladyship, but we better not stop.'

'What are we doing this far north? Who were those people?'

'Don't know, Ladyship. Papist-hunters seems like. But don't you worry now. Boller didn't like the looks of things on the way up; came this way to avoid trouble.'

'Well, he didn't avoid it, did he? You'd better drive straight to Spring Gardens. I'll walk to Mistress Behn's from there.'

Geoffrey's face disappeared for consultation and came back. 'Boller says he ain't letting you out 'til you're got where you're going. It ain't safe. We'll go High Holborn way and get to Mistress Behn's through the back way.'

Penitence sank back. She was still smarting. She'd forgotten she was somebody's whore. She'd heard there'd been unrest in London, but had imagined it was on the lines of the usual apprentice riots. The flares of the crowd became twinkles in the distance, and fields gave way to houses as they approached High Holborn where she'd been chased that night.

Don't remember. Don't remember. She was Rupert's whore because of That Night. Hurriedly, she checked the contents of her overnight bag to keep her mind out of reach of an abasement so absolute that she still couldn't tolerate its memory. Her body was less obedient; she felt the flesh move on her bones in revulsion.

They were stopped again at the top of Farringdon; scowling, Penitence presented herself for examination as Boller explained that she was Prince Rupert's Protestant woman.

The streets had an atmosphere different from any she

remembered. Some windows were brightly lit and crowded with people watching the activity below. In other houses they were shuttered.

The Militia was conspicuous by its absence. Groups with torches battered on Catholics' doors or clustered round some suspect asking questions. One house was burning while men held back the desperate householders. There was a business-like sense to the violence as if the men and women committing it had fallen into routine.

At St Bride's Street, Boller and Geoffrey wouldn't leave to return to Rupert's town-house in Spring Gardens until Aphra's door opened. 'Maister'd flay us anything happened to you.' Her temper was not improved by the temptation to go back with them; there she could have a quiet dinner brought by servants who appeared at the ring of a bell, a bath, a comfort-able bed and a book, whereas Aphra's house was less comfort-able and invariably full of people, often the wits whom Penitence preferred to avoid. But Aphra would be mortified if she didn't stay with her, and she didn't want her friend to think she'd become grand.

Sure enough, the room overlooking the Fleet Ditch was occupied by Nell Gwynn, who was fencing with Otway to the danger of a gentleman asleep on the rug, an actor Penitence recognized as one of the Duke of York's players; the artist, John Greenhill, sketch-book propped and paint-brush raised, who was squinting at Aphra's chair, drunkenly oblivious of the fact that his subject had gone to greet her guest; and a gibbering figure in a corner, the playwright Nathaniel Lee, who was mad.

Penitence told her tale of woe. 'What's happening for God's sake? They seemed to think I was Castlemaine or somebody.'

'It's the coat of arms, Peg,' called Gwynn. 'Same thing happened to me. They thought I was Charlie's new French bitch. They got me as I was coming past the Cross. Bloody near turned the rattler over. I told 'em. Put my head out the windy. "Peace, good people," I said, "I'm the *Protestant* whore."'

Removing a cat from Aphra's sagging couch, Penitence sat

down. 'But I don't understand. *Was* it Papists who murdered this magistrate?'

'It doesn't matter who murdered him,' said the depressed actor at the other end of the couch, whose name she couldn't remember. 'It's who people *think* murdered him that matters. They think it was Catholics, so it's Catholics will pay. I'm expecting to get arrested any moment.' He handed a sheaf of pamphlets to Penitence: 'Look at these bloody things.'

'Nobody's going to arrest anybody,' said Aphra. 'Have some more milk punch. Penitence dear, try some of my milk punch.'

The pamphlets were varied in style but their message was uniformly and virulently anti-Catholic. One had a woodcut of a Jesuit priest under which was the legend: 'My Religion is Murder, Rapine and Rebellion.'

Another drew a word-picture of what Londoners could expect when the Papist armies joined with indigenous Catholics 'to ravish your good Protestant wives and daughters, spill out the brains of your babies against the walls of your own houses . . .' etc.

Penitence squinted hard at this particular pamphlet, holding it to the light of the fire to examine it better. 'May I keep this one?'

The actor said she could keep them all. 'My death warrants.'

Aphra fed him more milk punch. 'The town's gone lunatic,' she complained to Penitence. 'One would have been tempted to get oneself a horse-pistol if one knew how to use it. I wrote some doggerel to counter all this nonsense the other day – "A pox on the factions of the City" – and, damme, if some Member of Parliament didn't accost me in the theatre and accuse me of eating baby Whigs. One had to be quite sharp with him. "One is a vegetarian," I said. "So blurt to you, sirrah."'

The atrocity stories went on. Titus Oates had become so bold he was pointing at the Queen's physician, implying that even the Queen was in the plot to kill the King. Magistrates were advising Catholic widows to marry Protestants to confirm their patriotism. The King was helpless in the face of such rage to help those he knew were innocent.

Worst of all was the emergency's effect on the theatre. 'You'll have a sad audience for *Othello*, I fear, Penitence,' Aphra told her. 'Shakespeare was no Whig, and if the plays ain't Whiggish, nobody comes to see 'em.'

But the company consisted of theatre people so gradually conversation reverted to the really important topics: Killigrew's financial problems; the emergence of the new actress at the Duke of York's, Elizabeth Barry, with whom the Earl of Rochester was besotted; the raging argument over rhyme versus blank verse.

Soothed, Penitence joined in, caught up on the gossip and watched Aphra with an admiration that grew at every meeting. Tonight her hair was escaping from a turban, her wrap was torn at the hem, and the toe of one of her Turkish slippers had developed a droop. She squatted on a stool, scribbling her latest play in a notebook without missing a word of the conversation she stoked so effortlessly, her pleasure in her disparate guests stimulating an answering affection which encompassed each other.

Anybody who was anybody and in trouble repaired sooner or later to this room with its second-hand furniture and its smell of cats, to receive Aphra's milk punch and unlimited support. It was poor Nat Lee's asylum. At first Nell Gwynn had been scathing about Aphra, as she was about anyone she suspected of pretension. That was until her mother, a famous drunk, staggered into the Fleet Ditch in an alcoholic stupor and drowned. Aphra's own mother had recently died in terror of the pink snakes crawling over her death-bed and the bereaved daughters, sharing a tragedy which everybody else considered comic, had drawn together.

And Thomas Otway – even Penitence had advised Aphra not to give him a part in her first play. There were enough risks for a woman dramatist without hazarding a stage-struck, stammering amateur. 'One mustn't be ungenerous in success, Penitence dear,' Aphra had said.

Penitence was nervous for her: 'You're not a success yet.'

'I shall be.'

And, despite the total silence when Otway stared in manic

stagefright at the audience, unable to remember his lines – he had to be replaced in the last act – the play had run for a phenomenal six performances. Otway had subsequently turned his genius to writing plays, and was doing well – but not as well as Aphra.

It would have distressed Aphra, had she been aware of it, that she had been the subject of the first and only quarrel between Penitence and Rupert. He'd been shocked at the idea of a woman writing at all, but after attending Aphra's second play, *The Amorous Prince*, he'd said to Penitence over dinner at Spring Gardens: 'It is to be hoped, my dear, that you will not be tempted to appear in any of this female's productions.'

'And why not?'

'The first act should have told you why not. It was a seduction scene. The couple just risen from the bed were not married, they weren't even affianced.' He was at his most pompous.

'Neither are we.'

'We are not on the stage.'

'Rupert, for goodness' sake, you've been to a dozen plays more scandalous than that.'

'They were not written by a woman. Your friend she may be, but she writes too loose for the modesty which should distinguish her sex. Were her work more influenced by the Matchless Orinda, I should have no objection to your appearance in them.'

Penitence got cross. 'The Matchless Orinda didn't have to earn her living, which is just as well because nobody'd want to go to a Matchless Orinda play. They turn up in hundreds for Aphra's. What do you want her to do? Go modestly into obscurity and a debtors' prison? Go modestly on to the streets?'

'She could marry, or find a protector – if anyone would have her.'

'She doesn't *want* to.' His imperturbability was suffocating her. 'She likes what she's doing. She's good at it. And if she ever asks me for one of her roles, I'll jump at the chance.' Even as she slammed out, she knew she wouldn't. Even as she locked the door of her bedroom that night, though Rupert had been too offended to knock on it, she knew she wouldn't. When she'd sold herself to Rupert she'd promised to protect his honour with her own, and his honour, it seemed, could not survive his whore's appearance in an Aphra Behn play. It was in the contract of sale.

By God, if it wasn't for Benedick, I'd leave him now. Live with Aphra in freedom and self-respect. She'd scrambled into bed and glared round a room in which every lovely surface, every candlestick and pot-pourri jar, every velvet curtain returned the soft sheen of the moonlight coming through the open lattice. *Freedom and self-respect.*

And dog-shit.

No, she wouldn't. She didn't have the courage.

Sitting opposite Aphra now, Penitence envied and pitied the woman still fighting the battle she herself had deserted. Hardly a day passed but Aphra was rolled in the verbal equivalent of excreta. Fops came deliberately to her first nights to disrupt what must be a bad play because it was a woman's. Churchmen who accepted bawdiness when it was written by a man condemned her 'immodesty' from the pulpit. Male playwrights were savagely jealous enough of each other's success; when the success was a woman's they were merciless. As it dawned on them it wasn't just novelty value that brought in her audiences, the wits went for Aphra with squibs and lampoons. Wycherley wrote a poem full of *double entendre* about her showing 'her parts' just to get 'a clap'. Her championing of women's right to marry whom they pleased and her plea for their sexual freedom if they were in love brought attacks on her private life by those who assumed that she took a different lover every night.

She had to struggle against publishers who were honoured to print Rochester's four-letter-worded poems but delayed Aphra's gentle erotica for fear it would be considered indecent.

The more she answered her critics back – and she did – the more publicity she got. The more publicity she got, the more she was reviled.

But Davenant at the Duke's Theatre kept putting on her

plays, and her plays kept running beyond the vital third day —
which was when the author took the box-office receipts. She
was getting over £100 a play, besides what she earned from
her poems, her editing and her panegyrics to various members
of the royal family.

What she did with the money was a mystery to anybody
who first encountered the shabbiness of the room over the
Fleet, but Penitence suspected that most of it went to Aphra's
brother and all the other lame dogs she was supporting.

'What's that? Dear Lord, what's that?' From outside came
the crack of a firework, shouts and the tramp of feet.

'It's early for Guy Fawkes' Night.' Frowning, Aphra got up
to go to the door, but the nervous actor stopped her: 'Don't
open it. Don't open it. They've come for me.'

'Better not, Affie,' said Nell Gwynn. 'It's all right, Neville
lovey' — *That's his name. Neville Payne* — 'it's the Pope-burning.
Some of the procession'll be coming past here on its way to
the City, is all.'

'All?'

Tenderly, Aphra woke up the drunk who'd been asleep on her
carpet, introduced him as 'Master John Hoyle of Lincoln's Inn',
and they all went upstairs to watch from the window of Aphra's
bedroom, which had a view over the Fleet Bridge to Ludgate.

The procession was just a tributary from the West End on
its way to join the main anti-Catholic demonstration being
organized in the City, but it was impressive enough. Even
Neville Payne, convinced it was directed against him, pressed
forward to see the cheering crowds and the floats, some
bearing mitred papal effigies surrounded by women dressed as
nuns but displaying their breasts and placards which read 'The
Pope's Whores'. One of the floats carried a white-faced, life-
sized puppet with a sword through its middle, representing
the murdered Sir Edmund Berry Godfrey. Round its neck was
a placard with the words 'Revenge Me'.

'Good, innit?' asked Nell Gwynn, beating time to the music
of the bands.

'Will you get back, woman?' begged Neville Payne. 'You're
attracting attention.'

'They ain't after you, my duck,' said Gwynn. 'It's Dismal Jimmy, Duke of York, as they want the balls off.'

The procession was piling up against Ludgate's bottleneck. To pass the time one of the floats' attendants erected a scaffold and hanged one of the effigies, then set fire to it. As its straw caught fire, the sack which formed its body began to squirm and then yowl.

'Oh God, oh God,' whispered Aphra. 'They've put cats inside.'

The amiability of the crowd was shocking; the display on offer diffused the earlier physical violence with the violence of its entertainment. Traffic still jammed the city gate as a young man on a magnificent horse, accompanied by outriders with flares, rode up to it. It was difficult for the watchers in Aphra's window to distinguish features, but they could see that the long cloak which hung from his shoulders and over his horse's rump was the royal purple which only the King, the Duke of York and Prince Rupert were allowed to wear. But the young man wasn't any of these.

Delighted, the crowds shouted his name as if it were an incantation: 'Monmouth! Monmouth!'

'Gawd, it's little Prince Perkin,' said Nelly, gravely. 'My Charlie ain't going to like this. He ain't king yet.'

Neville Payne clutched at her. 'He's not going to be, is he? Tell me he isn't.'

'He'd like to be,' Nelly Gwynn told him. 'Shaftesbury and the other Whigs is spreading the tale as his ma was secretly married to Charlie. There's supposed to be a Black Box somewheres as contains the marriage papers.' She snorted. 'Black box my arse. If Charlie married Lucy Walter, I'm the Great Cham of China.'

Beside Penitence the unshaven, drink-sodden figure of John Hoyle of Lincoln's Inn spoke for the first time: 'The boy has delusions of monarchy. If I don't mistake me, he's touching for the King's Evil. A prerogative of your lover, Nelly, surely.'

A circle which had cleared around Monmouth allowed them to see figures kneeling within it and Monmouth himself laying his hands on the bowed heads in the traditional royal gesture to cure scrofula.

Nelly shook her head. 'Charlie ain't going to like it,' she said again. 'He's not a bad young limb, ain't Perkin, but Charlie's a great one for the rightful succession. He won't stand for a bastard being king, even if it is one of his own.'

'He'll be dead by then, anyway,' said Penitence. She was tired and wanted to go to bed.

Hoyle said: 'I agree. Down with all tyrants. What does it matter who's king? They're all the same. Though I fear we shall all live to see that it matters a great deal. Mistress Behn, isn't it a somewhat long interval between drinks in this establishment?'

Unlike his appearance, Hoyle's voice was beautiful and educated and the moment he addressed it to Aphra Penitence knew they were lovers, a fact confirmed when at last the streets fell quiet, the party broke up and he and Aphra retired to bed together.

In the small guest bedroom, Penitence worried more about that than the kingdom's future. *Here's another one.* Aphra was not a promiscuous woman, though her generosity in giving houseroom to male as well as female friends down on their luck led people to believe that she was. Her trouble lay in being attracted to men who inevitably took her money before leaving her for somebody else.

Her last lover, another young lawyer, Jeffrey Boys, was always in debt, and Penitence was present when his creditors turned up on Aphra's doorstep demanding payment for notes she had signed on his behalf.

'What can I do?' Aphra had said, when they'd received their money and gone. 'I love him.'

'Do you have to love him quite so much? He's bleeding you dry.'

'What would love signify if we did not love fervently?' sighed Aphra. 'It is the one matter in which excess is a virtue.'

Obviously Jeffrey Boys had believed it was; a month later he had transferred his affections to a younger woman.

Penitence went round to comfort Aphra, who was scribbling away at the table which had a book shoved under one leg to keep it from wobbling and which served her as a desk. 'What are you writing, Aphra?' she'd asked, gently.

'It's a poem, my dear, to *her*.' Aphra wiped the tears from her eyes, leaving an ink-stain across her cheek. 'Warning her. She's so pretty, Penitence. One can see why she out-rivalled me. He had a right to go, of course, love must always be free, but one wouldn't want her heart broken too.'

'Oh, for God's sake, Aphra, stop being so damned *generous*.' But Aphra never learned, and went on loving and being betrayed.

Because none of them had been sure what a vulture looked like, the Vulture Press had been renamed the Cock and Pie Press, and, thanks to the recent legislation lifting the ban on unlicensed printers, was at last legal — and successful.

The medallions on the Cock and Pie's frontage had been freshly painted, as had its door, putting it in line with the rest of the Rookery which was coming up in the world with the influx into it of hard-working Huguenot refugees. The sign still showed a cock standing on some unlikely-looking pastry, but underneath it bore the legend: 'Printers by Royal Appointment'.

'What royal appointment?' asked Penitence as she entered.

'Well, you're a sleeping partner as is sleeping with a prince, so that's royal,' said Dorinda, 'and we're doing King's playbills and posters now, so that's royal. Want some of this new tea?'

'*Tea*,' said Penitence. 'My, my, we must be doing well.'

'Special occasion,' said Dorinda, nastily, 'when Prince Rupert's lady deigns to visit us poor printers', and went off to make it.

Why do I bother to come? Mostly she didn't. It was weeks since she'd last set foot in the Cock and Pie, and it was only out of a sense of guilt that she'd come this time. Rupert, who disliked coarseness in women, made it clear that, while he would not forbid the friendship, he approved of Dorinda even less than of Aphra. 'She isn't worthy of you, my dear.'

Penitence protested Dorinda's staunchness in times of adversity but she was relieved to make Rupert's disapproval a private excuse not to see the woman so often. Dorinda was undeniably common and she made too many references to a past Penitence was trying to put behind her.

The mock marriage with which the Earl of Oxford tricked Dorinda had done for her on the stage; or rather, she'd been jeered off it by wits who found her humiliation amusing. Her friends rallied round; Penitence had given her a half-share in the Cock and Pie printing business, MacGregor had taught her to read and helped her run it. Aphra, Rebecca Marshall and some of the actors sent her work.

How much she minded the loss of her theatrical career was difficult to gauge because she never spoke of it. She had become a tradeswoman with the same bravado she'd shown as a prostitute, as if she didn't expect anyone to believe it unless she acted and dressed the part. Her tongue was sharper than ever and in the spectacles she wore for reading, her hair scraped under a cap like a muffin and her figure hidden under an even more frumpish apron, she was daunting. But customers apparently expected a lady printer to be eccentric and spread the word that her printing was workmanlike and her prices low.

With MacGregor's help she'd branched out into books as well as pamphlets, so that the bank draft for Penitence's share of the profits, which MacGregor took to Awdes each Lady Day, was larger every year.

The salon was now a printing works. The press Penitence had liberated from Goat Alley stood on the spot where Francesca and Job had once formed a tableau. The couches and gilded chairs were for customers and had been pushed back against the walls to make room for setting tables among the painted pillars.

A businesslike smell of paper, lead and ink exorcized stale scent and sickness. A new skylight in the roof let in the morning sun.

To keep her eyes away from the doorway where, for her, sheeted bodies were always lying, Penitence strolled the room casually reading proofs that hung from the drying lines. She stopped being casual and read more closely. Nearly all the sheets were pamphlets and nearly all the pamphlets screamed hysterical anti-Papism with titles like *The Whore of Babylon's Poxy Priest* or *Jesuit Assassins: the Popish Plot further demonstrated in their murderous practices,* or *Conspiracy for the destruction of the Protestant Religion.*

A couple were downright seditious: *The Growth of Knavery and Popery at Court.* One was a song:

> A Tudor! A Tudor! We've had Stuarts enough,
> None ever reigned like old Bess in a ruff . . .

She raised her voice: 'What the hell's all this?'

Coming back into the salon from the kitchen, Dorinda put down the tray, adjusted her spectacles from the top of her head to her eyes, and came to look. 'That's a bit of old Marvell,' she said. 'He goes well nowadays.'

'And this?' Penitence held out the sheet Neville Payne, the actor, had given her saying it was his death warrant. It looked as if it might be. Nell Gwynn had sent word round to Aphra's that he'd been accused of being involved in the Popish Plot and arrested when he'd arrived back at his lodgings.

Dorinda peered at it. She still tended to move her lips as she read. Penitence helped her out: 'It says Papist armies are coming to rape all Protestant women and dash out their babies' brains. Recognize it?'

Dorinda shook her head. 'Nah. Drink your tea.'

'For God's sake, Dorry, of course it's ours. I'd know that chipped "P" anywhere.'

'Yes, well,' grumbled Dorinda, 'we've ordered new type from Holland. MacGregor's gone to fetch it.'

'Never mind the type,' said Penitence, 'the point is what the hell are you doing printing inflammatory stuff like this? You're going to get yourself royally appointed to the Tower if you're not careful.'

'Not us, Prinks. It's ballocking Papists going to the Tower nowadays and there's nothing the King can do about it.'

'I know,' said Penitence grimly. 'A harmless Catholic, a friend of Aphra's, has just gone there, and bills like yours helped put him in it. They're whipping people into a frenzy.'

Dorinda put her spectacles back on her head: 'Aphra should

choose her ballocking friends more careful, then, shouldn't she? She always was a bit on the Romish side. Drink your tea.'

'"Romish".' Penitence was scornful. 'Who's teaching you these terms? You didn't used to care if they wore rings in their noses. So who's turned you Puritan all at once? MacGregor?' She was using irony, but suddenly she caught up on what Dorinda had said. 'Holland? MacGregor's gone to Holland? Oh Jesus, that's who's commissioning this trash – you're in touch with those damned Levelling exiles.' 'Levelling exiles' was a phrase of Rupert's, who saw little difference between the Whigs' aim to exclude James from the throne and down-right republicanism.

She stood up. 'Well, you can tell MacGregor that I'll not stand for the Cock and Pie Press printing sedition. I've Prince Rupert to think of.' And found herself pushed back into her chair.

'Don't you,' said Dorinda, whose face had suddenly acquired a new angularity, 'don't you *dare* come poncing in here first time in I-don't-know-how-long with your perfumes and parasol and tell *us* what to print and what not to print. Prince Rupert don't like our pamphlets, eh? Well, hoo-ballocking-rah. Rocked your and Nelly's carriages, did they? Oh, I heard. Hoo-bloody-rah again. We're going to rock more than that. We're going to rock that ballocking James right out of the succession, the bastard.' She put her hands on her hips. 'We're going to rock dear Charlie and all the rest of his stinking Papist boot-lickers into thinking a bit less of their pricks and a bit more about their country. And if you and your ballocking Prince don't like it you can stuff it up your arse.'

'How *dare* you!'

Dorinda waggled her shoulders in mimicry. 'How-dare-you, oh, how-dare-you? You weren't so fond of the King yourself once, not 'til you started fucking his relatives.'

'You were happy enough to fuck an earl.' They were both out of control. Penitence could hardly think of anything to shout that was bad enough. 'That's who you're getting back at, isn't it? You don't give a damn about politics. Because one of the court made you look a fool you're getting back at all of them. You're jealous. You always were.'

386

'Get *out*. Get OUT, you Popish ballocking whore.' Dorinda was looking around for something to throw. 'Coming in here all lady of the manor visiting the poor. Don't forget I remember you when you was spreading your legs for a bloody turnkey.'

'And I remember you when you were spreading yours for *anybody* and I'm GOING.'

Ribbons of paper clippings wound themselves round her right heel as she stalked up the salon, and she kicked them away.

Common bitch. Past the couch that had been Phoebe's death-bed. *I should have cut the connection years ago. Rupert wanted me to.* Past the place where they had sat together watching over the dying Her Ladyship. *He said she'd try and drag me down to her level.* Where Dorinda had nursed her, kept Benedick safe while she was in prison . . .

She was at the doorway now where, together, they had dragged so many precious corpses. *If I leave now it's ended.*

She turned and said petulantly: 'I'm pregnant.'

Dorinda took in a deep breath and cupped her hands round her belly. Gruffly she said, 'Oh, come and drink your bloody tea. So'm I.'

For a moment Penitence was dumbfounded. '*Dorry*, I'm glad.'

'So'm I,' said Dorinda again and burst into tears of sheer pleasure.

Penitence was taken aback by how happy for this pregnancy she was, happier even than for her own. God had at last given something to this woman whose life had been so deprived and who deserved so well of her. *How could I have been so ungrateful?*

God and who?

Sitting over the teacups with her partner in parturition, Penitence tried to think of a polite way of asking, and couldn't. 'Who's the father?'

'Cheeky bitch,' said Dorinda without heat. 'MacGregor, of course.'

'Mac*Gregor*?'

'And why not?'

Penitence said hastily: 'No reason. I just never thought of MacGregor.'

'He ain't as old as your Rupert,' said Dorinda, defensively.

'I'm sure not.' She'd never thought of MacGregor as being old or young, or, for that matter, having a sexual existence; merely as someone with an aptitude for printing and drink, hovering on the periphery of life.

'He's off the booze. He's respectable. We're getting married.' She cocked her head to listen to her own words: 'I'm going to be a married woman.'

Penitence said: 'Congratulations. He's a good man.' *Is he a good man?* To judge from what he was printing, his politics had become revolutionary. She was ashamed she knew him so little.

'He'll do, Prinks.' Dorinda was smiling wryly; they both knew they weren't talking about love. 'He's trustworthy. He'll look after us, the sprog and me. Whore like I was, I'm lucky to get him.'

'He's lucky to get *you*.' Penitence was working herself up into anger again. 'And you make sure he doesn't drag you into the Tower.' She nodded towards the proofs. 'Who's commissioning all this rabble-rousing?' It was too much of a coincidence that *every* client wanted the Cock and Pie Press to print anti-Papism. There was organization here. MacGregor was working for somebody, a group.

Dorinda nearly answered. 'It's —' She stopped. 'You just never listened to him, Prinks. He's a political little bugger, is our Donal. Comes of being Scotch. Something to do with all them "C"s.'

'Seas?'

'Letter "C". All them "C"s up in Scotland. Conventiclers, Covenanters, Clans. He's tried to explain 'em but I can't understand half what he says. All I know is, Scotch religious quarrels make ours sound like a ballocking madrigal. The government there don't just ban Dissenters, they hunt 'em down and cut their tripes out. His family's Dissenters. Some of his cousins got rounded up the other day, taken to Edinburgh and booted.'

'Booted?'

'It's a torture. They put their feet in an iron boot and hammer in wedges.' She leaned forward belligerently. 'And your ballocking Duke of York there, apparently, watching like it was entertainment.'

'He's not my Duke.'

'He's your Rupert's ballocking cousin.'

'I don't believe it. James is too stupid to be cruel.'

Dorinda sneered. 'You're too close to the treacle, Prinks. But MacGregor believes it. And I believe MacGregor. He says William ought to succeed because James ain't fit to rule and I agree with him.'

Penitence was confused. 'William?'

'The Dutcher. The prissy little bugger we met that day at Newmarket. Of Orange.'

Light began to dawn. 'Is that why MacGregor's gone to Holland? He's working for Prince William? All this is to get William on the throne?' She was too concerned now to feel angry. 'You listen to me, Dorry. He's got to stop it. MacGregor is *not* to use the Cock and Pie Press for this. I don't care if James lopped his mother's legs off, I won't have it. He's to leave politics alone, it's too dangerous. For me and you. We've got babies to consider. I'm not having mine born in the Tower.'

Dorinda bridled but it was obvious that she had been conscious of the risk MacGregor ran of offending the King to the point where it was dangerous. Penitence's alarm infected her into promising to tell MacGregor that they must revert to printing more normal commissions. 'But he's a stubborn little bugger, Prinks. You don't know him.'

Thinking, as she walked from the Cock and Pie to the theatre that afternoon, of the position he had put her in – owning a press which was advocating a policy which not only her lover but her king would regard as treason – Penitence had to agree that indeed she did not know MacGregor.

She'd begun to wish she never had.

By Act IV, Scene ii Rupert was still not in the theatre. She knew it with the tiny remnant of awareness she kept for the audience. It wasn't like him to be late. The friend he was bringing must have delayed him.

'Swear thou art honest,' raved Othello.

'Heaven doth truly know it.'

'Heaven truly knows that thou art false as hell.'

As Aphra had predicted it was a poor house, but the play's spell had gripped it. She felt its nerves with hers. Hart pulled her to him, rocking in agony, and went into his affliction speech.

As he put his hands round her face – 'Turn thy complexion there' – she registered that Rupert was standing in the auditorium doorway, another figure behind him.

'By heaven, you do me wrong.'

'Are you not a strumpet?'

'No,' she told him, 'as I am a Christian:

> If to preserve this vessel for my lord
> From any other foul unlawful touch
> Be not to be a strumpet, I am none.'

Rupert had moved towards the boxes. His companion stood where he was, his face to the stage.

'What! not a whore?'

'Nnnno. A-as I shall b-b-umm-bb . . . as I shall b-bb-b—'

Othello grabbed her to him again so that his mouth was by her ear. 'What's the matter, Peg?'

'As I sh-shall b-b-b . . .'

'As-I-shall-be-saved,' came John Downes's prompt.

She didn't hear it. There'd been a change of pressure in her ears, a sensation resembling deafness. Somewhere there was an audience and poor Hart subsidizing Shakespeare with frenetic fill-ins of his own, but she stood outside time, opposite the figure in the doorway. Perspective was altering the distance between them as if they were being blown towards each other, like ships on a collision course.

'What!' roared Hart. 'Do I hear you say you are NOT a whore?' He pulled her to him once more. 'For Christ's sake, Peg, say *something*.'

The line was out there. Desperately, she hooked herself on to it. 'No, as I shall be saved', and heard Hart continue in relief: 'Is it possible?'

She threw back her head. 'Oh, heaven forgive us.'

As they changed in the tiring-room after the play was over, Becky Marshall said: 'I've seen you give performances, Peg, but tonight's topped them all. You were magnificent. Win a pair of gloves.'

'Two pairs,' agreed Anne. 'What happened in Act IV, Scene ii, though? I thought you were going to die. Hart nearly did.'

'I was distracted.'

'Funny thing,' said Becky, 'so was I, when I came on just after. A man in the doorway reminded me of Henry King. Do you remember Henry, Peg? No, he was before your time.'

Hart came in. 'Marvellous, my dear. Truly a performance to make the gods applaud.' He was exultant. 'Wasted on that pitiful crowd, of course, but we had them in the palm of our hand. Did I notice the teeniest lapse of concentration in Act IV, Scene ii? We nearly lost them, dear. I thought we were going to get goosed.'

'I'm sorry, Charlie.'

'Never mind, never mind. Your good Rupert has given me a benefit purse that will do much for my retirement, like the true prince he is. He asks me to tell you he awaits you in his chariot.'

Outside in Drury Lane the carriage lamps shone fuzzily through a cold drizzle. Boller was holding open the door.

Rupert's hands grasped hers as she got in. 'My dear girl, what a performance. Always you have moved me, but tonight as never before.'

He made the introductions between Penitence and the dark figure in the corner of the carriage. 'The Viscount is an old friend. He has been abroad for many years on the King's business, and I fear his health has suffered for it. He protests he will go to an inn tonight, but I have overridden him and said Hammersmith air and my lady will make him well.' He was delighted at what he'd done: 'My stratagem surprised him. You did not know until tonight that my lady and

England's finest actress were one and the same, did you, Viscount?'

'I didn't,' said the voice of Henry King.

'And what do you say to it?'

'I congratulate Mrs Hughes on her performance.'

The journey passed in Rupert's triumphantly gloomy summation of the state of England. When an answer couldn't be avoided, the Viscount of Severn and Thames gave it, shortly. His voice was tired.

Penitence didn't speak at all. In four miles she had only one coherent thought: *Thank God Benedick isn't home.*

Chapter 3

PETER stood between the Corinthian pillars, the open doors behind him casting a wide path of light up the steps. 'Welcome home, Your Royal Highness. Welcome home, Your Ladyship.'

'Thank you, Peter.'

'Hello, Peter,' said the Viscount.

For the first time since she'd known him, the major-domo showed emotion: 'Lord, Lord be praised. This is good times come again, Lord.'

For some reason it seemed a terrible thing that Peter knew and loved him. Her anger activated her legs sufficiently to cross the great black and white floor of Awdes' entrance hall and mount the staircase to the Long Gallery at speed ahead of him.

Like a good hostess, but without looking at him, she opened the door of the main guest apartments and said: 'I hope you will be comfortable, my lord. I shall send the housekeeper to make sure you have all you require.' He bowed. She curtseyed and left.

In her room, she went to her looking-glass, wondering if she'd aged, wondering if the force of anger she felt would splinter the glass; the face of a hag stared back at her. How *dare* he come back. How *DARE* he. How dare he know Rupert and Peter and re-enter her temperate, equable life where, if there was no passion, neither was there pain. *Why isn't he dead?* How *dare* he not be dead. Where had he *been* these thirteen years? And what did she care where the hell he'd been?

I don't. She collected herself, pulled back her shoulders and folded her hands in her lap, controlling her breathing. There was no necessity for this turbulence. He was a man she'd known long ago, and that was all he was. True, he was the father of her son, but he was not aware that he was, nor was anyone else except Dorinda, Aphra, MacGregor and ... *Oh God, Mistress Palmer.* She had a nightmare vision of Henry King and the former Rookery laundress meeting on Awdes' stairs.

It won't happen. Palmer was usually in bed by this time of night. I'll see it doesn't happen. Nothing will happen — nor should it. Two people who were once acquainted have encountered each other again by chance, that was all it was.

But if that was all it was, why this fury that suffused her even to the tips of her hair? *You left me. You thought I was a whore and you left me. Because of you I brought up a baby alone. Because of you I became the whore you thought me.*

For sure, he had never intended to re-enter her life. When she'd seen him in the theatre doorway, when he'd seen her on the stage, the shock had been mutual, she could tell from the way he'd stood ...

The outline of his head should not have been so familiar after all this time, she should not have been able to tell the set of his shoulders from all the other pairs of shoulders in the theatre ... God, God, what a mess.

A knock on the door made her tense. It was Rupert. 'You look tired, my dear. I apologize for inflicting a guest on you tonight, but Torrington deserves well of us. I don't doubt that later he will tell us all he has been through.'

She nodded. 'Rupert.'

He turned back. 'My dear?'

'I have something for you.'

Smiling, he said: 'Another birthday present?'

'In a way.' She went to the chest where she kept her old beaded satchel and took out the letter she'd found in Her Ladyship's box. 'I think you'll recognize the writing.'

'What's this?' He took it to the candelabra and read it, holding it at arm's length. 'And how did my lady come by this?'

'You wrote it to my mother. Captain Hoy was my father.'

He folded the letter with great care and put it down. 'I remember Hoy. A good man and a brave soldier. He had a stutter.' He took her in his arms. 'Why didn't you tell me before?'

'I don't know. Tonight seemed appropriate. I wanted you to know that we've always been connected. We always will be.'

'My dear, my very dear.' He kissed her, then became brisk. 'We'll speak more of this. But for now, shall we go down?'

At dinner Peter hovered, ensuring that the guest, who hardly touched them, was served enormous portions. Penitence found this irritating almost to screaming point, though she didn't know why, any more than she knew why tonight of all nights she had told Rupert about her father, except that he had suddenly seemed so vulnerable that she'd wanted to make him a gift of reassurance.

For that matter, she wasn't sure why she hadn't told him before. Perhaps it was because he'd been so careful never to enquire into her past that it had taken on an aspect of forbidden territory and his questions might have led to the fact that she had spent two years of it in a brothel. It would hurt him, even while he accepted her explanation that she had not been one of its whores.

Something you never believed, Henry King. For the first time that night she looked straight at the Viscount Severn and Thames.

For the first time the Viscount looked back at her. *And you still don't, God damn you to hell.* The Viscount was smiling and, with her capacity to understand him still alarmingly alive, she knew he, too, was angry. And, *DAMN him,* proprietorial.

Bad health, not age, made him appear older than the intervening years warranted. His skin was near yellow and his eyes bloodshot. But, apart from a touch of grey in his hair, he looked as he always did, damn him again.

Talking happily, Rupert ate his way through the interminable courses with an appetite ensured by the Stuart immunity to weight. It was Peter who picked up unease from hers and the actor's silence. He paced softly from Henry King's side of the table to hers to watch their faces. *Time to put on the mask.* 'And how did you and my lord first encounter each other, Viscount?'

It was Rupert who answered. 'In Ireland, it was. The wicked year of '49. Anthony here was a sprog not sixteen year old and sent like a parcel by his father that he shouldn't be raised in a regicide country. I took him aboard the *Antelope*. The *Antelope*, good little ship. Remember her, Anthony?'

'Very well, Highness. I remember Her Majesty pawning her jewels to buy her ordnance.' The Viscount nodded towards Penitence. 'I am happy to see the pearls at least were redeemed.'

Penitence put her hand to her throat. The pearls had belonged to Rupert's mother, Elizabeth of Bohemia, and were so magnificent that only Rupert's insistence overcame her terror of wearing them.

Rupert beamed. 'Her Majesty would have been happy to see them inherited by such beauty. By God, we had to pawn our eye-teeth to sail at all, and we did so as much to provide our living as to fight the King's enemies. The Cavalier fleet we called ourselves, though others provided less flattering epithets − "buccaneers" was one.' He smiled. 'And not without some justification. If we needed to refit, we first had to capture some passing ship and sell her, like damned corsairs, though I trust we eschewed those rogues' cruelty.'

'You were never cruel, Your Highness,' said the Viscount.

Penitence experienced a wave of relief. *He loves Rupert. He won't hurt him.*

'What days. Portugal, the Azores, the Indies, Africa. Remember, Peter? We gained you, at least.' He frowned. 'And lost him I loved best in the world.'

Rupert's brother, Prince Maurice, had drowned in a West Indies hurricane. Rupert never mentioned him without crying.

In the silence, the Viscount broke the spell of reminiscence.

'And how did *you* and my lord first encounter each other, Mrs Hughes?'

Again it was Rupert who answered. 'My lady' — he emphasized the words gently — 'was making her first appearance as Desdemona, a role she has since made her own, as you saw today. I was hard put to win her, but eventually she was persuaded to grace me these eight years.' He raised his glass to Penitence. 'And yet has the ability to surprise me.'

'I'm sure she has,' said the Viscount.

At the end of dinner, she was glad to withdraw to her parlour. The whiff of tobacco smoke and port came from the dining-room. She heard the men go out into the garden to do what men did out there, and return to Rupert's library. She wanted to go to bed: she couldn't go to bed.

The sound of raised voices brought her to her feet. They were quarrelling. *He's told Rupert.* This must be faced at once. As she entered the library, both of them were on their feet, the Viscount doing some heated talking. Rupert was surprised to see her, but courteous as ever. 'Please sit down, my dear. A glass of port.' To Henry King he said: 'I have no secrets from my lady.'

The Viscount, it appeared, did. He slammed his hand on the mantelpiece and stood with his back to the room, staring at the fire.

Rupert, tight-lipped, handed her the port. 'The Viscount has returned from abroad on a mission, my dear. He is come to offer me the throne of England.'

Penitence sat very still and waited.

Rupert took a chair near hers and faced her, though she wasn't the one he was talking to. 'He seems to be ignoring three things: firstly, that it is not his to give away; secondly that I fought a war to preserve the rightful succession of the crown, and thirdly that Charles is my cousin to whom I have sworn eternal loyalty.'

'Charles can keep it,' said the Viscount to the fire. 'It's James who must not have it after.'

'James too is my cousin.'

'And a Catholic.'

'His religion is immaterial.'

The Viscount turned round. 'Is it? His personal faith isn't in question, I grant you. He could salaam to Allah three times a day as far as I'm concerned. But the man will try and impose it on the country. I tell you I *know*. If the English would accept it, which they won't, could you see them in slavery?'

It was an added strangeness to this night that here, within twenty-four hours, was someone else prophesying that James would be a tyrant. Reluctantly, Penitence turned her gaze away from Rupert's face to the Viscount's, where it stayed.

'And it is slavery,' he was saying. 'Spain is crumbling under her monasteries' weight. France is trying to whip the world into submission with it. You're a man of science, Rupert, for God's sake, would you see all progress stopped because the Pope doesn't like it? Rome still holds Galileo a heretic and pretends that the sun revolves round the earth.'

I thought it did, I thought it did. I thought I knew you. Where was the actor in Mistress Hicks's window? This wasn't him; this was some other man.

'He would not impose it,' said Rupert stubbornly.

'I happen to know that he will. He's a fool and he will. And the English won't stand for it. They fought against absolutism before: they'll do it again, and we'll have another bloody revolution on our hands. The people I represent are trying to prevent it. Why won't you?'

'James would not impose it,' persisted Rupert.

'He'll sell us out to France. Charles has already done it.'

Rupert stood up. The fire cast his shadow across the rugs and floorboards to Penitence's feet, where it mingled with the other man's. 'You are a guest in my house, or I should run you through.'

The Viscount stood where he was. 'Your Highness, seven years spent in a French prison have earned me the right to say that. They've earned me the right for you to listen.'

Rupert sat down.

Agonized, Penitence thought: *Seven years in prison.* And then she thought, ignobly: *Where's he been for the other six?*

The Viscount picked up a stool, carried it over to them and

sat at Rupert's feet, leaning forward. 'You must believe me, my lord. This has nothing to do with Charles's personal betrayal of me. I've long forgiven him that. I swore fealty to him as you did — at the same time, if you remember — and I'll keep my oath. It's James I won't serve. But the fact remains that Charles signed a secret treaty with Louis in '70. His sister was the go-between.' His long fingers were outlined against the light of the fire as he counted on them. 'The parties to it were Louis, Charles, James and Madame, nobody else.'

'I fear you have taken pains for nothing, my lord,' said Rupert. 'The Cabal knew of it. Even I knew of it eventually. The treaty with France is no secret. Charles was merely insuring his country against all eventualities, as a cunning monarch must.'

'There was a treaty within a treaty. The Cabal only thought it knew the terms. What it didn't know was that Charles has promised not to oppose Louis' domination of the Netherlands. Nor did it know the very considerable sums Louis is paying him for his compliance. Nor did it know that, for more money, Charles has promised to go over to the Church of Rome.'

'No!' Rupert rose to his feet, almost pushing the Viscount off his stool as he stamped across the room. 'I'll not believe it.'

The Viscount followed him, relentless. 'I was a better secret agent than Charles thought I would be, and the information was given to me. I didn't believe it at first; like you, I didn't want to. Then my informant was found murdered and I thought: *Hello, hello.* When the secret police arrested me the next day, it began to look as if I knew something Louis didn't want me to know. By the time I'd spent seven years in La Reynie's prison, it had become a bloody certainty. *Especially as Charles never lifted a finger to get me out.*'

'We didn't know where you were. I sent to Louis myself—'

'Charles knew. He may have had enough compunction to stop Louis having my body weighted and dropped down an *oubliette,* but he knew.'

Oddly the anger in the room had dissipated. Rupert poured himself and the Viscount more port from the open tantalus and the two men sat down facing each other on opposite sides of the fire, stretching out their legs as if they'd come to the end of a long, not unpleasant, day.

'You have been hardly used, Anthony. I'm sorry.'

The Viscount held up his glass, and twisted it, watching flames shine through and turn it to ruby. 'So is the King. It was, he tells me, all the fault of his Scoutmaster-General. I'm to be given a handsome pension.'

A log crashed down on to the hearth and he put out a leg to kick it into the grate. 'I'm not complaining, Rupert. I was serving my country, and England is greater than her individual kings and certainly greater than her viscounts. It's England I'm frightened for. Charles thinks he's playing a subtle game – he calls it the Grand Design. But he's a child compared to that monster across the water. It's Louis who's playing with him. As for James, Louis'll eat him and spit out the pips. Louis XIV is a genius and if he's not stopped soon, he will rule all Europe – England included.' He tossed back his drink and got up. 'So I'm not serving James. He'd not mean to allow it perhaps, but Louis would have this country in his pocket before breakfast.'

Suddenly he leaned forward until he was almost kneeling. 'Your Highness, there need be no bloodshed. Half England already wants James excluded from the succession, and if it were known that you were prepared to take his place, the other half would come over. I beg you to consider. Allow your country what she needs, a king of moderation and common sense.'

Penitence knew the answer before it was made. To Rupert kingship was sacred and inviolable. An uncomplicated man who lived by the rules of precedence, he clung to tradition because it had provided the only certainty in a world of revolution and toppling thrones. His anger when someone of lower rank, like the Prince of Orange, was given preference over himself arose not from vanity but from a terror of disorder.

Bless him, he was singing:

'Loyalty is still the same,
Whether it win or lose the game:

True as the dial to the sun,
Although it be not shone upon.'

The deep bass voice dragged out the last note, and Rupert smiled. 'Remember, Anthony?' Kindly, he patted the Viscount on the shoulder. 'Tell them I am flattered by their offer. But it is not theirs to make.'

The Viscount gave in. 'I told them that's what you'd say.'

They accompanied him to his door and bade good-night.

To her relief, Rupert merely took her on to her bedroom and didn't come in. He kissed her hand.' You need your sleep. Don't think hardly of Torrington. He is not the revolutionary he seems, and will settle when he has time to recover from his hard experience. Indeed, he has served the King better than the King deserves. Did you know Charles took his wife?'

He nodded at her surprise. 'The woman died in childbirth and it was hushed up, but Torrington is no Roger Castlemaine to accept honours in return for being royally cuckolded. He disappeared for a while, and returned to the King's service only because his country needed him.'

And I know where he went to.

As he always did when he'd been badly disturbed, Rupert kept touching the wound on his forehead.

'Does it ache again?' she asked him. 'Come in and I'll bathe it.'

He wouldn't. She wondered what had upset him most; turning down the kingship, or learning of Charles's perfidy in secretly treating with the French against his Dutch allies.

'Do you know, my dear,' he told her, 'that worse than all is the knowledge that the King could stoop to treat any friend as he has treated Anthony Torrington. Having fouled the wife, how could he then further allow the husband to suffer imprisonment? The man was on Charles's service.'

'*Because* he fouled the wife,' said Penitence. 'David sent Uriah the Hittite into the forefront of the battle for the same reason.'

Rupert shook his head. 'It bodes no good. "And the thing David had done displeased the Lord."'

She said, and meant it: 'You would have made a splendid king.'

In her room she slumped into the window-seat looking out on the ornamental garden. *Why did you come back?* Except, he hadn't. There'd been no trace of Henry King in that would-be kingmaker with his weighty past, with his loyalties and even more terrible disloyalties.

'Your father is dead,' she had told Benedick, according to plan. But the actor who had woven enchantment across a dirty alley in the midst of poverty and plague had never quite died for her until now.

Now he was dead. Some grand soul inhabited Henry King's body, an aristocrat who had no need of common theatre because he strutted on the stage of the world, a Uriah the Hittite generous enough to return from the dead and forgive his particular David, who offered thrones as another man might say 'Take a card,' and irreconcilable with the mountebank in the Rookery.

That man had been merely a facet of this one's multi-sided personality, a character produced for the occasion, to fill out time while the real person within recovered from humiliation.

Henry King had bereaved her twice, once in leaving her and now again by proving that he had never existed in the first place. The flimsy weave of resentment and hurt and fury with which for thirteen years she covered over the abyss he'd left behind him gave way. She hadn't known she could feel such grief. *God DAMN you, Henry King.*

She had to rock, to walk, ease the pain by physical movement. Beyond the dark knots and loops of the ornamental garden hedges was lawn shadowed by splayed branches of cypress. She twitched a cloak over her shoulders and went downstairs.

On her way across the hall, she saw through the open library door that Peter had neglected to cover the fire with its night-time elm logs. She went in to see to it. As she put the guard in place, a voice to her right said: 'Hello, Boots.'

As easily as it had once crossed the alley between two windows, the voice crossed thirteen years to make her young and fragile again. She wanted to hello him back, bridge the distance in time just for a minute, but she didn't. This man had abandoned her; it was Rupert who had picked up and protected the pieces he'd left.

'Good-night, Viscount,' she said, and turned to go.

'You've done well for yourself, Boots, I'll say that. Pro . . . proud I saw the potential.'

He's drunk. He was sitting in a watchman's chair on the other side of the fire, his face in shadow, but the decanters in the tantalus on the table by his hand were considerably more depleted than they had been. *He was drunk when we first met and he's drunk now.* She plumped up a cushion and kept on her way.

The voice pursued her. 'Why don't you run away with me?' As she spun round he staggered up to his feet and wagged a tremulous finger at her: 'Mean it. We'll run away. You with the Queen of Bohemia's jewels and me with my pension, we'll be in clover.'

The temptation to hurt him was too strong to be resisted. She took the chair opposite. 'Thank you,' she said, 'I'm already suited.'

'Aren't you though? Done well for yourself. I used to worry about you. I used to say to Boots — she was my pet rat in prison — "Boots," I used to say to her, "if I'm ever out of here, I'll go back and see how your namesake's getting on, poor little trollop." Nee . . . needn't have worried. Here she is, dripping pearls in a prince's bed. Whored her way right up the social ladder. Did you fuck Charles in the process, or is he the next rung?'

What bliss. She felt a ferocious, combative joy. He'd wanted to return to the gutter-rat he'd left and be magnanimous to it. She yawned, patting her mouth and letting her rings flash in the firelight. 'He didn't offer enough,' she said. 'Like you.' *Take that.*

What he took was another drink, though as he sat down again he seemed to have sobered. 'I'm offering now,' he said, 'if you'll leave Rupert alone. And I'm offering marriage, which is more than the others did, I'll bet.'

'Marriage?'

'Certainly. My first wife was a trollop, why change a noble tradition?'

She ignored the insult as she tried to work out what on earth he was trying to do. Underneath the drink and the irony and the sheer bloody rudeness there was purpose. 'I see,' she said slowly. 'You think Rupert turned down the kingship because of me.'

'Practically said so. You've got the poor old sod besotted, anyone can see that. "I'd not replace my lady for the greatest queen in Christendom." Very words. He'd have to, you see. Low as England's fallen, she hasn't stopped ... stooped to making harlots queens – not unless nobly born, anyway.' He lurched forward in his chair so that for the first time since entering the room she saw his face. 'Leave him alone, Boots. You come away with me. Now.'

Did he honestly think he could hold out a tastier bit of meat and the bitch would follow him? He didn't understand her any more than he understood Rupert. He didn't understand anything. If ever there had been a moment when she could have told him about herself, she wouldn't wish it back now. This was war. She wouldn't tell him she hadn't been a harlot when they met if they stuck red-hot coals under her fingernails. She wished she had been. She wished she'd whored with every man she'd ever met because it hurt him.

She was exultant. *It hurt him*. He'd felt something for that stuttering wench across the Rookery alley. He'd created a passable woman out of the clay he'd found to hand and been proud of it. He'd patented his Galatea and resented the use other men had made of it.

What a fool. She could hurt and hurt him. 'Marriage?' she said. 'With you? Viscount, you're nowhere near my price.'

She turned to exit left as he lunged at her, side-stepped so that he staggered against the fireplace. *Drunkard*. He was shaking and mumbling, then he dropped. *Oh God, he's ill*. She dragged him away from the flames and ran to fetch Peter.

'*Mal aire* the French call it,' said Rupert, 'from the noxious mists of swamps. I've seen it before, in Africa, though you don't have to go that far to get it. His Majesty's recent illness was not unlike.'

'It doesn't matter what it's like or unlike. What can we do for it?'

Infuriatingly, Rupert tapped the footboard of the Viscount's rattling bed. 'It *is* the point, my dear, forgive me. Charles was cured not by doctors — as if those meddlesome idiots could cure anybody — but by the powder of a bark from a South American tree. It was brought back from there by the wife of the Viceroy of Peru, who was successfully treated with it after the manner of the natives of those parts . . .'

Penitence clenched her teeth. It was no good hurrying him. She pulled the blankets higher over the shaking figure in the bed and gestured to Peter to fetch more. If this bark was any good Rupert would have access to it; the King's illness had occurred at Windsor when Rupert, as its Constable, had been in attendance. *But quick, quick. He's dying.*

'. . . and is named *Cinchona* after her. Both Charles and I experimented with Robert Talbor to find the right dosage and . . .'

'Can we *get* it?'

'Indeed. I have some in my laboratory at Windsor. I shall ride there this minute. But, my dear . . .'

'Yes?'

'I shall have to stay on, I fear. The forest court is due to sit and I must take my place on the bench; then the King is coming down for the races. May I ask of you to remain here and take care of our poor friend? He is too recently in England to have gathered his own household, and it's too long a journey in his condition for him to be carried to his family seat down in the west.'

'I'll stay, Rupert.'

'It is not infectious, or I wouldn't ask. It will be merely a matter of instructing the servants and overseeing their nursing. Do not overtire yourself. Peter shall come with me to bring back the cinchona.'

'You take Boller,' Peter's deep voice came from the doorway, where he'd been hovering again, 'I ain't leaving here.'

Penitence looked up. As Rupert's oldest retainer, the black man got away with liberties allowed to nobody else, but he was showing a suspicion that alarmed her. Rupert didn't notice.

At long last she stood at his stirrup waiting to say goodbye when he came to the end of the numerous instructions about the estate he had for Peter and Samuel, the steward. His strictures always ended with the same words: 'In all things you are to obey my lady as myself.'

'Take care, my lord,' she said. They were formal in front of servants. 'If the headaches return you are to come home.'

He bent down to kiss her hand. 'We have not yet had time to discuss your father. I have been thinking of the matter. Did you know he was heir to a manor?'

'Was he?'

'The manor of Hoy. An old family. Somewhere in Somerset, I believe.' He nodded to himself. 'I shall investigate further.'

She watched his erect back as he rode away down the chestnut avenue, with Boller following on his palfrey. At the gates, he turned and doffed his hat, swinging it above his head like a boy in a gesture the royalist cavalry would have known well. *Bless him, oh, bless him.*

By the time she'd got upstairs to the sickroom, Peter was installed by the Viscount's bed. 'I'll be staying here,' he said. And it was more a threat than a promise.

Chapter 4

SHE TRIED to confine herself to the hundred duties implicit in the running of a big house. Nevertheless, the compulsion to be with the patient fretted her nerves when she wasn't, and took her back to his room at every spare moment. There was a wrangle with Peter when she proposed to watch through the night.

'I'm staying. Ain't seemly for you to spend the night here.'

'You need your sleep, Peter. Go to bed.'

'Ain't seemly.'

'Don't be so prudish. I need no chaperone. He's my lord's friend. And if he weren't, he's in no condition to accost me.'

Peter's big lower lip was stuck out as it always was when he was being stubborn. 'I'm staying.' The implication in the flat, curiously well-spoken words was that she might do the accosting.

'It's an order.' She feared rebellion, but though the lower lip stuck out further than ever, he went. *Does every damn male but Rupert think me a whore? It's my duty as hostess to nurse the man, that's all.*

It wasn't all. For years she'd been recommending his death to God, and now that God seemed to be obliging, she was surprised by a desperate pity. He lay curled up like a foetus, his hands clasped over each other, his nails blue with the cold that made his teeth chatter, as if he was in an open field in winter instead of a bed piled with blankets.

She went to the fireplace and stoked it to subdue the impulse to cuddle the poor creature back to warmth as she'd cuddled Benedick in coal-less winters.

Memories which had been superimposed by his desertion began to surface. He'd sat by her sickbed once and nagged her back to life. 'I've worked hard on you,' his voice had said, 'you miserable item of humanity.' He'd called her his achievement in Gethsemane. The Rookery had been the Place of the Skull for them all then, but for him there had been the special refinement in remembering his wife's adultery. Not for him the satisfaction of calling out his rival – you couldn't challenge a king to a duel – instead, escape to the bottle and the grim reflection of his own humiliation in the most degraded part of London. All women must have seemed prostitutes to him then, so how could he have believed her anything other than a whore? But he'd meant to come back. So he said.

'Thirteen years to come back across the channel,' she told the shivering figure on the bed. 'You shouldn't rush about so. Tired you out.'

Very well, if Charles made his treaty with France in 1670

and Henry King had spent seven years incarcerated through learning of it, that left time unaccounted for. 'You'd have been too late in any case.'

Too late for what? To scatter a few pieces of gold into the grateful claws of a street wench he'd remembered to be sorry for? That he'd named a pet rat for? *Ho, ho, Henry King.* There *was a surprise for your homecoming.*

A moan of 'Cold' came from the bed.

'Serves you right,' she said.

Emotions came and went too fast to be analysed. Resentment subsided, rose again, subsided, became panic when the shivering fits gave way to fever and delirium. The back of his neck was hot against her arm as she raised his head to give him the cinchona infusion, and she had trouble getting him to drink. Glaring, he grabbed her hair and shouted: 'But that was in another country.'

The notes Rupert had sent her were not reassuring:

> After the fever will come great sweating and some relief until he be taken cold again two or three or four days after. If the ague do reoccur every day then he will be so weakened that he may be collapsed and die. These rallies and relapses may so continue if it be he lack vitality.

The 'great sweating' occurred towards dawn.

She called for fresh sheets too soon and had to summon more. Watching Johannes and Herbert, two of the footmen, bundle the perspiration-soaked linen ready for the laundry, she gave a sudden start. She left them sponging the patient down with marjoram water and, leaving instructions that on no account was he to get cold, scurried off.

She found Mistress Palmer haranguing the laundry maid who was hanging out clothes in the yard. She took her into the kitchen garden.

'What, that mummer as put on the play for us that time?' Mistress Palmer was intrigued.

'Yes.'

'As lodged with old Ma Hicks?'

'Yes.'

'Him as is Benedick's——?'

'For God's sake, keep your voice down. Yes.' Mistress Palmer was the only one of her household who'd recognize Henry King — the Reverend Boreman had never met him. 'I just don't want you catching sight of the Viscount of Severn and Thames and launching into Rookery reminiscences.'

'A-course I won't,' said Mistress Palmer stoutly, 'I want to keep my position, same as you. It's nice here.'

'It's not a matter of keeping our position. I don't want him knowing about Benedick and I don't want the Prince upset.'

'Shouldn't think you do. Who wants to go back to the old Yard, and them times? Remember that night when you come crawling home covered in the sticky? And look at you now, sparklers on your fambles, fart-catchers behind your chair at dinner . . .'

Penitence left, feeling more a Jezebel than before.

Peter was back in the sickroom, sitting on a stool by the door with his arms folded. Her patient was awake but querulously weak. He gagged when she gave him the infusion. 'I escaped prison to get away from better stuff than this.'

'You escaped?' It was indicative of her interest that she added: 'When?' rather than 'How?'

'I don't know,' he said irritably. 'A year ago? Forced to take the pretty way home, via the Americas. Only ship I could get.'

Thirteen years accounted for. One layer of resentment peeled away, to be replaced by another. *He could have written.*

She sent down to the kitchens for invalid food and left Peter to spoon it into him while she went to rest. In the afternoon, which was overcast, she ordered the torchère lit in his room and sat near it with her embroidery while he slept. On his stool, Peter's head dropped on his chest as he dozed.

There was a shout from the bed. She dropped her frame and ran to him. He clutched at her. 'I dreamed I was back.' He was shaking, though not from cold.

Seven years. For the first time they became his years, not hers. Appalled, she got a glimpse of wasted day after wasted day dragged out under a tomb's lid which he could have had no expectation of lifting. 'There,' she said, 'there. You're safe now. You're home.'

He tucked her hands under his cheek and went to sleep on them. So as not to shift him, she knelt awkwardly on the bed-steps, not caring what Peter thought. For her those same years had been showered with applause and achievement, thanks to him. Tears were dropping down on to her arms, and, gently, she extricated one hand to wipe them away.

In the evening, after more cinchona and some broth, he became revived and spiteful. 'Did I tell you I had a pet rat in prison, Peter?'

'No, lord.'

'Pet rat. Called it Boots. Taught it tricks.'

'A clever rat, lord?'

'A very clever rat, Peter. When she came to me, all she could do was squeak. By the time I'd finished with her she could talk, what do you think of that?'

'You're joshing me, lord.'

'I'm not. She could even sing. She used to sing Balthazar's song.'

'What happened to the rat, lord?'

The Viscount lay back on his pillows. 'Oh, she went off to another's cell where the crumbs were better. You know what rats are.'

Penitence bit off her silk, jabbed her needle into her embroi-dery and got up. 'Good-night, my lord.'

'Going?'

'Yes.'

'Sing to me. Balthazar's song. To remind me of Boots.'

'I only sing professionally, my lord. I'll send you our lutist. That's what he's employed for.'

It was soothing to walk in the knot garden. As she paced round the tortuous pattern, the light from the terrace's flam-beaux showed up the hedges as black, raised stitching against the pale background of the gravel.

He definitely thought his tuition of her had established some sort of chattels-right. What she couldn't fathom was whether he resented Rupert's possession of the chattels which were more rightfully his, or whether, as he saw it, the same chattels were proving a stumbling block between Rupert and the crown.

Like the knot garden, their relationship had a repeating pattern. Its form depended on the illness. On the third day he began shivering again and was reduced to being pitiful. In the fever that followed his mind wandered away into Grand Designs and prisons. Afterwards he was exhausted and pettish until the the cycle started once more three days later.

When the second fever, which was very bad, was at its height, he shouted out again: 'But that was in another country.'

She and Peter were fighting to hold him down. This time she finished the quotation for him. 'And besides, the wench is dead.'

He stopped struggling.

'That's his wife is dead,' said Peter, wiping his forehead with his arm. 'Fair as the moon, she was. Song of Solomon.'

'Tell me.'

He shook his head. 'The wages of sin is death.'

'Romans 6, verse 23,' she said, automatically, causing the black man to look up in surprise. 'What *happened* when the King took her away from him?'

Peter looked sadly at the head tossing from side to side on the pillow. 'He wailed, he gnashed his teeth. We thought he'd go mad, the Prince and me, and we kept him a-locked up in Spring Gardens in case he injured the King. Or himself. And him cast out by his pappy for a-marrying her in the first place.'

'His father had cast him out?'

'For she was a Roman. And the King said: "Don't you mind your pappy, Anthony, you and her you come live with me in Whitehall until your pappy's dead." But the King he lusted for the fair lady and she lusted for him. And the wages of sin is death.'

His white-rimmed eyes looked meaningfully at her, and although she had more questions, he would say nothing.

So he married a Catholic, and his father cast him out for it. Some of the man's history was becoming clear. With no money, and refusing to accept payment for his wife's infidelity, as had Roger Castlemaine, he'd wandered drunk and singing along an alleyway in the Rookery and rescued a girl being set upon by ruffians for her boots.

The fever left him in a depression: 'Send me a confessor. And a lawyer to draw up my will.'

'You're not dying.'

'Yes I am.' He had a discontenting thought: 'Bloody Cromwell died of malaria.'

She grinned, but as Peter was momentarily out of the room, she took the opportunity: 'Why join the theatre?'

'What?' he asked, irritably.

'When . . . when your father cast you out. Why did you choose the theatre? Why King's?'

He closed his eyes. 'Mind your business, madam.'

As his health improved, so did his manners. It was a moving away; they had been nearer the truth of what was between them when he'd been insulting. There was no reason — she faced it, there was no excuse — for an attendance on him that could be performed by servants. She visited him each morning, after the barber had shaved him, to make polite enquiries and receive polite replies, and once again in the evening. She oversaw the preparation of the food sent up to him, she stuffed a pillow with herbs to sweeten his room and quizzed Peter on his needs.

Fervently she wished for his departure — in two more weeks the boys would be home for Christmas — and struggled not to admit the knowledge that every moment since his arrival had thrummed with a significance she hadn't known since the days of life and death in the Rookery.

The only place that gave her an illusion of peace was the herb garden. It was her creation, the only place in all of Awdes' grounds that hadn't been designed by somebody else. She knew herbs; her grandmother had used them for everything from cooking to curing constipation, but the plot at the trading post had been typically utilitarian. Not until she'd begun visiting great houses with Rupert had Penitence dreamed that herbs could be grown in anything but a plain patch. Inspired, she'd read every treatise on the subject she could find and begun transforming a disused area of ground on the far side of the stableyard.

Though she said it herself, after trial and many errors, she

411

had created something so pleasing that she and Rupert sat there to enjoy it as often as they did on the terrace over the knot garden. It ran down the length of the high stableyard wall which was of rose brick and which she had softened with apothecary roses and a quince tree. Paths of brick to match the wall were laid in chevrons and edged the formal centre where neat little grey hedges of cotton lavender made a lacy pattern filled with cushions of thyme and parsley. Mop-headed bay trees stood at the four corners, like sentries, guarding the standard honeysuckle which commanded the middle.

The bed running along the wall contained the untidy but useful plants like borage, sage and rosemary against a misty background of fennel. Rupert had given her a sundial for the garden and she'd stood it in an archway cut in the yew hedge which marked off the far end.

On the opposite side to the wall was a bank leading off under three great oaks to the enormous park and her present project was to make a small flight of grass steps in it. Dunstan, her gardener, had cut out the levels but she was laying the turves herself.

It was a cold, bright day and she'd wrapped up warm, covering her hair with a cloth. The activity of trundling back and forth, cutting and patting, absorbed her and she sang in bursts. '*Jackie boy. Master? Sing ye well? Very well. Hey-down, ho-down* . . .' The garden's robin watched her from the top of the spade Dunstan had left stuck by the turf pile. ' . . . *Derry-derry down. Among the leaves so green-oh.*'

Somebody else was watching. She got up from her knees and saw the Viscount standing beautifully in the wall gateway, a cloak swung round him as it had been when she'd first set eyes on him.

He's an ornament. Like the sundial. He should stand there always. 'Why did Peter let you out? It's too cold.'

'I escaped. May I talk to you?'

As she crossed the garden she was aware of what a fright she looked in her gardening boots and enveloping, pocketed apron. She dragged the cloth from her head and shook her hair out. He watched her every move, like a man studying a stranger.

412

They sat down on the lichened stone bench against the wall as far away from each other as its length permitted. Her hands were grubby with soil. She always started working in gloves, but unwarily stripped them off. She stuffed her arms under her apron.

He stared straight ahead and she had to make the running: 'I wish you could see the garden in the summer. I'm vain about it then.'

He looked around at the muted greys and greens. 'It is pleasant enough now.'

The robin flew across to one of the bays and eyed them. 'He's quite tame,' she said in desperation.

'I have come to apologize,' he said, stiffly. 'I have said unpardonable things.' He addressed himself towards her half-laid steps. 'I was unsighted by illness and the past.' He waited for a response and glanced irritably down at her fingers, which were tapping on the bench, when she didn't make one. It wasn't the reaction he'd expected, but he pressed on: 'You have been not only my hostess but my nurse, and have deserved infinitely better than I have given.'

The words were handsome but delivered without emphasis, like a schoolboy made to apologize for a lapse in manners to a rich aunt. 'Prince Rupert is wiser in his generation than I in mine. After all,' he added, 'a rose is no less a rose because it was originally rooted in a dunghill.'

How to hurt him. How to hurt him badly. 'Thank you, Viscount. Do you think I should terrace the whole bank, or only that section?'

'Did you hear what I said?'

'Yes. But we mustn't sit here chattering, you in danger of catching cold, and me with work to do. Shall I see you at dinner tonight? I look forward to it.'

When he stalked off, she returned to the turves in misery. Why did they react to each other's gambits? Why use gambits at all? After all this time, why couldn't they hold converse without running through every emotion in the human experience in as many seconds?

She knew why. She'd known from the moment he'd appeared in the doorway at the theatre. She wondered if he did.

Penitence looked around the garden, towards the sundial, the oaks that made a mystery of the park beyond them. Only a week or so before she had worried because she had not earned the munificence Rupert had showered upon her.

She had to earn it now. God had stretched out His hand from that clear, cold sky and demanded settlement of her debt. It was time to pay.

They emerged into the dining-room from different doors and carefully, like tortoises testing the air. They sat at opposite ends of the table and called remarks on health, weather and gardens.

The length of the table enabled her to whisper to Peter: 'Don't keep refilling my lord's glass. It's bad for his condition.' But it was too late; the decanter was down his end, and he made sure it stayed there.

Half-way through dinner she thought how silly this was. Defiantly, she moved down to the chair on his right; she wanted to know more of his political views, and since they had already proved to be high treason, their elaboration could hardly be exchanged at a distance of twenty feet.

'I'm curious, Viscount,' she said, quietly. 'If not James to succeed, then who now? Monmouth?'

'Monmouth?' He was incredulous. 'Monmouth?'

Not Monmouth. 'Who, then?'

He shrugged. 'If Rupert won't, it must be the next legitimate heir. Mary.' He tossed back his glass and muttered, 'Monmouth', disgustedly to himself.

Into her mind came a picture of James's elder daughter as she'd seen her a year before; round-faced, ordinarily pretty, young and sobbing. It had been a large family party at Whitehall – as usual, Rupert had insisted that 'my lady' be included as family – and fifteen-year-old Mary had suddenly burst into tears at the mention of her forthcoming marriage to William of Orange.

'Can't wonder at it,' Barbara Castlemaine had murmured to Penitence as they hovered in the consoling circle around the girl. 'Married to a dull, Dutch dwarf. A *Protestant* dull, Dutch dwarf. What a fate.'

'My dear,' Queen Catherine had said to her niece, trying to be kind, 'at least you've met the young man. When I came to England I had not even seen the King.'

'Madam,' Mary had blubbered, 'you came *into* England. But *I'm* going out of it.'

Penitence said now: 'She's not Elizabeth Tudor.'

'She doesn't have to be. She's acquired a consort who's the next best thing.'

She smiled. She still treasured the picture of William of Orange in a skirt after the débâcle at Newmarket. He and Rupert regularly exchanged a correspondence into which she slipped the occasional note and in which he included replies. *Viscount, if you have your way Penitence Hurd will one day be able to say of her king that she knew him when he didn't have any breeches.* It was unlikely.

'Don't underestimate him.' The Viscount filled up his glass again. 'That youth is all that stands between us and Louis. If our children are not to be speaking French and worshipping the Pope when they grow up, it'll be thanks to young William.'

That didn't seem likely either.

They wandered into Rupert's library. Peter fussed about the fire, set decanters, plumped cushions, but eventually ran out of things to do and had to leave them together, though he also left the door to the hall wide open. Penitence didn't close it.

They sat on opposite sides of the fire. Having kept to neutral ground through dinner, he was easier in her company; she felt he wasn't having to concentrate so hard in order not to insult her. For her part, she'd done a good job on bringing him back to health and it was luxury to look at him. She'd cropped his hair after the first fever to husband his strength, and the barber had fitted him with a wig which, with his elegant clothes, moulded him into the standard gentleman-about-town. She had a sudden anguish for the patched, funny man in Mistress Hicks's window. Perhaps he was there somewhere, under the lace and brocade, but neither of them could afford to call him back.

Carefully she said: 'Viscount, may I ask, what are your plans?'

'I thought of having some more of this excellent port, then of going to bed, and tomorrow taking my departure. Thanks to you, I'm well enough to go.'

The mask was well and truly on so she was able to incline her head to the compliment. 'You must stay as long as you wish. However, I didn't mean that. I just thought . . . you have had trouble enough. Must you get involved in more politics?'

He smiled. 'Politics have a way of involving themselves with everyone. It's inherent in the word.'

'But yours seem . . . personally inspired.'

He was angling his glass, as he had on his first night, so that it gleamed like the bezel on a ring. 'If you mean do I oppose my king because he slept with my wife, then no. I admit I didn't take kindly to it. In fact, to answer another of your questions, that's why I went and joined the mummers at King's.'

'Why?' It was good of him, she thought, after her assumed indifference this morning to treat her to an explanation. He must still feel he owed her something.

'Oh, he was trying to tempt me out of the country with ambassadorships and the like so that he had a clear run to the bed of the late Lady Torrington.' He took a drink. 'And I wouldn't take them. We cuckolds have our pride. And I like the theatre — I spent time with Molière and his troupe in my youth — *and* I had some puerile idea of capering in front of him, like Scaramouche, so that he'd be reminded of what he'd done. Perhaps I even thought of leaping off the stage into his box and stabbing the bastard.' He stood up and leaned against the mantelpiece, looking down at her. 'God, what fools we mortals be. Believe me, the late Lady Torrington was not worth it.'

Good.

He yawned. 'As it was, events overtook me. My grievance diminished in the face of all that death. England, I discovered, was more than courtiers dressing up as shepherds to leap in and out of each other's beds. It was poor and brave, like Ma Hicks, and MacGregor, and the girl in the window opposite mine. So when my country called me back to duty because it wanted me to keep an eye on the Dutch threat, I went.'

'The *Dutch* threat?'

'So it was believed at the time, but when I delved deeper the threat manifested itself not as the Dutch, but as Louis XIV and England's own king. Oh no, madam, my concern is not personal, I assure you. I happen to like my country's balance. I do not wish it shaken.'

'But is Charles shaking it?' she asked. 'It seems at the moment as if *it's* shaking *him*. Accusing poor Catherine of treachery and making him arrest all those Catholic lords.'

He was dismissive. 'Ebbs and flows, mere ebbs and flows. Oates will overreach himself – men like him always do. The danger is deeper. With the *pourboires* Louis is giving him, Charles may soon be in the happy position of not needing Parliament to vote him money. He can increase his standing army all by himself. And there, madam, lies the beginning of absolute rule.'

'I see.' She didn't. The state of the country was here, in Hammersmith, with its seasonal rhythm and its bucolic, unimaginative Squire Brewsters and its dairymaids and smiths and its regular attendance in the parish church to celebrate that pleasant compromise, the Anglican communion, a beautiful, unchanging and unshakeable solidity.

'I see I don't convince you. Let us hope nothing ever does.' He sat down and poured himself another glass. 'I understand you have a son.'

'We have two.' To head him off, she hurried out the first thing she could think of: 'Do you have children?' And remembered.

'Most unfortunately,' he said steadily, 'the late Lady Torrington died in childbirth and the baby with her. It is doubtful, in any case, that it was mine. No, I have no children.'

Once again she had a horrified glimpse through his eyes. If it hadn't been for her debt to Rupert, she would have told him then that he had a fine son, offered Benedick up as a restitution for the man's suffering. But it was time to pay. 'I'm having another baby in the spring,' she said, and in that moment saw that he'd lulled himself into believing Rupert so old that their relationship was platonic.

She thought he'd attack her. *He's drunk.*

'Ah, how charming,' he said. 'A small stranger, a patterer of tiny feet. Let's drink to the little bastard.' He aimed his glass into the flames and it shattered against the fireback.

Jesus, how primitive they were. Like rutting stags with their harems. He'd slept with her once and he still hated the idea that she should be impregnated by anybody else. Yet it hadn't occurred to him that the son she did have might be his.

With disdain she knew he'd return to the old theme, and he did. 'By God, Boots, you've come a long way since the Rookery.'

She flashed back: 'I have. You haven't.'

Anger always seemed to make him drunker. He put his finger to his lips. 'Naughty Viscount,' he said. 'Mustn't disturb the happy scene. Mustn't upset the cosy little nest, the *rich* cosy little nest. We don't want memories from our past vomiting all over our nice carpet, we've forgotten the dead in the Plague and the dead Indians, left them all behind, haven't we? Requiescat in oblivion. Boots has moved on.'

She got up to go, but stopped. 'What dead Indians?'

'Seem to remember some young whore telling me she'd been brought up American Puritan among Indians. Don't think about them, don't think about the Rookery. They're dead. All dead like Ma Hicks an' rest of unsavoury past.'

'Dead? Why are the Indians dead?'

'Massacre.' He'd taken her glass to pour himself another drink. 'Thought the Prince'd have told you. Or too busy in bed, was he?' He staggered towards her. 'A war, mistress. Between settler and Indian. Massacre. Don't concern yourself. Been over a long time.'

'Which settlers?' She hit the glass out of his hand, so that it joined the other in the fire. 'Damn you, which Indians? The Squakheag?'

He stared at her, sobering. 'Don't know. We anchored in the Connecticut estuary on my pretty way home. Things not so pretty. War was over an' the Indians were being rounded up and transported to the West Indies.'

They had been transfixed in her mind as in amber, both

Puritan and Indian; white-collared women sitting on their porches in the sun in the act of spinning; a canoe on the shining Pocumscut, its occupant with a paddle raised in a stroke that didn't come down.

The Viscount's voice came from far away. 'I'm sorry,' he was saying, 'I'm sorry. I'm a fool.'

Massacre.

She felt him hold her for a moment before he guided her to a chair and left her to call Peter to fetch her maid.

In the morning, they bade each other polite goodbyes in front of the gathered household and he rode away. She heard later that he had gone to Holland.

Rupert was obdurate. 'My dear, you must see that such a voyage at this time, in your condition, is impossible.'

'Why? Why is it? You've got ships that go over there.'

'Hudson's Bay and Rupert Land are a considerable distance from New England, and even if they were not, there is no question of your making the journey. I am astounded you should think of such a thing.'

'Why didn't you *tell* me?'

He pulled her to him so that she was sitting on his knee. 'Since I was unaware of your connection with the Americas, there was no cause for it,' he said, reasonably. 'It seems I have been entertaining a Puritan unawares.'

She couldn't stop crying, her wet face and nose were making a mess of his velvet coat. 'Please, Rupert. I *must* go.'

'My dear, what could you do if you did? The war has been over two years or more. Peace has been restored. You have no family there. I cannot let you risk either your health or that of our child. If you wish I shall have enquiries made.' He fumbled in his sleeve and produced a lace-and-lawn handkerchief. 'Look at you, you are not well now. Your valiant efforts in nursing Torrington back to life have worn you out. Blow your nose. There, see, you are upsetting Royalle. He's concerned for his little mistress.'

Penitence put an arm round the poodle's curly black neck and sobbed on. 'I beg you.'

'I shall not countenance your going and there's an end of it. No.'

Rupert sent orders to his Hudson's Bay agents to discover what they could from survivors of the war in New England, white or red. In the meantime, as a result of enquiries in the home ports, a varied and bewildered stream of men began arriving at Awdes to be greeted by the awesome figure of Prince Rupert of the Rhine, conducted to a drawing-room and questioned by his pregnant mistress.

Mostly these were sea-captains who had their information second-hand and at first Penitence thought they were exaggerating the scale of the horror that had overwhelmed New England. It had ruined all trade, they reported, aggrieved, except in slaves. 'And they ain't no good for slaves, Indians,' one jolly-faced captain told her, 'most on 'em wounded or starving when I takes 'em aboard at New Haven, and half of 'em dead by the time I off-loads in Jamaica. Don't hold their price, Indians.'

All the captains referred to it as 'King Philip's War' after the Indian who, they said, had started it.

'But who *is* King Philip?' asked Penitence again and again. The captains didn't know the tribes. An Indian. Now a dead Indian.

Rupert procured copies of documents for her from the Duke of York, who was holding a watching brief on the New England settlement for his brother. And it was from these that she learned just how terrible the war had been. Of the region's ninety towns, fifty had been razed or destroyed, thousands of lives had been lost, and with agriculture destroyed the war debt would take fifty years to pay off.

There were complaints from the surviving settlers to the Duke of York against the peace treaty his representative, New York's governor Edmund Andros, had imposed on them and the Indians the year before; 'a patched-up thing which do leave lying, cheating, murthering savages still in possession of no little part of the country and the massacring of us unavenged.'

In one document there was an eye-witness account of what had happened at Lancaster. The Indians, it said, had swooped down on their peaceful settlements inflicting untold violence and horrible torture 'whereof some of their victims were flayed alive, or impaled on sharp stakes, or roasted over slow fires'.

Rupert came over and took the paper from her hand. 'If you distress yourself like this, my dear, I must forbid you reading.'

She stared up at him. 'My Indians wouldn't have done this. Not Awashonks's people. Rupert, what went wrong?'

The next day she received a visitor who could tell her. His name was Fitzwilliam; he was young, well-bred and highly intelligent and Rupert had prevailed on him to come to Awdes because he had been one of James's agents sent out from England to take stock of the New England situation.

He was also a flirt. 'Most honoured to meet you, ma'am. Fell in love with you when I was fifteen. Saw your Desdemona, and your Beatrice. Based me ideas of womanhood on 'em ever since.'

She was too concerned to be flattered. 'How did the war start, Master Fitzwilliam?'

'It *started* in 1620, ma'am, when the first pilgrim set foot on New England soil, if you'll pardon me saying so – I understand from his Royal Highness that you are Puritan-related.' There was an echo of the Viscount's 'Done well for yourself' in the young man's amused look around Awdes' sitting room.

'Please,' she said. 'Just tell me.'

He shrugged. 'It don't work, ma'am. Two different peoples, civilized and savage, livin' side by side. It don't work. Now I liked the tawnee, what I saw of him, and if I'd been there with him and he'd been open to argument I'd have told him the moment the *Mayflower* hove over the horizon to slit his own throat. Quicker in the long run. Cut out the middle man. He was doomed, d'ye see.'

She opened her mouth to reprove his flippancy, then shut it. He was right. Even as a child, without knowing why, she'd cherished her Squakheag as one might cherish the last pieces of some wonderful, exotic fruit before being condemned to an eternal diet of bread.

'We used to understand each other. We used to live side by side,' she said, helplessly, as if by saying it she could make it true. But as Fitzwilliam talked Penitence recognized the small quarrels which she remembered between her grandfather's white neighbours and the local Indians grown into an explosive inability of two inimical cultures to coexist.

With their nomadic form of agriculture, the Indians needed sixteen or twenty times as much acreage as did settler families. With *their* system of agriculture, the settlers allowed their animals to roam, trampling the Indians' cornfields, and blocked with their river nets the supply of fish to the natives' traditional fishing sites.

'And the beaver hat's gone out of fashion, ma'am, you see,' Fitzwilliam told her, raising astonished eyebrows that it should ever have been in, 'so the Indian's fur trade went. Actually, the beaver's gone now, anyway. The Puritans don't need to trade with the Indian any more; they're exporting to England and the Continent. Good old pounds, shillings and pence've replaced wampum as the medium of exchange. Your Indian chiefs had begun selling off land in exchange for cloth, and axes and kettles and such. Puritan population up. Indian population down.'

More and more Indian land went under the Puritan plough, more and more protesting, trespassing natives were tried by a court they didn't recognize in a tongue they didn't understand and fined sums in sterling they had to sell more land to raise.

New white settlers flooding into Massachusetts Bay were prepared to be violent in a way the original pilgrims and their descendants had not been.

Indians began to die in incidents which Fitzwilliam put down as much to ignorance as cruelty, as when some English sailors spotted a squaw canoeing herself and her baby across Dorchester Bay and decided to test the story they'd heard that all Indian babies were born with the ability to swim. They'd rammed the canoe with their boat and upset it, causing the baby to be thrown overboard. The anguished mother had dived in after him and eventually managed to bring up her son's body. 'Dead of course,' said Fitzwilliam, and then said with contrition: 'His Highness will horsewhip me for upsetting you. But that's the sort of thing that built up tawnee resentment, d'ye see.'

'I need to know.'

'Turned out the squaw was the wife of an important sachem and the baby was his son. Well then,' sighed Fitzwilliam, 'after that, the soldiers of the Plymouth settlement went to arrest for some infringement the sachem of the Pokanokets, a young brave they called Alexander, and marched him off at gunpoint.' He looked puzzled. 'He was taken with an inward fury at the humiliation. He died.'

Penitence nodded. Indians, capable of enduring any physical hardship, died easily from shame.

'And it turned out he was *another* important sachem.'

On top of all the other injustices his people had suffered, to Philip, Alexander's brother, this was one too many. He made his declaration of war: 'The English who came first to this country were but an handful of people, forlorn, poor and distressed. My father was then sachem, he relieved their distresses in the most kind and hospitable manner. He gave them land to plant and build upon ... they flourished and increased. By various means they got possession of a great part of his territory. My elder brother became sachem ... he was seized and confined and thereby thrown into illness and died. Soon after I became sachem they disarmed all my people ... their land was taken. But a small part of the dominion of my ancestors remains. *I am determined not to live until I have no country.*'

It began in local skirmishes that led to bigger attacks and counter-attacks until it encompassed all the territories of the Wampanoag, the southern federation of which the Pokanokets were a part, releasing years of repressed anger, then on to Nipmucks, the Narragansetts, spreading north along the Connecticut River to the Nowottocks and the Pocumtucks, until it set alight the entire Algonquian nation.

Springfield, where Penitence had gone to school, had burned, so had Lancaster, Sudbury, Marlborough, Mendon, Chelmsford, Warwick and many others. Little wooden towns named out of homesickness went up in flames, and with them the slashed Bibles and bodies of their men, women and children.

'I fear the savagery weren't only the Indians', 'Fitzwilliam told Penitence. 'Friendly Indian communities were slaughtered by Puritan soldiers who didn't care whether their tribe was innocent or not if it was red. Red men, women and children were rounded up, taken to the coast and sold for slaves.'

'The Squakheag? Did you hear of an Indian called Awashonks? Or Matoonas?'

He shook his head. She could see that she had disappointed him; she hadn't been actressy enough; it was eccentric of her to know individual Indians. His account of the war had been more balanced than most, but it was an historian's. He had seen the inevitable rise of the white English Christian and the decline of the red savage; he might have been remarking on the disappearance of a species of mammal.

After he'd gone, she kept up her search among the documents for names and places she knew, like a woman looking for the remains of her family among ruins, but the disaster had been too huge for mention of individual neighbours or of the lodges of Awashonks's people.

She stopped reading. The slaughter had taken place two years ago while she, with her ears shut to politics, had lived soft. The screams and war-cries and flames had quieted. The dead were long buried, and she hadn't known. She hadn't thought of New England for years.

Yet she should have. She owed little to the Puritans of her childhood, though it distressed her amazingly that their or-dered society had suffered such horror, but she owed a great deal to its Indians. Apart from an affection she hadn't found among her own people, they had probably saved her life by helping her escape from the Reverend Block and his accusations of witchcraft. Not only had she never repaid them, it was likely she had done them positive harm by involving them. However innocently, she had added one more layer to the distrust between red and white along the Pocumscut River.

What can I do? What can I do?

When Rupert came in, she ran to him. 'We've got to see if they were sold as slaves. Help me find them, Rupert. I must go back.'

He was kind but firm: 'My dear, your most immediate debt is to the child. I shall make what enquiries I can, but with that you must be content.' She saw that he was certain they must be dead and she would never find them. All that his enquiries would uncover would be more horror; more babies dying, more mothers screaming.

In any case, as she could tell, he regarded the Indians as another species and her anguish merely as an hysteria caused by her pregnancy. Wearily, she went back to the table, folded up the documents and tied them. 'I don't want to know any more,' she said.

She was thirty-two years old now, not eighteen, and the pregnancy was difficult, made more difficult by dreams that increased her sense of guilt and betrayal. Sometimes the dream was of Henry King and she would wake up feeling disloyal to Rupert. Other dreams took her back to her New England childhood and she'd wake to find herself sobbing. In these dreams her Indians were always running, not after something nor away from anything else, just running in the unhurried ease of movement the young braves used when they travelled long distances; she'd hear the gentle thud of their moccasins along the worn, forest tracks, see the sun shining through the leaves to dapple their bodies as if they moved through water.

They'll die. If they'd been netted, put into the dry fields of slavery, they would die gasping like fish for the freedom of their element. They could only breathe if they had unlimited space in which to do it. They wouldn't survive in chains.

And what of New England now? What would it be if this wonderful dimension was for ever gone from the forests leaving them impoverished and empty? Whiteness would spread through what had been shot through with colour like a wildflower meadow as the delicate balance that had held for a thousand years gave way under Puritanism.

How could you make them slaves? You went there to escape from slavery.

After she'd had a slight haemorrhage, Rupert, with desperation overcoming his aversion, sent an invitation to Dorinda to come and stay at Awdes 'so that you may deliver your own child into healthful air and be a companion to my lady, who is in sore need of your comfort', and issued another to Aphra Behn.

The two women were just what Penitence needed – Dorinda bracing and in the same parturating boat as herself, and Aphra the only person in the world who could appreciate her horror for the plight of the Indians.

She listened carefully to the outpouring. 'I really think one is going to have to speak out against slavery.'

Penitence grabbed her hand. 'When?' If one voice – and that her friend's – was raised against the concept that any human being should own the life of another, she could be eased of some guilt at least.

But Aphra had become a realist. 'When I've got time, and when I know it can sell,' said Aphra firmly. Penitence pressed her no more; perhaps because she had failed in her bid to support herself she had an almost mystical admiration for Aphra who had succeeded.

They turned to other matters. Aphra, as usual, was a source of all news. 'The tide's turning against those fearful Whigs at last,' she said. '*Nobody* believed Oates about the dear Queen planning to poison the King. And executing all those poor Catholics, well, it nearly killed His Majesty to have to sign the death warrants. Even the mob cried when poor, dear Viscount Stafford went to the block. It shouted out "God bless you, my lord, you are a murdered man."' Her face was as near vicious as its amiability would allow as she added: 'A pity it didn't think of that months ago when it was believing everything Oates said and was howling for Papist blood. Poor, dear Neville Payne is only now out of the Tower.'

'Mob?' asked Penitence.

'Oh my dear, we have two new words invented this terrible year. "Mob" and "Sham". And now Shaftesbury and his Whigs are not only trying to exclude the poor, dear Duke of York from the succession, but their more extreme faction is trying to persuade Charles to name Monmouth as his heir, which he will not do, of course. Reading all those horrible pamphlets that are maligning poor James, one is so happy that one dedicated *The Rover* to him.'

Penitence realized too late that in Aphra and Dorinda she was storing gunpowder and match under her roof.

'Malign poor James, eh?' asked Dorinda. 'Ballocking crippler. Do you know what he done to MacGregor's family?'

'Where *is* MacGregor?' interposed Penitence quickly. She had been surprised that Dorinda had accepted Rupert's invitation so easily, leaving the Cock and Pie Press in the charge of an apprentice.

'Away,' said Dorinda curtly, and turned back to Aphra.

Aphra's stout defence, that Scotland's barbarities were committed by its government and were not the responsibility of poor, dear James, led to a quarrel that Penitence only calmed with difficulty. At last, with Dorinda puffing and Aphra exuding a stubborn sorrow, she turned the conversation to the theatre, though even here they were on dangerous ground since the playhouses had become microcosms of the political divisions outside them, and fights were breaking out between Tories and Whigs in the audiences.

After dinner they sat in her drawing-room and Aphra read them selections from her plays and poems. Penitence was startled by how good they were. Aphra had mastered her craft; she was funny, a brilliant plotter and she was pulling in the crowds. But the theme that ran through almost all her work was a plea for equality of love between the sexes. Time and again she attacked the property-marriage system, her most usual heroines battling not to be married off against their wishes.

It was a brave stance. The loose-living aristocrats of Aphra's audiences were rigidly old-fashioned when it came to trading their daughters for enhanced lands and prestige. 'The critics savage one for encouraging daughters into rebellion, but I shall attack slavery where I find it. In New England's forests. Or old England's parlours.'

'You tell 'em, Affie,' said Dorinda, invigorated.

Aphra smiled over at her hostess. 'There is slavery for women, too, Penitence. One has to earn one's bread, and one can only fight one form of slavery at a time.'

'I'm beginning to think it's indivisible.'

The evening ended with love-poems. Outside the windows snow was falling on the knot garden, making it into white embroidery. Inside, Aphra's warble was of an erotic, Arcadian spring:

> 'Your body easy and all tempting lay,
> Inspiring wishes which the eyes betray.'

'Give us "Amyntas led me to a grove", Affie.'

> 'His charming eyes no aid required,
> To tell their softening tale;
> On her that was already fired,
> 'Twas easy to prevail.
> He did but kiss and clasp me round,
> Whilst those his thoughts expressed:
> And laid me gently on the ground.
> Ah, who can guess the rest?'

In the silence, Dorinda heaved a deep sigh. 'Gawd,' she said, softly, 'I can.'

So could Penitence. She became brisk. 'It's time for bed, ladies.' Both women looked as tired as she felt. Dorinda had already confided that she was tormented by a fear that the venereal disease she had contracted in her prostitute days, though it seemed cured, might affect her child.

Aphra was drawn and thin; the indignation with which she talked of her critics she made amusing, but Penitence knew they hurt her. 'One sends off one's plays with . . . "Va, mon enfant! Prends ta fortune", . . . only to see the poor things stabbed like Hypatia by male pens. "A woman make a play? Burn it for immodesty!" One could almost be vexed.'

The Earl of Rochester, her adored patron, was dying a profligate's death, and her poems revealed that her love-life was unhappy. According to Dorinda, who kept up with theatre gossip, her lover John Hoyle was being unfaithful with men as well as other women.

They were all tired, she thought; three tired women worn down by the attrition of being women. *Damn men.* Damn them for starting wars, for their politics and plotting and most of all for making women love them.

After Aphra went back to Town, there was no less tension. Dorinda behaved herself when Rupert was around, but in Penitence's company she sneered at their richness of living. '*How* many cooks? Forgotten the time when all we had was poor old Kinyans, ain't you?'

'Three cooks,' said Penitence, patiently, 'five scullions, and a lad to turn the spits. And I haven't forgotten Kinyans.'

Or: 'Nice taste in ruby earrings your Queen of ballocking Bohemia. We was in the wrong end of business, Her Ladyship and me.'

She'd finally touched a nerve. Penitence dragged her out into the herb garden where they couldn't be overheard. 'One more word,' she hissed, 'one more word implying I took up with Rupert for his jewels or his cooks or any other bloody thing, and I'll kill you.'

'What was it for then? His vibrant young body?'

Peace, good people. I'm the Protestant whore. 'Leave me alone. Leave me *alone.*'

Desperately, she waddled off to the stone bench where she had sat with Henry King. After a moment, Dorinda waddled after her, sat down and took her hand. 'You looked like your ma, just then.'

'I got tired,' Penitence told her quietly. 'After that night, after they covered me in the dog mess, I couldn't fight any more. I took the easy way out.'

'Yeah, I know. I didn't mean it.'

'Yes, you did. And you're right. It was still whoring. But I do love him. Not like he wants me to, but I'm good for him.'

'I know. Don't take no notice of me.'

The turf steps had taken well. Dunstan had scythed them. Achingly, her robin hopped around their feet while blackbirds flew in and out of their nests in the yew hedge in the endless business of feeding their young.

Penitence rallied. 'And because you and MacGregor have turned republican, it doesn't mean that all this' – she waved her hand round the lovely garden – 'is wrong. Rupert's a very *good* man.'

'I know he is, Prinks. And I ain't republican neither. I don't understand what MacGregor's going on about half the time. But he's a good man and all, and he thinks if that ballocking James gets to the throne, it's England as'll be rolled in the dog turd. And I believe him.' She took in a breath of herb-scented air. 'Oops, I'm going to have to pee again.'

They helped each other up, and went back to the house, discussing the more pressing business of what late pregnancy did to the bladder.

Dorinda's was a terrible labour; after over forty-eight hours of it a panicking Penitence, two weeks away from her own, sent Boller and a coach to St Giles-in-the-Fields to fetch Apothecary Boghurst, the only medical expert she trusted. Because he charged less than doctors, he'd attended many a difficult birth in the Rookery.

Outside the door of Dorinda's bedroom, she warned him not to mention hers or Dorinda's connection with the Cock and Pie. The little man hadn't changed one iota. 'I am no doctor, madam, but I comply to the teaching of Hippocrates.'

'Was he any good with babies?'

Dorinda's bed was surrounded by women. Besides Mistress Palmer there was Mistress Dobbs, the Hammersmith midwife, Annie the dairymaid, whose child had died and who was present in her capacity as the coming baby's wet-nurse, and three maids.

The room smelled of the butter with which the midwife had been trying to grease the baby's passage out into the world, and tangy earth.

Apothecary Boghurst sniffed. 'Hollyhock roots?'

'Yes, Doctor,' said Mistress Dobbs, 'I been pounding 'em small.'

'Have you stuffed any up her yet?'

'I was just about to, Doctor.'

'Out.'

Mistress Palmer and Penitence were allowed to stay. The midwife's complaints to her companions diminished down the hall.

Dorinda's hair was wet with sweat and she bit convulsively at the leather pulling-strap. From under the mattress knife-handles stuck out, making it look like a giant slab of meat prepared for cooking. Apothecary Boghurst drew out the knives and threw them into a corner.

'Put 'em there to cut the pain, 'pothecary,' protested Mistress Palmer.

'They haven't.'

Ashamed, Penitence put out her bruised hand once again for Dorinda's dreadful grip. Witnessing the suffering without being able to alleviate it had so demoralized her that she'd followed the midwife's lead like a sheep. Even so, she demurred when, after the examination, Boghurst put the coal tongs into the fire and then plunged them into the bowl of briony water warming near it.

'You're not going to put those in her?'

The apothecary took her to one side. 'It's the mother or the child,' he said. 'I doubt if we can save both. If I don't act now, we'll save neither. Tie her hands to the bedhead, and both take a leg each.'

Gripping Dorinda's foreleg to her chest, Penitence prayed, hopelessly, for God's mercy on her. The shrieks echoed screams from the Plague and New England. *Why isn't there more kindness in the world when delivery into it is torment like this?*

The cord was cut and the bloodied scrap that was the baby was taken away by Mistress Palmer while the apothecary delivered the afterbirth. The silence of the room settled like wool on their ringing ears. With her forehead still resting on Dorinda's white knee, Penitence began to doze.

There was a tiny choke and a mewl of tentative complaint.

Mistress Palmer whispered a Magnificat: 'The little bugger's alive.'

Another whisper came from the bed. 'Is it all right?' Apothecary Boghurst got up to look and nodded. Incapable of surprise, Penitence watched tears roll down his cheeks as they were rolling down hers. 'You have a brave daughter, mistress,' he told Dorinda.

When Penitence went down to send up the wet-nurse, she was crying for the baby's bravery, Dorinda's, the apothecary's, Mistress Palmer's, her own, the courage of creation in the face of insuperable odds. 'There is a God,' she sobbed to an alarmed Rupert. 'He's upstairs.'

He took her to the Awdes chapel to give thanks, and she gave it to the God who had appeared in Dorinda's bedroom, something neither male nor female but a raw, squirming, indomitable amoeba of both.

She couldn't stop sobbing. Dorinda's travail hadn't been only in her labour but in every minute of her progress from childhood to womanhood in a world organized for her obliteration. 'Make it easier for her baby,' Penitence prayed. 'Make it easier for mine.'

Dorinda named her baby Penitence, though the child was always known to her intimates as Tongs.

Penitence's daughter, born sixteen days later, was called Ruperta.

Chapter 5

AGAINST the fashion of the class to which she now belonged, Penitence not only insisted on breast-feeding her daughter but spent every available minute with her. Their first separation came when Prince Rupert decided to take Penitence on a visit to a destination he refused to name.

Penitence didn't want to go. 'It's no good saying she must stand on her own feet, Rupert; she's still only toddling.' She was surprised at him wanting to leave the child; his adoration of Ruperta was almost painful. Even the King of England had

been summoned to worship at the cradle-side, and had obediently pronounced the baby 'wondrous appealing, a thief of
future men's hearts'.

'She has already stolen mine,' Rupert told him. 'I think my
Lord Burford would not prove an unsuitable match for her.'
The Earl of Burford was Charles's elder son by Nell Gwynn.

But it was an unsatisfactory visit; the King refused to
commit himself on the proposed marriage, and was even more
elusive on Rupert's other request — that Dudley and Benedick
be given titles.

Rupert was beside himself with rage. 'He ennobles the
bastards of every adulterous punk in his bed, while I, who
fought for him and his father before him, see my fine lads
remain commoners.'

'You seem prepared to marry Ruperta off to one of those
same bastards,' said Penitence, coldly.

'Gwynn is an honest trull,' he told her — he'd always liked
Nelly, 'and young Burford an honest boy. None of Monmouth's pretensions to the throne there. And yes, yes, my
dear, Ruperta shall not be wed against her wishes. I merely
wanted to establish the principle of her worth, but Charles
wouldn't know a principle if it bade him good-day.'

Penitence nodded. 'I heard you tell him.'

'Well, what would you have? Mop and bow and hold my
tongue like a damned courtier? Here I support, from my own
pension, honest tarpaulins he should have paid years ago,
while he lavishes a hundred thousand pounds on that new
French harlot. Where does he get the money, eh? Eh? Torrington had the right of it. The King of England's in the pay
of France.' He was stamping around the drawing-room, holding
his head.

Penitence became frightened. 'My dear, you'll make yourself
ill. Come and sit down.'

It was because his health was becoming as unstable as his
temper that she agreed to go with him on the mysterious
journey, though it was agony to leave Ruperta. She hadn't
been in any condition, let alone had the time, to enjoy
Benedick's childhood; she didn't want to miss a minute of this

one. And Ruperta was an especially rewarding child: healthy, chuckling and with the promise of an extraordinary beauty discernible in her chubby face — Stuart beauty; the cleft of the chin was there, and the large eyes, though in her case they were blue. As the King had said when he looked at her: 'You'll not dispute this one's paternity, cousin.'

Ruperta was another in the long list of debts she owed Rupert. *Paying again*, Penitence thought, miserably, as she waved goodbye from the coach. Dorinda, who was to stay at Awdes during Penitence's absence, stood on the steps to watch them go, Ruperta holding one of her hands and Tongs the other, both of then waving.

'Has that woman no home of her own?' asked Rupert as he frequently did, sometimes as a joke, at other times with something like resentment that he so frequently returned to Awdes from Windsor Castle to find Dorinda in residence. Whenever MacGregor was away — and he was away a lot — Penitence invited her to come and stay.

'She's my friend,' said Penitence, firmly, as she always did, 'and Tongs needs all the good country air she can get.'

'A poor little thing.' He was in good humour today. He enjoyed patronizing Tongs, his goddaughter, mainly because she was a scrawny, colicky baby who, with her frequent illnesses, highlighted his own child's looks and splendid health.

To Penitence as much as to Dorinda she was a miracle, and she loved her.

'Where are we *going*, Rupert?'

'West.' It was his little secret. Wherever it was, a contingent of servants had been sent ahead a week before.

'The Americas?' She had a fantastic moment of hope that he had found Awashonks and Matoonas and the rest and that she would see them again.

'Not so far, madam. Ask no questions and you'll be told no lies.'

Penitence sulked. *I want my baby*. Men always pushed you in directions you didn't want to go.

But as the coach rattled on westwards, she became enlivened by the change of scene. She hadn't, after all, left Awdes in over a year, partly afraid that Rupert's suggestions that she accompany him to Town might involve her in another meeting with the Viscount of Severn and Thames to the disquiet of her emotions. She had allowed motherhood to overwhelm her, neglecting her looks, current events and, more importantly, Rupert himself. *Pull yourself together*. Her milk had been drying up in any case. With Dorinda, Annie, who'd been promoted to nursemaid, Mistress Palmer, the Reverend Boreman and the rest of the Awdes household to look after her Ruperta would be safe enough.

It was a fine late April. Along the firm roads the countryside was regaining colour and patches of interesting shade from the unfurling leaves of trees and the cow parsley frothing in the banks. They stopped at inns where Rupert had hired all the accommodation for the night so that they could have privacy and only their own staff to attend them.

She began to enjoy herself. On the second day they were crossing the sweep of Salisbury Plain and made a detour to see Stonehenge. Rupert twitted her Puritanism for making her uneasy in the presence of the great pagan stones. 'How my Cavaliers would rub their eyes to see me now in thrall to a Roundhead.'

He'd fought over nearly all the territory they passed through and had an anecdote for every mile of it. Penitence had heard most of them before, but to see the location renewed their interest.

After the plain the country grew less neat, more jumbled with trees and colour. Increasingly their progress was slowed by the declivity of a hill and the steep rise of the one after it.

For Dorinda, who considered that civilization stopped outside a five-mile radius of London, this would be here-be-dragons country. *She'd make her will*. Yet, though the villages and towns they passed through were increasingly remote, they were often impressive and prosperous, even if their traffic was halted by slow men driving flocks of even slower sheep, and the buildings were preponderantly Tudor, or earlier.

'This was for Parliament,' Rupert would say of one town, or 'There were brave Royalists here,' of another, and left her with a confused sense of political geography that the nearer a place was to sea-level the more it had supported the Roundheads, whereas if it had been set on a hill it was certain to have declared for the King.

'We are in Somerset now,' Rupert said, and pointed north. 'Somewhere over there is the ancestral home of your former patient.' He mistook her alarm for blankness. 'Anthony, my dear. The Viscount of Severn and Thames.'

'We're not going to visit him, are we?'

'No, no. Though it is a remarkably fine house. But we should never get away; he would wish to fête his nurse.'

I don't think he would, Rupert. Immediately the countryside took on significance from being in *his* county, but because it was his county she knew she would for ever be uneasy in it.

By the evening of the fourth day they had reached very strange countryside indeed, a land that was almost uniformly flat, so flat that anything which interrupted the straight line of the horizon, a gaggle of pollarded willows, a church tower, attracted the eye with an almost mystical significance. Their road became a causeway over reedy marsh where the hooves of cattle made sucking sounds as they grazed, leaving dark pools of water in the deep prints they left behind.

The landscape was the loneliest they had passed through, alien with the song of birds she had never seen before, rustling with strange grasses, and yet she was teased by a feeling that if the carriage wheels would only stop their rolling she would be able to speak the place-names, or know what was the medical use of the little catkinned myrtle that spread over the bogs, or tell Rupert the local nickname for the tiny, bearded bird fluttering in the rushes. It was like being haunted by a phantasm that flickered just beyond the range of vision.

'Is this still Somerset?'

'Still Somerset.'

'I feel very strange, Rupert.'

'Not long now, my dear. We're nearly there.'

But she was far from tired; as the carriage left the causeway and began to negotiate a slight climb, she clung to the window frame so that she could look behind her to the apparently endless, level expanse of varying greens. 'What is that place?'

'Those are the sedgemoors, my dear.'

Sedgemoors. 'The Levels.'

He was surprised. 'Yes, the Somerset Levels. Have you heard of them?'

'I can't remember.'

The carriage was proceeding through a winding avenue of horse-chestnuts which looked as if it might be going somewhere grand and instead debouched them into a farmyard. Penitence thought they had come the wrong way but they drove on, scattering hens, through an archway and along a track. The carriage halted.

'I think perhaps we should walk from here, my dear,' Rupert said.

Now she knew, though not for anything would she have spoiled his surprise. *Bless him, oh bless him.*

In front of her was a moat where the arch of an uncompromising, square, stone gatehouse made a tunnel's entrance on to a flat wooden bridge that led to the moat's island.

And the house.

From here there were only glimpses of stone and tile and chimney through the trees. As she crossed the drawbridge, the corresponding gatehouse on the far side framed a courtyard. She walked through the archway, along a drive skirted by overgrown lawn. Immediately in front of her was a crenellated rectangle of a hall in the warm oolite of Ham Hill, as plain as the gatehouses except for the stone-traced quatrefoils at the head of its three long windows.

It was an old-style hall with what had once been an undercroft where animals were kept, now a habitable ground floor with its own front door.

To make up for the hall's starkness some early Tudor adventurer had enclosed the courtyard on north and south by two wings of the then latest trend, crazily timbered, deep-tiled, gabled, lattice-windowed buildings whose upper storeys leaned over towards Penitence like tipsy revellers. The sun setting over the Levels behind them shone straight into the courtyard to make a ragbag of architectural textures into a mellifluous collage, honey-coloured stone, cream-and-mushroom timbering, tiny oaken doors, diamond-paned windows that winked reflected amber. Even the cushions of lichen on the tiles of the many-angled roof were a matching grey and gold.

Rupert was tutting with disapproval at weeds and dilapidation. Penitence didn't see them. The tilting upper storeys of the Tudor wings gave the impression of packed theatre galleries; the house was making a statement only she could hear; she wasn't just being welcomed but applauded.

A door set in a surround of worn carving opened and Peter stood in the archway looking curiously in place, as if they had gone back to the time of Crusaders and Saracen servants.

'Furniture in?' snapped Rupert.

'Yes, lord.'

Inside she was almost blinded as her eyes adjusted to the darkness of a passage formed by two screens of black oak panelling. The stone floor had been polished and gently hollowed by centuries of feet and reflected a triangle of daylight at its far end where a door stood open at the back of the house. On the left was a staircase with a newel post carved in the shape of a Saracen's head. Peter, candelabra held high, led the way up the staircase which made a dog-leg into a passage, and then stood back to allow her to go first through a door. She went into the hall.

Space and God. Those were her first impressions. It was sparsely furnished and somewhere Rupert was apologizing for not yet having procured suitable pieces for it. The hall's dimensions had managed to incorporate into themselves the cool beauty of medieval holiness. The lattice panes of the three tall windows were so old that their amber and green glass threw the sunlight on to the stone floor in the effect of a honeycomb. Over the plain and enormous rectangle that was the fireplace were carved the arms and roses of the first Tudor.

Rupert stopped talking as he glimpsed her face. Instead he smiled and came to stand formally in front of her, holding a ring on which were a set of huge keys, and a scroll hung with seals on ribbons.

'Madam, I have the honour to present to you your own home. Your good father was born here. It is fitting that now it is yours.'

'Mine?' She had guessed it to be her father's home but had expected only that they were paying a visit.

'The ownership was in dispute since your grandfather's death. Both parties were pleased to resolve the quarrel by selling outright.'

'Mine?'

He looked pleased with himself. 'It is not, perhaps, as beautiful as the birthday gift you awarded me, and certainly not in as good condition, being nearly five hundred years older, but it is nevertheless a present, though one which, I had hoped, would evince some other reaction than tears.' He mopped her eyes with his handkerchief.

It was called Athelzoy Priory. She tried the name on her tongue; an apple-tasting name, beautiful with an undercurrent of the comic, like the combination of dignity and exuberance that had met her in the courtyard.

Rupert strode to the fireplace. Across its top was a white stone beam inscribed with Latin. 'Quod Olim Fuit Meminisse Minime Juvat,' he read out. '"There is little joy in remembrance of the past."' He bowed to her. 'I intend to have it changed, if you will permit, my dear. I trust that for you, as for myself, there has been joy in these past years we've spent together.' He had his hat in his hand, and the colours of the last of the sun coming through the panes turned his exquisite black velvet coat into motley.

She crossed the floor of her hall and put her arms round him.

The next day they examined everything together. Rupert himself had only been here once before – to see if Athelzoy was worth buying. 'As it is, my dear,' he assured her, 'though I fear your grandfather and his forebears were not the men to exploit its possibilities. Gamblers all. Like your father.'

'Was my father a gambler?'

'Renowned for it throughout the regiment. We loved to

play him, I remember; he so invariably lost. Poor fellow, poor, brave fellow.'

The manor had stood empty since her grandfather's death, he told her; he had procured the basic furnishings in London and sent them down in carts for the servants to arrange. He had chosen well, selecting plain but excellent chairs, settles, beds, presses and tables from the time of Elizabeth. Modern pieces would have looked out of place.

The servants, too, had done well. The interior was spotless and had been burnished within an inch of its life with beeswax and soap.

In the Tudor wings jars of buttercups threw yellow reflections on to the dark wood of the window-sills, pewter dishes glowed severely along the sideboard and the creaking flights of stairs to the upper floors were lethal with polishing.

'The Glastonbury priors owned it from time immemorial, but it fell to the crown in the Wars of the Roses and Henry VII gave it to his henchman, d'Haut, from whom you are descended, my dear. It was modernized in 1521, and damn all done to it since.'

It was so unusual for Rupert to swear that she knew how much the manor's disrepair was upsetting him. The roof leaked in parts, there was woodworm in some of the timbers of the north wing, the drawbridge wouldn't work because its chains were rusted into their grooves, jackdaws nested in the twisted brick chimney-pots. 'And as for the sanitary arrangements . . .'

Even Penitence, who found new enchantments every way she turned, had to admit to the insanitariness of those arrangements which were a large privy built into the wall of the solar at the back of the house with a channelled drop down into the moat. The five bottom-shaped holes in its seat — two large, three small — over the drop showed that the Hoys' privy-going had been familial, though the state of it also showed their aim to have been terrible. The fact that at the same time they had allowed the springs and streams of the moat to block up caused Penitence to wonder not only at her paternal family's hygiene but also at their insensitivity to smell.

Never mind, Rupert had called in modern builders and

drainage experts and brought down from Awdes a selection of close-stools with their removable pots, carved lids and padded seats. She was more concerned that the topiary of the life-sized yew chessmen in the south garden had been allowed to outgrow to the point where their shapes might be lost.

Her yew chessmen. Her timbers with their fine graining like the wrinkles in the skin of a very old woman. Her square, lead drainpipes, each one carrying the 'H' of the Hoy crest. Her White Room in the north wing with its superb plaster ceiling moulded into pendants and strapwork.

She circled the house in a saraband of disbelief, touching and stroking. *Her* ancient chestnut trees coming into bud. *Her* slit to the left of the gatehouse arch for parleying with the enemy. *Her* fishponds beyond the moat, her fields beyond that, her stretch of the sedgemoor turbaries, her section of the River Minnow. *Her* rowing boat moored against steps going down into the moat at the back of the house.

'Well?' Rupert asked her.

'Very well. Very well. Very, very, very well.' She butted her head into his chest. 'Is it really mine?'

'Completely. It is a small manor, I fear, but totally yours. Nobody can gainsay you, my dear. Not now nor when I'm gone.'

She stood back, frightened by the elegy in his voice. 'Where are you going?'

'My dear, in the nature of things . . .'

'No.' She had to stop him saying it. 'I can't do without you.'

He was pleased and roused and took her to bed.

Afterwards, triumphant, he was full of solicitous plans. 'We shall entertain my lady's neighbours.'

She protested. 'It will tire you too much; the house isn't ready.'

'I'm younger than I thought, it seems,' he said smugly. He was anxious that she be established as part of the country scene 'while I am yet here to introduce you'. He knew, as she knew, that without the protection of his name she – and more importantly, Ruperta – would find entry into Somerset society difficult if not impossible.

441

She rested her head on his arm and stared up at the tester, ashamed all over again at having had to simulate pleasure when Rupert deserved not only his own sexual fulfilment but hers. She'd prayed a thousand times for her love for him to be as physical as it was emotional. It would have made things easier all the way round. *Damn Henry King*. How could the memory of the night with him, one single night, nearly twenty years ago, still come between her and a man so much worthier?

An old complaint; she watched it entwine itself in the riot of carved oaken creatures and swirled designs that decorated the tester. They had chosen the biggest room in the north wing for their bedroom but even so it was dwarfed by this bed, a huge, shining, black, muscular edifice that sprouted carving on every surface. It was the only piece of furniture that had not been removed from the house by Penitence's grandfather's quarrelling heirs — presumably because it was too heavy to shift. Perhaps her father had been born in it.

'Don't leave me, Rupert.' She wasn't thinking of herself. For his sake she wanted this Indian summer of his to last for ever now that he had his daughter and a home life where he was looked up to and didn't have to suffer the rudeness of young men who had taken the place he should have had at the side of his fickle king. 'I can't do without you,' she said again.

She could; she could bear anything. But it would be a ruder, lonelier life without him. 'And don't let's bother with entertaining.' Not only did she not care a damn for Somerset society, there was also the risk that entering it would involve an encounter with the Viscount of Severn and Thames; already Rupert had put him at the head of the list of people to be invited to a series of dinners.

But that evening Peter was put in the carriage and sent back to Awdes with detailed instructions from Rupert to fetch more kitchen staff and pack up sufficient glassware, silver and napery.

In the meantime *noblesse* had to be *oblige*'d. On Sunday they walked across the drawbridge and followed the moat round to the back of the house where a track led them through orchards to the surprisingly beautiful parish church to attend a less impressive service conducted by a hurried curate for whom the souls of St Mary's, Athelzoy, formed only one of many congregations he had to lead in worship that day.

Outside in the churchyard, where sheep nibbled the grave-side grasses, the congregation gathered in a respectful ring to listen to Rupert's carrying voice introduce himself and his lady. It was a small number for such a large church, forty or so adults, the majority of those elderly. Ancient bonnets on fair or greying hair, jerkins and skirts matted from too much washing, lovely complexions even among the old, the necks of the men engrained with earth, the hands of the women calloused from perpetual spinning. Some of the younger women carried a distaff resting on the belt round their waists, and spun as they listened. The children – she especially studied the children to see if this place would be a salubrious home for Ruperta and Tongs – seemed healthy enough.

She liked the young people she'd met so far: Mudge and Prue Ridge, the son and daughter of the farm that encroached on the Priory's frontage. Both seemed intelligent, were hand-some and very strong. It was Prue who brought the Priory's milk each morning, carrying it from the farm in a pail balanced on her head. Once, when she'd left it in the kitchen, Penitence had surreptitiously tried to heft the pail, and failed. 'A full five gallons on her head with the same ease I wear a hat,' she told Rupert, amazed.

'Her Ladyship wishes me to hope,' finished Rupert to his audience, 'she finds you as loyal and willing as she will be your true liege lady and ever bear you in her heart and mind.'

There was a cheer. 'Do be she give us work, ull she?'

'Indeed,' said Rupert, nodding, 'I am sure my lady will be needing staff she can trust.' Loud cheer. 'And I am instructing the landlord of the Hoy Arms that anyone wishing to drink Her Ladyship's health tonight may do so at my expense.' Cheer so loud the rooks came out of the churchyard elms and circled, cawing, in the breezy blue sky.

Together she and Rupert moved away. 'They are suffering,' Rupert told her. 'Time was when every household in this area kept its own sheep, sheared its own wool and spun it for sale to the clothiers. That and harvest work kept them going. Now the clothiers have better profit from putting their spinners in something they call a *"factory"'*

'The old ways are the best,' she teased him.

'And so quite frequently they are,' he said seriously. 'These "factories" will loosen the bond that exists between high and low on the land. Look, now, at these cottages, half of them empty. Good peasants who loved their lord and their land gone to work in a box.'

Rupert still hankered after the feudal system at its best, and tended to regard as dangerously revolutionary anybody who didn't. Penitence refrained from pointing out that only extreme hardship or strong incentive could have tempted anybody away from Athelzoy to work in a box. A stream ran down both sides of the street under flagstone bridges that led to fat, white, mud-and-plaster cottages with deep windows and even deeper thatch. Almost every back garden had a well, hazel or apple or pear trees and a vegetable plot. A morning shower had added the smell of damped dust to that of cows and spring.

Yet it was true, half the cottages were deserted. Her Priory had provided much of the employment on which this village depended and the death of its master, her grandfather, had thrown out of work the labourers who had gathered in his harvests and the servants who had manned his household.

Further down the track widened to become the nearest thing Athelzoy could boast to a village square; sheep and cattle pens encircled a cross that was quite as big and almost elaborate as the Eleanor cross in London's Charing. A thin man dressed in Puritan black suit and hat stood on its steps, intoning from a Bible.

Opposite the east side of the cross was the Hoy Arms. Built in the same style as the Priory's timbered wings, it reminded Penitence of the Ship back in Dog Yard; the same air of unwarranted jollity, the same architectural nudge in the ribs to its neighbours.

As the inn's landlord emerged from his door to greet them,

wiping his hands on his apron, the man on the steps of the cross shuffled round so that he faced in their direction.

Penitence tensed and tightened her grip on Rupert's arm. She had a sudden sense of *déjà vu*.

'Whoso loveth wisdom rejoiceth his father, but he that keepeth company with harlots spendeth his substance.'

She'd known it. The tone was the tone of Titus Oates, the Reverend Block, the sing-song that Puritan saints considered necessary to the expression of righteousness. She hated it. But it was the timbre of the voice, the long-drawn aaa put into 'harlot' that took her back to another time and another country. For a moment she was confused, then she put her whole weight on Rupert's arm to stop him as he pulled foward towards the man, waving his cane in fury. 'No!'

'I'll whip the rogue, I'll have his skin off.'

'No. Leave him. Rupert, he's not worth your attention.' He dragged her on, intent to kill. Frantically, she gestured to the landlord to come and help. Between them they turned a puffing, shouting Rupert round and, by confiscating his stick, got him through the door of the Hoy Arms where the landlady added her considerable weight to sit him on a settle.

'Excuse me a moment.' Penitence hurried outside and over to the man on the steps of the cross. He was being verbally attacked by villagers returning from church for having insulted a royal prince and source of future employment. A few were throwing handy lumps of manure as if they'd only been waiting for an excuse. *Not a popular man.* He wasn't trying to protect himself but had closed his eyes in martyrdom, his lips moving in prayer. The crowd encouraged her to join in the fun. 'You give un what for, Ladyship, proper paain in the bum, they old Presbyters.' Someone suggested the stocks.

'What's your name?' asked Penitence, quietly.

The man's eyes opened. He couldn't be more than sixty, though he looked older. It was uncanny to see on this face the same bitter lines as on another face she'd once known well.

'My name is everlasting,' he said.

'I'll wager it's not,' she told him, 'I wager it's Hughes.'

'He that keepeth company with harlots spendeth his substance,' he said, sulkily. 'Proverbs 29, verse 3.'

'Verily the publicans and the harlots go into the kingdom of God before you,' she told him. 'Matthew 21, verse 31.' And went back to the inn.

Distracted by the bad impression made on his royal visitor, the landlord and his wife were trying to mollify him with words and best ale. Rupert ignored both. Under control now, he sat upright, white with rage.

He wouldn't reprove her in public – he rarely reproved her even in private – but she'd shamed him by not letting him defend her and by going to talk to her detractor.

She ignored him. 'Who is that man? Where does he live?'

The landlord turned to her in relief. 'Not one of ours, I tell ee. Comes from over by Sallycombe. Whole viper's nest on them preachifiers as says its their duty to din a respectable body's poor ears every Sunday.' The landlord spat into the sawdust of his floor. 'Sallycombe folk, every one. Why Lady Alice do tolerate un I don't know. I don't. Roundheads and Dissenters they was. Roundheads and Dissenters they still be.'

'What's his name?'

'Martin Hughes, Your Ladyship. A teaseller. Oh, what a viper.'

Mudge Ridge put his head round the inn door. He'd brought his cart to the smithy to have a wheel straightened and was now going home. Would His Highness and lady like a lift?

Penitence accepted; Rupert's hands were still shaking. He didn't speak during the journey back, but sat on the bouncing seat of the farm cart with the dignity of a Cavalier on a charger. Penitence sat beside him and talked to Mudge who walked ahead, leading the horse. He too was apologetic but saw further than the landlord.

'Somerset now,' he explained – he pronounced it Zummerzet – ''tis divided twixt Royals and Roundheads, church and meeting-house. Always is, always was. And what with the gentry becoming richer and the Church more Romish, poor folk are turning to Dissenting. Not so much farm folk, mebbe, but weavers and spinners like.'

Weavers and spinners like her maternal grandparents had been before they left for a new world.

Come to that, she hadn't seen either Mudge or Prue Ridge in church this morning either, though their parents had been. Casually she said so.

Mudge glanced over his shoulder at her and she realized that in the old days her grandfather, royalist and churchgoer, would have punished his tenants for non-attendance. She winked at him, and saw his white-lashed blue eyes widen first in surprise and then in relieved amusement.

Back at the Priory she sat Rupert down in the room to the right of the screen passage that they had made into a parlour, poured him a brandy and then knelt at his feet. 'I'm sorry, Rupert.'

'The man shall be whipped despite you. If such unmannerliness goes unpunished there will be revolution come again. The magistrate shall be informed. You shall not be insulted in broad daylight.'

She doubted whether a magistrate could pillory someone for an insult, but perhaps in Somerset it was possible. 'Please, Rupert . . .'

He held up a hand. 'You shall not speak for him. Such tenderness is out of place. I'll put the vermin in the stocks myself.'

'I hope you won't, Rupert.' She took his hand. 'I'm fairly sure he's my grandmother's brother. The vermin's my great-uncle.'

Chapter 6

THE Viscount of Severn and Thames, it transpired, was in the Low Countries and would be unable to accept the kind invitation to dine with His Royal Highness Prince Rupert and Mrs Hughes on May the 4th.

'They say he's thick with Prince William,' Rupert told her,

troubled. 'I wish I may not hear he has become a Whig.' Whigs upset him; not only would they exclude James from the succession but their extremists called for the Protestant Duke of Monmouth to be legitimized so that he could be the next king – something Rupert would as soon see done as enthrone the Devil.

'But would you want him a Tory?' she asked and then regretted it as she watched his indecision; she hated seeing Rupert, a man who had always been clear as to where his duty lay, struggling with doubt in his old age. His cousin's rule worried him – not least by suspending Parliament. Every day he received letters from his London financier and merchant friends complaining of the King's gerrymandering to gain political control of the City and its juries. Rupert's loyalty to England's institutions were almost as great as his loyalty to its throne, and he became upset that each was threatening to abolish the other.

No doubts bothered the neighbours who came to dine at the Priory. Church of England Tories to a man, magistrates, sheriffs, *nouveau riche* clothiers, they expounded the damnation of Whigs in their rich, drawn-out, heavily diphthonged accents. Their equation was crudely simple: Whigs were Dissenters and Dissenters were damned.

Penitence, who knew many aristocratic Church of England Whigs, realized that this far from London she was in a different world; the sons of men who had fought for the crown still despised the men whose fathers had fought for Parliament. Toryism reigned supreme. To be successful was *ipso facto* to be a Tory. Whiggery, on the other hand, flourished among the defeated Nonconformists: insignificant but independent artisans; weavers, small farmers, craftsmen.

If Martin Hughes was an example of Somerset Whiggery and these local landowners who were her guests and who displayed their wives, wealth and prejudices in the absolute assurance that Prince Rupert would approve them, were typical Tories then she – and she realized for the first time that she was the result of a mating between a representative of both – didn't like either of them much. She felt more in tune with the countryside than its people.

'Y'ear there was naastiness twixt yourself and one of they dang blue-nail preachers, Your Highness,' brayed Sir Ostyn Edwards, Penitence's nearest neighbour and the local magistrate. The news had spread with speed; even the Cartrights, a couple of strong but likeable Tories at Rupert's end of the table, had heard of it – and they lived at Crewkerne, a good ten miles away.

Rupert played it down. 'There was a fellow spouting some foolishness. It was of no matter.' He made no mention of Penitence's presumed relationship with the preacher just as he did not tell the guests that on her paternal side she was a by-blow of Captain Hoy, their contemporary. It was none of their business.

'Trouble-makers and revolutionaries,' pronounced Sir William Portman, the MP for Taunton. 'They're Whigs, sir, weaving, thieving Whigs. You should send 'em down, Ostyn, send 'em down.'

'Ah do,' said Sir Ostyn, indignant. 'Then you gennulmen complain as ah'm taking away your workers.'

'They Hugheses is no workers of maahn,' complained Sir Roger Pascoe. 'Too danged independent. Teasellers. You want to kick 'em off your land, Alice' – he raised his voice; Lady Alice Lisle was deaf – 'I say you want to kick 'em off your land and into my factories, Alice.'

'I don't want to do no such thing then,' said Lady Alice. 'Ah'm not saying they ain't bothersome preachifiers, but ah'm not seeing they starve at your looms for four shillings a week when the going rate be seven and well you know it, Sir Roger.'

Sir Roger beamed, not at all put out. 'And find their own harness, size and wind their own quills. If 'tis good for the trade, 'tis good for the country.'

''Tis good for thy pocket,' scolded Lady Alice. 'Commerce uz made for man, not man for commerce. And I do mean *all* men, young Maister Pascoe.'

Alice Lisle was the only unaccompanied woman there and the only woman whom Rupert had been advised to invite in her own right. She was a local institution, a widow of seventy or more who ran her manor farm two miles away with efficiency. Born and bred in the area, part of the landed gentry, she was not only the widow of a Cromwellian but a Dissenter herself. Yet she had outlived disapproval to become a respected part of the landscape. Because they'd known her all their lives, the Tory gentry accepted her and her inconvenient philosophies as they accepted Barrow Mump or Glastonbury Tor, those eccentric hills which rose out of the flat countryside like altars.

'What is a teaseller?' asked Penitence. She'd heard the word twice now in connection with Martin Hughes.

Every head at the table turned in her direction as if in anticipation, though of what she wasn't sure. She had kept silent during most of dinner unless urging her guests to eat. Women, all except Lady Alice, were not encouraged to do more than admire and agree with the male conversation, and most of the wives kept their elaborately dressed heads down and did just that.

Rupert had done his best to make it clear that Penitence was the giver of the feast: 'Is it your wish that I carve, my dear?' and 'Her Ladyship has not yet had time to furnish her table as she would wish, have you, my dear?' But his guests refused to follow his lead. They found the situation peculiar. For years they'd listened with horrified delight to tales of what happened at court, they knew the lechery of princes and the wantonness of actresses and had prepared themselves to witness *goings-on*. When what went on was a domesticity only unusual in its harmony they were not just wrong-footed but disappointed.

Now they stared down the table at Penitence like boys at a fair watching a sword-swallower who was taking his ease between acts. She fought down the impulse to snap a garter, to appal them as they so obviously wanted to be appalled, and stared back.

'Eh?' grunted Sir Ostyn. He was the local magistrate and recently widowed; there had been much jollity from his friends about his search for a suitable wife. The linenfold panelling of her dining-room made the perfect background for his over-curled fair wig and upturned nose. If you could frame him, thought Penitence, you'd have a fine portrait of a pig. The candlelight shone on richly polished board and silver and was kinder to the faces round it than most of them deserved. *Why do I have to bother with these people? I want to go home. I want my daughter.*

'Her Ladyship asked what a teaseller was,' prompted Rupert.

'Oh, teaseller,' said Sir Roger, triumphantly. 'Don't know that then in Lunnon. Teaseller's a man as grows teasels.'

She caught Rupert's eye and rose. 'Shall we leave the gentlemen, ladies?' *I'm damned if I ask what a teasel is.*

Chairs were pushed back as the gentlemen stood up and the ladies exited.

'Do we have our hostess's permission to smoke?' asked Rupert.

Bless him. 'Of course.'

She led the ladies along the screen passage to the north wing and showed them where to find the close-stools in the room Rupert had insisted on for a bathroom, then afterwards led them back to the passage in the hall's undercroft and along it to the parlour. 'I thought we could gossip over our coffee in here,' she said brightly, 'it's small, but warm on this chilly night.'

Lady Pascoe, disconcerted by the Priory's bathroom when her own, larger mansion had none, scrabbled for reascendancy. ''Tis small, iss fay,' she said. 'You want to get your man to build un out. My parlour's twice the size.'

It would have to be. 'Coffee? Tea? Or chocolate?'

If she'd been in a more tolerant mood, she'd have realized they were intimidated as much as disapproving. For all she was a fallen woman, she was a *sophisticated* fallen woman, the intimate of princes, an habitué of wicked London and its even more wicked court. They had to impress on her how little they were impressed, how much bigger their houses were than hers, how much better acquainted they were with local matters, with the Priory itself.

'Ah used to play with the Hoy children when I were a

babby,' said Lady Portland. 'Knew every inch of this place. Have ee found the secret room yet?'

Penitence sat up, intrigued for the first time that night. 'No. Where is it?'

'Old Maister Hoy, he'd tease us and never let on. But 'tis yere somewhere.' The plumes in her hair nodded as she looked around the panelling.

The word 'tease' stimulated Lady Pascoe into telling Penitence about teasels, a thistle-type plant apparently, its bristled head much used in the clothing industry for carding. Didn't she know what carding was? Mercy me, they didn't learn 'em much in Lunnon, did they? Well, carding was . . .

Lady Alice, the only one of them Penitence really wanted to hear, slept openly and enviably through the whole discourse until the glorious sound of men's boots released them all to follow Rupert and the male guests up the staircase to the hall where Peter was waiting with further trays and trolleys of savouries, sweetmeats and marzipans which, Rupert had assured her, were a necessary topping-up of Somerset stomachs before everybody went home.

The hall, rarely warm and on that early spring night positively chilly, was lit by a fire. Apple logs six feet long filled the grate and sent out scented flames that sparkled the guests' jewellery and changed the expressions on the faces of the gargoyles, one at the bottom of each of the roof's great trussed arches.

Rupert, however, had opened one of the lights so that his guests could see the swathe that he had ordered cut through the woodland where it sloped down towards the Levels.

Sir Ostyn approved. ''Bout time this place had a decent approach. You want to line it with logs, corduroy like.'

'Not corduroy,' scoffed Sir Roger. 'Setts. You want setts, Your Highness. And dang great gates at the entrance.' All the men joined in to tell the Prince what he did or didn't want on the Priory's approach.

I don't want it at all. Penitence had protested when Rupert revealed his plan to make a wide, straight drive from the track up to the house, instead of the winding tunnel that snaked around the rise to the Ridges' farmyard. She liked the secrecy of that approach, the way it hid the house so that it came as a beautiful surprise. But Rupert had accused her of over-modesty — 'Thou shouldst not hide the Priory's light under a bushel' — and she had given in because, though the deeds might be in her name, he was the one who'd paid for the place.

Now that the three lights of the hall blazed out into the darkness, she felt less that her Priory was being displayed to advantage and more that it had been stripped to reveal its nakedness. It could be seen by traffic using roads across the moors between Glastonbury and Taunton. Benighted travellers would be attracted to it, thieves and robbers . . .

Behind her Lady Pascoe said: 'I got one like that, only mine's bigger.' Penitence turned, wearily expecting another piece of her furniture to be denigrated. But the woman was pointing at Peter despite the fact that the steward was less than three feet away.

'Mine's younger,' said Mrs Cartwright. 'Got mine in Bristol.'

Unable to bear it, Penitence left them to compare slave-trade goods and took the opportunity to sit next to Lady Alice. 'This Martin Hughes,' she said, 'Martin HUGHES, Lady Alice. Where does he live? LIVE, dear.'

If she mentally put a white linen cap on the head of the man who'd stood at the steps of the cross, she saw her grandmother; the same piercing eyes, the same lips thinned in dislike of everything human. Even coming from a man's throat, the voice had the exact timbre of the one which extolled the younger brother who'd stayed behind 'to fly the Lord's banner in the battle against sin'.

And so had his great-niece encountered him, standing on the steps of a cross in Athelzoy, still flying it.

There was nothing wrong with Lady Alice Lisle's memory; over the years both Hughes and Hurds had been in service to the Lisle family. 'We was all zealous workers for the Lord, but they Hugheses, and especially Tabitha and her brother Martin, they was hot for it. Sour little madam, Tabitha, mind. How she ever caught the eye of that 'andsome Ezekiel Hurd I'll never know. *Never* know.' Lady Alice glowered. 'She made un join the brethren, so's they could accuse everybody else of lustful thoughts. Oh ma dear Lord, to they the naked truth was a lustful thought to be done penance for. Managed three lustful thoughts, though, to ma certain knowledge — Martha, then John, then . . .'

Penitence's lips formed the shapes. 'Margaret.'

'Margaret,' said Lady Alice. 'Poor maid. Lovely maid she was.' She gestured Penitence close. 'Caught the eye of the son of this very house. More than the eye, too. Mad for her, young Jack Hoy. Might even have wed her, though t'would have been against his fayther's wishes, but the poor lad got heself killed in the war.'

'What happened to her?'

'Oh.' The wrinkles in the fuzzed skin round Lady Alice's mouth deepened as if drawn in by purse-strings. 'The Hoys they turned her away. And Tabitha, hard-hearted besom, took the poor maid's babby off her. Threw her own daughter from her house. I said to her: Give the poor maid back her babby and *I'll* take un in, I said. Let her who is without sin among you, let *her* cast the first stone. I did. But Tabitha's heart *were* stone. "The strumpet brought shame on our house," she says. "Let her pursue the path of wickedness while we follow the Lord in righteousness." Oh, that woman's heart were stone. Like her eyes.'

I remember. Age had petrified it harder. Affection was a fissure in the dyke of righteousness which might let in the flood of sin; it was cemented over; there was not a smile, not an indulgence, not a cuddle her granddaughter could remember. And good daughter Martha had slavishly copied that same Christless Christianity. *Poor Martha.* In a rush of pity, Penitence forgave the woman who'd passed as her mother for so many years. Had Tabitha realized it, all her strength of character had been inherited by bad daughter Margaret.

'She took un all off to the Americkies — babby, Martha, poor Ezekiel — and left that sad maid to fend alone. Many's the time I've wondered about that maid.'

She became a successful brothel-keeper.

'And you her spitting image,' said Lady Alice, craftily. There was nothing wrong with her eyesight, either. 'Same surname as Tabitha's, too.'

Penitence smiled at her. 'May I come to call on you tomorrow? TO-MOR-ROW?' There was still a great deal she wished to know. It had been a long time since she'd had a family; perhaps there were other members less righteous than Martin Hughes who would welcome her, reminisce, show her where her mother had met and fallen in love with the son of Athelzoy Priory.

Whether she would tell all to Lady Alice she hadn't decided. The old woman obviously guessed something. But even Rupert didn't have the whole story yet; not what had happened to her mother after her abandonment, nor where her daughter had been reunited with her.

Perhaps it was time she told Rupert about the Cock and Pie.

As it turned out, she didn't get the chance. That night he developed a headache which didn't go away. When she took off his wig to help him to bed, she saw that the wound on his forehead was suppurating. He insisted on getting up next morning, but by the afternoon admitted defeat and went back to bed. 'Take no notice of me, my dear. You've had no time to enjoy your new home.'

She ignored him and went downstairs to discuss with Peter the feasibility of making the coach journey back to Awdes.

'He'll refuse a doctor, wherever we take him,' Peter pointed out.

She was frightened. Somerset had become the end of the world; unfamiliar and resourceless. 'He might have Apothecary Boghurst. We'll make a bed for him in the coach.'

It frightened her even more that Rupert put up no opposition as Peter and Boller half-carried him to the coach. He lay with his head on her lap and she tried to shield it by tensing herself against the jolts, not even noticing until it was five miles behind her that she had left Athelzoy Priory without a goodbye glance. By the time they reached the outskirts of London three days later, Rupert was so ill Penitence risked the extra miles and took him on to the house in Spring Gardens so that Apothecary Boghurst could get to him quicker.

Chapter 7

IT WAS a long-drawn-out death. Rupert partially recovered for the summer but in the autumn relapses became frequent until recovery ceased altogether. When Penitence pulled back the curtains each morning she resented the rumble of carriages and the street-cries, a world persisting in going about its business while its great warrior was dying.

He knew he was. At the beginning of November he made his will. When the lawyers had gone, he was tired and she sat beside his bed while he dozed. He woke up with a start and didn't seem to know where he was. Then he asked: 'Will you marry again?'

The 'again' nearly undid her. 'No.'

The Earl of Craven, for whom she thanked God, called every day but, apart from him, those who kept the vigil with her were mainly the servants, and her own friends like Aphra and Dorinda, the Reverend Boreham and Apothecary Boghurst, and the dog Royalle, who refused to leave the bedside.

The King didn't attend, though she kept him informed.

On her instructions the secretary wrote to the remaining children of James I's daughter and Frederick V of Bohemia. The Elector Palatinate had just died but in any case had ceased correspondence with his younger brother, furious that Rupert had given their mother's jewels to a mistress — though the only filial support their mother had found in her old age had come from Rupert. Sophie was now the Electress of Hanover, Louise was in a convent, and neither could find time to come.

Only in the bedroom of the house in Spring Gardens did the age of loyalty right or wrong persist while the prince who'd personified it relived it in his confused mind. Weeping, Lord Craven and Penitence hung on to his hands as he tried to wave a ghostly cavalry into battle and shouted orders to long-dead men.

When they'd got him to sleep she would sit and and wait for Craven's remembrances of his friend. They always began: 'You should have seen him . . .' and they always ended with him crying.

'You should have seen him outside Bristol. Clad in scarlet and silver lace on his black barbary horse. The "Dragon Prince" Cromwell called him, but he respected him, oh yes, even that rogue respected him. These royal drunkards that command us today, what respect is due to them but ropes to hang themselves?'

Through Craven's eyes she watched the young Rupert and a handful of half-armed Cavaliers scattering the steel hauberks of the Parliamentarians at Powick Bridge, riding against the imperturbable pikes of the London trained bands at the first battle of Newbury. 'Time and again he saved the Cause. Endangered it once or twice, too, but always extricated it again, always. It was not his fault it was beaten.'

She asked the question she had never thought to ask Rupert. 'Why did he settle in England?'

Craven smiled. 'Do you know, my dear, I sometimes think it was for his enemies. He was never a political man, nor did it occur to him to question the rightness of his uncle's quarrel with Parliament. But he told me once the fortitude of the Roundheads impressed him. Just before the end of the war, he wrote to me that if he rode so he broke his neck, he would not be unhappy that England have his bones.' The Earl was crying again.

If he was reliving his old campaigns, the wounds they'd inflicted reanimated so that he could suffer them again. Every morning and evening when Penitence or Peter soaked the dressings from his legs and head, pus oozed out from flesh that was turning green. Ruperta complained of the smell when Penitence lifted her on to the bed to kiss him and for the first time got a smack from her mother. 'Kiss your father.'

It was only Ruperta who brought something like coherence into Rupert's ramblings. In a lucid period he managed to convey to Craven that his Order of the Garter must be sent to the King with another request for a marriage to be arranged between her and Burford.

Charles ignored it.

On the 27th of November he began to cough. Master Boghurst said: 'It won't be long now. Fetch your sons.'

457

The boys knelt at the end of the bed, but as the coughing and the night dragged on Penitence had chairs brought for them to sleep on. Only she and Peter stayed awake. In the morning Rupert was still alive.

She lost track of time and place. Sometimes it was Henry King's hand she held, sometimes Dorinda's. Once Her Ladyship's. She dreamed of Awashonks and woke up with a jump and thought that the dark eyes staring reproachfully at her were those of the Squakheag's sachem. They were Peter's.

It was still dark the next morning, the 29th, when Peter's scream set Royalle howling.

Downstairs in the drawing-room the Earl of Craven, as executor, read the will to the household. Rupert had left nothing to his legitimate family. There were bequests to the servants, Dudley got his property in Germany, the rest was left to Penitence and Ruperta 'with his wish,' said Craven, 'that Benedick shall share in his mother's fortune'.

Attached to the will was a special, loving message to Ruperta, which the Earl solemnly read to her in her high chair, that she be a good girl and always obey Lord Craven and her mother.

Penitence was not consulted about the funeral, which was organized by the Earl Marshal. Rupert's body was taken out of the house in Spring Gardens to the Painted Chamber at Whitehall for a lying-in-state and from there to Westminster Abbey for interment.

Two companies of foot led the cortège, followed by Rupert's male household servants, followed by barons' younger sons, viscounts' younger sons, Privy Councillors, eldest sons of barons and viscounts and earls' younger sons, through the panoply of precedence to the officer carrying Rupert's coronet on a cushion in front of the coffin.

The Earl of Craven, in a cloak with a long train borne by two supporters, was the chief mourner. Behind him were more earls and viscounts, Yeomen of the Guard and Rupert's outdoor servants, gunsmiths, Boller and the other coachmen, and watermen.

Peter should have headed the procession of household staff but by the time the funeral took place he was dead. They'd had to lift him away from Rupert's death-bed and carried him upstairs to lie him down on what turned out to be his own. Penitence had carried food to his room every day and beseeched him to eat but the black man's will had suspended every process which kept his body animated. Oddly, he emanated no grief; just a stubborn refusal to live. His lower lip stuck out as if he were sulking, only retracting when Penitence tried to force a spoon into his mouth.

It seemed vital that he should live; Penitence's bereavement had brought with it guilt that she had never loved Rupert enough or in the way he'd wanted. She hoped he'd not known that she didn't. *But I knew.* Her sexual pretences she remembered not as attempts to please but as the grubby simulations of a brothel. She'd short-changed him; even now, perhaps, she could make up something of the lack by preserving this, his loved and loving servant. Besides, Peter was woven into the fabric of over ten years of her life and she couldn't bear to lose any more of it. 'Try and eat, Peter. What will I do without you?'

She was holding his unresisting hand and realized it had gone cold. She threw herself on his body, weeping; his death emphasized Rupert's in a way nothing else had; it added to her guilt that she hadn't been able to keep him alive. He'd been so much more loyal to Rupert by dying than she had in living.

'Nonsense,' the Reverend Boreman told her sharply. 'What are you about, woman? Are we heathens that we have to die because our lord does?'

'Peter wasn't a heathen,' she sobbed.

'He was a slave. He didn't want to live any more. Are you a slave?'

Yes. I sold myself. Rupert bought me.

Dorinda was even more contemptuous. 'So he bought you. It was a fair trade; you made him happy. What they want for their ballocking money? Get some sleep, for Christ's sake.'

Women were allowed no part in Rupert's funeral, neither

were illegitimate sons – who had not been ennobled. Penitence, Dudley and Benedick watched the service by peering over heads from the public's end of the Abbey nave. They weren't invited to the funeral meats either.

They ate their own at a small gathering in Spring Gardens, mostly of theatre people.

'They could have given you a place at the front of the Abbey,' said Aphra Behn, indignantly. 'Everybody knows how important you were to him.'

'What now?' asked Nelly Gwynn. 'You staying on here?'

'I can't. I'm being evicted.' Spring Gardens was in the King's gift which had been extended only to Rupert. Awdes, which had been leased for Rupert's lifetime, was also closing to her.

'Always got a home with me, Peg.'

'She'll come to St Bride's,' said Aphra.

'She'll bloody come to the Cock and Pie,' said Dorinda.

Becky Marshall also proffered her house. Penitence thanked them all, and promised to visit. 'But for now I'll go to Somerset.'

She was still being tortured by the guilt of the bereaved. *I didn't love him enough. Why didn't I take better care of him? Could I have taken better care of him?* Somerset was hideously far away from her friends and everything she knew but it was the home Rupert had bought for her and she felt she would be expiating something she owed him if she stayed in it.

'Never mind, Peg,' said Charles Hart. 'It was a fine funeral. Lord, I hope as many weepers line the streets when the Great Prompter calls me. The miles of black under overcast sky. Muffled drums. What theatre.'

'Yes,' said Penitence. 'He'd have loved it.'

On her way out Gwynn said: 'You don't want to bury yourself in the sticks. Get back on the stage, ducky. You've kept your looks and being skinny suits you.'

Rupert didn't want me to go back. She knew Nelly's reaction if she told her that, so she gave another, though equally true, excuse: 'Killigrew won't have me. The King has indicated I'm not wanted.'

Nell Gwynn was apologetic. 'He's a bit miffed about old

Rupert's will, Peg. You mightn't think it, but my Charlie's a great one for legitimate family. He'd have put poor old Catherine away and married somebody with babies in 'em years ago if he wasn't. He can't understand why Rupert left it all to you.'

'Neither can I.'

Gwynn looked at her sharply: 'Oh my Gawd. Let's all enter a nunnery.' She had no time for self-doubt, in herself or others. 'He left it to you acause you made him happy. He liked fucking you. That's what it's all about, Peg. Wars and politics don't keep men warm in bed. He got good value for his money.' She patted Penitence's cheek and became brisk: 'James'll be happy enough to have you at the Duke of York's. You stay, Peg. Buy yourself a town-house and a nice young lover. You earned 'em.'

Penitence kissed her. 'I'll think about it, Nelly.'

'Well, don't think too long. Ain't either us of getting younger. And any time you want to sell Elizabeth of Bohemia's pearls I'm in the market.'

When everybody had gone, Penitence took the boys into her drawing-room, sat them down and stood by the fireplace. 'I thought we ought to discuss your future,' she said.

'Have we got one?' asked Benedick. Of the two, he was showing his grief more openly. Dudley was trying to hide his for her sake.

'Well,' she said, 'in view of the King's attitude, your advancement may be delayed. In England at any rate, and for a while.'

'I want to join the army,' Benedick said.

'You want to join any army,' pointed out Dudley.

She'd been afraid of that. *And Dudley will because he thinks he ought to be military like his father.*

She kept her voice mild. 'I have a suggestion. I have written to the Prince of Orange to ask if you may attend his court for a year or two. He is a relation, after all. He has written back to say he would be delighted.'

Dudley smiled for the first time since his father's death. 'Seeing the world.'

'Fighting the French.' Benedick was on his feet.

No you won't. William had written back to her: 'Had I not known of their connection with my revered late kinsman, I should yet welcome the two young gentlemen for your sake. Do not concern yourself, dear madam, that they shall be endangered of body or soul.'

She'd done her own checking. William's furious defence of his country had given Louis XIV pause; for a while at least the Dutch Netherlands were at peace. Reports from The Hague were of Mary's domesticity, visits to the opera and church, garden-planning, home-building.

If the boys didn't break their necks hunting − which they could do just as easily in England as in Holland − their bodies would be safe enough and their souls much safer in his care than tasting the debauchery of Whitehall.

What a fool you are, Charles Stuart, preferring dissolutes to splendid young men like mine and Rupert's.

The boys wouldn't lack money. She was going to share between them the 1,694 guineas that Rupert's iron chest had contained.

The only hesitation she felt in sending them to the Netherlands was caused by a letter in her pocket that minute. It was a polite condolence on the death of His Royal Highness, Prince Rupert. It was signed by the Viscount of Severn and Thames and its address was The Hague.

There was a lot to do. Rupert had left pensions to members of his household who were old enough to retire − and most of them were. Good positions had to be found for those who remained and who didn't want to accompany Penitence into the wilds of Somerset.

To her surprise, the Reverend Boreman and Mistress Palmer were quite prepared to be uprooted again and replanted in Somerset. Boller, the coachman, and Johannes and Annie, the nursemaid, were also willing to go with her.

Penitence watched almost everything she'd known for the last eleven years go under the hammer during the sale of Awdes' contents. She remained dry-eyed until the last lot, an old hunting mare of Rupert's that had gone blind years ago.

Squire Brewster bid a pound and bought her. 'No, no,' he said with surprising concern for Penitence's anxiety. 'She shall live out her days in high grass. He'd have wanted it so.'

In the spring Boller drove the last unsold coach through Awdes' gates to take the Great West Road. Inside it were Penitence, Mistress Palmer, the Reverend Boreman, Dorinda, Ruperta and Tongs. On top sat a lot of cases. Beside it ran a large black poodle.

Without anything being formally said, Dorinda had now so infiltrated the household that she and Tongs were part of it. The Huguenot apprentice was successfully running the Cock and Pie Press; MacGregor was longer and longer away in the Low Countries and Dorinda referred to him less and less often.

The arrangement suited Penitence sufficiently for her not to ask questions. Tongs and Ruperta were excellent playmates and, while Dorinda could be a screaming irritant, hers was the down-to-earth voice that saved Penitence from becoming too maudlin in her bereavement.

Behind the coach came a luggage wagon with Annie and Johannes. The outriders consisted of a large troop of the Earl of Craven's musketeers which the Earl had insisted on sending along to see her safely into Somerset: 'Suppose word got out to highwaymen that you were carrying the dear Queen's necklace, Mrs Hughes. No, no, Rupert would never forgive me.'

It seemed to Penitence that the coach would attract a good deal more attention with a troop of outriders than without them; Elizabeth of Bohemia's necklace was assuming the weight of a millstone. On the other hand, it was Ruperta's dowry.

I must find Athelzoy's secret room. Put the damn necklace in it for safety.

It struck her that she wasn't safe any more. Rupert had protected her, her child and her goods but now she could be preyed on – and not just by thieves. Already the King had shown his pique at her inheritance of his uncle's money by banning her from the stage of his theatre. He might positively punish her. Try to marry her off, perhaps. He would be unlikely to defend her against the harassment of men like Charles Sedley.

Penitence worked herself up into such a panic that she felt again, as she hadn't in years, the terror of the night when she'd been pursued along High Holborn. Once again she was a hare and any dogs who cared to were free to run her to ground. Only this time she was even more vulnerable in having a leveret. *I'll turn and fight this time. They shan't hurt Ruperta.*

'Told you them oysters was crapped,' Mistress Palmer shouted above the rattle of the coach.

Penitence looked across at her. 'What?'

'Them oysters. Back at that last inn. Turned you green.'

'You all right, Prinks?' asked Dorinda. 'You been snuffling.'

She was being idiotic. She wasn't *that* important; Rupert hadn't left her so much money that she'd automatically become prey to robbers and fortune-hunters. 'I was worrying about the necklace,' she said, 'with all these soldiers, every thief in London will have gathered I'm taking it down to the country.'

'Country?' Dorinda put her head out of the window and regarded the green view unfavourably. 'Tunbridge Wells is country. This is ballocking jungle. Any poor sod of a thief as tracks us down here is going to need a restorative. Where are we?'

'Not far now.' Dorinda was right. If she was a hare, at least she was returning to her forme. She would creep into it. Athelzoy, Rupert's last gift to her, would become a shrine to his memory and she the keeper of its flame, paying the debt she owed him with chastity, devoted motherhood and good works. Sacrificially, she stared out of the window, waiting for the coach to begin its slight climb through secret trees along a winding track

She'd forgotten the driveway that Rupert had ordered to be blazed through those secret trees. Unfinished, it cut a swathe as ugly as if a Titan had scuffed his way through her woodland to get to the house.

But as she looked up towards the Priory, Penitence fell in love all over again. Too exposed, yet built to be exposed, its square gatehouses at this remove resembled outcrops against the lovely rectangle of the hall, while the crazed, inspired

Tudor wings tipped their chimneys like hats to see her back again.

She gathered Ruperta and Tongs to her so that they could stare out. 'We're home, my pippins.' They would be safe here. Deep in Somerset where nothing ever happened. Far away from the epicentre of politics and kings and courtiers.

And at long last she could be virtuous; this was Rupert's true legacy to her, independence. Her body was her own. She didn't have to trade it for food or shelter. For her, the supreme luxury that so few women ever knew — sufficient food in the larder and solitude in her own bed.

No more loving Rupert yet dreading the moment when his ageing hands moved over her skin. Again guilt stabbed her. *I didn't love him enough.*

Instinctively her head turned to the north in which general direction lay the ancestral home of the Viscounts of Severn and Thames as if she would direct her decision towards it. *But I shall atone. I stay faithful to his memory for ever and ever.*

BOOK IV

Chapter 1

CHARLES II was struck by illness on 2 February 1685.

The only one of his numerous illegitimate children not called to gather about his bed was the Duke of Monmouth who had been forced into exile after the discovery of the Rye House Plot.

This latest plot had been in many ways the Whig version of the Popish Plot, except that in this case it was a real one. It was a Protestant plot within a plot. At its core was a plan for killing Charles and his brother James as they passed near Rye House, Hoddesdon, on their way back from Newmarket.

Unknowing that fanatics in the inner plot were contemplating regicide as a way of protecting the Church and liberties of England, Monmouth had nevertheless been on the fringes of the outer plot and keeping company with men who thought these things could only be saved by insurrection. Shocked, Charles had called his son 'a beast and a blockhead' and sent him away.

But the King, and especially James, Duke of York, profited from Rye House. Overnight popular feeling went Tory. The public's loyalty, which had been diminishing as Charles's reign became harsher, turned to him and against the Whigs. And he'd used it.

James, no longer seen as a would-be tyrant but as a victim, was brought back to court. The Whig Party that had called for his exclusion from the throne was all but destroyed. Those who had defamed him went to prison. Old enemies were executed. The Whiggish City of London had its franchises withdrawn. Other boroughs, where there were Whig officers and which regularly returned Whig members to Parliament, were remodelled to put Tories into the ascendancy.

Now, at the age of fifty-three and after a reign more like a twenty-five-year Bacchanalia, Charles was dying.

With considerable courage — one virtue the Stuarts never lacked — he endured four days of treatment by his doctors, who, it was said later, 'tortured him like an Indian at the stake', before death released him. It is certain that just before it did he was received into the Roman Catholic Church.

People wept in the streets when tolling bells announced the death of King Charles II but there was no outcry against the accession of King James II and James turned this equanimity to goodwill. Mary was already married to William of Orange. His second daughter, Princess Anne, was now married to the equally impeccably Protestant George of Denmark.

Thus, the English reasoned, however Catholic this new king proved himself to be, they could at least look forward to the throne passing into safe Protestant hands when he died. And he *was* fifty-one years old. And he couldn't be *that* bad, could he?

Standing in the high pulpit of St Mary's Church, Athelzoy, its vicar announced: 'I shall now read the accession speech of our new and beloved King James the Second.' He glanced nervously down for permission from a slim, middle-aged lady in a large hat sitting at the front of a crowded congregation . . .

His patron took Prince Rupert's time-piece from her pocket, polished it, shook it, read it and suggested in a clear, carrying voice: 'Perhaps only the *relevant* parts, Vicar.'

'Very well, Your Ladyship.'

'We could then dispense with a sermon.' Beside her, Sir Ostyn Edwards nodded a vigorous head.

'Very well, Your Ladyship.'

Dorinda leaned over Tongs's head and hissed: 'Is he speaking English?' Dorinda had continual trouble with Somerset dialect.

'Yes. He's going to read King James's coronation speech.'

'Affie and me already heard it.'

'Then hear it again.' It was all very well for Aphra and Dorinda, newly arrived from London, to be blasé about the speech but it had taken time for copies of it to reach Somerset's county town of Taunton, while illiterates – like most of her parishioners here – had to wait until it was read out from the hundreds of Somerset pulpits, as it was in hers today.

Penitence turned her head to estimate how many of her congregation could read and counted four: Mudge Ridge, Sir Ostyn, of course, just, Hurry Yeo, the landlord of the Hoy Arms, and Hurry Yeo's eleven-year-old daughter who went to school in Taunton and whose immortal soul was considered to be imperilled by doing so, not just because it flew in the face of Nature for girls to read but also because she was doing so at a school run by a couple of women Dissenters.

Perhaps I should found a school.

She was the most important person in Athelzoy; therefore it had become her responsibility. *Her* congregation, *her* parishioners. The Bishop of Bath and Wells might consider them his but without the wealth Penitence had brought to it the church couldn't support a vicar of its own.

The whole village had been as dormant as a bulb, potentially fertile but unable to flower until it received the requisite warmth and moisture of cash. Long before the Civil War, and certainly since the death of its only son, the Hoy family had lacked money to vitalize Athelzoy's capability to grow. Penitence, unrealizing at first, had brought the first necessary shower by employing some of the villagers as household labourers and groundsmen.

The young people who'd left their homes in search of work came flooding back, irrigating themselves and Hurry Yeo's business by patronizing the Hoy Arms, thereby forcing Hurry to employ a tapster.

Under the guidance of young Mudge Ridge, who'd only needed the capital to turn his own and the Priory's farm into profit-making concerns, Penitence's herd of dairy cattle was improved by the acquisition of a Devon bull. 'And now you'm a dairy farmer you got to have pigs,' said Mudge. Sure enough, within the year two spotted Gloucestershire sows had littered thirty-three hardy piglets which grew up into tasty – and profitable – bacon, chitterlings, puddings and sausages on the waste whey and milk.

But the biggest money-maker of all, and one fast becoming an industry, was teasel-growing.

Penitence had been dubious; she barely knew what teasels were, let alone how to grow them. Or, come to that, what to do with them when grown.

'Let me, let me, Your Ladyship,' Mudge begged. 'You got the soil, over by Sallycombe you got heavy girt clay. Ah pleaded with Old Maister but he were a stubborn old . . . gennulman . . . and couldn't see what I see.'

'I thought they grew teasels at Sallycombe already,' Penitence said. 'The Dissenters, those Hugheses' — *my family* — 'aren't they teasellers?'

'Piddly liddle plots,' said Mudge, scornfully. 'Could'n grow a bunyan. We, you, got fifty, sixty acre pleadin' for teasel.' Splendid young man that he was, his huge, soil-engrained hands were pumping the air. In another moment he'd shake her. 'Can't ee see what I see?'

Though she let him have his way on twenty of the acres, she couldn't. For two years she couldn't see. The teasels were sown, planted out, weeded with long-bladed, thin spades, then replanted in prepared ridged and furrowed soil, and all Penitence could see was that if it rained too much in June her teasels would be ruined for their purpose, and if she went on paying wages for such intensive labour, *she* would be ruined. And all for a plant that couldn't be touched with the naked hand, had no scent and reminded her of a stiff-backed, bristle-headed Dogberry.

It wasn't until the following August's harvest that she'd seen Mudge's vision — wagons taking 250,000 teasel-heads along the Sedgemoor track to the clothiers in Taunton, 250,000 teasels for raising the nap on broadcloth, 250,000 so packed on to staffs that they looked like fuzzy loofahs, thirty staffs to a pack, each pack selling at £15.

The next year she'd rented ten acres to Mudge for himself and gave the entire village of Athelzoy employment in planting fifty of her own.

The only people less than pleased with her teasel triumph were the Dissenters who rented the few acres of clay favourable to teasel-growing on Dame Alice Lisle's land. In effect, Penitence's mass production was putting her own great-uncle out of business.

And by this day in early summer, in *her* church, surrounded by *her* villagers, the sun coming in coloured dapples through the new rose window dedicated to the memory of Prince Rupert of the Rhine, Penitence didn't give a damn for her great-uncle. *Serve him right*.

She listened carefully to James's accession speech, giving nods of approval at its repeated reassurance that the King wanted confrontation with nobody. Yes, he affirmed, he was a Roman Catholic, but there need be no concern; on oath he would maintain the Anglican Church and the laws of England. He would not relinquish his own rights, but he would respect the rights of others. 'Just as I have already fought for my country, I shall go on supporting her liberties.'

Beside her, Sir Ostyn also nodded: 'Ah told un when ah wrote to un to go easy. Upset the liberties ah told un and upset trade.'

'I'm sure the King found your advice most valuable,' said Penitence. Sir Ostyn was an idiot. *Still, I agree with him.* She didn't want riot and revolution now that she was about to increase teasel production and expand her outlets, this time to clothiers in the North of England.

Here, in Athelzoy, she was in a pocket of Toryism which, like the country as a whole, was delighted with James's speech. Sir Ostyn had joined a rush of magistrates, burgesses and merchants to promise King James their loyalty and assure him they would never put up as a member to the House of Commons anyone who had voted for his exclusion.

But elsewhere Somerset's non-agricultural working population consisted for the most part of Dissenters — Baptists, Presbyterians, Puritans, Fifth Monarchists, etc. — to whom James's Papistry was anathema. Families like her grandmother's, the Hugheses, the labourers and artisans of this area, had fought hard for Parliament during the Civil War and, despite Charles's promises of magnanimity on his restoration, had suffered for it ever since. James could proffer them rights of worship until he was black in the face; as far as they were concerned he was a Catholic and therefore Beelzebub. *They could cause trouble.*

Vicar Lambert finished reading the King's speech in triumph at its happy message and that he'd got most of the words right. 'There, good people,' he said, 'we have now for our Church the word of a king and of a king who was never worse than his word.'

Penitence raised her eyebrows; Vicar Lambert wasn't usually so felicitous in his phrases. He must have heard it from somebody else.

'That's a good un,' she heard Sir Ostyn say. 'Good watchword, that 'un.' Sir Ostyn was going to do as well out of King James's reign as he had out of King Charles's.

And Sir Ostyn wanted to marry her.

Partly it was because he lusted after her, but then, Sir Ostyn lusted after anything with a hole in it, but mostly because he wanted the Priory and her fortune. He made no bones about it and took no notice of her refusals. The only good thing about him was that he was no Charles Sedley, thank God; she could keep him at arm's length and he, in turn, kept off other suitors.

At the end of the service he tried to get out of the pew door ahead of her, but she swivelled past his bulk so that she could go down the aisle without him. Her hands gently nudged Ruperta and Tongs ahead of her, conscious that every woman in the congregation was taking note of what the three of them were wearing, and knowing it looked superb.

Out in the churchyard she and the others stood under the stiff branches of its enormous and ancient yew tree while the congregation filed past her. At a lift of Penitence's finger Mary Claymond stepped to one side and waited until Her Ladyship should be ready to talk to her.

Dorinda mimicked her, holding up a hand in papal blessing and bestowing a 'Nunc, nunc' on each one who passed. Aphra had gone into the throes of composition and was staring at the sky, swaying and muttering.

After the villagers had made their curtseys or forelock-tugs they gathered by the lych-gate until Penitence left, watching

Dorinda and Aphra with expectancy. At first they had been so floundered at the visits of Penitence's theatrical friends that they had reacted by deciding they weren't there at all. The clothes, accents, mannerisms had been too strange. When Aphra tried to stimulate a love of literature by quoting poetry at them they were forced to the conclusion that she was mad — an opinion they hadn't changed.

Dorinda they'd put down as Penitence's personal and female jester.

Penitence turned to the waiting girl: 'Mary, I wish you to tell your parents that Mudge Ridge will be calling on them at dusk tomorrow with my blessing.'

Mary gave a bob. 'What bist ee coam vur, Leddyship?'

'He's to ask for your hand, as you well know, Mary Claymond.' She gave the girl a smile. 'I'm told it's a cool hand at pastry.' In the Somerset villages that was the highest praise a girl could expect.

Mary bridled. 'Ah don't know if ah'm willing. Maister Ridge be chapel, not church.'

Penitence was instantly cross. 'It doesn't matter. Haven't you just heard the vicar telling you your king is for tolerance? Do you consider yourself better than your king? I'll have no such nonsense. Mudge is an excellent fellow and you'll be lucky to get him.'

Leaving the churchyard Penitence paused for a second beside a tiny new headstone which simply read: Royalle, AD 1671–1684. She'd had to fight the diocese to get the dog buried in the churchyard, but she'd won. *Rupert would have been pleased.*

As they walked Aphra said: 'One never learned Zummerzet, but do I gather that child just now isn't willing to marry Mudge?'

'Of course she is,' snapped Penitence. 'She's just playing bashful. It will be a splendid match for her. And Mudge could do with a good dairymaid for a wife.'

'No impediment for true minds there, then,' said Aphra, idly.

Penitence looked at her suspiciously. *Was I overbearing with*

Mary Claymond? No. It would be a good marriage for them both.

A May breeze touched the candles of the chestnut beside the duckpond, and sent a shower of tiny white and pink petals on to the water. Ruperta and Tongs, who had sustained adult dignity through the long church service, were being urged by Sir Ostyn to climb the tree after a squirrel's drey he said he'd spotted – and didn't need asking twice.

'Really, Ostyn,' said Penitence, lifting Tongs down from his back and brushing down the child's bottle-green velvet jacket, 'they'll get their clothes dirty.'

'Nothin' wrong with a peck of dirt. They don't want to grow up namby-pamby Lunnon ladies. They want to be strong, Zummerset maids. Eh, my boodies? Want to come hunting along of I?'

'Yes, please, sir,' answered Ruperta immediately, and Tongs echoed her a second or two later. Penitence looked at them with pride. Springs and summers spent in Somerset had put roses in their cheeks, and flesh on Tongs's delicate bones. Nothing namby-pamby about either. Ruperta took after her father in having no physical fear at all but Tongs was the one with courage; she had to overcome terror, and did, every time she mounted a horse.

They reached the Hoy Arms where Hurry was waiting with the tankard of ale Penitence had ordered him to have ready for Sir Ostyn before they resumed the walk back to the Priory and dinner.

Dorinda looked over towards the market square. 'That poor bugger called you a doxy again?'

Civilization had come to Athelzoy in the form of a proper pillory with its articulated yoke that fitted over neck and wrists, instead of the whipping post and rings which had adorned the village in the old days.

Today, as more often than not, the offender stuck in it was Martin Hughes. She noticed with satisfaction that the man's thin lips were compressed tight in the martyrdom of real pain. The height of the pillory was designed to put maximum strain on the spine.

'He has been sentenced for condemning the King's coronation,' she pointed out. It was partly true but Sir Ostyn's
attention wouldn't have been attracted to the offence if Penitence hadn't complained of it.

Great-uncle or not, Penitence's patience with the man had
run out. The fact that she was cornering the market in teasels
had turned his insistence on holding her up as an example of
Satan profiting from sin into persecution. Every Sunday he
came to Athelzoy to preach against her.

His thin black figure haunted her, just as she had been
haunted and persecuted by the Reverend Block back in Massachusetts. Three months ago, when he was preaching in Taunton's Parade, he'd glimpsed her and pointed her out to the
crowd as 'that harlot actress, mistress of the dead dragon
prince'.

But this time the malevolent forces of Puritanism had
mistaken their prey. *I'm not poor and frightened any more.* This
time her friends weren't Indians but powerful admirers, like Sir
Ostyn Edwards, JP. This time the hare had turned round and
bitten the dogs, and it was the shade of the Reverend Block
whose head and hands pawed through the pillory yoke as well
as Martin Hughes's.

Watching the scene from the doorway of the Hoy Arms
while Sir Ostyn downed his tankard, she muttered to Aphra
and Dorinda: 'That'll teach him to accuse me of wallowing in
the fruits of sin.'

'Let's face it, though,' said Dorinda, 'the bastard's right. You
are.'

It was meant as a you-and-I-remember-when, a reminder of
war from one survivor to another, but it rumbled at the
foundations of a structure Penitence had worked hard to build.
Without Dorinda and without Martin Hughes Penitence could –
and would – have forgotten that she'd ever been anything but a
woman of good standing.

She turned away sharply to continue the walk.

She always suggested this walk to her visitors on Sundays;
it took her to the village, her village, past her bean- and
wheatfields to the view over the sedgemoors where her black,

Devon cattle grazed the marsh meadows and where, in the distance, hung the flat, mauve cloud that was her teasel crop.

Expecting to be shunned and not greatly caring as long as she could quietly sacrifice the rest of her life to serving Rupert's memory, she had been surprised how her neighbours' attitude changed towards her once they found that, thanks to her Hurd grandfather, she made a competent farmer and, thanks to Mudge Ridge, was earning a fortune from her teasels. English country gentry, she discovered, hated Frenchmen, Italians, Scotchmen, Irishmen, Papists, Presbyterians, Independents, Baptists, Quakers and Jews, but they were tolerant to a fault of their own kind.

They farted, belched, played hideous practical jokes and had much in common with the beasts in their own meadows but they were too interdependent to be scandalized by each other's naughtinesses, even if that other was a woman. Viciousness was not in them. Courtiers like Charles Sedley expended wit on the buffoonery of such rustics but they could have taught him a thing or two about group loyalty.

Not for them the luxury of who's in, who's out, not when they sought each other's permission to hunt over each other's land, not when the Levels flooded and left their manors isolated islands needing neighbourly rescue, not when their best plough broke, or a wheel came off their carriage, or the birth of their baby was proving difficult. Then they needed the help of whoever was nearest, and if whoever nearest had an undesirable past it took a back-seat to the usefulness of her present.

Graceless and bucolic, Somerset gentry yet had an oyster-like ability to smooth over irritants until they were acceptable. Finding that Penitence was not to be dislodged from the Priory by rudeness, cold-shouldering, advice, or offers of marriage, her neighbours mentally labelled her an oddity, as Lady Alice Lisle was an oddity, and absorbed her. Their labourers helped with Penitence's harvests as hers helped with theirs. When a Pascoe child died the Reverend Boreman was just in time to save its soul by baptism. Some of Rupert's cinchona preserved the life of another Pascoe baby. Sir William

Portman's contacts were enabling Penitence to sell to the northern clothiers.

It wasn't to be expected that they'd treat her with kid gloves; their heavy winks were incessant, they made rutting motions with their brawny forearms, but in the company of anyone they considered above or below their class, or with anyone who came from further away than Glastonbury, they included Penitence in their ranks – and closed them.

As for the lower classes themselves, they were brutal realists. Leddyship was vurrin and touched to boot, but she paid good wages and she paid them regular. QED she had their loyalty.

So Penitence became Lady of Athelzoy.

She would have liked not to be a vurriner, to reveal that she was a Hoy, of the same stock that had ruled the village for centuries. But to do so would inevitably revive the scandalous love story of her parents, put her midway across the class divide and link her with pestiferous, trouble-making, Dissenting Hughes.

And that she could not allow. For the first time in her life Penitence was rich, respectable and in control. It was a giddying sensation. People watched her in case she was displeased. Vicar Lambert consulted her about his sermons. Tradesmen solicited her custom.

Even at the height of her fame on the stage, she had been vulnerable to the assaults and insults of the tiring-room. Now she could punish her detractors by asking her good neighbour, Sir Ostyn Edwards, JP, to put them in the pillory. She wasn't going to compromise all that by claiming blood kin with those very detractors.

As the fact that she had been a notorious mistress faded from other people's memories, so it faded from her own. At first she had desired respect because 'Rupert would have wanted it for me'. Then she desired it for its own sake, then she demanded it. The amused voice which, in her first year at Athelzoy, said 'Act the fine lady', had faded to be replaced by a sharp 'You *are* a fine lady.'

Dorinda kept spoiling it.

They crossed the bridge over the Minnow which rushed down to join the more sober Cary which in turn joined the River Parrett as it made its sprawling way towards Bridgwater and the Bristol Channel. Here the land fell away in the varying greens that Penitence loved, the prickled olive of her osier beds, a breeze turning willow leaves silver-green side up, the dark of rushes.

The sedgemoors called to her in a way she could not account for unless they had provided the bed for her conception — which they probably had. Unattractive in winter, treacherous with quagmire, they nevertheless had drama. Perhaps it was the sky dominating the flatness, or the way the setting sun turned the pools and meres into amber, or the fact that you were dangerously close to sea-level, a speck on a vast green solitude that rolled unhindered and empty to the Bristol Channel.

Hardly a day passed but she'd taken the opportunity to walk them or ride them on her pony, taking Barnzo, the farrier's son, with her as a guide until now she could look out at them and discern the hidden causeway that led from the track at the bottom of the rise to the Taunton road, and know where she could pick sphagnum moss and which turbary produced the best peat bricks for the Priory fires. It was said of her that she could 'ride the marshes' — the local phrase for knowing them well.

'The Levels,' she said, breathing them in.

'Lovely,' said Dorinda. 'Can we go home now? I'm breaded.'

'You'll never make a Zummerzet maid,' Sir Ostyn teased her.

'Thank Gawd for that.'

From the first Dorinda had taken against Athelzoy, and not only Athelzoy but the whole of Somerset. It was too far from London, it had too many smells, was too quiet, too lush, too dark at night, too hot in summer, too full of insects that flew, crawled and buzzed their way up from the marshes. She couldn't understand a word the ballocking cider-suppers said. Teasels did not excite her.

What kept her returning to it was the benefit and obvious

enjoyment her daughter derived from sharing Ruperta's life. Tongs pined when she was anywhere else.

When Becky Marshall, on a visit, had suggested Dorinda should leave Tongs at the Priory and return with her to join the company at the Duke of York's as a dresser-cum-character-actress, Penitence had seen the gleam of footlights reflected in her friend's eyes, and encouraged her to go. At the same time she resented it on Tongs's behalf and said so to Becky: 'How can she plan to abandon that dear child?'

And Becky had said: 'I think if I may say so that she's displaying great love in leaving her behind. You're mistress of the household. It's you, not Dorinda, Tongs turns to for instruction. That dear child is more yours than hers.'

So Dorinda went, mercifully unrecognized by a new generation of theatregoers, to take Sisygambus parts first in one play then another, until she was staying longer in London each year than in Somerset.

They turned right along the deep, narrow, fern-fringed lane that connected the bottom of the village with the bottom of the Priory drive and came out between oaks on to a green which commanded the Levels on the left and the great wrought-iron gates to the right.

'Barnzo, Mother.' Ruperta was pointing at a distant horse and cart crawling over the causeway that led from Taunton to this end of Sedgemoor, bringing Athelzoy's Nonconformists from their meeting-house service.

'I asked Barnzo to call in at Tidy's and see if there was a letter from my son,' explained Penitence to Sir Ostyn. Tidy kept the post office. 'Otherwise the carrier wouldn't bring it until tomorrow.'

'What malevolent spirit named the man Barnzo?' asked Aphra.

'His head's on crooked,' said Penitence, absently; quite suddenly she was struck by a fear of the horse and cart. Rationally the protuberances from its sides were fleeces being brought for Athelzoy women to spin into yarn, but they made the shape of the cart into a winged hornet swelling bigger as it crawled towards her.

'There's one in every village,' Sir Ostyn was explaining to Aphra, tapping his temple. 'His yeead's on crooked. He were barnzo. Barnzo.'

'Born so,' said Penitence at Aphra's incomprehension. 'Children, escort our guests to the house and tell Johannes we're ready for dinner. I'll just wait and see if there's a letter.'

The girls put their hands into Sir Ostyn's and Aphra's, curtseyed and pulled them towards the house. Penitence, watching them go, saw Sir Ostyn's free hand goose Aphra's backside – and his jump as Aphra goosed him back.

Dorinda stayed with her. Awkwardly, without talking, the two women watched the cart, holding their fluttering hats to their heads against the strengthening breeze that mixed the smells of grass and marsh with the elusive tang of sea.

Let there be a letter. Benedick was a hopeless correspondent. Until a few weeks ago she'd received news of him every month from the faithful Dudley, but now Dudley had joined the Christian army's crusade against the Turk and his letters came in batches after long intervals. She worried about him, and about Benedick left behind in the Netherlands without his foster-brother's common sense to steady him. She hadn't heard from either for six weeks.

He's dead. They're both dead. She was having a premonition of the news, the sting of the insect as it crawled towards her, ever bigger. Having seen it as monstrous she couldn't dislodge its misshape from her eye. Barnzo's poor face and leather cap became a head with mandibles and multi-faceted eyes. Then he waved – 'Letter from Holland, Leddyship' – and reverted to a simpleton driving a cart full of people and fleeces.

She snatched the letter from his hand, and frowned her disapproval at his passengers: her own dear Mudge and Prue Ridge, Jack and Mistress Fuller, the Mackrells, the Yeo child, Jan and Betty Creech and their baby. Good people all of them, but Dissenters from the mainstream religion that Penitence was beginning to consider essential to the well-being of the country's economy.

Barnzo's ever-nodding head nodded with deliberation at her: 'King Monmouth be coming to Somerset.'

'Shshhh.' Mistress Fuller put her hand over her son's mouth, and Penitence sympathized. 'If Sir Ostyn heard you, Barnzo, you'd go to prison.' She looked at Mudge: 'What set this off?'

'Oh, there's rumours at meeting.' He was reluctant.

'There's always rumours,' she scolded. 'And people like you stupid enough to encourage them. Monmouth won't dare come. Not after the Argyll fiasco.'

The Earl of Argyll had invaded Scotland in what had been supposed to be a two-pronged attack against James's Catholic reign – the Duke of Monmouth to provide the other prong by landing somewhere in England to raise a Protestant rebellion. In view of the fact that Argyll had been captured after a month of incompetence it was not expected that Monmouth, who was known to be unable to raise sufficient men or money from his fellow-exiles in the Netherlands, would make the same mistake.

'They be arresting our friends in Taunton,' burst out Barnzo.

'They're rounding up trouble-makers all over England,' said Penitence, who'd been told so by Sir Ostyn. 'We don't want silly men making trouble, do we.' She looked squarely at Mudge: 'Do we? Not with the teasel harvest coming on.'

Mudge grinned at her. 'Won't be, Leddyship. Not from I.' There were nods from the others in the cart.

'Good.' She slapped the tired horse's rump to set it on its way towards the village and turned to her letter.

'That's mine,' said Dorinda.

Penitence stared at her, slipping her nail along the sealing wax. 'It's *my* letter. It's from Benedick and Dudley.' She had to hold the letter in the air to foil Dorinda's grab for it.

'It's mine. Look at the ballocking name on it.'

'You heard. It's from Holland. Of course it's for me.' To tell Dorinda she was a jealous slut was a warm and beautiful temptation she would give way to any moment.

Dorinda gave way to her own: '"Leddyship", "Leddyship",' she minced. 'Everything's for Leddyship.' Her voice dropped: 'You've got too big for your boots, you. Poncing about like the virgin of the manor just because a lot of turnip-pickers have to do what you tell 'em.'

'You're jealous,' screamed Penitence. 'Your man's left you with nothing except what I give you. You're jealous because Tongs loves me better than you.' She was back in the attic of the Cock and Pie; she felt her hands reaching for Dorinda's hair and stopped, appalled.

'Perhaps,' said Dorinda in a court accent, 'you would be good enough to regard the superscription on that there letter.'

Penitence looked down and, shamefaced, handed it over.

Dorinda turned her back to read it. MacGregor had taught her to read, but she still moved her lips. The back of her head and shoulders made the same shape as on the day she'd carried Benedick away from the window of Newgate prison.

How could I say those things to you? You, who sheltered my son for me. Penitence said, gently: 'Is it from MacGregor?'

'Yes.'

'Is he well? I didn't know he was back in the Netherlands.'

'Don't know everything, then, do you?'

When it came to MacGregor, thought Penitence, she knew nothing. Twenty years on and off she'd been acquainted with the man and all she could relate of him was that he was a radical Scotsman never radical in her presence. It was as if her interest had glissaded over him without picking anything up, as if he withdrew to make himself invisible. *He must have opinions.* She knew he had opinions; otherwise why did he care to publish the anti-Catholic, anti-James ravings of crackpot exiles? But he'd never expressed them to her. Dorinda had once said it was because he was afraid of her. *Henry King liked him. Damn it.* Who cared who Henry King liked or didn't?

Now she was sorry she hadn't taken more trouble to know the man. Obviously he was still important to Dorinda. Come to think of it, he'd been an important, or at least constant, part of Benedick's childhood, a male presence insubstantially but for ever there in the chaotic scramble that had been her efforts to feed them all.

She tried again. 'Is he coming back to England soon?'

'Mind your own business.' Dorinda's tone was not so much rude as abstracted.

If you won't, you won't. But later Penitence was always

grateful to remember that she ignored the snub and edged across the distance between them to take Dorinda's hand.

Dorinda took hers away but, again, not with hostility. She folded the letter and carefully tucked it in her pocket.

Ahead of them the house and the lovely jumble of its roofs and chimneys lifted Penitence's heart as it always did. How right Rupert had been about an approach that set it off. In silence they walked towards it.

Over dinner Sir Ostyn entertained them with a hoof-by-hoof account of the twenty-six-mile pursuit of a hind by the Acland Staghounds in which he'd taken part the day before. After the meal, in the hall, when the women took the opportunity to duck beneath his sentences and exchange their own news — they hadn't met together for two months — he listened, rapt, as if to Scheherazades. That they were independent women — rare cattle in Somerset — intrigued and appalled him. But if they paused he took up the chase again, certain they would be spellbound.

As he talked, Penitence tried to keep her eyes away from the gargoyle opposite her. *Don't stare at it. They'll see.*

She had found the Priory's secret room. At least, she knew *where* it was. She just couldn't get into it.

Three years it had taken the house to yield even that much of its secret. Three years of increasingly dispirited search for that holy grail of the householder, a safe hiding-place, until, at last, she'd thrown in her hand and taken Elizabeth of Bohemia's necklace back to London in a hat-box and lodged it in the Earl of Craven's bank. Then, of course, she'd made her discovery.

It had been the night of the flood, when the Bristol Channel had broken through the coastal defences and come snaking across the moors, almost to the bottom of the Priory's drive. She had been in the hall, playing spillikins with Ruperta and Tongs, trying to keep the children's minds off the terrible sound of the wind while the rest of the household scurried from one window to another to fasten the shutters more securely.

The candles had guttered in the shrieking draught and she'd looked up and noticed for the first time that the mouth, nostrils and eyes of the gargoyle in the north-east corner of the hall were an empty black.

On hands and knees, to the girls' delight, she'd crawled until she was opposite one of the other gargoyles and glanced up into its leer. Its nostrils were grey, not black. They were stopped up.

A crawl back to the corner gargoyle. *Very clever*. Of the six gargoyles in the hall, this was in the deepest shadow and the one the eye shied away from. Not because it was ugly — the others were uglier — but because it pervaded unpleasantness; this was a gargoyle who wished you ill, knew your future and waited with watchful attention for it to happen.

When the girls had gone to bed, she'd fetched a stool and some tapers. Standing on tiptoe she put a taper up the gargoyle's nose and wiggled it about. The face was a mask; at the back it was hollow — she tied on another taper to the end of the first and inserted it further — very hollow.

The noise of the wind covered the scrape of the ladder as she dragged it up to the hall then searched the house for withies.

She'd approached her face to the gargoyle's with reluctance. But to be close to it was to wonder at the artistry of the stonemason who'd made so repellent a thing with a few digs of a chisel.

The mask slanted downwards at an angle of forty-five degrees to the floor of the hall, making it difficult for her to peer through its apertures. She bound two withies together with string, constructing a rod about four feet long, and fed it through the gross mouth, then added another.

It was impossible to estimate the full dimensions of the space she was investigating, but she pushed six feet of withies through without coming against any obstruction.

She tried twisting the gargoyle to see if it moved but it was all of a piece with the wall. The air from its holes smelled of stone and age, but not damp. When she put her mouth to the gargoyle's mouth and said 'Hello' she nearly fell off the ladder as she heard her voice deepen and reverberate back at her. *'Hallooo.'*

She had found the room. But how to get into it?

That night and subsequent nights Penitence measured and paced. The length of the passage between the hall and the solar corresponded with the other side of the wall. So did the height. The room wasn't in the long side of the hall, then, but somewhere in the end of its rectangle, built into the north wall, perhaps between the fireplace and the corner.

But that was where it got difficult. At that end the hall dovetailed into the later wing, the Tudor north wing, where the floors were not on the same level as the hall's. Indeed, there were so many corners, cupboards, tiny flights of stairs, that it was almost impossible to spot any discrepancy which would indicate the secret room's whereabouts.

Eventually she thought she'd tracked it down to behind the south wall of her bedroom which backed on to the north-hand side of the fireplace end of the hall. If her reckonings were correct, somewhere between the two was a damn great gap. But there was no door.

She could have screamed with frustration. There was no point in being the proud possessor of a secret room if you had to employ labourers to break down a wall to get into it but all her tappings and furtive removals of suspected panels revealed nothing.

'Have you read my play, Penitence?'

She'd had to wait until spring until she could reasonably order the hall fire to be allowed to go out and she could creep into the grate to examine the right-hand side of its flue. Taking what the locals called a 'pickass' with her, she'd inflicted considerable damage to the brickwork before coming up against the infuriating solidity of more stone.

'Have you read it, Penitence? Penitence, *dear*, have you read *The Widow Ranter*?'

'I'm sorry, Affie, I was miles away. Yes, I read it. All last night. How did you think of her? It's wonderful.'

And it was. It wasn't Shakespeare, but it was marvellous entertainment and moved at a gallop. Set in Virginia during the Indian Wars, its dramatic meat was a conventionally tragic love-story between an English soldier and the native queen.

But what was new in this sort of drama was the eponymous comic heroine, Widow Ranter herself, lusty, hard-drinking, smoking, cursing, prepared to fight for and with the man she loved. In every other play such a virago ended with a submissive speech to her lover. Not the Widow Ranter. Unreformed, impenitent, she and her man went off into the sunset to a comradely happy ending.

'When is Duke's putting it on?' she asked.

Aphra sat back in her chair: 'When can you play her?'

'How'd it be if I came to one of they old mummeries of yourn one day?' asked Sir Ostyn. 'Ah ain't never seen a play.'

'They wouldn't let you in, dear,' said Aphra and turned back to Penitence, who'd been struck dumb.

'You want me for the Widow Ranter?' It was a part to murder for. It stole the play. And it could be played by an actress *d'un certain âge*.

'Betterton's asked for you. He saw you in the old days.'

Thomas Betterton was the leading light of the new generation at the Duke of York's and Aphra must have pressed him to ask for her; her stage appearances had been few enough when Rupert was alive; since his death they had ceased altogether.

To go back. Shall I? Can I? The thought that she would never act again had been bitter, but she had laid it on the altar of Rupert's memory with a self-sacrificial: 'He wouldn't want me to.' Anyway, her role as lady of the manor had called for acting and she'd played it to the hilt. *Should I?* Perhaps it wasn't worthy of her present status to return to that raffish world, that seedy, degenerate, *delicious* world.

Those watching Penitence noticed the hauteur that had become natural to her expression relax into something wistfuller and certainly more human. Aphra took advantage of it. 'Come back with Dorinda and me,' she said. 'Three weeks' rehearsal, six performances — you can be back here at Athelzoy before the teasels whelp, or whatever they do.'

'Not me,' said Dorinda, 'I'm staying on here for a bit.' She half-raised herself from her chair to bow at Penitence: 'With your permission, Your Ladyship.'

'Of course.' Penitence ignored the sneer; she was puzzled. But it made her decision easier to know that Dorinda would be here to help the Reverend Boreman and Annie keep an eye on the girls. 'In that case . . . Affie, yes please.'

As luck would have it, Penitence found the door to the secret room two days before she journeyed to London – or, rather, Ruperta and Tongs found it.

Because Penitence was keeping Annie busy helping her to pack, the two little girls were making their own amusement and had ventured into forbidden territory to bounce on Penitence's bed.

She heard the protesting creak of the tester's great timbers from downstairs and was hurrying to put a stop to the horseplay when a crash and cry alarmed her into a run. Two guilty pairs of eyes regarded from the bed, the blue squeezed up with pain.

'She didn't mean it.' Tongs had her thin arm round Ruperta's neck, protecting her, as usual. 'She fell over and it came off.'

'It' was the central panel of the bedhead which hung askew.

Sternly, Penitence examined her daughter's bruised leg, pronounced it fit to walk on and banished her and Tongs to the kitchens.

Left alone to examine the damage to the bed, she saw that nothing, in fact, was broken. Although it was carved to look all of a piece with the bedhead, the heavy two-and-a-half-foot-square panel was actually a separate piece of oak tongued at the top and bottom to slide aside along concealed grooves in the panels above and below it. Ruperta's fall had shoved the wood sideways and dislodged part of it out of its runners.

Penitence was so busy fitting it back that she only noticed what was behind the gap it left when it was too late. There was a click as the panel slid into place, covering up the section of wall it had exposed – in which she'd seen part of a door.

, Trembling with excitement, she tried to slide the panel sideways again, but it wouldn't move. Damn. The click had been a catch dropping back into place. She pushed and tugged uselessly, she stood up on the pillows and tried reaching over the top of the bedhead to feel down the back, but the bed had been made to stand flush against the wall and she couldn't intrude more than her fingertips. Damn. *Damn.*

She sat down to think. She could get an axe and whack the panel open or she could get a team up from the fields and pull the bed out. *And sell tickets while I'm about it.* There seemed little point in a secret room that was public knowledge. No, there was an easier way to open the panel, the way its designer had intended; she just had to find it.

Penitence sat back on her heels and looked at her bedhead, its carving shining a rich black in the morning sun, like an encrusted cliff still wet from the tide. Two rows of smaller panels surrounded the one that moved – or, at present, didn't – each one a biblical story depicted by stiff-legged figures in early Tudor dress. Hunting between the panels, floppy-eared dachshunds sniffed the trail of a hare, gazehounds lolloped after stag, until the round was reversed and the stag hunted dachshunds and the hare the gazehounds. It always made her smile.

Across the top was an inscription in Welsh – 'KYFFARWTH AIGWNA HARRY AP:LL'. Rupert had given her a rough translation: 'An Expert was Harry ap Llewellyn who Wrought this.'

Now she knew why the Hoy who commissioned the bed brought a Welshman to carve it, doubtless sending him back to Wales when he'd done it with instructions to keep his mouth shut as to what lay behind it.

'Very well, Harry Ap:Ll,' said Penitence. 'Where do I press?'

The central panel was of Adam and Eve. Adam stood on one side of the Tree of Knowledge with his left hand coyly hiding his genitals. On the other side, a convenient tress of her long hair hid Eve's. Coiling round the Tree was a dragon-like serpent, teeth exposed in a grin as its snout pointed towards Eve's bare breast.

The apples on the Tree, or Adam's belly-button, might be the knobs that would release the panel's catch but Penitence was afraid she knew Harry Ap:Ll better than that. She extended her finger and gave a quick jab at Eve's jaunty nipple, heard the click, watched the panel slide to the left and saw the door she had been trying to find for nearly four years.

It was of carved pine and bigger than the panel, though she couldn't see by how much, and its sill corresponded with the panel's bottom rim. It was already opened a few inches into the room behind it. She thought it probable that before the north wing was built there had been another stone room where her bedroom now was and this door would have been hidden behind an arras.

And why sit here working out such things instead of going in?

She was getting fanciful in her old age. First her dread of Barnzo's cart the other day, and now this reluctance to explore a marvel. *There could be treasure in there.* Well, yes, but treasure wasn't the only thing they walled up.

First she locked her bedroom door. She fetched and lit a candle, then she put a pillow across the sill of the panel, not just to form a bridge for her knees to the sill of the secret room, but to block the possibility of the panel clicking back into place and her finding no mechanism at the rear by which she could open it again. The thought made the palms of her hands wet.

Holding the candle ahead of her she crawled across the pillow into the room and, because its doorsill was a foot above its floor, had to do some complicated leg-work before she could stand up inside.

It was a nasty room. There was nothing in it except a bench, but malignity had got trapped in its dimensions. It was too high and too long for its seven-foot width. There was no window in the stone walls and the only light came from the door and a collection of holes in the wall opposite against which the bench stood. She couldn't understand the room's function; it was over-large as a hiding place for jewels and the air-holes indicated it was for habitation of some kind. A priest's hole? But why? The Hoys had been Protestant since Henry VIII; there was no need for their house to have a room for the practice of forbidden Mass.

It was when she examined the holes in the wall facing her that she got an inkling. They were irregular, two round ones side by side at the top, two more below, equally round but smaller and closer together, and a slit beneath the lot. All were

491

in a concave recess and were actually tiny tunnels sloping downwards in the thickness of the wall.

She put her eyes to the recess and saw familiar colour which, for a moment, she couldn't place until she recognized the Isfahan rug that had once adorned Rupert's study at Awdes and now lay in front of the fireplace in her own hall. *Of course.* She'd forgotten. She was staring through the eyes of the gargoyle.

Not a priest hole, a peep-hole. A place for spying. A voyeur's room. Some old Hoy had sat here on this bench and observed his household without their knowledge. Who had he spied on? His wife? No, of course not; in the time this room was built the hall had been a priory. The prior had sat here, dirty old man, his gargoyle's eyes watching his unknowing flock, recording sins, overhearing plots, listening for things his monks did not tell him in confession.

A figure moved into her field of vision – Joan, a slow-moving daughter of Athelzoy, employed to sweep. The gargoyle's encircled view gave her interest and significance. Lazily, she brushed up the ash of the fire where it had spilled over the grate. As she carried it away in her bucket her skirt sent some of the fine, white powder blowing on to the rug. Joan paused, then rubbed it in with the thick sole of her shoe.

You and I are going to fall out, miss. Penitence pulled herself up; spy-holes had fascination as well as horror. She must resist it. With an effort she also resisted giving an eldritch screech of 'Your sins have found you out, Joan Pedder'. The shock would probably kill the slut. Instead, she held up the candle for a last look round the room, found nothing else of interest, and crawled out of it.

She supposed she was glad the room was there but she felt none of the thrill of secret possession she had expected once she found it. She could lodge such jewellery as Rupert had given to her in it, but since robbery was almost unknown in this part of the county it was probably as safe in the heavy chest where she usually locked it.

Oh well, you never knew when a hiding-place would be useful. But she wouldn't mind at all if she never went into the unpleasant place again. And she would certainly have a word or two with Joan Pedder.

Chapter 2

THERE were still just irregular, though rising, walls of masonry where St Paul's had been, but the rest of the City was elegant in its resurrection and its populace hurried familiarly along the neat streets and in and out of the shops as if they had always been there.

Nevertheless, Penitence found London peculiarly oppressive. It was hot, of course, and she had grown used to the unlimited space of Somerset, but a town that had once been relaxed to the point of disorderly was now become tidy, almost prissy.

On her first promenade she wondered what was different about the merchants who passed her before realizing that the thread of moustache which prosperous men had worn in imitation of Charles II had gone. Now they were fully shaved in imitation of James II. Gone too was the relaxed dress; coats were narrower and stiffer. There were fewer ribbons, and shoes were decorated with buckles.

Women's fashion had changed as well. *And not for the better.* She didn't like the elaborate caps which rose in a wired pleated frill at the front nor the formalized drapery of the gowns with their bustles and trains. The effect wasn't so pretty nor so comfortable as in her day. She caught the echo of the thought. *Oh God, I'm getting old.*

The theatre was in a bad way. King's had died of Killigrew's poor financial management. The only playhouse in London now was the Duke of York's and even there attendances were down. 'The King has no enthusiasm for it,' Otway told her, 'you'd think politics, hunting and Catherine Sedley were the *only* things to concern him.'

The biter had been bit with a vengeance. Sir Charles Sedley, it was said, raved furiously at the King's adultery with his daughter. In the tradition of James's mistresses, Catherine Sedley was plain but she had her father's brilliant bitchiness and confessed herself puzzled at James's fascination with her. 'It cannot be my beauty, for I have none; and it cannot be my wit, for he has not enough to know that I have any.'

Other old friends were in trouble. John Hoyle was drunker than ever. Dryden had found it politic to turn Catholic. Charlie Hart was dead.

Nevertheless it was delightful to be welcomed into Aphra's soirées, and to be greeted as an honoured Thespian when she visited the tiring-room. Thomas Betterton bowed over her hand and said: 'I was privileged to see your Beatrice, ma'am.'

When, acting modesty, she protested she was too old and too rusty for the Widow Ranter — *but try to take her away from me* — he said earnestly: 'Age cannot wither you nor custom stale your infinite talent.' Having just seen his Macbeth, the compliment moved Penitence almost to tears. Close to, he was of unexceptional height with a face like a cottage loaf; on stage he'd been seven feet tall.

Aphra also insisted on effecting an introduction between Penitence and the King's recently appointed Chief Justice, Sir George Jeffreys: 'A fine, forceful man and a wonderful play-goer. One can't have too many friends in that class. He's saved several plays by his frequent attendance. One's dedicating one's translation of *The History of Oracles* to him. You must recall him, dear. He was often backstage at King's. He was *ravished* by your Desdemona.'

He was brought to the next soirée to meet her.

'And I tell you, dear madam,' roared the Lord Chief Justice, 'that Othello is a fool. Magnificent, but a fool. Had he brought his case to my court, your Desdemona should have gone free as a bird and that lying, snake-tongued knave Iago should have been whipped at the cart's-arse as Titus Oates is whipped now, 'til the blood runs. I'd have pinned his slanders to his shoulders, I'd have discovered the rogue.'

Penitence batted admiring eyelashes: 'How illuminating to have a great legal mind view the play, my lord.' As Aphra said, you couldn't have too many friends in Sir George's class.

But I still don't remember him. If, as he was telling her, he'd come to the tiring-room after one of her appearances in Desdemona, he hadn't made much of an impact.

He was immoderately clever, it was said, and his roots were humble. Perhaps it was only when James, to whom he seemed devoted, came to the throne that he had been given room to spread his extremely large personality. His somewhat unremarkable face was charged with blood and power so that it was difficult to look away from it. He heated Aphra's hot, untidy front room with his energy and his enormous, surprisingly musical, bass voice. He was about forty years old, a heavy drinker, and still greedy for flesh — his hand was constantly touching Penitence's — for attention, for everything. They said he was unhappily married.

For all his exalted position, he was finding it thrilling to be among theatre people and on familiar terms with men and women he had before merely watched from the gallery. His prominent blue eyes searched round for reactions every time he spoke. *He's an actor manqué.*

He took her hand to his huge breast. 'Make me a promise that you play Desdemona for me, or I'll not live. Betterton here shall be your Othello, will you not, Tom? A special performance for the Lord Chief Justice. Indulge me.'

Penitence saw that Betterton was attracted to the idea; his attempts to put on *The Widow Ranter* were being frustrated by increasing rumours of a Monmouth invasion. In times of disquiet James wanted his audiences watching trusty old plays with patriotic themes, like *Henry V*, not untried Widow Ranters.

Every day there were reports of a rebel fleet gathering on the Texel across the Channel, and Penitence had decided that if nothing came of *The Widow Ranter* soon she would have to go back home. If there was going to be trouble she didn't want to be so far away from the children.

On the other hand, it would be deflating to return to the West without having appeared on stage at least once more.

She said: 'Can we please Sir George, Tom? It's so rarely we poor actresses are on the right side of a judge.'

The Lord Chief Justice was amused. They could tell by the way everybody's glass vibrated in the roar. Betterton nodded.

The conversation turned inevitably to the latest news from the Netherlands. 'Worry not your pretty heads, ladies,' said Sir George, capturing Penitence's hand again. 'If the rogue lands, we have our defences. We're watching the North-West and Scotland. Traitors and those obnoxious to the government are being rounded up.'

'The North-West?' asked Penitence, relieved. 'Monmouth won't be troubling my neck of the woods then?'

'No, no, ma'am. Lancashire, Cheshire, or Scotland is our information, if the rogue comes at all. Mistress Hughes's neck of the woods is safe — a pretty neck I'll warrant. We'll debar Monmouth from it, but may your Chief Justice see this little neck when he travels the next Assize in the South-West?'

'You are always welcome, my lord,' said Penitence. She wondered whether her cellar could cope with a visit from Sir George. She wondered if she could.

On 11 June 1685 the Duke of Monmouth made landfall near Dorset's Lyme Regis in the South-West with an expeditionary force some eighty-odd strong.

Two of the Duke's most important lieutenants fell out immediately, one shooting the other dead.

But the invaders could not be relied on to continue wiping themselves out; already Nonconformists were rallying to the Duke's Protestant banner. King James called out his standing army and alerted the Dorset, Somerset and Devon militias.

Penitence wanted to return to the Priory immediately but was persuaded against it. The rising was in Dorset, if it could be called a rising. Even if it strayed over the border into Somerset, what could the Duke do with eighty-odd men? It was only a few days until the performance of *Othello*. Would she disappoint the Lord Chief Justice, a more dangerous enemy than a thousand Monmouths?

It wasn't easy to get a coherent picture of what was happening in Somerset; some reports said the whole county was rising to join the Duke, others that he was making little impact on any but the disaffected. Ominously, there had been no word from Dorinda or anybody else at the Priory for over a week.

By the time Penitence made up her mind that whatever was happening she had to get home, she couldn't get a seat on a coach. 'All reserved for military and official personnel,' she shouted at Aphra, as if it was Aphra's fault, when she returned from the Flying Coach office. 'Monmouth's raised his banner in Taunton – *Taunton*, that's only ten miles away across King's Sedgemoor – and thousands flocking to it. The bastard's requisitioning houses and horses.'

She panicked. Monmouth would be stealing her stock. The household was starving. He'd burned the house down. They were all dead. Monmouth was a murderer, a rapist and killer of little girls. He . . .

'Calm *down*, dear,' said Aphra. 'We've not heard of anybody being hurt, not a piece of furniture splintered, there hasn't even been a battle.' She administered milk punch and common sense. 'Why not put it out of your mind – yes, I know, but *listen* – give the performance of your life on Saturday and ask our dear Lord Chief Justice to give you a chitty making you an authorized person, or whatever it is. Please him, and he'll refuse you nothing.'

Penitence began to steady. 'But I want to go home now.'

'Be sensible, dear. It's only two more days, and Monmouth's not a monster who eats little girls. Even if he was, he'd never get past Dorinda. No, no, he's just marching about.'

Penitence kissed her. 'He'd better not march over my teasels.'

Those who saw Thomas Betterton's *Othello* with Peg Hughes as Desdemona were to tell their grandchildren of it with the superiority of those confident its like would never be seen again.

'Decus et Dolor,' said Becky.

'Decus et Dolor.' She gulped a breath of the old, unique theatre smell, King's or Duke's, and entered, swishing her cloak around her, to give the last act of what she knew would be her finest – and last – performance.

For one thing, she would never surpass the heights to which she had risen this night because her greatness was due to Tom Betterton, not the other way round. She hadn't witnessed such acting before. For another, she didn't have the courage any more to face cowering in the tiring-room with a sick bowl and fighting down terror each time she stepped out from the wings. She couldn't go back to a life that was like a boxing booth, where victory over one challenger only meant that you were still on your feet to meet the next. She felt pity, as well as envy, for Duke's new luminary, Elizabeth Barry – and gratitude; the girl was beautiful and talented but had agreed to understudy her for this performance. Also she made Penitence feel old.

The tiring-room mirror was polite to her years; if there was grey in her hair, it was hidden among the blonde and her skin was lasting well. But the indefinable something that was age would mean she'd soon look ridiculous playing the part of a young bride.

And the stinkards wouldn't be slow in pointing it out. She'd forgotten the appalling strain they added to the already nerve-racking life of an actress. There they'd been, flooding into the tiring-room in the interval; another generation, as aggressive and persistent, as rude – though definitely less witty – as the courtiers of Charles. One had already called her 'Auntie' as he tried to snap her garter.

Through the throng Becky had caught her eye: 'Makes one remember Sir Hugh Middleton kindly, don't it?'

But above all what had brought home the realization that she was no longer an actress was the anxiety not only for her children, but for her house, her people and her livestock as Monmouth's army marched closer and closer to them. She offered her acting career up to God in exchange for their safety, and feared He would not find it acceptable because it was too favourable a bargain on her side.

Thanks to the presence of Sir George the fops were passably well behaved during the performance. There was absolute silence as she sang the Willow Song, except for the sobs of the Lord Chief Justice.

At the end, Betterton's hand holding hers high, she bathed for the last time in that lambent, auditory love that was the audience's applause and bade a silent 'Goodbye'.

Sir George was still weeping as he came backstage – and very aroused. 'Oh, dear creature, that I could whisk you to dinner and Paradise ... that the King had not sent for me this very moment.' He was waving a piece of paper carrying the royal seal.

She had to work fast. 'I am flattered, sir, that you have delayed to see the play out. If I have pleased you, grant me a boon.' She leaned forward so that he could look down her cleavage. There wasn't time for subtleties.

'My withers are not stone, Mistress Hughes,' he breathed wine fumes in her ear, 'they are flesh, and you have wrung them. Ask of me what you will.'

She explained, watching calculation enter his light blue pop eyes.

He said: 'Shall I lose you now I have found you? We may not dine tonight, but there is still tomorrow.' He patted her bare shoulder, and appeared to forget to lift his hot hand. 'No, no, dear lady, it is too dangerous for you to go home.'

'I can think of nothing else but my children until I can see them,' she said warningly. *You can wring your own damn withers.* She appeared to melt: 'Did you not say you will soon be entering ...' She fluttered her eyelashes. '... my, er, neck of the woods? Give me a docket to travel, my lord, that I can prepare my house against your ... *coming*.'

Out of the corner of her eye, she saw Betterton, who'd just come in, run a finger round his collar as if he found it too tight. Anne Marshall was grinning, Becky had raised her eyebrows and Elizabeth Barry was interestedly picking up points.

Sir George's mouth was wet. 'If the King commissions me to bring these rebels to book when they are caught, I shall travel the south-west circuit like the scythe of doom. Shall you fall before me too, madam?'

'My fields will be standing ready,' she whispered back. She could be ashamed of herself later. *Just give me the docket.*

She got it. He called one of his men to bring his travelling writing desk and wrote it out there and then, instructing whomsoever it concerned that Mrs Peg Hughes was to be assisted to the utmost, signed George Jeffreys, Lord Chief Justice. As he sealed it he shouted: 'Monmouth, thou standest condemned that thou didst come between this woman and myself. For that alone shall you be disembowelled when at last you face your judgement.'

Becky paused in taking off her make-up. 'And when will *that* be, my lord?' It was July now. Monmouth had been marching the South-West virtually unchecked for nearly a month.

But the Lord Chief Justice had gone, leaving his wine-flavoured saliva all over Penitence's arm.

'*Well,*' said Anne, 'talk about highway robbery.'

'So that's what they mean by "*Stand and deliver*",' said Elizabeth Barry.

'I needed the docket,' Penitence said defensively. She regretted her performance now that it had gained its end, not least its hamminess. She was aware she had promised the man more than she intended to pay, but consequences had overridden immediate need; he might die, she might die, the world could end before they met again.

'You certainly went bail for it.'

'Let's hope Sir George isn't too severe on her when she surrenders her person,' said Anne. 'They say he's got a very big Assize.'

'Oh, shut up,' said Penitence.

Even with accreditation from the Lord Chief Justice, the journey down to Somerset was a nightmare that lasted a week. The flying coaches flew only as far as Salisbury and after that she had to ride post, clinging on to the stout waist of a Bridgwater merchant who was hurrying back from Scotland to take charge of his troop of militia.

At Yeovil there was no change of post horses. The Post Office rule was that, if it had no mounts available, passengers were free to hire their own after half an hour. Penitence and the Bridgwater merchant waited half a day at the inn while its ostler made fruitless enquiries among the local farmers who were reluctant to hire out such horses as they'd managed to hide from the requisitioning agents of both King and Duke. The streets, too, were empty of horseflesh. Eventually Penitence rushed out and captured a mule and a donkey from two countrywomen on their way to market, and offered them a price they couldn't afford to turn down.

It meant parting with much of her luggage as well as the Bridgwater merchant, who was taking the mule and a different way to his home than Penitence's route. He was worried about her; they had developed the comradeship that comes to benighted travellers. As she packed her saddle-bag with a change of clothing, he knocked at her door to give her – in return for the mule – a cartridge belt, a flintlock cavalry pistol and a lesson on how to use it. 'She's old but she's trusty is Bess. See, she's rifled and can fire more than one shot. The pan-cover and steel are in one piece, here, and this is the safety catch.'

He refused to listen to Penitence's protests that she hadn't far to go, she had friends along the way, she wouldn't want to shoot anybody, that the last heard of Monmouth's army was that it was miles away, camped outside Bristol. 'War be dangerous to women, no matter which,' he said. 'If you spots Monmouth, you shoot un.'

She paid the ostler three shillings to accompany her on the remaining twelve or so miles home and set off the next morning into a July dawn. The bells of Yeovil's churches told her it was Sunday.

The ostler deserted her when they caught up with heavy royalist artillery lumbering along the Somerton road, telling her he must answer a call of nature. What made her cross was that she waited half an hour before realizing he wasn't coming back from behind his tree.

The guns were dragged by oxen and blocked the road; her difficulties in getting the little donkey past were compounded by men constantly catching its bridle so that they could eye Penitence up. They weren't so much lustful as unhappy. She

gathered that the royalist commander, Feversham, didn't understand artillery or the needs of artillerymen, would benefit
from having a round of shot stuffed up his person and what
was a pretty woman like her doing on a road like this.

They were heading for Bridgwater. Latest intelligence put
the enemy just outside it. Penitence was relieved. Bridgwater
was too near for comfort, but it was at least further away than
Taunton. With luck, the battle — if there was a battle —
wouldn't touch Athelzoy.

As soon as she could, she left the main road with its traffic
and roadblocks for the hill tracks. She was becoming tired and
desperate. She kept mishearing birdcalls as a child crying —
it was Ruperta, it was Tongs. She kicked the donkey and
rode on, blinded by the lowering sunlight as she came into it
out of trees, knowing that if she faced it she must sooner or
later come down into the Cary valley from which she could
find her way home.

All the cottages and huts she passed were shuttered. No
smoke came from their stacks, no hens scratched in the empty
runs. When she saw horsemen in the distance she took the
donkey into some trees and hid until they'd passed.

The ground began to slope consistently downwards and
the donkey stumbled. Penitence got off and walked with it,
realizing that her eyes were becoming stretched with staring
to keep the track in view. By the time she'd got down to the
Levels they had gone into sepia with the banks of the rhines
reflected as smudges in water still touched by gold and old
rose. At long last, and far away, she glimpsed Athelzoy's
church tower, its weathervane caught gold by the last ray of
sun, and sobbed with relief.

She found a path that would take her home, though slowly —
its apparent aimless meandering avoiding the quagmires that
lay in wait under the thin crust superimposed by a dry
summer. It was just possible to make out the dip it made
through the grasses, but she went ahead carefully. If the
donkey got mired she'd never get him out.

There was a crackle as of somebody lighting dry twigs, no,
letting off fireworks a long way away. It died down, started

again, became brisk; a busy, innocent sound — until she realized it was musket fire. It came from directly north but if there were twinkling lights in that direction they were difficult to distinguish from stars.

What was eerie was that the noisier it became to the north, the quieter went the marsh around her. Usually a night walk was full of the carping of frogs, the booming of bitterns and the rustle of reptilian traffic through the rushes. Now everything had stopped.

The path shimmied gently under her feet and she heard a whine, then a *crump*. Somewhere north a cannon had fired. There were more explosions, until the tremor coming up through the soles of her feet became a continual palsy. She'd heard artillery before — she'd been present when the Fleet gave Rupert a twenty-one-gun salute, and had thought then that the scream of the shell represented the terror of those it was about to fall on, just as the *keek* of the hunting owl imitated the squeak of the mouse before the talons ripped it open.

Flashes lit up part of the northern sky now — flame roaring out of cannons' mouths.

The long-promised battle between Monmouth and his uncle's army had begun.

Stop it. Stop it. You're too near my children. Damn you, go and fight somewhere else.

What puzzled her was a thin pencil of light that made a path over some willows ahead of her. It came from the direction she was aiming for. Not musket nor cannon fire, a steady beam. The Priory should be over there. It *was* the Priory.

What are they doing?

The three windows of the hall that should have been in decent obscurity shone out to make a triptych, a Christmas welcome, a beacon, an invitation cast over the moor: come and fight here, rape me.

Dorinda. I'll kill her.

Something was very wrong. To be on the safe side she led the donkey along the old track to the house, the one that led to the Ridges' farm. The farmhouse was shut up, hurdles that had once penned pigs lay on their side in the yard – in the gloom she tripped over one and grazed her ankle. From what she could see there was no other damage but the silence of a place that had always been busy with fowls and a rootling pig unnerved her and she began to run, dragging the donkey with her.

The bridge over the moat was floodlit by the hall windows and it wasn't nice to be exposed as she crossed it, the donkey's hooves making a loud, hollow reverberation. She kept her eyes away from the shapes of the yew chessmen on the north lawn in case one of them moved.

The light gave the courtyard normality. Mounting block, tubs of flowers, the lichened stone lions crouching against the steps, all reassuring. But no dogs came to greet her. No maids appeared at the windows to bob the mistress hello, no groom walked bandy-legged through the stableyard arch to take her horse ... donkey. She let go its bridle and left it by the trough, taking the pistol from its saddle-bag.

The front door swung open when she touched it and then creaked to behind her so that she had to feel her way along the screen passage until her eyes were accustomed to the dark. Heat came out of the kitchen and there was a glow from its fire reflecting on copper pots.

The girls are dead. The household was keeping vigil upstairs in the hall. The lights from the windows were candles round their catafalques. Sobbing with dread and fatigue she threw herself at the stairs and pounded up them.

All the light in the hall came from three candelabra standing on the sills of its windows, the rest was in shadow. The noise of her ascent still hung in the air and covered some other quick and furtive movement. Penitence set her back against the nearest wall and brought up the pistol while she listened. It wouldn't hold still but wavered up and down.

There was no sound now except the distant battle's. Straining, her eyes travelled from piece to piece, the black mouth of the fireplace and the portraits of Rupert against the lighter walls. *Bless him*, he *wouldn't cower in his own house*. 'Come out,' she called, making herself angry. 'I know you're there.' Her voice echoed; she wished she'd kept quiet.

Something emerged out of the fireplace and walked towards her, brushing itself down and speaking in the creamy, comforting diphthongs of the Somerset accent. 'You never did then,' said Prue Ridge.

For all her assumed nonchalance, the girl was shaking and so was Penitence. They clutched at each other's hands. 'What's happened? Where are the girls and Mistress Dorinda?'

Mistress Dorinda, it appeared, had instructed Johannes and Boller to take the two children, Annie, the Reverend Boreman and Mistress Palmer out of the danger zone a week before to stay with the Cartwrights at Crewkerne. Boller had brought back a note to say they'd arrived safely, had gone off the next day to fetch supplies from Taunton — and hadn't come back. Staff from the village had run to their homes to secrete their stock in the marshes, out of the way of army scavengers.

It took time to learn these things, mainly because Penitence relaxed when she knew the little girls were safe and didn't catch all that Prue said. Then again, Prue thought Penitence knew more than she did. 'Miss Dorinda and Mudge gone looking for un.'

Who? Who had they gone looking for? Where? When? Why?

'This minute gone.' Prue didn't know the name of the person seached for: 'She couldn't rest still. 'Twas her man seemingly.'

What man? Who had been so important as to lure her friend and this girl's brother out into the marsh when they heard the noise of gunfire?

The bombardment had increased and the crackle of musket fire sounded as if the marshes were burning. She went to the windows; the flickering in the northern sky was like lightning that didn't go away. She began to blow out candles, but Prue stopped her: 'I was to keep they alight so's if they missed un he'd find the place.'

'"Her man" . . . MacGregor? You can't mean MacGregor?' Oh God, MacGregor had been in the Netherlands; he *couldn't* have been so silly as to join Monmouth's invasion.

Prue shrugged. But, yes, the man referred to was in the battle. She slapped the side of her head, her face clearing, then started to undo her shoe. *It's been too much for her*. But Prue was producing a letter that had been tucked under her foot. 'She said show ut you when you came.'

It wasn't from Dorinda to her, it was a letter from MacGregor to Dorinda, the one they'd quarrelled over when Barnzo brought it across the marshes from Taunton. At the top it said: 'On the island of Texel'.

It was very short, dated 14 May, nearly a month and a half ago. 'Dear Wife', it began:

> The lad is determined on it: I would have told all to his unknowing father trusting him to be as inclined as ourselves to wish his son's retreat from this business of Monmouth but my lord Henry King has left the Netherlands. All the caution the boy will use is to call himself by the name of Hurd. Stay by his mother at the Priory as I shall stay by the lad when we get to England to direct him in need. We are committed to the venture now. Pray the Lord He smiles on the Duke's endeavour so that you and I be reunited in life before we are in Heaven. But as He wills. Yr loving husband, Donal MacGregor.

For a second her mind drew back as if full understanding would scald it. The Duke was the Duke of Monmouth. Did he mean Henry King was the unknowing father? Because if he did . . .

'There, there, my 'andsome. Don't take on so.' Prue Ridge was holding her on to a stool with one hand and waving a smouldering taper under her nose with the other.

'M-my-s-ss-son,' said Penitence, 'I have a s-sson.'

'That's what 'twas then,' nodded Prue. 'Would un be a Benedick? Iss fay, she mentioned a Benedick. Would MacGregor be his pappy?'

Penitence shook her head. Her lips had gone so stiff she had difficulty enunciating. 'He's D-Dorinda's husband. They were very f-ffond of Benedick.' *My son, my son*. She began to get up but Prue stopped her. 'Where be going?'

'My son. He came with Mon-monmouth. He's out there.'

'Iss and a thousand others with un. You'll never find un.'

'Neither will Dorinda.'

'Mebbe not,' Prue said, truthfully, 'but she made a . . . a rendezvous, she called it. Mudge'd told her to tell her man if he ever got lost on the moor to make for the west side of the Poldens and turn south. That's where they gone, I reckon.'

Penitence's knuckles pressed against her cheeks. She was trying to comprehend the chaos of a battle but could only see the dear body of her child amongst those throbbing lights and knew there must be a thousand impediments to her son finding his way to the Priory – death, for one. 'It's hopeless.'

Prue shook her head: 'There's Mudge with her.'

Penitence seized on the girl's faith because there was no other counter to despair. She built on the flimsy optimism: 'And Dorinda's been sensible.' For if you were lost on the moor you could always see the Poldens – not very high hills by normal standards, but on this flat terrain they stood out like a mountain range – and if you made for the western side of the Poldens and turned south you would be unlucky not to see the light from the Priory hall windows eventually.

She stood up. To keep busy might, just, keep her sane. 'We'll get bandages ready,' she said, 'and food. And tell me everything.'

She tried to concentrate to keep her mind away from the battle; even so she kept losing the thread. Eventually, however, chronology and events and personalities became linked into some sort of coherence.

Three weeks before, practically the entire population of Athelzoy and the marsh villages had crossed the ten-mile causeway to Taunton to look on this son of Charles II who had come to challenge his Papist uncle and raise the Protestant rebellion standard in the market square.

It had been difficult to glimpse him, Prue said, so great was the crowd that had come in from all over the countryside. Dressed in purple with a silver star on his breast, he was besieged by people trying to kiss his hand and shouting 'A Monmouth! A Monmouth! The Protestant Religion!' Prue had listened to his 'Declaration' read aloud by cryers. There had been some interesting bits, as when the Duke accused King James of having burned down London and murdered King Charles. But it was very long and when Prue asked one of the men standing by what it meant, he said: 'We come to fight Papists', which it was a pity the Declaration hadn't said in the first place.

Then twenty-seven girls from the town school — 'little Rachel Yeo was there,' Prue said, proudly — had made a pretty procession and presented the Duke with a flag they had sewn themselves.

Men had come from all over the county to enlist. So many, said Prue, that she thought the whole world must be for Monmouth. 'Five or six thousand foot and a thousand horse, people do say.'

But the next Sunday Sir Ostyn Edwards, JP, had ridden over to tell the Athelzoy congregation that it mustn't aid the Duke with men or food. '. . . and if us did we'd be traitors to our lawful king. None of the gentry were joining him, Magistrate Edwards said, and we mu'n't neither. But after he'd gone comes Master Hughes to the village cross and says the good old cause of God and religion as had lain dead is risen again. And who cared what the gentry did anyhow.'

Martin Hughes. Benedick and Martin Hughes. How strange that two such dissimilar relatives should be on the same side; the fanatical old man from conviction; but what could have tempted the young one to Monmouth? Romance, of course. And love of a fight. She heard Dudley's voice saying that Benedick wanted to join an army, *any* army.

Her son would almost welcome that the cause was lost as long as he fought for it; he would see himself as another Rupert. *Oh, Benedick, why didn't you tell me?*

She went to the window and held on to the sill, feeling it vibrate with the percussion of the guns. *I've been here before.* A long time ago she had stood at a window, just as helpless. Then, as now, it was to Dorinda that she'd had to entrust her son's safety. *I thought it was I who'd changed while she stayed the same. But all I did was become rich. I haven't been paying attention.*

It was Dorinda who'd paid attention to the people who mattered where she had let them go, too busy — as Dorinda had said — to find out what they were feeling.

MacGregor's letter to Dorinda had argued a depth to their marriage that Penitence had never guessed at. Never tried to. It was Dorinda who had kept in closer touch with Benedick, through MacGregor's frequent visits to the radical exiles in Holland, than she had. Dorinda had known it was in her son's mind to sail with Monmouth, and tried to change it.

A moth singed by one of the candle flames fluttered on to the back of Penitence's hand and she stared at it. *I don't know what to do. I don't even know what to do with this moth.* It rolled off her hand to the floor and she turned away.

Together they tore up an old sheet for bandages and prepared soup. Prue was full of her own and Mudge's cleverness in having concealed so much of the harvest from 'they old wreckers', as she called army requisitioners. Her complaint was against James's men, who had occupied the area when the Duke had marched off towards Bristol and done little to endear themselves by demanding, then forcibly taking, supplies. The Duke's quartermasters, on the other hand, hadn't had to requisition food; it had been brought to them in cartloads, flocks, herds — a gift from the common people of Somerset to their Protestant saviour.

She had thought she knew what her village thought and did, but she suspected Prue's narrative of concealing that many of its men had joined Monmouth, or certainly sympathized with him. *I didn't pay attention.*

The candles in the windows were low and they fetched others to replace them. They burned without flickering in the heavy air but there was a tremor to the flame. The noise of bombardment was getting louder and it seemed to Penitence that she could distinguish out of it the racket of drums and trumpets.

'How far away is it, do you think?'

Prue joined her. 'Five mile. Six. I reckon 'tis round about Chedzoy.' For the first time her self-possession gave way. 'If you get killed, Barnabas Turvey, don't you come crying to me.'

509

'Barnabas?'

'Chedzoy chapel,' wailed Prue, 'and a girt fool. Couldn't wait for Monmouth to get to Taunton, oh no. Has to leave his tidy little loom in Chedzoy and tramp all the way to Chard to enlist.'

'Nice lad?' Penitence put an arm around the girl's shoulders.

'I seen worse,' sobbed Prue. 'What for do they do ut, Leddyship? Eh? Answer me that.'

'I don't know.' Young men, perhaps Benedick, perhaps Barnabas, had their limbs blown apart. Wheatfields were trampled and soaked in blood. All the good, growing things mangled because somebody thought their religion better than somebody else's. *I did once.* And then she had met Her Ladyship, and come to know Dorinda and the Cock and Pie, and found that, basically, it didn't matter what you believed as long as you didn't hurt people and you let the corn grow. *Stop it. Stop it.*

It was impossible to stay still. She went out and led the donkey round to the farmyard, fed and stabled him. She walked down the driveway to the gates, her eyes checking but not registering the dark rows of young chestnuts which would one day line its avenue.

She stood, keeping her eyes away from the flashes so that her sight could distinguish between the blacks and not-so-blacks of the near moorland, trying to hear local sound beneath the barrage. The moon was coming up; she could see the outline of the Poldens against the sky. *Make for them. Come home and be safe.*

She couldn't bear to watch any more. She turned round and went slowly back to the house.

Chapter 3

THE NIGHT was so long that Penitence kept taking out Rupert's time-piece and shaking it, believing it had stopped, until it did. She fell asleep and woke up to find she was clutching the time-piece to her chest. Prue was still standing at the window. 'Ladyship.'

Penitence went to stand beside her. The artillery had stopped, though sounds of musketry had become widespread. And the sky had changed, losing the deepest layer of black. 'Dawn.'

They went out into the expectant air of a July dawn, crossed the moat and went down to the gates. Firing was much closer now and they could see the occasional tiny stabs of light that went with it. The first scream they thought was an owl's until it lasted too long. There were others, shouts and splashings, travelling easily over the flatness from differing distances.

Cordite tinged the air which grew lighter until the landscape revealed itself as if dipped in milk; white at the bottom where the mist was thick and then in opaque gradations so that the top branches of willow and alder stuck up like flat scenery artistically arranged between a muslin haze. It was going to be a beautiful day.

The sharp kik-kik-kik of a water-rail in the reeds woke up the land birds in the Priory trees. A marsh harrier began quartering his hunting ground, waiting for the mist to clear.

With the birdsong came the ragged shouts of men, still some way off but unmistakably swearing in panic.

'Where are they?' It was like being marooned on a mountain top trying to penetrate cloud cover below them.

'Heading for Scaup rhine,' said Prue. They couldn't see the men, only the dislodgement of the haze made by their running. What they could see was the horsemen who chased them because eerily, almost ridiculously, the horsemen's hats were the only things visible. Ten or so hats, mostly brown, one black with a high feather, zigzagged through the marsh like hounds. Once a sabre rose up above the haze to gleam in the dawn sun before it flashed down. There was a scream.

Giggling even as she wept, Prue said: 'Which is which?'

'It doesn't matter.' It only mattered that the hidden foxes should escape those dreadful, millinery hounds. Even if it was

Benedick under one of those hats, she still prayed that the men he was chasing got away.

The mist was clearing and the bank of the rhine was high so that they could see the running men as they topped the bank and fell down into the trench of fog on the other side. 'So many.' Twenty or so. They were too far away to distinguish faces, for which Penitence was always glad, but they could see the fear. They could tell that one didn't attempt the bank but ran along it, because the figure of a cavalryman bobbed in a horizontal direction on his invisible horse until his sabre swept in a beautiful movement along the line of his gallop. They saw him come trotting back.

The cavalrymen dismounted and ran to the top of the bank. This time they had pistols in their hands.

'Oh no,' said Prue, ''tis too deep.' The men in the rhine would be dragged down by mud, trying to climb up, slipping, clawing. She began to jump up and down shouting, 'Leave un be.'

'They won't.' They were too far away to hear Prue's light voice anyway. Still Penitence joined her, waving her arms, yelling, because if it was useless, it was also against nature not to protest.

The cavalrymen used the men in the ditch for target practice. They made an elegant frieze along the bank, perfectly etched now in the sun that had burned away the mist, taking aim, once or twice pointing out an escaper to each other.

Penitence dragged Prue away as the shots began.

The two of them ventured back out of the gates when the firing was over. If the royal army had won the battle, two of the men in the ditch might be Benedick and MacGregor. *Whoever* had won the battle, there might be somebody still alive in the rhine.

But though the cavalrymen had gone, the Levels were busy and they didn't dare venture into them. Here and there knots of mounted men rode the causeways. Sometimes they dismounted to slash at clumps of reeds with their sabres. Every hut and haystack on the marshes was burning. Once, the two women saw a line of men roped around the neck being driven

512

north along the Taunton causeway. *At least they're taking prisoners. But who's taking who prisoner?*

The morning wore on while they dithered and did nothing until it became afternoon. 'I can't bear it. I'm saddling the damn donkey. I'll ride over to Ostyn's. I've got to know.'

Together they went towards the farm, Prue protesting it was dangerous to go. Then she said: 'There's some'un behind us.'

They had come the old way to the farmyard rather than up the house drive; it was quicker. Behind them the deep ruts of the track disappeared round a bend dappled with cowpats and the shadow of leaves. As Penitence listened she heard a dislodged stone rattle away from a foot. 'Get into the trees.'

But lumbering round the bend with a body across his shoulders was Mudge. The body's dark hanging hair hid its face and funnelled blood down Mudge's jacket but Penitence knew who it was. She ran to him. 'Thank you, Mudge. Oh, Mudge, oh Mudge, thank you.'

She steadied her son's head as Mudge lowered his body on to the track. 'Is he all right?' She could see he wasn't. Around his forehead a piece of lace she recognized as the bottom of one of Dorinda's petticoats had dislodged and was allowing blood to seep out of a wound that had torn across the back of his head. His skin was yellow-white.

'He'll live.' Mudge straightened and put his hands to the small of his back. 'He's a tidy weight.'

'Where did you find him? Is Dorinda with you? Where's MacGregor?'

'Miracle 'twas.' Mudge addressed his sister. 'There's King's men all over but the man MacGregor'd got un in a dip on Yancy Hill. Miss Dorinda weren't pleased we had to go so far. "I told you further south, you ballocker," she says to her man as she kissed un and he smiled like, then he fainted. Broken ribs, I reckon.'

'Who won, Mudge?' On reflection it was a stupid question. If Monmouth had won MacGregor and Benedick could have stayed on the battlefield and waited for the ambulance carts instead of dragging themselves to a dip in the Polden hills.

'The Devil,' Mudge told her. He kissed his sister. 'Can 'ee drag the boy from here? I'd better get back before the patrols get un other two. Miss Dorinda can't manage alone.'

'Be careful, Mudge. Thank you, Mudge.'

Penitence didn't even watch him go, and didn't allow Prue to, but called her to put Benedick's arm round her shoulders and help her get him to the house. He was completely unconscious and his weight was fearful; he'd grown. The toes of his boots dragged wavy lines in the dust of the track. Once across the other side of the moat, the women had to prop him on the bench inside the gatehouse tunnel while they rested.

They'd reached half-way across the courtyard when they heard hooves trotting up the drive. Prue began to pull towards the hall door, but Penitence pulled to the left. 'In here, in here.' The north wing door was nearest and stood open. Doubled up under their burden, they almost fell over the threshold and Penitence kicked the door shut behind her.

'Upstairs. Quickly. Quickly.' Whoever it was would try the hall first – the more impressive door and the first to be seen on entering the courtyard. She had her son's hands in hers now and was hauling him from above while Prue pushed from below.

Benedick's boots caught on every rise with a loud click but the sounds of hooves and voices in the courtyard covered it – whoever it was, there were a lot of them. The door to her bedroom was only a yard away now. The staircase was narrow but, thank God, well polished.

The men were in the house now. Even from here she could hear boots and spurs in the screen passage and somebody shouting in the name of the King.

'Go round,' she panted to Prue. 'Go round the hall way so they don't think you've come from here. Keep them there. Offer them ale.'

'Wreckers took that last week.' Prue let go Benedick's legs and squeezed past him up the stairs to the tortuous passage that eventually bent round to run between the hall and solar to the stairs.

'Offer them anything. I need a few minutes.'

'They'll look under the bed,' Prue warned her.

Not behind it. 'Go, for God's sake. Before they come up.'

How she did it, she never knew. Later that day she was hobbling from lifting a weight half as much again as her own on to her bed, clambering through the panel, then pulling the body through after her. At the time she didn't notice pain. She had to do it anyhow, no time to consider the boy's wound. The elegant frieze of figures standing on the bank of a rhine taking aim at men floundering below kept moving through her mind. *They'll shoot him.* She tugged fiercely at her son, furious at him, ready to kill for him, until his legs scraped over the sill and they both fell backwards on to the floor of the secret room.

No time to see him comfortable. Even above the sound of her own panting she could hear boots coming along the corridor towards her bedroom and Penitence's voluble protests: 'Her Ladyship's sleeping.'

Penitence dived for the square of light that was the opening in the bedhead, got herself through, squirmed round and dragged the panel back. It clicked into place, she got off the bed, the bedroom door opened – all simultaneously.

She patted bits of her dress and herself into place, and the man who came through the door saw her do it. *But that's all right. If I'd just woken up I'd do the same.* It was an actress's response: yes, my character would do that. She knew she was going to have to act to the top of her bent for this man.

He was bleach-haired, thirty-odd, not bad-looking and he didn't believe anything; not that the earth went round the sun, not that the sun went round the earth, not in God, not in non-belief. From the moment Penitence set eyes on Nevis she knew he lived in a vacuum.

'Major Peter Nevis, mistress.' His eyes roamed the room before resting on her: 'Search it.'

So exactly did the last words match the tone of his greeting that she thought he was addressing them to her but, as he said them, two soldiers leaped forward and pushed her out of the way to kick open her clothes press, tear down paintings, overturn her mirror and shake out the contents of her scent bottles and powder boxes. While one ripped through the bed-hangings with his sword the other dived under the bed and came up with the chamber pot, shaking it over the floor and then, as if disappointed it was empty, throwing it against the wall, where it broke.

She remained calm. *Would my character remain calm?* It would have to; she was shaking too hard with relief at having got Benedick hidden to simulate anger. Anyway, the destruction was being perpetrated less as a search – who would hide in a scent bottle? – than to get her frightened. And this much she already knew: if she showed fear to Major Peter Nevis he'd want more.

She showed dignity instead. 'And why is this being done?'

'Guess.' He was tossing robes out of her clothes press with the end of his sword, idly, not looking at them. His eyes were directed at the bed.

'I guess it is because you are a lout, sir.'

'Not a bad guess.' He sidled over to the bed and sat on it with his sword point-down to the floor between his knees and his hands crossed on its hilt. 'But my guess is you're hiding somebody, Mistress . . .?' He raised an interrogative eyebrow.

'Hughes.'

'Mistress Hughes. In fact I know you are. A man carrying another was seen coming up this rise from the marsh.'

Is that all? There was some abatement to her terror. 'Oh well,' she said with sarcasm, 'that proves it. He wouldn't have been going to the village, or the church, or the farm, he'd have been coming here. What an idiotic fellow you are.' Play the grand lady, the royalist, make him ashamed of suspecting her, *her*, of hiding a rebel.

'Yes,' said Major Nevis, 'he would. You see, Mistress Hughes, I have a wonderful instinct. The Arabs used to say I had a third ear. That may be because I cut off so many of theirs, of course, but I like to think it was because I hear the things people aren't saying.'

His left hand was feeling in the rumpled bedclothes. 'For instance, the first thing your abigail didn't say to me when she met us in the hall was that she had something to hide. Now you aren't telling me you are concealing someone.'

He had wonderful instinct right enough, but he wasn't sure. *And I'm an actress.* She could feel his mind probing her stance, looking for weakness and disconcerted at not finding any. Time to bring in the big guns. 'Fellow,' she said, 'you will regret this nonsense when I tell Lord Chief Justice Jeffreys of it.'

'Tell the King while you're about it, mistress.'

'I could,' she said, 'I know him too.'

He brought his hand out from the bedcovers and sniffed it. 'And explain to the King why there's fresh blood in your bed?'

Her toes curled with the effort not to show shock. She'd dragged Benedick to the bed, then climbed on it and hauled him so that his head and trunk rested across it while she got the panel open. *That's when the blood went on the covers*; after that she'd put a pillow over the two sills and sledged him through on it. He'd bled on the pillow as well, but by the mercy of God she'd just had time to put it between his head and the floor of the secret room.

'You humiliate me, Major, if you force me to explain what happens to women at certain times of the month.' She ought to blush but her face was bloodless. It might shame him.

It didn't. He nodded — more at an opponent scoring a hit than if he believed her. She braced herself. He was capable of having her stripped to make sure she was menstruating.

Slowly, like a puppet's, his head began to turn to the left as if it was being drawn to consider the bedhead. He brought up his sword and casually began digging its point into bits of the carving and flicking it out again. Penitence stood frozen, unable to think, just watching as the swordpoint went into the eye of a hare, then flicked off the nose of a dachshund, stabbed Adam's navel, waiting for the inevitable when it pierced Eve's nipple.

There was an altercation at the door; somebody shouting, Nevis's lieutenant was shouting back. She heard the word 'wounded'. *Pay attention to them, not Eve.* The man had powers but perhaps she could will them towards something else. *Not Eve. Not my son.*

He was looking at her. 'I'm going to find him, Mistress Hughes. Wherever he is, I'm going to find him.'

And she believed him.

'Bring her down.' He stood up and went out of the door, and the soldiers took Penitence's arms and marched her after him.

In the courtyard a standard hung above the archway of the gatehouse tunnel painted with the Paschal Lamb. Beneath it, two horses were coming in, the wheels of the cart they pulled still sounding on the bridge. Sir Ostyn Edwards in the red and yellow uniform of the Devon and Somerset Militia was striding ahead of it, shaking his fist at Major Nevis: 'I ain't leaving the wounded waiting in that dang marsh no more. Fly-blown, poor 'andsomes. They needs good water and good women to nurse un.' He turned to Penitence: 'Ain't that so, Mistress Hughes? Good water and good women.'

She could have kissed him. 'Bring them in, Sir Ostyn.'

Mollified, the magistrate gestured to red-and-yellow-clad soldiers to start lifting down the men who lay in the cart and the one behind it, grumbling to Penitence and the world in general as he did so. ' "Wait" he says. "There's rebels in that house," he says. "May be Monmouth," he says. "Wait 'til I go and ferret un out," he says.' He turned on Major Nevis, looking like a gaudy bantam cockerel. 'And I told you Mistress Hughes was a good friend to Prince Rupert hisself and as like to shelter Monmouth or his rebels as my arse.'

Major Nevis addressed his lieutenant: 'Nobody to go in the house until you've finished searching, Captain. After that nobody to go in the house without they're accompanied by you or Canto.'

'Yes, sir.' Nevis's lieutenant had long black hair, olive skin and an earring but he looked capable. *Of anything*, thought Penitence.

'I'll be back.' Major Nevis swung himself up into his saddle and rode out with his mounted troop behind him. He hadn't so much ignored Sir Ostyn as seemed unaware of his existence.

The magistrate shook his fist after him. 'I'll write to the King, iss fay. Just because we'm militia, don't mean you can treat us any old way.' He nudged Penitence and repeated, 'Just because we'm militia.'

But Penitence was watching the major doff his hat in a salute to the standard hanging from the gatehouse as he rode under it, or rather, she watched the hat. It was black and had a high feather. It had been predominant among the hats that had hunted down the men in the mist that morning.

'Good riddance to un.' Sir Ostyn wiped his top lip with a hand that shook, and Penitence knew it had taken courage even for a magistrate to stand up to Major Nevis.

'Who is he?'

'Colonel Kirk's second-in-command. One o' the Lambs.' At her incomprehension he jerked his head towards the standard embroidered with the Paschal Lamb. 'See them colours? Never thought I'd see men scared of a danged sheep but that un'd frighten its own side, never mind the enemy. Kirk and Nevis, just back from the garrison in Tangier. Ask me, they've learned nasty ways from they danged Tangerines. Very nasty. Still, the King do love un.' He turned to his wounded who were being helped off the carts. 'Well, Jem, there's a cut to be proud of. Missus would have complained if ut was an inch higher, I reckon.'

Nevis's second-in-command, a lieutenant with the unlikely name of Jones, interpreted his superior's orders meticulously; Prue was only allowed to enter the house under guard, Penitence wasn't allowed in at all, and the wounded lay on the cobbles of the courtyard in full sun all the afternoon. More and more injured were brought to the Priory gates as word spread that it had been designated the casualty post for the southern end of the Levels.

'You thank God it's royal troops mostly down yere,' Sir Ostyn told her. 'Up by Weston Zoyland they got all the injured rebels in the churchyard. Thousands, they do say.'

'How do they know which is which?' she asked furiously. Not all the militia were in uniform, having run straight from their fields and jobs to answer the call to arms. Blood mixed with mud rendered it impossible to tell the original colour of the cloth Penitence cut away from wounds that day. Army, militia, rebel, they were all suffering. She got up from her knees to face Lieutenant Jones: 'Will you let me go to my room for more bandages?'

He surprised her: 'Yes.' He chewed tobacco — a habit she hadn't come across before. When he smiled, as he did now, his teeth were tan-coloured. He spoke very little, probably so as not to betray a foreign accent, but he listened a lot. As she'd bent over a dying man to catch his last words, Lieutenant Jones was there, catching them too. Soothing a patient's head with a cold cloth, her arm was obstructed by Lieutenant Jones as he listened to the delirious babblings.

'Good.' She pushed past him to the north door, found he was going with her and changed direction to go in by the hall instead. The Tudor wing stairs might have blood on them.

She strode ahead, desperate. She begrudged nothing to the men she was nursing, except that her own son lay without help a few yards away. This was the first time she'd been permitted to enter her house since . . . she looked back over her shoulder and saw that it was evening sun lighting up the screen passage . . . since midday. Prue had been allowed in, but always under guard. Even had Prue known how to enter the secret room she was too closely watched to help Benedick. The girl looked as desperate as Penitence felt; on top of the worry for Benedick was the anxiety for Mudge, Dorinda and MacGregor out on the marshes. The activity around the Priory would warn them not to come close, but on the other hand where could they hide? Royal troops were scouring the Levels for fleeing rebels. Every so often some half-dead scare-crow was flung into the courtyard to be patched up by the doctors before being marched off to the prison carts.

If she had not lived through the Plague and seen what it did to the human body, Penitence would have been no use to the men who lay in rows across her courtyard. Prue had kept retching each time the surgeons uncovered an anemone-coloured bit of bowel or liver or revealed a piece of bone glistening white among the blood. Penitence, fighting sickness herself, had kept her busy fetching water from the pump.

Flies were attracted by the stench and heat. There was no shade. Time and again, Penitence appealed to Lieutenant Jones to let his soldiers take the men into the cool of the hall but he refused.

She was trying to bandage a stomach wound when some militia soldiers began dragging her patient away towards their cart. 'He's a Monmouth, Ladyship,' explained their sergeant, pointing to the white cockade pinned to the man's jacket.

'He's hurt,' she screamed. The sergeant – a local man, she knew his face from somewhere – was not unsympathetic. 'Better let me have un, Ladyship.' He cocked his head towards the mild woolly shape sewn on the standard over the archway. 'He's a rebel dog, but tid'n pretty to see dogs torn by Lambs. That old boy Nevis, he don't take prisoners.'

His subordinates didn't leave stones unturned either. As Penitence passed through her house she couldn't see a chair standing upright. Cupboard doors were off their hinges, every tapestry cut from its pole. All the portraits, even the two of Rupert, lay face-down in the hall.

But the greatest destruction was in her bedroom. Nevis had returned to it to inflict more. Her down quilt had been stabbed so that the place was snowed with feathers. Her needlework which had been stretched on a frame by the window was slashed across and across.

The devastation had a message. Nevis's instinct was telling him the room concealed something. It was also a display of sexual hatred; her shifts and under-petticoats had been hung from the tester rail of the bed and a hole gouged out from the front of each skirt at pelvic level. Most serious from her point of view was the door's smashed lock which stopped her from securing it.

Lieutenant Jones's dark eyes were on her face to see how she reacted. She almost forgot to – she could only think of the boy in his hiding-place. He could have bled to death or choked on vomit. He'd been in darkness without food or drink for over four hours.

It was an effort to keep her eyes away from the bedhead. It was an effort not to pick up a torn piece of wood from her tapestry stand and stab the leering pig to death. *They'd hear if he screamed*. It was her only reason for not doing it.

The bandages from her medicine chest were spilled on the floor. As she gathered them up she caught a glimpse of her face in a shard of her looking-glass. It was dirty. Now she came to think of it, she hadn't done anything to her appearance since she left the inn at Yeovil ... incredulously she counted back ... only yesterday morning.

God damn them all. I'll be clean if the skies fall. 'Will you leave while I wash?' she asked.

She glimpsed his brown teeth as he spat. Deliberately, she went to her toilet cupboard and washed. She balanced the sliver of glass on her scored dressing-table, searched among the wreckage for her hairbrush, righted a stool and sat down to brush her hair.

'You want change your robe I don't mind.' Lieutenant Jones's voice insinuated down from somewhere above her head. He was behind her. She could feel the heat of his groin against the back of her neck.

Will it help Benedick if I do this? It's how I saved him once before. She calculated. Was there the remotest possibility that this man would allow her to tend to Benedick for services rendered? *No.* Her body wasn't sufficient incentive now for a man like this to betray his superiors for long. She studied the dark eyes reflected in the mirror and knew they had looked on excesses she couldn't even think of. Benedick was better off dying unconscious in his hole than in the hands of this man.

'Get away from me,' she said.

For a moment she rested her head in her hands, her fingers threading her hair. How had all this happened in a *day*? This was war, then, this thing arbitrated by other people, those poor men out there, her son dying in his hole, this sudden collapse of all structure, this lady of the manor transformed back to actress and then to calculating whore.

Hooves clattered in the courtyard and Jones moved over to the window to see, then jerked a thumb at her. 'Down. Now.' He was suddenly in a hurry.

She began gathering up ointment jars from the floor in the hope that he'd lose patience and go without her. He lost patience but drew his sword instead. 'Down.' Hastily, she swept jars and bandages into her apron and preceded the man down the stairs.

'Evacuate this place. Get these men down to the ambulance carts.' It was Major Nevis's voice. Some of his soldiers were already joining the militia doctors in carrying stretchers across the bridge.

Not until she saw him again did Penitence realize what fear Nevis had left in her. His figure on his horse was outlined against a glorious sunset — and turned it grey. She might cope with everyone else to bring herself and her son out of this situation intact — Sir Ostyn, bless him, the lustful Jones, even Monmouth if he found his way here — but Captain Nevis was beyond anything that she could manage. He had no bounds.

The men with him were of similar, though paler, stamp. Uniformed, they still gave the impression of irregulars: thinner, quicker, more wolfish than standing army soldiers.

Jones crossed the courtyard, stepping over the stretchers, and his commander bent down so that the man could whisper in his ear. *Is it about me?* The men surrounding Nevis's horse were fixing bayonets. The click of the knives fitting into the muzzle of muskets brought up the head of each man in the courtyard capable of lifting it.

With Jones leading the way Major Nevis, still mounted, followed to one of the wounded lying in the shade of one of Penitence's flower urns. Their men came behind, lifting their feet like cats to avoid the bodies stretched on the cobbles. She heard Jones say: 'He's one.'

It was the wounded man who'd been delirious and babbling while she cooled his forehead and Jones listened. She'd known even then that he was a rebel who'd been mistaken and brought in for a royalist soldier — he'd kept raving of 'King Monmouth' as she tried to hush him and hope that Jones didn't understand his thick Somersetshire.

She watched Nevis nod, saw the right elbows of two of his men crook as they brought up their muskets, then straighten. She saw the bayonets go into the body of the man at their feet, and still didn't believe what had happened. The steel went in so easily. There'd been just a twitch then, again so easily, the man was dead.

Penitence found herself running forward. 'What are you doing? He was *alive.*' Sir Ostyn was behind her, backing her up. 'You varlet, you villain. I protest, sir.'

'Do you?' asked Nevis. 'The man was a rebel. Perhaps a spy.'

'You dog, sir,' shouted a militia surgeon from the other side of the courtyard. 'He was entitled to trial.'

'Trial?' said Nevis. 'You want a trial?' He was looking towards the gatehouse. The setting sun was shining through its tunnel in an arch of orange light that made the eye blink. Black figures stood against it, one dumpy and still with a distorted collar round its neck and what looked like a lead snaking upwards from it.

Penitence couldn't make it out. But from the other side of the courtyard she heard Prue gasp: 'Barnzo. Barnzo, what they doing to ee?' She watched the girl run into the light and be pushed to the ground by one of the guarding figures.

Penitence turned to the man on the horse. 'It's Barnzo,' she said, as if he'd know.

Nevis's voice was negligent but it carried into the silence. 'Stands accused of obstructing His Majesty's soldiers when they were searching the village for rebels and of shouting epithets against the King. Ask the prisoner if he has anything to say, Harris.'

There were villagers on the other side of the moat. From his height Penitence recognized Jack Fuller, who was the tallest man in Athelzoy and Barnzo's father.

'He says Bur, bur, bur, sir,' called back Harris, and somebody laughed.

It was a trick of Major Nevis that as he talked he looked elsewhere than at the person he was addressing until his last sentence. He did it now, turning his head as if considering the upper windows that looked down at him from three sides. 'Anything to say in this man's defence, Mistress Hughes? Like who was being carried up this rise this morning and by whom?' Now he looked at her. 'And where he is now?'

He's trying to make me an accomplice. The sun through the tunnel turned the gatehouse entrance into a proscenium arch against which actors stood in perfect, black silhouette. *It's a play. It isn't real.* She said: 'He's a simpleton. You can't hang him. Please don't.' It wasn't the right line. Too feeble. *It is a play. But it's real.* Even if she could trade Benedick's life for Barnzo's, she had no right to trade Mudge's.

Nevis nodded to the silhouettes around Barnzo and Penitence shut her eyes. She heard the screams from Prue and the villagers.

When she opened her eyes again the silly round face of the Paschal Lamb looked down on a bundle that swung beneath its embroidered hooves. Beneath them both carts with wounded were trundling across the bridge and down the drive. On the other side of the moat the relief of villagers was kneeling, all except Jack Fuller who stood upright and still.

A shocked Ostyn Edwards lectured Nevis. 'No harm in that poor soul, 'twas sheer cruelty to hang un. I'm going to report you to the King.'

Nevis stretched. 'You're going to take the wounded to Taunton.'

Penitence said quickly: 'Don't leave me, Sir Ostyn.' The thought of being alone with Nevis terrified her.

'I won't, maid,' he said stoutly. 'I take my orders from the Duke of Somerset and from the Duke of Somerset only.'

'Captain Sir Ostyn Edwards?' said Nevis.

'I am, sir.'

'In charge of the Cary Valley troop of the Somerset Militia?'

'And proud of it, sir.' Sir Ostyn put his arm around Penitence.

'Ordered by Commander Feversham four days ago to destroy the bridge over the rhine at Chedzoy so as to deny it to the enemy and still deliberating on how to do it when the enemy crossed it yesterday?' Nevis's eyes regarded the sky.

'T'wasn't . . .' Penitence felt Sir Ostyn's stout arm slacken.

'Mistook a hollow tree trunk in a hedge for artillery and called on his men to retreat, as it turned out, into real enemy fire?'

Sir Ostyn's arm dropped away from Penitence's shoulders.

'Poured rapid fire into advancing enemy all night to discover when dawn broke that he'd peppered the sails of Somerton windmill?'

Sir Ostyn said nothing.

At last Nevis looked at him. '*Now* fuck off to Taunton.'

Lieutenant Jones and some of the Lambs lined up to cheer a destroyed Sir Ostyn as he and his troop disappeared into the last of the sun underneath Barnzo's still-hanging body.

Penitence tried to remember where she'd put the Bridgwater merchant's pistol. She was going to be raped or killed, probably both. Her death would mean Benedick's. She had never felt so frightened but if she could remember where she'd put her pistol she'd go down fighting. She was as terrified for Prue as for herself and her son; the girl didn't deserve what was going to happen to her now. Nobody deserved what was going to happen . . . *In the kitchen chimney*. That was it. She'd become irritated as it clanked against her knees while she'd helped Prue prepare soup during the long hours of waiting for Dorinda to come back.

Stay away. At the thought of Dorinda, Penitence felt tears come to her eyes. *Keep safe. But I wish you were here. You and me together*.

Leaning over the pot she'd felt the pistol hit her knees again and had put it on the sooty shelf inside the chimney. If Nevis's men hadn't thought to look in the chimney, it was still there.

She heard a whimper. Prue had been pushed into the middle of the courtyard in a circle of soldiers.

Penitence staggered as the shoulder of Nevis's horse nudged her forward. She looked up. Nevis's hands were on the pommel of his saddle. He was apparently riveted by the condition of his horse's right ear. 'There's two ways of doing this, Mistress Hughes.'

'I'm not hiding anybody,' she said, and knelt down. 'Please, sir, please, I'm not hiding anybody.' She had turned liquid with fear. There wasn't anything she wouldn't do if he would only not let happen what he was going to let happen.

'One way,' he said, 'is to give your abigail to my men until you tell me where and who you're hiding.' He smiled and

526

turned his head so that he looked at her. 'Or I can set fire to the house.'

'Please,' she said, 'please.'

From somewhere came anger. An odd, almost unrelated anger, for the reduction decent people suffered at the hands of monsters like this man on the horse above her.

How dare he unman poor, amiable Sir Ostyn and his militia because they couldn't kill? They were crop-growers, children-raisers, they *made* things — they didn't have time to learn how to destroy efficiently. How dare he take away a harmless life like Barnzo's, how dare he threaten atrocity on Prue, on her. How *dare* he hate women.

'You bastard,' she said and ran for the kitchen.

She got to the chimney in time to see that the pisol wasn't there before they caught her and dragged her back to the courtyard. Her bolt had released the men to action and Prue, lost somewhere under a crowd of them, was screaming. Penitence screamed with her as she kicked and spat at the two men who held her back.

And stopped.

'That's not nice, lads. Don't do it,' said a voice that managed to carry and remain conversational at the same time. Somebody new had ridden, unheard, into the courtyard.

'I heard women screaming,' said the voice, chattily, 'and I said to the Brigadier: That must be old Nevis up there, let's call in. And he said: It looks a decentish place, why not spend the night there? He'll be here in a minute, by the way. Help the lady up, Muskett.'

Prue, clutching the torn basque of her dress to her breasts, was helped to her feet by a sturdy soldier in buff uniform. Nevis's men edged reluctantly back, wild animals driven back from a carcase by flame. They looked from the speaker on his horse to their major on his. The newcomer had the red and yellow flashes of the Somerset Militia on his collar and sleeves but he was no Sir Ostyn; there was a whip behind the sociability of his tone; besides, he held a pistol — carelessly and as if he didn't know he had it, but steadily — pointed in their direction.

527

Unnoticed in the shadows, a great peace descended on Penitence. The other soldier who'd come in with him held a flare which lit up his face; she was eighteen again and he looked as he'd looked in a Rookery alley, smiling on her attackers as if he loved them.

And I loved you. *Then and ever since. So much.* With incredulity and pain she couldn't remember why she'd wasted twenty years away from him. *Oh, God, what do I look like?* She so forgot the situation they were all in that she put up a hand to adjust her hair — and found two of Nevis's soldiers still trapping her arms in theirs.

They might be on the same side but these two limbs of the army weren't losing any love for each other. The Viscount of Severn and Thames was holding off a nasty situation with personality, two men and a pistol. *It isn't over yet. Take care, my dear.* She'd caught a glimpse of Nevis's face. *He hates you.*

At that moment Henry received reinforcements. A younger man on a handsome horse came trotting into the courtyard at the head of a cavalcade of officers: 'Is supper ready, Torrington? Where is this place? Who owns it? Ah, Nevis; the corpse told me it must be you.' Somebody was already taking down Barnzo's body.

She knew this man too, though not enough to recall the name — a theatregoer, had done something disgraceful. She was saved. More important, Benedick was saved — if she could manipulate the situation aright. To do that she had to contrive what she longed for anyway, to be alone with the Viscount of Severn and Thames.

Nevis was sullen: 'The owner's a hell-hag. She's hiding a rebel. I was just going to get her to say where.'

The *name.*

She took a deep breath and pitched her voice across the courtyard. 'Sir John Churchill.' This was James's second-in-command in the West.

He looked round and squinted in the attempt to place her. At his side the Viscount of Severn and Thames had become very still. She shook off the men who held her and walked forward into the light of the flare, trying to look like the actress she had once been and not the exhausted harpy she felt now.

'Peg Hughes, by God. What by all that's wonderful do you here?'

'This is my house, dear,' she drawled. 'The Prince bought it for me. And I have been trying to convince this deranged oaf that I am not entertaining Monmouth in it. Win a pair of gloves, my dear, and send him away.'

He was charmed to hear theatre slang. He had been stage-struck, she remembered now. Always at the theatre. He'd attacked an orange-girl one night and Otway had called him out for it. He was introducing her to his staff: 'Gentlemen, the dearest *friend'* — he winked — 'of our hero Prince Rupert, and finest actress of her generation. The stage's not been the same since she and Nelly left the boards.' He made her feel ninety, though he was about the same age. 'Your precious instinct led you astray here, Nevis. Peg, may I also present Colonel Oglethorpe of the cavalry? And Viscount Severn and Thames? You were interested in the theatre at one time, Torrington. You must remember Peg Hughes.'

There was a pause. 'I do indeed.'

Penitence looked up into the face of Henry King, and fainted.

She came to as he carried her up the stairs. Prue was lighting the way and the soldier Muskett was bringing up the rear. *This is ridiculous.* She was, she knew, near exhaustion but to become so weak when she looked at him as to faint . . . nevertheless, the sheer luxury of being in his arms was something she wasn't going to forgo by insisting on walking. Everything had gone out of her but the physical remembrance of him. She put her cheek against his neck and felt his throat move. *And you remember me too.* The air about them thrummed.

'You've got fatter,' he said.

She grinned because she hadn't. She moved her head so that her skin brushed against the stubble of his chin. He was breathing hard, and not just from expending energy: 'Jesus Christ.'

Prue opened the door to the bedroom and a small snow-storm of feathers rose up in the draught.

'What the hell's all this?'

Lust subsided as the nightmare of the situation came back. He put her down. She said: 'Major Nevis was searching for the rebel.'

'What did he use, cannon fire?' He caught sight of the petticoats with their obscene holes still hanging from the tester rail. 'I'll kill him.'

'Henry, I need help.' She struggled for coherence. Muskett was standing in the doorway, Prue was lighting candles in the room. 'I want Prue to go downstairs and bring me some food and drink. I want Muskett to go with her; it's not safe for her to be left alone.'

Prue looked dreadful. A trickle of blood from her nose had dried on her top lip. She'd managed to tie her torn basque together enough for decency but it showed bruises on her shoulder. 'Are you all right, Prue?' Penitence asked. 'Did they hurt you?' *Of course she's not all right. Of course they hurt her.* The girl was suffering reaction; the candleholder in her hand was shaking but she was regarding the man who'd saved her from rape with something approaching worship.

Penitence lowered her voice so that Muskett shouldn't hear: 'And the bandages, Prue. I left them in the courtyard. But don't let anyone see you bring them.'

The girl nodded and left. With a glance at the Viscount, Muskett followed her.

As fast as she could Penitence began heaping on the bed the things she would need in the hidden room; light, covering, water ... 'Hold this please.' She passed the Viscount a bowl and ewer.

Slowly he set them down on a table. 'I gather from this that you lied, do I? You *are* hiding a rebel?'

'Not Monmouth,' she said. 'It's your son.'

She was in a hurry and desperate to recruit his help or she would never have told him like that. She'd had dreams in which she told him. Sometimes it was as retribution: *This is the son you abandoned when you abandoned me.* Sometimes with sorrowful bounty: *See the son I have been nurturing for you.* But if the son wasn't to be dead when he discovered he had one she must move fast. She didn't even look to see how he took the news, but tied everything except the ewer in a sheet. She just said: 'When I knock to be let out, press Eve's nipple', pressed it herself and started clambering through the hole, dragging the bundle after her.

She heard him say: 'Won't she mind?' as, once in the room, she turned, took the ewer of water off the bed and shut the panel.

The cluster of holes in the wall showed that candles were lit in the hall where she could hear the great table only used for feasts being dragged to the centre of the room. There must be so many officers to be given supper that the dining-room was too small for them. *I hope they've brought their own food.* She wondered if her taper would be bright enough to cast a beam through the gargoyle's orifices that could be seen in the hall. She had to risk it. She needed light.

Benedick lay where she'd dumped him; his breathing was irregular and he was very cold. The room smelled of urine and vomit. For a moment she dithered, undecided which of his needs to deal with first, then set to work.

After a while the panel slid back and the Viscount's long legs came over the sill followed by the rest of him. 'Muskett's guarding the door.' He looked around. 'God Almighty.'

'Shh,' she begged, though the noise from the hall below where army sutlers were setting the table would cover any exclamations coming from a gargoyle's mouth. 'Lift him up.' As she put a folded blanket on the floor to act as a mattress under the still-unconscious Benedick, she saw the three of them in a delayed nativity: Joseph, Mary and a large baby Jesus in this taper-lit stable. It was another irreplaceable moment she had no time to savour. 'Look at his head. How bad is it?'

She'd cut the boy's hair away from the wound showing a straight path of torn flesh.

He held the taper near the wound and peered. 'I think he was lucky. The bullet grazed his skull, probably cauterizing it as it went. But it gave him a hell of a thump. He'll not be *compos mentis* for a bit.'

'He swallowed some sips of soup,' she said. She took the rolled strips of cloth he'd brought and began bandaging, watching him studying Benedick's face. Her movements made the light from the taper flicker, distorting the boy's features. *He'll see the resemblance.* It was too marked not to be noted. She saw it all the time. 'Will he be all right?'

'Dark room, rest, liquid food.' He shrugged as he looked around. 'You seem to have thought of everything. Except what they'll do to the two of you if they find you sheltering a rebel. *Have* you thought of that?'

She didn't understand him. 'He's my son,' she said. 'Our son.'

The noise from the hall coming through the air-holes was getting louder as officers gathered to eat. They heard Churchill's voice calling for the Viscount of Severn and Thames: 'Where's Torrington? Still tending our hostess?'

'Fucking the bitch more like,' said somebody else. It was Nevis's voice. Penitence noted that, though Churchill had reprimanded the man for his treatment of her, he hadn't sent him away.

'I thought he was courting the Portlannon girl,' said somebody.

'No marriage contract says you can't fuck a beautiful actress.'

'Turns my stomach just to sit down with militia.' Nevis again. 'If we'd left it to them, the King would've lost his bloody throne.'

'Most, I grant you,' said Churchill's voice, 'but if it hadn't been for Torrington and his North Somerset men I'd have lost my life.'

By her side, the Viscount grunted. 'I must go. I'll leave Muskett on the door. You'll be safe enough.'

So he's going to get married. She watched him squirm through the panel. 'Henry.'

His face appeared in the square. 'Yes?'

'Is the rising all over? Has the King won?'

He nodded. 'It's all over.' His eyes went to the figure on the floor. 'Bar the killing.'

She sat staring at the square of light long after he'd gone away. *He didn't even ask Benedick's name.* If she thought about it she would weep. But she couldn't think about it; she was too damned tired.

Gently, she laid her son's head on its side on the pillow. He was warm and clean, at least; it was as much as she could do for now. She took up the taper and crawled through the hole with it. She put the panel back, blew out the light and fell asleep.

Hours later she woke up to the sound of horses and men moving in the courtyard below her window. There were low voices outside her door, then it opened. 'It's me.'

She knew it was. She brushed feathers out of her face and hair. He came and sat on the bed. 'We're being deployed to chase what's left of the rebels. Monmouth's been sighted heading for the New Forest. I'm ordered after him.'

'You're not leaving me here with Nevis.'

'No. Nevis is to join the rest of the Lambs at Taunton.' As she sighed with relief, he said: 'Just who is it you've got in there?'

'Benedick,' she said. 'He's known as Benedick Hurd.' She thanked her God that he'd used the name by which he'd been christened rather than the Benedick Hughes which was how he'd been known at court. It was unlikely that anyone would identify the Major Hurd who had allied himself with Monmouth as Peg Hughes's son and Rupert's foster-son.

'For God's sake, Boots. Hurd's one of Monmouth's cavalry commanders. Half the country's hunting for him.'

She'd had no idea. Her son still seemed a child to her. 'What are we going to do? How can I get him away?'

'You're not — until he's conscious. Then we'll see.'

'You'll come back?'

'It looks as if I'll have to.' He slammed his fist on the mattress, and feathers fluttered around them. 'For Christ's sake, Boots, there was no need of all that cock and bull to present him as my son. I wouldn't have given you away.'

'But he *is* your son.' She heard her voice, ineffective and whispering, a snake's hiss, the echo of women down the ages foisting somebody else's child on to the innocent, trusting, helpless male.

And he said, the Viscount said, Henry King said: 'How could you possibly tell?'

She looked at the line of his head and shoulders against the glow from the window. Twenty years had taught him nothing. His distrust of her was so great that the attraction he felt for her must be regarded as an aberration. He'd spent all his years in Louis XIV's prison — and probably most of them since — fighting the memory of the whore he'd been ungentlemanly enough to fornicate with, yet unable to forget her.

I knew who you were the moment I saw you. How could you not know me? There was no act she could perform, no display of virtue that he would ever believe, because he *wanted* to believe her and the very wanting damned him in his own eyes and society's as a fool.

When he'd looked at Benedick he'd looked in a mirror that had reflected his own face made youthful again. But he must not believe his own eyes because he'd found the mother in a brothel. Therefore she'd been a whore. Therefore her child was anybody's.

She was suffocating; the misery of Newgate, the toil, the responsibility, the nights spent pacing the floor during measles, the croup, teething, all the fight to keep his son alive and he asked how she could possibly tell.

Anger lit twenty years of suppressed resentment and became a bonfire. 'You *stupid* b-bba-b—' It wouldn't say itself. She was hitting her cheeks so that the word would come out, she was drumming her heels, she clawed at him. 'You b-bbaa—'

'Bastard,' he said. 'For God's sake *breathe*.' He caught her hands to hold them away.

Their faces were close, the heat of each body reflecting back on to the other's. His body and hers. His breath on her mouth blowing the fury higher until it was transmuted into an intolerable passion.

'Oh Christ, Boots,' he said. And that was that.

How *nice* it was. How lovely men were, thick, inflexible branches sheathed in silk. She remembered from twenty years. The bedhead was creaking rhythmically, somebody was trying to get in. *In* . . . 'They'll hear,' she said.

'Let 'em,' he said.

She couldn't bear for it to finish, she couldn't stop it finishing. Cartwheeling, vortexing, whirlpooling, panting, she came back to a ruined bedroom in an occupied house and a man who thought she was a whore. *And I've just proved it.* Respectable women weren't as abandoned as that. *Poor respectable women.*

As she watched him begin to dress, she was returned to the Rookery. 'Last time you apologized and never came back,' she said.

He was pulling on his boots. 'You remember.'

'Oh for God's sake. Of course I do.' *Think what you like. Think anything. Only don't leave me again.*

'It's only Monmouth this time, not Louis. I'll be back.' He arched over her, leaning on his hands so that he could look at her. 'I'll leave you Muskett. You can trust Muskett. But for Christ's sake be careful or you'll be hanging from your own gatehouse like that poor sod earlier.' He kissed her hard. 'And do something about this bloody bed. I'm covered in feathers.'

She snuggled into it as he went out, picking down off his shoulders. When she heard his step in the courtyard, she had to pull a sheet round her shoulders and rush to the window. He was still brushing feathers off his uniform. Churchill and some of the other officers were joshing him about her. He shrugged them off and waved his hat at her as he rode away with the others.

She stayed where she was, trying to glimpse him coming out of the gatehouse before he disappeared down the drive. *The doxy bidding the night's soldier goodbye from her window.* Nearly the oldest scene in the world. She didn't care.

A hoof stamped below her and she looked down. There was one horse left in the courtyard. Its rider came out from the doorway immediately below her window. Nevis. He swung into the saddle looking round at the house, an owner checking that everywhere was secure, as his horse clattered towards the tunnel gatehouse. She saw that the Paschal Lamb colours had been taken down.

Just before he entered the tunnel, he reined in and turned his horse round. Instantly she drew back. NO.

Nevis smiled, took off his hat and waved it — exactly as the Viscount had done. Then he went.

Chapter 4

THE DECISIVE factor of Monmouth's rising was that the gentry did not join him. Tories were satisfied with James II, and few Whig landowners at this stage were prepared to go against the legitimate successor to the throne, even if he was a Catholic, in the cause of a bastard, however Protestant.

The thousands of artisans and poorer men who flocked to Monmouth's banner had done well in the battle of Sedgemoor, executing a difficult night advance and fighting bravely when the action began, but without modern weapons and training they could not hope to stand up for long against disciplined troops, especially those under that rising commander of men, John Churchill.

Once their lines broke, panic took over and they ran. The death toll was large. The churchwardens at Weston Zoyland in charge of clearing the battlefield alone listed 1,384 corpses which were buried in mass pits in the marshes. Many bodies lay unrecovered.

Monmouth was discovered three days after the battle, hiding in a ditch where he'd been gnawing on a handful of peas. He was taken to the Tower of London and executed.

A lucky few of his officers managed to escape to the Netherlands, some 1,300 men were taken prisoner, the rest — about a third — were hunted across the moors and hills of Somerset like deer. Militia officers who had not distinguished themselves when Monmouth was a force to be reckoned with became enthusiastic hounds of human quarry, offering their troopers five shillings per rebel taken — or their victim's goods if he were propertied.

But as in war so in rounding up fugitives the militia proved amateur in comparison with Kirk's Lambs. Corpses hanging from shop-signs became synonymous with the Tangier regimental colours and spread such terror that people who gave shelter to fugitives were frequently betrayed by their neighbours to avoid reprisals.

The gaols of Hampshire, Dorset, Somerset and Devon became overcrowded as they waited for the Lord Chief Justice, Sir George Jeffreys, and four other judges to deliver them of their rebels in what was to go down in history as the Bloody Assize.

At the end of every market day those merchants and squires who owned land in and around the Levels gathered at the White Hart in Taunton to drink cider together before they went home. It was an unofficial gathering but time-honoured; womenfolk were rarely present. It had surprised Penitence, while in Taunton on her own business, to receive an invitation. And also, on attending, to receive news of the latest arrest. 'Lady *Alice*?'

''Tis so, I tell ee.' Sir Ostyn was irritated.

'But . . . *Lady Alice*. How could you do it?'

He stamped so that the floor of the inn's upstairs room shook. 'Dang it, tid'n nothing to do with me. 'Tis martial law. The preacher were up her chimbley and into prison she do go, magistrate or no magistrate, neighbour or no neighbour.' He poured Penitence and the others a beaker of cider. 'Yere, sup that.'

''Tis a cruel shock, I know, Peg. But she shouldn't a-been a-hiding of rebels,' Sir Roger Pascoe pointed out reasonably. There was a general nod of agreement.

'She's old. She gets confused. Who found this preacher up her chimney? Nevis, I suppose?'

There was silence. The major's sixth sense had made him

the Black Shuck of the Levels and the islands round about. Villagers evoked his name to frighten their children and told stories of how he had turned his horse aside from the causeway and directed his men to where a rebel hid in Middlezoy Ditch a mile away. 'Could'n've known, he could'n. Must have sniffed un, like a dog.' Infected with fear of him as she was, Penitence tried to be rational and had pooh-poohed Prue's hysterical accounts of seeing the man watching the house at nights — until she herself saw a horseman wearing a hat with a high feather standing on the moat bridge in the July moonlight making no attempt to hide.

'I don't like un, I admit,' said an innkeeper from Middlezoy. 'Nearly a month now and he won't have they corpses taken down from my sign, making it unsalubrious for trade. But he's keen for the King and I admire that in a man.'

'God bless the King, God love un,' said Sir Ostyn. There was a general: 'God bless King James.' Penitence blew out her cheeks but added a slavish 'Amen'. Royal devotion was the order of the day

'Let's get on with ut,' said Mayor Cranbourn. 'Oh, the burden the Assize do lay on us loyal burgesses you would'n believe.' He handed her a well-thumbed letter. 'You know Sir George's mind, Peg. See here. Would you say he means a gallows to be erected in *every* market square? Or only the greater markets? Or cattle markets? Or poultry markets? Or which markets?'

'I've no idea. Ask him.' Unhelpfully, Penitence handed the letter back. Since it had become known through the Clerk of the Assizes, who had come ahead of his master, that Sir George Jeffreys wished his favourite actress, Mistress Peg Hughes, to be included in the arrangements for his welcome, she had been consulted on every aspect of the Lord Chief Justice's likes and dislikes. It was why she'd been invited today.

'Suffering something wicked from the stone, he is, Peg, and very hasty with ut they do say,' explained the Mayor.

''Tis all very well but do judge and King know the expense we're put to?' Sir Roger took over the reading of the letter.

'"Halters to provide for the rebels, faggots for the burning of their bowels, a furnace and cauldron for the boiling of heads and quarters, salt for the preservation of the pieces – half a bushel each man." Do he *know* the price of salt? "Tar, oxen, drays and wains."'

'They haven't even been tried yet.' She looked wonderingly about her. These weren't cruel men; good husbands, fathers and neighbours. Like her, they knew some of the rebels personally, their shoes had been mended by them, wool from their sheep had been woven on the now-deserted looms. Yet they could consider the provision of instruments for such people's destruction in the same manner with which they discussed a coming storm.

Sharply, she turned to the reason she'd accepted the invitation. 'Can I rely on your tenants in my fields next month, Sir Ostyn? Sir Roger?' With so many casual labourers in prison, field workers were at a premium and Penitence was worrying for her teasel harvest.

Sir Roger looked at her craftily. He was a Somerset man. 'How about this yere acting, then?'

She had a deep reluctance to meet Sir George Jeffreys ever again, let alone put on a performance for him, but it would undoubtedly be politic to do so; nobody would suspect a woman in favour with the greatest judge in the land of harbouring a rebel. And she needed her teasels harvested. *But damn.* 'A short performance, then,' she agreed.

They shook hands. 'And yere,' Sir Roger was back to his letter, '"sufficient number of spears and poles to fix the heads and quarters." How many do ee think's "sufficient"? I wonder, would His Lordship mind if we stuck un on palings?'

'For God's sake.' She turned away and took Sir Ostyn to one side. 'Any sign of her, Ostyn?'

He shook his head. 'I've searched every list from every gaol this side of the Poldens and I've not found un.'

'What about MacGregor? Perhaps she gave her name as Dorinda MacGregor. Ostyn, there can't be that many women in gaol in Somerset.'

'You'd be surprised, maid. They be rife, *rife.* Silly girt besoms like the schoolmistress—'

'That reminds me.' Penitence turned on her neighbours. 'Who's going to speak to Sir George about the Maids?'

They might be prepared for the execution of troublesome rebels, they might not stand up for poor Lady Alice Lisle but, surely, there wasn't a man in the room who wouldn't protest against the imprisonment of the twenty-seven little girls whose only crime had been to present a flag to Monmouth. Poor Hurry Yeo of Athelzoy's Hoy Arms, whose daughter was among those in the gaol at Taunton Castle, had solicited her support, and she'd been sure that she'd find a sympathetic hearing from even the strongest Tory.

Until now. 'Who's going to speak?' she asked again. After a long silence she said: 'I see.'

'He do know thee, see, Peg,' said Sir Roger.

Angrily, Penitence turned back to Sir Ostyn. 'And Mudge Ridge? He's not on a prison list either?'

'I'm sorry, Peg.'

What am I going to say to Prue? What am I going to say to Tongs? It was as if Dorinda, MacGregor and Mudge had disappeared off the face of the earth. She had tried to pretend to herself that the silence with regard to Dorinda and MacGregor had been because they'd got away, had managed to avoid the aftermath of the battle and find a boat to Holland. But Mudge's absence since he'd gone off to bring them to the house made this explanation unlikely. Every day that passed reinforced the obvious: the three were dead or captured.

The trouble was that the captured had been dispersed among prisons all over the county and beyond, with little record of who had been sent where. Henry had made enquiries for her at Weston Zoyland where most of the rebels killed during the battle had been buried in huge pits, but nobody remembered the corpse of a woman. *Oh, Dorinda.*

'They'd've given false names I dare say. Protect their families, like,' said Sir Ostyn, kindly. 'Don't ee despair, my beauty. They'll be safe in gaol, depend on ut.'

No comfort there; reports from the prisons said conditions were so bad that if the Assize didn't start soon there'd be no rebels left to try.

Her voice quavered. 'They shouldn't be in gaol at all. They haven't done anything.' As far as Dorinda and Mudge went, this was true. She'd seen no reason to tell the magistrate that Dorinda's husband had been with Monmouth's army.

After the cool of the dark upstairs room of the White Hart, to step into Fore Street was like opening a kiln; heat rushed at her, ferocious for late afternoon. Further along the moony eyes of the Paschal Lamb stared at her from the standard hung on a bracket from the door of the inn where the officers of Kirk's regiment had made their headquarters. She couldn't bear to look at the thing. She noticed that pedestrians hurried their steps to pass it. Already the area of Taunton where the non-commissioned Lambs were billeted was known as 'Tangiers' and its formerly mild, provincial alleys had attained many of the less savoury aspects of that city.

It was not likely that James II's troops would be kind to the people of Taunton, which had been called by succeeding Stuarts 'the most factious town in England'. It had been steadfast for Parliament through the Civil War, withstanding two royalist sieges which had destroyed two-thirds of it. A breeding ground of Nonconformism, it had supplied a regiment of men for Monmouth and its prisons now held over five hundred awaiting trial by Judge Jeffreys.

She turned in the direction of the Castle where the parents of the Maids of Taunton kept a vigil outside the prison; she'd brought Mrs Yeo in the donkey cart and must now collect her to take her home. The woman's dreadful anxiety was infectious. Penitence knew that tonight she would again send Boller over to the Cartwrights at Crewkerne to see that Ruperta and Tongs were safe, despite her assurance that they would be; the Cartwrights, nice people, had absorbed them as well as most of her staff and even her dogs into their own, huge family, thrilled to be able to tell their neighbours that they were fostering Prince Rupert's daughter for the duration.

Penitence missed the girls badly. The reason she had given for not allowing them to return yet was that, with the Priory so near Sedgemoor, there was still a likelihood of rebel activity in the area, to say nothing of unpleasantness from the proximity of Kirk's Lambs. Even in Crewkerne, they shuddered at the name of Kirk's Lambs.

What worried her more, what kept her awake at nights, was the consequences to them if it was discovered that the Priory was concealing one of Monmouth's commanders. At best Penitence's estate would be sequestered and Ruperta thereby deprived of her inheritance. Tongs would have lost not only her mother, but a home.

'Mistress Hughes?'

She spun round. The man following her down the short cut to the Castle was ordinarily dressed but she recognized a Dissenter; there was something Puritan in the rigidity of the neck and shoulders, the way the fingertips of each hand were prinked together, as if relaxation might lay him open to the accusation of being human. 'Yes?'

'A word, Mistress Hughes.' He was looking around to see if they were observed.

'Yes?'

'I bring thee opportunity to serve the Lord and save thy soul, mistress.'

She was relieved. Just a more sophisticated form of begging. 'My savings are my own,' she said neatly, walking on.

He was a typical Puritan preacher; the more rebuffed the more persistent. 'Lady Alice willed thee a carpet, mistress, afore she was taken. 'Twill be delivered tonight. Thou art advised not to unroll it until thou art alone. Nor to inform the authorities that thee has it.' His eyes narrowed to look significantly into hers.

'What carpet?' She was suddenly frightened.

'Lady Alice said thou wouldst recognize the pattern,' the man said, and turned.

Penitence walked on, trying to calm herself. A harmless madman, that's all. Or perhaps it was poor Alice who'd been sent mad by her arrest and begun willing carpets to her neighbours. This fear she felt was groundless; a result of hiding Benedick; she saw menace everywhere.

She couldn't think. It had been a long day. Taunton, pleasant town that it had been, was now an occupied zone, too full of the Tangier regiment and preparations for death. It was so *hot*. She faced so many problems: How to handle the Lord Chief Justice when he came, after she'd so deeply compromised herself the last time they'd met. How to bear Mrs Yeo's pain all the way back to Athelzoy. How to bear the journey itself, the mosquito-ridden hiatus that lay between her and a bath. How to bump over those miles and miles of marsh and not become frantic for Dorinda, Mudge and MacGregor. How not to worry about Benedick and what to do with him. How not to fear for Ruperta and Tongs.

Yet in the midst of all this, she had the assurance that God was a loving God. For occasionally, sparingly, ensuring she didn't get used to joy, and almost always at night, He opened His hand and allowed Henry King's return to the Priory and her bed.

She heard his horse's hoofbeats while they were still on the track and was standing at her window to see him turn in through her gates.

Frogs were croaking in the marsh and a harvest moon lit the sweep of the drive like an enormous street lamp and put a yellow tinge on the lawn where the yew chessmen cast geometric shadows. She thought she saw one of them move. *Nevis?*

Then she heard Muskett's challenge and Henry's invariable answer: 'It's me, you silly sod', and everything else went out of her head as she went downstairs to greet him so that he could carry her up again.

This time, as he prepared to go into the usual bedroom, she stopped him and said: 'Next door.'

'What's wrong with this room?'

'Benedick's recovering,' she told him, 'I don't want him to hear us.' It was part of the truth, not all of it.

He shifted her over his shoulder. 'As long as there's a bed.'

The bed was the trouble; the milk-flowing, honeyed land it had become for both of them was Rupert's bed. It made her feel guilty. With Rupert she'd tried, gratefully, to return his love-making because she owed him so much. She had promised fidelity to his memory. And now, here she was, foaming with a passion that came free and much less deserved for somebody else. The least she could do was choose another bed to foam in.

The bedroom next door was smaller and its bed meaner but, as he said, it didn't matter.

Abruptly, he'd asked her once: 'Did you get this much pleasure from Rupert?' And then said: 'I'm sorry.' She knew he wanted her to say 'No'. Yet it would have been shameful to tell him that she'd felt nothing when Rupert touched her but guilt and a hope it would soon be over. The least she could do for a man who'd given her all that Rupert had was to keep the secrets of his bed. *We mistresses have our ethics.*

Instead she told him Helen hadn't known so much pleasure from Paris as Penitence did from Henry King, that she drained the world's supply of pleasure every time he took her to bed. And that was true.

She suspected such extravagance confirmed his suspicions even while it delighted him. It was the sort of wanton response men expected from whores. It couldn't be helped. It didn't matter any more. She'd lost her pride. He could take her on any terms. Just as long as he took her.

He did.

A long time later, when she was breathing normally again, she nudged him in the ribs. 'Who's the Portlannon girl?'

'Who?' He was drifting off to sleep.

'The Portlannon girl. The one you're courting.'

'Oh, her. Nice girl. Rich. Good family. Not a trace of stutter. I'm considering her as the next Viscountess of Severn and Thames.' He yawned and looked at her from the corner of his eyes. 'Jealous?'

'No.' And she wasn't. *No good being bitch in the manger.*

'I thought I ought to have . . . children before I'm too old.'

'Of course.' *He meant to say 'a son'.* But she didn't protest that he'd got one. Like everything else, whether or not he believed Benedick to be his had lost its importance. It was as if the two of them had stepped into a walled garden outside ordinary life, created from previously unknown textures, with its own weather, in which they were the only inhabitants.

When he couldn't get away from Bridgwater where he and his militia had been stationed, she went through the processes expected of her, spoke, moved, worried, discussed her crops, while all the time her soul clawed at the gate in the wall to be let back in. Once she set eyes on him again the lock turned and music that was like no other music floated through the gate as it slipped open in invitation.

There was no past in the garden. Because he grew restive when she mentioned the past he refused to talk about his own though she would have liked to know more. He only said: 'The late Viscount, my father, was pleased to exercise *droit de seigneur* over every female on our estate, probably not excluding the sheep. But, by God, when I brought home a Catholic wife – suddenly he was the outraged Puritan. He threw me out. He said no good would come of it.' He closed his eyes. 'And he was right, the venal old bugger.'

Knowing the uniqueness of what they shared – and she knew he knew – it was a wonder to her that her past mattered so much to him. It exasperated her that it did. But it did.

It was time to leave the garden. 'Shall we go down to supper?'

'I thought you'd never ask.' He began to feel about for his clothes. 'All this pleasuring makes a man hungry.'

'It's very good of you to do it,' she said politely.

'I'm like that. No thought of self. You say Benedick's better. How much better?'

'He worries me, Henry. Sometimes he's confused and other times he's just bad-tempered.'

'To be expected after a concussion like that. He's got to be fit two nights from now. He's riding to the coast to catch the tide at four-thirty a.m.'

She put her head against his sleeve. 'How did you get the boat?'

'Yacht, woman. She's a yacht and she's mine, crewed by my men.' She kept forgetting he was a viscount. 'She's moored in a creek in the Parrett estuary, which by impure coincidence is guarded by Severn and Thames's North Somerset Militia, bless 'em. I'll put him in a basket or something and tell them he's smuggled goods. All my men are smugglers. The place is about fifteen miles from here as the crow flies.'

'We haven't got a crow, Henry dear. We haven't got a damned horse since the requisitioners took the last one. We've got a donkey cart.'

'I'll bring another horse with me.' He ushered her out of the door and along the corridor. Their footsteps echoed as they went down the newel staircase, emphasizing the quiet. There was no staff now, except Muskett and Prue; the rest were helping out at Crewkerne.

She'd told the village servants not to come, ostensibly because there was no work to be done but actually to give Benedick a chance to move about unseen when he was well enough.

Prue had left cold meats, bread and preserves on the kitchen table. With the influx into the area of soldiers, and now all the officials and clerks necessary to the Assize, food was in shorter supply than ever. Tonight Henry had brought a bottle of Bordeaux and some smoked venison which had been sent down from his estate in the north of the county.

Penitence couldn't eat. 'How can you get Benedick through? You said yourself the Levels were full of regular army still looking for rebels.' She'd be sending off two precious eggs in one basket.

He crammed his mouth full of venison and dismissed the problem: 'Ay owe ee.'

'I beg your pardon?'

He swallowed. 'They know me. Every roadblock on the causeway knows I have this insatiable woman to ravish. They give a cheer as I go by. It's very touching.'

'They don't know Benedick.'

He pulled her to him. 'Boots, I'll get him there. He'll be wearing Muskett's uniform. I don't know any other way to do it. We've got to be there two nights from now or the tide's wrong and we'll be seen by the guardships in the bay. Just make the boy fit to ride and I'll get him there if it kills me.'

That's what worries me. She couldn't think of what else to do either and being close to him didn't encourage concentration. 'Still no news of Dorinda and MacGregor? Or Mudge?'

'No, I'm sorry.' He let go of her. 'Jesus God, how could MacGregor be such a fool as to throw in with Monmouth? I'd only seen him at The Hague a week or so before and he made no mention of it then.'

'You knew MacGregor in the Netherlands?'

'I knew MacGregor in the Rookery, if you remember, drunken Scottish bugger. He was on the wagon when we met again in The Hague – saved by the love of a good woman, if you can describe Dorinda as such. So I employed him. He was one of our agents, he helped organize the English distribution of pamphlets for Bentinck and me.'

'Bentinck!'

'Prince William's right-hand man.' He looked at her curiously. 'Do you know Bentinck?'

'I met him once, a long time ago.'

Immediately he was restive. They were in the dangerous territory of her past. 'You seem to have met a lot of men in your time. Bentinck. Churchill.'

She shrugged and began preparing a supper tray to take up to Benedick and Muskett. *And how many women have you met in your time?* He was slouched in a carver with one of his legs up on the table and he still looked very much as he'd once looked in a Rookery window. His hair, long then, short now – his wig was somewhere in her bed – had gained some grey but not much. The light from the kitchen fire caught a throat the years hadn't thickened. He was as attractive as all hell, and he could make her crosser than any man she'd ever met with his doubts of her and his digs at Dorinda.

If Dorinda's dead, it's because she tried to help your son. She hadn't told him that.

For one thing, *if* he believed it he would be under such a burden of debt to the MacGregors for his son's life that he wouldn't rest until he'd found them, and thereby bring more suspicion on himself. She'd already heard murmurs against him from the county gentry; he'd spent too long in Holland with Orange William; he'd been heard to make caustic comment about King James. Churchill admired him, but Churchill was back at Whitehall by now; the county was at the mercy of Kirk's regiment and both Kirk and Nevis hated him, mainly because he had contempt for them and showed it. *Dorinda, I'm sorry. I can't let him try to find you.* To have a son with a price on his head was killing her; for his father to fall under suspicion would break her nerve completely.

She said: 'So you're working for William.'

He caught her every inflection. 'Good God, him too?'

'I have met Prince William,' she told him coolly. 'Merely met him.' *He was without his breeches at the time.* 'Are you putting him on the throne of England now? Last time it was Rupert.'

'Rupert was in the clutches of some harpy,' said Henry. 'William's got Mary trained. He's the better bet.'

She went round the table and knelt by his chair. 'Darling, no more battles. They hurt people. People disappear or they get hanged. What does it matter which king's on the throne, or if nobody's on it at all?'

He was appalled at first, then over his face came the toleration shown to idiots and children. He lifted her up on to his knee and tapped her nose with his finger as he made his points: 'There's got to be a king, you see, Boots, because otherwise coins would have blank spaces where the head should be. And you can have a king who's a fool, like Charles I. And you can have a king who's a Catholic, like Charles II. But if you've got a king who's a fool *and* a Catholic, like James, sooner or later you're going to have a revolution. And that's when William comes in.'

She stroked his face. 'The first thing you ever said to me was how you couldn't trust kings. Not any of the buggers, you said.' A million years ago. A prissy, innocent, voiceless thing she'd been, crawling along a Rookery gutter to get away from attackers as poor as she was. And from the clouds had descended this jaunty *deus ex machina* to save her not only from the attackers but from prissiness, innocence and voicelessness.

'I said don't trust them, I didn't say do without them.' His mouth went lop-sided as he remembered. 'That was a cold old day, Boots. I can see you now. You looked like a miniature Guy Fawkes.'

And we let each other go. And now I've got you back. Peacocks and ivories, gold and sapphires, were in her kitchen in the shape of this man. Penitence wriggled herself closer into his lap and felt him instantly go hard. 'Oh no you don't,' she said, though God knows she was tempted. 'You'll wear yourself out.' She clambered off him. 'I'm taking supper to Benedick and Muskett.'

He sighed. 'Oh, very well.' To Penitence he complained that Benedick was a fool, that anybody who had joined Monmouth was a fool, but the boy intrigued him. Once she'd seen him put his hand on the bed next to Benedick's to compare the two. To her they'd seemed facsimiles, narrow and strong, but she hadn't said so. *Go ahead. Let suspicion ruin the next twenty years as they've ruined the last.* He made her so angry. She loved him so much.

As they entered the bedroom, Muskett, who was playing cards with Benedick at the bedside table, stood to attention. 'Suh.'

Henry looked at the piles of coins on the table. 'I shouldn't wager too much, Major Hurd. My sergeant is known through the length and breadth of North Somerset as Machiavelli Muskett.'

Penitence loved Muskett. He was as dependable as he was solid and his humour made him more attractive than many a man with better looks. She had hopes of him and Prue. He was staring straight at the wall. 'The major is an honest cardplayer, suh. Which is rare for cavalry, suh. And officers. In my experience. Suh.'

'Does your mind ever dwell on the kisses of the gunner's daughter, Muskett?'

'No. Suh.'

'It should.' He turned on Benedick. 'How are we tonight, Major?'

'I don't know how you are, but *my* bloody head's pounding.'

'Benedick!' Penitence could have killed him. He didn't know

Henry was his father — until Henry was prepared to claim him, she had not considered it right to tell him — and had shown increasing truculence in his presence, but he'd never been outright rude like this. 'The Viscount has been good enough to come here tonight to inform you of the arrangements for your escape.'

'That's what he's come for, is it? Nothing else?' Benedick was gaunt. Physical weakness was presenting his anger as petulance. Shaking, he held on to a chair-back to help himself up. 'I would like to know why the Captain Viscount is helping a rebel escape in the first place. Or perhaps it's a question I should ask my mother. Sir, I demand to defend her honour by calling you out.'

'Do you, by God,' said Henry.

How could I have raised a boy so stupid? He'd adored Rupert, of course. And he was ill. She supposed that as a single woman, much gossiped about, her honour must appear to need defending. Looking at her son, Penitence caught her breath at the resemblance to his father. The candlelight emphasized the hollows of the eyes and the new line down the long cheeks. *He's aged.* She was so sorry for him. By this ridiculous parade he was attempting to pretend that medieval chivalry still existed when, in fact, he had seen it blown to pieces during that night on Sedgemoor. She knew he had. She'd heard what he raved of in some of his nightmares.

She caught at the Viscount's sleeve and dragged him away to whisper: 'Deal with him gently, Henry.'

'Don't worry that I shall deal with him at all. He's probably a better duellist than I am. He's younger for a start. And as tall. Besides,' he added querulously, 'the little bastard outranks me.'

'Something on the drive, sir,' said Muskett who'd been diplomatically looking out of the window.

Henry went over to put his hand on Benedick's shoulder and force him back into his chair. 'You shall have satisfaction later, Major. Stay out of sight.' He joined Muskett and Penitence at the window.

They could just see over the gatehouse roof to the bottom

of the drive, a still, white river under the light of the huge moon. From here Muskett's 'something' looked black and softly rolled, like a slug. But if it was a slug, it was man-size.

'Stay here.' Henry was priming his pistol as he went out. Muskett, who kept one to hand, was seizing his: 'Best stay here, mistress.'

Whose house is it? She took Benedick by the arm and helped him up. 'Time to go back in the hole, I'm afraid.' When he had Muskett to guard him, she allowed him the run of the bedroom – as long as he kept away from the windows.

'No.' Peevishly, he shook her off. 'I want to see what it is.'

He's overtired. How many times had she said that during his childhood? They never changed. 'Benedick,' she said, 'you're weak enough and you're still young enough for your mama to slap you if you don't go back in that room.' And she meant it.

He grinned. She'd forgotten he could. *You're your father's son.* She helped him through the bedhead then ran to join the two men. They were standing back to back, Muskett with his pistol pointed at the slug, Henry covering the left-hand side of the drive. 'Muskett didn't see the cart drive up, but he heard it go. And he thought he saw a shadow over there.' After a minute he relaxed. 'All right, Sergeant, let's see what they've brought us.'

Penitence already knew. 'Lady Alice's carpet.'

It wasn't just a carpet; as the men jerked at the fringed end it unrolled and the body of an elderly man flopped on to the gravel.

Laboured, noisy breathing told them he wasn't dead or the face, which was ghastly in the moonlight, would have suggested it. As a child Penitence had been made to join her community in filing past the coffin at the funeral of august Puritan preachers, and they had looked like this man; dressed in black with their Bible between their hands.

This man's hands still moved and he smelled rather worse than the dead preachers, but he was of the same ilk. She knew it too well.

'A rebel,' said Henry. 'With congested lungs from the look of it.' He ran his hand over the man's broadcloth black coat.

'Damp. Been lying out in the reeds possibly. Somebody doesn't want to hide him any more, and I can't say I blame them. What do you think, Muskett?'

'I agree, sir.'

'And what do you think we should do with him?'

'Personally, sir, I'd find the nearest hole in the marsh and throw him in.'

'I agree. Wrap him up again.'

'No.' Every instinct screamed at her to overlook the claim of common humanity and let the men rid her of this bane, to quickly turn her head and be left unburdened. *What did you and your like ever do for me? Why should I take in one more male who thinks I'm a whore?* Wearily she said: 'Bring him up to the house.'

'Boots, you have trouble enough.'

'I know, but he's a relative of mine. His name's Martin Hughes.'

While Henry and Muskett took the unconscious man to the scullery to strip him of his damp clothes and wash him, Penitence went up to the main north-wing bedroom to find more blankets and some clothes of Rupert's. She opened the panel and helped Benedick out of the secret room, explaining what had happened.

'Did you come up here just now?' he asked. 'I thought I heard somebody moving about the room.'

Penitence looked around uneasily. There was a rule that he wasn't to make a noise until the panel was opened and, knowing the risk to her if he was discovered, he'd carefully obeyed it, though to avoid the worst horrors of claustrophobia he always kept the door behind the panel open.

She looked under the bed and in the cupboards and locked the door behind her before she went downstairs to tell the men. Martin Hughes lay on the scullery table, wrapped in a blanket.

'Shall I search the house, sir?' asked Muskett.

'What's the point?' said Henry, wearily. 'The bloody place has got more ins and out than a weevilled cheese. Get upstairs and guard the boy.' When his sergeant had gone, he turned on

Penitence. 'I want you out of here,' he said. 'Muskett will escort you to Cheynes, that's my place, and you can stay there until we get rid of all these relatives you keep collecting.'

'No. I can't go.' She began preparing a poultice to relieve Martin Hughes's chest; she was fast running out of sheets to tear up.

'Look.' He was getting angry. 'This old spindleshanks was planted in the drive to draw us out of the house while they searched for the boy. They suspect you.'

'No,' she said. 'It was Nevis was in the house.' She heard her voice rise in hysteria and brought herself under control. 'Nevis was in the house. He watches. He's suspected me from the first but as long as he can't find the secret room he has no case. It was Lady Alice who sent . . . the carpet.'

'Lady Alice Lisle? I thought she'd been arrested.'

'She has. She willed it to me. She saw the family resemblance.'

There was goose grease in a pan in the larder and she fetched it. While it warmed by the fire, Penitence told Henry King what she knew of her mother's story. 'They took her child, me, to the Americas leaving her to starve. Only she didn't. She went to London and opened the Cock and Pie instead.'

'Her Ladyship was your *mother*?'

She wondered if this confirmed his suspicions. Like mother, like daughter. She slapped goose grease on to lint, lint on to the cloth, and the cloth on to Martin Hughes's bony, hairless chest. His skin was hot and his thin mouth was open to suck in air.

'Very well,' said Henry, 'but none of this says you can't get out of the firing line. If you insist on heaping coals on this nasty old bastard's head, leave it to me and Muskett. We'll get him away.'

'There's Dorinda,' she explained, 'I can't leave without knowing what's happened to her.'

He was getting angry. He'd never held any brief for Dorinda. Apart from that, Penitence knew he was impatient to take her to bed again before he returned to Bridgwater. 'The wench is dead or in clink. Either way, what could you do?' He was dismissive.

'I'd go to Jeffreys,' she said, unguardedly. 'He'd give her to me.'

'Really? Another admirer?'

She looked up from tying the poultice into place and saw the polite interest fixed on his face, and began to get angry herself. 'Yes, as a matter of fact.'

He nodded. 'You actresses cover a lot of ground.'

'No,' she said. 'We don't. We stay still and men come around *us*. Being on the stage doesn't necessarily mean a woman's a whore. Being in a *brothel* doesn't necessarily mean she's a whore.'

'Really?'

She thought of the industry which men devoted to seducing women and the industry with which they then defamed them. She thought of Aphra, traduced for earning her own bread. She thought of Dorinda made a laughing-stock for believing a man loved her. The man before her stood for the entire genus of exploiters. 'Really,' she agreed. 'She becomes a whore later, when she's left holding the baby and is put in Newgate for debt. *That's* when she becomes a whore. And when she's trying to earn a living for them both and a man says she can't unless she sleeps with him. *That's* when she becomes a whore.'

Twenty years' resentment fed her fury; it had the bit between its teeth and was unstoppable. The exhilaration of hearing the truth come out of her mouth at last was like a trumpet to a battle-charger; it went the faster. She let Martin Hughes's body flop back on to the table so that she could lean over it and shout at the man opposite, the enemy. 'And if Lord Chief Justice Jeffreys wants to tumble her in return for letting her friend free, then it's a small price to pay because she's *used to being the whore you made her*.' She screamed the words.

Then she was sorry. It was no time go into all this when she was overburdened and overfrightened and they were both too tired. *I love you. I only ever loved you.*

But it was too late now.

He bowed. 'Obviously I cannot help you, madam. May I suggest you bring back some of your staff to protect you and yours.'

She had to call Muskett down to carry the old man upstairs. She could hear the spurts of gravel as Henry's horse took the drive at a gallop. As she was lighting Muskett through the door of the bedroom, the eyes of the sick man over his shoulder opened and focused on her. 'Jezebel,' he said. It was automatic, a response to any woman not buttoned to the neck. He probably wasn't even aware he'd made it. *Why am I doing this?*

And as she threaded the skinny old body through the hole in the bedhead to Muskett on the other side, Benedick chose to protest: 'It's bad enough in that hole without having to share it with the likes of him.'

Wearily, she fetched bedding, climbed through the panel and helped Muskett make the old man comfortable. Then she climbed out again.

'That's your great-great-uncle,' she said. 'That' – she pointed to the drive – 'was your father. And *that*,' as hard as she could she hit her son across his face, 'is for growing up like them. Now I'm going to bed.'

Most of the casual labour which Penitence had used in previous years to harvest her teasels had come from Somerset's Dissenting male population, a large proportion of which had either been killed in the Monmouth rising or now lay in prison awaiting trial.

Even augmented by such labourers as her neighbours could spare, only eighteen men filed into her courtyard at dawn to receive their harvesting instructions.

Penitence looked from them to the early morning mist hanging over the marshes and wondered if the heatwave would last long enough for so few to harvest so much before the rains came. Already wiseacres in the village were prophesying storm, and the air was becoming heavy. The Levels had gone quiet as if heat was squashing the life out of them.

Waterfowl kept to the shade of the reeds. The only sound was a persistent hum of insects and the unexpected buzz past the ear by a dragonfly.

She looked back to the men. They were waiting to be given the teasel knives and the blood-summoning, sinew-stiffening speech which, by tradition, Mudge had always delivered to them before they went out to the fields.

'Do your best and do it quickly,' she told them clearly. *What do they expect in this heat? St Crispin Crispian's?* 'There'll be a bonus for any man who can finish his three acres first.'

The incentive put a sparkle in the men's eye that Shakespeare couldn't have produced and they shuffled past her table in goodwill as she handed out the teasel knives which were always kept in a locked case in the hall cupboard. These were expensive, being especially made for teasel-cutting; small, lethally sharp blades which fitted inside the curve of a man's forefinger so that in using them a teasel-harvester's gloved hand looked as if it was picking the bristled heads rather than cutting them.

Impatient but true to her duty as lady of the manor she asked after the men's families and gave back news of her own. Yes, thank you, Miss Ruperta and Miss Tongs were well and she hoped they would be returning soon, once the Assize was over. How are the little ones? *Please hurry and go.* Yes, thank you, she was managing quite well with Sergeant Muskett and Prue to look after her.

If the teasels bring in enough profit, perhaps I can buy Benedick's pardon. Perhaps, if Dorinda and MacGregor were alive, she could buy theirs. It was being said that Lord Grey, one of Monmouth's few aristocratic lieutenants, had already been allowed to purchase the King's forgiveness with £7,000 and the betrayal of all his former comrades. Even from the sale of Elizabeth of Bohemia's necklace — half of which belonged to Ruperta in any case — she could not hope to raise such a sum. But then Benedick, being younger and less well-born, would not fetch so much as Lord Grey.

Yes, thank you, Miss Ruperta and Miss Tongs were well. No, there was still no news of poor Mudge Ridge, but thank you for asking.

'Do ee miss him, Ladyship?'

She looked up because this was not a polite enquiry, but had the tone of a message. The man who gave it was heavy-set and middle-aged. She could not remember seeing him before.

'Very much,' she said. The other seventeen men had retreated into the shade of the gatehouse preparatory to marching off to the teasel fields. She handed the man before her the last knife on the table, but he didn't take it.

'Did ee hear about the escape at Ilchester gaol, Ladyship?' He was looking about casually, acting insouciance so hammily that Nevis would put him down a suspect right away if he saw him. *Don't let Nevis see him.* She felt a spasm of fear put her heart into an a-rhythmic beat. She suspected Nevis of being everywhere.

No, she hadn't heard of it.

'Sixty men, Ladyship. Sixty got away. We reckoned you'd be interested and you'd want to tell Prue Ridge.'

'For God's sake,' she snapped, 'if Mudge was among them, tell me.' She couldn't bear this furtiveness, these cryptic 'carpets'. Even if Nevis *was* watching, he couldn't overhear. 'Do you know anything of a man called MacGregor? Or Mistress Dorinda?'

The man shrugged, then he was gone. She saw him join the others to cross the moat, but then break away across the moorland.

When she looked down at the table, she saw that he'd left the teasel knife behind. She picked it up and put it in her pocket before she went to tell Prue what had happened. She found the girl sweeping out the hall.

'Is that what he meant, Prue? That Mudge was in Ilchester gaol and has got away? But how could Mudge have got to Ilchester?' The village was six miles to the south-east and well away from the battle.

'They put un in prison all over the place.' Prue's once-plump face had brightened. 'And they damn Lambs wouldn't keep Mudge Ridge locked up for long, iss fay. I reckon that's what 'tis. Mudge's got free.' She began to cry on Penitence's shoulder. 'God preserve un for a good brother and keep un safe to get home.'

'Amen.' *But not yet.* Fond as she was of her bailiff, Penitence profoundly hoped he would make for somewhere else other than the Priory or the farm. The secret room was definitely getting overcrowded, and she was already at risk. Nevis suspected her of hiding one of Monmouth's commanders and whoever it was that had delivered 'the carpet' *knew* she was hiding the rebel preacher, Martin Hughes.

If whoever-it-was got captured he might very well betray her to save his own skin. Somebody had betrayed Lady Alice Lisle for the same reason.

I shall be ill. Nobody could live on such a knife-edge of anxiety for so long without amassing bad humours in her body. *I haven't got time to be ill.* She must investigate the possibilities of escape for her son and for his damned great-great-uncle, if the man survived.

And now, added to her woes, was the thought that she had locked herself out of the secret garden by telling Henry of her whoredoms. He'd believed those, all right. Happy enough to believe truth that damned her; unable to hear truth that didn't.

She was defiant nevertheless. *I'm glad I told him.* How had he thought she'd survived any other way? What did he expect? What did all men expect? That women keep themselves pristine, like new flower pots, for men to plant their own, exclusive seed into? *I bet he didn't spend all these last years in self-denial.*

It was the late Lady Torrington's fault in cuckolding him with the King that he so mistrusted women. *If he was as suspicious of the late Lady Torrington as he is of me, then I'm sorry for the poor dead slut.*

But if his jealousy meant that he wasn't coming back to smuggle Benedick to the coast and freedom, she didn't know what she would do.

I shall be ill.

She pulled herself together. *There's no time to be ill.* The problem with problems on this scale was that they absorbed your time in a stomach-clenching rotation that led nowhere except to madness. 'Go and get some breakfast ready for the men,' she said to Prue.

'There in't much.' Prue wiped her eyes. Food was becoming scarcer than ever now that what had been left after army requisitions was being commandeered for the invasion of judges, clerks, barristers and servants necessary to the Assizes. The Levels' marshes were empty of cattle and the Levels' islands of sheep.

'Do what you can.' *The Assizes.* There was another horror waiting to be faced and faced this very afternoon. In her escritoire in her bedroom was an embossed, be-sealed, be-ribboned letter which read:

> Dearest Madam, I saw your performance. Will you not come to see mine? We shall dine after. Your humble servant, Jeffreys.

She crossed the hall to put the teasel knife back in its case, and stood still.

Somebody was breathing.

She looked round; Prue had left for the kitchens, the hall was empty, the morning sun coming through its windows in three patchworked stripes. Muskett was upstairs in the bedroom, guarding the two fugitives. There was no one else in the house. Yet somebody was breathing. A wheezing intake of air. A long, shaky expulsion. She was taken back twenty years to the condemned cell at Newgate and George's heavy panting as she undressed before him, chattering her nonsense.

Nevis. She fought down panic as she whirled around. There was an explanation. Must be. *Drains. A cat. Something up the chimney.* It was loudest when she was close to the interior wall, and louder yet at the fireplace end. *Of course. The gargoyle.*

She expelled her own breath in relief as she looked up. It was gasps from the still-delirious Martin Hughes she could hear coming through the vents from the secret room. Yet, even as she took in the rational explanation, she was shaken by superstitious horror of the life given to the gargoyle's malevolent face by the air that whistled through its mouth and nostrils.

She ran through the hall door, along the passage to the main bedroom. 'For God's sake, Muskett, can't you keep him quiet? Where *is* Muskett?'

Sitting by the window, her son directed a thumb over his shoulder towards the bedhead where the panel was open. Penitence clambered through, struck again — as she always was — by how drearily the shape of the room acted on the spirit, her spirit at any rate.

Muskett was kneeling beside the palliasse on which lay the heaving body of Preacher Hughes, bathing his face and neck. A rushlight burned in the pincers of its holder, casting its unflickering light on the old man's slack, stubbled chin. Magnified by the high, sloping walls of the room the noise of his breathing was louder than ever.

'Hear him, can you?' Muskett had already recognized the problem.

'They can hear him in Taunton.'

'Sorry, mistress. I'll stop up the vents. I got me some clay.' Not for the first time Penitence wondered how much Henry paid Muskett and decided, as always, that it wasn't enough. He handed her the cold cloth to continue cooling Martin Hughes while he began stuffing clay into the holes that led to the hall. 'But if the panel's closed, mistress, these'll have to come out. They'd suffocate else.'

She examined Martin Hughes. He was still in crisis. 'He's no better, Muskett, is he?'

'Him?' Muskett appeared not to approve of Dissenting preachers. 'His sort'd survive the Last Trump.'

'Prue will bring breakfast soon. Muskett, I'm grateful to you. Muskett, will he come back?'

'His Lordship?'

'He said he'd be back tomorrow night to fetch Benedick.'

'If he said he will, he will.' Was rain wet? Did birds fly?

Penitence looked at Muskett with envy that any human being could rest such absolute trust in another. 'Have you known him long, Muskett?'

'As long as me teeth, mistress. My father served the old Viscount.'

'So you knew the first Lady Torrington?'

'I did.' The tone was non-committal.

'I knew him during the Plague.' She heard her voice softening and couldn't help it.

'Yes, mistress. I gather. We was all worried where he'd gone to.'

'Major Hurd is his son.' She didn't know why she said it.

'Is he, mistress?' She'd caught Muskett looking from Benedick to Henry and back to Benedick and she knew the resemblance had not escaped him, but, as far as Muskett was concerned, if the Viscount didn't acknowledge Major Hurd as his son, then no son of his was Major Hurd.

With the twinkling lights in the wall blanked out, the secret room became more unpleasant than ever. Penitence left Muskett with his patient and eased herself out of it to sit on the bed. The room had been tidied, though it still showed signs of its wrecking. 'Benedick, there are things I should tell you.'

They'd had little time to talk since he'd been fit. She hadn't yet found out what sort of person he was now, what change the battle of Sedgemoor must have wrought in him. He'd become a cipher for the baby he'd once been. She felt the same protective agony, had the same cat nightmare she'd known when she'd been in Newgate, as if he was the mewling, helpless little thing he'd been then instead of a grown man.

She said abruptly: 'Why did you join Monmouth?'

He didn't turn round from the window. 'Prince Rupert would have done the same.'

'Prince Rupert would never have tried to unthrone a legitimate king,' she said.

He didn't want to discuss it. Instead he pointed to the slanted view beyond the courtyard over the western Levels where the rising sun was turning the early morning mist into a golden rose. 'Where is that?'

'King's Sedgemoor.'

He hadn't connected it to the night flashed with gunfire. He fell quiet. She could have wept for him. Well, he was going to have plenty to distract him. 'Benedick,' she said again, 'I must tell you things.'

So she told him. First about MacGregor and his Aunt Dorinda. To her amazement, instead of being distressed for them, he was angry: 'Aunt Dorry? God damn it, can't a fellow go off to war without all his female relatives running after him?' He was ashamed, of course, but Penitence could have hit him again. *They've no idea.* They thought of the world as a ringed-off space with women circling it, like an audience, with no other involvement than a spectator's. 'Where is she? With MacGregor?'

'We don't know.'

'Then we'll just have to go and find them. Where's my sword?'

From far away, somewhere among the infinitely changing green of reed and meadow came the boom of a bittern.

'Benedick,' said Penitence. Her voice failed and she had to try again. 'Benedick. Out there is a river called the Parrett. On its estuary tomorrow night a boat will be waiting to take you back to the Netherlands. Tomorrow night you will be aboard the sodding thing. I want that clearly understood. To the Netherlands. You and your father.'

He'd been almost smiling until then. 'What father? Why do you keep on about my father? He's dead.'

She didn't make it elaborate, just told him that during the Great Plague she and his father had been thrown together, that he had been called away on service to his country, most of it spent in a French prison, without knowing he'd left a son behind him.

He was quiet for a long time, digesting it. She began to worry that she wouldn't be ready for when Sir Ostyn Edwards came to fetch her to take her to the Assizes, but she dared not interrupt the boy's thoughts.

'Do you know,' he said, 'I always knew my father wasn't dead. Your voice would change as you said it. I thought he might be Prince Rupert.'

'No.' *How sad.* You never knew what was harboured in the mind of your child.

'Oh.'

She said brightly and ridiculously, 'The Viscount is very nice. His family name is Torrington. Anthony Torrington. I call him Henry.' *He's got good teeth.* She began to get irritated. *I'm not selling a horse.*

'Why?'

'Does it matter?' *Do you want a father or don't you?*

'Will he make an honest woman of you?'

'I beg your pardon?' She was furious now.

'Is he going to marry you? Will he acknowledge me?'

That's all she was to her own son, a chattel to be passed around for his benefit. 'No,' she shouted, 'because I won't marry *him*. I'm going to stay a dishonest woman like I've always been, and if you don't like it you can go hang yourself and save King James the trouble.' She stalked over to her dressing-table, adjusted the sliver of silvered glass that was the only decently sized piece left of the mirror, and began to brush her hair.

After a while she felt her son's hands on her shoulders and looked up at him. He was as tall as his father. 'I suppose,' he said, 'you haven't done badly. For a dishonest woman.'

'Thank you.' She patted his hands. 'And no more nonsense about trying to find Aunt Dorinda. I can do that better alone. You're a risk to me as long as you're in the country. I'll fare better when you're out of it.'

'Yes, I see that. But it was typical of her, wasn't it? To risk her life for mine? She and MacGregor were always so kind to me.'

'Was it? Were they?' How unheeding of other people's virtues and relationships she had been as she'd plotted and clawed her way through her life.

'A viscount,' mused Benedick. 'Not so bad a choice for a father after all. What does that make me?'

She couldn't resist it. 'A bastard.'

Chapter 5

'PROPER little maypole,' said Sir Ostyn admiringly as he helped Penitence into his carriage. 'A sight for sore eyes, you are, my 'andsome. Us'll have a tumble together on the way.'

Penitence stood on the step and looked down at him. 'I'm prepared to go in my donkey cart,' she warned him. He'd recovered some of his confidence since the trouncing it had taken at the hands of Nevis. She was glad for him, but not enough to have to put up with being fumbled all the way to Taunton. 'Besides, Prue's coming with us.'

He was not put out. 'Tumble the maid too, if ee like.'

She had dressed carefully in her best and known as she did it that she was inviting trouble. She had so overplayed the coquette for Jeffreys the last time she and the Lord Chief Justice met that he would more than likely wish to bed her after their dinner together tonight.

She'd stood a long while in her shift before her pier glass holding up first one robe then another and calculating like a Treasury clerk.

If Henry has deserted me ... *plus* more importantly, if he has deserted his son ... *equals* me to save Benedick from the gallows.

The man with the authority to free Benedick ... *plus* Dorinda and MacGregor if they should so need ... *equals* me offering my body to same man in exchange.

She subdued revulsion and in doing it realized that she had achieved true whoredom in looking beyond the act to the reward. *I must save my son. The hanging of my son would not be a survivable event. I am my mother's daughter. She whored for her survival: if it proves necessary I shall whore for mine.*

In the end she'd chosen the dark blue cotton; it showed up her still-excellent skin.

Sir Ostyn and Penitence didn't arrive at Taunton Castle until eleven o'clock but they had only missed a few minutes of the Assize's first case. Most of the morning had been taken up by the ceremonial attendant on the opening of the Assize. Trumpets had been blown, red carpets laid, nosegays exchanged, speeches given. Everybody who was anybody in Somerset was displaying his or her loyalty to King James by his or her attendance and best clothes.

So crowded was the court that at first Sir Ostyn was

refused admission, despite his magistracy. It was Penitence who got them both in by displaying the Lord Chief Justice's letter, which so impressed the usher that he flung himself into the courtroom at a crouch and came out dragging two protesting gentry whose places she and Sir Ostyn took.

The first case was Lady Alice Lisle's.

It was like being mummified. The deep sills of the Castle's high windows were filled by spectators who refused the ushers' pleas to descend and who blocked out so much sunlight that candles had to be lit. The heat, the smell, the gloom enclosed Penitence so that she almost panicked, until she was drawn into the drama being enacted at the other end of the long hall where candles illuminated two protagonists like footlights.

Jeffreys was lit while the wigs of the two judges on either side of him merely made grey frames around faces that had disappeared.

And the aged woman in the dock was lit, her white cap and Puritan collar brilliant and sharp-etched.

A disembodied voice was mumbling from the witness box, cut short by the carrying bass of Sir George Jeffreys. 'They block the light. Hold up a candle that we may see his brazen face.'

A candle was held up to reveal a male witness doggedly muttering as tears rolled down his face. Penitence knew him; it was Lady Alice's steward.

'That is all nonsense,' said Sir George. 'Dost thou imagine any man hereabouts so weak as to believe thee?'

'She thought them only Presbyterians, my lord, not rebels. She thought they was mere in danger for preaching.'

Lit from below the Lord Chief Justice's mouth seemed to sprout tusks. For the first time Penitence heard an echo of the Welsh accent he had tried to lose. 'There is not one of those snivelling, lying, canting Presbyterian rascals but, one way or other, had a hand in the late horrid conspiracy and rebellion. I hope, gentlemen of the jury, that you take note of the horrible carriage of this fellow. A pagan would be ashamed of such villainy.'

'Oh ma dear Lord,' whispered Sir Ostyn to Penitence, 'if he can treat a witness so, what will he do to Lady Alice?'

What would he do to me? She was committing the same crime.

The captain who had found the two rebels hidden in Lady Alice's house was called to give testimony. The prosecutor was redundant; it was the Lord Chief Justice who did the questioning.

What a performance. She hadn't seen a Richard III like it, not even Lacy's. The man posed, varied his tone, sometimes making his audience laugh, lulling it with gentleness, causing it to jump, repelling, attracting, displaying a brilliance of grasp that kept it stunned.

The play — Penitence corrected the thought — the *case* rested on whether or not, when she gave the two men shelter, Lady Alice had known they were rebels. Lady Alice protested that she had not. Penitence wished she would say so with more emphasis; she had aged since the two of them had last supped a dish of tea together, her head shook and her deafness caused her to cup her hand round her ear. Jeffreys had allowed a court official to stand beside her in the dock to repeat everything that was being said. Penitence wished too that Alice had worn less starkly Puritan dress. But she was proud of her; her neighbour was conducting herself with dignity; her face had the blinking composure of the very old.

Now Jeffreys was summing up — lethally. How could the dame not have known the men were rebels? 'And if she knew,' rang out his wonderful voice, 'neither her age nor her sex are to move you. I charge you, good jurymen, as you will answer at the bar of the Last Judgement, deliver your verdict according to conscience and truth.'

When the judges and jury retired, the court became bedlam. Penitence heard fors and againsts all around her.

'Always for Dissenters, she was.'

'Kindly old besom yet. And wept for the King when he died.'

'She knew they to be rebels though.'

''Course she knew, but hiding hunted deer ain't the same as poaching. 'Tis only womanly. They'll never burn her.'

Penitence turned to Sir Ostyn. 'Burn her? They mean to burn her?'

His piglike face was miserable.

''Tis the punishment, Peg.'

She shook his arm. '*Burn* her? For an act of charity?' She had forgotten that Alice's crime was her own, only being able to picture judicial flames scorching up that frail wrinkled body. 'They'd be too ashamed.' The witch-finding bonfires of the Interregnum had produced a reluctance among sophisticated people – and, surely Jeffreys, monster though he was, was a *sophisticated* monster – to return to such barbarism. This was a new age. For all his faults, Charles had encouraged toleration and science. James could not, he could *not* put the clock back.

Sir Ostyn hushed her. The court rose as jury and judges came back.

'Yes?'

'My lord,' the chairman of the jury was perplexed and nervous, 'the men Lady Alice was accused of hiding, they'm not convicted yet. What we'd dearly like to know, my lord, is if 'tis treason to hide a man as hasn't yet been proved a rebel?'

'It is all the same,' Jeffreys assured them.

'But we're not sure she did know them to be rebels, my lord.' It took great daring.

In the silence of the court it was possible to hear the bell of St Mary's Tower ring for one o'clock. There had been no adjournment at midday and the Lord Chief Justice Jeffreys was shifting on his bench. The chairman of the jury flinched as if wishing to take cover.

'I cannot conceive,' shouted Jeffreys, 'how, in so plain a case, you should even have left the box. If I have not an instant decision, I shall adjourn the case and you shall be locked up all night.'

'See, Peg,' said Sir Ostyn, as jury and judges left the court again, 'this is the pity of ut. I'm frit as he'll have to make an example of the old soul. He's got more to try at Dorchester, more at Exeter, *before* he do move on to Wells and Bristol. He's got to make an example of un here.'

She didn't understand. 'It's Lady *Alice*. She's your neighbour.'

An usher was trying to edge along the close-packed row of public seats in which they were sitting. He leaned over and whispered: 'His Chief Lordship asks if Mistress Hughes would wish to take refreshment with him at his chambers in the break.'

No, Mistress Hughes wouldn't. But the respectful glances that were being cast at her by all those within range of the whisper brought her to her senses. Whatever happened to Lady Alice, Penitence had her own neck to think of, and the closer she was to Jeffreys, the less likely that same neck – and Benedick's, and Martin Hughes's, and Dorinda's and MacGregor's – would be subjected to the axe or the rope. She nodded, and got up. 'Give un my regards, mind,' said Sir Ostyn.

Despite the usher clearing the way, it was slow-going through the press to the doors. The noise of conversation and argument stopped as the jury filed back again into its box and the judges to their dais.

Reluctantly, Penitence turned round. The scene was still a stage-set; Jeffreys with his wide, red face and scarlet robes might have emerged, steaming, from a trap door to Hell; Lady Alice a study in dry white and black, her head nodding, her eyes focusing perhaps on memories of her long life or her arthritis, everybody's grandmother.

'Guilty, my lord.'

Jeffreys sentenced her to be burned alive.

'By the Lord, madam,' said Jeffreys, waving a capon leg, 'but it refreshes the eye to rest it on your sweet face. What say you, my lords?'

Justices Wythens and Levinz agreed that it did and got on with eating and drinking at the well-stocked table of the inn next door to the Castle.

Penitence refused all food, but accepted a glass of wine, hoping it would settle her stomach and stop her hand shaking. She drew the Lord Chief Justice to a corner. 'Can nothing be done? Can I do nothing to persuade you?'

Jeffreys frowned. 'You regret Lady Alice, mistress?'

'I do,' she told him.

He said unexpectedly: 'So do I. But I am the King's servant and he must be protected. I have pronounced the legal sentence for a traitor, which is what she is.'

'She is so old.' Penitence took a deep breath. 'There are neighbours,' she said meaningfully, 'perhaps even one's friends, who have become innocently, maybe foolishly, embroiled in the ... the rebellion. If one appealed to you for mercy on them ... one's gratitude, my lord, would be undying.'

Their eyes met. She knew her timing was wrong; the proper moment to offer him her services would be tonight, after he'd dined well. But the dreadful sentence had added Lady Alice to Penitence's list as another brand that must — this time literally — be plucked from the burning. She could think of nothing else. Subtlety and craft deserted her with the picture of that harmless old body tied to a stake flickering constantly in her brain. It could be Dorinda's. It could be Benedick's.

'Mistress.' He was no fool. His yellow-streaked eyes held a warning. 'It is to be hoped you have no such neighbours or friends. Should they be my own brother, I would pronounce guilty men guilty. The King was most grievously endangered. Blood must form such a moat around him as nobody shall cross again.' His red face approached hers. She could smell sweat and the dust of his wig. 'However lovely the supplicant, she should make no difference to the sentence. Whether or not it is carried out rests with the King.' He winked. 'In *that* matter, mistress, I shall always be your friend.'

He began ushering her back to the table. 'As for Lady Alice, I have ordered her to be given pen, paper and ink and told her to employ them well.'

'She can appeal to the King, you mean?'

'She knows what I mean. It is out of my hands.'

Penitence felt better. There was no doubt that with any other judge than Jeffreys Lady Alice would have been found not guilty. But as the man saw it, he was doing his job. At least, he'd enough humanity to advise Alice to appeal. James would surely show clemency. And she herself now knew where she stood; Jeffreys had indicated clearly that he could not be bribed to alter a decision by money or fair words, but that, after he'd made it, his influence with the King might yet be employed – for a consideration.

He was waiting for her reaction. Aphra's words on Jeffreys came back to her: *You can't have too many friends in that class*. She feared the man but in her circumstances she could not afford him as an enemy. She employed her best stage smile; she wasn't an actress for nothing.

He was delighted. 'This lady,' he announced to his fellow-judges, 'is an oasis for us travellers in this benighted desert. Let us drink of her. She shall sing to us, pour her song like nectar over our parched souls.' Their apathetic response irritated him. 'If some of us have souls.' He turned to her. 'Do we dine together tonight, my dear?'

Oh God. 'I fear you may be too laboured, my lord.'

'Too laboured? I would say we are too laboured. We are lighting such a candle of justicial labour as shall never be put out. Some thirteen hundred rebels yet to try and I vow we'll have sentenced them all within the month if it kills us which, what with constant travel, the smell of rogue ever in our nostrils, and plagued by the stone, it may well.'

He was using the royal 'we' since his companions looked fit and well. He didn't. His hands clenched occasionally and he winced from pain. The usher had told Penitence that Sir George's valet had told *him* that the great judge suffered terrible from the stone. 'Pissed sixty-three stones on the journey to Taunton. Sixty-three.'

The amount he was drinking – 'On doctors' orders, madam, doctors' orders' – was adding a purple tinge to his face. 'We shall see how many we can try before the day ends. And Lord send they plead guilty. If all the dogs plead not guilty we shall be trying them till Doomsday. We must attempt the blandishment of the King's mercy offered to them if they plead guilty to save precious time.'

Justice Wythens, a dry little man, shifted in his chair. 'I would challenge the legality of offering men an inducement to plead guilty.'

'Would you? *Would* you?' Sir George Jeffreys leaned forward.

Justice Wythens of the King's Bench leaned back. 'In view of the fact that some will be sentenced to death just the same . . .'

'Presbyterians,' shouted Jeffreys. 'These are no men but Presbyterian dogs who bared their teeth against their king. There's no promise binding to such as they. I tell you, we make an example here and now or stand condemned ourselves of failure of duty to our country.'

The other two judges rose. 'Time for a whiff of tobacco before we return to the pillory,' said Levinz. 'Excuse me, my dear.'

To be alone with the Lord Chief Justice was alarming; sick or not, the man radiated appetite: 'And when do you sing for me, Peg? I shall never be too laboured for thee.' He was reaching for her hand.

'There is an entertainment planned by the burgesses for tomorrow night, my lord.'

'Pox to it. A hall with draughts and tinny trumpets, I know them, I know them. In London I was given an invitation to your house.'

Sir George's clerk came in bowing, saying that the court was ready when Sir George was.

To Penitence's relief, he rose. 'Alas, dear madam, this nose must be applied once more to the grindstone.' He walked her to the door. 'God give me the strength to do what must be done and do it quickly. Did you hear the Lord Keeper is dead?'

'No. Poor Lord North.'

'Amen. Were I in the King's sight at this moment the position would be mine. Yet here I drudge among the savages while lesser men conspire against me. Shall I be Lord Keeper, my dear?'

'I know you will.'

He nodded. 'And Lord Chancellor hereafter?'

He is *aiming high.* 'I wish you success, my lord.'

His farewell kisses on her hand went on up her arm, leaving it chicken-flavoured. 'We shall dine well tonight.'

Oh, help.

Back in court it was hotter than ever. The accused, mostly

men, though some women, came in batches of a dozen, manacled and chained from foot to foot, four batches an hour for the rest of the afternoon. Some wore the clothes they'd been captured in, others had gangrenous wounds that added to the fetor of the hall. Sir Ostyn sniffed at a pomander. Penitence put her scented handkerchief to her nose and over it scanned the faces carefully in case one of them should be MacGregor's so changed that she might have difficulty recognizing it.

None of the women was Dorinda.

After a while the faces blended into one, a country face stolid with uniform courage. The reading of the charges became a monotonous formality in which only the names changed. Jeffreys lifted his face from his nosegay, and after the barest of consultations with his two colleagues, said over and over again 'Prisoners at the bar, we find you guilty. Sentenced to death', and closed his eyes until the next batch came up. The court became restive; wigs of barristers clustered together for chats, like fungi, prosecutors laughing with defenders. 'Could've stayed at home, they buggers,' said Sir Ostyn, shifting. 'For all the good they're doing they could've left ut to their clerks.'

Penitence saw that Prue had somehow struggled through to the crowd at the door and beckoned her over, but she was unable to move for the crush and after a while Penitence lost sight of her again.

'NOT GUILTY?' With the rest of the court Penitence jerked at the Lord Chief Justice's shout. He seemed to have been dozing himself; with his wig awry he'd only just become sensible to the plea of the man in the dock before him.

Penitence had missed hearing the man's name, but whoever he was he was brave to put forward a plea that would take up Judge George Jeffreys's time.

'Not guilty?' He glared at the offender. 'On what grounds do thee plead not guilty, you viper?'

The prisoner protested that the witnesses appearing against him weren't credible. 'One a Papist, my lord, and one a prostitute . . .'

'Thou impudent rebel,' bellowed Jeffreys, 'to reflect on the King's evidence. I see thee, villain, I see thee with the halter round thy neck.'

The accused said he was a good Protestant.

'Protestant?' shouted the Lord Chief Justice. 'You mean Presbyterian. I can smell a Presbyterian at forty mile.'

A character witness for the accused came forward, an immaculate but pitying Tory: 'My lord, this poor creature is on the parish.'

The Lord Chief Justice was pleased to grin. 'Do not trouble yourself,' he assured the witness, 'I will ease the parish of the burden.'

The man was sentenced to death. Jeffreys had got into his stride. He was almost turning up his sleeves. 'Do we have more not guilties, Master Clerk?'

Most extraordinarily, they did. With the example of the sentence pronounced on the Protestant pauper, not to mention on Lady Alice Lisle, there were yet dogged men in the cells of Taunton Castle who believed that they were innocent and that Judge Jeffreys would find them so.

With relief Penitence realized that if the court was to work through today's list it would be sitting far into the night and therefore too late for her to dine with the Chief Justice. It was also too late for her to get home across Sedgemoor before dark.

'Not to worry, my boody,' said Sir Ostyn. 'Your 'andsome lover's arranged it. We'm invited to stay at Sir Roger's. 'Tis more convenient. Prue and all, more's the pity, or we could have shared a bed.' He gestured around the courtroom. 'Wouldn't want to miss tomorrow's show by going back home, would us?'

Penitence accepted gratefully and smiled at his perpetual joke that they were lovers. The Pascoes had a splendid house not far away from the Assize Hall in North Street. She even forgave Ostyn's description of men and women on trial for their lives as 'a show' because she too felt the elements of its drama. She had not seen wretches clinging to the dreadful bar of judgement; she had seen actors.

But she could stand no more of it. Tomorrow she would return to the Priory, unsuccessful in her feeble attempt to seduce the chief actor himself, but only too grateful that she had not had to undergo the ordeal of his tiring-room.

Later that night Prue came to her room at the Pascoes' in tears, begging her to plead with Jeffreys for the life of Barnabas Turvey, the young weaver of Chedzoy.

'I love un, oh I love un,' wept Prue, 'I didn't know until I saw un in the dock looking so pale.'

'He was in the dock? Today? Did he plead guilty?' She couldn't remember the name, but there had been so many. 'Prue, I'm so sorry.'

'That bull of Bashing dared sentence un to death. You got to save un, Penitence.' No more 'Your Ladyship'. It was the democratic appeal from one woman to another, implicit in it the reminder that Mudge had saved Benedick.

Penitence told the girl about Jeffreys. 'He said if it were his own brother who'd been proved guilty, he could do nothing. And your Barnabas pleaded guilty.'

Unworthily, she thanked her God that she'd had that conversation with Jeffreys. If she hadn't she knew that, for Prue's sake, she would have had to approach him again tonight.

'He were told to plead.' Prue had managed to persuade a gaoler she knew to let her speak to her beloved through the bars of his cell. 'Deputy prosecutor he said he was, offered un his life if he spoke guilty, all of them their lives. To save time, he said.'

Penitence put the girl into her bed, and climbed in with her. 'Then he'll keep his life. Some prison, perhaps, and then he'll be free.'

'But they sentenced un to death,' wailed Prue.

'A formality,' said Penitence, believing it. Also she was tired. It had been a long day, one of many long days since her secret room had become occupied. She had so many people to worry about that Prue's weaver came well down the list. She stroked the fair curls off Prue's forehead to persuade her to sleep, and slept herself.

In the morning the girl had gone, and when Penitence,

574

eager to get home, came downstairs to search for her, Lady Pascoe evaded her questions. 'Ah think the maid did see somebody she knows.'

'Who?' *Damn the wench.* This was no time to be renewing acquaintances.

There was noise and bustle in the street outside, more than usual for such an early hour. Penitence peered through the bottle glass of the Pascoes' dining-room window to see green distortions of figures hurrying past in the direction of the Castle.

'Ah should'n go, my soul,' said Lady Pascoe, ''twon't be pretty. They're starting executing.'

Penitence stared at her. 'But they were only sentenced yesterday.' No interval? No appeal? Even the highwayman Swaveley had been given right of appeal.

''Twon't be pretty,' said Lady Pascoe again. Her face was pale. It was said she'd been a Dissenter herself before Sir Roger married her. 'I should'n go.'

Penitence had already gone. The crowd along North Street filtered into the cattle market which was normally held on the green outside the Castle. The crush was so great that Penitence had to ask some people on the steps of a mounting block outside a house if she could stand on it for a moment so that she could look for Prue.

Over the heads of the crowd she saw a covered market place — there was one like it in every town, a slated lichened roof supported on stone pillars to keep the weather off the auctioneer. Militiamen were holding the crowd back from a space in front of it in which stood an empty gibbet and, beside it, a dais which had been set with a red table gleaming with badly applied new paint.

Around and about the square were other spaces where men and women hung with their heads and arms through pillories like still, inelegant statues. In London the crowd would have been pelting them for the joy of throwing things but Taunton had lost its sense of fun. These were the lucky ones from yesterday, the ones who hadn't been sentenced to death. Nobody was looking at them.

Penitence squinted into the early morning sun to make out the design of the yellow flashes on the militia uniforms and saw, with relief, it wasn't the North Somersets'. *Henry wouldn't let his men do this.*

The attention of the crowd — she had never seen one so quiet — was focused on a cart at the side of the square. A harvest cart, huge, long, rough-wooded, with sloping slatted sides containing a dozen or so men in chains. Around the bottom of the cart, standing on tiptoe so that they could touch the hands of the men through the slats, were women, some screeching, others not. The men were singing.

Within the shade under the market roof, busy shapes were moving. Smoke issued out into the clear air with the sound of bubbling and the smell of tar, reminding Penitence of fences.

She got down from the mounting block, and a man, doffing his cap, took back his place. *Run away. Let me run away.* But one of the women crying around the cart was Prue Ridge.

It took a while to get to her. People in the crowd were so crammed together and so intent that it was like struggling through a close plantation of saplings. Eventually, she was spewed out in front of the line of militia and had to sidle past their pikes. Edging her way along she stumbled against one of the statue's plinths and automatically apologized. The man's head drooping through the hole in the hinged plank about his neck had its eyes half-open. A large piece of paper pinned to his cap, which still bore the rebel green ribbon, read: 'I am a Monmouth.'

At the next pillory along — 'A Monmouth I will love' — Penitence avoided seeing the face of the girl by passing behind her and saw her back instead. Flies had landed on the blood oozing through the slashes in what had been a flowered cotton dress. An older woman was trying to fan them away with her cap and muttering over and over in a monotone: 'Don't fret, maid, don't fret.' But her eyes, too, were on the cart.

Once again, the scene had been designed for theatre; the placing of the statues, the raised podium, the crowd, but in true theatre there were no flies. This, then, was the epilogue to the virtuoso performance she had witnessed yesterday by the white-wigged, scarlet-robed actor on his bench. He gestured and spoke his lines – and the flesh of lesser men and women was torn open and real blood ran out of it.

There was nowhere she less wanted to go than towards the cart but the soldier guarding it made no move to stop her reluctant approach towards Prue. Behind the cart, down a side road, she glimpsed horses and the uniform of dragoons, ready in case of trouble.

Just then the executioner climbed up on to the dais from the shadows of the market and shouted: 'Next.' Two militia let down the rear gate of the cart and one of the men in it was made to descend. The singing of the remainder grew louder as he was shuffled towards the dais.

'Come away, Prue.' Penitence took her by her arm.

The girl's other hand was through the slats of the cart, clutching the hem of a young man's coat. She turned to Penitence, dazed. 'They promised his life,' she said. 'You said as he'd be saved.'

Some of the men in the cart were wounded but all were singing. Penitence looked up at Prue's lover and saw a white face that had been nice-looking only a few weeks before. *He's so young*. Barnabas Turvey's splendid throat moved as he shouted the hymn. His eyes, looking down at Prue, were agonized.

There was an involuntary sound from the crowd as if it were trying to gasp for the man from the cart, now being hauled up by three hangman's assistants on a rope thrown over the gibbet arm, his legs kicking in the air. They'd undressed him down to his breeches and taken off his chains. The executioner in his black leather hood watched from the dais, inclining his head slightly at the movements and scratching his armpit, like someone having to make a fine judgement.

As the kicking became feebler he nodded and his assistants eased the rope until the hanged man's feet touched the ground, then caught him as he buckled, and lifted the half-conscious body on to the table.

Penitence later remembered that she was surprised the table

wasn't red any more. Somebody had thrown a bucket over it and washed the paint away ready for its next glistening coat.

Two assistants knelt, holding the hanged man's legs. The third took the arms and bent them back so that the ribs formed a ridge above the hollow of the man's belly. At another nod from the executioner, the breeches were pulled off.

The singing above Penitence grew louder to cover the screams. She buried her head against Prue's shoulder but heard the rip of the knife, the slap of entrails as they were thrown into a bucket, then the chopping — sounds she'd heard a hundred times in the kitchen back in Massachusetts as her grandmother quartered a chicken.

She had heard of people being hanged, drawn and quartered but the true enormity of what it entailed had not crossed her mind. *I am fearfully and wonderfully made.* She cowered before the sacrilege of God-fearing men who dared to take to pieces such a communicating, perpetuating, functioning miracle as another man's body.

'Next.'

'Wait on,' came an aggrieved voice from the shadows under the roof, 'brine bucket's full. We'm filling another.' But the cart tail was already being lowered and another man taken to the gibbet. Two more and it would be Barnabas Turvey's turn.

'Missus.'

She looked up. The boy was kneeling down so that he could speak through the slats. Her tears blurred her view of his face. It could have been Benedick's.

'If you've pity, missus, take her from here.'

She sobbed and nodded. His manacled hands were gently peeling Prue's fingers from his coat, and with all her strength Penitence tugged the girl away. They heard his voice call: 'Lord bless thee, Prue, and tell un I died a Monmouth.'

In Fore Street, amazingly, a brightly dressed man approached her and doffed his cap as if he and she lived in a normal world.

'Sir George's major-domo, dear lady,' he said, and said it again. With her arm around Prue she looked beyond him, unhearing.

'. . . I see what it is, dear lady, you fear for your provisions. It's often so, but we bring our own, and a staff.'

'What?' she said.

'Have no fear. It will all be arranged. Sir George enjoys his little surprise visits, but in my experience the lady likes some warning to pretty herself.'

'What?' she said.

'Mistress.' The man was becoming agitated and officious. 'Your attention would be appreciated. The Lord Chief Justice intends to surprise you for supper this night. He was pleased to say that, since Mahomet would not attend on the mountain, the mountain must come to Mahomet.'

'What mountain?'

It was only as she and Prue walked the ten miles home across the moor that she became collected enough to understand that the Lord Chief Justice of England had asked himself to the Priory for dinner.

'Will he come, Muskett?'

Tired as she was from the long walk home, Penitence paced the main bedroom because she couldn't keep still. After what she had witnessed in Taunton's market square that morning she could not look on her son where he sat by the window without seeing his body torn apart as the bodies of the men on the cart had been torn apart. She couldn't even rejoice that Martin Hughes was better. What was the point of his old carcase recovering if it too was to be quartered? He lay on the bed, the panel behind his head open in case they needed to use it quickly, and grumbled at Prue who was feeding him gruel because now and then she fell into a trance and stared at the spoon with sightless eyes.

I want Henry. She was as helpless now as she had been on that day in the Rookery when he'd rescued her from her attackers. Mentally she crawled as she had then, a deer writhing from the dogs on its back.

'He'll come, missus,' said Muskett.

She was unreasonable in her panic. 'What if he does? He can't get Benedick away with the house full of Jeffreys' men. He'll miss the tide.'

'There's other tides.'

Muskett was a rock, but she was unnerved by the sense that a destroyer was approaching her house with hastening, predestined steps. *We'll be betrayed*. The risk increased every second. They'd been lucky not to be betrayed before. And now, since the horror displayed outside the Castle today, who wouldn't scruple to tell the authorities that she was hiding a Dissenting rebel? After all, Lady Alice, held in higher esteem and greater affection than she was, had been betrayed, sold to the authorities by a woman in return for a husband who'd been arrested after Sedgemoor. How much easier to betray the former mistress of Prince Rupert and her canting uncle. Even those who'd originally given the old man shelter hadn't liked him enough to go on giving it. She didn't blame them. *I don't like him much myself.*

He was grumbling again that Prue was withholding the next mouthful. It was the voice that had called damnation on her head a hundred times.

'Shut your noise,' she snapped at him.

She wouldn't care if he were captured, she wouldn't care if *she* were. It was Benedick that concerned her, only and totally her son.

He was also grumbling. 'Mother, find me a sword and I can shift for myself. I'll make for the coast on my own.'

'You shut your noise as well,' she told him. Still weak, in a countryside overrun with royalist troops, he'd be picked up in a day. *Deliver my soul from the sword: my darling from the power of the dog.* How exactly the psalmist had known her situation. Would Henry come? How would it help if he came? *I just want him here.* He was her *deus ex machina*. He'd delivered her from her enemies before, though then the enemies were simple robbers, not the ranged forces of the State.

'Sit down, missus.' Muskett's square hands took hers and led her to the window-sill. 'You can watch for His Lordship and tell us what Judge Jeffreys plans for tonight. See if us can work out a plan of our own.'

She hated to think what plans Jeffreys had for tonight. She tried hard to recall what his major-domo had told her. 'He's sending over his own household that travels with him to prepare the house and the dinner. A small affair, with a few friends.'

'Ah now. *That's* the way to go. Sneak the major down the north-wing stairs, like, when they're at table.'

'It'd be terribly dangerous,' she said. 'Jeffreys' staff is large and I know he has a detachment of dragoons to guard him wherever he goes. They'll station men at the gatehouse to stop comings – and goings.'

'A idea, though.' Muskett licked his finger and drew a line on the glass. 'Keep that un for later. What then?'

'Well, then I suppose I provide the entertainment. Jeffreys wants me to sing. And, oh that's right, he wants me to do some Shakespeare.'

'Play-acting?'

'A soliloquy or two perhaps.'

'And where'll you do that, missus?'

She'd got his drift. The years passed her back to another time of horror, when another child had needed to be rescued. 'Oh, Muskett. We did it once. Your master and I. We lured the watchmen away from their posts.'

'*That's* the way to go.' Muskett never smiled; everything he said was straightfaced, but she could tell he was pleased by the way he drew another, longer line on the glass. 'Put up a stage round the back. Away from the gatehouse, like. You and the captain do your luring. I'll get the major across the moat and away to the captain's yacht quick as a ferret.'

Penitence said quietly: 'And the other gentleman?' She jerked her head towards the bed and Martin Hughes.

'No,' said Muskett firmly.

She didn't blame him. The old man was too old, too ill and definitely too unpredictable to make such a journey, especially at the speed at which Muskett and Benedick would have to travel. Well, she'd think of what to do with him when the crippling load of Benedick's danger was lifted off her shoulders.

Muskett turned to Benedick. 'Fine actor, the captain. You ought to see him, Major.'

'I'm not so bad myself,' said Penitence. The preciousness of the moments on the Cock and Pie balcony when she'd played Beatrice to Henry's Benedick were back with her. The horror of the Plague had eroded over the years; the memories strongest now were of human courage. She could recall in perfect detail the scene on the roofs opposite as she'd sung Balthazar's song: Mistress Palmer's face, Mistress Hicks's, the child attached to the chimney. They made her braver.

'For the visage mask of actors do but hide the skull of sin,' shouted a voice from the bed. One of Martin Hughes's set responses had been stimulated by the word 'actor'.

'We should have left him in the marsh,' Penitence said to Muskett. She was feeling better.

The sergeant paid her no attention. He was regarding the old man with interest. 'Isn't there a play where there's a blackamoor masked?'

'Othello? He's not played in a mask any more. We use lampblack. As a matter of fact . . .'

She stared at the sergeant. He'd just spat liberally on his finger and wiped a large smear across the entire window. He bent down to put his impassive face directly opposite hers. '*That's* the way to go, missus.'

They had a few minutes to discuss the way before Judge Jeffreys's major-domo arrived at the head of a procession of carts bringing provisions and staff. Followed by Major Nevis with Sir Ostyn Edwards and a warrant to search the house. Followed by the Rt Hon. Viscount of Severn and Thames. Followed by the Lord Chief Justice of England, Sir George Jeffreys and friends.

Nevis's men searched the house again under the apologetic aegis of Sir Ostyn Edwards. 'Proper sorry I be, Peg, but some bugger says old Martin Hughes is hiding hereabouts. Ah told that danged Nevis as you'd as soon shelter Old Nick. "Her's had him put in the stocks afore now," I told un but would he listen?'

They stood in the hall, watching cupboards emptied, soot brought down the chimney, bayonets inserted between the stones of the wall to see if any could be dislodged. 'Proper pig of a man, and I told un,' said Sir Ostyn, 'but 'tis the military makes the law now. Of course, who he's after is the rebel Hurd. Bagged all the others, Wade, Ffoulkes and Goodenough, but not Hurd. Last seen being carried off the field in this direction, seemingly.'

Penitence's hands clenched. The magistrate, puzzled, took one of them in his to comfort her and exclaimed at its coldness. He cocked a lashless eye at her face. 'Bain't seen any such animal, have thee, Peg?'

'No,' she said, and he nodded in relief.

I should be indignant. She should be protesting at Nevis's suspicions but she had to concentrate so hard on suppressing panic that she had no energy left for even spurious rage.

A crash and shouts from upstairs told her that Nevis's instinct had again led him to concentrate his search on the main north-wing bedroom. She ran upstairs, followed by Sir Ostyn.

Muskett, shouting, was being restrained by two of Nevis's men. If possible the room was in even worse condition than it had been after Nevis's previous search. The sliver of looking-glass had been ground under somebody's boot, every drawer lay scattered, the bed had been stripped down to its frame and her newly mended mattress once more torn open. The crash had been caused by the tester which had given way under the weight of one of Nevis's soldiers as he crawled into the space between it and the ceiling of the room. The bedhead, however, was still untouched.

Now she was angry. Or panicked. Or both. She strode to the bed and pulled the soldier off it. For good measure she kicked him. Then she turned on Nevis. 'By what right do you do this again? I would remind you I am a loyal subject of King James and his late cousin's good friend. I shall inform the King of your repeated vandalism, and complain to the Lord Chief Justice when he dines here tonight.'

'And so I will too.' Considering his previous reduction at Nevis's hands, Sir Ostyn was showing courage.

Nevis was not impressed. She wondered what *would* impress

Nevis. His face was not unpleasant but it was unmemorable. Away from him, when she tried to recall it, she couldn't bring it to mind because it was unrepresentative of the animosity she felt streaming from the soul behind it. There was no way to reach the man because he took no sustenance from people around him, apparently desiring nobody's goodwill but his own, following some route he had set for himself. She had impeded him; set up a block between him and the man he was hunting down. But he had the antennae of an ant, and like an ant would find a way up, round, down or across to his goal without ceasing, until he was squashed.

He terrified her.

He looked straight at her. 'He's here. I fucking know he's here. And I'm going to find him.'

'Don't you swear to a lady, you varmint,' shouted Sir Ostyn, nostrils gaping. 'Ah'm going to speak to your colonel about this behavin' of yours . . .'

'Three,' said Nevis. He wasn't looking at the magistrate. He looked at Penitence. 'One. Hurd. Two. Martin Hughes. And now a man called Mudge Ridge. Three.'

She swallowed. 'What about them?'

'I've questioned a lot of people, lady. And people answer my questions when I ask them.'

She could imagine his method of questioning.

'Witnesses saw Hurd being carried in this direction. Witnesses saw a cart containing the man Hughes coming in this direction. And now, after a break-out at Ilchester gaol, the man Ridge, your bailiff, madam, is seen. By witnesses. Coming in this direction. Today.' His voice was flat; he used pauses as emphasis. He turned on the magistrate: 'Coincidence?'

'Certainly 'tis,' said Sir Ostyn stoutly.

'No.' His voice held the certainty of the world. 'There's a hidden room in this house. I'm having mallets fetched and I'm going to reduce these fucking walls to rubble 'til I find it.'

'Not tonight, my dear man,' said a voice from the doorway. '*What* a mess. Like a hen-house. But this is still the best bedroom in the house. What*ever* you're going to do, it'll *have* to wait until tomorrow.'

It was Jeffreys's major-domo, a willowy, middle-aged man in primrose brocade who kept cupping his face in his hands. He carried the Lord Chief Justice's authority but, more effectually, his concerns were so trivial that it was as if his limp fingers had snuffed out a lighted fuse. Neither Sir Ostyn nor Major Nevis could cope with him. Nevis gave Penitence a last look: 'I'm putting such a ring round this house tonight as a mouse won't get out. And tomorrow the walls come down.'

When he'd gone, her legs gave way and she sat down on the bed to gather herself for the next fight. The major-domo had already set his minions on cleaning up the room. 'We'll need our mattress, and our sheets ... We'll cover the tester with a curtain.'

'This is my bedroom,' she told him.

The major-domo's eyes opened wide: 'If Sir George stays, we'll need the best bedroom.'

'Why would he be staying?'

'Dear lady,' the major-domo wriggled his shoulders, 'if you don't know I'm sure I don't.' He plucked at his chain of office. 'We'll need a place to change after our day in court, regardless, so a bedroom we must have.'

'Not this one.'

He flung out his arms and huffed, but gave way. 'Oh. Very well.' He chose the bedroom next door instead.

She had a horror of Jeffreys's arrival that was not only fear of its complications in getting Benedick away. Until this morning, she had thought of the man as a bully and tyrant, but nevertheless as faintly amusing in his delight at his prowess, an over-acting actor. Since the trial of Lady Alice and the sights and sounds of Taunton's market square the man had grown monstrous to her. She had seen the reality of his sentences, heard it, smelled it, known that he wouldn't scruple to apply it to her own son.

I beg you, God. Don't let him come.

She was thrown into another panic as the major-domo ordered the hall table to be set for dinner. 'Why not the dining-room?' she asked. The gargoyle's orifices had been unstopped to allow the two men in the secret room to breathe now that the door had to be shut on them. Every time she passed it she fancied she heard muttering.

'Too small, dear lady,' said the major-domo immediately.

'How many people are coming for Heaven's sake?'

The major-domo's hands pressed together under his cheek, like a child sleeping. He had the most meaningless set of gestures she'd ever seen. 'It depends what mood we're in. I've known us bring near a hundred.' He caught sight of her face, and showed his first bit of compassion. 'If you're worried for your supplies, dear lady, we've brought all with us.' He spoke no less than the truth. His people were already setting out epergnes and cutlery produced from green baize bags.

A little of Penitence's self-respect as a householder came back. 'I have my own silver. We will use that.'

'We only like the best, dear lady.'

'I have the best.'

Rupert's silver, brought with her from Awdes, opened the major-domo's eyes. '*Madam*. Why didn't you *say*?' From then on he treated her more courteously, which was a mixed blessing in that he tended to consult her on every point, which in turn meant that, in order not to seem on intimate terms with Muskett, she had to dismiss that invaluable sergeant from the bedroom.

She employed the age that followed in dressing meticulously and employing every artifice and paint she could think of to make her face less haggard. Every few minutes she went to the window to look for Henry. *He's not coming. It's useless.* She watched the sun set and the moon rise. She watched Nevis throw a cordon round the far side of the moat and heard the frogs in the marsh begin their monotonous, bellowing court-ship. She lit candles and went back to her mirror because fear had brought out beads of sweat on her top lip. She looked passable. She reminded herself of every ageing actress's rule: *Keep your back to the light.*

The smell of the night grasses in the marsh was being subdued by the smells coming from the kitchen where she could hear Jeffreys's French cooks shouting at each other. The major-domo himself had taken the rest of his staff out to the

586

grounds where, after consultation with her, the entertainment was to be held.

Prue had been sent to stay the night at the vicar's house in the village. She had wanted to stay and Penitence had wanted to keep her, but as soon as Nevis and his men had arrived at the house the memory of the night she'd almost been raped had rendered her incapable of doing anything but tremble. Penitence missed her.

The rest of the house was quiet. She heard a creak on the tiny flight of steps that led to the passage between the hall and the solar. It did that sometimes. When she went out to check that nobody was outside the room, the corridor was empty.

Returning, she opened the bedhead panel and pushed the door behind it. 'Are you all right?' Stale air came out at her.

It was Benedick's voice. 'The old man won't stop praying.'

'Stop up the holes.'

'Then we can't breathe.'

Damn the man. Why had she taken him in? What had Puritans ever done for her except threaten her life, and now that of her son? She said quite seriously: 'Smother him if you have to.'

She heard her son give a grunt of amusement. 'Is he here yet?'

'No,' she said. 'Jeffreys isn't either.'

'I meant Jeffreys.'

'Oh.'

'I'm sorry I called the Viscount out.' *Bless him, he's trying to please.* 'I can see that you wouldn't want me to kill him. If he is my father.'

'I do know, Benedick,' she said coldly.

A bony-wristed young hand emerged out of the panel, felt about and found her hand. 'It'd be like that Oedipus fellow. Killing your father, I mean.'

'Not quite,' she said. Eton education had done little to instil the full implication of Greek tragedy into her son. 'Oh, Benedick. I don't know if Muskett's plan will work. I don't know if he'll come. The grounds are full of soldiers.'

'I'm a bother, aren't I?'

She was transported back twenty years. Who'd said that and nearly broken her heart in saying it? *Job.* Her Ladyship's poor, brave Job. *It's an omen.* Job had died. Benedick would die.

She cradled her son's hand against her cheek.

'For God's sake, Boots, what's going on?' The Viscount had to bend his head to get through the door.

She had wanted him to come so much and been so afraid that he wouldn't that she was disconcerted now that he had. 'Where have you been?'

'Busy.' He looked down at her without warmth. 'So, from the looks of things, have you. What have you been doing, selling tickets?'

While she was telling him, Muskett came marching into the room. 'Lights of Lord Jeffreys' retinue seen on the causeway, suh.'

The Viscount walked to the window. 'We could evade that old tub of lard and any of his people. It's Nevis who worries me. Why's he here tonight of all nights?'

'I think it's because Mudge Ridge has escaped. They think he's heading this way. And Nevis only wants an excuse. Henry, he *knows* Benedick is here. I don't know how he knows, but he knows. He's talking about battering down walls tomorrow.'

'So we've got to get the boy away tonight.'

'Muskett's got a plan,' Penitence said. 'Tell him, Muskett.'

She watched his face as Muskett told him, committing it to memory in case the desperate, autumnal sadness that had settled on her was a true foreboding of loss. His nose was still too big; he wasn't handsome at all yet she only had to look at him to want him. She saw his eyebrows go up. 'Othello? I know the words but . . .' He turned to Penitence. 'I've never played Othello in my life.'

'Oh yes, you have,' she said, and if she knew anything she knew this: 'You've played him for the last twenty years.' He was taken aback. She stood up: 'I must go. Will you do it?'

Instead of answering, he looked at Muskett. 'Think up this little gem all by yourself, did you, you bugger?'

'Suh,' rapped out Muskett. 'The old carpet gentleman gave us the idea, suh.'

His master nodded. 'Thank him for me.'

Penitence went downstairs to greet the Lord Chief Justice.

As Penitence, standing at the gatehouse, swept her curtsey, Jeffreys's major-domo muttered at the sight of his master: 'We've got the stone bad again. My, look at us. Want to piss. Can't piss. Think we can booze it away. There'll be tears before bedtime.'

Judge Jeffreys had come prepared for a Bacchanalia. He'd brought nearly forty people with him, only a few of them respectable like Sir William Portman, the local Member of Parliament, and his wife, and Sir Ostyn, who'd invited himself. They already looked as if they regretted coming.

The rest were soldiers such as Colonel Kirk of the Tangier Regiment, who was joined by Nevis and Lieutenant Jones, and Assize luminaries like the Prosecutor and Deputy Clerk, or lesser courtiers who'd travelled down from London – Penitence recognized a couple of the fops who'd attended her farewell performance at the Duke's.

Kirk greeted her with over-familiarity. 'We remember the old days, don't we, mistress?' As if they'd slept together. In fact, it was his sister, Mal, a fervent theatregoer, who'd known her. She'd been a maid of honour at court – a title she lost by sleeping with James when he was the Duke of York. Now that Penitence came to think of it, Mal had also slept with Monmouth himself. It was thanks to her that Kirk got his first commission. Monmouth had given it to him. Apart from long eye-teeth which gave him a wolf's smile, Kirk radiated amiability where Nevis didn't but it was from Kirk that the Lambs had gained their reputation for terror. He had two women hanging on to his arm who, from the look of them, had been trawled from the stews of Taunton. There were more attached to some of the other male guests. All of them were drunk.

Their behaviour, even as they stepped down from their coaches, showed an expectation of later sexual activity – with whom seemed unimportant.

Do they think I'm a trollop? The insult, she felt, was to Rupert and Rupert's house. By the time dinner was half-way through she felt more offence than fear and from her end of the table — she'd had to fight the major-domo, who'd wanted her next to Jeffreys, to take her place at the head of her table — was inhibiting her guests' worst excesses with an expression of hauteur that might have caused Elizabeth Tudor to wonder if she was using the right knife.

She had no help from Henry. Half-way down the right-hand side of the table, he was absorbed in eating and staring down the cleavage of a dark-haired female who sat between him and Nevis and who appeared willing that he should. His was the only head not turned in the direction of the Lord Chief Justice at the other end of the table from hers.

Penitence knew she was inhibiting an orgy, but only just. Soon most of the guests, including Jeffreys if he kept drinking as he was, would be out of control.

She had managed to turn the conversation away from sexual badinage, only to have it concentrate on the day's trials, which, as it turned out, were grosser. Jeffreys was boasting. 'She was pleading for him to be handed over unmutilated. And I said to the woman, "Certainly, madam, since you plead so eloquently, you shall have what part of his body you love best and I shall direct the Sheriff accordingly."'

Sir Nicholas Fenton, whom Penitence remembered from Charles II's court, laughed inordinately and patted the Chief Justice's hand: 'Wonderful, my lord. Give her the prick. Give 'em all the bloody prick. How many today, my lord?'

Sir George's mouth emerged black and glistening from his wine cup, leaving Penitence with the impression that he had been drinking blood. 'Two hundred and seventy-two.'

The Deputy Prosecutor stretched. 'A number to go down in the annals as never has been, never will again be tried in one day.'

'Two hundred and seventy-two,' quavered Sir Nicholas. 'Wonderful, wonderful.'

Colonel Kirk shouted: 'What of the Maids, my lord? When do you try the Maids?'

Penitence stopped pretending to eat and listened. She had

hoped to appeal to Jeffreys to order the children's release. Poor Mrs Yeo traipsed over the moor every day to visit her daughter in Taunton prison.

The Lord Chief Justice drew himself up. Kirk had over-stepped the mark. 'They shall stay where they are. I am not in the business of trying schoolgirls.'

'Schoolgirls. Bloody wonderful.'

'Nevertheless, my lord,' persisted Kirk, 'they'll fetch a pretty penny. I hope you'll remind the King to reward his soldiery with some of the profit.'

Jeffreys shrugged. 'The judiciary as well as the soldiery need reward. But let their canting families buy them out as they will. It's no business of mine.'

Penitence turned to Sir William Portman who, seated on her right, was looking increasingly uncomfortable. 'What can he mean? What's to happen to the girls?'

Lady Portman leaned across her husband: 'It's rumoured that they'll stay in gaol until their parents buy them out. They're to be given to the Queen's maids of honour for the profit.'

'Maids to maids,' said Penitence, 'I see.'

'Shshh,' said Lady Portman, warning her to lower her voice, but Sir Nicholas Fenton took up the phrase. 'Maids to maids. Wonderful.'

What have I to do with these people? She could not bear that they were here in her hall, not just for the danger they posed but for their butcher-shop souls. Behind Jeffreys's head hung Rupert's portrait and she imagined it reproached her. He had given her this house and she had desecrated it with these vulgar people, even, God help her, with the physical joy she'd found in bed with another man.

The clarity of this beautiful room was being drowned by the profane conversations and the languorous tunes now played by the Lord Chief Justice's musicians in a corner by the stairhead. The great, pure line of its shape was confused by the bowls of flowers and resined torches in their sconces with which the major-domo had seen fit to decorate it, overcoming its elusive scent of incense.

The only indigenous thing that was in accord with the swine at her trough was the north-east gargoyle. It gibbered at her, trying to attract her attention, and theirs. She could swear she heard the thing whispering.

The sight of the table itself made her gag; she'd not seen such food in weeks. There was too much meat, too few sallets. Blood and fat oozed, glistening, out of the baron of beef, the mound of pickled pigs' feet ('our favourite' according to the major-domo) had been knocked so that trotters rolled between the dishes, the fried sweetbreads and liver of veal overflowed their rich, dark red sauce.

'Not eating, dear madam?' boomed Jeffreys down the table at her.

'I have no stomach for it.'

Strangely, he understood. 'My 'domo tells me you were disquieted by Jack Ketch's work in the market this morning.'

'Yes,' she said. The rest of the table had gone quiet.

'Regrettable, regrettable.' Gravy and wine dripped on his chin. 'But an example had to be made here, now, at the start, though the tender heart of a lady cannot see it. Tender heart.' He lingered over the thought as if he'd eat it. Then he shook his lace cuffs at her. 'But I promise you, madam, there'll be sound sense to show mercy in other towns of the Assize, now the point is made.'

'And a sound profit.' There was absolute silence. *What are you doing?* She couldn't believe she'd said it. *You may need this man.*

Jeffreys's little eyes became smaller. He wasn't pleased but he allowed himself to be diverted by Sir Nicholas Fenton's guffaw: 'Sound profit. Wonderful.'

Kirk brought attention back to her. 'Talking of profit, my second-in-command suspects Mistress Hughes of kidnapping rebels that she may claim the reward. He says three such have been seen near the precincts. One of them Hurd, no less.' He was joking; he didn't believe it. She'd seen him arguing with Nevis.

'Kidnapper. Wonderful.'

'What's this? What's this?' Jeffreys had picked up a scent.

'I've extracted a description of Hurd's likeness from some of the rebels he commanded.' Nevis was delving down the side of his boot. He was producing a piece of parchment. 'He was seen being carried off the field in this direction.'

From somewhere Penitence produced a shrug. 'The major has seen fit to search my house twice, my lord, with no result. And I protest, my lord. It's hardly likely I'd shelter the enemies of Prince Rupert's nephew.' *Remind them of who you are.*

But the parchment was going the rounds of the table.

'Not unlike you, only younger, Viscount,' said Sir Ostyn, the fool.

Henry stretched out a hand for it: 'Not as handsome.'

When it reached Penitence she managed a creditable sneer: 'He looks like Hamlet's ghost. Perhaps you should look for him on the ramparts, Major. Except that we have no ramparts.'

'Wonderful. No ramparts.'

'Come, Major,' said Jeffreys. 'You've searched the place and done your duty as you see it. Now let this sweet soul be. I order it.'

For a moment, Penitence thought Nevis would persist; for all his instinct, the man had no perception of how to be graceful even when it was in his interest to be so, but he saw the sense of bowing. 'I'll keep a ring of men round the house nevertheless.'

Kirk slapped him on the back and turned to Jeffreys. 'No harm in that, my lord, just for the night. The man could have hid out in the grounds. Nevis has a nose for these things. It's your safety we think of.'

Over in the dark corner beyond the fireplace the gargoyle gibbered and chattered.

Jeffreys nodded: 'Very well. If it does not interfere with our entertainment, hostess?' It wasn't really a question.

Penitence rose. 'On that matter, sir, I must go and prepare it.' As she passed his chair to go to the stairs, Jeffreys put out a hand and grabbed her arm, pulling her down so that her face was close to his. She smelled the wine and meat on his breath. He'd become amorous. 'Play Desdemona for me. 'Twas when I loved thee first. Dost love me, Peg?'

'Who could not?' *Keep it playful.* 'Will you be my Othello, my lord?'

He whispered: 'A pox on Othello. Green-eyed cur. Give me a kiss. I'd not kill thee on that bed, Peg, except with love.'

She couldn't tolerate being near him. Heat rose out of his big body and enveloped her. She smiled down at him, kissed his sweating cheek and stared into his eyes. 'Until then, my Moor must be more murderous. Who 'tis will surprise you, I think.' *This sounds like Dryden at his worst.*

She was pulled down further and nearly toppled as his mouth tried for hers and found her chin instead. 'Play Desdemona for me. 'Twas when I loved thee first.'

Lord, how she loathed drunks and their reiteration. But as she scurried along the passageway to her bedroom, she could have sung. She'd thought she might have to manœuvre the Lord Chief Justice into requesting an excerpt from *Othello*; instead he'd done it voluntarily. *So far so good.*

Muskett had found two more looking-glasses and set them on to tables. Her dress, cloak, wig and shoes were laid out on one. On the other was a jar of lampblack, a long piece of bed-curtain and Rupert's best travelling cape lined with scarlet sarcenet. 'The theatre lost a fine dresser when you went into private service, Muskett.'

'Thank you, mistress.' He went outside. With him guarding the door while she changed, it meant that she could open the bed-panel. 'Are you ready? Let me see you.' She studied the head thrust through the hole, kissed it and echoed Sir Nicholas Fenton. 'Wonderful.' *Is it?* Would it fool Nevis? 'And once you're back in the Netherlands, stay there.' She slammed the panel back in place as the door opened.

It was Henry. Immediately he sat down at the dressing-table. 'Where's the sodding looking-glass? God Almighty, I'm too old for this.' Smearing lampblack on his face, he squinted over at her: 'And so are you. Did my eyes deceive me or did you just now encourage the dishonourable intentions of the gentleman in the ruby flush?'

She was busy before her own glass. 'He's got to be kept sweet. We may need him before this night's out.'

'How?'

'I don't know.' How could she know? 'If Benedick's discovered . . . we could plead his connection to Rupert.'

'Boots, the King has just beheaded his own nephew. Jeffreys isn't likely to overlook your son's treachery merely because the boy got on well with Rupert. Or because you tickle his fancy.'

You don't know. She'd got herself out of one of the worst parts of the worst prison in England by selling herself to a man. She'd become an actress by selling herself to another. *You don't know what men will do for lust.* The heat rising from Jeffreys's body wasn't different from the heat of George, or Killigrew.

With a start she saw he was watching her. 'Great God Almighty,' he said. 'You'd do it.'

And she would. The thought made her flesh creep, it wiped all colour out of present and future, but if it came to it and Benedick's life was the prize, she would do it.

She could hear her name being shouted from the hall. Her audience awaited her.

'Decus et Dolor,' she said and went out.

Chapter 6

THE SETTING was wonderful. As she'd begun to explain that afternoon what she wanted for the entertainment, the major-domo had patted his nose: 'If there's one thing we know about, dear lady, it's drama. We've seen enough. Leave it to me.' There'd been little time to do anything else and the man had flung himself into the role of theatre manager with abandon.

They'd agreed the stage should be the grassy platform that formed a natural terrace to the south side of the house before sloping down to the yew chessmen, the lawn and the moat. Tonight it looked as if it had been invaded by giant fireflies. Chinese lanterns imported by Rupert through the East India

Company hung from branches and the spears of yew horse-men. Jeffreys's musicians played softly and unseen from the moat edge where lampions hung over the water, showing up the white of its water-lilies and adding their reflections to the moon's bigger one.

On the platform itself had been ranged urns of flowers. The children's sea-shells, collected during an excursion to the coast, formed the reflector of the footlights and the back set was provided by the open french doors to the lit interior of the room in the south wing that had been Rupert's library.

A couch trailing silk shawls and rugs had been set centre back and was causing ribald comment from the members of the audience as they took their seats on the cushioned benches.

Penitence and the major-domo stood in the wings — a curtain hung between the yew Red Queen and one of her pawns. He had his elbows together and was banging his fists, like a child afraid of thunder. 'Listen to the *noise*. How can you quell them, dear lady? Aren't you *quaking*?'

She was, but not from stagefright. 'What's your name?'

'Gilbert.'

'Gilbert, I've quelled audiences that make this one look like Puritans at prayer.' Compared with the stinkards in full cry from Charles II's court, these were amateurs.

Down by the moat the musicians were waiting for her signal. She raised an arm, a trumpet blared, the audience on the benches whoo-hoo-ed, and Peg Hughes stepped out before the footlights once again.

Had she gone straight into the serious speeches they'd have goose- and cat-called as a revenge for the disapproval she'd radiated during dinner. She wrong-footed them. She'd pinned her hair into a cap of curls, décolletaged her basque until it almost showed the nipples, and in Cockney sang them:

> 'My lodging upon the cold floor is,
> And wonderful hard is my fare,
> But that which troubles me more is
> The fatness of my dear.'

At the familiar song, those who were theatregoers burst into spontaneous applause. 'Nelly,' called Fenton, 'Nelly to the life. Wonderful.'

Penitence strutted, swishing her petticoat and winking at Jeffreys.

> 'Yet still I cry "O melt, love,
> And I prithee now melt apace,
> For thou art the man I should long for
> If 'twere not for thy grease."'

It brought a laugh at Jeffreys's expense which was dangerous, but it got the rest of the audience on her side to play with. Gradually, teasingly, she led them along the gamut from sauciness to the maudlin, picking up Jeffreys along the way by a heart-rending appeal to him as she sang:

> 'None ever had so strange an art
> His passion to convey,
> Into a list'ning virgin's heart,
> And steal her soul away.'

It was inviting a cat-call for 'virgin' but each time she took a bow she inched her basque a little higher and they listened more soberly. During Balthazar's song she dared switch her attention for a second. White buttocks pumping up and down behind a yew knight were Sir Nicholas Fenton's on top of a Taunton whore. *Her Ladyship wouldn't have let a Cock and Pie girl be so sluttish.* On the benches Nevis himself was the only one sober. He sat upright, his head turning from her to the moonlit garden, as if he knew she was up to something. Beyond him she could see he'd ranged his men and Jeffreys's dragoons round the far side of the moat at twenty-five-yard intervals, dark statuary in the moonlight.

Several of them leaned on their pikes, listening, instead of holding them at the slope – but that didn't matter. For the purposes of Muskett's plan, it was what was going to happen in a moment that counted.

597

She went into Portia's 'The quality of mercy', kneeling and holding out her arms to Jeffreys. *And you listen, you pig.*

It was time. Somewhere in one of the upper windows, Henry had been waiting for his cue. From the far side of the house came screams and shouts. Somebody loosed off a musket, one or two on the benches sprang up groping for their swords.

Round the corner of the house, pursued by Muskett with a clapperboard, capered a tall figure dressed in stuffed pantaloons, full-sleeved shirt and a wide-brimmed hat with a feather so drooped that it curled under its owner's nose. Its face was black and its codpiece was the size of a plum pudding from which stuck an enormous dildo. It was a clown straight from the Harlequinade out of Scaramouche via the Mysteries and, automatically, the benches laughed.

One of the sentries, a sergeant, was apologizing to Kirk. 'Gave us a start, sir. Black face an' all, came rushing out at us like and Davis let off a shot. Thought it was the Devil, sir.'

Kirk was still laughing, it was Nevis who snarled: 'Get back to your post and stay there.'

The black-faced clown fell on its knees at Jeffreys's feet:

> 'Is it the law? When he knocks on the door?
> For poor old Nick? Merely showing his dick,
> In the cause of farce? To get shot in the arse?'

The Lord Chief Justice twitched the clown's hat off. He'd been put out when he arrived to find Henry *in situ*, regarding him as a rival, but now he collapsed with laughter. 'The man shall suffer the utmost rigour of the law, Viscount.'

Penitence retired to the wings to unpin her hair while the major-domo draped Desdemona's cloak around her. As she brushed out her hair, Henry joined her. Muskett helped him change, put Othello's cloak around him and exchanged the hat for a turban made of Penitence's green brocade bed-curtain pinned with a brooch of brilliants that Rupert had given her after the birth of Ruperta.

Henry said: 'All right, Muskett, get back to the bedroom

and stay there. Major Nevis may try to search it again. From the sight of him he's unimpressed by our hostess's display.'

He didn't look at Penitence as he added: 'Though she seems to have seduced the rest.'

'Oh for God's sake,' she said, irritably, 'I'm lulling them.'

'Is that what Her Ladyship called it? Go and get on the bed. Let's finish the farce.'

'Decus et Dolor,' she said, but he wouldn't answer.

The french doors to Rupert's study had been closed. After a minute they opened, revealing the bed and, this time, Desdemona in her nightgown and her hair down, singing her willow song. There were no bed-jokes now. As she finished and lay down to sleep the garden was quiet except for a nightingale singing in the woods behind and, again, the Lord Chief Justice's sobs.

I did lull them. Why *are you always jealous?*

She heard him pad on to the terrace and begin pacing as he went into the great soliloquy from Scene ii of the last act. It was a long time since he'd been on a stage, but the emotion he shared with the man he was playing added a vibrancy to his Othello that even Betterton wasn't capable of. She realized how much he hid from her by humour. *I'm so sorry. Why don't you believe I love you?* Perhaps he did but, like Othello, like all men, he was incapable of understanding that a woman could be sensual and faithful at the same time. If she felt passion she must be passionate. If passionate she could not be faithful. Eve, she thought. *It's all the fault of Eve.*

How had the two of them evolved from Beatrice and Benedick to Desdemona and Othello? Whatever he thought she had done, however many men he thought she'd had, why couldn't he accept it and take what happiness they possessed now? Men were such egotists, such exclusivists. They had to possess things to love them.

> 'Yet I'll not shed her blood,
> Nor scar that whiter skin of hers than snow,
> And smooth as monumental alabaster.

Yet she must die, else she'll betray more men.
Put out the light and then put out the light.'

Henry, I'm so sorry. Until now she hadn't penetrated how deeply she'd tormented his soul.

It was too late to change her interpretation of Desdemona as a sensual woman. It was the way she had played her when Rupert had brought him to the theatre. He'd stood in the doorway at King's and seen her abandoning herself to love in Hart's arms.

I was acting then. You must know I'm not acting now.

When he woke Desdemona, she put out her arms and pulled him down on her like a woman used to making love the moment her man came to bed. She heard the hiss of Jeffreys's breath. So did he, and dragged away so that she was thrown back down with her hair across her face.

As she pleaded for her life, she stroked his face. As Desdemona and as Penitence she tried to show how much she loved him.

'Think on your sins,' he commanded. *Remember the Cock and Pie.*

'They are loves I bear to you.' *I do remember. I lived twenty years on the memory. Don't leave me.*

'Ay, and for that thou diest.'

He forced her down on the bed, calling her a strumpet, and as the pillow went over her face she knew it flashed through his mind from some barbaric reservoir within him to press until she couldn't torment him any more. He mastered it within the second.

A high falsetto spoke unseen from the wings telling Othello that Iago had contrived the situation from malice and that Desdemona was innocent. The major-domo had offered his services as Emilia and was reading from a précis composed by Penitence allowing Othello to go into 'Behold! I have a weapon' and then to 'I kissed thee ere I killed thee'.

The body she knew so well fell on hers. 'No way but this, killing myself to die upon a kiss.' And he *was* kissing her; no professional actor would have kissed like that — it was too

600

distracting, let alone being barely decent. She was aware of nothing but him, the applause was a background, like far-away thunder.

Her body was so part of his that she felt the tap on his back, somebody knocking at the gate of their secret garden. It was Jeffreys trying to get in. The scene had inflamed him; it was his right to lie down on Desdemona – he'd provided the dinner. 'You have maddened me, my dear,' he said, as he helped her up. 'Let us steal away for some time to ourselves.'

The Viscount got up, stretching: 'I fear it *would* be stealing, my lord. I see Mistress Hughes and I must reveal our secret. Come, madam.' He pulled Penitence to her feet and put his arm round her, bringing her to centre stage and raising his voice: 'Mistress Hughes has consented to be my wife. We are to marry as soon as my duty is over at Bridgwater. Aren't we, sweetness?'

She knew what he supposed he was doing; protecting her with his name when he left her with Jeffreys and his retinue, as he would have to in a minute if their plan was to succeed. It was past two o'clock already.

She doubted if he knew what he was doing in fact; marking his territory so that nobody else should have her in his absence. Worse, he'd humiliated the Lord Chief Justice in public. He didn't see Jeffreys's face – in accord with the plan, Muskett had come up saying the horses were ready and they were late returning to Bridgwater for duty. From this moment everything must be conducted at a rush.

Only she saw Jeffreys's furious blush of humiliation that his plan for the night had not just been foiled, but foiled in front of all the friends who'd known what it was.

Jeffreys wasn't one of the court wits who could seem to shrug off the fickleness of one woman – however much he might punish her in verse later – as long as there was another to take her place. That a woman was affianced had meant nothing to such as them; they would take her just the same. But Jeffreys came from a lower-class, higher-church stratum of society than theirs; he was a bourgeois; his women had to dote on him while he had them, and on him alone – they must not have given their hand to another man practically under his nose. *He'll never forgive me.* She saw the hatred come into his small, boar's eye, not for the Viscount but for her, who'd led him on.

The Viscount was speaking to Kirk, laughing and slapping his back like a boy: 'See me frighten the sentries, Percy? What do you say? I think I'll stay in costume and frighten all the ones who've fallen asleep on duty as I ride back. That'll make the lazy sods sit up.'

Jeffreys bowed to Penitence. 'Madam, be good enough to order my carriage brought to the door.'

It was apparent to everyone that such entertainment as there'd been was all the Priory was going to provide. The night's fornication was cancelled, unless it could be had in the carriages on the way back to Taunton. Perhaps this was why the Viscount's suggestion was appealing. Everybody was for dressing-up and scaring the sentries on the roadblocks across the moor. Lampblack was produced and most of the men and at least two of the women were smothering their faces in it, winding their scarves round their heads in imitation of Othello's turban.

Sir Nicholas Fenton had gone so far as to take off his trousers and, to the horror of Lady Portland, was blacking his penis. 'That'll fright the sentries.'

Everyone repaired to the courtyard where the carriages waited. Jeffreys clambered into his. Penitence ran to it to say goodbye but the Lord Chief Justice refused to look at her. He called to Kirk, who was standing nearby: 'Withdraw your men, Colonel, we shall need them in Taunton tomorrow. Leave this mistress to be guarded by her husband. I wish him well of her.' He jabbed his coachman in the back with his staff and was driven off, leaving the other drunks to crowd in the three remaining vehicles.

Nevis was shifting from place to place, checking faces.

Penitence had set aside a punch as a stirrup cup. She ran to fetch it and in going with it from guest to guest kept their attention away from the Viscount and his casual remark that he must fetch his sword from his tiring-room. Out of the corner of her eye, she saw his robed and turbaned figure retreat into the screen passage and disappear up the newel staircase.

It came down a minute later, buckling on its sword, the black face invisible in the dark of the passage and only the brilliants in the turban catching the reflection of the carriage lamps in the courtyard.

Muskett helped him up on his horse and then got up on another. Penitence handed him the stirrup cup. 'Good luck with the sentries,' she said. When he'd drunk, he gave her back the cup and she felt his fingers stroke the back of her hand for a second before he shook the reins and his horse walked forward to join the queue of departing guests at the gatehouse.

Nevis stood on one side of it and Lieutenant Jones on the other, both of them with a lantern held high, scanning the faces as they went by. Kirk was arguing with him: 'If you've been through the house, then he's not here. We'll need the men in Taunton tomorrow – from the look of Jeffreys' complexion he'll hang the whole town. It's an order, Nevis.'

Servants carrying lampions were riding ahead of the carriages, each one slowing down until Nevis nodded them through and Jones slapped their horses' rumps to send them on their way. Behind the next carriage Othello and Muskett were approaching the gatehouse.

The Portmans and Sir Ostyn bade subdued goodbyes. 'You didn't tell me as you were betrothed to a viscount,' Sir Ostyn reproached her.

'I didn't know I was,' she told him.

He peered at her. 'You don't look too viddy, maid. Do ee want me to stay?' He meant it kindly, and she refused as courteously as she could. *Just go*.

Gilbert the major-domo was supervising the loading of his wagons by the kitchen and came teetering in and out of the courtyard to tell her what couldn't be found and what would have to be fetched the next day. He was worried and as affronted as his master: 'You've upset him. I *said* there'd be tears before bedtime. It's all very well, dear lady, but it isn't you that gets Gilbert you're a varlet and a boot at your head.'

She peered over his shoulder to see what was happening at the gatehouse. There was a delay. Nicholas Fenton leaned down from his carriage – it was the last – to scream his thanks and show her his black genitals. She nodded at them, 'Very nice, Sir Nicholas,' her eyes on the hold-up where Nevis's lantern was practically scorching the lampblack on Othello's face as he examined it.

Please God. If they were discovered now she had added Henry to the list of those who would stand before Jeffreys in the dock.

They were through. The lantern had lowered. Nevis had nodded. Jones had slapped the rump of Othello's horse and now the rump of Muskett's. Kirk was following the two of them. Nevis was following *him.* His men were forming into a phalanx ready to march off. *Thank you, God, thank you, thank you, thank you.*

She stood on the bridge of the moat waving as the last of the major-domo's wagons lumbered through the gates at the bottom of the drive to join the cavalcade as it wound its way to the moonlit causeway. She watched the twinkling line until distance extinguished its lights one by one. At Middlezoy, with luck, two of its riders would peel away from it and ride like hell towards Bridgwater and the coast. There would be so many roadblocks to negotiate. Most of the sentries would know Muskett – and they knew the Captain-Viscount's horse. Would they let them by?

She wondered how she had the strength to go on worrying. She was empty; no emotion left, yet the part of her that had gone with the man now crossing Sedgemoor still had the ability to be afraid.

The quiet of the night was soothing; her ears vibrated with the noise she had lived with for the past few hours.

She had regained her Priory. She should have had the drawbridge chains repaired so that she could shut out Jeffreys's brutish world for ever. As it was, she bolted the gatehouse before she did a circuit of the house to make sure Nevis had left nobody behind. The topiary chessmen had retained some of the heat of the day and exuded the sweet smell of yew; the tobacco flowers Rupert had imported from the Americas to remind her of Massachusetts came into their own at night and added to the scent of roses and lavender and bruised grass.

A white shape was peering out from behind one of the chessmen. She made herself run at it – and found it was a pair of drawers. Sir Nicholas's. Further on she stumbled over a snake and gasped. But it was the dildo.

She had disturbed a bird; she heard a rustling in the bushes down by the moat, and found herself hurrying. She shut the terrace doors of Rupert's study and locked them, then walked quickly round the rest of the house until she'd regained the courtyard. It was dark, the major-domo had removed all the candles he'd brought and lit none of hers. The moon was still high, but under the shadow of the eaves she had to feel for the lock on the doors of the two wings and try a couple of keys from her chatelaine before she turned them. She had left the doors unlocked on purpose – it showed she had nothing to hide.

She groped her way in through the hall door, locked it behind her and ran her left hand along the screen until it touched the newel post of the stairs. Her high heels clacked loudly into the silence of the house and the top rise of the stairs creaked, as it always did. She put her feet more carefully in obedience with the growing instinct to keep everything quiet.

Unusually, her hall was hot – the major-domo had insisted on lighting the fire – and smelled of meat, tobacco and scented resin. Moonlight curved over her feet as she stepped through its reflection on the floor to open one of the lights and let in the night air. She stood at the window looking over Sedgemoor, wondering how Benedick would feel crossing the moor where so many comrades lay buried. *Make sure you don't join them, my son.*

A barn owl flapped past on white, lazy wings, causing her to start back, and behind her the gargoyle screamed.

It kept on screaming as she hared along the passage to her room, threw herself on the bed and ran her fingers over the bedhead searching for Eve's nipple.

There was a flickering light when the panel drew back and she could hear movement. 'Henry? What's the matter?'

'Your bloody uncle or whatever he is, that's who's the matter.'

She could see into the room now. A rushlight stood on the floor near Martin Hughes's bed. Martin himself had hunched himself into a corner and was uttering monotonous screams, his eyes bulging as he stared at what Penitence had to admit, if you'd just woken up, would be a shock. In an up-thrown light the Viscount looked a tall demon from Hell. She wriggled into the hole, seized the rushlight, emerged with it and lit one of her bedroom candles. With its aid she found a pot of lanolin grease and some lamb's-wool which she took back with the rushlight and handed in to the Viscount. 'It's all right,' she said soothingly to her great-uncle. 'He was disguised. You're safe now, thanks to him. We'll get you away soon.'

'Did the boy get away?' Henry scrubbed lampblack off his face.

'He got away from *here*. Oh, Henry, there's such a long way for him to go.'

'He's got Muskett. Muskett'll see him through.'

'Yes. I miss Muskett.' She'd become dependent on the man.

'He'll be back. He'll see the boy on to the yacht and then he'll come back for me.'

'But when you go back to Bridgwater they'll know you hadn't made the return journey. They'll have only seen Muskett riding back.'

'Good God, woman, where's your faith in the English militia? For one thing they're too bloody inefficient to know I haven't already slipped by them. For another, they'll have changed the sentries. The morning duty will think I came back for more you-know-what the same night. Which,' he winked at her — he'd recovered his poise — 'is not a bad idea.' He finished wiping the lampblack of his face, and turned to Martin Hughes, whose screams had subsided to a chesty wheeze. Henry poured him a beaker of water from the ewer and held it to the old man's mouth. 'Look well on me, Master Hughes. I am to be your great-nephew-in-law. God help me.'

'Shshh,' Penitence begged him. 'Keep your voice down.'

'Why? Didn't you check the house? I heard them all go.'

'I don't know why, just keep your voice down.'

'Is there any food left? We'd better get this poor old sod fed.' He was pleased with himself. She'd seen similiar euphoria in Hart and Lacy and Kynaston after a good performance. Known it herself, for that matter.

She had to force herself down to the kitchen. Never before had she felt afraid of the house, but her recent guests had left it menacing and alien.

Jeffreys's cooks had been charitable enough to leave some scraps and she took them, with a jug of wine, back to the bedroom where Henry had got the old man out of the panel door and laid him on the bed, gently talking to him to reassure him after his fright. From the way Martin fell on the food it was obvious he was better. With a shock, Penitence realized she had fed neither him nor Benedick all day. It seemed dreadful to her that she'd sent her son into such danger on an empty belly.

'And I got Jeffreys off your back, didn't I?' Henry was still triumphant. 'Or off your front — whatever the bastard's preference.'

'You did.' He had no idea. Jeffreys would hate her for the rest of his life. *And you can't have too few enemies in that class.*

'Why didn't Rupert marry you?' Henry asked idly. 'Left it to me to make an honest woman of you, I expect.' He stretched. 'Well, tomorrow we'll go to my place and get married in the chapel.'

She knew she should keep her mouth shut — they were both too tired for argument — but even in this predicament she could not leave him deceived. 'I can't marry you, Henry.'

'What?' That he would be refused hadn't occurred to him.

'I promised Rupert I would never marry. He was dying.'

'And now he's dead. For God's sake, Boots, you were hardly the bride of Christ. He wouldn't marry you: I will. It's a good offer.'

He sounded so aggrieved she almost laughed, but his mouth was thinning into the line it took when he almost hated her. She pleaded: 'Henry, Rupert gave me everything. What difference does it make? You know I'll be honoured to be your mistress.'

He got off the bed, grabbed her arm and hurried her to the window; he couldn't bear that even such as Martin Hughes should hear her talk like that. Until that moment she hadn't seen how conventional was the core under the unconventional exterior. Perhaps, she thought, it's all of a piece. He defied everything his father stood for by marrying a Catholic, by becoming an actor, by choosing to serve his country as an agent rather than the more usual politician or soldier. But equally he was the opposite of his promiscuous father in believing firmly in the honourable estate of marriage. *And both your choices have been a disappointment: the late Lady Torrington, now me.* She knew what it must have taken for him to fight down all his suspicion and jealousy and offer to marry her. It made her love him more, even while she was irritated. *He could have asked nicely.*

At the window, he shook her. 'Will you stop thinking like a trollop? I want legitimate heirs.'

Nobody could move her to anger quicker than he could. 'Is that your reason for marrying?'

'It's the usual one.'

Below them moonlight flooded the courtyard, reducing the shadows of the flower pots and the mounting block to dark pools around their bases.

'For God's sake,' Henry was saying, 'Rupert had no right to demand such a thing. He didn't marry you himself.'

'He would have,' she said sharply. *How dare he attack Rupert.* 'But he couldn't. And he didn't make me promise. I gave it freely.'

'Then you're a—'

Their voices rising, they still heard the creak in the bedroom doorway and then the voice: 'A fornicators' quarrel is it?'

Nevis stood there.

It took time for Penitence to register that the man was dripping wet from his cloak to his boots and had a horse-pistol in each hand. The triumph in his eyes was awful. A lamb

608

saw the same expression before the wolf leaped; the slavering joy of a predator about to kill. For the moment she experienced such despair that she was rocked and nearly fell, as if the world had stopped turning.

'Major Nevis,' said the Viscount. 'How nice. Swam the moat, I see.' His voice was as steady as when he talked to Muskett.

'But kept my powder dry.' Nevis must have put the guns in his hat; it was the only thing that wasn't wet. Its long feather gleamed. He edged to the bed and put the mouth of one of the pistols against Martin Hughes's forehead. The old man's eyes were shut and he looked, as he'd looked for days, at death's door. Nevis didn't give him a second glance. He turned his head and peered into the hole from which the rushlight inside still glimmered. 'I *knew* there was a secret room.'

Penitence's hand, gripping Henry's, felt him bunch his muscles to leap across the room and attack the man, then relax as he saw it couldn't be done before the pistol fired. *Thank God*. He was being sensible. Nevis would kill him, and Martin Hughes too.

'Nobody in it,' said Nevis. 'I suppose Hurd's gone?'

Penitence said: 'Who?' She didn't know what else to say.

Henry said: 'He didn't enjoy the company.'

Nevis nodded. 'He was the blackamoor. You changed places. I was near half-way to Taunton when I realized. So I came back.'

'He won't be sorry you missed him.'

Nevis smiled. 'Neither am I. I've made a better catch. Much better. I've got Prince Rupert's doxy for one.' He switched his attention to Penitence, whom he'd largely ignored. 'You'll burn, mistress.' It gave him pleasure, but not as much as telling Henry: 'And I've got the Viscount of Severn and Thames. And you're for the block, master. I'll see you get the same executioner as Monmouth. He took five strokes of the axe and then had to finish the job with a knife.'

She said: 'The Viscount had no part in the escape. He came back to spend the night with me, as he often does. He knew nothing of my plan to substitute my son in his place. He was in the next bedroom, waiting for me. Why would he help one of the King's rebels? He's not been concerned with the rising. He's a loyal subject.'

She heard herself chattering on and knew that neither of the protagonists was paying her attention; she was that marginal thing, a woman. This was male territory, two stags circling, but of the two it was Nevis, the one with the advantage of a weapon, who was the challenger. She wondered how Henry could have inspired so much enmity, then she thought that it was because he had everything while Nevis, without humour, charm, or connections, survived by hating those who had.

'Why should he help one of the King's rebels?' Nevis picked up her question to play with. He was looking at the Viscount. 'Because the rebel Hurd is his son, that's why.'

He waited for their reaction. He got more from Penitence than the Viscount. *How does he know?* How *could* he know? He looked so ordinary yet radiated such omnipotent ill-will. The element of sorcery was added to the shadows of the room.

'Do you know how I know?'

She shook her head, though he wasn't looking at her.

'A little gargoyle told me.'

He'd been in the hall, listening. The spy-holes of the secret room worked two ways. He'd heard her and Henry talking. She tried frantically to think of what they'd said.

'And a little letter.' He was becoming confident now, shifting to make himself comfortable on the bed. With a glance down at Martin Hughes, he put the right-hand pistol down on the table to the right of the bed and felt inside his coat. Penitence could practically feel her lover willing the old man to make a move, now, to grab his enemy's arm. She willed equally hard that he shouldn't. The other pistol was aimed without a tremor in their direction.

Nevis had a letter in his hand. It was the one MacGregor had sent to Dorinda. After Prue had given it to her she'd kept it in a box on her dressing-table. He began to read, carefully, like a boy showing off to a favourite teacher.

Dear Wife. The lad is determined on it. I would have told all to his unknowing father trusting him to be as inclined as ourselves to wish his son's retreat from this business of Monmouth but my lord Henry King has left the Netherlands. All the caution the boy will use is to call himself by the name of Hurd. Stay by his mother at the Priory as I shall stay by the lad when we get to England to direct him in need. We are committed to the venture now. Pray the Lord He smiles on the Duke's endeavour so that you and I be reunited in life before we are in Heaven. But as He wills. Yr loving husband, Donal MacGregor.

He looked up. 'You're a sad slut, Mistress Hughes, you lock up nothing. I've moved around your house by day, by night. I've found keys, pistols, letters, all for the taking. And this one. It proved you Hurd's mother. I knew the bastard would come. And just now I heard a gargoyle speak in a woman's voice, I heard it call a man "Henry" and prove him Hurd's father.' He put the letter back in his coat, and the pistol once more against Martin Hughes's head. 'Old fornicators. Did Prince Rupert know his drab was employing a mere viscount to fill her twat?'

Penitence barely heard him. She stared straight ahead, every nerve intent on the man beside her who had gone as still as death. *Now you know because a man has told you so. You wouldn't believe me.*

Nevis was still trying to get a rise out of Henry. 'The King'll be interested to know one of the peers of his realm has got a son that's a Monmouth.'

She felt Henry bring his attention back to the present. 'But you see,' he said reasonably, 'we were afraid he'd disgrace the family name and join the Lambs.'

Oh, bless him. She saw Nevis's thumb cock the left-hand pistol. *Don't shoot him.* The man stayed where he was for a while. He seemed to be thinking. He laid the uncocked pistol carefully on the table. He stood up, felt above his head to the tester rail, levered himself up on the bed and kicked backwards.

His boot heel stabbed into Martin Hughes's head. Blood spurted in the old man's grey hair. It was the most calculated, casual bit of violence Penitence had ever seen. Nevis's face didn't change: 'To keep him quiet while we go to the hall,' he said. 'Jones will come soon and we'll take you two fornicators to Taunton.'

It was odd to hear the Puritans' much-loved denunciation 'fornicators' in the mouth of a member of a regiment renowned for its colourful cursing. It seemed to be the worst Nevis could call them. *He was brought up like I was.* She'd placed him. He was that most dangerous thing, a revolter against his background; he had thrown in his lot with the sinners, but could find no joy in their sinning unless it was cruel.

The Viscount offered her his right arm and she took it. Waved on by Nevis's pistol they crossed the bedroom to the door.

Like her, the Viscount appeared to be dwelling on his death for he suddenly shouted: 'Whatsoever thy hand findeth to do, do it with thy might; for there is no work, nor device, nor knowledge, nor wisdom, in the grave, whither thou goest.'

'Ecclesiastes 9,' said Penitence automatically.

'Shut your mouths. I'll not have fucking preaching, I'll not have it.' Unable to see that bland face, Penitence could hear the hysteria in Nevis's voice.

Now Henry had switched to the Psalms. 'Length of days is in your right hand.' He'd got it wrong. It was 'length of days is in *her* right hand'. He had her arm pressed tight against his side and was steering her too far to the right so that she stumbled against the bedside table.

She got a glimpse of Martin Hughes's pained, open eyes and the blood on his hair. Henry's right hand let go of her left one and jerked before taking it again.

Nevis came behind them. The candle he was managing to carry threw the shadow of the feather in his hat on to the wall ahead of them. 'The pistol's pointing at your doxy, Captain,' he said.

Among all the fears of what would happen, Penitence felt an unexpected and searing regret that she was to end up notorious. It seemed to her at that moment that all she'd ever wanted was respectability. Like a wood in bowls she had been thrown down life's alley askew; instead of a straight run she had wobbled from side to side, inevitably ricocheting from one disaster to the next. She wouldn't even die married. *A doxy. Ruperta, I'm so sorry.* Aphra would write a play of it. Oh God, this was one's life flashing before one's eyes.

'Well, well,' said Henry. 'A son.' He was speaking only to her.

Immediately she stopped drowning. It was the two of them alone in a boat. Nevis's filthy monologue behind them was the background sound of sea.

'Why didn't you tell me?' He was aggrieved again.

'*What?*'

'Right away when you knew.'

'I didn't know where you were. How dare *you* reproach *me.*' Of all times, how could he infuriate her like this.

'You could have made enquiries at court.'

'We d-d-d-didn't move in c-court circles in Newgate.' *Oh damn.*

The muzzle of a pistol poked into her spine so that she stiffened. 'Get into the hall.' Once in, Penitence was made to go and light the candles in the windows while Nevis kept one pistol against the Viscount's back and the other trained on her. Her hand trembled so that she could barely strike the steel. When she'd succeeded, she was told to open one of the lights 'so's we can hear Jones'. The Viscount was sent to sit down under the window next to her while Nevis stayed by the stairhead. 'There'll only be two horses, you fornicators. Mine's down by the gates. Jones has got his. You'll be taken across the moor and through Taunton on the end of fucking ropes.'

'Newgate?' asked Henry of her.

'For debt.'

'Ah.' She waited for him to say he was sorry for all she'd suffered, instead he said: 'That's two swords the boy's had off me. What happened to the first one I gave you?'

'We sold it,' she said and was glad to say it. Incongruity

613

added to unreality. Did she sit under the beautiful windows of her own hall, talking of the past with a madman while another waited to lead her to infamy and death? Or was it a dream?

Would I have gone to Newgate if it hadn't been for him? She had blamed him for it so long that it was difficult to remember. It didn't matter now anyway.

'It was a good sword,' said Henry. Now she realized. He was trying to keep her cross in order to stop her being frightened. He was failing. Every nerve was listening out for the sound of a horse outside.

'Shut your fucking fornicating mouths,' said Nevis, disconcerted at losing his audience. 'One more word from you and the bitch is pulled into Taunton naked.'

'Spanish,' said Henry. 'Or did I get it in Morocco? Anyway' – he settled down more comfortably against the wall – 'I remember the swordsmith telling me what a fine regiment the Tangiers was, considering it took only those who didn't have the brains to join any other. Insisted on shagging only the best camels, he said . . .'

No, don't. He was deliberately trying to enrage the man, as he had her – for what purpose this time she couldn't imagine.

Nevis's face stayed as neutral as ever but out of his mouth came a stream of vituperation, much of it against militia captains who'd never seen a shot fired in anger and ran when they did.

Penitence was amazed that two men could consider the denigration of each other's regiments an insult. *What does it matter?*

It was then she noticed the rat. A wavy rat, which was impossible, but grey like a rat. It bobbed for a second against the ornate banister of the stairwell next to Nevis's foot where he stood at the top of the stairhead. A wavy rat was no more extraordinary this night than anything else. She didn't question it. She was very tired. If she went to sleep perhaps she would wake up to find herself back at well-regulated, well-respected Awdes, with Rupert. *I'm so sorry, Rupert.*

'Goats now,' said Henry. 'They weren't so particular about goats . . .'

Stop it. He'll kill you.

The cocked pistol in Nevis's hand shook as he stepped forward. The hole of its muzzle became larger and so magnetic that as it bobbed her eyes went up and down to follow it. 'You arrogant bastard. You never had to work for anything. All your food and your carriages and your commission, what did you do for it but fornicate.'

He was inching forward all the time, and Penitence knew he would shoot if Henry wasn't quiet.

And Henry wasn't quiet. He was spouting Proverbs at the top of his voice, louder than ever: 'Steel sharpeneth steel; so a man sharpeneth the countenance of his enemy. Sharpen it in the name of the Lord.'

Again he was misquoting but by now she'd spotted the rat again. She saw it rise up and become Martin Hughes's grey head. He was coming up the stairs behind Nevis. *The top stair creaks.* She tried to will the information towards him. *He'll hear you.* Of course, that was why Henry was making such a noise.

'Whosoever shall smite thee on thy cheek, smite him on his.'

The Lord never said that. Besides, the old man held no weapon. What could he smite with? She wanted to join in the diversion by shouting something, anything, but she had gone back twenty years. Her words had blocked and her head nodded like a fool's in the effort to get them out. Instead, she stamped on the floor.

Now it was they who were frightening Nevis. His eyes had widened and she could see hers and Henry's wildness reflected in them. There was a sort of power in losing control and she no longer tried for words but screamed, the scream of the lamb before the wolf, the terror beyond terror.

And she saw her great-uncle tiptoe unsteadily up behind Nevis and stroke him on his neck. It appeared almost a touch to attract the man's attention, so gentle a movement that Nevis didn't shoot. He put up the uncocked pistol as if to brush something off his collar. It disappeared in an outburst of blood. Some bung seemed to have shot out of Nevis's neck under pressure. The blood sprayed black in the moonlight;

they could hear it rapping against the pistol and splashing on the floor. Martin Hughes fell back to avoid it.

Then Nevis pulled the trigger; a reflex action. The shot was towards the fireplace but he was already sinking to his knees like a slaughtered ox. He looked puzzled.

Henry leaped forward and pulled up Nevis's cloak as a shield against the blood. 'Well done, Uncle.'

'I smote the son of Belial with the edge of the sword,' said Martin Hughes.

'You certainly did.'

He's been expecting this. She couldn't understand what had happened. Her lover and her uncle congratulating each other.

'Is he dead?' she asked.

'Don't stand there like a sodding lily, Boots. Get a bucket of water. Lots of buckets. We've got to get rid of the blood before Jones comes.' He looked up at Martin Hughes who was still clinging on to the stairhead. 'We can't kill Jones too, unfortunately. We couldn't explain two deaths. We're going to have enough trouble explaining this one.' He turned back to Penitence. 'Move, woman. And don't step in the blood, for God's sake. We don't want footprints all over the place. Go on, move.'

'But *why* is he dead?'

He looked pleased with himself. 'Show her, Uncle.'

Shyly, as if proffering a sweetmeat, Martin Hughes held out his hand. Set in the bend of his forefinger was a curved, steel blade. For a moment she couldn't see what it was; his whole hand was blood. 'I have cut down the unrighteous.'

'It was on the table next to the bed,' said Henry. 'How the hell Nevis didn't see it, I'll never know. It was practically sitting up and waving. I managed to knock it near Uncle's right hand as we went out of the door.'

She'd put it there. She'd picked it up off the table on the day she'd handed out the other knives to the harvesters and received the news that Mudge Ridge had escaped from Ilchester gaol. Meaning to put it back with the others, she'd been interrupted by ... what was it ... hearing Martin Hughes's breathing coming from the gargoyle, and run upstairs. It had been on the table so long it had become a fixture she hadn't noticed.

She was sent to loose Nevis's horse from where it was tethered by the gates, but though she slapped its rump time and time again, it wouldn't gallop off. For the time being she took it to the farm, until they could think what to do with it, then joined the others in the hall.

Nevis was wrapped in his cloak and then the lovely rug that had lain near the fireplace. Henry checked the house to see where the man had got in and repaired the damage while Penitence lit more candles in the hall. They all three worked frenziedly, chucking water over the blood, mopping, then squeezing the pink water into the buckets, fetching more water. It was impossible to understand how a man's body could have held so much blood. It had shot everywhere, on to the stairhead, the walls, into the moulding of the banister rail. Diluted by water it was gradually lifted from the floor, though at the cost of making the boards look as if they'd come up from the sea, but it would take days before every splash of it could be found in the cracks of the walls.

And there was no time. Already she was amazed that a night could last so long. If Jones hadn't come yet, he would certainly come at dawn.

While they worked, Martin and Henry argued about what to do with the body. Penitence wasn't consulted. Death was men's business. They talked about it in a businesslike way. She was amazed by her great-uncle's composure. She supposed she had no idea of him. *He could teasel a son of Belial before breakfast every day for all I know.* She laughed at the thought even as she shook.

Henry King shot her a look. 'There's no time for hysterics.' He leaned on his mop. 'All right, we'll put him in the secret room.'

'No!' She screamed it.

Henry said: 'Boots, there isn't time for anywhere else. We'll wall it up tomorrow, tight as a tomb.'

'Not in my house. Not in my house. Not in my house.'

'All right. All *right*, Boots. It'll have to be the moat. And it'll have to be quick.'

She held the candle while the two men dragged the carpet down the staircase and then along the screen passage to the front door. By the time they'd got there Martin Hughes was puffing so badly she had to help him push while Henry pulled the body up over his shoulder. Her hands were splayed in the effort of forcing them to touch the carpet. *Out. Get out of my house, you thing, you dreadful thing.*

'We'll need a weight.'

Between them she and Martin rolled one of the heavy flower urns along on its base across the cobbles, spilling earth and marigolds. Its crunching was so loud she couldn't hear anything else. *What if Jones comes now?* Outside the courtyard she looked to the east. It might be her fear, but it looked one transparency lighter than the rest of the sky.

At the drawbridge she kept a cowardly look-out so that she didn't have to see the business of lashing the urn to the body.

She heard the splash and saw the ripples waft the water-lilies below the drawbridge up and down.

It wasn't until then that she could think. 'You must go,' she said to Henry. 'You're supposed to be in Bridgwater. Jones will know you killed him. They'll find his horse at the farm. Go now.'

'Jones won't *know* anything. It depends what Nevis told him. We can bluff it out.'

'We can't bluff the horse,' she sobbed. 'Take it and go.'

'No.'

She pulled herself together. This was going to require cunning. She wiped her eyes and smoothed back her hair. 'If we can get them to think Nevis has never been here . . .'

'He would have told them where he was going.'

'It doesn't mean he arrived.' *We're actors. Deception is our middle name.* They had fooled everybody – everybody except Nevis – once. How to repeat the trick? *Think.* Into her head, God-sent, came a deep, ungodly voice from long ago. 'Do you remember Ma Hicks?'

For a second the tension on his face faded. 'The only woman I ever really loved.'

'Do you remember when they were shouting for an encore,

she said: "Never mind about 'encore', make the buggers do it again?" Let's do it again.'

She began running back into the house. Questions and answers chased through her brain. Where had they put Nevis's hat? Would it be bloody? It was a black hat, blood wouldn't show. They both wore the same sort of cloak. Henry is taller. You can't easily assess the height of someone on a horse. He's dark. Nevis is fair. *Was* fair. Mist, we need a morning mist.

Reaching the hall, she raced to the window. It had got just chilly enough towards morning to create vapour; there was a veil-like quality to air that was slowly achieving greyness.

Nevis's hat had rolled off his head as he fell and lay against the banister of the stairwell. On the underside of the brim there was a gleaming splash on the matt felt but with luck nobody would be near enough to notice.

Outside, the two men were brushing away the spillage from the urn. Panting, Penitence began pulling Henry across the drawbridge. 'Get the horse. Get the horse.' The drive seemed like a lit stage-ramp pointing straight at them.

Henry swung her back to the shadow of the gatehouse. 'Don't be a fool, Boots. I'm not leaving.'

'You've got to.'

'There'll be suspicion. You can't face that alone.'

'There won't be if Nevis is seen riding away from here.'

'There'll be suspicion,' he said again. 'Questions. They might drag the moat.'

'They won't.' *How to make him go. How to get him safe.*

Then she knew.

She pulled away and looked up at him: 'You've got to go. You're putting me in danger.'

'Don't be a fool.'

'I'm better off without you,' she said. 'Martin Hughes goes back into the secret room until the countryside is quieter. Nevis is seen riding away from the house, so he can't have died here. I shall be safe *if you go now*. Jeffreys will protect me.'

He hadn't seen Jeffreys's face. She could work on his jealousy. Anything, anything to get him away.

Immediately he became casual. 'I suppose he will,' he said, 'for a price. It depends on whether you want to pay it.'

'It's a small price.'

'Not to me.' He had never admitted his jealousy, for that matter he had never said he loved her. He was telling her now. 'Boots, not to me.'

'Well it is to me,' she said. She smiled. 'I've paid it before. It's nothing. It doesn't matter. It's a sale. It keeps food on the table and people out of prison. It got me this house. It means I can keep this house and my daughter.' The tension broke and she was hammering on his chest and screaming. 'You're putting my daughter in danger. Why don't you go? I don't want you here. I'm a whore, don't you see? It's what I'm good at.'

She couldn't see his expression because the wobble of reflected dawn light on the water played through the floor-boards of the bridge up on to his face.

He began to walk away from her towards the drive and she dragged along behind him. *Well done, Peg Hughes. Welcome another twenty years without him.* She doubted if she'd survive them.

They turned right towards the farm. She found herself shivering. The dawn was the first presage of autumn after the long, dry summer. She noticed spider webs strung between the bushes with sliding globules of dew on their filaments. There was a satisfactory mist rising from the marsh, lying in curtains like the finest gauze between willow and hazel.

The farmhouse had been wrecked from too many searches but a comforting smell of cow manure and poultry lingered in the farmyard. Nevis's horse looked round at them from where she'd slung its reins over the gatepost.

The Viscount began tightening its girth. 'I do understand,' he said, reasonably. 'You're probably trying to save me as well as yourself. I can imagine you are being brave. But I'm taking my bow because I can't go on like this. I need peace.'

He let the saddle-flap fall, put his foot into the stirrup and swung himself up. He put out his hand for Nevis's hat and she gave it to him. He looked at it, twisting the brim until the blood showed.

He said: 'I think it's true — you will be safer without me. But I should have to leave anyway. Whether you sleep with that monster or not isn't the point at issue. What is, what's irredeemable is, that you can plan to do it. You've been a whore too long.'

It was what she wanted but it was so painful that she reacted. 'Who made me one?'

'I presume that I did. There's no blame for what you've become.' He looked down at her at last. His voice was almost kind. 'You are a remarkable and beautiful woman, Boots, and I admire you. Actually, I love you. But it appears I'm a creature of my past as much as you and I cannot face a future with a woman whose first thought in any difficulty will be to fuck her way out of it. And there's the truth.'

He put Nevis's hat on his head and shook the reins.

She walked back to the house without watching him go. There was no need for goodbyes. He'd said his.

In fact Lieutenant Jones didn't turn up until late morning; even then he came more out of force of habit than suspicion. On his way over to the Priory he and his troop had been diverted by sentries' reports that Major Nevis had gone by at the gallop in the mist, heading north. Wonder he didn't break his neck. Yes sir, unmistakably the major; they knew by the hat.

'Did he say where he was going?' Lieutenant Jones asked Penitence craftily.

She was huffy. 'I never saw him. He didn't come here. And if he had, after all the trouble he caused searching the place when I had guests, he'd not have been welcome.'

In the hall the servant Prue was equally aggrieved. 'Look at this danged hall and the mess you gennulmen make with your vittles. Taken buckets, buckets, to get the danged grease out of this floor.'

For the look of the thing, Lieutenant Jones searched the house and grounds but was interrupted by a militia messenger who carried the news that Major Nevis's hat had been found by Ticky Hole, a quagmire on the other side of Sedgemoor with the reputation of never yielding up its dead.

Nobody ever found out what he'd been doing there. There was a strong suspicion that he had been pushed rather than fallen but to question suspects, let alone take reprisals, was difficult because Ticky Hole was far away from any habitation. In the end it was decided that he had been chasing an escaper who had overpowered him. King James made a graceful allusion to his courage and loyalty but was unable to reward the major's next-of-kin because, like the major's body, they couldn't be found.

Two weeks later Sir Ostyn Edwards discovered the whereabouts of Dorinda and MacGregor. Both had been taken to the tiny, beehive lock-up at Glastonbury on the other side of the Poldens after capture, where a semi-literate clerk had entered Dorinda on the prison roll as Mags Roger and MacGregor as M. Rigger. Under those names they had been transferred to Wells to await the coming of Lord Chief Justice Jeffreys and the Assize.

When Penitence reached Wells the next day the trial was over. MacGregor had been sentenced to transportation.

Dorinda hadn't come to trial. Six weeks in an overcrowded prison during the height of summer had been too much for her and she had died ten days previously of gaol fever.

BOOK V

Chapter 1

IT WAS in the aftermath of the Monmouth rebellion that King James II showed the same inability to understand the English character that had taken his father to the block.

Until then he'd done well, mobilized his army quickly, dealt a swift and exemplary punishment to the rebels. Whig opposition to his monarchy was in disarray to the point of being non-existent. Parliament, shaken by the uprising, was James's creature and voted him more money than it had ever voted his brother – and he had the power to keep this Parliament for as long as he wished.

There were mutters against Jeffreys's Assizes but nobody had expected the rebels to be treated merely as naughty boys. Many wished the King could have answered Lady Alice Lisle's appeal more mercifully but instead of pardoning the old woman whose crime had been to hide a fugitive, he merely commuted the sentence from burning to beheading. Nevertheless both Church and Commons felt that here was a stern, forceful, sober, hard-working king, quite unlike his frivolous brother, who had made it clear to waverers from Toryism what they could expect if they caused trouble. If it was that same king's peculiarity to be a practising Roman Catholic, well, let him.

That should have been that.

Then, after Jeffreys's return, the King suddenly ordered the death of another 239 rebels. Even Jeffreys seemed to have thought that enough had been enough; 'I was hated by the kingdom for doing so much in the West, and was ill received by the King for not having done more,' he said later. The blocks, cleavers, stakes had to be got out again. Gallows were re-erected. More wagons brought more salt to the towns for the pickling of more men's quarters. Once again the smell of human entrails pervaded market squares. Towns and villages which had got used to the sight of the head or haunch of somebody they knew on top of the flagpoles found a new piece of tarred anatomy staring at them from a signpost. Some people had never got used to it; the West wasn't London where the head of some traitor or another always decorated the Bridge. Lord Stawell, a loyal Tory, protested at the distribution of limbs across the countryside and was rewarded by having three more men hanged and dismembered at his gates.

Now, when everybody had thought the killing over, it was begun again. Bits of bodies were broadcast over Dorset, Somerset and Devon, a strewing of death that went on through October and into November until everybody, with the possible exception of Kirk and his Lambs, was sick of it and recalled the suffering of the Protestant martyrs under Bloody Mary.

Then there were the transportations. Transportees went into exile for ever and were usually made to serve as slaves for the first five years. In the case of the Monmouth rebels this enforced labour was increased to ten years by royal decree.

Again, it wasn't the punishment that was considered outrageous nor even, this time, the scale; it was the royal greed. The profit from selling nearly 1,000 transportees as slaves to the sugar plantations of the West Indies at from £10 to £15 a head was given not to those who had dealt with the rebellion but to nine courtiers, including the Queen, some of them (like the Queen) Catholics.

The Maids of Taunton, the schoolgirls who had proffered a flag to Monmouth on his arrival, were not tried or sentenced but it was considered that a royal pardon was needed for their misdemeanour — the pardon's price to be set and collected by the Queen's maids of honour and the children to be threatened with outlawry until it was. Most of the children's parents being propertied, the court agent acting for the maids of honour set the figure at £7,000.

After months of pleading and haggling the maids of honour

accepted a price based on £50 to £100 per girl, the children's value having dropped after the death of one of them in prison.

Not only in the West Country was it perceived after all this that the greater sufferers had been those who had done least in the rebellion while those who had helped to organize and lead it had, with the exception of Monmouth himself, been allowed to buy their freedom.

On a crisp mid-November morning, a horse pulling a cart of teasels with a countrywoman on its driving-seat plodded up to the small stone bridge that crossed the Cary near Chedzoy.

The militiaman guarding the bridge, who'd been watching its approach across the Levels, shifted his pike and transferred his weight from one foot to the other to deliver his challenge: ''Marning, Ladyship. On our own today, is ut?'

Penitence got down for a chat and adopted the local dialect which was her *langue de guerre*. 'What's going to come of trade Ah don't know, Matt Fry. Not a driver to be had; poor zouls 'm either on their way to the sugar plantations or weeding the rhines or guarding their arses, like you.'

'Folk needs protecting, missus.'

'Lord's sake, who from?' She pointed up at the gibbet on the other side of the bridge's foot from which hung an iron-bound, unidentifiable, tarred piece of human meat of which the shiny black surface had been worn away here and there, enabling a couple of rooks to peck at the baconized interior. 'Can't even scare crows, so ee can't.'

'Bridgwater again, is it?' asked Matt Fry, unperturbed. 'Thought you'd sold all your middlings.'

'These be piddlings.' She led him round to the back of the cart and picked up one of the staffs to show him the smaller teasel heads that had been rejected from the first-class batches. 'Don't fetch the same, but 'tis all profit.'

They chatted some more before Penitence got back on the driving-seat, shook the reins and moved off, removing Nevis's horse-pistol from the pocket under her apron back to the space under the footboard.

The moors were more populated at this time of the year

than any other; the drains and rhines which took away at least a little of the winter floods had to be cleared. Gangs of men, women and children made straight lines along the hidden ditches with dark weed forming a tideline at their feet, and called out a greeting to Penitence who called it back. Against a great, colourless sky skeins of geese flew in, also calling, to their winter quarters. The low scrub which covered the uncultivated stretches had its usual grey touched with frost to contrast with the startling emerald of its mosses, the scarlet hips and the infinitely variable yellow carpets of willow and hawthorn leaves. The air smelled of rich, autumnal compost.

After a mile there was a rustle from the hedgehog stars that filled the back of the cart and Penitence spoke, apparently to her horse. 'No you can't. We're still the wrong side of the Poldens.'

She spoke again: 'Well, think of it as improving your soul by discomfiting your body. "Make not provision for the flesh, to fulfil the lusts thereof." Romans something. All right, 13. Hush now, we'll be passing more drainers in a minute.'

They weren't, but it was a good way of ensuring peace.

Further along she pulled up the cart at a signpost and addressed the air once more: 'To the left it says Bridgwater and to the right Woolavington. Is this where we turn?'

She nodded and pulled on the right-hand rein, turning the cart north. The signpost was decorated with a head around which had been tied a ribbon with the words: 'A Monmouth'. At the foot of the post somebody had lain a posy of rose-hips and old man's beard.

She wondered if the old man in the back of the cart would recognize whose it had been. *It might be that young lad of Prue's.* Anger she would never be rid of came over her again in a wave. How dare they pull apart what they could not put together. Lady Alice's dignified old head toppling into the executioner's basket. *I am wonderfully and terribly made.* How much suffering there had been. What had Dorinda gone through? What was MacGregor going through at this moment? She was so lonely.

A letter from Benedick, signed O. Moor, had enquired

earnestly after her health, told her of Mr Moor's safe arrival in the Netherlands and mentioned making the acquaintance of a certain Henry King, Esquire. It hadn't been safe to say more. While she rejoiced they had finally found each other she would have given a lot to see how father and son got on together and felt all the lonelier at the thought that she never would. For a moment she was so overcome by pity for herself and humanity in general that she nearly let her great-uncle arise from the prickles of his prison to join her, but not quite. You never pitied Martin Hughes that much. His patroness beheaded, his congregation decimated, a fugitive in his own countryside, forced to kill a man to save himself and others, even these awful experiences could not lend the man pathos. For once, he was at her mercy.

So, as they lumbered up one side of the Poldens and descended down on to the causeway that crossed the wet meadows of the Glastonbury vale, she told him what was to be done about her Indians. 'First MacGregor, of course,' she said, 'and then the Squakheag. They'll have completed their five years. No, I do not want them converted; they are a good deal nearer the Lord than you are.'

For good measure she told him about the Reverend Block. 'A prating, bigoted, lustful hypocrite who'd have watched me burn,' she shouted to the air, getting angry as she remembered. 'If it wasn't for him, I'd never have left Massachusetts.'

What would I have become? The narrow-minded wife of some Puritan farmer? Eccentric Indian-lover? Dead in the King Philip War? 'You remind me of him,' she told the teasels.

Actually, she doubted if Uncle Martin Hughes had lusted after anybody his whole life long, but she paid him the compliment of letting the insult stand.

At first she had begged him to tell her about his niece, the girl who had become Her Ladyship, but he'd refused to discuss the sinner who had not only borne a child out of wedlock but borne it to the son of the hated family which had fought his own during the Civil War.

'Didn't you ever wonder what happened to her after you all cast her out?' she'd asked him, but he had shaken his obstinate grey head and for a moment she had seen her grandmother in him and known that his loveless form of Puritanism was a homage to the one woman whom he had ever found worthy of affection, his sister Tabitha, and that she had been a stronger influence on him than he on her.

The only other person he seemed to hold in esteem was, surprisingly, the Viscount, for whom he felt the camaraderie of men who'd overcome a common enemy. 'Thee should have married un,' he'd told her, 'I heard un offer. Wilt play the harlot like thy mother?'

'Yes,' she'd said. 'And proud to.' He provoked that sort of response. The fact that she'd taken him in, nursed him and was now attempting to get him out of the country, had not brought a word of gratitude. True, he'd killed Nevis but that had been to save his own life as much as hers and Henry's and had anyway overlaid her feeling for him with an irrational aversion. Her eyes tried to avoid seeing his right hand; for her it was always covered in blood. Nevis had to die, she would tell herself, yet the casual way in which her uncle and her lover had combined to cause it and then cover it up still shocked her. Even now she was reluctant to go into her own hall, and more reluctant yet to go near the moat. As for eating fish from the stewpond fed by the spring that ran from the moat . . .

That apart, the presence of a man in her house for whom the authorities were still hunting meant that she dared not bring the children and staff back to it but had to beg the Cartwrights to keep them at Crewkerne a bit longer, while she camped out in the Priory with Prue and a staff from the village that went home at night. Which meant being unable to tell Tongs of her mother's death, a task she was dreading and therefore wanted to put off no longer.

Yet how could she expect a child not yet seven years old to take in what she herself couldn't absorb? She and Dorinda had survived the Plague together, childbirth together, the woman couldn't be dead. She was at the Cock and Pie, cursing Penitence for not going to see her. It wasn't bearable that she'd died. And suffered before she'd died. And died for Benedick.

Given the opportunity of this cart ride, Penitence explained all this to her uncle at length and in detail. 'And,' she ended, 'you're costing me a lot of money, you miserable, canting, hypocritical, ungrateful old man.'

She'd had to go up to London to confide in the Earl of Craven. Elizabeth of Bohemia's necklace had been sold to Nell Gwynn, and half the proceeds put in trust for Ruperta; the rest, Penitence's half, was dwindling fast. Part had been out-laid on Martin Hughes's behalf, but while in London she had also encountered Hurry Yeo, the landlord of the Hoy Arms, his wife and the other parents and representatives of the Maids of Taunton trying to buy their daughters' pardon from the King.

They were pitiful. Unused to London, its ways and its prices, they had already run through most of the money with which they'd hoped to free their children. At Whitehall they were being passed from secretary to secretary, made to wait outside doors – sometimes for days – for agents who never attended to them, or might tomorrow. And all the while the thought of what was happening to their little girls in prison was sending them mad.

Landlord Yeo had lost so much weight Penitence almost hadn't recognized him, while Mrs Yeo's colour was bad and her feet and ankles had swelled alarmingly. 'Iss fay, there's ache in that danged old Whitehall,' she said tiredly to Peni-tence, not meaning her own pain only, but that of the hundreds of rebels' relatives battering their heads against Whitehall obfuscation in an effort to purchase their loved ones from death or, what was often the same thing, transportation.

Penitence offered the Yeos and some of the other Maids of Taunton parents free accommodation at the Cock and Pie, procured the assistance of the Earl of Craven and John Church-ill in the prosecution of their pleas, and advanced them £100 each. *Damn Monmouth*. 'Damn Monmouth,' she shouted. A pheasant dithering on the bank decided not to cross the track after all and rustled back into the scented, rusty-coloured bracken.

The teasels rebuked Penitence as a foul-mouthed harpy and

for that she let them remain undisturbed while another five miles went by before allowing her great-uncle out of them.

At Lower Langford they spent the night with a fellow-preacher of Uncle Martin's. There couldn't have been more double-knocking, passwords and general secrecy than if the man been putting up Monmouth himself. Penitence, tired, demanded her bed which turned out to be in the hay loft of the barn but was at least quiet. The next morning she also demanded hot water and repaired with it back to the barn to make up her face and dress herself in her best blue velvet and sapphire earrings. There were still ten miles to go, this time on horseback, but there would be no opportunity to change before Bristol where she must make a good impression.

She looked carefully into her travelling mirror in the bad November light which was reluctantly seeping into the barn. Stress had caught her up and was showing itself in hollowing cheeks and temples. *Old. I'm old. No wonder he doesn't want me. He's making jealousy his excuse to marry somebody young enough to give him children.*

'Jezebel,' said Uncle Martin Hughes without heat, coming into the barn, his invariable response to seeing her regard herself in the looking-glass, to her powders and perfumes on the dressing-table, or when she wore earrings or her hair uncapped.

'Fop,' answered Penitence for once. She had provided him with some of Rupert's clothes altered to fit his shorter frame. The black embroidered coat hanging down to his skinny knees with the lace gorget at his throat, the feathered hat and silver-buckled shoes, wore him rather than he them. She grinned.

He said: 'Shamed in the sight of the Lord I be.' But his great-niece detected an interrogative note as if he wanted to know how he looked.

She put Nevis's pistol into a saddle-bag: 'Just in case some highwayman fancies my earrings or your buckles.'

'By the Lord, let un try.' He surprised her. For a moment she was warmed by a sense of comradeship which went as she placed the fur-edged, satin-lined hood of her travelling cape over her hair and he called her 'Jezebel' again. She supposed it was a compliment of sorts; it meant she had committed the sin of looking pretty.

They were leaving the cart until Penitence returned – the teasels were payment for their night's accommodation and the risk the preacher had taken in giving it to them. Martin mounted the horse and Penitence got up behind him and they took the road for Bristol.

Penitence was surprised by the beauty of the houses. Though smaller than London, Bristol ran the capital close in its foreign trade. The shop windows displayed fine hats, silvers and pewters, gilt leather trunks, beaten gold jewellery. Best of all were the cloths: the silks, the various cottons, niccanees, cuttanees, buckshaws, nillias and salempores thrown over chairs and counters glowing like flower gardens behind the dark glass of the shopfronts. 'Jezebel,' intoned Uncle Martin, as he peered in with her.

The inn was called the Blackamoor and Elephant, and, so that illiterates wouldn't miss it, its balcony was decorated by two enormous plaques, one bearing the head of a negro, the other an elephant's. Inside it consisted of corridors, tiny rooms and doors, a puzzle of black wood, redolent with beeswax and old wine. At the mention of her name, a bowing landlord showed them upstairs to the parlour, where a softly spoken, carefully smiling gentleman and his pretty wife were waiting for them. 'Mrs Hughes, a pleasure. I am John Spragge, secretary to the Royal African Company. My wife, Henrietta.'

As Penitence was about to introduce Martin, Mr Spragge held up a hand and smiled her back into line. His whisper was one used by reassuring doctors at a death-bed: 'And this must be Master Smith for whom we are pleased to be arranging a passage.'

'It's kind of you,' she said humbly. The cost of the passage alone was £500 – the Royal African Company wasn't being all that kind – but that it was smuggling out at all a man it must suspect to be a rebel against its king was a cause for gratitude due to the intervention of the Earl of Craven and the fact that Rupert had been a prominent shareholder.

'Not at all, Mrs Hughes.' Mr Spragge beckoned with his discreetly be-ringed fingers at a lurker in the shadows and ordered it to show Mr Smith to his cabin on the *Bonaventura*. 'You shall have time to say your goodbyes later, Mr Smith,' he confided, 'but perhaps you would like to settle in for now. You will be sailing on the afternoon tide.' His soft voice hoped that would be suitable, but Penitence saw that it didn't matter if it was or wasn't. *He wants Uncle Martin away as quickly as possible*. She was impressed.

She accepted a dish of excellent coffee from Henrietta who asked vaguely if she'd come far and told her that she and Mr Spragge had four children and lived in a sugar house in Prince Street.

'Sugar house?'

Henrietta looked around for help. 'Mr Spragge says it is a pleasantry to call it so. I think because this is a sugar town built on the sugar trade.' Henrietta seemed spun from sugar herself with her fair, frizzy hair and light, frosted-blue, absent-minded eyes. The pastel flowers appliquéd on to her dress looked like marzipan roses.

'On that matter,' said Mr Spragge, soothingly, returning from the door, 'I have the Earl of Craven's permission to try and interest you in investing in our enterprise, Mrs Hughes.' He sat down and paused. Penitence wondered which smile he was going to use now. He seemed to have a selection. It was admiring. 'We in the Company know how much trust our late patron, Prince Rupert, put in you, Mrs Hughes.'

She translated 'put his trust in you' as 'left you a lot of money'. *Elizabeth of Bohemia's necklace*. Lord Craven hadn't seen fit to mention to the Royal Africans that it was sold. She inclined her head.

'Have you ever thought, Mrs Hughes, of how even princes in these troubled times can no longer rest assured of traditional income but, like that dear, modern-thinking man, Prince Rupert, must invest in the life-blood of this great country of ours, trade?'

She hadn't, but she knew that for the next hour or so she was going to. Well, it was not unrestful to be plied with coffee, cakes and compliments and listen to ways of earning money with what remained of her inheritance. It had been an expensive year.

The Royal Africans not only made money, it appeared, they practically minted it. They couldn't fail. If one ship in three came in a man . . . begging her pardon, a woman . . . sustained no loss. If two came in she was a good gainer. If all three, she was rich for life. And on an average only one ship in five miscarried.

Mr Spragge's smile bared his soul. 'Even I, Mrs Hughes, invested my widower's mite . . . beg pardon, Henrietta, a little pleasantry . . . and though the cargo was indifferent and reached the West Indies in poor condition, the profit on the venture was 38 per cent. Thirty. Eight. Per cent. What think you of that?'

He stifled her answer with a benediction from his hand. 'Wait, Mrs Hughes. There is no need to make a decision at once. Come, bid goodbye to your uncle, look over the *Bonaventura* – she is the latest addition to our fleet, just commissioned – and then you may wish to meet some other partners of your . . . of Prince Rupert.'

Like most people, Penitence had always been excited by dock quaysides. On these Bristolian wharves it was like passing through an olfactory rainbow to walk past the barrels of spices, tobaccos, sugars and wines. In a strange way the unimpressed dockers unloading ivories, apes, tea, coffee and peacocks as if they were everyday goods highlighted the exotic, like the grey, English water lapping against the ornamented, foreign hulls.

But it was from these docks that the transports had left for the Atlantic crossing, packed with rebel Englishmen being carried to their ten years' bondage or, more likely, their death. MacGregor had been among them and his difficult-to-remember face haunted Penitence's mind's eye more, not less, as the days went by, as if Dorinda's ghost were etching it there to remind her of her debt to him.

The *Bonaventura*, a big ketch, was gleaming new and smelled of wood and lanolin. Uncle Martin Hughes's stern cabin was well fitted; she would have thought it a sight too good for him if she hadn't found, to her consternation, that she was having pangs at the thought of his going.

He, however, was surly: 'These tarpaulins baint going to the West Indies,' he said, accusingly. 'You told me West Indies.'

She turned on Spragge. 'I paid for the West Indies.'

The smile was understanding but held reproof. 'Anxious as we are to oblige a protégé of our dear departed prince, Mrs Hughes, you must realize that the *Bonaventura* has been built to ply between the Guinea Coast and the West Indies. First she must pick up her cargo in Africa before taking it on to Jamaica. It will make but a week or two's difference to Mr Smith's arrival.'

She turned back to Martin Hughes where he had sat himself down on his bunk and got out his Bible. This, then, was the moment of their goodbyes. With thunderous proper feeling, Mr Spragge whispered that he and Henrietta would wait outside while she said them.

Penitence and her great-uncle were left alone. The boat rocked in the wake of some passing ship and she heard the slap of water against the hull. It reminded her of the sound she wished she could forget, of entrails being thrown into the executioner's bucket. *I saved you from that at least.* 'You'll write and tell me,' she begged him. 'MacGregor first and then the Indians. You'll let me know if you haven't enough money.' Irritating to the last, he put his finger on the line he had appeared to reach, looked up and nodded before returning to scripture.

Impulsively she found herself saying, wishing she wasn't: 'Won't you bless me before you go?' Of all people she had reason to know that water was thicker than blood but, with Martin Hughes's departure, the last of her mother's family would be gone from her for ever and she no nearer to understanding them than the day she left Massachusetts.

'Thee were a colicky babby,' he said, and because she'd been expecting a rebuff she didn't hear what he said for a moment.

'Was I?'

'On this very quayside I bade thee goodbye before thy grandmother took thee to the Americas and thee did sick bile on my best broadcloth.'

'Did I?'

'Admit thy transgression, come to repentance and thee shalt have my blessing.'

All love must be for the Lord; the more affection one saint of the Pure Church felt for another human being, the greater his responsibility to save that soul for the Lord. She supposed he must be admitting some sort of fondness. He'd probably felt the same for her mother. She hadn't come to repentance either. 'Goodbye, Uncle Martin,' she said.

To her chagrin she was blinking back tears as she rejoined the Spragges on deck where sailors were stowing and lashing casks. Above their heads men with bare feet curling like a monkey's ran up and down the ratlines. Spragge busied himself to expound the ship's seaworthiness. It was probably still short of investors. Penitence nodded dumbly as he suggested she might like to see the cargo hold – 'We pride ourselves it is the most up-to-date in the trade' – and followed him down a ladder into a hole that smelled of a carpenter's shop where curls of wood brushed her feet as she stepped down on to planking.

She found herself in a narrow passageway formed by the bulkhead on one side and slatted shelving that took up all the space on the other. If the shelves hadn't extended back so far she would have thought them built for a library – the height between each would have taken a large book although the uprights occurred, apparently unnecessarily, every sixteen inches and had a ring screwed into them which corresponded to a ring in the slats some six foot further in.

The effect of the cubbyholes and new wood would have been pleasant if it hadn't reminded her of Flap Alley *My God, in Newgate human beings used to have to sleep in cubicles only a little bigger than that*. She nearly said it aloud, but thought that Mr Spragge would be shocked at a potential investor who'd been in Newgate. Or perhaps he wouldn't. Rebels, criminals –

if they had money, the Royal African Company seemed prepared to do business with them.

'Do note, Mrs Hughes, that on a ship of this size we can carry as many as 516. Note too the ventilation overhead . . .'

Five hundred and sixteen? She felt goosebumps go down her arms. '*What* is it you transport?'

Mr Spragge expelled a what-have-we-been-talking-about breath and fixed on a patient smile. 'Our cargo is slaves, Mrs Hughes. That's the trade. Slaves to Jamaica. This is where we stack them.'

'Excuse me,' she said, 'I meant the cargo you said you'd be plying from Africa to . . . oh, my God.'

Mr Spragge's smile was playfully tolerant of women's ignorance of what wagged the world. 'Mrs Hughes, how do you think the sugar grows, is cut, refined?' He bobbed his raised finger forward, like a schoolmaster. 'Ships, slaves, sugar. Sugar, ships, slaves, the great triangle of navigation. Since 1680 the Royal African Company has shipped 5,000 a year and hopes to . . .'

As he went on talking his voice faded against the sickness rising in Penitence. *This is where we stack them.* Unwillingly, she was lifted up and squeezed into her allotted space on the shelves. *Her right hand and leg were shackled to someone else's left hand and leg. She lay in a space smaller than a corpse's in a coffin. The wood of the shelf above hers almost touched her nose. Her body bucked with the rise and fall of the ship, water poured in through the holes in the cargo cover and ordure from the slave above dripped down on to her stomach and legs . . .*

She was clawing at the ladder, fighting to get into the air, holding on to the canvas on a boom, retching.

When she could next take notice of anything, Henrietta was wafting a handkerchief back and forth in front of her face as if lack of air had been her trouble while Mr Spragge, more astute, was explaining that such over-sensitivity was unnecessary; that discomfort wasn't the same for blacks as for whites. 'They don't feel the same privation. And when they get to the plantations they are so happy. Henrietta, dear one, tell Mrs Hughes of our voyage to the Barbados and how happy the negroes were in their new home.'

Henrietta looked around as if trying to recall the voyage. 'Yes, indeed,' she said. 'They were very happy. Except that I thought it very odd to see the black cooks chained to the fireplaces.'

'You see, Mrs Hughes, they're not the same as us . . .'

'They are,' she whispered. 'They are.' She could see Peter's black suffering face as he watched with her over the dying Rupert. She turned on Spragge so that he recoiled and bumped his head on the boom. 'You would not do this if Prince Rupert were alive.'

He blinked, genuinely puzzled. 'Why would we not? I don't think you understand, Mrs Hughes. Slaves, sugar, ships – they are the *raison d'être* of the Company. Your . . . His Highness was one of its founders.'

'No,' she said, 'Rupert didn't know of it.'

As he protested, she pulled herself together, pushed him and Henrietta away, wiped her mouth, tied the ribbons of her hat more firmly under her chin and set off for the gangplank. At the taffrail gate she swayed for a moment. 'He didn't know of it. Not Rupert.'

Penitence never remembered finding the livery stable and her horse, though the houses she passed stayed in her memory.

Sugar houses, pretending their roofs were gingerbread and their mullions sticks of barley-sugar when in fact their foundations stood in human blood, like the skeletons of baby-sacrifices found under ancient hearthstones.

Not Rupert.

She stayed a wordless night in the barn at Lower Langford and didn't remember that either. She hitched the cart to the horse and drove it south, only vaguely aware of what she was doing or the countryside she passed through.

What has happened? Why do I feel like this? It wasn't as if she had not known of slavery, but it had always been *out there*, as drawing and quartering had been *out there* until she had been present at its execution. Now, whatever damned thing it was that had assisted her to become part Indian, or part eagle, the same thing that had enabled her to become Beatrice and

639

Desdemona, had entombed her. For one moment she had been slid into a living coffin and seen the lid slam.

Matoonas. Awashonks. *Forgive me*. She should have given up everything to go and find them, left behind child, protector, comfort, house ... Nothing she sacrificed would have been too much payment to save them from those human stacks. Blocked into a space of inches when they had run free through a thousand square miles, they would shrivel into dust.

In that moment she knew her Indians were dead.

Rupert always knew. She faced it.

Fifty times he must have told her the story of Peter, when he and his brother Maurice had moored in the bay of a village on the Guinea coast and gone ashore to find the villagers fled and a small, bewildered, black boy scrabbling at his knees. 'They thought we were slavers, you see, my dear,' Rupert would always say.

And you were. You took Peter home, Christianized him, you knew he could feel pain, happiness, jealousy, love – above all, love – and you could still join other men in an enterprise to market his brothers and sisters in the same way you would sell cattle or coal.

The cargo was indifferent. Arrived in poor condition.

Rupert rose up before her, stiffly dignified, loving, the most decent man of his generation.

She longed to forgive him but it wasn't her wrong to forgive. *If you can't see how great a wrong it is, who else will?*

Nobody was equipped to see what she saw. *She* was the freak. It was her peculiarity to have spent a childhood learning that people of one colour could suffer the same pain as those of another. Her adolescence in the Rookery had seen women bought and sold. Forced from one country to another, from one man to another, the struggle she and other women had waged and lost against their rightlessness opened a window on to universal injustice.

Consignments. Profit. Trade. Applied to human beings, the words were ultimate blasphemy. She knew it. Dorinda had known it. Now, if MacGregor was alive still, he would know it. But who else?

The devastating loneliness of her knowledge dwindled her into an ant crawling across the table-top of the Somerset Levels.

'Aphra.'

The November air took the word from her mouth and froze it into vapour. She watched it drift to join the steam rising from the horse's back. But Aphra would know, *had* known. The strange woman had divined the indivisibility of freedom; that unless it applied to both sexes and all races it was not freedom at all. Aphra would speak out for it. Nobody would listen, of course, but the great truth would have been said and perhaps one day somebody would hear it.

Still she was as lonely as when she'd first stepped off the ship from Massachusetts into the slums of London. The pale, lowering sun gleamed on bare branches and, along the route, tarred, iron-bound pieces of flesh swung in the light, cold airs with a not unmusical reverberation. She wanted Aphra, the only person in England who would understand her misery. And she wanted MacGregor. *Stay alive, MacGregor.* With MacGregor saved she would be less lonely for Dorinda and might pay back at least part of the appalling debt she owed them both. She wanted the camaraderie of the Cock and Pie days to rush in and fill the vacuum in which she now lived.

And now she had lost Rupert, or at least the assurance in ultimate human decency which is what Rupert had meant to her. *Oh my dear, how could you?*

Trundling through her winter landscape, Penitence became colder and freer as the last shackle of her own bondage fell away and she recognized the great and true simplification; that all men, all women, were flawed and that all power, therefore, should be checked and balanced with no person having absolute rule over another

She absolved Rupert; how could he have been expected to see the world as she saw it? But she also absolved herself; the agreement between them had been honoured by both sides during his lifetime but now, in not being what she had thought him, he had forfeited his right to her fidelity after his death.

The light was going fast as she reached the bridge over the Cary at Chedzoy. The rebel piece of flesh on its pole was a dim ornament, like a deformed stone pineapple at the gates to a great house.

'Tickle up that old nag, Leddyship, or you'll be spending the night in the Levels,' Matt Fry said to her as she passed.

Penitence neither saw nor heard him.

God damn it, she thought wearily, I could have married Henry after all.

Chapter 2

IN ASKING Parliament to vote him extra money for a bigger standing army, James hit a nerve for the first time.

For one thing, the House of Commons had a traditional suspicion of kings who had their own, strong armies. Also it was full of gentlemen who were proud of the militia, who liked nothing better than putting on their breastplates at weekends and drilling their servants up and down the countryside.

For another thing, during the emergency, the King had appointed army officers who were Roman Catholics. Under the Test Acts — those same laws which had forced James himself to resign as Lord Admiral when he was Duke of York — they held their posts illegally. Not only did James declare that he would *not* remove such men from their posts, but he wanted the Test Acts and other laws against Dissenters repealed.

Parliament might have nodded at allowing Protestant Non-conformists, Presbyterians, Baptists, Quakers and the like to worship as they pleased, but abolition would also give Roman Catholics freedom. Didn't the King know the country wouldn't stand for that?

The fact that the country's Roman Catholics were well behaved, that there were barely enough of them to form a regiment let alone rule, and that the Pope himself had told his representatives in England to pursue only a moderate and constitutional policy, none of this mattered; no dread went quite so deep into the English psyche as fear of Popery.

The appearance on the throne of the Prince of Darkness himself couldn't horrify the English more than the thought of Roman rule. Indeed, they couldn't distinguish between the two. The massacre of St Bartholomew, the numerous Catholic conspiracies against the life of Good Queen Bess, the Gunpowder Plot, now Louis XIV's assault on his French Protestants after the abrogation of the Treaty of Nantes – all these terrors were attributed to a faith which was seen to free its members from the rules of morality as long as they advanced their Church. It was why Titus Oates's fabrications of Jesuits-under-the-beds during the Popish Plot scare had spread such panic.

Much depended on James recognizing that this deep-seated antipathy of English men and women, high and low, was not to be dispelled by reason nor force.

It appeared that he couldn't. When Parliament proved evasive he showed his displeasure and dissolved it. He was, he said, 'resolved to give liberty of conscience to all Dissenters whatsoever, having ever been against persecution for conscience' sake'. It was a noble sentiment and he backed it up by issuing a general pardon which released 1,200 Quakers as well as Anabaptists from prison.

But a darker strain showed in James's toleration. Protestant ministers, commissioners, administrators and army officers – especially army officers – were finding themselves dismissed and replaced by Roman Catholics.

The alarm bells began to ring.

For a while Society buzzed with the news that the former actress Peg Hughes, Rupert of the Rhine's mistress, had been cast off by the Viscount of Severn and Thames after a brief affair and that the Viscount had also quarrelled with the King and gone across the water to offer his services to Prince William of Orange. Then, other more important matters attracting its attention, Society forgot them both.

Penitence spent the next three years on her Priory estate trying to attract as little attention as possible. While it could not be proved that she'd had a hand in helping Monmouth rebels escape justice, the events of the summer of 1685 had done her reputation no good and she needed to retrieve it if her daughter and foster-child were to be received into Society without the doubtful repute of their mother staining their chances.

Mistress Palmer took the news of Dorinda's death with the philosophic detachment of the aged. 'Lord keep her. There's another Dog Yarder gone. Well, we all got to go some time.'

Tongs, however, grieved more deeply for her mother and father than Penitence had expected, considering that in the last year or two she had seen them so little. It was no good promising her that MacGregor would return one day — he hadn't. No good, either, to put up a memorial to her mother in order to give the child a focus for her grief since Dorinda's body had gone into a quicklime pit along with other prisoners and, as she'd died a suspect rebel, was refused commemoration.

It took two years, the intervention of Aphra Behn, the Earl of Craven and £300, for Penitence to receive permission to put up a tablet to her friend in the church at Athelzoy.

The Reverend Boreman, who was becoming old and inflexible, wanted it inscribed with the words: 'He that is without sin among you, let him first cast a stone at her.'

Penitence's anger was remembered by all those who witnessed it: 'I won't have her judged. I won't *have* her judged. Do you hear me?' More and more it seemed to her that if their only choice was between starvation and sale, the lot of poor Englishwomen was no better than a slave's. 'Let anybody, *anybody*, fling a stone at her and it'll get flung back right in their bloody eye.'

In the end Dorinda's tablet bore the legend: 'No greater love than this'.

Penitence was becoming as short-tempered as she was short-staffed. The blood-letting of the Assizes, the transportations and deaths in prison had taken their toll of the young, male population, while feeding a billeted army was costing the West Country dear. There weren't enough labourers to keep the Levels well drained and that first winter after the rebellion saw the Parrett flood the moors as it hadn't for years, drowning cattle and winter crops. Penitence was only able to plant a few acres of teasels with the manpower available which meant that she was going to lose her markets in the North of England. She watched her yew chessmen become merely untidy bushes because there was nobody to topiary them.

Worst of all, she had to watch Prue's young face set into intolerant and bitter lines as the girl found her only comfort in the Lord of vengeance who was being increasingly worshipped in the chapels around Sedgemoor.

The one bright beam into their greyness came through the same grapevine which had informed Penitence of Mudge Ridge's escape. Now she received word that he, too, had reached Holland. Penitence sent back some of her fast-dwindling money and Benedick's address.

After eighteen months she received another letter, this time from across the Atlantic. Once she had waded through the obligatory exhortations for her repentance and recommendations to the Lord for her unclean soul, Uncle Martin settled down into a surprisingly communicative, if unpunctuated, style.

There was much about the rigours of the voyage and the resultant looseness of his bowels, a long description of eating turtle-meat, none at all of Africa itself, but a good deal about the slaves the *Bonaventura* had taken aboard there. He was indignant at the condition in which they travelled 'in that so many do perish' but only because it deprived him of potential converts. Uncle Martin Hughes, it appeared, had found a new vocation; 'to bring to the Lord the poor benighted creatures so that the trade can encompass good not evil'.

His account of Jamaica covered one side of a page, mostly concerned with the number of black girls who adorned the houses of the plantation owners and managers and the sin thereof.

Not until Penitence was nearly screaming as she read did he come to it:

The law here being unobserved I did find little hindrance in discovering and after much haggling in purchasing the Scotchman we spoke of and procuring his passage on a Dutch ship which may arrive there afore this letter though his master was reluctant to let him go since he has proved trustworthy in business which is a rare occasion among so many miscreants.

For a moment, Penitence sat down and held the letter against her cheek. *MacGregor*. One brand out of the burning.

But there was another page of Uncle Martin's crabbed writing and, sewn into the one she was holding, a protuberance.

She read on:

After much enquiry I found no trace of thy Squakheag and no hope of it in that overseers here do despise Indian slaves for that they die too soon so I took ship for the Americas to find spiritual comfort in my brothers and sisters in the Lord and to look for thy people and mine but though at this moment I sit in the midst of mountain and plain on the edge of the river called Pocumscut there is no sign of heathen habitation nor none else except burned grass as if it caught fire and only this bead which I do send thee.

Penitence unstitched the paper where it had been sewn over at the edge and extracted a faded red and blue bead, a necklace bead, scorched on one side.

For a moment she stood where her uncle had written his letter beneath the twisted mountain of Pemawachuatuck under which the lodges of Awashonks's people had rested beside the river. Through his eyes she looked out at a smokeless, blackened ring, soundless except for the call of the circling eagle, and knew not only that her Indians were dead but that their way of life would never be seen there again.

Gently, she folded the letter around the bead and took it upstairs to put it in a silk fichu in her dressing-table drawer.

Then she went downstairs to find Tongs and tell her that her father was alive and on his way to freedom.

It was one of those periods of hiatus. In the pauses when Penitence had time to feel anything other than exhaustion it was a sense of suspension. Surprised, she discovered that her neighbours, those assured Tory men and women, were in a similar state. When they met together the topic of conversation that dominated even fatstock prices was the four Roman Catholic lords who'd been sworn into the Privy Council. Posts which Anglican churchmen could have expected to hold were going to members of the Church of Rome.

Under Charles I, Somerset royalists had faced conflict but never a divided mind. In fighting for the royal cause they had known they were upholding King and Church in one symbolic body. Now, for the first time, their grandchildren stared at the prospect of a terrible choice. King *or* Church? What if James made it impossible to be true to both?

'Ah tell ee,' roared Sir Ostyn Edwards at her, 'he'll be loyal to the Church, iss fay.' But he was obviously shaken after a trip to London during which he'd seen friars walking its streets, openly fingering their rosaries.

Pamphlets were being sold with royal approval which purported to prove that Charles II had lived and died a Roman Catholic.

'Old Rowley whored like a Papist, we'n't deny ut,' said Sir Ostyn, stoutly, 'but we *know* he were a good Protestant.' His tiny, white-lashed eyes slid sideways at Penitence. 'Weren't he?'

'I don't know,' she said. 'Did you see Aphra?'

By introducing Sir Ostyn to the brief but dynamic influence of Aphra and Dorinda, Penitence had unleashed another devotee to the theatre. His yearly visits to London had become quarterly and this time he had spent four nights watching successive performances of Aphra's latest play, *The Lucky Chance*. 'Naughty,' he said, 'I never seen a naughty old play like ut.' He was the only person she knew who actually held his sides when he laughed.

Yes, he'd gone round to Aphra's house and she'd entertained him and given him a copy of the play to bring back for Penitence to read. 'Poor old soul now, though, with her rheumatics.'

Ostyn's conversation was combative and Penitence dismissed his remark as an attempt to provoke her. Aphra was her senior but had always retained the youth of a contemporary. Her letters were as sprightly as ever and gave her reasons for not accepting Penitence's invitations as having too many commissions to finish. Penitence, trying to keep her head and — often literally — her crops, above water, had sent back similar apologies.

She enjoyed reading *The Lucky Chance*, a fast-moving comedy in which penurious heroines decided to marry wealthy old men. Where most plays dealt with the rich, this one drew on Aphra's experience of being hard up. Its glory, however, was her portrait of the impotent old lechers her girls had chosen to marry — not the usual run-of-the-mill creations but endowed from Aphra's experience with a dreadful vitality. *Mr Behn*, thought Penitence.

With the play Sir Ostyn had also brought back some of Aphra's other work, among them her fighting defence of *The Lucky Chance*:

> They charge it with the old never-failing scandal — that 'tis not fit for the ladies. As if the ladies were obliged to hear indecencies only from *their* pens. Had it been owned by a man, though the most dull, unthinking, rascally scribbler in town, it had been a most admirable play.

'Poor old soul?' demanded Penitence of Sir Ostyn. 'You tell 'em, Affie.'

There was also Aphra's long Pindaric for James and his Queen on 'The Happy Coronation of His Most Sacred Majesty' which Penitence didn't bother to read. What she did read in bed one night, what transfixed her, was Aphra's poem to John Hoyle, 'To Mr J.H.'

All Heaven is mine, I have it in my arms,

> Nor can ill fortune reach me any more.
> Fate, I defy thee, and dull world, adieu.
> In love's kind fever, ever let me lie,
> Drunk with desire, and raving mad with joy.

Damn you, Affie. She too had held Heaven in her arms in this very room, this very bed, and let it go.

The laws against Popery were still unrepealed but the King took matters into his own hands. Without waiting for a Parliament that would repeal the Test Acts – one would never have been elected in any case – James made his own Declaration of Liberty of Conscience.

The reaction was extraordinary. One by one the Protestant Dissenting churches, groups that had faced prison for their faith, preachers who'd lost their livings by refusing to follow the Articles of the Church of England, men who'd been driven out of their homes by the Five Mile Act, all these people told James that they didn't want his permission to worship legally if it meant that Roman Catholics were to receive the same indulgence.

It made no difference. James ordered that his Declaration be read from every pulpit on successive Sundays.

Six bishops went to Whitehall carrying with them a petition signed by the Archbishop of Canterbury, assuring James of their loyalty but most courteously pointing out that he couldn't do it; the King couldn't dispense with statutes – that was the privilege of Parliament. They must therefore refuse, if the King would graciously forgive them, to allow his Declaration to be read in any Anglican church.

The King didn't forgive them: 'This is the standard of rebellion.'

On their knees the bishops swore it was not. 'Sir,' said Bishop Ken of Bath and Wells, 'I hope that you will grant to us that liberty of conscience which you grant to all mankind.'

James persisted furiously: 'This is rebellion. This is the standard of rebellion.'

'We have two duties to perform,' answered Ken. 'Our duty

to God and our duty to Your Majesty. We honour you, but we fear God.'

The bishops were sent to the Tower.

And the Queen was pregnant.

The five-aisled church of St Mary Magdalene took some filling but on a Sunday in June 1688, the population of practically the entire Taunton Vale formed its congregation, including Dissenters who wouldn't have been seen dead in an Anglican church at any other time and wouldn't have been tolerated if they had. By being sent to the Tower, Bishop Ken of Bath and Wells and Bishop Trelawney of Bristol had become everybody's bishops, even anti-episcopates'.

The congregation's eyes were on the preacher as he climbed the steps to the carved pulpit. In almost all the churches in the land the eyes of the congregation concentrated on the preachers at that moment climbing into a thousand pulpits. Would he? Wouldn't he?

In St Mary Magdalene he didn't. Some two thousand Somerset men and women sat back in satisfaction to listen to the usual sermon.

In a hundred City parish churches Londoners too folded their arms and settled down to the accustomed hour's nodding and/or dozing. Even in St James's Palace chapel the Anglican priest refused to read out its present royal owner's Declaration of Indulgence.

In Westminster Abbey, however, as a more obedient preacher began to read what his King commanded, his voice was drowned by the sound of his vast congregation walking out.

Outside St Mary Magdalene's, under the budding lime trees, Penitence's neighbours gathered about their carriages.

'That'll show un,' said Sir Roger Pascoe.

Sir Ostyn nodded. 'Teach un to gaol our bishops. By God, Ah've a good mind . . .'

'Can we go home now?' asked Penitence. She'd already been waiting for the half-hour since the service ended while her fellow-worshippers congratulated each other as if they had personally defeated the forces of Rome single-handed. She had her teasels to see to.

'Teach un to pass off any old Papist babby on us,' said Sir Roger.

Lady Portman and Lady Pascoe both nodded with the authority of parturient women. 'Her's too old and lost too many babbies to have un now. Smuggling the poor little mite into the bed in a warming pan, wicked.'

Penitence sighed; if they got on to the royal birth she'd never get home. At thirty Mary of Modena was younger than both Mesdames Portman and Pascoe and, as queens usually gave birth in a room filled with at least forty weighty witnesses and as those witnesses on this occasion had included the entire Privy Council, Lord Chancellor Jeffreys among them, she herself was inclined to believe that James had at last been vouchsafed his much-longed-for legitimate son and heir.

But it was an indication of how much trust his subjects had lost in James that they refused to believe it. It was an impostor baby, a lie, a Jesuit fraud, a plot to deny succession to that good Protestant, Princess Mary of Orange, and put some Papist's brat on the throne.

In fact, thought Penitence, they dare not believe it. They had been prepared to put up with James's Catholicism when it was likely to die with him but the vista of an unbroken succession of Romish kings had put the wind up the English people. And as a sign that the gods first sent mad those whom they wished to destroy, James had asked the Pope to be the baby's godfather.

From somewhere among the knots of people gathered outside the church a whistle rose above the general chatter. The tune was catchy but it was its effect on her friends that attracted Penitence's interest. They pricked up their ears like hounds at the hunting horn.

'What is that?' she asked. 'I keep hearing it.'

'King goes on like he do, you'll be hearing a danged sight more of it,' said Sir Ostyn, bundling her and the two girls into his carriage. ' 'Tis called "Lillibullero". Hush now.'

On the way back across Sedgemoor he talked of Prince

William of Orange. 'Reckon that's the sort of lad as'd do us. Protestant wind to blow away Catholic muck.'

Penitence couldn't get excited about it. Only three years ago these same people, Bishops Ken and Trelawney among them, had been happy to countenance the executions of men who'd backed just such another Protestant wind to blow James away. She said so.

''Tis a very different thing,' Sir Ostyn lectured her. 'Monmouth . . .' He glanced behind him to see if Ruperta and Tongs were listening. The name still had power. '. . . he were a bastard, like this babby they're trying to foist on us is a bastard. William, now, he's legitimate, married to legitimate Mary. He's the sort of lad as'd do us. Protestant wind.'

'I'm sick of James,' she said, 'but I'm sicker of seeing men try to get rid of him. It would mean killing. There's been enough. I'll not listen to any more.' She maintained her refusal to discuss it and so forgot to ask him what it all had to do with the song 'Lillibullero'. In the days that followed she learned that it sang of a Protestant wind:

> O why does he stay so long behind?
> Ho! by my soul, 'tis a Protestant wind.
> Lero, lero, Lillibullero . . .

The ridiculous words and skipping, cheerful rhythm tangled themselves up in the Protestants' hope of William of Orange so inextricably that the song became a signal and a defiance. The tune was heard coming from Whiggish coffee-houses, apprentices whistled it as they went about their trade, it was said that it had even been heard in Whitehall where the beleaguered Protestant Princess Anne was steadfastly defying all attempts by the Jesuits to convert her and her household to Roman Catholicism. To wear an orange favour was dangerous but, so far, royal authority had not yet grasped that opposition was consolidating in the form of a song.

On the day that Penitence took her boar across the marshes in order to oblige Lady Pascoe's sow and stayed for tea, Lady Pascoe was heard to hum the tune as she passed out the cups.

My God. Lady Pascoe too. If James had lost the devotion of this snobbish, fat, honey-cake-making, likeable woman he had lost England.

Into Penitence's memory came Henry's voice: 'You can have a king who's a fool and you can have a king who's a Catholic but if you've got a king who's a fool *and* a Catholic, sooner or later you're going to have a revolution. And that's when William comes in.'

In her own view James had to go, not because he was Catholic or foolish but because he'd said: 'I know the English. One must not show them at the start that one is afraid of them.'

It was the remark of an alien, someone who not only *was* afraid of the English but didn't regard himself as one of them. And as Penitence recrossed the moor with a June breeze flipping the willow leaves white side up, ruffling the blue surfaces of the rhines and scenting the air with the smell of bean flowers, she realized it had become vital to her that, if England had to be personified by a monarch, then that monarch must feel for the country what she had come to feel for this area of Somerset. Nationality had nothing to do with it; Rupert, born in Bohemia, had been English to his finger-tips. James was English-born and as removed from his people as if he came from the moon.

Mary, she thought. Mary had wept when she'd had to leave England to be married to the House of Orange. *Mary will do.*

As much as she ever would be, Penitence was now rehabilitated into her community and, even if she was still seen as a threat to wives, she was at least trusted to be part of the same political scene as everyone else, which meant that her neighbours, with a wink and a nod, handed her the leaflets being secretly distributed throughout the country and expected her to pass them on. Who was doing the distributing, nobody was sure, but there was no doubt the pamphlets originated in the Low Countries. Some were anti-Catholic, hysterically so, some anti-James, some pro-William and Mary. All demanded that the King release the bishops from the Tower and make concessions to the established Church.

The most persuasive of the pamphlets was an open letter to the English people written by one Caspar Fagel, Grand Pensionary of Holland, setting out what would happen if Mary was allowed to succeed to her father's throne. It was a calming, reassuring document saying she would not permit the persecution of anybody because of their manner of worship. English Roman Catholics should be allowed the considerable degree of freedom they enjoyed in Holland, as long as they were excluded from both Houses of Parliament and from public employment.

If James isn't a madman, thought Penitence, he'll not only *not* take exception to what his daughter says, he'll follow her example. But she was beginning to suspect that James *was* a madman who carried obstinacy to the point of derangement.

It was Sir Ostyn who brought her the next pamphlet one evening: 'Got a mention of your friend in ut.'

This had been written by a Dr Gilbert Burnet, a name increasingly appearing on propaganda from the Netherlands. Penitence's eye latched on the words 'Aphra Behn'. 'She's your friend too,' she told Sir Ostyn, taking the paper to the light.

Dr Burnet bewailed the state of England under James and cited as symptomatic of its moral decline that the King encouraged 'such a poet as Mrs Aphra Behn, so abominably vile a woman, who rallies not only all religion but all virtue in so odious and obscene a manner'.

Penitence put the paper to the candle-flame and turned on her neighbour: 'Who the hell is Dr Gilbert Burnet?'

Ostyn loved seeing her riled. 'A fine propounder of liberty, so they tell us. A good friend to the Prince and Princess of Orange and none to your Aphra seemingly.'

'Whose liberty?' She advanced on the man, furious, brushing cindered pieces of paper from her dress. 'Eh, damn you? Whose liberty does he propound?'

Sir Ostyn retreated. 'I'm not speaking agin Mistress Behn, poor soul, but she's strong for the King and she writes danged naughty plays.'

'I don't care if she's strong for the Great Cham of China. She's earning her living. She hasn't had to get married, or whore, or beg, or do anything she doesn't want to do. She doesn't take in laundry and sew. She writes. She doesn't write pious tracts. She writes popular plays. She's good at it. That's what she's chosen to do and just because no woman's earned her bread by doing it before, this B-B-Burnet wants to stop her.' Aphra Behn had entered a race in which the prizes were reserved for male runners. She'd won and kept on winning but, because winning meant fame and 'fame' as applied to women was synonymous with notoriety, an idiot like Burnet was free to call her every dirty name he could lay his tongue to.

'Never knew you stammered, maid,' said Sir Ostyn, and made Penitence so cross she showed him the door without offering him refreshment.

Damn them. Just as she was beginning to think that for William to topple James would be an advance for freedom. She could tell what would happen. They'd bring in this new ruler in the name of freedom and out would go the freedom of women like Aphra Behn.

In October the Prince of Orange declared his intention to come to England with an army to see 'a free and lawful parliament assembled as soon as possible'.

In his declaration distributed all over England, William listed the violations of his wife's kingdom by 'evil counsellors'. Parliament had been set aside, judges replaced by time-servers, an avowed Papist was on the High Commission to which the Church of England had been entrusted. Every borough had been told it must vote for the repeal of the Test Acts or have its franchises taken away. For no crime but that of proffering a petition to their sovereign, fathers of the Church had been imprisoned.

'Therefore it is that we have thought fit to go over to England and to carry with us a force sufficient, by the blessing of God, to defend us from the violence of those evil counsellors.'

Immediately James realized his danger he changed tack, putting back in power men he'd deprived of it, returning charters to boroughs, issuing a proclamation in which he solemnly promised to protect the Church of England.

But it was too late. Loyal Cavaliers had been forced to make their choice. James's *volte-face* merely confirmed that here was a king who would only obey his country's constitution under threat.

More and more letters poured over to The Hague assuring William of the support of great men when he landed.

James's one ally was the wind. It blew from the west, keeping William's ships in their Dutch harbours. In the streets of London apprentices gathered to stare up at the weathercocks on church spires and whistle the wind round to the opposite quarter. The tune they whistled was 'Lillibullero'.

At Athelzoy a late harvest was gathered in. The last sheaf in the cornfields was raced for with cries of 'A nek! A nek!' and placed on top of the loaded cart. After gleaning, Michaelmas geese and poultry were put out in the fields to work over the stubble. After that it was time to gather the small scented Rusticoat apples which in the Levels were known as 'jayzees' and cart them to the mill in the Ridges' farmyard.

On November the 1st, as Penitence watched the cider pony tramping patiently round the stone trough turning the crushing wheel until the pulp was the right consistency, she was startled by Prue's yell of triumph: ''Tis changed, look.'

'What's changed?'

Prue was pointing to where her washing hung on the line. The breeze which had been blowing the smell of apples on to it had fallen, then picked up unexpectedly cold.

'Wind's changed to the east. Now he'll come. Now he'll give that danged James what for.'

A week later the Prince of Orange landed in Torbay in Devon at the head of a large force, much of it formed by English exiles.

The King and his army marched to Salisbury to block his son-in-law's advance. The country waited, expecting to hear of the great battle in the West which would decide whether

England was to be ruled by a Catholic king or his Protestant daughter.

But there wasn't one. Instead each day brought news of powerful men abandoning James and crossing the no-man's-land between his army and William's to join the Protestant cause.

Here was no repeat of the Monmouth affair with William attracting only the underprivileged and downtrodden to his banner. This time the ground had been carefully prepared; he'd waited until he was invited by some of the greatest names in the land, with secret promises of support from many others.

The first to leave James was Lord Colchester, next the son of the Earl of Bedford. After them it was the Lord Lieutenant of Oxfordshire, a man previously loyal to James and who had helped to put down the Monmouth rebellion but was unable to stomach the King's treatment of his Church. Next the commander of James's garrison at Plymouth, the Earl of Bath, made his escape and put himself, his troops and his fortress under the Prince of Orange's command. Then came Sir William Portman, the most influential Tory in the West of England and one of the men who had captured Monmouth.

Slowly the two armies approached each other but it was as if James's proceeded down a steep hill and his men were tumbling away from him. It didn't help that the King was suffering violent nosebleeds and his men kept seeing blood on his face.

They brought him the news that Lord Churchill, his greatest general, was missing from his quarters. Churchill had left behind a letter. In it he said he owed everything to the King but he was a Protestant and he could not draw his sword against the Protestant cause. He had gone over to the Prince of Orange.

James retreated back to London and on the way his other son-in-law, the stupid, amiable Prince George, husband of Princess Anne, rode off to join his brother-in-law in the Dutch camp.

Back at Whitehall the King was greeted by the news that Princess Anne herself, with her great friend, Sarah, the wife of Lord Churchill, had stolen away in a hackney coach.

The King wept. 'God help me! My own children have forsaken me.'

As William's army moved slowly but inexorably up through the West towards London, two of its members broke away and rode across the Somerset Levels to call at Athelzoy Priory where they were received with much celebration by the household and its children.

The mistress of the house, however, was absent. 'Gone up to London,' Mistress Palmer told Benedick and MacGregor. 'Had a letter from a friend of that Aphry Behn's. She's dying, poor soul.'

Penitence drew back the curtains to look out on to St Bride's: 'Who's Dr Gilbert Burnet, incidentally?'

Behind her, Aphra sucked in enough breath to reply. 'One of the great and good. Or an outlaw and a rabid Whig. Depending on your point of view. He was supposed to have converted Rochester. On his death-bed. Heard his confession.'

'That must have been worth hearing.' Penitence crossed back to the bed. 'Can you shift over while I straighten this bit?'

With difficulty, grunting with pain, Aphra hotched to one side of the bed while Penitence made the other. 'Yes. Burnet wrote an improving tract on it. Poor Rochester. Promise, Penitence, promise, promise, promise. No divines wanting to save my soul at the end.'

'Don't talk about ending. You've got years yet.' Her reassurance fell into a room where most of the guests had departed. Otway, discovered dead in his garret; Buckingham dead in a lonely Yorkshire farmhouse, bewailing that he had been a shame and a disgrace; Nell Gwynn dead; John Hoyle on trial for buggery; Becky Marshall, defeated, married to a wealthy grocer.

Now the hostess was making her own agonized, protracted departure from the room where she had listened and written and administered milk punch and where she now lay in bed. The old Aphra was in the voice and eyes, the rest had twisted, as if her bones had been in a fire. Most appalling were her hands, claws with fingers aligned sideways from the huge knuckle of the thumb. At forty-eight, she had suddenly passed from her prime to senescence in a matter of months.

'Hardly, dear.' She smiled. 'One would have liked to end up in the Abbey with the other poets, but they're not likely to let a woman in.'

As Penitence tidied up the room she noticed many of its ornaments were missing. *She's pawned them.*

An untidy young woman came rushing in. 'I overslept. Did you manage to sleep at all, my poor dear? No, Mistress Hughes, we don't like our pillows like that. Like *this.*'

The young woman's name was Chloe and it was with some reluctance that she had allowed Penitence to take her place at Aphra's bedside while she herself got some much-needed sleep. Even now, Penitence suspected, she would try to ban her from the house if it wasn't for the money Penitence had given her to buy medicine and nourishing food.

The girl fussed about, establishing her prior right, pouring out the medicine, putting paper, pen and ink to Aphra's hand as if they were as necessary as the physick. With it all, she was careful not to touch her. Last evening, on her arrival, Penitence had tried to embrace her friend but, at her wince, stood back. Obviously the slightest pressure was painful, yet seeing her manoeuvre herself was awful.

At last they made her ready to face the day. 'Is there any movement outside?' she asked. 'What do you think is happening? Penitence, do go and find out what's to do with the poor King.'

Nothing loth, Penitence put on her cloak; 'And wax,' said Chloe sharply. 'It eases Aphra's hands to put them in warm wax. A pound of best beeswax from Partridge's up by the 'Change.'

As Penitence left the room, Aphra Behn scooped up her pen, holding it between her hands to write.

There was less traffic in Fleet Street than she'd ever seen before and when she turned down towards Blackfriars to look upriver she could see smoke smudging the sky towards Whitehall. Its smitch was in the air along with something else — a London unsure of itself, lacking the usual chestnut-vendors and the warm, Christmas smell of their popping pans, half its shops shut, none of the usual people doing the usual things, apprentices gathering ready to riot, women shouting questions from first-floor windows, be-wigged men to be seen in discussing groups through the archways to the Inns of Court.

The coach from Somerset had set her and its other passengers down at Aldgate last night, refusing to enter the city; at his previous stop the driver had received reports of anarchy. She'd had to get a waterman to take her to the Blackfriars steps and then make the uneasy walk to St Bride's and Aphra's house, with sounds of shouting in the distance, and the glimmer of fires in the western sky and nervy watchmen ushering her along and refusing to tell her if King James was still on the throne or not — probably because they didn't know.

Well, there were only two places in London to go for news. One was Whitehall, which was where the trouble was; the other the Exchange and she had to go there anyway to get Aphra's beeswax.

It wasn't until she entered the colonnades of the Exchange that she realized how she'd let herself go. Once she'd turned every head in the place. Now she saw faces that then had recognized her go by without a sign that they'd ever known her. Sir Walter Legge, he who had waylaid her at the Drury Lane entrance every night for weeks, actually pushed past her as if she were no more than the flower-seller who had her pitch by the East India Company stairs. *Am I so old?* She was thin from hard work, her hands were calloused and her nails ragged, her dress was out of date and, anyway, faded. She saw Sir Charles Sedley in the distance and shrank back. *At least I've not got fat. Or bald.*

But if she was commonplace she was invisible. Hanging around on the edge of groups, asking questions and being patronized with a 'my good woman' in the answer, she learned the reports as they came in.

The embassies of Catholic countries had been attacked and

set on fire last night; the Spanish ambassador's library had gone up in flames. A mob had got into Whitehall hunting for Father Petre, the royal Jesuit adviser. Parks were being ravaged, deer killed, roads blocked by self-appointed police who stopped every traveller until he'd proved he wasn't a Papist.

Yes, my good woman, the Queen and the baby Prince of Wales had gone – her informant was a contemptuous young clerk. No, he knew not where. They'd been smuggled to Gravesend and aboard a boat. Now, if she would step aside . . .

Yesterday, Tuesday, it appeared, the King had ordered the Lord Mayor to attend Whitehall with the Sheriffs of London and exhorted them to be vigorous in their duty. He would stay at his post. He'd found it necessary to send his wife and child out of the country, he'd told them, but he himself was calling a Parliament and negotiating with the Prince of Orange, whose forces were now stationed seventy miles from London.

Back once more at Aphra's house, Penitence learned the sequel to this – from Dryden. It was symptomatic of the extraordinary time they were all living through that yesterday the playwright had been able to stride into Whitehall Palace, assured of his right as Poet Laureate, and now skulked for reassurance in the faded familiarity of Aphra's room, afraid not just for his Laureateship but for his life. Having written an attack on the Dutch under Charles and converted to Catholicism under James, he could not look forward to being popular with a new, Protestant regime. At the moment, it was hurt at his king's defection that he felt most.

'He told Lord Northumberland to guard his bedchamber door and call him at the usual time today,' he said. 'I was there with all the courtiers and lords waiting to make the morning bow, and the bedchamber was empty. He'd gone in the night – down a secret stair. And taken the Great Seal with him.'

The country could cope with a runaway king but its machinery was seriously disturbed by the loss of the Great Seal, which was later dragged up out of the Thames by a fisherman. Without it law and order could not be maintained. The head had parted from the still-running chicken. Government buildings were suddenly full of constitutional lawyers, ministers, clerks busying themselves in laying out documents and searching archives for a precedent that would tell them what to do and wishing the crowds in the street outside would stop singing long enough for them to find it.

> English confusion to Popery drink.
> Lillibullero bullen a la.

The Lord Mayor was seen to faint in panic when they brought before him a low-looking fellow in sailor's garb who turned out to be the Lord Chancellor, Sir George Jeffreys, formerly Judge Jeffreys, apprehended in a Wapping tavern trying to escape on a boat.

Jeffreys had been manhandled by the mob who'd caught him and it was said by those who rescued and marched him to the Tower where he had sent so many others that his shaking lips kept forming the pout of a 'w' as if he would ask 'Why?'

At last news came from Whitehall to say that poor Lord Northumberland, Lord of the Bedchamber who was also commander of the palace troop of Life Guards, had done the only thing he could — declared for the Prince of Orange. The remaining officers of the army had met and passed a resolution to submit to William's authority. Such peers as were still in London were repairing to the Guildhall to form a provisional government.

Nobody slept that night. People ran to and from each other's houses carrying news. Aphra insisted that her door be left open so that she could know what was going on but the continual, chattering consternation of her friends tired her out, as did her grief for the king she had loved. At dawn Chloe locked the door and insisted she rest.

It was then, going upstairs to her own bed and seeing the thin winter sun washing the street outside, that Penitence realized what she had witnessed in the last twenty-four hours. *I've seen a revolution.*

Pride in her adopted country suffused her. In all the reports she'd heard that day, not one had mentioned loss of life.

There'd been kerfuffle, damage, insults – it would take considerable diplomacy to soothe the heads of countries whose embassies had gone – but no loss of life.

There was a revolution. And nobody got killed.

William marched into London with the drums beating 'Lillibullero'. Penitence didn't go to see him do it; Aphra was too ill and Chloe too worn out with nursing her for them to be left. Besides, it poured with rain all day, turning the orange ribbons strung across the streets into brown strings.

From the window she watched people carrying oranges stuck on sticks splash up Fleet Street on their way towards St James's Park for the welcoming parade and found the rain symbolic; already London felt like the aftermath of a party whose guests had sobered.

Her only gesture to the new order had been to go out and buy some clothes; it was time to revive what looks she had left – in case Aphra had visitors.

It was years since she'd had time to study her reflection, and the shops' looking-glasses were brutal. Her facial skin had weathered and contrasted too sharply with the white of her shoulders and chest to wear anything low-cut. There were crow's-feet by the side of her eyes and, oh God, a close examination of her hair showed an occasional silver thread. The hairdresser's assistant, who worked on her nails, tactfully suggested she wear gloves.

Wildly, Penitence laid out money on paints, hair washes, creams, scents and dresses and reverted to sleeping in an oiled mask. Betterton was hoping to put on *The Widow Ranter* and Aphra still earmarked the part for her. Even playing a harpy, Penitence had no intention of going on stage looking like one.

Titus Oates was out of prison, calling down the Lord's retribution on those who had put him there, and rabid Protestants were enjoying revenge on those they regarded as collaborators. While Aphra had never turned Roman Catholic, her house was becoming a daytime refuge for those who had, and she was well known as a supporter of the disgraced King; accordingly refuse was thrown at her door. Both Penitence and Chloe had been threatened in the street by fanatics as 'Papist sluts of that whore of Babylon'.

Dryden, Neville Payne, Betterton, all the old set who had done little to earn the approbation of the new regime, came under cover of darkness to Aphra's to sit by her fire and talk and wonder what would happen to the theatre under Queen Mary. Aphra was their totem, the fulcrum on which they teetered, wobbling now, but with increasing cheerfulness the longer they stayed by her warmth and kept the door shut on the winter outside.

In her company, the old days came back, Nelly Gwynn was resurrected, Rochester, Buckingham, all the wits' stories and escapades were repeated, Charles's naughtinesses, Castlemaine's extravagances, the tarnished gilt was polished up and presented as solid gold.

Penitence remembered it differently and in any case they made her cross. *Can't they see how ill she is?* They drained Aphra's energy, as if hers was the only source available to them, as deeply as they drained her milk punch bowl, apparently uncaring where either commodity came from – the punch was provided by Penitence had they bothered to ask – or how much they cost.

Penitence restrained her impatience with them better than Chloe, whose scoldings they ignored, because Aphra would have been mortified if her guests were embarrassed. They gathered round her bed like a court round a throne, occasionally sitting on it, hammering it to make a point, not noticing that every jerk made her lips clench with pain. She pretended to them that she stayed in bed from choice – 'One grows lazy with age, my dears. Should Love come through the door again, here one lies – ready.'

In fact, she was barely able to walk; it wasn't only the arthritis that crippled her but breathlessness. Just getting up to use the pot set her gasping. Her colour was bad, her ankles and legs swollen. When her guests were gone, she sat in a stupor of exhaustion and came out of it chiding herself for having wasted writing time.

She wrote continually; Penitence went to the publishers

every week with some new work — the last volume of *Love Letters*, verses for a collection of poems she was bringing out, translations, histories, and long stories which were in a form new to Penitence and which Aphra called her 'novels'.

Emboldened by the thought that Aphra would not flourish under a queen as straitlaced as Mary, her enemies redoubled their attacks. 'Sappho, famous for her gout and guilt', was a poem accusing her of subsidizing her writing by prostitution. Penitence told Dryden to burn it, but Aphra learned of it. 'Well, my dear, one should be honoured; they said the same of the original Sappho.'

Another was anonymous and referred to Aphra as:

> That lewd harlot, that poetic queen,
> Famed through Whitefriars, you know who I mean . . .
> Plagued with a sciatica, she's besides lame,
> Her limbs distortured, nerves shrunk up with pain.
> And therefore I'll all sharp reflections shun,
> Poverty, poetry, pox, are plagues enough for one.

Does she still have to put up with this? Hadn't twenty years of pleasing the public earned her some respite?

There was none. Aphra didn't give herself any either. When it was Penitence's turn to sit up with her, she heard Aphra's pen scratching away until the early hours.

The first visitor from the victors' camp was Benedick, ringleted, in velvet and triumphant. Penitence spent a long time hugging him, and he her, before taking him in to Aphra, the woman who had taught him to read and whom he still called 'Aunt'.

He marched in: 'Make room for the victor of Wincanton.'

Penitence guided him away from Aphra's bed, which he was about to sit on. 'What happened at Wincanton?'

'The only damned engagement we had all the way from Devon. We were outnumbered by James's troops, but as it turned out they were only Irish. We fought over a hedge. Actually, it could have gone badly — there were four of them to every one of us, but some of the Somerset locals gave out that the rest of the Prince's army was coming up, at which the Irish fell back. So we carried the day, and the hedge, and William congratulated me later on my superb courage.' He looked modestly down at his nails. 'I should be surprised if I'm not *Sir* Benedick when the Prince comes into his own.'

So like his father. The very inflection of the voice was the same; his son had spent the last years modelling himself on Henry. *Well, he could have done worse.* He was waiting for her to ask where his father was, but she had her pride.

'How they loved us in the West. I suppose, after Monmouth, poor things ... Those luscious cream-fed girls. I tell you, ladies, one had to fight to maintain one's virginity, but, no, no, I said, my heart belongs to one more beauteous than you.' He bowed to Aphra, and she fluttered her eyelashes back. She was still susceptible to handsome young men.

But it must be hurting her, thought Penitence, to be entertaining one, however handsome, who'd fought against her beloved king. She'd have to get used to it; the Lords Temporal and Spiritual who'd formed the provisional government had judged that by his flight — to Louis XIV — James had not only abdicated but deprived his son of the right to to be proved his true heir. Thus the throne devolved on his elder daughter Mary, the Princess of Orange.

Benedick, however, kept talking as if it was a foregone conclusion that William would be asked to take the crown.

For the first time Aphra bridled. 'He can't be king, my dear; he has no right. Mary is a Stuart and the next in line. William is only her consort.'

Benedick shook his head. 'He's not a man likely to content himself with being his wife's gentleman usher.'

Penitence interrupted to keep the peace: 'Where and how is MacGregor?'

Her son smiled at her: 'He's very well. He's gone to Scotland with the Viscount of Severn and Thames to help him prepare a report for William on the situation up there.'

'Ah,' she said. 'Good.' *Damn the boy.* Would he say nothing else?

He turned to Aphra. 'The Viscount is my father. I am his acknowledged son.'

'So I hear,' said Aphra. 'I knew him first as Leander. Do you remember telling me about him in Newgate, Penitence?'

Benedick said: 'Did I tell you that on the way from Torbay MacGregor and I called in at Athelzoy looking to see my old mother? The girls and everybody else are well and send their best love.'

As Penitence showed him out, she asked: 'Do I look old?'

'You look sixteen.'

She said with indifference: 'I hope your father is well.'

'Ah *ha*.'

'Ah ha what?'

'Just ah ha. I don't think he wanted to go to Scotland.'

She became interested in a piece of fluff on his coat and flicked it off. 'Indeed.'

Benedick's hands took her shoulders and squared her to face him. 'Mama, I know you promised Prince Rupert never to marry, but do you think he'd have wanted you to remain lonely for the rest of your life?'

'Is that what your father told you?'

'I asked him why you two didn't marry and that's what he said.'

How nice of Henry. And how nice and romantic of their son to believe him, though it left her looking the culprit for the estrangement. Nor could she disabuse the boy. *Benedick, your father has good reason to believe your mother a harlot and cannot stomach the thought.* Hardly.

'Won't you marry him? He's a very fine man, you know.'

'I know he is,' she said. 'But I think you'll find he won't ask me again. The mountain doesn't really go to Mahomet.'

Whether the throne should be occupied by Mary as queen or regent, with William as consort, king or regent, or any combination of the foregoing, was solved by the Prince and Princess of Orange themselves. Mary, still in The Hague, wrote to say she had no wish to rule without her husband.

William, who had held aloof from dictating terms, now explained himself. He esteemed his wife, he said, as much as it was possible for man to esteem woman, but not even from her would he accept a subordinate place. He did not desire to take any part in English affairs, but if he did consent to do so there was only one part he would play. He must be offered the throne for life, or go back home.

It cleared the air. It was now obvious that William and Mary must be King and Queen; the head of each must appear on the coin of the realm, writs must run in the names of both.

However, to make sure the excesses of previous Stuarts were never perpetrated again, it was thought necessary to set down the fundamental principles of the English constitution. No money to be exacted by the sovereign, no standing army to be kept up in peacetime without permission of Parliament. There must be rights of petition, of electors to choose their representatives freely, to debate, to a pure and merciful administration of justice.

As documents go the one drawn up in a few hours by a committee under the chairmanship of a low-born young barrister named Somers didn't look particularly impressive. But no other country had it.

It was called the Declaration of Rights.

While arrangements for the Coronation went ahead, the little house in St Bride's received another visitor from the court.

Penitence opened the door to a large, fair-wigged clergyman radiating such bounciness that just looking at him was tiring.

'Gilbert Burnet at your service, mistress.' He was a Scot and had an orange ribbon on his hat. 'And begging audience with Mistress Aphra Behn, if you please.'

'*Doctor* Gilbert Burnet?'

He was delighted. 'Indeed, mistress. I see my fame has preceded me.'

'It has. What do you want?' If this was the man who had assailed Rochester with exhortations to repentance on his death-bed, the Earl had paid for at least some of his vices. Dr Burnet was not someone you'd want at your lowest ebb.

'Mistress Behn will wish to see me.'

'She's ill and she doesn't. I'm not having her pestered for a conversion, and certainly not by someone who called her vile.'

He wasn't disconcerted. 'Whom do I have the honour of addressing? Is it Mistress Peg Hughes? I know these things, d'ye see. And I was a great admirer of Prince Rupert, nor have I heard anything to tarnish the name of his mistress. Apart, of course, that ye lived in sin.' He beamed at her.

Penitence's eyes opened wide. A bubble of amusement, the first in weeks, had to be suppressed.

He was assuring her of his good intentions. 'No, no, Mrs Hughes. I've come on another mission – for the King, not the Lord this time. I have been his right-hand man in exile, I have marched with him from his landing, I have advised, cajoled, argued with and for him, and now I wish him celebrated.'

'Oh, come in.' It was like allowing a pack of panting, piddling, happy puppies into the house. 'But you go when I say you go.'

He lowered his voice in what Penitence suspected he believed to be a whisper. 'Is it the pox the poor soul has?'

'No it isn't. How dare you?'

He was pleased. 'I never believed the story.'

He was a primitive, Penitence decided, whose thoughts slid immediately to his tongue but he radiated a naive goodwill that would have been endearing if there hadn't been so much of it.

She had to leap at his arm to stop him giving Aphra's hand a vigorous shake. 'Is it the gout, Mistress Behn? I'm heartily sorry. My granny died of it. But I'm unconscionable glad to meet ye. There's some of your pieces, though not all, have given me pleasure. I'm a bonny writer myself and I know one when I see one.'

It was one of Aphra's good days and she was amused. 'In what can I serve you, Dr Burnet?'

'Serve your King, mistress, serve your King. I'm here to give ye a commission, which I'm pleased to do since I see from the state of your hoose that you've fallen on hard times.' He shot his cuffs in admiration of himself. 'I've criticized ye, I know, though for your own good, but I need ye to write a coronation ode for our new King Billy, a panegyric surpassing the one ye penned for the unworthy James.'

Penitence was triumphant. Whatever could be said against this man, he wasn't unintelligent; he'd hobnobbed with crowned heads all over Europe, he'd written histories, his prose style was that of a considerable journalist – and he'd come to a woman, a despised woman, to set the seal on William's victory. *Oh, Aphra, the whirligig of time certainly brings in its revenges.*

'D'ye see, ma'am, I'll be frank.' *Do you mean you haven't been?* 'Our new king has every virtue but that of pleasing the masses. He has a cold way. I've had to speak tae the man and he took it ill, but you're a crowd-pleaser, Mistress Aphra, they'll listen to ye. Will ye laud great Caesar as he should be lauded? Ye'll be well rewarded.'

Aphra was charming but immediately Penitence knew she wouldn't do it. Her eyes showed anguish but she wasn't going to do it: '*Dear* Dr Burnet, one recognizes the Princess Mary and her right to succeed, but not her husband's. The breeze that wafts o'er the cheering crowds leaves me unpitied, on the forsaken, barren shore to sigh with echo and the murmuring wind.'

Burnet worked on it. 'Ye'll not do it?'

'No.'

He was a tenacious man and by the time they got rid of him, Aphra was gasping for air, as if Burnet had used up the room's supply. Tears dripped down her cheeks. 'The first commission one has ever refused.'

'I can call him back. Affie, are you sure? He'll be a good thing, William, I think. There's been no killing, no war, it must be the most peaceful revolution the world's ever seen.'

Aphra's shoulders heaved with the effort to speak. 'He's a usurper. One doesn't pass kings back and forth like lumps of sugar. Good or bad, James is one's king.'

You stupid female. Penitence's anger surprised herself. *The divine right of kings is over and the right of people is beginning.* She had to turn away. Why couldn't the woman apply some of her romanticism to a concept greater than drawing a sword to fight for a man because he had a crown on his head?

Behind her, puffs of breath managed to shape themselves into a sentence. 'One is not a whore, Penitence.'

And I am. That was why she was so angry. Of all them who had battled to enter some other profession than prostitution, only Aphra hadn't failed. The theatre had beckoned her generation of women and they'd run through the doors, clutching such talent as they had in the hope of using it for the first time in a way that didn't involve dependence on a man's bed. It had been too difficult; Nelly, Dorinda, Knipp, the Marshalls, herself, all of them, had been forced back into the market as mistresses or, what was little different in terms of sale, wives.

Only Aphra had never sold her flesh. She'd chosen her men badly, but she'd chosen them out of love pure and simple. And now the same independence that had performed the miracle of earning her own living had rejected the accolade which belonged not just to her but to her weaker sisters who'd reached for it.

The Whigs aren't going to forgive you, Aphra. They'd stamp on her memory until it disappeared into the mud they'd spent years preparing for it. *And neither will I.*

Unforgiving, Penitence went on nursing her friend through agonies so resembling a drawn-out drowning that even Chloe prayed for her beloved to die, and on the last day went to Westminster Abbey.

'Wait there,' she told the hackney coach driver.

She'd never liked the Abbey much. Its enormous, marble-plaqued, gold-encrusted walls held less sanctity in her view than the parish church of Athelzoy. In the first place you had to pay threepence a head to get in, except for services. And inside lurked the official tomb guides, waiting to be tipped for intoning the Abbey's history. It was too close to Whitehall Palace, too far from God. If it had been left to her, Rupert would have been interred at Hammersmith. As it was, they hadn't let her into Henry VII's chapel to see him buried.

At the huge house in Dean's Yard, she made short shrift of the servants who tried to tell her Dean Sprat was resting from his efforts expended during the coronation of William and Mary four days before. 'He will see me.' It was a command.

'My dear Mrs Hughes, how nice to meet you again. In

671

what may I serve?' The attractive young man who'd procured Aphra's and her release from Newgate when he was chaplain to the Duke of Buckingham had expanded into overweight middle age. He'd shown agile footwork to keep his position at all under the new reign: he'd collaborated too much with the old one.

Like his abbey, Thomas Sprat had been too close to the centre of power for his soul's good. The eyes that had once been amused were careful. Assessor's eyes.

'I should like you to come with me. Aphra Behn is dying.' Penitence watched the name resurrect the mad, bad days when it had been less important to serve God than create a good aphorism, when he'd helped Buckingham write and perform *The Rehearsal*, when he'd wiled away the nights on Aphra's milk punch and discussion of rhyme versus blank verse. 'She's asking for you.'

In the place of the stately dean was a young man, vastly daring: 'Then I'll come.' He regretted it, because Penitence made the hackney's driver go like Jehu. 'Mrs Hughes, is this pace necessary?'

'Yes.'

She and Chloe sat on the stairs while he administered the sacraments; they could hear the whistle of Aphra's breath as she dragged it in to speak, but her voice, like his, was a murmur. 'He's got to allow it,' said Chloe. 'He must.'

There were tears in Dean Sprat's eyes when he emerged, but also anxiety. 'She wants to be buried in Poets' Corner,' he said.

'I know,' said Penitence. 'What did you tell her?'

'I told her "Yes". At that moment what else could I do? Death was looking at me. But . . .'

'That's all right then,' said Penitence, firmly.

'Mrs Hughes, it is not all right. I must excuse myself from a commitment when it was merely a word to ease a dying woman.'

'Why?'

'It was not a promise. How could it be? The decision as to who should or should not be buried in the Abbey is not mine alone. The Chapter, let me tell you, will not allow it.'

'Why?'

'Mrs Hughes, the days of King Charles are over; the Protestant wind is blowing with an almost Puritan vigour and will find our friend a less ... shall we say, less *worthy* figure than those of us who understand these things.'

'Well, I *don't* understand these things,' said Penitence. 'She's going to be buried in the Abbey with the other poets. That's what she wanted. That's what you promised. That's what she's getting.'

The Dean had recovered his poise; before her eyes he was ageing back into the pompous cleric. 'Do not make me regret I came, Mrs Hughes. I did it from sentiment for times past. For one thing, Poets' Corner is not a place for women and never will be, despite Mrs Behn's magnificent effrontery. To put her alongside Shakespeare's memorial? Spenser? She goes too far.' He was justifying himself by whipping up indignation, but Penitence's was the product of a lifetime. He backed away from her, fumbling for the door-latch.

'P-ppoets Corner, Sprat. She's going to Pp-pp-oets' Corner.'

Chapter 3

APHRA struggled above the rising tide in her own lungs until the early hours of the next morning when her heart stopped.

The sudden quiet of the room magnified the dreadful breathing that had gone before it so that, as they laid her out, the first tweet of a bird waking outside seemed to break through wool.

Penitence pulled Chloe away from the body and sat with her in the window-seat watching the dawn come up over the rooftops behind Aphra's small, overgrown back yard.

'We were lovers,' said Chloe.

'I know.' *Phoebe and Sabina. Aphra and Chloe.* Her friend might have lost the love of men but in her great need she had found the love of woman.

By mid-morning they had assumed the briskness that goes with the strange comfort of death's arrangements.

'She's left me the house.'

'Good,' said Penitence.

'And George Jenkins is to see to publishing *The Widow Ranter* and Betterton's to put it on.'

'Good.'

'And she asked me to give you this when she'd gone. She said she hoped it would do.'

'This' was a manuscript written while she could still hold a pen, though its last pages were scarcely legible. It was in novel form, she'd called it *Oroonoko*, and it was about a slave.

Penitence had to read it twice before she realized it was a masterpiece. The first time she was disappointed; it was coolly written and at the same time fantastically romantic. Aphra had made her slave not one of the poor thousands shipped from Africa to Jamaica, but an educated prince of his African country, Coromantien, in love with a black general's daughter, and betrayed by an English sea-captain to be sold in the slave-market of Surinam.

Once Aphra got her hero to Surinam the descriptions of place and people became sharp. The white men who ran the country, she wrote, were worse than transported criminals. It was the native Indians who lived in the first state of innocence. 'Religion here would but destroy the tranquillity they possess by ignorance; and laws would but teach them to know offences of which they have no notion.'

There was the feel of authenticity in the details she gave of the slave trade's organization in Surinam: the quayside sales, the overseers of plantations, the auctions and the shame of it.

Oroonoko harangued his fellow-slaves. 'An ass, or dog, or horse, having done his duty, could lie down in retreat, and rise to work again, and while he did his duty, endure no stripes', Aphra made him say:

But men, villainous, senseless men, such as they, toiled on all the tedious week 'till black Friday; and then whether they worked or not, whether they were faulty or meriting, they, promiscuously, the innocent with the guilty, suffered the infamous whip.

Of course, Oroonoko's love, Imoinda, arrived in Surinam a slave and the couple were reunited, revolted against their masters, suffered terrible fates. *Then she died and then he died*, thought Penitence. It was stirring, crowd-pleasing stuff.

It wasn't the tract Penitence had hoped for. It was more: a good story, a blast against the moral savagery of slavery and it was Aphra's testimony against the concept of human beings as property. *Oroonoko*'s subject was a black man, but he was an extension of everything Aphra had ever written about the human soul, male and female: it was about freedom. The first blast of the trumpet.

It will do, Affie. It will do very well.

Attached to the final page of the manuscript was a verse from a poem Aphra had written to the laurel tree:

> And after monarchs, poets claim a share
> As the next worthy thy prized wreaths to wear.
> Among that number do not me disdain,
> Me, the most humble of that glorious train.

As a sop, Dean Sprat had a grave dug for Aphra in his Abbey's east cloister. Chloe was prepared to opt for that. 'She's the first female commoner to get into the Abbey on her own merit, Penitence.'

'It's not good enough.' Penitence was angry. Angry *at* Aphra, *for* Aphra, *with* Aphra; she could feel anger lapping against her sanity, fed by the thousand insults thrown at her friend, at all her friends, at herself, all the women who'd made a break for freedom and been brought down by the dogs of male hatred and rolled in their dirt. 'She's to go in Poets' Corner.' It all depended on that. If she could see Aphra resting where she belonged this slopping, rising fury inside her might subside enough not to burst the mental restraint only just holding it back. 'She wrote *Oroonoko*.'

Then, on the day of the funeral as mourners gathered in Aphra's room, an Abbey messenger knocked at the front door and handed Chloe a letter. It said that Aphra couldn't be buried in the Abbey at all.

> In the absence of the Dean, and in the presence of his deputy, we, the Prebendaries of the Chapter, are in agreement that the interment of Mistress Behn in the Abbey is not suitable. Therefore we have sent to her parish church of St Bride's and received back word from its priest that her obsequies may take place there this afternoon.

Penitence tore up the letter, dragged the weeping Chloe off the open coffin, told Betterton to screw down the lid, and when he'd done, plonked Aphra's pen and inkwell on it. 'All right,' she said, 'who's carrying the damn thing to the Abbey?'

Benedick, Betterton, Neville Payne and young Thomas Creech, a promising poet whom Aphra had befriended, heaved the coffin down the steps to the crêpe-clad cart drawn by black-plumed, black-caparisoned horses. Chloe, who had chosen to wear the most peculiar of Aphra's peculiar caps, took her place behind it as chief mourner. The driver assumed a mournful expression, the drummer began beating his muffled skins and they set off.

It was a windy day with occasional scurries of rain. Orange flags and decorations still hanging from some of the balconies flapped sideways and paper rosettes rolled along the streets, making the horses shy, jerking the coffin so that the pen and inkwell fell off and Penitence had to carry them.

While the blowing detritus lodged itself in conduits, the funeral procession picked up the eccentric pieces of humanity that had loved Aphra Behn.

Jacob Tonson, her publisher, emerged from his bookshop, suitably clad in black – he always was. As they passed along the Strand they were joined by a gaggle of actresses who'd been rehearsing at Duke's. Holding on to their hats, skirts lifting, ribbons whipping their faces, they pulled a hobbling John Downes along with them. The proprietor of Will's

Coffee-House standing at his door, wiping his hands on his apron, said: 'Aphra?' and fell in beside Betterton. Sam Bryskett and Dogberry with some of his theatregoing butchers came in from Covent Garden; so did two flower-sellers and a stationer. John Hoyle, coat-collar up, hat down, sneering, lurched into the ranks from the Red Lion, and Rebecca Marshall ran up from her house near Charing Cross, bringing her grocer with her.

Just before Whitehall a small crowd that had gathered round a tree to stare up into its branches fell back as a figure swung down and ran towards the coffin, making the horses swerve. Dressed in a nightshirt, his head wrapped in brown paper tied with string, Aphra's fellow-playwright, Nat Lee, had come from Bedlam. Penitence had visited him in it. He smiled beautifully at her. 'I escaped.' He was shaking with excitement and cold and there were scars on his wrists. 'I've brought *Nero* for her.'

'Nero?' said Dogberry, nervously. 'That bugger's not coming too, is he?'

'It's his play,' explained Penitence. 'He wants to put a copy in Aphra's grave. I said he could.'

Benedick put his cloak round the madman and the cortège moved off again. Penitence held Nat's hand as he trotted beside her on bare feet. 'I loved her,' he said. 'But I never told her.'

'She knows now.'

At the avenue to Whitehall the gravel became too much for Nat's feet so they perched him on the end of the funeral cart. The crowd at the Holbein Gate gaped as they went through. Windows opened and some of the Palace servants, thinking they were mummers, sent up a cheer. 'Not far wrong, either,' said Betterton, waving his hat.

By the time the procession reached the Great West Door of the Abbey it had grown fifty-odd strong. A Yeoman of the Guard, who was throwing dice in the porch with a tomb-guide, swore when he saw it. 'They never told me there was a burying today. They tell you, Charlie?'

'Well there is,' Betterton said in his best grand manner. 'Open the doors, my man.'

'Once we've got her in the hole, they can't shift her,' Becky Marshall was explaining to Sam Bryskett. 'Penitence read the rules that she got from the Dean.'

'They shifted Cromwell,' said Sam.

They watched the Yeoman of the Guard unhook his keys from his belt. He was sorting through them. He was putting one in the enormous lock.

And then a prebendary came round the corner from the entrance to the Cloisters and asked them what they thought they were doing. Within minutes the Yeoman of the Guard had his pike levelled at them, the tomb-guide had been sent running to fetch the rest of the Abbey guard and prebendaries were pouring through the Cloister door, having celebrated the ending of Chapter with a large meal at the house of the Archdeacon who'd partaken freely of his own port.

Benedick put his hand over his mother's mouth and held her arms so that the argument could be left to Thomas Betterton: 'Why may she not, Venerable Sir? The Dean gave his permission.'

'Dean's absent,' said the Archdeacon, flapping his hand in a direction which indicated that the Dean was in the Thames. 'Chapter's decision. No actresses in the Abbey.'

'Mistress Behn was a playwright.'

'Same thing,' said the Archdeacon. 'All whores and topers.'

A soberer prebendary stepped in front of him. 'With respect, Archdeacon.' He turned to Betterton. 'My good sir, you must understand our position as keepers of this most holy place. Mistress Behn was an enterprising woman but hardly an ornament to her sex and it was felt she would lie more comfortably in some other resting place.'

The Archdeacon wagged his finger. 'Won't have her in. Put her in St Bride's with other scribblers. Good enough for her.'

'Such playwrights as we honour here,' went on the soberer prebendary, shaking his head at the Abbey's indulgence in giving any of them houseroom, 'wrote to the glory of God, in sacred language, Shakespeare and, um, Chaucer.'

'Have you read the "Wife of Bath" lately?' shouted Becky Marshall.

678

'Didn't have her in either,' shouted back the Archdeacon, sure of his ground.

The Abbey guard was filing into the space between the funeral party and the West Door, most of them old soldiers who came cheap. Penitence's eyes pleaded with her son and he took his hand off her mouth. 'Keep everybody here,' she told him. 'I'll be back.' She gave him her purse. 'Buy them wine. And get some food for Nat Lee.'

'Where are you going?'

'To see the King.'

She began to run. Apart from the ranks of agitated men round the Abbey door it was surprisingly quiet; over towards the river neither House of Parliament was sitting, and only a few lawyers and their clerks were pausing to stare on their way in and out of Westminster Hall; the whole place was resting after the efforts for the Coronation. It had stopped raining. It was getting dark and the carved, square gatehouse leading to the bridge over the Tyburn ditch had a wet sheen that reflected back the torches in their holders on either side of its passageway.

Then she was out of the Middle Ages and running towards Whitehall. From the suffocation of the Church she ran into the suffocation of Government; she saw it rolling towards her like fog, ready to muffle her in its obfuscation as it had so many petitioners before her. Some sanity returned. *They'll never let me near the King; it'll take days*. She advanced through the murk towards the light of the Holbein Gate where a gentleman was wearily dismounting from a horse. As he turned he saw her and stopped in mid-stretch. It was the Viscount of Severn and Thames.

After a moment she said: 'I want you to take me to the King.'

And he said: 'They don't usually let you in with a weapon.'

She looked down and saw she was holding Aphra's pen like a dagger. 'I'm burying Aphra in Poets' Corner, you see,' she said reasonably. 'They won't let me, and the King's got to make them.'

He nodded. 'The Buttery first, I think.'

679

'I want to see the King.'

Carefully, he took the pen away from her. 'You shall have it back later,' he said as she snatched for it. 'And you shall see the King. But the Buttery first.'

They served excellent ale in the Palace Buttery and he made her sit down at one of the tables and drink a frothing pint of it. In between gulps he fed her with morsels of equally excellent bread and cheese. 'When did you last eat?'

She tried to think. 'What day is it?'

'That's what I thought.'

'I must see the King.'

'Finish your ale. He's waiting for us; at least, he's waiting for me. For the Scottish report.'

Some form of normality was returning as she ate, but with it came a lassitude. In a while she'd have to return to the fight and Aphra's unburied coffin and leave this man for the last time.

With Aphra dead, Dorinda dead, her stage career over, her energy gone, there would be no occasion for her to visit London again; she would stay in her backwater, subsumed by its minutiae. One day, perhaps, she would hear that this man had married a young heiress and produced healthy tributaries for the viscountcy of Severn and Thames.

I shall wither. The thought of hearing it withered her now. She hadn't fully realized the fortitude necessary to face life without him, the pressure every minute imposed because he wasn't sharing it with her.

Do I love you that much? She did. Had. Would. They had known each other for, what, twenty-five years? A generation. Literally, a generation of love seeded into them both the moment they'd met. Given the greatest gift life had to offer, greater than talent, greater than pride, certainly greater than wealth, they had left it untended. And that – she saw it now – was true sin. She was a sinner not because she had whored to stay alive but because she hadn't pursued her lover – how beautiful that word was and how dirty they had made it – and not only forced him to see her as she was but open his eyes to the fact that he loved her as much as she loved him. *Because you do.*

Such waste it had been.

She felt a tear drip down the side of her nose and rubbed it, pretending it was an itch. 'How's MacGregor?' she asked.

'He had to stay on. I think he's arranging to give you Scotland. Tell me about Aphra.'

She told him and anger for Aphra re-energized her in the telling. 'Why shouldn't she be commemorated with all the other poets? They've got somebody called Casaubon in there and who was he, I ask you? Did he write for freedom from slavery like Affie did? And Michael Drayton who only wrote one line worth saying, and Thomas Triplet. Who the hell's ever heard of Thomas Triplet? I'll wager those p-p-pprebendaries don't know.'

'Let me get this clear. You're trying to bury Aphra Behn in the Abbey's Poets' Corner?'

'Yes. But the prebendaries are trying to stop me.'

He leaned back, fingering his chin. 'Have you tried fucking 'em?'

'Ah.' She shouldn't have lowered her guard. John Downes used to tell her time after time when she was learning to fence. She sighed and stood up. 'Not yet. But it's a thought. Shall we go?'

He took off his cloak and wrapped it around her to protect her from the damp of the courtyards. She could feel desperation emanating out of his flesh into hers. *I can't help you, my dear, dear man.* Only he could transcend the rules men made for themselves and choose the greater maturity of love.

You have to realize for yourself. It has to matter more than anything else.

The Palace was still in disorder from James's flight; every Dutchman they saw was gloomy and every English servant resentful of the Dutch. The usher taking them to the Royal Apartments complained to Henry as to a fellow-sufferer. 'Won't have his hand kissed, if you believe it. Won't even let us *kneel*. Won't touch for the King's Evil, just wishes 'em better health and less superstition. And *she's* everywhere, taking gruel to the poor and checking the accounts. Checking the *accounts*.'

The Grooms of the Bedchamber were hanging about in the vestibule outside and apologized in advance for the lack of ceremony. 'He says would you suffer him to receive you *déshabillé*, Marquis. He has the cough.'

One of them muttered: 'When ain't he?' They showed no interest in Penitence.

Marquis. Oh well, good luck to him.

King William III of England was crouched over the Bedchamber's fireplace, coughing. He was in his slippers with a shawl round his shoulders. Like the great bed, the red and gold room had been stripped of its hangings and faded marks on the walls showed where they'd been taken down. The windows were open.

'Anthony.' He stretched out a hand but as Henry took it, said quickly: 'No need to kiss it. How was Scotland?'

'Chaos, Your Majesty. But first, may I take the liberty of introducing Mrs Peg Hughes, an old acquaintance of mine? She asks a boon.'

The King turned away from the fire and looked at Penitence. Then he crossed the floor and kissed her hand. 'An old acquaintance of mine as well,' he said slowly. 'I am deeply in her debt. You look well, Mrs Hughes.'

'So do you, Your Majesty.' She hoped she was the only one to be lying. He looked ghastly; she hadn't remembered him as so small. How old was he? Thirty-eight?

'Better than the last time we met.' They still understood each other. A second's worth of amusement touched the pinched, white face and went again. Holding her hand he took her to the window — 'I can't breathe in your London' — leaving the Marquis staring. He gasped some air into his concave little chest. 'Perhaps the Marquis would not understand that then it was also in a bedroom.'

She whispered back. 'I don't think he would. He's not an understanding man.'

Together they looked out on the Thames; the tide was in and to both of them the lap and smell of water brought longings for other waters; she for the streams and rhines of Somerset, he for his canals. 'I would give ten thousand pounds to be in Holland now.'

'You were homesick then.'

'I shall always be homesick. And now I cannot go home.' He'd got the stoop of a pedlar, as if England made a heavy pack.

They stood nodding at each other before he had a fit of coughing and hurried her to the fire, indicating that the Marquis could join them. 'You once did me great service, Mrs Hughes,' he said formally. 'In what may I serve you?'

She explained.

'Aphra Behn?' He connected the name with something disgraceful. 'One of my good Uncle Charles's favourites?'

'Not in that sense. He liked her plays.'

'The woman playwright.' He'd remembered. 'I hear she was bawdy.'

It will be her epitaph. Penitence was overcome by hopelessness. Well, if she couldn't get Aphra buried in the bloody Abbey on Aphra's merits, perhaps she could get her there through her own. 'I want her in Poets' Corner. That's the boon I beg.'

'Poets' Corner?'

'The South Transept. In Westminster Abbey.'

'Ach, Westminster Abbey.' The King turned to the Marquis. 'You missed a comedy there, Anthony. The Coronation was virtually a Popish ceremony. In my shirt to the waist, kneeling I was. It was very draughty. And too much music.'

'Sire,' said Penitence, sharply, 'my friend lies unburied outside the West Door. Give me permission to inter her in the South Transept.'

'Ask me for something else.'

'*What?*' She'd rescued this little Dutchman from ignominy. Damn it, she'd held his head while he was sick.

'Ask me for anything else. Ask me for Devonshire. Ask me for a duchy. Ask me for jewels, for the hand of this Marquis in marriage. You shall have them all.'

'But I don't want any of these things. I want the little bit of earth my friend has deserved.'

'No, you don't.' He sat back down in his chair. His face had become impassive. 'Mrs Hughes, you are asking me to interfere with the Church of England. My uncle lost his throne for that and I will not follow him. I told you once that the overriding principle of my life is to oppose the advance of France, and that I cannot do if I am fighting the Church of my own realm. No.'

'Thank you, Your Majesty.' She swept him her best theatre curtsey and turned to go, but the Marquis's hand reached out and gripped her arm.

'Your Majesty,' he said, 'the Abbey is a Royal Peculiar.'

William III's face remained expressionless. Penitence didn't like it any more. 'It is peculiar certainly. In what way Royal?'

'It means that it is under the jurisdiction of no bishop nor archbishop, only the King's. It is the sovereign's free chapel and exempt from any ecclesiastical jurisdiction but the sovereign's.'

'Therefore?'

The Marquis turned to Penitence. 'The grave's dug?'

'Yes.'

'And you think that once the coffin's in they won't move it?'

'Yes.'

'Therefore, Your Majesty, you have the right to give permission for a subject . . .' He raised an eyebrow at Penitence. '. . . fifty subjects to enter your own Abbey. What they do when they get there is something else again.'

'It will cause trouble, Anthony.'

'William, you must get used to trouble. You're in England now.'

Coughing, the King went to his table, scribbled some lines on a piece of paper, came back and gave it to Penitence. 'There.'

She didn't say thank you. The paper wasn't that big.

'Show Mrs Hughes out, if you would be so good, Marquis. Then return. We have to deal with Scotland.'

She went out frontwards and without a word. In the vestibule the Marquis handed her Aphra's pen from where he'd put it on a table.

She was numbed by the ingratitude of kings. 'I should have left him without his breeches.'

'Good God, not him as well!'

'Oh, Henry,' she said. 'When are you going to let yourself off the hook?' and left him staring after her.

Penitence had a stitch in her side by the time she reached Westminster and paused to catch her breath. Across the square the coffin lay surrounded by flares on the green in front of the Abbey. Nat Lee was sitting on it; beside him was a hogshead of wine from which he was refilling beakers with a ladle. With their capacity for enjoying any occasion, the players had turned the cortège into a party. The funeral cart and horses had gone, but the drummer had stayed and been joined by a fiddler and some of the mourners were dancing, Benedick with one of the actresses – it looked like Elizabeth Barry – Dogberry with Becky Marshall, Payne with Chloe. Passers-by, mostly beggars and street-walkers, had come up to sample Nat's generosity.

Further off the prebendaries had gathered by the entrance to the Cloisters in a watchful, disapproving group, though Penitence glimpsed a leather bottle doing the rounds there as well. The Archdeacon, who was showing a tendency to lie down, had been propped against a mounting block.

The only people who weren't enjoying themselves were the string of Abbey Yeomen disconsolately guarding the West Door.

Penitence was relieved; no soldiers or constables had been called in; the City of Westminster was administered by the Abbey and the Dean and Chapter were careful to guard its rights without outside help.

In that moment the scene resembled a beach, the invader's camp lit by flickering lights, the defenders standing with their backs against the towering cliff of the West Front covered with the barnacles and roots of its elaborate carving. The battle-lines were drawn, old enemies, the Arts versus the Church.

Such solid ranks against her, so untroubled by doubt or amusement, so certain of others' sin.

Such a rag-tag army, her side. Tipsy entertainers, beggars, writers, a gibbering escapee from Bedlam, publicans, whores.

Aphra would have approved.

So, now she came to think of it, had Jesus.

It went out of control, like wars do — unexpectedly. A ghostly line of small white surplices issued from round the corner on invisible feet, snaking towards the West Door. It was time for Evening Service. Automatically, one of the Yeomen of the Guard unlocked the door and opened it to allow the choir entrance, showing the candle-illuminated interior of the nave.

Penitence began to cross the road.

Nat Lee stood up on Aphra's coffin, shrieking and pointing at the light. Somebody's trained voice shouted 'Decus et Dolor!' and Aphra's army went into the attack.

By the time Penitence had got to the green, the coffin had gone, borne up like a battering ram on many shoulders; she thought she saw her son's among them.

'Decus et Dolor!' Elizabeth Barry was beating back a Yeoman trying to bar its way with her heavily loaded pocket, two more actresses and Chloe, Aphra's cap over one ear, had jumped on another and were clinging round his neck.

Penitence ran to join the battle. So did the prebendaries, two of them trying to restrain Nat Lee who was hammering a third of the group with its own bottle.

The coffin's rush had got it through the door, but the pallbearers had been forced to put it down and Betterton, Creech and Payne had their backs to it, swords out, defending its position against a contingent of guards.

It was amazing how many weapons the Abbey held. Such prebendaries as weren't armed already were wrenching halberds from the fists of statuary warriors and throwing funerary vases. But the armoury was open to all; Rebecca Marshall was standing on the bent back of a street-walker and reaching up for a lance holding regimental colours. Dogberry had grabbed a candle-holder from the Chapel of St George and was wielding it like a pike.

The noise went up a hundred feet to the vaulted roof, whipped across tombs to echo back off the gilded figures of saints. Grimacing faces ducked and shouted behind the calm of marble effigies.

All masks were off. Penitence had expected the hatred of the Church, but what amazed her was the ferocity of her friends, as if Aphra was just a rallying point for a hundred years of condemnation. Some pent-up element was loose in the Abbey; licence against censure, restriction against liberty, the acceptable against the possible, both sides were released in the pagan joy of hitting. The original cause of the fight was forgotten.

The choir, escaped from the Master, had relapsed into boys who were joining in with yells in high trebles. One had butted Sam Bryskett's stomach and another was impartially biting a prebendary's leg. She jumped on to the coffin and heard her own voice ridiculously shouting: 'On, on, you noblest English. To Poets' Corner.'

There was an answering roar and she was tipped off as beggars and Betterton, yelling more Shakespearean war-cries, swept Aphra towards the choir. But the forces of the Church rallied half-way up the nave and, with the gates of the Henry VII Chapel forming a backdrop, pressed the coffin back to the side door to the Cloisters.

Penitence's head had hit a pillar and she'd lost interest for a moment, until she heard the rasp of a sword and saw the soberer prebendary advancing on her, glaring. 'On guard, whore.'

The man's mad. But so was she. She crouched in the position John Downes had taught her with her left hand quirked out and Aphra's pen upraised. The soberer prebendary lunged and his sword-tip slashed her sleeve, scratching her arm as she parried with half a pen. 'God damn it,' she shouted, 'you're not supposed to do that.'

No appreciation of theatre, this man, a killer. *Oh my God, he is.* The man's eyes gleamed. There was froth at his mouth. He wasn't going to stop when the curtain came down. She dodged behind a sarcophagus. After all she'd been through she was going to die in a farce. There was blood on her hand as she raised it to protect herself. He was about to lunge for her chest.

Another figure stepped in front of her. 'That's not very

nice,' said a voice to her opponent. It had said the same thing to her other opponents.

She collapsed on to the sarcophagus. The soberer prebendary didn't like the change but was out of control and didn't mind who he killed. 'Whoremonger,' he screamed.

'Oh, really,' said the Marquis of Severn and Thames, crossly, 'I haven't got time for this.' He pressed the man back between the pillars of the triforium into the shadows. She heard a clang and they came out again, the Marquis clutching the soberer prebendary by the collar, pulling him towards Penitence. 'Mrs Mahomet, I presume?'

Tears were falling down her face as her gratitude for the man streamed upwards in prayer. He'd come when, if his jealousy had been stronger than his care for her, he would have stayed away. His presence was an acknowledgement. He'd let himself off the hook.

He looked down at her. 'Have you ever thought of taking up a quiet pursuit? The army? Gun-running? Something contemplative?'

She shook her head and closed her eyes for a moment. 'I love you, Henry,' she said.

'That's all very well, but every time I have to come and rescue you I offend some king or another. William was put out that I cut him short to come and get you out of trouble – yet again. We're running out of kings.'

'Never mind,' she said. 'This time you get to keep me.'

'Do I?'

'Yes,' she said, 'you do.' She looked into his face. What had done it she didn't know but something in him had won a battle over something else; his love had overcome the whatever-it-was – jealousy, masculine pride – that had kept him from surrendering to it until now. He was amused but rueful. After all, if one thing wins another is defeated. *She* knew it was the better part of him that had gained the victory but he had yet to be persuaded. Well, she had the rest of her life in which to persuade him. It was a nice thought.

He said, peering at her arm, then at the tomb, 'Do you know you're bleeding over Lady Jane Clifford?' He helped her to her feet and supported her as they went towards the noise that had transferred itself to beyond the Cloister door which stood open amid a litter of broken urns.

As they made their way towards it, the Archdeacon staggered in from the western end holding his head. The wreckage of his abbey sobered him. 'Sacrilege!'

Henry bowed and introduced himself without letting go of the prebendary's collar. 'This lady is entrusted with a letter from His Majesty, who has now sent me to express his disquiet at this business. Show him, Boots.' He regarded the paper Penitence produced from her sleeve. It was indecipherable with blood. 'Ah. Well. Perhaps you would permit me to tell you what it says.'

He was rescuing her. It would have been impossible to succeed without male authority in this bastion of maleness. Still, if she could only get Aphra honoured as she should be honoured, the female sex would have won a victory. *And you'd have liked Henry, Affie.*

'What it *says*,' he was saying pointedly, 'is that the King expects the Chapter of Westminster Abbey to honour the promise of its Dean and bury Mistress Behn in the South Transept.'

'Does it?' asked the Archdeacon.

Did it? She hadn't read it, but she was damned sure it didn't.

'It does,' said Henry. 'Perhaps you would inform the Chapter.'

'Don't do it, Archdeacon,' yelled the soberer prebendary. 'The King can't dictate to us.'

Penitence was sick of him. 'Yes he can.'

Henry placed his sword-tip against the prebendary's spine and bowed to the Archdeacon. 'Lead the way.'

The battle in the Cloisters was going badly for Aphra's side. The Church had brought in reinforcements in the shape of beadles and adult choristers. The street-walkers and beggars had wisely disappeared. The actresses were inflicting damage, though running out of ammunition; nearly all the men had been forced to surrender. Creech and Benedick still struggled with three Yeomen and John Downes, panting with age, was fencing beautifully with a beadle. Betterton's sword, however, lay at his feet as he displayed open palms to two muskets aimed at him and Dogberry. Payne had been wounded in the leg. Sam Bryskett's arms were being held behind his back by assorted prebendaries.

The most interesting situation was Nat Lee's. His brown paper hat had unravelled and hung in folds round his head which was the only part of him to be seen, the rest being down the hole dug for Aphra, and he was flinging up stones and earth at anyone trying to get near him. He looked like an angry rabbit.

'Pax,' shouted the Archdeacon. He didn't have the voice.

Henry did. 'PAX.'

All bodies stilled, all heads turned. After one look, Nat Lee scrabbled on.

The Marquis gestured to the Archdeacon. 'Your scene, Venerable Sir.'

The Archdeacon rose to it: 'Bury the bloody woman,' he said, 'King's orders.'

There were protests from the Church's army.

And one from Aphra's. 'She's going in P-pp-poets' Corner.'

But at this the enemy ranks raised their weapons again with a chorus of 'No'. The Archdeacon shook his head: 'Here or nowhere.' The soberer prebendary said: 'Over my dead body.'

The Marquis rescued him just in time by standing between him and those from the theatre prepared to take the man up on his offer. 'Look around you, Boots,' he pleaded. 'If you go on somebody's going to get killed.'

She looked around and saw that her years of accumulated fury at women's wrongs had sent her sufficiently insane to believe she could right them, reducing her and Aphra and Aphra's friends into fools. Colours which had illumined the last few minutes muted into the grey shadows of a stone passageway where bruised and tattered misfits stood in the grip of eternal authority.

I'm proud of them. They couldn't win. Would never win. It was only because they had spent their lives in illusion that they had even dared to try. Henry was right. The play was over; the audience hadn't appreciated it – to the point where it was prepared to kill them. Already she and Neville Payne were bleeding, nearly all the others hurt.

'Boots,' said the Marquis, 'you've got her this far. Settle for it. Learn to compromise, for God's sake.'

She looked at him. He was proffering medicine that he'd already had to take. Even now he wasn't reconciled to her past; he never would be. He had compromised with it to gain their future. In her turn she would have to overcome her resentment of *his* resentment. She would have to compromise, not just over Aphra, but over the rest of her life. Well, there were worst fates than a compromise. England itself had just made one. Extremists had held back from killing each other for the first time and instead had agreed to put on the throne that narrow-chested, coughing little Dutchman. William, the compromise king. If England could do it, she could. Actually, she was too tired to do anything else.

She nodded.

Eventually they found the coffin skewed under a pew in the Chapel of St Faith. Creech's shoulder was dislocated so they needed another pallbearer. Penitence wanted it to be the soberer prebendary but he'd been sick and gone home.

The Marquis went into earnest consultation with the Archdeacon, receiving assurances, paying out moneys. The Abbey's chief organist was sent for and came gladly – Purcell had been fond of Aphra.

Elizabeth Barry tore a piece off her already torn petticoat and bandaged Penitence's wound, then together they wandered into the South Transept to look at the memorials of Poets' Corner until everything was ready. 'Who's Thomas Triplet?' Barry asked.

'I've no idea.'

'I'm glad Affie's not going in with *him*.' Idly drawing a moustache on Abraham Cowley with a finger that had been dipped in Aphra's inkwell, she said: 'Chloe says Affie left you *The Widow Ranter*.'

'Yes.'

'It's a wonderful part.'

You're too young. The girl was beautiful; she'd only been sixteen or so when she'd become Rochester's mistress. He'd taught her how to act and made a fine job of it according to Betterton who'd told Penitence: 'Next to you, she's the best Desdemona I've ever seen.'

No. It's me who's too old. Penitence said: 'You can play her if you like.'

Barry twirled round. *'Can I?'*

'Yes. This was my last performance. I'm getting married.'

The funeral party had gathered itself and put Chloe's hat on straight. They lifted Nat Lee out of the grave so that Aphra could be put into it. He cried on Betterton's shoulder all the way through the interment.

The wind of Purcell's Te Deum reached them even here, in this far, dark corner, and the choristers sang like angels. 'I heard a voice from heaven,' declaimed the Archdeacon, 'saying unto me, Write; Blessed are the dead which die in the Lord; from hencefourth: yea, saith the Spirit, that they may rest from their labours.'

They sprinkled the Abbey's dust on to the coffin and held Nat Lee back from following it. Since there were no gravediggers, Creech and Dogberry filled in the hole and when the earth was level there was a rush of prebendaries to help them tamp it down.

The churchmen went first and one by one the mourners followed until only the Marquis and Benedick and Penitence were left. The son winked at his parents and ran to catch up with the retreating form of Elizabeth Barry.

Penitence looked down at the earth. 'People will tread on her,' she said.

Henry took her good arm and led her back into the nave where a prebendary was snuffing the candles. She turned towards the Henry VII Chapel. 'I ought to go and say goodbye to Rupert.'

He tightened his grip. 'You've said goodbye to him.'

She considered. 'I have, haven't I? I'm going to marry you.'

'Wait until you're asked, woman.'

Together they stood in the great doorway, looking at the

green where Aphra's army was finishing the wine. They saw John Hoyle emerge from the direction of the Abbey Arms and rejoin it. 'He deserted.'

Henry said: 'If the King hears I lied about his permission, I'm not likely to get my ambassadorship.'

'Did you want it?'

'Not really. I thought I'd settle down and spend the rest of my old age in Somerset.'

She put her hand on his. 'I thought I would too. We've done enough. We'll leave the rest to William and Mary. Theirs should be a sensible reign.'

As they crossed the road to join the revelling mourners, he said: 'But duller.'

'Oh yes,' said Penitence. 'Thank God. Much, much duller.'